RADLEY'S CHRISTMAS FOR HORNY MONSTERS

HORNY MONSTERS

BOOK SIX

ANNABELLE HAWTHORNE

WET LEAF PRESS

First Edition published 2023

RADLEY'S CHRISTMAS FOR HORNY MONSTERS

ISBN: 978-1-949654-37-0 (ebook)

ISBN: 978-1-949654-38-7 (paperback)

ISBN: 978-1-949654-39-4 (hardcover)

Written by Annabelle Hawthorne

Published by Wet Leaf Press

www.wetleafpress.com

Interior Design by Wet Leaf Press

This book is for those who celebrate Christmas
those who do not
and those we will miss this holiday season

CONTENTS

'TWAS THE NIGHT BEFORE CHRISTMAS

The crisp morning air of late December filled Mike Radley's lungs with a chill that was tough to contain. He had to fight the urge to cough, and the stray hair sticking out of his scarf that kept tickling his ear wasn't helping matters. Kneeling in the snow, he contemplated the small map of his front yard that he had drawn with a gloved finger.

"Tink think pincer move still best attack." The goblin across from him was bundled up in a thick winter jacket that she had altered for herself. Her voice was muffled by the yellow gaiter across her face. Between the magical goggles and the aviator hat she wore, only a small patch of green flesh could be seen along the bridge of her nose. "Surround invaders, bust heads."

"It won't work," Kisa growled. "There're too many of them." The cat girl wore white ski pants and a dark-red sweater with a black vest. Her tail twitched behind her as if tuned in to a demented metronome.

"We need to succeed." Mike looked up at them from behind a pair of ski goggles. His eyes had long ago adjusted to the blueish tint. "The consequences if we fail…" He shook his head in disgust.

"You can't hide forever." The woman's voice had a mocking tone and came from several different places at once. "We already found your pet rock, by the way. She's down for the count."

"Damn it!" Mike smashed his map with a fist. Abella had been hiding in the hedge maze, ready to spring an ambush once the intruders moved past her. Right now, he was hiding in a gap beneath the gazebo, a structure in the center of the maze.

"Caretaker…" A masculine voice with a low growl taunted him. "I'm going to find you."

"Not if I find you first," Mike muttered, then looked over at Tink. "They're in the maze. No pincer attacks. There were four of them left at last count. Are you up for this?"

"Tink show no mercy!" She saluted him so hard that her red braids bobbed across her chest, and then she picked up a thick wooden club and ducked out the hole.

"I'll see what I can do," Kisa added. "I don't know how they keep spotting me though. I think they've found a way to counteract my magic." The cat girl had a natural gift for being forgotten, even in plain sight.

He reached out and put one hand on each of theirs. "Be careful out there. If we lose…never mind. C'mon, let's go." Mike got on his belly and slid out of the hole. Around them, the frozen hedge maze had formed icy trenches they now used for defense. Tink and Kisa were short enough that they could hunch over and run without being spotted, but Mike had to crouch to remain hidden.

Heavy footfalls to his left had him holding still while Kisa ran ahead. Mike tilted his head to peek through a gap in the bushes but was startled to see a large pair of eyes looking back.

"Found ye!" The figure leaped over the hedges with little

effort, landing in a crouch with the buckles on his leather outfit jingling. Thin wisps of black smoke drifted from the gap in his neck as he threw a pair of snowballs at Mike.

Mike's magic surged forward, leaping from his outstretched hands to cause both the snowballs to explode in midair. His precognition triggered, and he jumped hard to the left as a massive snowball crashed down where he had been crouching moments ago.

"Nice trick!" He grabbed a double handful of snow and tossed it into the air, his magic striking it with miniature bolts of lightning. The snow vaporized and then froze in the air, the icy mist hovering like fog as he ducked around the corner and then dove over the top of another hedge.

"Ye can't run forever, Caretaker!" Suly called to him, but Mike ignored it. He needed distance right now, and the only way to get it was—

Turning a corner, he saw Asterion standing there with a large snow shovel full of snow. The Minotaur was wearing a thick black scarf and winter pants. His torso was bare, with little flakes of snow catching on the edges of his exposed body hair.

Asterion bellowed and swung the shovel, launching the massive amount of snow. Mike slid under it but lost his footing when his boot got caught in the branches of a nearby shrub.

"Shit," he muttered as he tried to free himself without losing his boot.

Asterion shoveled some more snow and held it high, ready to dump it. Kisa leaped from between the shrubs and pulled off her hat, which she pushed over Asterion's eyes.

"Save yours—" she managed before Asterion accidentally dumped the load of snow on himself and Kisa. Both of them went down with a thud.

"Asterion, Kisa, you're out!" Yuki sat on top of an ornamental throne of ice by the front door of the house. She held a steaming cup of hot chocolate in one hand as she surveyed the grounds and acted as the referee.

Mike cursed, then moved away from the spot. He moved through the hedges until he came upon a massive pile of snow with a pair of stony wings sticking out of the top.

"Abella?" He scraped away the snow from where he thought the gargoyle's face would be. When he got to her, she spat out some snow and frowned. "Who did this to you?" he asked.

"I would hate to ruin the surprise," she told him with an emotional smile. "Also, Suly is right behind you."

Mike grabbed a handful of snow and threw it as he turned. The dullahan leaned sideways and allowed his head to drop to the side so the snowball missed. Suly's gloved hand grabbed tightly onto his hair as he threw a snowball with his free hand. The snowball struck Mike in the leg but didn't count for an elimination.

"You missed," Sulyvahn declared with a grin as his head swung like a pendulum.

"Maybe," Mike replied. "But she won't."

Sulyvahn's body turned just as Tink leaped on top of the nearby bushes, her club held low. She swung it as hard as she could, firing a packed snowball from the scoop she had carved into the top. Her aim was amplified by the magical goggles on her head, and she hit Sulyvahn between the eyes hard enough that he dropped his head in the snow. His body spasmed dramatically and fell backward into a drift.

"Suly is out!" Yuki declared.

"Tink crush enemies!" she yelled while packing her club with more snow. "No have mercy!"

A massive snowball almost a foot across shot through the air, smashing into Tink so hard that she vanished, her hat and gloves ripped free by the shrubs as she fell. Mike got to his feet to see Bigfoot standing on the other side of Abella's snow pile.

"Tink's out!" Yuki shouted.

"That was a little overboard, wasn't it?" he asked, knowing that Tink was okay. The goblin was tough as nails, and he could already hear her swearing from the other side of the hedge.

"Little booger can take it," Bigfoot told him as he scooped up another massive snowball. "As for you? Let's find out."

When Bigfoot lifted the snowball over his head with both hands, Mike unzipped his jacket and pulled it open. Strapped to his chest was an antique doll with eerie features. The air filled with maniacal laughter as the snowball Bigfoot held smashed onto his head.

"Maybe if you were a Yeti, these things wouldn't happen to you." Mike winked.

Bigfoot responded by flipping off Mike with both hands before falling over backward dramatically, which sent a cloud of powdered snow up into the air.

"Bigfoot is down," Yuki declared with a grin. "It's one against one, folks!" At the base of her throne, the fairy quartet watched eagerly, all of them cheering in delight. At the windows of the house, several rats spectated the event, including Reggie. They had already put together small flags with the letter *B* on them that they waved excitedly.

"Technically, it's two against one." Beth's voice came from two separate directions. "Cheating with a doll! Have you no shame?"

"We will not go quietly into the night!" Mike declared dramatically as he scrambled over the hedge and found Tink. He put her hat back on and handed her back her gloves as she pulled off her goggles.

"Get big revenge for Tink," she told him with a wink.

"You know it." He pulled off his ski mask and slid the goggles over his face. The stark whiteness of the world immediately mellowed as several tiny lenses flicked out of hidden locations and dropped down over his eyes. With the goggles on, he could see the most recent tracks in the snow with ease, but that wasn't the best part.

He scooped up a generous handful of snow and packed it. Holding it in his hand, he cocked his arm back and watched the trajectory line form in front of him. It took some getting used to, but it would give him an important edge against his foe.

His magic warned him of inbound danger, and he ducked under a volley of snow that came from behind. Months of training had enabled him to fine-tune his danger sense, and being able to convince his magic that losing a snowball fight was bad showed just how far he had come. He dodged forward as more snow missiles came from the front, then did a small cartwheel to the side to avoid yet another volley. It wasn't just his magic that he had trained. If not for spending the last several months training his body to move, he would have been hit.

And how was Beth throwing snowballs from several directions at once? Unless she had unlocked some magical ability he was unaware of, it shouldn't be possible. It was almost as if Jenny was attacking him…

"Jenny?" He pulled the doll out of her harness. "Are you secretly a double agent?"

The doll blew a psychic raspberry at him, so he planted her head down in a nearby snowdrift. It didn't surprise him at all that she had played both sides.

"I guess Jenny is out," Yuki declared as Mike pulled Jenny free and then ran for cover. The rules for elimination required that snow touch someone's head or face, and he didn't dare risk her wrath by leaving her buried.

"Now it's one on one," Beth declared from multiple directions. However, Mike caught movement from the corner of his eye and threw a snowball in a beautiful arc toward Beth. She ducked behind a hedge, and the snowball exploded into powder.

"It's over," Mike asserted. "You may as well come out and —shit!"

The air over Beth's head filled with spiraling balls of snow that rocketed toward him. He crouched behind the hedge and watched them all smack into the Abella pile.

"That's how she got me," Abella informed him. "Sheer quantity."

"Quality over quantity," he declared, then picked up some snow and formed it into a sphere. He watched for movement again and saw the top of Beth's hat. Standing up, he threw the snowball and used his magic to push it out of his hands as fast as possible. It smashed into Beth's head, revealing that she had stuck her hat on a stick.

"Ah, shit," he muttered as Beth stood up to his right. She whirled her hands around dramatically, pulling moisture from the air and forming it into several snowballs all at once.

He dodged the attack, his magic shattering the few that would have struck him. Beth kept moving forward, her gloved hands glowing as she kept him pinned down. It was only a matter of time until she made a mistake, and he saw his opportunity when she tripped on a root buried beneath the snow.

He ran toward her, scooping a handful of snow as he went. Realizing she was in a tight spot, Beth summoned snowballs above him that fell as he slid to one side and readied his own snowball.

With a grunt, he pitched the snowball at Beth's face. She responded by summoning another ball of snow in front of her, and the two balls collided in an icy explosion, which filled the air with snowflakes. Beth dove through the cloud of frost, a snowball held tightly in her hand as she tackled Mike to the ground.

"It ends now, Caretaker!" She went to smash the ball in his face, but he caught her by the wrist. Beth maneuvered herself so she was sitting on him, her ass pressing directly into his crotch.

"N…never!" he stammered, distracted by the feel of her weight on his body. His magic swirled through him, making him hard, but he imagined the sensation was dampened by the fact that they were both wearing snow pants.

Beth grunted as she tried to shove the snowball into his face. Her dark eyes were wide, revealing the golden flecks that had appeared in her pupils over the last couple of months. They were a result of the magic she had gained, and he wondered what else about her was now different. "Never… underestimate…a woman…who…doesn't want to do the dishes!"

As they fought, her ass rubbed against him hard enough that his magic started to activate. Beth's eyes sparkled as if she was casting a spell, and his concentration finally slipped. She smashed the snowball into his face, sending a chill through his whole body.

"Victory for team Beth!" she declared, sitting up and holding her arms in the air. As she pumped her arms, her hips gyrated against his, and he gritted his teeth as he commanded his magic to calm the fuck down.

With the others in the house, getting zapped by his magic wouldn't be that big of a deal. While he could now use it for defense, its primary function was for transferring sexual energy. But he and Beth didn't have the same relationship that he did with the other women. With the others, he could sense their intent and motives like it was second nature, and it was just easier somehow. With her, he was always in the dark, as if there was a mental block.

If he were still in therapy, it would definitely be a hot topic.

"Looks like you're doing the dinner dishes," she declared moments before she was bombarded by snowballs from the side.

"The game is over, Jenny," Yuki warned, then leaned to one side to dodge a snowball that slammed into her throne.

But I'm the house champion! Jenny stood waist-deep in the snow, her arms raised as chunks of snow ripped free from the ground and targeted everyone. The fairies screamed in panic as they fled the scene.

"Okay, you," Bigfoot said as he stood, but an icy maelstrom frosted him from head to toe. He wiped slush out of his eyes and blinked, his dark eyes buried beneath thick fur.

Freeze, freeze, all of you! Jenny's laughter filled the air as everyone ran for cover. It wasn't uncommon for Jenny to take things too far, and Mike leaned around the corner of a hedge to help pull Beth to safety.

"You realize she's getting coal for Christmas?" Beth wiped the snow off her face. "Giant sack of it."

"How about a dream car? I find that giving Jenny anything flammable in large quantities is a terrible idea." Mike grinned, then handed Beth his hat. "Temporary truce?"

Beth smiled, then put his hat on her head. "Truce. But you're still doing dishes tonight."

The front yard filled with playful screams as everyone moved to safety from the impending ice storm. Yuki descended from her perch and landed next to Jenny, her tails swishing behind her.

"We may as well do this right," she declared, then summoned a fortress of ice that was six feet tall. She plucked Jenny off the ground and set her on the upper walls. "There, now you can see them."

"Yuki!" Mike stared at the kitsune through a gap in the hedges. "You're siding with her?"

"Indeed." She held her hands over her head and summoned flurries from the sky. "After all, you guys wouldn't let me play earlier. May as well get in on the action."

"So it's treason, then." Mike looked at Beth, then over his shoulder where Tink had appeared. "Gather the others!" he yelled with a smile. "It's time to take down the snow queen, and her little doll too!"

Mike pushed open the door to his bedroom, his cheeks bright red from the cold. He peeled off his soaking-wet pants and walked through the bathroom to throw them in the closet hamper. Tink had stripped her wet clothes off in the living room and taken them straight to the dryer while the others dispersed to change in their respective rooms.

"Having a good time, lover?" Naia was sitting in the tub, her breasts on display. Steam rose from the surface of the water, blotting out the windows.

"Indeed I am." He stripped down until he was naked and put the rest of his clothes in the laundry. The edge of the tub was warm to the touch as he stepped into the water. "Thanks for getting it hot for me."

"It's not the only thing that's hot." She winked at him as he sat down next to her. "Maybe you need something more than a bath?"

"I…uh…" He laughed. "Sorry, I was trying to think of a clever response. All the blood must have rushed somewhere else."

"I know how it is," she told him as she moved above him. "Someone gets you all bothered and you can't think straight for days."

"That obvious?"

"It is." Her groin was pressing against his, the shaft of his cock lying along her labia. "I can feel your magic all knotted up inside. I'm curious how that came about."

"Gee, I don't know. Do you really want me to talk about how hot and bothered a certain friend of mine gets me?" He touched her face, then brushed some hair out of her eyes. "What if you get jealous?"

"It just means I have to work that much harder to hold your interest." She moved her pelvis against his, and his cock grew hard. It almost felt like the heat of the water was being pushed into his body. "Would hate to find out I'm second best," she said with a fake pout.

"You're second to no one," he told her. "And this is, by far, way better than warming up with hot cocoa."

"Is that what the others are doing?" She winked at him. "There's plenty of room in here if anyone else wants to join us."

"Oh, I kind of snuck away. Beth convinced the others to come join her at the hot springs, and…" His voice trailed off as he shook his head sadly. It had been a special place for him and Velvet, and he still couldn't bring himself to go see it. Beth had arranged for a pair of portal sheds in Oregon to connect the springs to the cabin.

"It's okay," she told him, laying her head on his chest. "You don't have to talk about it if you don't want to. But I'm here to listen if you need me."

"Thanks." He held Naia against his body and inhaled her scent. It was the smell of the ocean in his dreams, a private island populated by the women he had swapped soul fragments with. He ran his fingers through her hair, curling the thick blue strands with his fingers. It was like petting silk, and due to her aqueous nature, he never had to worry about tangling it.

"It's not something I'm trying to avoid. On the contrary, I've spent a lot of time confronting it." In a way, he had to. He and Velvet had produced an egg from their union, and it would hatch sometime next year. But taking care of the future was a separate beast than dealing with the past. "The last time I was at the springs, I was there with her. If I picture them in my mind, she's there automatically. It's like I've saved that special moment and filed it away for a rainy day."

"But if you see it without her, it's like letting her go one more time."

Mike smiled, then rubbed a tear from his eye. "I couldn't have put it better. It's something I want to hold on to, if just for a little while longer." And when he finally did confront that magical meeting place, he definitely didn't want to do it in front of everyone and possibly ruin their good mood.

"You've been through a lot this year, but that was definitely the worst of it." Naia leaned away from him and traced the scar tissue on his right arm. "Speaking of, has this been hurting lately?"

"Only if I overdo it while practicing magic." He had channeled enough magic through his arm to shatter the bones, and it was sore on occasion. Some people had old football injuries; he had an old magic one. "Oh, before you make me forget, Ratu wanted me to tell you that she thinks Opal will be ready to come home in a month or so."

"That's great news!" Opal was a slime girl who had been injured in a fight with an angel. Over the course of several weeks, she had lived in Naia's bathtub while Mike had fed her magic in an attempt to help her regain her proper shape. Eventually, Ratu and Tink had built a special containment unit in the Labyrinth for further treatment. Opal was one of a kind, a being created from the raw elements that angels and demons had been forged from.

Mike hadn't understood the process itself, but once Ratu was finished, Opal would gain her independence. In the meantime, he had made sure to stop by every couple of days to visit both women and ensure they had everything they needed.

"Yeah, I thought so too. I'm not sure about sleeping arrangements, but that's just because she turns into a puddle when she sleeps. I feel bad buying her a giant bucket as a bedroom set, you know?" He slid his hands along Naia's thighs, sending tiny streamers of energy into her body. Naia sighed in pleasure, then resumed grinding her pussy on his cock.

They took their time, sharing tender kisses as she pressed against his throbbing shaft. He grabbed her by the hips and adjusted her aim so he could penetrate her on the next thrust, then let out a moan of delight as he sank into her warm depths.

"I'm not in a rush to finish," he told her. "Slow and easy sounds really nice tonight." It would also take his mind off Velvet. Though time was capable of healing all wounds, grief was often an unwelcome visitor.

Naia smiled demurely as she rode him, her hips undulating slowly above his. Her vagina swirled around his cock in a maelstrom of sexual energy, teasing him with its suction. Naia was able to manipulate her innards, and her inner folds shifted in stages as her exterior went still. To an outside observer, it would look as if nothing was happening, but Mike was experiencing the best parts of a blow job while buried deep inside Naia.

She kissed him as she ran her hands over his chest, pausing to tease his nipples. His hands went to her breasts, and he gave them a playful squeeze. He closed his eyes and buried his face in the crook of her neck, a small orgasm building up inside his body. His magic demanded to be released, but he held back.

Sometimes it was nice to take things slow.

"Ahem."

Mike opened his eyes to see Yuki standing there, her gaze to the side. He tried to ignore the burning sensation in his cheeks. It wasn't uncommon for the others to spot him having sex with someone else, but they rarely spoke up about it unless they wanted to join in.

Naia turned her head around so far that if she had bones, they would have broken.

"Hello, Yuki. Are you here to join us?"

It was the kitsune's turn to blush. "Um, no. I knocked, but nobody answered. I thought I heard something, but it was so quiet, I thought that maybe I was wrong."

"We're just taking it slow tonight." Naia's calm voice was antithetical to the sensation of fingers and tongues suddenly teasing the head of his cock. The nymph could tell he was close, and was using his embarrassment to her advantage. "What's on your mind?"

"I can come back," she said.

"Nonsense. Mike doesn't mind, do you?" She turned to face him and smiled coyly. Her pussy clamped down on his shaft, and he couldn't remember what the question was about.

"Uh…no?" His heart pounded in his chest as he was stealth fucked in front of Yuki. What was the etiquette for such a situation? Naia had given the invite and been declined. Was he supposed to pull out?

As if sensing his distraction, Naia gripped him tightly with her thighs and pulled him even further inside her.

"I was hoping I could use your bath tonight." Yuki took a step backward toward the door. "After…after you are done."

"Um, yeah. Yeah, okay." Mike fought to keep his voice steady as Naia buzzed all around him. Something was tugging at his balls and teasing the sensitive skin just below them.

"Oh, we won't be long." Naia winked at him. "Will we?"

"No?" His eyelid was twitching, but he wasn't sure if anyone could see it.

"Thank you, I'll just…wait in my room." Yuki moved toward the door and paused for a second, as if about to ask something else. Shaking her head, she turned and left.

"What was that about, do you suppose?" A naughty grin fixed itself on Naia's face as she lifted her ass and slammed it down onto his thighs, sending a burst of water up the sides of the tub. He didn't worry about the potential mess—Naia pulled any spills back into the tub with little more than a thought.

"Don't...know..." Mike grabbed her by the hips and channeled a surge of energy through her body. "But that was very naughty. Santa might not leave you any presents."

"There's only one thing I want coming down my chimney tonight." Naia tilted her head back far enough that he could feel the tips of her hair brush against his thighs. Her pussy squeezed him so hard that he groaned. "I'm just worried about how such a massive thing will fit through it!"

Mike really wanted to make a joke about opening his package, but it was too late. Naia's pussy was squeezing him in stages, and he blew a massive load deep inside her. Her eyes lit up from within as she came in response, her whole body rippling in delight as she clung to his body and moaned his name in his ear.

They sat this way for several minutes, her pussy milking every last drop of cum out of his body. He sighed as all the tension left his muscles, then relaxed completely as she shifted her weight off him.

"I should probably clean you up," she told him with a grin as she kissed her way down his chest.

"You're made of water," he pointed out. "I'm already clean."

"I'll double-check just to be sure." She winked, then slid down his torso and took his still-rigid cock in her mouth.

"Definitely want to be sure," he muttered, closing his eyes and leaning back. Naia made cute little mewling sounds as she sucked him hard once more.

THE ELEVATOR RIDE TO THE TOP OF THE SIXTY-FOUR-FLOOR Manhattan building was long, but Lily endured it. The man standing in front of her winked over his shoulder as he tucked his security card into a pocket.

"We'll get some food in your belly soon enough," he told her. "You can make it another minute or two."

"Thank you so much, mister." She hid a smile. The man, Anton Lee Dalles, was watching her in the reflection of the doors. She clutched the snow-dusted blanket tighter around her body. "I thought I might freeze to death out there."

"And you might have," he replied. "It's supposed to dip into the single digits tonight. I'm surprised you weren't at one of the shelters."

"There was someone there I would prefer to avoid." She gazed adoringly at Anton's back, knowing the man was watching her every movement. "But I didn't expect it to get so cold."

He licked his lips, and she noticed the fingers of his left hand flexing. He shifted it out of sight, but he couldn't hide his desires from her.

The elevator doors opened, revealing a small lobby with some chairs and a set of double doors. He pulled a key out of his pocket, unlocked the doors, and pushed them open.

"Thank you," she said as she walked in, making sure to drip extra snow on the floor. The suite was enormous, and a large tree had been decorated, by the window overlooking the city. Down below, the world had been blanketed in snow. If not for the last-minute rush for gifts, the streets would have been largely deserted. "Wow, you must be loaded, mister!"

"I do well enough for myself," he told her as he walked over to a minibar. "Would you like something to drink?"

Lily shook her head, allowing thick auburn curls to tumble free of her blanket. "I'm only nineteen," she told him. "I don't want to cause you any trouble."

Anton chuckled, pouring two glasses of scotch. "This is the penthouse suite," he told her. "Anything that happens here will stay between us."

Lily crossed the room and accepted the drink with a

gloved hand, the fingertips of the glove gone. She sniffed the scotch. "Wow, it smells so strong!"

"It's fifty years old," he told her, then sipped. She mimicked him, letting the liquid fire roll across her tongue. When she swallowed, she coughed dramatically, and he took the glass from her with a smile.

"It can be an acquired taste," he said, then gestured to the kitchen. "Are you hungry? I could fix you something."

Lily nodded, allowing him to go through his nice guy act. He spent almost forty minutes preparing her an amazing meal as the sun vanished behind the nearest buildings. It was a gourmet soup made from pork broth with plenty of fresh vegetables chopped up in it. He encouraged her to try some more scotch, and she obliged. A warm buzz filled her body as she allowed the alcohol to combine with whatever he had spiked the soup with.

"You have such a lovely home," she told him as she finished up her meal. "Are you sure I can stay the night? I would hate to get it dirty with these clothes."

"It isn't a problem," he told her with a smile. "If you're worried about it, you can take a quick shower and change. I have some clothes your size that you can wear."

"Um…" Lily played coy, crossing her arms. "Why do you have women's clothes?"

He chuckled as he picked up her dishes. "They belonged to my daughter. She's all grown up now, they're left over from when she lived here. I never got around to redoing her bedroom is all. I'm always busy with other stuff." His voice was reassuring, but she could practically smell his arousal.

"Is there real soap?" she asked, making her voice as hopeful as possible.

"Of course. The maid refills everything, and it isn't like anyone uses that bathroom anymore." He gestured down the hall. "It's the one at the end, on the left."

"Thank you." Lily stood and giggled as she walked down

the hall. It was hard to tell what he had spiked her food with, but it wouldn't matter in the long run. It was easier to let the drugs work on her and play along than try to fake it.

Once in the bedroom, she stripped out of her clothes and took a shower, making sure to ignore the pinhole camera in the showerhead. She put on a pretty good show of looking pathetic while washing grime out of her hair, knowing Anton was watching her right now. If he had been watching closely, he would have noticed the small seams along her calves that revealed she wore a pair of boots that were the same color as her skin. The one limitation of her shape-shifting was her inability to hide her cloven feet, but this trick was simply a scaled-up version of a magician's fake thumb tip. By the time she was naked, nobody seemed to care about the sudden rigidity of the skin around her ankles.

When she came out of the shower, she picked up her dirty clothes and tossed them into the laundry hamper before looking through the rest of the closet. There were plenty of full outfits next to each other, but she picked the blue Christmas dress that had been put in the front. She picked out white tights and pulled them on slowly in view of the camera that had been installed in the nightstand clock. In total, she had noticed three cameras in the room itself by the infrared sensors on them. Demons could see outside the visible spectrum, which helped them immensely when it came to hunting. She wondered if the cameras had been installed before Anton's daughter had moved out, but figured she would know soon enough.

The bedroom itself was pristine, as if Anton's daughter had left for college one day and never returned. Maybe it was a time capsule of another age, or perhaps something he had staged. She would know more once she was inside his mind.

After she left the bedroom, the waif's clothes in the hamper evaporated beneath the lid and turned back into demonic essence before returning unseen to her body.

"Wow," Anton told her, a big smile on his face. "Anyone ever told you that you clean up well?"

Lily smiled demurely, then accepted some hot cocoa from him. "I almost feel human again," she told him as she sat on one of his leather couches.

"I bet." He drank from his own mug, so she did the same. He had spiked this one with something else. "But that's what Christmas is about, right? Being kind to your fellow man?"

"Or woman." She smiled weakly, the muscles in her face going numb.

"I agree." He moved to sit next to her. "Bet you're feeling sleepy, aren't you?"

"A little bit," she admitted. "I think it's all the food I ate. My tummy hasn't been so full in a while. You've been so nice to me, I don't know how I can thank you." Her whole body was flooded with heat as the chemical cocktail pushed her brain into overdrive. Was it some type of Ecstasy? It was a signature blend; that was for certain. Her mind was easily able to disconnect from her body, allowing the drugs to do their work without her cognitive functions being impacted.

Anton reached over her shoulders and gave her arm a squeeze. It was gentle at first, but she could feel the iron teeth of a predator behind it.

"If I'm being honest, I'm just grateful to have company for Christmas Eve." He sipped at his cocoa, then set it down on the glass table. He picked up a remote and clicked a button, causing the nearby fireplace to turn on. Mechanical gears whirred as curtains drew themselves across the large windows. "And you even look a little bit like my daughter, so it's a bonus for me."

Lily laughed, her lips sloppy as they didn't move quite right. "Was she daddy's little girl?" she asked, her voice slightly slurred.

"Very much," he replied, his voice tender.

"I have daddy issues," she blurted out, letting tears flow.

"We had a big fight, I haven't seen him in a very long time. I wish I could show him how much I loved him."

Anton squeezed her against him, and she gave him a token resistance at first before giving in. As she leaned her head on his shoulder, she manifested her tail and stabbed him in the neck.

The descent into the Dreamscape was almost instantaneous for her. While his soul struggled to piece together the world, she guided it into place. It was a carbon copy of his penthouse, and she led its completion to mimic how it had been in the real world. It was an almost seamless transition—she felt him tense up for a moment, as if suspecting the change, then relax when she leaned into him.

In the real world, she unzipped his pants to expose his cock.

"So you miss your father?" He placed a hand on the back of her head and ran his fingers through her hair.

"What are you doing?" she asked, keeping up the act.

"Sorry, I guess you remind me of my daughter. I forgot myself." He removed his hand, but she could feel the tension in his soul. It was a simple matter to flit through his memories, to see exactly what he had planned for her. Lily smiled in the real world as she sucked his cock into her mouth and bobbed up and down.

"It's okay," she told him in a meek voice. "It makes me feel like I'm home. When things weren't bad."

He grinned, his soul blazing in triumph. His thoughts floated in the background of her mind, and she altered the dream to match. The straps of her dress slipped down, revealing her shoulder, and she pushed her arms together so he got an eyeful of cleavage when he looked down at her. It was easy enough to add a small freckle on the inside of her left breast. His daughter had one, and she could feel his pulse quicken when he noticed it.

In the Dreamscape, her body went limp from the drugs he

had slipped her. In the real world, her wings extended behind her as she purged her body of toxins while blowing Anton on his couch, eager to harvest both his seed and his soul.

Anton guided Lily to the couch, listening to her incoherent mumbling as he pulled up her skirt to reveal faded white panties. Lily watched with disinterest from a different point of view as he ripped the clothes off her and put himself between her legs.

"So what do we have here?" Mike stood in the kitchen now, sniffing the pot the soup had been cooked in. It wasn't actually Mike but rather a fragment of his soul that lived and grew inside her.

"Serial killer," Lily replied, joining him at the counter. Anton was taking his time with her body on the couch, undressing her in stages as he snapped pictures with his phone. "The bastard kills and rapes women who look like his daughter."

Mike paused, a deep frown on his face. "Don't you mean rapes and kills?"

She shrugged. "According to his memories, it's interchangeable."

"Disgusting." Mike swirled the pot around, summoning up a fresh batch of soup. "Decent chef though. So why his daughter?"

"Repressed sexual whatever. The why doesn't really matter, I give him two minutes tops in the real world." As she spoke to Mike in the Dreamscape, she could sense the beginning of Anton's orgasm in the real world. "But Christmas Eve is special. He finds a homeless girl or a hooker who reminds him of his daughter, spends all night with her here at his home, then dumps the body in the river on his way to spend Christmas Day with his daughter and her family. It's pretty disgusting."

"Agreed." Mike poured himself a bowl of soup, then made one for Lily. "How did you find him?"

"A predator's instincts." She accepted the soup and sat with him. "I was on the hunt, and so was he. Was curious what his vice was, and now here we are."

"Horrible. He deserves what's coming." He ate his meal, ignoring Anton's actions in the background. Mike's soul fragment was almost always present in the Dreamscape now and had witnessed some pretty terrible things from her choice in prey. Ever since Mike had become her master, she could only feed on the wicked.

Not that she minded. It was far preferable to the innocents she had been forced to prey upon for the last few centuries.

Anton had posed Lily a dozen different ways, snapping pictures the entire time. Though seconds had passed in the real world, it had been a few hours in the Dreamscape. He was stroking himself while taking pictures, the muscles on his abdomen flexing as he blew his first load on Lily's chest. In the real world, Lily began swallowing Anton's load, pulling his soul with it.

"That's my cue." Lily stepped away from the counter and hopped back into her dream body. She fast-forwarded the dream until it was almost sunrise. Anton, thinking he had spent an evening violating his prey, was ready to seal the deal by strangling her.

He put on a pair of black gloves and squeezed Lily by the neck. She took a few wheezing breaths, then opened her eyes and seized him by the throat. When she squeezed, his eyes bulged in his head at the sheer strength of her grip.

"Wh…what?" Anton struggled for air as the lithe thing beneath him cut off the oxygen to his brain. He stood, and Lily followed, wrapping her legs around his waist so he couldn't escape. Anton was strong from years of preparation, working out to ensure he could dump a body without getting exhausted.

But this was the Dreamscape, and Lily was fully in charge. No amount of CrossFit would help him here. Anton flung Lily around helplessly, unable to knock her off or escape as she continued to squeeze him by the throat.

"Are you gonna rip off his balls?" Mike asked.

"Nah," she replied casually. Anton couldn't hear her when she spoke; all he could see was the face of his own daughter as Lily transformed the rest of the way into her. "I've got something better planned for him. It is Christmas, after all."

Anton managed to break Lily's grip by slamming her into a chair and fled for the lobby. She gave chase with no intent to catch him, delighting in seeing the relief in his eyes as he got into the elevator and managed to close the doors before she could get there. A dial appeared over the elevator with a number at the top.

"Is that for my benefit?" Mike asked as he sat on one of the couches.

"Nah, he'll spot it eventually." The number was 666, and the dial slowly did a full rotation before settling at the top once more. Lily waved her hand, transforming the private area into the lobby of the building.

With a loud ding, the elevator doors opened, and Anton stumbled out.

"Help me! Somebody help!" His face was covered in scratches as he ran for the revolving door. It was snowing outside, and as he pushed his way through the door, the world transformed into his apartment.

"Ooh, clever." Mike watched with interest as Anton sprinted back into the lobby so fast that he tripped and fell, landing on his face. A lobby attendant appeared from behind the desk, and she ran over to assist him.

"Sir, are you okay?" she asked.

"Please, help me, I…" His eyes widened when he recognized the lobby attendant.

"Sure, I'll help you." The attendant herself was one of the thousands of souls Lily had consumed, forced to do her bidding for all eternity. The soul was wearing the face of a young woman named Michelle who had been murdered by Anton almost twenty years ago. He had gone through his collection enough times that all his victims were burned into his brain. What he had considered a treasure trove of memories was about to become the arsenal that undid him.

Anton shrieked in horror and crawled free before Michelle could do anything to him. He made it into the stairwell and let out a primal scream.

"What's in there?" Mike asked.

"He's back in his apartment." Lily licked her lips as her mind flitted to the real world. Anton's soul stretched like a rubber band from his body to her mouth, then snapped free so she could consume it. Over the days ahead, she would strip him bare, consuming his very identity until his soul was little more than a tortured husk that would do her bidding. "Only this time, he's a girl, and I'm going to make him relive each of his murders from the woman's point of view."

"Fitting." Mike screwed up his face in contemplation. "But is it enough?"

She shrugged. "What is true justice? If I steal twenty dollars from someone, I could be forced to give it back. It undoes the deed but not the harm itself. But when it comes to a life, what then? Does killing this man undo the harm he's caused to the girls he murdered? Do their relatives miraculously feel better? An eternity in Hell is, for most people, the best they can ever hope for."

He shrugged. "I guess not. It's probably a question for someone higher up."

"Yeah, well they aren't talking to anyone." Lily stepped out of the Dreamscape and back into the real world. Anton lay reclined on his couch, his eyes locked on the ceiling as his body continued to live on without him. Doctors would be puzzled, and experts would be brought in to evaluate his condition. His daughter, wherever she was, would probably spend her life savings keeping the man alive.

After consuming a soul, Lily became privy to all its secrets. Sifting through Anton's memories revealed he had been a devoted father with demented tastes. He had shown nothing but care and kindness for his offspring, and his eventual decline would cause no small amount of worry and financial destruction.

"But not if we pull the Band-Aid off," Lily muttered. She wandered through Anton's home until she found his collection. It was hidden behind a plate in the back of his closet that was held shut by magnetic locks. Inside the hole was a small box with several solid-state drives, each one labeled with the initials of a woman he had murdered.

Anton's daughter would no doubt come looking for her dad once he failed to show up for Christmas. Based on Anton's warped memories, Lily couldn't be certain whether his daughter would do the right thing and attempt to bring closure to the families of the murdered women.

"Damn it, Romeo, you're making me soft." She reached into her corset and pulled out a small clamshell phone. She typed out a quick message as she stacked the drives next to Anton's laptop, then set the phone next to them.

Eulalie would know what to do with all this. After Lily hit send, Eulalie would have one of the rats chew a portal to Anton's apartment to retrieve the computer and the drives within the hour. It wasn't the first time they'd done this—in fact, it had become part of Lily's routine to try to out the murderous people she consumed. Since Lily knew all Anton's passwords, Eulalie wouldn't even need to break into his files. Any digital evidence of Lily's intrusion would be erased, and the rest would be turned over to the authorities.

Eventually, the police would know who the murdered girls were, which might bring closure to their families. Satisfied that she had done her part, Lily sauntered back into Anton's living room and contemplated the man on the couch. She straddled his body and grabbed his head with both hands.

She twisted his head around hard enough that it faced backward. His daughter would be horrified to discover Anton had been murdered, but now the poor girl wouldn't go broke trying to fix the piece of shit.

The deed committed, she wandered over to the minibar and contemplated the selection. There were some very fine spirits here, and she picked up an unopened bottle of whiskey.

"Pappy Van Winkle," she read aloud. She knew from Anton's memory that the shit was expensive and would probably be a decent present for Mike. Of course, she was looking forward to giving him his real present later. He had always been very careful not to ask her to shape-shift during sex, so she was curious what kink he would have her enact.

Satisfied that her work was done, she walked over to the curtains and pulled them open to reveal the city. Down below, the world kept moving as it always had, the inhabitants of New York unaware that she had cauterized an unseen cancer from it.

"Merry Christmas, you worthless bastards. You're fucking welcome!" she yelled as she smacked her hand against the glass. Smiling, she contemplated opening the whiskey and drinking some of it. After all, she had done her good deed for the holiday. Smirking, she sank into the Dreamscape to check on Anton and make certain he was adequately miserable.

His soul cried out in agony as if on fire, and she slowed time in the Dreamscape to a crawl. Minutes in the real world would become days in here, which meant Anton would experience a lifetime of torment before Lily finished feasting on him. Satisfied that his demise wouldn't be quick, she stayed to watch as he experienced the murder of Michelle from her point of view. Hours passed as Anton was eventually strangled by a copy of himself, and Lily smirked as the dream faded and he was escorted in again by his clone. His second victim had taken hours to die from strangulation, and she couldn't wait to watch as Anton gasped for breath while hanging in his own bedroom closet.

A powerful cramp formed inside her physical body, causing her to drop the bottle of whiskey. It fell in slow motion, then shattered in a burst of glass on the cold marble at her feet. With her mind half in the Dreamscape, she watched as the falling snow outside slowed to a crawl. Down below, moving cars froze in place on the streets, as if someone had hit pause on a movie.

Was she under attack? What was going on? If not for her accelerated state of mind, she doubted she would have even had time to respond to whatever was happening. Her thoughts were muddy as she dug deep into her core and activated the magic that would take her directly to Mike. The world outside went still as Anton's apartment disappeared in a puff of smoke.

THE FIRE CRACKLED IN THE FIREPLACE AS MIKE SAT IN HIS NEW recliner. It had been an early gift from Eulalie, who was spending a quiet evening with Bigfoot. It was her first Christmas without her father and her sister, and she had decided that a quiet evening with her uncle at the cabin was the best course of action.

The house was quiet. Sofia had dropped by long enough to make dinner for everyone, then had gone back to the Library while Mike, Tink, and Kisa started working on the dishes. There was apparently a rush on new stories being published right before Christmas, and she was already behind in cataloging them.

Kisa and Tink shared hot cocoa by the hearth, wearing package bows that they had stuck to each other. The Christmas tree was packed with presents underneath, most of them from Mike to the others. Even though many of the members of the house didn't celebrate the holiday, Mike had gone ahead and bought them gifts anyway. To him, it had always been more about giving than receiving.

"Do you think we'll see Santa tonight?" Death sat in a recliner of his own. It was far narrower than Mike's and made of black leather. He had a plate of biscuits in his lap and would occasionally toss one into Ticktock's mouth. The mimic was currently imitating a large present with green wrapping paper and would lick its lips with a ribbon-shaped tongue.

"I don't know. You might fall asleep too soon." Mike tried to hide his smile.

"You know that I do not sleep, Mike Radley." Death turned his gaze back to the fireplace. "Though, do you suppose that I'm a liability? Perhaps he will know I'm awake and choose not to descend our chimney tonight. Mike Radley, this was mentioned in one of your Christmas songs!"

"Those songs are for children." Yuki walked into the living room with a towel wrapped around her head. She was wearing a thick white bathrobe that matched the bushy tips of her tails. "The whole holiday is a scam."

Mike frowned. Yuki struggled with Christmas, but he didn't blame her. The few Christmases she had celebrated with Emily had been poisoned by later deeds. Last year, she had locked herself in her room and refused to come out. He had been extremely happy when she offered to judge the snowball fight earlier while Sofia finished up Christmas dinner for everyone, and even more so when she had joined Jenny in the free-for-all that had frozen him half to death afterward.

"It is not a scam," Death replied. "Surely the whole world isn't in on the same conspiracy!"

Yuki rolled her eyes. "Look, you all have fun sucking on candy canes, but I'm going to bed." She looked over at Mike and gave him a small bow. "Thanks for letting me use the bath tonight."

"No problem." He gave her a smile. "You sure you don't want to join us?"

The kitsune's eyes scanned the room, then settled on the tree. She snorted, then shook her head. "I'm good. Guess I'll see you all in the morning."

"Good night, then." He watched as she ascended the stairs, then waited until he heard the telltale click of her bedroom door above. "Wish she enjoyed the holiday like we do."

"Ah, but if everyone was the same, then nobody would be different!" Death chuckled to himself, then sat forward. "But perhaps you can enlighten me on why she called Christmas a scam?"

"Tink, maybe ease up on the booze," he said, desperate to change the subject. Tink giggled by the fireplace, then poured some more alcohol from a flask into her hot cocoa before offering some to Kisa. The goblin's cheeks were flush and her eyelids drooping.

Kisa abstained. Her cat biology didn't pair well with alcohol.

"Christmas is Tink's favorite holiday!" Tink declared while waving her mug around. "Get big presents, sometimes eat too many cookies and get big sick."

At the mention of cookies, Kisa grabbed the nearby plate and moved it somewhere else. The pom-pom on her Santa hat hung over her shoulders, bouncing along her collarbone as she stuck her head under the tree and rearranged a few of the presents.

"Boo!" Cecilia appeared from the tree, her ethereal body passing through its branches. Kisa hissed and scrambled backward, her hair standing on end. The banshee waved her hands around menacingly over the cat girl. "I'm the Ghost of Christmas Past!"

"Fuck you," Kisa replied, then ripped off her hat and threw it at Cecilia. The banshee caught the hat and stuck it on her head. While she adjusted it, the red streak in her hair poked out from beneath, and she swept it behind one ear. Tink cackled where she sat, spilling some of her hot cocoa.

"Are we playing *A Christmas Carol?*" Death tossed the last of the biscuits to Ticktock, then leaned forward in his chair. He let out a raspy breath as he pointed dramatically at Kisa.

"Ew, stop that shit." Kisa hopped into Mike's lap and put her head on his shoulder. "If you don't protect me, I'll bite you."

He hugged her tight. "Okay, everyone, lay off. That goes double for you, Tink."

Tink bared her fangs at him. "Husband kiss Tink's butt. Maybe kiss something else too." She turned around and bent over, revealing her bare ass.

Mike hoped nobody bought Tink underwear. If so, it was money wasted. Cecilia leaned down to kiss Mike on the cheek, then gave Kisa her hat back. With a wink, she faded from sight.

"I think Christmas may be my favorite holiday." Death sat back in his chair and stared at the ceiling. "I think it's all the bright lights that people put out. I'm rather surprised you didn't put any up."

"You can blame Quetzalli for that," Mike responded. By some twist of fate, Tink and the storm dragon had discovered that sticking a plug in Quetzalli's nostrils would allow her to power the lights. This had led to an experiment to see how many lights Quetzalli could power, which had eventually resulted in the destruction of thousands of LED lights. There was a shortage now, and he had been unable to find suitable replacements in time.

"Is that why she isn't here tonight?" Death had spent most of his time the last week wandering the city to look at decorations. Most people couldn't see him, and the few who did often turned away and forgot. The visage of Death was rarely a welcome sight, doubly so right before Christmas.

"No. Dana wanted to reconnect with her family and took Quetzalli with her for emotional support. She's posing as the new girlfriend to account for all the time she's been missing, which will probably cause problems."

"Because of her horn?" Death asked.

Mike shook his head. "Ratu enchanted a napkin ring to hide it. As long as Quetzalli doesn't headbutt somebody, it'll stay hidden. It's the fact that she looks like she's twice Dana's age that could rile Dana's parents up." When Quetzalli had been transformed into a human by the fairy queen, she had been given the form of a woman in her mid-to-late forties.

"I am uncertain why her parents would mind," Death replied. "Even though the relationship is a farce, wouldn't they appreciate that their daughter has found somebody with wisdom and maturity like their own?"

"I think, for most people, it's the fear that the wisdom and maturity are being used to manipulate the younger partner. Think about when you first arrived at the house. There were so many things for you to learn, you probably would have believed anything we told you."

Death nodded in understanding. "Not anything, but yes, I think I see your point. I would have been easy to manipulate."

"You still are," Kisa grumbled. "Have you found the Krampus yet?"

"What?" Mike looked at Kisa. "What are you talking about?"

Death frowned, then set down his tea and folded his hands. "Tinker Radley informed me that the Krampus was a demon who would steal toys from children. I regret that I have been unable to find him these last few days."

"Tink!" Mike leaned forward far enough in his chair that Kisa had to slide out. "Did you tell Death he had to save Christmas by sending him on a snipe hunt?"

"I was unable to find the snipe this summer," Death added. "But luckily, it never ate all the roses in our garden."

Tink cackled so hard that she fell over on her back. "Bone face try so hard to save Christmas, scare way more kids in the process!"

"Scared children? How?" Mike looked up at Death. "What did you do?"

"Tinker Radley told me that the Krampus preyed on vulnerable children." Death nodded sagely. "So she suggested I look at the Children's Hospital, and so many of the kids there could see me, and—"

Mike was out of his chair, ready to grab the troublesome goblin, but she saw him coming and scurried under the tree.

"Too far, Tink! Too far!" He crouched and pushed some presents out of the way. Tink had pressed herself against the back wall beneath the tree and was just out of reach. She blew a raspberry at Mike and tried to stand up behind the tree.

The back door slammed, and Beth walked into the living room with a bundle of packages under her arms. Behind her, Suly carried in several more, both his arms full.

"Sorry 'bout the door," he said. "Gettin' right windy out there, can hardly see."

Mike looked up at Suly, then cursed when Tink bolted from behind the tree and disappeared up the stairs.

"Is there room under that tree?" Beth sat down with her knees folded beneath her and handed Mike the gifts. He couldn't help but notice the cream-colored tights under her burgundy sweater dress.

"Uh, yeah." He shifted packages around and helped Beth place hers. They were meticulously wrapped with shimmering bows on each. He paused when he got to a bright silver one with yellow stripes. It had his son's name on it, but Zel's foal had been terrified of Mike every time he had come to visit. Apparently, only having two legs was akin to being the monster under the bed for some centaur children, and his son was only a few months old. Centaur infants were more like human three-year-olds, which meant that logic and reason didn't always line up as they should.

He hoped the gift would thaw the ice a bit, but turned his thoughts toward the woman in front of him. Dwelling on being his son's personal boogeyman would only bring everyone else down. "Looks like you went all out."

"Only a bit. It's hard to buy gifts for people who don't really believe in physical possessions." She lowered her voice to a whisper. "Most of it is candy and treats."

He nodded. It wasn't a bad strategy. His gifts were mostly practical, like a new pair of shears for Suly to use, or some new drill bits for Tink. Truthfully, he could have blown thousands of dollars on each person, but Beth was right about them not really caring about things. It was experiences that mattered, and if he could give them something that would make their day-to-day lives easier, it was a no-brainer.

"So does that mean I got candy too?" he asked, seeing the gift with his name on it. He picked it up and gave it a shake, but Beth snatched it away.

"No snooping," she told him, then stuck it somewhere else. "Unless you'll let me shake what you have for me."

Kisa snorted hard enough to startle him. Beth's cheeks turned red as she restrained a laugh. Mike tried to keep his face neutral as he picked up an oblong package hidden tucked far beneath the tree.

"Go for it." He handed the gift over. "Shake it all day, you won't guess."

The golden flecks in her eyes sparkled as she shook the box up and down. He could sense her magic now, hovering around her like a perfume. Not sure what sort of spell she was using to see inside a box, he put his middle finger beneath his thumb to summon a tiny spark, then flicked it in front of her face, where it sparkled like a tiny firecracker. Distracted, her magic disappeared and she nearly dropped the gift in surprise.

"No cheating," he told her.

"How did you know that wouldn't hit me?" she asked, her tone suddenly serious.

"Because you have my full attention," he responded. The air in the room suddenly felt hotter than usual. "I mean, uh, I'm not distracted. I'm in control. That's what I mean."

Beth bit her lip for a moment, as if contemplating his answer. It almost looked like those gold flecks of hers were moving. "What if I said I wanted it to?"

"I'm gonna check in on my sister," Suly announced. "I can sense her out front. Maybe sit with her awhile and watch the flurries fall." With that, he left through the front door, letting in a cold blast of air that ruffled Beth's hair.

"Let's go find Tink." Kisa grabbed Death by the hand and pulled him out of his seat.

"But I wish to stay by the fire," Death protested.

"I'll let you open a present early."

"Then my hand shall not be stayed!" Death slammed the rest of his tea and stood, the tinsel garland around his neck shimmering in the firelight. He practically dragged Kisa out of the room as her stockinged feet slid on the smooth wooden floor.

Mike couldn't help but notice that everyone had vacated the room, and felt his pulse quicken. Beth sat across from him, her eyes glittering with liquid gold. Magic had changed her in so many ways, and he wondered how many of them were similar to his own. If there was anything Beth had been good at, it was exuding confidence. It was a trait he felt lacking in himself, and though the attraction had always been there, it was kind of a relief that she was making the first move.

"You…do know what would happen if it did, right?"

Beth smirked, leaning in close. "Oh, I'm aware. If not for the geas, the whole neighborhood would be aware."

"I…" He chuckled, amazed at how awkward he felt. "I have to admit something first."

"Oh?"

"I've always thought you were pretty. Even before, well, all this." He gestured around him, referring to not only the house but everything that had happened. "When we first met, I was kind of a nervous mess around you. Maybe that carried forward, I don't know."

"You don't say." Beth arched an eyebrow.

He laughed. "Yeah, I'm sorry about that. It's just, for me, I always worried that I might be crossing a line. I'm aware of my effect on people, and I never wanted to take advantage of that, especially not with you. But you're different now, so maybe it wouldn't be an issue, but..."

"You sure do talk a lot for a man who's about to get laid." She moved toward him, and he put a hand up to stop her.

"Lily, I swear to God, if that's you, I'm going to be so pissed," he whispered. Beth had never been this direct, and the succubus had mocked him endlessly over his inability to move on his attraction to Beth. On numerous occasions, she had even offered to turn into the beautiful lawyer during sex, but he had always declined.

Beth pushed his hand away. "I've had a lot of time to think about the things I want. And I've decided that one of them is you, and I'm tired of waiting for it. If I need to throw a shout-out to Jesus or God while I'm riding you to make this happen, then so be it."

Mike's mouth went dry at the realization that this was the real deal. Lily was well known for her dislike of the divine to the point that she abhorred even the mention of God.

"Why now?" he asked, his voice barely audible. Even after all this time and everything that had happened, there was a small part of him that still didn't believe. Perhaps it was because they had met back before the magic had become a part of him. In his eyes, she had always been amazing, and was even more so now. With so many magical men in her own life, the idea that she would still desire him this much had his heart racing.

"I always felt like you were so far ahead of me," she replied in a whisper. "But now I've finally caught up."

She leaned forward into him, her lips pressing into his. The magic inside him swelled up and washed over both of them, hissing as streamers formed along his skin. He closed his eyes and allowed the magic to carry him away, savoring the soft touch of her lips.

Beth held perfectly still. He tried to part her lips with his tongue but was puzzled when she held them firmly together. Opening his eyes, he saw that her own eyes were closed, but she was frozen in place.

"Um..." He backed away, wondering what had gone wrong, then noticed that Beth still hadn't moved. Her lips were frozen in mid pucker, with a slight gap in the middle. "Beth? Are you okay?"

Worried that his magic had done something weird, he stood and backed away. The temperature in the air dropped, and a low rumbling sound filled the air. It became louder, making the whole house shake.

"Hey!" He fell backward into his chair, but Beth remained motionless, as if glued to the floor. The ornaments on the tree didn't even sway as Mike fought to regain his footing.

The fireplace groaned, as if about to burst from the heat. The bricks of the hearth glowed from within as if superheated, and the flames changed colors and shot sparks into the living room.

"Tink! Kisa! Someone!" He tried to move toward Beth to pull her to safety, but when he grabbed her by the wrist, he couldn't budge her. The world tilted sideways, and he fell away from the hearth as the flames in the fireplace exploded in intensity. A loud scream filled the air as a massive object shot out from the flames, barely missing Beth and destroying the living room table along the way. It slid through the room and slammed into the doorway of the office, cracking the plaster around the frame.

Mike rose to his feet, the air crackling around him as he summoned his magic. Something had just violently invaded his home, and he wasn't about to let it start trouble.

The object was red, with gold and silver runners on the sides. It was far too massive to have fit through the fireplace, and he grabbed the poker from the fireplace and used the hook end to grab the runner and pull on it.

"Mike Radley, what is going on?" Death stood on the second floor, looking down at Mike over the railing with his hands clasped around Tink's ankles. The goblin tried to kick him but paused when she saw the object blocking the office. Her skirt had fallen down to reveal her ass and bare pussy. If not for her tail, her dress would be over her face.

"Get ready for a fight," he told them as he yanked on the runner. The wooden object creaked as it tipped over, revealing an ornate sleigh covered in silver bells that emitted no sound when it struck the ground. In the back of the sleigh was a giant red bag tied shut with a golden rope.

A tiny figure stood, her red hat knocked sideways. Long blonde braids hung behind pointy ears, and her hair and shoulders were covered in snow. She tried to stand but fell over the front of the sleigh and landed hard on her butt. Her red dress was rimmed with white velvet, and she wore candy-cane tights above curly-toed shoes. Shaking her head, she squinted up the stairs.

"Tinker?" Her high-pitched voice was filled with both recognition and hope. Her bright-green eyes flitted to the dark figure holding the goblin, then back to Tink, her pupils widening as she gasped. The pale skin of her cheek looked as if it had been brushed with golden glitter, and she raised a gloved hand to her mouth. "Oh my Santa."

Her eyelids fluttered as she fainted, her head thunking against the sled and knocking off her hat. She went limp on the floor, her splayed-out limbs making her look like a large doll.

"Tink? You know this person?" Mike looked up the stairs.

Kisa had appeared from the hallway, her mouth agape as she gazed at the scene.

"Tink don't know," she replied, still upside down. "Maybe familiar? Can't remember."

The stench of sulfur filled the air, and a pair of hands wrapped protectively around him from behind.

"Romeo, something's wrong, I..." Lily went silent, and he turned to look at her. She was glaring at the scene before them, her lip twitching. Different emotions crossed her face, but chief among them was puzzlement. "What the hell is this?"

"You know as much as we do," he told her, waving his hand at the sleigh. The whole scene was unbelievable, but maybe he should have expected it. If Bigfoot, the fae, and the Jersey Devil were all real, then why not one of Santa's elves?

Death dropped Tink on the ground with a thud and put both hands on his cheekbones while doing a little dance.

"Mike Radley! Do you know what this means?" Death's eyes blazed with unholy fire. "We are going to meet Santa Claus!"

NOT A CREATURE WAS STIRRING

Yuki sat in bed with her knees pulled up against her chest. In one hand was an old copy of *Alice in Wonderland*, and in the other was a handful of fox fire. Her bedroom light was off, since the fox fire provided plenty of light to read by.

Alice wasn't even open. Instead, she ran her fingers over the well-loved cover, tracing the portrait in the middle. It had been a gift from Emily, the only true love of her life. The two had been inseparable until Emily had fallen under the influence of the shadow and locked Yuki in a tower world. The last time she had seen Emily alive was when the former Caretaker had returned to steal her eye for a magical ritual.

A single tear fell on the book, and Yuki wiped it away, smearing condensation across the cover. Her relationship with Emily had been a lifetime ago, in human terms, anyway. The hurt was still there, but time had a habit of helping old wounds scar over.

She opened the book and ran her fingers over the pages. There was once a moment where she had opened this book for the first time. Its pages would have seen a young, vibrant kitsune that was hopeful for a future filled with love and laughter. Later, it bore witness to heartbreak followed by inconsolable rage. The book was like an old friend. It had seen her both at her best and her worst.

Moving the fox fire closer, she wondered how long it would take the book to burn away completely. It was just one of many tendrils remaining that connected her to the past, but it was easily the one that hurt the most.

Her conversation with Naia had been a long one. She hadn't wanted to have it in the backyard, where anyone could listen in. However, walking in on Mike and Naia having sex had definitely thrown her off. It wasn't the first time she had seen it, but it was perhaps the longest she had actually watched.

"What do I want?" she wondered aloud, then set her book down on the nightstand. She closed her hand, extinguishing the fox fire and plunging the room into darkness. Yuki lay back on the bed, her gaze on the ceiling. More than once, it felt like she was still trapped in that other world while this one kept spinning without her. It was easy enough to put on a brave face, to act like nothing was bothering her. Out of everyone in the house, it was Mike who had seen through the mirage. He seemed to understand exactly what she was going through.

Sighing, she pulled a pillow over her face and groaned as she went over her conversation with Naia.

"Is it okay that I'm ready to move on?" she asked as she stared blankly at her feet. She sat naked in the tub, her back pressed against Naia's knees as the nymph rubbed her shoulders.

"That's something only you can know," Naia replied.

"It's strange, but I feel like I should be happier about it. Forgiveness hasn't been easy, but..." Yuki shrugged, which sent ripples through the water. "It's like that gaping hole in the middle of me is finally...okay. It's not great, but I no longer feel like I'm one step away from falling apart."

Naia stopped rubbing Yuki's shoulders and started braiding her hair just below the ears. "I think it's wonderful that you feel that way. It's been over a year since your return. I often thought it would take you much longer to get to where you are today."

Yuki flicked the water with a finger, releasing just enough of her magic to freeze the water droplet as it formed. It plunked back into the bath, then floated from her and melted away.

"Realistically, it should have," she replied. "But I think you know part of the reason I feel this way."

Naia leaned into Yuki, hugging her tightly from behind. "It's him, isn't it?" she asked in a low whisper.

Yuki said nothing for several moments, then nodded. She had spent so many years with Emily and the others of the house. Her continued sense of loneliness was further aggravated by the fact that she was the only one who had retained memories of their years together. As the only witness to Emily's time as Caretaker, she felt uniquely qualified to assess it. Personal betrayals and corruption aside, Emily had provided a home that was far safer than anywhere else on the planet, to Yuki's knowledge.

Comparing Emily to Mike, though, was a no-brainer. Even though Mike's world seemed to be far more dangerous, his successes already far exceeded anything Emily had ever been capable of. Emily's home had been safe, but she had definitely played favorites. The love in Mike's home was palpable in the way he treated everyone and went out of his way to make time for them. He gave selflessly and treated the others like equals.

"He gives me hope," Yuki finally replied. "I'm still scared that he will fall from grace, but after what I saw in the spring…"

She didn't have to finish the statement, because Naia knew exactly what she referred to. There had been a moment in Oregon when Mike had been surrounded by all the power of the forest. His magic had gone wild, forming behind him like an ominous set of black wings. The darkness had come, ready to twist him into a being of power and fury—if he survived the process. Leeds had taken something precious from Mike, killing a woman he loved for no other reason than to hurt him.

Steeped in such power, Mike had diverted the killing blow at the last moment and poured his magic into revitalizing the land instead. She alone had seen that raw power form above him, spreading apart into wings made of shadows, eager to be unleashed and do his bidding. In the grip of such anger, he had not only found mercy but had also acted on it.

"True strength comes from within," Yuki whispered, hugging herself tightly. "It's an ancient lesson that is hard to truly understand, and yet he does. He proved it to me on the day he saved my life, the same day he gave up a wish for his heart's desire to not just save my life but restore my heart and mind. He did so again in the forest while gripped by a terrifying wrath. He shows the others a kindness I can't fully describe, giving of himself whenever he is able. I want to be strong like him, to find it in my heart to keep moving forward."

Naia ran her hands through Yuki's fur, then filled the tub with more hot water while the two sat in comfortable silence for nearly an hour. Yuki's thoughts were like the tendrils of water vapor rising from the water, easy to see yet difficult to grasp.

Even now, hours later, she still didn't know how to move beyond her past to become a better version of herself. She was stuck.

A loud banging sound from downstairs had her instantly on her feet. She slid into her robes, the fabric cool against her bare skin. Opening the bedroom door, she ran down the hallway. Below, she could hear the others talking, and paused at the railing to take in the sight of a small woman slumped on the ground next to a massive sleigh, with Mike squatting over her.

"I'm just saying, Romeo, that the big man is going to be pissed at you for killing one of his cookie makers." Lily stood behind Mike with her arms crossed. Though her tone was comical, there was a defensive set to her shoulders that Yuki didn't like at all.

"What's happening?" Yuki demanded as she descended the stairs. "Are we under attack?"

"If we are, it's a weird one." Kisa stood next to Death and Tink, who was busy adjusting her dress. "That weird little bitch down there crashed her sled and passed out."

"Where did the sled come from?" Yuki asked as she made it to the bottom floor.

"The fireplace," Mike replied. "And that's not all. Look."

He pointed into the living room. Yuki narrowed her eyes at the sight of Beth frozen on her hands and knees. Her lips were puckered together, but she was like stone.

"Is it a spell?" Yuki asked as she moved closer to Beth. She knelt and poked Beth with a candy cane from the tree. It broke apart without so much as making an impression in Beth's skin.

"If it is, it's a big one." Lily knelt beside her. "I was in New York when I felt everything coming to a halt. Would have missed it if I hadn't been balls-deep in the Dreamscape having a snack while watching the snow falling outside. Teleported back here in time to see this. I think whatever is happening isn't just occurring here."

"There's one way to find out." Yuki moved to the window and looked outside. Swirling flakes of snow were frozen in the air as if the whole world had become a painting.

"Oh sparkles." The tiny figure on the floor shifted, then pushed herself up to her knees. Yuki blinked when she realized the figure was dressed as one of Santa's elves. "Is Tinker's dress back on? I saw…everything." She shuddered and then opened her eyes to look at Mike. "You shouldn't be here," she said.

"I think you just stole my line." Mike pointed the poker at her. "Who the hell are you?"

The elf looked woozy for a moment, then held her hand against the sleigh to steady herself.

"My name is Holly," she said, then rubbed at her ears, which had gone red. "And please don't use naughty words around me. I don't want to get—"

"Shhhiiitttt." Lily stretched the word out as she said it. "Fuck."

"Oh!" Holly tipped over as if losing her balance. "No, really, this isn't a—"

"Asshole." Lily grinned as Holly hyperventilated. "Oh, you are too pure. You wanna see a perfect pair of tits?"

"Lily." Mike's tone of voice was serious. "Let her talk, please."

Holly nodded, the pom-pom on her hat ringing as if it had a bell inside. "I don't have much time. Well, I have all the time I need, but maybe it's not enough."

Mike cleared his throat and knelt by the elf. "I just want you to know that you wrecked my living room with a magic sled. I request that you be very direct with me in regard to what is going on and how you got in here. The geas should have kept you out, and I need to know how you bypassed it."

Holly nodded, then adjusted her hat. "Okay, where to begin?"

"Is this Santa's sled?" Death was running his fingers over the velvet fabric on the seat. "And is that his bag? Does it have presents inside?" He reached for the bag, his eyes burning brightly.

Holly scrambled up onto the sled and slapped Death's hand away from the bag. "That is not for you," she declared. "So you stay away from those presents!"

"But I've been good this year!" Death hopped up and down, his hood bouncing along his back. "And the rules say you get a present if you're good!"

The elf rolled her eyes and turned to open the bag. "If it'll keep you quiet, here." She pulled a small box from the bag and handed it to Death. "To answer your questions, though, this is Santa's sled, this is his bag, and all the presents in the world are inside."

"Why are you here?" Yuki glared at the elf and was pleased to see her cower a little in fear. If Holly was indeed a threat, she was likely a weak one. Still, it wouldn't do to underestimate her.

"I came for her." Holly pointed at Tink. "There's a huge problem at the North Pole, and I know she can help."

"Tink help?" The goblin looked at Mike and shrugged. "Maybe. Good at many things, like trick Tink do with her mouth that—"

Holly pulled a pinch of something white from a pouch around her belt and threw it in Tink's face. Stunned, the goblin took a step back as Mike grabbed the elf by her collar with one hand and lifted her out of the sled to hold her in the air.

"If you just hurt her," he growled, the air around him rippling.

"No!" Tink grabbed the hem of Mike's shirt and tugged on it. "Pointy ears no hurt Tink, help Tink remember!"

Holly nodded, a terrified expression on her face. "That's all it was, it'll help speed things up! You see, Tinker has helped out at the North Pole a couple of times when the furnace broke down. It won't fix all our problems, but it'll help!"

"What problems?" Mike lowered Holly into the seat of the sled. "And why is everything frozen?"

Holly let out a relieved breath and pulled a thick crushed-velvet hat from beneath the seat. It was the richest red Yuki had ever seen and smelled like peppermint.

"Okay, so this is gonna be hard to believe, but here goes." She handed the hat to Mike. "Santa is missing, and the North Pole has gone dark. No elves, no reindeer. It's like everyone just...vanished."

"And so you came here?" Yuki looked into the living room. "And what did you do to her? Or everyone, for that matter."

"That's not me. It happens every year." Holly moved over to Beth and casually hopped onto her back. "It's a time lock. Santa activates it so he can deliver presents to the entire world in a single night. The whole world is frozen right now and will stay that way for, well, until we can find him and undo the lock."

Yuki frowned and knelt by Beth. She wasn't breathing, but her skin still held a healthy glow. If it was a stasis spell, she would have turned blue and died by now. "You say the whole world is frozen in time, but we aren't. You aren't. Explain."

"That's because of the sled. It creates a field. Anyone near it who isn't a human gets excluded. This lets Santa have extra helpers if he needs them. Anyone staying at the North Pole is also excluded—this is just an extension of that feature." She tilted her head at Mike. "Though, I'm curious why you aren't affected."

"Didn't pay my human union dues," Mike explained. "They took my card away."

"It's a compass!" Death had opened his gift and held it up proudly. It was a fancy silver compass that looked similar to a pocket watch and was inlaid with a white mother-of-pearl face with a nautical compass rose painted onto it. "I've always wanted one of these!"

"You have?" Mike asked.

"Well, I didn't know that until I had one." Death held up the chain that was attached to the compass and then looped it around his neck. "It is beautiful, thank you."

"Guys, focus!" Yuki turned back toward Holly. "Okay, so you needed help and came here…why?"

"Pointy ears come for Tink," the goblin declared proudly. "Tink fix furnace, big thing, lots of tunnels!"

"Tink is the only one who can fix the furnace, it's true. But the real reason I came here was…" Holly took a deep breath, then let it out. "Sheer desperation. I didn't know where else to go and brought the sled and gifts with me to keep them out of the hands of whoever shut everything down."

"If everything is shut down, how did you manage to escape?" Lily sneered at the elf, who backed away from the succubus. "What makes you so special that you didn't just get gobbled up like the rest of them?"

"I was on special assignment." Holly puffed out her chest.

"That new game console that everyone wants this year? I was busy returning one."

"Returning?" Mike raised an eyebrow. "Those things have been sold out for months. Why would you be returning it?"

"I had to borrow one." For a moment, Holly looked like she was going to be sick. "I took it from underneath someone's tree two weeks ago and temporarily replaced it with a dummy present. The elves spent several days figuring out how to replicate the design. I was trying to put the real one back but got stuck hiding it back under the tree. Elves have ways to be invisible to humans, but the family dog fell asleep on the fireplace because they had a lovely fire going. Whenever I got close, it would wake up and growl at me. I hear that we smell like butter cookies.

"Anyway, I was gone much longer than expected as a result. The dog got up to get a drink, and that's when I ran. Still, I was gone maybe three hours tops, which is why I'm so concerned. Usually, there's a big party while Santa delivers presents, and the only people working are emergency support teams, and even they don't have to do much. But to come home and find the place empty with the furnace shut down…" She shuddered. "Real scary stuff. I wandered for a bit and found the sleigh. I sat with it and waited, knowing that Santa would come. But when the alarm for the time lock went off and he hadn't, I knew something was wrong. The countdown is almost twenty minutes, so I pushed the sleigh into the fireplace just before the lock engaged."

"So the whole world is frozen in time until we undo that lock?" Mike looked over at Beth. "Is it like a switch, or…"

Holly shrugged. "I don't know. I have free access over most of the workshop, but I've never seen how Santa does it. A friend of mine might know how. He's very old and has seen pretty much everything, but we would have to find him first."

Yuki sat down on the edge of the sleigh and narrowed her

eyes at Holly. "And I suppose you want us to come back and help?"

Holly shook her head. "No. Someone has to stay here and guard the sleigh. It's usually kept in a secure location until Santa puts the bag inside. Only he can lift it. The sleigh was still locked up, which means whatever happened occurred right after Santa loaded the sleigh but before he could leave. I can't think of any reason he would do that. Whatever happens, we cannot let anyone else get their hands on this sleigh."

"Why?" Lily sat on top of Santa's bag, her arm nearly elbow-deep. With a grunt, she pulled out a box wrapped in red-and-silver ribbon and shook it next to her ear. "Afraid we'll flood the economy with shitty toys and upset the value of the dollar?"

"No." Holly climbed onto the sleigh and pulled the present out of Lily's hands. "This bag is special. If anything happens to it, then Santa can't deliver presents to children all around the world. This is his life's work, and we must preserve it."

"Um, correct me if I'm wrong, but…" Mike made a face. "I don't recall ever getting an actual present from Santa. It was usually just my mom."

The elf rolled her eyes. "Well, duh. That's how Santa's magic works! It keeps him hidden at the North Pole by changing people's memories. So when you find out that Santa isn't 'real'"—Holly held up finger quotes—"your parents are already under the belief that they bought everything for you, and Santa's secret is preserved."

"Makes sense," Mike muttered. "Always was surprised that she got me anything for Christmas, much less signed it from Santa."

"That sounds an awful lot like how the geas works." Yuki stood and looked at Holly. "Retroactively changing things to preserve the home's secret."

"That's right!" Holly stuffed the present back into the bag and pulled the drawstrings shut. "The same spell that protects Santa also protects this home. It was a gift from Santa to… to…" She scrunched up her face. "Well, to whoever built this place."

"He knew the Architect?" Mike looked at Lily, then Yuki. "That means he could tell us about who built this house!"

"Oh, fuck me." Lily rolled her eyes dramatically. Holly jumped as if burned. "As if we all don't know where this is going."

"Mike." Yuki moved toward him and put a hand on his shoulder. "I want you to keep in mind that whatever is happening here isn't a house problem. If Holly is right, the time lock happens every year and we've never even noticed. If you want to help, I'm with you a hundred percent. But if you want to sit this out, she'll leave and the lock will just end from our perspective. We don't have to get involved at all."

He nodded, then looked at Holly. "At the very least, you need Tink to get your furnace back online, right? If she goes, I go too."

"And me." Kisa crossed her arms. "Last time I stayed behind, everything went to hell and we needed all hands on deck."

"Ah!" Holly covered her ears. "Really, no swearing, please!"

"Bad words make pointy ears horny." Tink chortled with glee as she moved closer to Holly. "Tink remember special time with pointy ears, way better than fun with hammer."

"Bad words make you horny?" Lily laughed. "I have to see this."

"No!" Holly's eyes went wide in horror. "Absolutely not! Last time we had an outbreak of naughtiness at the North Pole, it was years before things went back to normal! And bad words don't make us…amorous. They make us mimic the behavior itself."

"It may be prudent of you to stay behind," Mike said to Lily with a frown. "As much as I'd love to have you with me…"

"I'm simply too sexy for the North Pole." Lily rolled her eyes. "I get it. Wouldn't want to start an orgy with a bunch of children."

"We are *not* children!" Holly stomped her foot and looked at Tink. "We're just petite! Tink, tell her!

"Stinky demon just jealous of small girls like Tink." The goblin threw her arm across Holly's shoulders. "Come. Go fix furnace, find Santa, get presents!"

"I'm coming with you." Yuki looked at Mike. "There will be no objections. Whatever took everyone is still up there, and I'm not letting you go alone."

"Wait." Lily frowned. "I'm not going to stay here and babysit this sled all by myself. If time is locked, I might be here for days while you get shit figured out."

Holly let out a low moan, then pulled a pair of earmuffs over her ears. "Just let me know when you're ready to go," she said in a too loud voice.

Mike nodded, then looked at Death. "Do you think you could do me a huge favor?"

"Indeed, Mike Radley." The grim reaper moved into the driver's seat of the sled, his fiery eyes now glowing green. "I shall make sure nothing happens to Santa's sled. You can count on me."

"I…thought you would argue, but okay. It should be safe inside the house. The geas will keep out any unwanted visitors. And since time is locked…" Mike frowned. Yuki could tell he was trying to figure something out, but had no idea what. "With any luck, we can get things sorted at the North Pole and you both won't have to wait long at all. If we find Santa, he'll have to come here for the sled, which means you'll get to meet him."

Death grinned, the fire in his sockets growing brighter as

he picked up the loose reins and held them in his hands. "You can count on me to do the right thing, Mike Radley. You have my word."

Now Yuki was suspicious but didn't know why.

"Holly." Mike waved at the elf, and she removed a muff from one of her ears. "Can we use the sled to unlock any of the others?"

Holly shook her head. "Whoever is with it when it leaves the North Pole is the only person who stays unlocked. Since I brought it through the fireplace as the lock went up, the field worked on everyone inside your house, but that's it."

"Bloody fucking convenient," Lily muttered. "If this turns out to be a trap, I'm gonna hook that elf's asshole with a giant candy cane and beat her against the wall like a piñata."

Holly's whole face turned a violent shade of purple as she tipped into the wall and dry-heaved, frantically adjusting her earmuff back into place. Yuki felt bad for the little elf but agreed with Lily. With most of their housemates locked in time, it had been dumb luck that Yuki had even been at home.

Last Christmas, the others thought she'd retired to her room for the night. Instead, she had gone on a long walk in the park and had spent most of the night staring at a frozen lake and listening to the ice crack as the sun came up. It had been hard being inside the house, remembering so many Christmases with Emily and the others. There were still moments she felt like a complete outsider, especially since she was the only one who held those memories. Christmas was particularly hard, and the only reason she had stuck around after the snowball fight was to talk to Naia.

"Okay, well, let's make sure nobody else here is caught outside of the lock just to be certain. Team North Pole, I need you to make sure you have everything you need before we leave." He looked directly at Yuki. "You're right that this isn't technically a house problem. Maybe it's stupid, but I feel like I ought to go. I'm a parent now and would feel like a major piece of shit knowing that I could have helped the big man himself and didn't."

Yuki frowned. Being honest with herself, she didn't want him to go. If she could get away with it, she would make him stay and go in his place. She would use her magic to force his obedience and would find some way to lock him up until she returned.

But then she wouldn't get a chance to see that strength of his once more. It wasn't enough to just remember what she had seen in Oregon. He had devoted the last several months to becoming stronger, to becoming the kind of Caretaker the house now needed. If she hoped to walk beside him, she needed to be stronger too.

"Team North Pole?" She raised an eyebrow. "Are we really doing teams?"

"They're the home team, we're the North Pole team." Mike tilted his head. "Which team are you playing on?"

"*Orokana ningen.*" Yuki crossed her arms. "You would be lost without me."

"Mike Radley could borrow my compass," Death offered, holding up his gift. "Then you could stay behind. Though, I suppose it wouldn't function that well at the North Pole." The grim reaper contemplated the compass, then tucked it back into his cloak. "She is right. You would be lost without her."

"Just let me get my coat." Yuki moved toward the stairs.

"Wait." Mike's eyes lit up when Yuki looked at him. "Why would you need a coat? I thought the cold didn't bother you anyway?"

She narrowed her eyes at him, annoyed at his stupid attempt at a joke. They had gotten worse recently, and she knew it wasn't because he had been spending time with the dryad, Amymone. Her love of a bad joke was already legendary, but she was in hibernation. No, it was likely someone else was egging him on, or he had decided that his new status as a father entitled him to sink to a new low in comedy.

"My coat has pockets," she told him. "I can't just pull stuff out of my ass like you do."

This got a genuine laugh from Lily, which brought a smile to Yuki's face.

Up in her bedroom, she gathered up her magical tarot cards and tucked away a few things she thought she might need. As she was about to head back downstairs, she caught sight of *Alice* sitting on her nightstand.

There was no telling how long she would be gone. She pondered the book for several long moments before picking it up and tucking it away into her coat. It felt heavier than normal, but she refused to let the past drag her down.

ONCE EVERYONE WAS READY, HOLLY THREW A HANDFUL OF glitter over everyone who was going and told them to run headfirst into the fireplace. Tink led the charge, her toolbox in hand. Kisa went next, followed by Yuki. Mike looked at Beth by the tree, frozen mid-kiss, and set his jaw. Was Beth's magic like his own? Would it trigger his desires, filling him with pleasure until he felt like he would burst as his own magic did the same to her?

"I'm coming back for that kiss," he muttered, then ran through the flames. They parted for him, revealing the dimly lit interior of a building that made him think of a conference hall after a convention. Abandoned boxes and tables lay scattered everywhere as if the inhabitants had simply walked away.

Mike noticed that it was cold. It wasn't so much that there was a chill in the air, but it almost felt like the heat was being sucked from his body through his feet. Each breath sent a puff of crystals into the air, and he even heard Yuki gasp at his side.

When he looked at her, she had sprouted more fur along her body to keep warm. Behind them, Holly came through the fire, her eyes gleaming with determination.

The space they were in was a giant dome with large glass panels, making Mike think of a snow globe. Up above, he caught glimpses of the northern lights frozen in place across the night sky while snow swirled around the building. He had so many questions about how the time lock worked. Clearly there was a limit to the field around the North Pole, but was it just time on Earth that was frozen? Or was it the whole universe? How could he even see light from distant objects if it could no longer travel to his eyes?

"Hey." Kisa gave his foot a playful kick. "You're making the face again."

"Yeah, sorry." He walked away from the fire, then looked back. It was a gigantic fireplace with hundreds, possibly even thousands, of stockings all along the top of the mantel. The names stitched into the stockings were mostly whimsical or Christmas related. The white marble floors beneath were decorated with silver inlays that looked like snowflakes, and he could see the fire's reflection in its smooth surface.

"I just want to point out that some of these are stripper names." Kisa approached one stocking and tapped it. "Candy? Star? Or what about this one?" She pulled the stocking down and held it up for Mike to look at.

"Crystal. Okay, point made." He felt a push as Holly shoved past him and snatched the stocking from Kisa.

"Don't touch these," she warned, then put Crystal's stocking back. "This is essentially our mail system, and each elf knows where their stocking is. Don't mess with them."

"Sorry, Holly." He looked at Kisa. "Let's keep our hands to ourselves for now."

Kisa snorted. "Speak for yourself." She moved to his side and leaned into him.

"Oh sprinkles." Holly hugged herself, rubbing her arms.

"The furnace has been off for too long! Much longer and this whole place will freeze!"

"Well, I guess we should head there first." He gestured for Holly to lead. Instead, Tink took point and walked across the large room over to a set of golden elevator doors.

"Tink remember," she proclaimed proudly. "Furnace this way."

"It's fucking cold in here." Kisa grabbed Mike's arm and hugged it. "You're way warmer than this coat I grabbed."

"That's not how heat transfer works," he replied. "I'm wearing layers, and so are you."

"Maybe it's a mental thing." She closed her eyes and rubbed her cheek against his bicep. "You warm me from the inside."

Holly watched the two of them with her mouth slightly ajar. Mike noticed that the frost that formed in front of her mouth often sparkled as if filled with glitter. What sort of creatures were the elves of the North Pole? Emulating naughty behavior seemed a little silly, and he wondered if they had been created that way.

Tink pressed the button outside of the elevator and bounced on the balls of her feet. She wore a tiny pair of fur boots she had made from a pair of Uggs Beth had given her.

"So this place is usually busy?" he asked.

Holly nodded. "When Santa leaves to do his deliveries, there's still work to be done. But a huge party starts, and we spend weeks celebrating while he does his deliveries while the world is frozen. This place should be full of elves right now."

"Weeks? Is that how long Santa takes to deliver everything?" Mike asked.

"At least. We think it might be longer for him, but nobody knows for certain. How do you keep track of time when, well, you can't?" She smiled sadly. "It's kind of scary wondering what happened to everyone."

Mike wrapped his arm around Kisa and squeezed. "Trust

me, I know that feeling all too well." He couldn't help but think back to what had happened in the spring, when he had left home and the apocalypse had almost started on his lawn. If not for the entire world being frozen in time right now, he wouldn't have even considered coming. "So time freezes like this every year? Is it something Santa does himself, or is it some kind of magic artifact?" He really hoped it was something simple, like a switch that could be flipped, though he supposed finding Santa was a priority.

The elf shrugged, then hugged herself. "I've heard rumors both ways, but I try to ignore workplace chatter. It's easy to get sucked into gossip."

"Elves gossip?" Yuki was standing off to the side, peering down a long hallway. "Doesn't sound very, well, nice of you."

Holly frowned. "It's not like human gossip. We focus on stories, or things we've heard around the workshop. It's never meant to be derogatory, if that's what you're getting at."

"Like who's dating who?" Kisa had one arm around Mike's waist now. When she spoke, Holly jumped as if startled.

"Wow, I forgot you were even there!" She shook her head in astonishment.

"I get that a lot," Kisa grumbled. She hooked her fingers in one of Mike's belt loops and pulled. "You don't forget I'm here, right?"

"I never do." In fact, Mike could have her stand anywhere in the room while closing his eyes and he would know exactly where she stood. He wasn't sure why she needed the reassurance, but was happy to give it to her. "You doing okay?"

"Place gives me the creeps," she said. "Has a bad vibe. Reminds me of when I was homeless."

He gave her another squeeze. While most of her memories were gone, she did have more than a couple regarding her time on the streets. Sometimes she would have a random one and share it with him. He had spent a few months trying to use what little she knew to piece together who she might have been when she was human, but there had never been enough information.

"Should the elevator be taking this long?" Yuki was watching Tink, who was zoning out in front of the doors. Mike wondered if the goblin was still drunk, because she stuck her tongue out at Yuki, let out a belch, and then pulled her goggles over her head before forcing the door open.

"Well?" Holly bit her lip, then moved behind Tink.

"Bad news," Tink informed them. "No power." She took a step back and let the doors shut. "Maybe take stairs?"

"Ugh, no!" Holly grabbed at her braids and pulled them tight. "Stairs aren't really a thing! The elevator is magic, it only looks like it goes up and down."

"Focus on the solution, then." Mike put a calming hand on the elf. "Is there some way to restore magic to the elevator?"

"Maybe, I don't know." Holly groaned and leaned against the wall next to the elevator, then slid down until she was sitting. "I don't know how these things work."

"Let me take a look." Yuki sighed and pulled the elevator open, then summoned a handful of fox fire that transformed into an orb. She tossed it into the darkness where it hovered in place, illuminating the shaft. "I see some summoning runes. With a bit of work, I could make the elevator come here manually. Will take some time though."

"Sounds like a plan." Mike looked at Holly. "Is there somewhere nearby where we could sit, or maybe warm up? Feel kind of dumb just standing here."

"Don't go too far," Yuki cautioned. She had summoned a sword with one of her tarot cards and was using it to scratch something along the side walls of the elevator shaft while Tink held the doors open. "I want you close by in case something happens."

"I know somewhere." Holly gestured to a nearby doorway.

"It's the Cocoa Lounge. It would be a great place to get some hot chocolate. In fact, I wonder…" She walked toward the double doors and pushed them open. Mike made to follow but looked at Yuki first.

"Should be fine," Yuki said. "Just stay in the front area and don't go looking for trouble."

"Loud and clear." He walked into the Cocoa Lounge with Kisa right behind him and did a double take. The lounge itself was the bastard child of a hotel bar and a Christmas party. Gaudy decorations were hung from the ceiling with care, and the walls were plastered in Christmas cards.

"Those are real," Holly said, seeing where Mike was looking. "When they get lost in the mail, they come here. We change them every couple of months."

"Interesting." He moved toward the closest wall for a better look. The cards weren't organized in any meaningful way, and they were written in different languages. "So all these people celebrate Christmas?"

"Sort of." Holly pointed toward the corners. "Santa is really big on traditional giving. It's just that Christmas is kind of his thing. If you look up there, we have some Kwanzaa cards as well as Hanukkah. It's never meant to be a competition. The staff likes to keep them organized by holiday so we can see them all together and appreciate the spirit of the holiday season."

Mike squeezed into a booth, then pushed the table away so he could comfortably fit. Based on Holly's dimensions, he supposed eight elves could sit there. "If Santa is real, does that mean the Easter Bunny is real?"

"A rabbit that poops eggs?" She shook her head. "Sounds kind of silly, doesn't it?"

"That wasn't an answer," Kisa replied.

"You're right, it wasn't." Holly winked and disappeared behind the bar. It sounded like she was rummaging around, then she stood with a smile on her face. "Aha! The cocoa lines are still warm! I can make you a drink if you'd like."

"Please." Mike watched Holly move around behind the bar, then turned his attention to the front window of the lounge. From where he sat, he could see Yuki and Tink working on restoring power to the elevator. If the cocoa lines were still warm, then everyone couldn't have been gone too long, right? "Holly, does this place have an intercom system?"

"We do." She sighed and put some mugs on the counter. "And Tinker is the reason."

"Oh?"

"Yeah. You see, the furnace has an enormously large set of vents that direct heat everywhere at the North Pole. She was doing things in the vents that triggered naughty sickness in multiple places at once. We realized an intercom could have been used as an early warning system."

Mike chuckled, wondering what sort of trouble the goblin had gotten up to. However, he went back to the idea of an intercom. What if an evacuation had been ordered and Holly missed it? Maybe if they could get to the control booth, they would find some answers.

"Hey, a jukebox!" Kisa jumped to her feet and moved toward the jukebox. It was carved out of dark wood and full of small vinyl records. She examined it and started pushing the buttons.

"Yeah, won't work." Holly hung her head. "The lights are self-sustaining for emergencies, but that thing runs on the same magic the elevator does."

"Are you sure magic isn't just elfin for electricity?" Kisa moved behind the jukebox. "Shit, never mind. No plug."

When Kisa swore, Holly dropped the mug she was holding, which shattered on the floor.

"Oh fudge!" Holly scowled at Kisa. "I'll be back. I need a broom."

The elf disappeared into the kitchen, and Kisa looked at Mike. "Hey, come check this out."

"Check what out?" He stood and walked to the jukebox. The names of the songs had been written in perfect penmanship on each button, and it was no surprise that they were all Christmas related.

"She said it runs on magic." Kisa threw him a mischievous look, then grabbed him by the hips and pulled him against her. On her tiptoes, her head was at the base of his sternum as she flattened her body against him, using one of her hands to tease his cock through his pants. "C'mon, let's see some sparks."

He was about to tell her that wasn't necessary, but he was still feeling a little frustrated by having his encounter with Beth interrupted. Focusing his magic into his hand, he held it over the jukebox and closed his eyes.

Unsure how the jukebox would respond, he focused on the idea of transferring energy from his body into the device. As the sparks danced along the edges of the jukebox, his senses expanded and revealed the device's inner workings. It wasn't composed of wires or sensors but a magical crystal in the middle that had gone dormant.

"Aha!" He concentrated, pressing his magic against the crystal and feeling it rev up. Immediately, the jukebox clicked to life, revealing Christmas lights that had been embedded in the wood.

"Yes!" Kisa exclaimed, then released Mike and perused the selection. He moved back to the booth and sat down. Out in the lobby, Tink and Yuki seemed to be hotly debating something. The goblin was pointing her hammer at Yuki like a magic wand while Yuki drew glowing sigils in the air that rotated. Tink smashed a couple of the sigils, then analyzed one and nodded profusely. Rolling her eyes, Yuki turned her attention back to the elevator.

The wooden arm inside the jukebox lifted a record free

and placed it on the turnstile of the player. When the needle hit, a familiar tune filled the Cocoa Lounge. It wasn't until he heard the words *Santa, baby* that he recognized the song.

This version had a modern sound with a steady beat, and Kisa swayed her hips from side to side while looking over her shoulder at Mike.

"Is the power on?" Holly appeared behind the counter, a broom in hand.

"Nah, I started this up." He kept his attention on Kisa as she danced to the song. Her lithe body moved beneath her coat as if it floated above her frame. "Who is singing this? It's really good."

"An elf," Holly replied. "We have an in-house band that records our own versions of the songs that mortals write. Each year, they redo all of them so we at least hear new versions."

"I see." It was hard to imagine such a rich voice coming from someone like Holly, but he knew better than to assume anything when it came to magic. As for rerecording the songs each year, he imagined it was for the best. If the elves had to listen to Christmas songs all the time, the least they could do was change it up.

Kisa continued her dance, throwing looks at Mike as she swayed. The song came to an end, and the record was replaced. "Last Christmas" started playing, this version sung by a man.

Behind him, Holly was singing along quietly as she cleaned up the broken mug. Kisa was doing some sort of impromptu interpretive ballet to the lyrics, her face twisted up in sadness as she reached for Mike longingly. She danced all around the lounge, nimbly moving around chairs and tables as she used the entire floor like a stage.

When the song came to an end, he applauded. Behind him, he heard Holly clapping in approval as well. He looked back to see that she was fidgeting with something under the bar, and steam was rising from a nearby vent.

When he looked back at Kisa, she was by the jukebox again. She winked, then chose the next song. There was a loud pop of static electricity when she touched the jukebox, and she shook her hand in response. She contemplated her fingers for a moment, a broad grin crossing her face.

It was "All I Want for Christmas Is You." Holly sat down next to him and handed him a pair of mugs. The drinks were decorated like candy canes and topped with whipped cream and sprinkles.

"The singer sounds just like Mariah Carey," he told her.

"Oh, this one is her," Holly replied. "It's Mrs. Claus's favorite song, so we leave it untouched."

That explains why I hear it every year. He took the mugs and set Kisa's aside before sipping from his own. The flavor was rich and warmed him up immediately.

"Magic cocoa?" he asked, holding the mug close so he could take in its scent. It was unlike anything he had ever smelled and reminded him of walking into a chocolate shop.

Holly nodded, her eyes on Kisa. The cat girl had moved toward Mike, allowing her coat to slide from her shoulders onto the floor. She put her hands on his knees and lip-synched the words as she gyrated her hips behind her. Kisa leaned forward until her face was inches from his own, then stuck her tongue out and licked some of the cream from the top of his cocoa.

He smiled, feeling her desire wash over him. Ever since she had become his familiar, their bond had been steadily growing. Not only could he sense her presence, but he could often feel her mood as well. Recently, her arousal had become a tangible thing that floated around in the back of his mind, and he remembered how she had grabbed his cock only minutes ago.

Moving forward, he took her by the hands and spun her around until she faced away from him. Pressing her ass against his leg, she ran her hands up and down his thighs.

Kisa spun around and hopped onto him, locking her legs around his waist as she gazed into his eyes.

"That's so…naughty," Holly whispered, her mouth hanging open. Mike couldn't help but notice that she wasn't looking away. The music had acquired a background hum that was almost imperceptible, and the elf's eyes were wide.

"Yeah, it is." Kisa wiggled her hips and playfully licked Mike's lips. "How about it, boss? You got any more cream for me?"

"Uh…" Mike threw a glance at Holly. It wasn't like they were home and could just find somewhere private. This was the North Pole, and they were being watched. And why was the jukebox making that sound? Could record players hum like that?

"Nah, don't worry about her." Kisa pressed her groin against his. "I think she likes it."

"Kisa." He tried to sound stern, but his willpower was fading. Feeling Kisa's soft fur against his skin was always a turn-on, but now she was practically humping him through his clothes. It didn't help that his magic was reacting to her, which meant it was two against one.

"C'mon, Caretaker. It's Christmas. What's a girl gotta do to get you to fill her stocking?" She buried her face in his neck and purred.

"Excuse me." Holly's cheeks were bright pink, and tiny crystalline shapes had appeared on her skin. "I can't see if you stand that way."

"Told you." Kisa's breath was hot in his ears. "I think she wants a show."

"Holly?" He looked at the elf to try to get a sense of what she actually wanted. Holly had shifted in her seat to get a better view and was clutching her cocoa mug so tightly that her fingers had turned white. Her lips were slightly parted, and her eyes met his. What if their actions had triggered the naughty sickness she had mentioned earlier? "I'm…we…do you want us to stop?"

"Don't mind me," she whispered with wide eyes. "I'm just…watching."

"Ooh, she likes to watch." Kisa was crooning in his ear now. "Wanna show her how you can fuck me without sitting down? I bet she'd like to see that. And don't tell me she doesn't excite you. I've seen you checking out those tights she's in, made me feel a little possessive is all."

Mike looked out the window to see Yuki and Tink still standing outside the elevator. Whatever they were doing seemed intensive, and he hoped he could finish before Tink walked in and demanded to join. The last thing he wanted was for poor Yuki to sit outside waiting while he satisfied the goblin.

He slid his hands beneath Kisa's shirt, lifting it enough to skim his hands along her sides. Her fur was soft and her body warm. Behind her, the multicolored lights of the jukebox had brightened in intensity as the record started the song over instead of turning it off.

"Yeah, that's it." Kisa's tail twitched behind her as he slid his hand down the front of her stretch capris, the tips of his finger teasing the upper folds of her pussy. "Let's show her how we do things at home."

His head was buzzing now, and it felt like he was lost in a haze. Kisa licked the side of his neck and nibbled on his ear as he teased her clitoris with nimble fingers. Holly was visible from the corner of his eye, the elf panting like she was running on a treadmill.

The volume of the jukebox increased, and a blue aura formed around it.

Ah, shit. Mike moved toward the jukebox as Kisa pressed herself into his hands. He recognized that blue glow, and when he moved his hand toward the jukebox, the air crackled around his fingertips.

It was his magic. What he had used to kickstart the jukebox had somehow intensified and was creating some sort of sexual feedback loop. It explained the weird sounds and why Kisa was suddenly all over him. Out of all the women of the house, his own familiar would be the most susceptible to his magic. In his attempts to activate the crystal, his magic was now being broadcast to anyone nearby who could hear it.

At least, that was his working theory. His brain was operating on a reduced blood supply on account of the massive hard-on he was now sporting.

"Hey," he whispered to Kisa. "So it looks like my magic is kind of doing a weird thing here, and I just need to—"

The jukebox let out a crack as the magical aura turned into a series of sparks that jumped into his outstretched fingertips. His muscles tensed up as the magic washed over him, and he sat Kisa down on the jukebox while pushing her legs apart. She was already shoving her pants down and managed to pull one leg free just as he buried his face in her furry snatch.

Her scent surrounded him, and he lapped from her dripping folds. The skin around her labia had a very thin layer of fur that was nearly invisible against her dark skin, and it tickled the edges of his mouth as he slid his tongue over the top of her clit while using his chin to push her open. The music distorted, slowing until the record came to a stop.

"Yeesss!" she hissed, her claws digging into the back of his neck without breaking the skin. "Oh God, that feels so good."

Mike couldn't see Holly and no longer cared. He heard the occasional gasp behind him but was riding the wave of his own magical backlash. His hands fit perfectly over the smooth contours of Kisa's ass, and he held her against his face as her legs folded over his shoulders and squeezed. Her shirt rode up, revealing the cream-colored fur of her belly.

The jukebox sputtered back to life as his magic activated it. The song changed, and when the record spun up, it was a familiar instrumental piece with an electric guitar. He tried to remember the name of the band, but that part of his brain no longer functioned. It had been a long time since he had experienced his own backlash, and he made a mental note not to try to infuse any more enchanted objects with his own magic.

"Oh fucking…fuck!" Kisa squeezed his head, her hands slipping up to the back of his head. Her claws dug into his scalp, but he let the pain fuel him as Kisa came on his face. Her thighs contracted hard as she crushed his head between them. The music was now muffled as he sucked her clitoris into his mouth.

With each spasm, Kisa scratched him. He winced but wasn't worried. The wounds were superficial and would heal in a matter of hours. What was on his mind, though, was how full his balls felt. His magic demanded release, and he wasn't about to be denied. Mike pulled his head free and tilted it back and forth to loosen the muscles.

"Whew." Kisa fanned herself with one hand. "Wow, that one came out of nowhere, it's almost like—"

With a yank, he pulled Kisa down and spun her around so her torso was lying across the top of the machine. He had already undone his pants, revealing his massively engorged cock. She made a goofy face at him over her shoulder, but he pressed himself into her so suddenly that her right eyelid twitched.

Biting down on her lower lip, Kisa held tight to the jukebox as Mike pounded her from behind. Her tail kept hitting him in the face, so he tucked it under one armpit and resumed his grip on Kisa's waist. She wrapped her legs around him, allowing him a better angle.

"Yeah, that's my good girl." He reached under the back of her shirt and scratched his nails down her furry back. Kisa moaned, then arched her back for him.

"I hate that I do that, but it feels so good." She purred as he fucked her from behind, her claws leaving gouges in the wood. He used one hand on her hip to keep them connected while the other did long, slow drags down her back. Occasionally, he would move a hand along her side and trace his fingers along the underside of her breast. If he thrust into her deep enough, he could briefly tease her nipples with a fingertip.

Mike heard Holly gasp. He turned and saw that she had her legs crossed with a hand pinned between her thighs. Her eyes were closed as she rocked back and forth, whispering, "I won't be naughty, I won't be naughty."

The visual pushed him over the edge. Grabbing onto Kisa's hips, he rammed himself into her so hard that the jukebox rocked beneath them. Her pussy gripped him tight every time he slid out, as if reluctant to release him.

"Yes, yes!" Her legs squeezed him so hard that his spine popped. He groaned as he felt that first wave of heat flood his belly, then release in a torrent of sticky cum inside Kisa's womb. His magic concentrated into a ball, then poured itself into the cat girl.

Kisa's ears flattened, and she let out a yowl of pleasure, then sank her claws into the jukebox so hard that she ripped some of the paneling off. Sparks shot from her body into the jukebox, and the arm malfunctioned, swinging around hard enough that smoke started rising from beneath it.

"Shit, shit!" Mike tried to pull Kisa away from the jukebox, only to fall backward onto his butt when she let go. Since they were still connected, this resulted in Kisa slamming into him so hard that it triggered a second, much smaller orgasm in him. His legs spasmed as she rocked herself back and forth.

"Yes, yes...yes...damn!" Kisa groaned, then looked over her shoulder. "That one got away."

Mike said nothing. His cock was still pulsating, filling her with microbursts of semen. Holly grunted, and he noticed that her teeth were clenched tight as she shuddered, her whole body going still. The Cocoa Lounge filled with the smell of burned wood as the jukebox let out a whine, and then the protective glass cracked. Tendrils of smoke rose from the speaker as the lights turned off.

"You really filled me up." Kisa wiggled her ass, then looked over her shoulder at him. "If I'm gonna wander around the North Pole, I'm not doing it with cum-soaked panties."

He nodded, then held his arms out as she dismounted and scooted back until she could sit on his face. Her pussy had taken on the musky scent of his spooge with just a slight hint of ozone. When he buried his tongue inside her, Kisa groaned as she did the same for him, licking his cock clean.

A year ago, the thought of doing such a thing had been foreign to him. However, Kisa absolutely loved doing it, and it wasn't like almost everyone else wasn't already eating his sperm for one reason or another.

It also didn't hurt that it had taken on a semisweet taste. He wasn't sure if that was his own magic or a trait he had taken on from someone else. His spooge shimmered like it had glitter because of one of the times he had come inside a fairy, so why not an improved flavor?

Kisa's rough tongue had him clean pretty fast, so she was content to suckle on his cock and moan as he ran his tongue along her inner folds in an attempt to get it all. He ran his fingers over her pubes, stroking them lovingly as he did his best to clean her insides. Her juices were mixed with his own, and the taste of them made him feel like he was floating.

"They're coming." Holly was looking outside as she wiped her hand off on a napkin.

"We already did." Kisa giggled as she squirmed off Mike and pulled her leggings back up. Mike stood and did his best to adjust his clothes. Holly handed him a napkin.

"Your face is all shiny," the elf told him in awe.

"Thanks." He wiped off his lips and chin, then crumpled the napkin up and threw it in the nearby trash just as the door of the Cocoa Lounge opened. Yuki held the door while Tink strolled in with a smug look on her face.

"Elevator fixed!" she declared. "Tink fix anything!" Her eyes were still a bit glazed over, but it was clear she was mostly sober now.

"Hey." Yuki looked at Mike, then Kisa. Her nose wrinkled as she sniffed the air, then rolled her eyes in exasperation. "Seriously? You didn't even make it an hour before fucking at the North Pole? And in front of poor Holly, no less."

"In my defense, it was kind of an accident." He gestured at the jukebox. "Who would have guessed that using my magic to activate the crystal inside would have caused some weird reaction that affected everyone in here?"

Yuki narrowed her eyes. "Uh-huh. Seems like we can't go anywhere without you wanting to stick some part of you inside something or someone else. We should probably put a warning label on you."

"To be fair, Holly didn't try to stop us." Kisa grinned, then winked at the elf. "I think she liked it."

Holly's face turned red as she coughed into her hand and slid out of her seat. "I just wanted to make cocoa for everyone while we waited."

"Cocoa!" Tink pushed past Yuki and stormed up to the bar. "Tink like it hot, with plenty of whipped cream!"

"We're short on cream right now," Kisa whispered with a giggle. Mike swatted at her playfully, not wanting Tink to overhear. It wasn't so much that she would get jealous but that she would demand a turn, and he didn't think now was a good time for it.

"Anyway, we can leave now." Yuki crossed her arms. "So let's see about starting that furnace back up, shall we?"

Holly nodded, then led the way. Mike picked up what was left of his hot cocoa and drained it. It was the perfect temperature, leaving a blazing trail of warmth all the way down into his belly. Kisa offered her cup to Tink, and the goblin frowned.

"All the cream is gone," she complained before drinking it. "Stupid cat."

"I'm not even mad." Kisa chuckled, then left the cocoa lounge.

Once everyone was out by the elevator door, Yuki had them all get inside. On the back wall of the car were a pair of glowing runes.

"We can power it with magic," she said. "I would have suggested you give it a try, but now I'm afraid of what would happen."

Mike nodded. Without a doubt, the last thing he needed to do was trigger an accidental orgy inside the elevator.

Yuki put her hands on the runes and closed her eyes. Motes of light hovered around her hands as the door shut. Tink pushed a button near the bottom, and the elevator hummed as it descended.

"So how big is this place?" Mike asked Holly. "And how does it not get spotted?"

The elf shrugged. "Nobody really knows how big it is. From the outside, it looks like rubble ice, and it's still way bigger on the inside. As for why it hasn't been discovered, nobody can come near without the magic chasing them off. Only those who are invited can breach the exterior, but a shortcut like the fireplace network can bring you here as well."

That sounded familiar. Mike's home was similar, only his front yard wasn't the arctic north. When people came knocking for trouble, he usually had to chase them off his lawn.

"But you're at the North Pole," Kisa argued. "People have specifically come to the North Pole before."

"Magnetic or true?" Holly grinned. "And what if I told you that neither of those places was at the top of the world? Kind of hard to pin a place down when it exists on a large chunk of ice, isn't it? It's rare, but sometimes humans get close. We almost had an icebreaker ship breach the perimeter one summer, it was very exciting."

"Wait, a ship?" Kisa's hair poofed out. "Is this whole place…just floating on ice? Like, there's nothing but ocean beneath us? We could sink?"

The elf put a calming hand on Kisa's shoulder. "Relax. This place is special. The ice outside is magical and wouldn't melt even on the hottest day. And floating really isn't the right term for it. If you dig into the ice, you'll just keep digging down and down without ever reaching water."

"Almost like it's a separate plane." Yuki nodded. "Think of it like the tower world. It's a separate place entirely but has been plugged into our world."

Kisa crossed her arms and glowered. "Doesn't make me hate it any less."

The elevator dinged at intervals as it continued its descent. Eventually, it stopped and the doors opened, revealing a chamber full of pipes and vents. At the other side of the room was a gigantic furnace surrounded by abandoned tools on the ground as if they had been dropped when work stopped. The group stepped out of the elevator.

"Tink come, save day!" The goblin smacked her hammer on an abandoned cart. The resultant echo made Mike wince.

"Tinker!" Holly clapped a hand over the goblin's mouth. "Someone might hear you!"

"Isn't that the point?" Yuki walked forward, her eyes on the ceiling. "Might help you figure out where everybody went." She took a few steps into the room, then turned to face the elf. "In fact, what are you worried about, exactly? You said that everyone vanished and you were afraid, but what exactly are you afraid of? It isn't like Santa eats elves or something, is it?"

Holly opened her mouth to respond, but a sharp metallic ping rang out against a nearby wall. In a moment, Yuki summoned a cluster of icicles and sent them across the room like daggers, pinning a small figure to the wall by the fabric of his overalls. A pair of earmuffs fell off his head and slid across the ground.

"Allie!" Holly ran across the room to the trembling figure. It was an elfin man with white skin and a massive wrench clutched in his right hand. His eyes were wide as he stared at the group, his gaze lingering on Tink the longest.

"Holly? Is that you?" His voice wavered as he struggled to free himself from the ice. "What are you doing here?"

"What do you mean, what am I doing here?" Holly moved to his side and helped him yank the icicles free. "Everyone, this is Alabaster. He's the head of security and maintenance here at the workshop."

"I'm not the head of anything right now!" Alabaster grumbled as he used his wrench to smash an icicle and free himself. He brushed some dirt off his overalls and then adjusted his hat, which had become crooked. His voice had a thick grumble to it. "As for what you're doing here, I thought maybe you were with the others."

"I'm not. I was out on assignment. Allie, what happened here?" Holly took Alabaster's hand in her own. "I'm really scared!"

"As you should be. Do you still have your earmuffs?"

Holly nodded, then pulled them out of the pouch on her belt. "I do."

"Good. Keep them ready at all times." The elf looked at the others as he moved to pick up his own. "You all probably won't be affected. If you hear that intercom click on, you make sure to get those over her ears."

"You aren't exactly telling us what's going on." Yuki's features had gone hard. "Or what we're up against."

"I'm not entirely sure," he grumbled. "I happened to be wearing my earmuffs because I was using the forge to repair one of Santa's runners for next year. I needed something from storage, so I didn't bother taking them off. It's a great way to avoid meaningless conversation.

"Anyway, I came out of storage and saw everyone else staring at the speaker like it was the big man himself. I was about to take off my earmuffs to hear what was going on, but their eyes!" Alabaster shivered. "It was the early symptoms of severe naughty sickness. They dropped everything right where they stood and started shutting things down. There were a few others like me wearing earmuffs, and they were held down, their earmuffs removed. I hid myself away, nobody knows the workshop like I do. When they shut the furnace down, I came here to see why, but that's when the power went off."

"Santa's missing too." Holly's eyes were full of tears. "The world is caught in the time freeze, so it must have happened right before he left."

"Does Santa have any enemies?" Mike thought it was a perfectly reasonable question and didn't expect both of the elves to laugh.

"Boy, does he ever!" Alabaster chuckled, then his face became serious. "Several, actually. He's got a good rep with you humans, but he had to step on a lot of toes to get to where he is today."

Behind them, the elevator dinged. Mike turned around to see that the dial above the elevator was now moving.

"That...shouldn't be doing that," Yuki said. "Unless somebody called it."

"Nobody should know that we're down here, right?" Mike looked at the others, then Alabaster.

The elf shrugged. "The power's out, so any surveillance would be magical."

The dial moved all the way to the right, then stopped at a cursive *L* for lobby.

"There are dozens of stops on this one," Holly explained. "Maybe they spotted the alterations but have no idea where we are?"

"I think we're going to find out," Mike replied as the dial began moving. It rotated through the other floors without stopping and was nearly on their floor when his whole body filled with icy dread.

"Everyone! Hide!" He grabbed Tink and Kisa by the hand and dragged them away from the elevator. Alabaster and Holly put on their earmuffs as they squeezed between a couple of pipes. Thinking Alabaster knew best, Mike helped Tink and Kisa squeeze into the same space.

However, he couldn't fit. Everywhere in the workshop had been built for someone smaller, and he couldn't think of anywhere to go.

"What are you doing?" Mike hissed at Yuki. She had summoned her magic and was using it to build a wall of ice in front of the elevator doors.

"I should be asking you the same thing!" She shot back. He turned around and realized the door to the furnace was big enough that both of them could easily fit inside. It seemed unlikely that someone would casually start it back up, but it also meant that nobody would look for them inside. "C'mon!"

He ran toward the furnace and was happy to hear Yuki right behind him. The elevator dinged on their floor, and there was a scraping sound as the doors tried to open. He and Yuki were inside the furnace now, and he saw that the walls were covered in large silver filters. Cold air blasted him from every direction as they ran into the darkness.

Behind them, there was a sound like someone taking in a deep breath, and Mike looked back to see the ice wall explode.

WHAT IN THE DICKENS?

"And then there were two." Lily scowled at the fireplace. While she had been more than a little angry that Mike had asked her to stay behind, the rational part of her understood why. Nothing would give her more pleasure than antagonizing that elf. Lily could tell that Holly had quite the body hidden underneath her Santa slave wear. Goading the woman into a sexual encounter sounded positively delightful.

The emotional part of her wanted to rip someone's face off and eat it.

"Not quite, my young demoness." Death moved toward the tree and knelt to pick up a package. "Ticktock is not human, so I assume he is in a wakeful state."

As if in response, the lid of the gift slid to one side and a ribbon emerged, hanging over the side like a dog's tongue.

"We got left behind, bone daddy. We're just warming the bench until they return. I'm surprised you offered to stay. Don't you want to see the North Pole? Meet your big, fat hero?"

Death chuckled. "Ah, but then I wouldn't be able to do this." He hopped onto the bench of the sleigh and set Ticktock next to him, then picked up the reins. "On, Dasher, on, Dancer! On, Francis and Plissken! On, Gromit, on, Stupid! On, Dahmer and Blumpkin!"

Lily scowled. "Those aren't their names."

"Those are the names Tinker told me." Death turned to examine Santa's bag. "I wonder if there are any other presents in here for me? Or perhaps there's one for you?"

"If the legends are any metric, I should have a nice big rock in there."

Death ignored her, his arm already buried deep in the bag. "How do you suppose he finds the presents? Is there some kind of order to them? Holly gave me that compass earlier without looking, so maybe I just need to think really hard…" The flames in Death's eyes swirled as he pulled a gift the size of a toaster out. "Aha, look!"

He tilted the present toward Lily, a smug look on his face as he tapped the label.

"No shit?" Puzzled, Lily took the box. "How do you know it's for me and not some other Lily?" She examined the label and saw *Lily the Succubus* written on the tag in golden calligraphy. "Okay, that's fair. It's heavy."

"Open it! Open it!" Death was gripping the side of the sleigh so tight that his fingers dug into the velvet upholstery. "Let's see what Santa got you!"

"This is ridiculous." She slid her finger beneath the wrapping paper to rip it, then stopped. A cold breeze moved across the back of her neck and tickled her ears. "Do you feel that?"

Death paused. "Feel what?" He gave the sleigh a squeeze. "It feels nice. I think it's mahogany."

In the kitchen, something fell on the floor with a metallic clatter.

"I thought there was no one else outside the time lock." Lily set the package down on the seat and walked toward the kitchen. The dining room was dark, as the lights had been off when time froze. However, the kitchen light was on, and she could see a moving shadow within. There was muttering, followed by a wet, slurping sound in the kitchen.

Turning the corner, she found herself staring at a large figure huddled over the sink. It had pulled one of the pans out of the drying rack and was licking it with a tongue the size of Lily's forearm. Its sloped, abnormally large face terminated in a bulbous nose, with thin slits for eyes.

Lily froze, stunned by what she was seeing. The window above the sink was cracked open a couple of inches, and she could feel the cold from where she stood. The creature hadn't noticed her yet, and she wondered briefly about the fluid dynamics of air in a time-stopped world. Was this creature an undiscovered local? Or had it snuck in somehow?

The lumpy figure grunted in disgust and threw the pan to the floor. It sniffed at the other pans, drool hanging from its lips.

Snapped from her reverie, Lily slapped her hand on the countertop. "Hey! Potato face!"

The figure turned to look at her, its mud-colored eyes going wide. Growling, it grabbed another pan from the drying rack, then threw it at Lily so hard that the impact knocked her to the ground. Before she could rise, the creature was on top of her, its thick fingers wrapped around her throat.

She tried to say something witty, but the bastard was squeezing too hard. Even if this thing ate mold from inside the walls to keep the house clean, it had officially earned an ass beating. She willed her tail to appear and stabbed the thing in the neck, injecting it with sleeping venom.

"Ur?" The creature blinked, then stumbled backward and fell on its butt, rubbing at where she had stung him.

"Yeah, that's right, go to sleep, asshole." Lily stood and rubbed her neck. The torn skin closed up beneath her hands as she waited.

The creature growled at her and jumped to its feet, shaking off her venom.

"Fuck me," she swore as the thing ran toward the sink. It jumped at the window above it and turned into mist, passing through the gap.

"Lily! Help!" Death's voice was filled with panic, so Lily grabbed a pair of knives from the knife block and ran back toward the living room. Death was sitting in the sleigh, trying to shove away a pair of figures similar to the one from the kitchen. One of them wore an ugly green hat, while the other had large teeth that protruded from behind its bottom lip. Both of them were fighting to pull Santa's bag from the sleigh, but Death was wrestling them away.

"Use your scythe!" she yelled as she held up the knives.

"It only works on spirits," he replied. "Also, these things are quite strong."

Lily leaped into the fray, aiming the knives for the figure in the hat. Both of the knives cut through the burlap vest the thing wore, but slid across its skin without injury. The creature spun around and clubbed Lily in the face with a meaty fist, knocking her away.

"No!" Death was now sprawled across Santa's sack, the drawstring pulled tight beneath his body as the creatures tried to pull him away. "These are not your toys!"

"Okay," Lily muttered as she moved toward the sleigh. "Let's try this again."

She stabbed both the creatures with her tail, knowing there would at least be a temporary effect. They both turned to face her, spreading their arms wide as if to catch her.

"If you think being pinned between two idiots frightens me, you've got another thing coming." She could see that Underbite's eyes were glassing over, while Hat's eyes were wide with rage. Crouching, she leaped into Underbite, pushing it to the ground and stabbing it several times with her tail. The creature moaned, its eyes fluttering.

One down, Lily thought with a smirk. *One to go.*

Hat grabbed her from behind by the tail and whipped

her into the sleigh. Grunting, she tried to grab hold of something as she was dragged across the floor, but the object came loose and fell with her. It was her present, and she couldn't help but grin when she saw her name glistening in the light.

"*Sæt stelpa.*" Hat grinned at her as it crouched over her torso. The smell of damp soil and mold was overwhelming, and its breath wasn't much better. Hat cocked a fist over his shoulder while grabbing Lily by the neck.

She smashed her present into its face, knocking its hat off. The creature yelped and clutched its nose as it stumbled away from her, leaking green blood on the floor.

"Now use this one!" Death cried as he picked up Ticktock and tossed it to Lily. She caught the mimic while still lying on her back, then took aim with both hands.

"You know the drill, toaster." Lily threw the mimic at the now hatless creature. Ticktock unfolded in midair, revealing bladed limbs that scratched and stabbed. Hatless cried out and ran across the living room, toward the fireplace. Like the creature in the kitchen, it folded into itself and turned into a green mist that shot up the fireplace.

"Oh, Lily." Death knelt to pick up her gift. "I'm afraid the package tore."

"What the hell was in this thing, a rock?" Lily took the remains of her gift from him and tore the paper away. "Oh, you've got to be fucking kidding me!"

"That…is a very big lump of coal." Death frowned. "I suppose it's the thought that counts?"

"Fuck that." Lily dropped the heavy piece of anthracite. It gouged a chunk of wood out of the floor, and she gave it a kick into the living room, leaving a furrow in the wood where it landed. "These assholes just broke into our home, Death. *Our home.* They aren't supposed to be able to do that, and I'm about to find out why." She moved toward the remaining creature on the floor and stabbed it a few more times for good measure. If the creature wasn't asleep already, it was faking it really well.

"I am worried for the others." Death sat down on the bench of the sleigh. "This was supposed to be fun."

"We have very different ideas of fun." Lily put her hand on the creature's head and frowned. Even though it was asleep, its dreams were impenetrable. Instead of sinking into its Dreamscape, she got only fleeting images, most of them of the sleigh itself, followed by the bag.

"Well?" Death sounded worried.

"They're here for the sleigh and the bag." Lily moved her hand away and wiped it off on the burlap vest. "If we leave it here, more of them will come. Since they aren't frozen in time, they must have come from the North Pole too."

"Santa's helpers?"

"Nope." While she hadn't understood most of the images, the intent had been clear. Whoever these guys were, they hated Santa with a passion. "And there are more of them, like one big ugly family."

"Beauty is in the eye of the beholder." Death reached down to the floor where Ticktock came waddling up on metallic legs. He picked the mimic up and set it on the seat. "We must not judge based on appearances. But yes, they would seem to be assholes."

"We need to move the sleigh somewhere else." She frowned as she contemplated her options. There was nowhere in the house that was airtight, and she certainly didn't want the place to get trashed. "How the heck do we even move it though? I'm strong enough to pick it up, but it's bigger than any of the doors."

"Ah, but Holly got it through the fireplace, did she not?" Death began searching the sleigh. "I am willing to bet there's some sort of user's manual we can look at."

"Death, I understand that this whole childish naivety thing is your schtick, but there's no way that Santa has—"

"Here it is!" Death had lifted the seat beneath him to reveal a small journal with a cover made of wrapping paper. He flipped through the pages and nodded to himself. "Oh, good. It has a table of contents."

Lily blinked in surprise. "Why the hell does Santa need a user's manual for his sleigh?"

"Have you not been watching all those Christmas movies? Santa is always getting in trouble, and someone has to come help him. It makes sense that he would—aha!" Death flipped through the pages and nodded. "Um…some of these words are too big for me."

"Let me see." She took the book from Death and looked at the page he was on. "In the event that the sleigh must be transported through confined spaces, it will automatically utilize the properties of relativity and length dilation to…" She felt her eyes glaze over as the description was followed up with a mathematical proof. "I think it's saying it will just fit, because reasons."

"Aha!" Death's voice was filled with glee, and Lily looked up to see that he had pulled a large red velvet coat from under the seat. He belted it over his robes, and the fabric draped awkwardly, the cut designed for a much thicker figure. "I knew he would have a spare!"

"Why would…y'know what? It doesn't matter. We need to get this somewhere safe, but where?" She looked at Beth, still frozen in place. "Do you think we need to take her with us?"

"Ms. Holly said that time is stopped everywhere but the North Pole and where the sleigh is. Once we leave, the house will be safe."

"But that also means those creatures must have come through when the sleigh did. So why didn't they do anything?" It occurred to her that they had only revealed themselves after everyone else had left. If that was the case, then was it just the three of them? Or were there more? Were those things now time locked outside the sleigh's range, or was there some other magic at work here?

"Everywhere else on Earth is frozen in time," Death informed her. "So we cannot expect to receive help from anyone on Earth. Perhaps the centaurs could assist us?"

It wasn't a bad idea, so Lily got behind the sleigh and pushed it toward the back door. When they reached the hallway, the sleigh narrowed down to fit. Death, while in the driver's seat, squeezed down as well.

"How fascinating," he muttered. "The whole hallway has become larger to accommodate us!" He turned to look at her and grinned. "And you are much wider as well!"

Lily ignored him. When they got to the door, a cold gust of wind came from nowhere and the door opened by itself while playing a sound like jingling bells.

"Ugh, enough of that Hallmark shit!" She pushed the sleigh outside, and the door shut itself as the sleigh expanded to its previous size. The shortcut to the centaur village was through a small hut that had been built near the edge of the property. The sleigh felt surprisingly light on the snow as she maneuvered it toward the hut.

Up above, she heard the scrambling of feet on the roof. She looked up to see six figures staring at her from above, each one glaring at her with malice.

Lily didn't like that she and Death were outnumbered and was concerned that the figures hadn't acted yet. It was like they were waiting for something, and it couldn't be good.

When she and Death got close to the hut, Lily opened the door and looked inside. A large rat portal had been chewed into the back of the hut, and she ran through the portal into the yurt on the other side. Shoving the flap open, she started to call for help but paused.

The centaur village was silent. At a nearby fire, the flames were frozen in place as a storyteller was in the midst of sharing a tale with a small group of centaur children. Across the yard, a tent flap was in mid curl behind a centaur woman who had just exited and was now frozen midstride.

Lily ran back through the portal, licking her lips nervously. The centaur village wasn't even on Earth; it was a pocket dimension. Did that mean time was frozen everywhere? How would such a thing even work?

"Centaur village is a no-go," she announced as she stepped back outside. Death was staring at the roof where more figures had appeared. There were nine of them now, including Hatless.

"What are they waiting for?" Death asked. He was answered by a low growl as a dark figure appeared over the roof. It blotted out the sky as it moved across the roof of the Radley home, then turned its head to reveal a pair of bright-yellow cat's eyes. They looked huge in the moonlight, and the darkness of the pupils sloshed like ink.

The giant cat hopped off the roof and landed on the snow without leaving so much as a paw print. Its dark, ashen fur was tipped with white, and it had the wild look of something feral. It bared its fangs and swiped at the sleigh with claws the size of daggers.

"No! Bad kitty!" Death summoned his scythe and swiped at the cat's paw. The cat hissed and pulled its foot back.

"I thought you could only hurt spirits," Lily said.

"He doesn't know that," Death replied.

The giant cat circled them as Lily moved next to the sleigh. The cat stood nearly twenty feet tall and had the stocky build of a lynx. Its tail twitched behind it as it looked for an opening.

"The village is time locked as well," Lily said. "We're on our own."

"Hmm." Death waved his scythe at the cat, then looked at Lily. "Maybe it's not that everything else is frozen in time but that we are trapped in a single moment."

"Sure, whatever." Lily didn't care about the how or why of

time locking and picked up a snowball and threw it at the cat. It exploded harmlessly against its fur. "But it doesn't help our current situation."

"Hmm." Death jabbed at the cat, but it was getting bolder. It was only a matter of time before it figured out Death couldn't hurt it. "I can think of someone who could protect us from a bad kitty cat."

"Cerberus?" Lily looked down the hill at the gate. "There are so many reasons that it won't work, but let's go to that single moment theory."

"The Underworld has never cared much about the proper flow of time. If something can be killed during this moment, then the Underworld would still let us in," Death replied, then swatted away a paw. The blade of the scythe passed harmlessly through it, and the cat pulled back its paw, eyes wide in shock. The cat lifted its foot and inspected the pads with discerning eyes.

The damned thing grinned.

"Oh. Oh dear." Death looked at Lily. "Perhaps you should just push us toward the gate and pray for a Christmas miracle?"

"Damn it, bone man, demons don't pr—" She ducked as a claw slammed into the side of the sleigh, making it slide across the snow. Death used the butt of his scythe like a pole to guide the sleigh. When the cat struck again, the figures on the roof began their descent, scrambling down the drains to get to the ground.

The cat batted at the sleigh, launching it forward. Lily tumbled into the back of the sleigh where the bag was. It pressed against her, pinning her in place and crushing a couple of ribs. She couldn't see anything but could hear the figures shouting to one another. By the time she pulled herself free, they were sliding down the hill toward the gate to the Underworld.

"This is much more fun than those saucer sleds," Death declared as he grabbed her and pulled her into the front seat. "I would advise you to hold on tight."

"Death, we're crashing!" She tried to unfurl her wings to fly away, but the cat was right behind them. With an outstretched claw, it tore a hole through the membrane of one of her wings. Pain lanced through Lily's body as she fell forward, her eyes widening as she held on tight to the sleigh.

Death didn't acknowledge her. Instead, the grim reaper loudly sang "Jingle Bells" as the world around them distorted, the bars of the gate spreading themselves far apart as Lily and Death slipped through an opening that was a couple of inches wide. Behind them, the cat's face looked like pulled taffy as it let out a growl of rage and raked its claws against the indestructible iron gate. Sparks sprayed into the air and danced in the snow, then the swirling mists of the Underworld wrapped around Lily and Death, obscuring the house from view.

THE ICE WALL THAT HAD BLOCKED THE ELEVATOR EXPLODED into large chunks that hovered in place. Yuki held her breath as she watched them rotate for a couple of seconds, then form into a giant archway. It wasn't so much that the ice had been re-formed; that didn't bother her. She had felt it react with excitement, as if eager to obey the commands of whoever was behind those doors.

Ice didn't do that. At least, it never had for her.

The elevator door slid open, and a cloud of fog billowed outward. Everything the fog touched frosted over with intricate patterns, and Yuki had to bite her lip to keep from swearing.

"I know you're down here." The speaker had a slight husk to their voice, but Yuki couldn't tell if it was a man or a woman. However, the frost patterns had her worried. The intricate nature of laying patterns in frost wasn't something casually done. It took tremendous amounts of effort for such an artistic endeavor, and the newcomer didn't look like he was straining himself by any means. "You made quite the mess of the Cocoa Lounge."

Mike pulled an air filter off and silently lowered it to the ground. He took Yuki by the hand and pushed her into the gap.

"What are you doing?" Her voice was so quiet she may as well have just mouthed the question.

"They're tracking my magic," he replied in sign language. His sign language was sloppy but passable. He had been working on it with Daisy for over a year now. His magical ability to understand it hadn't translated to being able to use it himself, so it was something he practiced regularly with the fairies.

When the figure emerged from the frost, it was a young man with pixie-cut hair, light-blue skin, and pointed ears. His hair was white, and he had sharp cheekbones that made him look aerodynamic.

There was a napkin balled up inside a crystalline sphere made of ice in his hands. Yuki nearly groaned when she realized it was probably a napkin Mike had used. With a single hair, a witch could track someone to the ends of the Earth. Whatever was in that napkin had made it easy for them to be found. The ball had a silver arrow hovering above it, which oscillated back and forth between where Mike stood and where Kisa was hiding.

"Now that's interesting." The man turned to look at where Kisa and the others were, when Mike cleared his throat. "How are you in two places at once?"

"Okay, you've found me." Mike had moved farther down the throat of the furnace, where the light didn't quite reach.

"Sorry, I got here a little while ago, and have no idea what's going on and kind of ended up down here. Care to explain where everybody went?"

The man looked taken aback, and his bloodless lips pursed together. "You're not an elf."

"Nope. I am definitely a human man," he replied while moving away from Yuki's hiding place. "Just an ordinary guy who fell through his fireplace."

"An ordinary human couldn't do that." The stranger pointed at the arch behind him. "Summon and command the elements. No, I suspect you are more than you seem, and definitely believe that you aren't alone."

"Now, now, no need for accusations. I'm just a random guy lost in a Hallmark movie, and you're coming off pretty strong." As Mike spoke, Yuki could feel the subtle pressure of his magic radiating down the length of the furnace. She felt a need to believe him, to take him at his word and trust that he meant no harm. It was an interesting extension of his magic, and she wondered how much was a conscious effort on his part. Or maybe it was just her own wishful thinking? She would have to ponder it when their lives weren't in potential jeopardy.

"Humans aren't allowed in the workshop." The stranger held up the ice sphere. "And why are there two of you?"

"Don't know. I'm not sure how that spell of yours works. If you explain it, maybe I can answer your question?"

The man walked toward where the others were hiding, little spheres of ice spinning around him like tiny moons. Yuki realized after a moment that he wasn't even walking—instead, he hovered about an inch off the ground and glided forward.

"We're not off to a good start to begin with, and you're about to piss me off." Mike's voice now contained an edge that was hard to ignore, and he was nearly at the entrance to the furnace. His magic filled the air, and the pressure in the room increased. The man stopped and turned his attention back toward Mike.

"Stop that," he said.

"Stop what?" Mike held his hands out, showing they were empty. Yuki felt a cold breeze inside the furnace. It was coming from the man with the crystal ball. She pulled the tarot cards from her pocket and began sorting through them to find the right one. Sometimes when she held the cards, a sixth sense guided her to the one that was right for the situation. Other times, like this, she was forced to rely on her own imagination.

"Whatever your magic is doing. Stop it." The man held up the crystal. "Or I will make you stop."

"Then have a proper conversation with me." Mike stopped at the entrance to the furnace. "My name is Mike, by the way."

The man mulled this over, then looked at the crystal ball. The arrow kept twitching away, his features hardening as a layer of frost formed over his skin.

"You can call me Jack." Jack lifted a hand and made a casual gesture, as if shooing a fly. A powerful gale of wind slammed into Mike, but he had crouched a moment before it hit and grabbed a seam in the floor. His legs nearly slipped out from beneath him, but he remained upright.

Mike conjured a spider made out of lightning and sent it running across the floor. It leaped up and clung to Jack's face, causing him to panic and back into his own ice arch. A couple of blocks fell loose, but the structure remained intact despite the gaps in its support.

Yuki jumped from her place of concealment and drew the Two of Wands. A staff appeared in each hand as she dashed toward Mike. When she made it to his side, she handed one to him.

"They shoot fire," she explained, then held her staff out and summoned a jet of fire. Jack dodged, summoning a sphere made of ice to deflect the flames. Dark-blue veins stuck out in Jack's neck as he hovered into the air and pointed at the two of them. The ice arch burst apart, with chunks of ice rushing toward them.

Mike ducked under the first one, then jumped over another. He had ignited his staff as well, and sweat beaded along his brow as the two of them tried to evade the icy projectiles while still attacking Jack.

"We can't fight this guy," she said. "Do you know who he is?" Instinctually, she wanted to summon a dozen icicles and turn the man into a pincushion but had a strong feeling that anything she made would no longer belong to her. Even now, she could feel the magnetic pull of his magic as the shattered ice slid back across the floor toward him.

"Jack fucking Frost, apparently." Mike's eyes flicked over to where the others were hidden. "Think a loud enough noise would make him drop that crystal ball?"

"Maybe." She pulled a pair of earplugs from a pocket in her sleeve and deftly jammed them in her ears. If they could destroy the ball, they could get away. But where would they even go?

Mike took a deep breath and unleashed the banshee's scream. The sound caught Jack off guard, and he covered his ears, causing his shield to drop. Yuki directed a stream of fire at Jack, concentrating it on his hands. The flames licked at his flesh, and when he dashed up into the air, he dropped the crystal ball on the floor.

Yuki turned her staff onto the orb. It melted in seconds, then the napkin ignited and turned to ash. She grinned, happy for the small victory.

The scream ended when Mike ran out of breath, and he was taking another deep one when Jack let out a howl of rage reminiscent of a blizzard. The whole room frosted over as gale-force winds shoved Mike and Yuki down the throat of the furnace. The floor froze beneath them, and they were now sliding on ice.

"Yuki!" Mike stuck his hand out and grabbed her tail as they slid down the tunnel. She didn't know how far they went, but the icy wind suddenly vanished as the world went dark.

KISA CROUCHED BEHIND THE BLOCK OF ICE NEXT TO THE elevator, her wary eyes on the back of Jack's head. She had moved away from the others the moment she realized Jack was using her and Mike's bodily fluids to track them. Now that the napkin was gone, she was safe.

As for Mike, he and Yuki had slid down the long hallway of the furnace and simply disappeared. This seemed to puzzle Jack, who was gazing warily down the throat of the furnace. He picked up a chunk of ice and contemplated it for a moment. When he threw it into the furnace, it slid into the darkness and then blipped out of existence.

"Hmm." Jack turned around and pulled something out of his pocket. It looked like a child's walkie-talkie. He held it to his mouth and pushed the talk button. "The intruders escaped into the furnace. Human man and a fox demon. They disappeared, I don't know why. Over."

The walkie-talkie emitted a piercing burst of static. Kisa winced and held her ears, but Jack nodded as if he understood the sounds.

"I see. Should I send the ghosts after him? Over."

Another blast of static, then silence.

"Understood." Jack put away the walkie-talkie and pulled a trio of Christmas ornaments from his pocket. He set them on the ground and took a step back.

From each of the ornaments emerged a single light, each one about a foot across. They circled over Jack in a tight spiral, changing colors like bulbs on a Christmas tree.

"Find them," Jack commanded. "Teach them the true meaning of Christmas. Then kill them."

One after another, the lights shot into the furnace and disappeared into its depths. Satisfied, Jack walked back to the elevator and pressed the button. Once he was gone, Tink and the others emerged from hiding. Alabaster was clutching his head as if in agony.

"Oh, they have the spirits, how did they get the spirits?" He groaned and looked at the furnace. "I'm so sorry about your friends."

"Why?" Kisa moved to get a closer look at the furnace, but Holly intercepted her.

"It isn't safe," Holly explained. "From here, it looks simple enough, but once you go past a certain point, you can end up anywhere. They could be hundreds of miles away already."

"What the hell? How?"

The elf shook off the minor swear. "We use a sunstone to heat this place. It's essentially a tiny star. The furnace is infinitely long and always changing. That's why Tinker has had to help us. Those goggles of hers are the only thing that can lead you out!"

"Tink go get husband," the goblin declared, pulling the lenses over her eyes. "Fix furnace too. You see."

"You can't go in there!" Alabaster shook his head. "Jack sent the spirits of Christmas themselves in there! How was he able to command them? Only Santa can do that! As for your friends, they're as good as dead. I'm sorry."

Tink rounded on Alabaster and grabbed him by the straps of his overalls. With surprising strength, she lifted him and slammed him into the wall. Holding him with one hand, she pulled the hammer from her tool belt and pressed it against his chin.

"Take back." Her voice was quiet, but her yellow eyes had gone wild, and she was breathing heavily through her nose. "Pointy ears wrong, take back wrong words!"

Alabaster scowled at the goblin. "I'm not afraid of you," he told her, then pointed up at the ceiling. "I'm afraid of whoever is up there, running the show. That voice is one of the scariest things I've ever heard, and the fact that Jack was taking orders from it is even worse!"

"I didn't hear anything," Kisa said. "It was just radio static."

Holly and Tink both looked at Kisa. "Really?" asked Holly. "It was all growly."

"Not growly," Tink added. "German." She set Alabaster down. "Tink go in furnace, find husband."

"You won't be able to find him. The goggles will guide you out, but they won't help you find him. And even if you do, the spirits will have gotten to him first. They will show him things about himself that he isn't willing to accept, and that will drive him to madness."

"Tink no care." She was already walking toward the furnace. "Husband come for Tink, now Tink turn to help."

"Hey, wait." Kisa caught Tink's tail and held it. "Is it even safe in there?"

"With the heat off? Yeah, sure." Alabaster shook his head. "You're more likely to starve to death though. Elves who've gone in almost never come out."

"Husband different." Tink whipped her head around. "Always beat odds. Pointy ears want Tink help? Husband first." She jabbed her finger in Alabaster's direction, then turned back to the furnace. "Fix stupid furnace after."

"Tink." Kisa tugged her tail again. "Hold up. If I come with you, I can sense where he is. That'll help us find him, and then you can bring us all out."

Tink nodded, then looked at the elves. "Tink go now."

"Wait." Holly reached into her pouch and pulled out an impossible length of Christmas garland. She wrapped it around Tink's waist and tied it off, then moved on to Kisa. "Don't get separated," she told them. "Even if you're only a foot apart, the furnace can split you up. Also, I have some cookies you can take with you. They'll keep you from getting hungry, at least."

Holly looked like she was going to say something else, but behind them, the elevator groaned. Everyone turned to look as the dial moved again.

"Are they coming back? Why?" Alabaster frowned as the dial turned. They watched the ornate arm rotate until a hideous screeching sound filled the air when the elevator was halfway there. The shaft vibrated as the lights flickered overhead.

The white elf slapped his earmuffs on and, with a panicked expression, took the garland from Holly. He tied a knot around her waist and gave her a push toward the furnace.

"Run!" He cried, then pushed them again. "All of you! Go, now!"

"Allie, what's happening?" Holly tried to undo the knot at her waist, but Alabaster shoved her toward the furnace again.

"There's no time. You have to get away!" Alabaster winced when a loud screech filled the chamber. The magical lights overhead dimmed to a glow as a low bass tone filled the room, then burst into a symphony of whispers. "One of us needs to survive, and it needs to be you!"

Kisa had heard enough. The sound itself reminded her of the time she'd fought an angel, and she half expected a winged abomination to burst out of the elevator shaft and demand revenge. She grabbed Holly around the waist and started running toward the furnace.

"No, stop, wait!" Holly tried to fight them, but Tink helped Kisa lift the elf as the two of them dragged her into the darkness of the furnace. Tink handed Kisa a flashlight, then snapped the lenses of her goggles into place.

Behind them, there was a loud whoosh, followed by sizzling metal. Alabaster had pulled out a welding torch that looked like a candy cane and was attempting to weld the doors together. The sparks that fell from the magical tool danced around on the floor and laughed like children before puffing into nothingness.

"Keep going!" he cried. "Don't let anything happen to Holly!"

The elevator door reached their floor, then buzzed loudly when the door wouldn't open. Something hit it from the inside, causing the doors to split apart and release a cloud of smoke.

Kisa looked back to see a long dark arm burst forth from the doors and grab Alabaster by the head. Long fingers easily palmed Alabaster's skull and dragged him toward the elevator.

"Mother of Kris Kringle!" Holly's eyes were wide with terror as the doors opened farther. Inside the darkness and the smoke, something laughed as Alabaster was pulled inside. "Run faster!"

Alabaster screamed, then went silent. The elevator doors groaned as they were forced apart by a pair of those dark, sinister hands. Kisa let out a shriek as the doors burst open, and then she slammed into a wall and fell. Everything went abruptly quiet, the air stinking of magic and sulfur.

"Ow, damn it!" She scrambled to her feet and tried to run, but Holly and Tink grabbed onto her and wrestled her to the ground.

"Safe now! Safe!" Tink pointed back the way they had come. "Look!"

Kisa looked past Tink and saw that a solid wall had appeared. "Won't that thing come out where we did?"

As if in response, a distant roar could be heard off to her left.

"No, but he's probably in here with us already." Holly shivered. "I've heard the stories, but I never believed he could come back."

"He who?"

Holly sat back on the ground and let go of Kisa, then hugged herself tightly. Instead of speaking, she broke into quiet sobs of grief.

IT WAS PITCH BLACK, AND THE GROUND WAS SLOPED ENOUGH that Mike slid at an accelerating rate. He kicked his legs out to try to feel a wall and felt around for something else to grab with his free hand.

He had a fistful of Yuki's tail in his other hand. Logic dictated that pulling her tail was an absolute no-no, but every fiber of his being screamed *Danger!* at the thought of releasing her.

Yuki grunted next to him, and he heard a loud pop, followed by the sound of screeching metal. As they came to a stop, he fell over a ledge and dangled by one arm in the darkness. Above him, Yuki howled in pain. He summoned another spider, having it jump and stick to the wall.

The spider provided enough illumination to see that he was dangling over a pit. He couldn't see the bottom, and bits of dirt and ash drifted past them from somewhere up above. Down below, a few tarot cards fluttered out of sight.

"Damn it, Mike! At least grab my leg!"

"Sorry!" Unburdened by a fear of heights, he pulled himself up by gathering Yuki's other tails into a bundle and climbing them. He was able to get a solid grip on her ankle. "What are you holding on to?"

"Summoned some swords," she replied. "But I can't let go or we'll fall."

"Understood." He summoned another spider and sent it up the wall and over the ledge. They didn't provide much light, but there was no other illumination to see by. "Better?"

"I see a ledge with a handrail." She grunted, and there was a popping sound from up above, followed by a shower of sparks. "I think I can get us there. Why don't you get a better grip?"

Unable to do much else, Mike obeyed. He pulled himself up to her waist and was chagrined when his head ended up inside Yuki's robes. The lingering odor of her bath with Naia clung to her skin, and if he weren't dangling over a bottomless pit, he would have chanced extricating himself to assume a better position.

"You're heavy," Yuki grunted, then said nothing else. Progress was slow, and he tried really hard not to notice how smooth her legs felt against his face. Kisa had a thin layer of hair over her entire body, but Yuki's skin alternated between fox and human, creating patches of fur along her form. Her thighs had no such deviation that he could feel, and he wasn't about to ask about her choice in fur distribution.

The process was only a couple of minutes, but it felt like hours. Yuki's movements had slowed significantly, and sweat now poured down her legs.

"You good?" he asked.

"No." She had stopped moving. "We're by the ledge, but I don't know if I can make it."

"We kind of don't have a choice," he told her. "Unless you want me to let go." He wondered if he would fall a few feet and teleport somewhere else in the furnace. It was better to take the chance than potentially kill both of them.

"Don't!" She grunted, then moaned in pain. "Even if you did, I don't think I can pull myself up. I'm sorry."

Mike sighed, his magic uncoiling inside him. "Don't be sorry, you're doing your best. I can get us back up. This is going to hurt, by the way."

"What?"

He summoned the magic, allowing the raw electrical charge to build up in his hand. This was going to be tricky enough, and there wasn't going to be enough time to explain it. Saying a little prayer, he clamped his palm down on Yuki's thigh and let it all loose.

The kitsune tensed up as the charge ran through her body and into the metal hilts of the swords, causing the muscles in her body to lock into place. With his other hand, he pushed her robes open so he could start climbing up her body. Her eyes were wide and her teeth bared when he moved his hand to her side and transferred the magic over. The current running through her body kept her from letting go, and he knew he could only hold out for a few more seconds before the magic was gone.

Two more transfers later, he saw that she had been summoning swords and stabbing them into the metal ducting to use as handholds. The blades were short like daggers but had gotten the job done. Mike and Yuki were now only a couple of feet below a catwalk.

It was difficult, but Mike managed to maneuver himself up onto the previous set of blades while holding on to her left wrist. He hooked his arm around the corner rail of the catwalk and then released the magic.

Yuki gasped and went limp beneath him. Mike pulled her up by pushing off the swords with his feet, then slipped his arm around her back once she was high enough.

With a shove, he was able to push her up onto the ledge. Yuki crawled away from the corner as he pulled himself up behind her. His limbs felt like they were on fire, and he lay on the cool metal, gasping for air.

"You…shocked…me…" It was both an accusation and a statement of fact.

"Sorry," he mumbled, feeling sick to his stomach. Quetzalli had taught him how to control the flow, but his mastery over it wasn't the best. He was nowhere near throwing lightning by any means and had accidentally given Tink a nasty zap one day while messing around. Luckily, the goblin had thought it was just kinky foreplay. "You okay?"

"Everything hurts," she whispered.

"I'll make it up to you." The little lightning spider nearby popped out of existence as his magic went dormant. Using it to run a current through Yuki had drained him to nothing.

In the dark, he reached for her. The soft fur of her robes felt good beneath his fingers. He crawled toward her, then groaned in agony as he sat up and leaned against one of the railing supports. Yuki said nothing as he pulled her between his outstretched legs and leaned over her protectively.

"Let's just rest for now," he told her, fighting back a yawn. It had been almost bedtime when Holly had appeared in his house, and he was officially tired. The darkness in the furnace was absolute, yet he felt like he was being watched.

They sat there for a while. Mystery lights flickered along the edges of his vision, but he realized they were still there even when he closed his eyes. There was a term for them, but the memory escaped him.

With nothing but phantom lights for company, he found himself nodding off more than once. The temperature of the room was fine for now, but it definitely felt cooler. Or was that just a side effect of strenuous climbing? It was hard to say.

He wondered how many presents Lily had opened. There was a small amount of guilt over leaving her behind, but clearly all was not well at the North Pole. If Santa's bag was in danger, she was well equipped to handle it. Death was probably keeping her out of trouble.

Romeo. Lily's voice echoed from the darkness, but he wasn't sure if he had imagined it. The succubus hadn't been around much lately and had seemed surlier than usual. He supposed it was related to the birth of Callisto, his son.

The centaur tribe had sent for him and Ratu on the day he was born. The pregnancy had gone well, but Zel had known the birth would be difficult. Her human vagina was never going to be sufficient to accommodate a centaur foal. Preparations had been made, and several of the herd's healers had been brought together to figure out how to deliver the child surgically.

Despite all their preparations, things had gone downhill quickly. Helpless, Mike had stood by and listened to the healers and Ratu debate how to remove the child quickly in case Zel didn't survive. The centaurs were capable healers, but major abdominal surgery was not an art they had brought with them from their former herd.

Salvation had come in the shape of Lily. Mike had left the yurt to pray when Lily had teleported directly to his side. Admonishing him for trying to involve a big hairy bastard who didn't give a shit, she had walked into the yurt and started barking commands. Apparently, she had used the Dreamscape over a year ago to take a class on veterinary medicine to stitch Dana up, and she also had a couple of souls in her collection with the knowledge to guide the healers through the complex operation.

Zel had survived, and Callisto had come into the world with his father's hair and his mother's eyes. Lily, usually uncouth, had spent several minutes silently casting sidelong glances at the child. Satisfied Zel would survive, she had promptly excused herself and vanished for two weeks.

"Mmph." Yuki stretched beneath him. "I fell asleep."

"It's fine." He rubbed the top of her head, right between her ears. "I've got a bit left in me, and who knows when we'll get another chance."

She sighed in his arms, then fell into another deep slumber. Mike waited a few minutes and tried to summon a spider for light. He couldn't even make the sparks appear, and a throbbing pain shot through his right wrist and forearm.

Fucking figures, he thought. *Nearly fell to my death after a pissing match with Jack Frost, and now I can't get it up.*

He put his hand back on Yuki's head and used the soft fur at the base of her ears like a worry stone. She mumbled something, then wrapped an arm around his leg and held him tight.

His thoughts drifted back to Callisto, then to Tink and Kisa. He could feel Kisa moving around somewhere beneath him, which made zero sense. Since they had essentially teleported away from everything, it was likely that she was in the furnace with them as well.

He thought back on the encounter with Jack. There was something nagging at him about the whole event, but he couldn't quite put his finger on it. He had been too worried that Jack would find the others to think past the moment. Now that he had the time, he would use it to analyze what he had learned. The North Pole hadn't just been abandoned. At a minimum, Jack was out looking for troublemakers. But why?

Somewhere in the darkness, water started dripping. He yawned, then scratched Yuki's head some more. The rhythmic rubbing of her head had become a form of self-hypnosis, and he felt his attention waning.

Shaking his head, he blinked away the sparkling lights that appeared once more. They shifted back and forth like a metronome, and he tried to look away but couldn't. He remembered learning about them in Boy Scouts, something about how lights would appear if you got lost in a cave with no light source. Cavers would chase those phantom lights, thinking escape was just around the corner. If they were lucky, they would slam into a wall rather than fall into a crack and vanish from the world.

Thinking about being stuck in a crack in the earth made him think of Leeds. That fucker had likely lost his mind months ago, but Mike had no way of knowing. Once a month, Abella would make a trip out that direction to make sure Leeds's living tomb looked undisturbed. Mike had considered going with her just to piss on the bastard's mountain but had spent the time at Velvet's grave instead. They had buried her next to her parents in a spot with a beautiful view of the valley.

The lights were closer now, or maybe just larger? It was so hard to focus; the chill in the air was making him huddle over Yuki, and she was like a tiny heater.

He rubbed his face, then shook his head. Falling asleep here was a bad idea, but he was just so tired.

"Callisto? Stop being like that, this is your father." Zel held her hand out to the foal standing behind the apothecary table in her yurt. Callisto shook his head vehemently. Newborn centaurs looked more like six-year-olds than infants. His unruly locks bounced across his shoulders as he grabbed a stack of Zel's journals and pulled them into a small wall so Mike couldn't see him.

"No!" Callisto shouted, then tried to duck down behind the book stack. "Scary monster!"

Mike's eyes snapped open, and he sat upright. Sleep had snuck up on him so quickly that he hadn't even had the opportunity to manipulate the Dreamscape. How long had he been out?

It couldn't have been long, right? He flexed his hand and tried to summon the magic once more. Even a little bit of light would help him stay awake.

The phantom lights now loomed overhead, and he looked up at them with a frown. He had never really thought about the fact that maybe they weren't a hallucination. He squeezed his eyes shut, and they remained. Still just a figment of his imagination. While his eyes were shut, he thought of Zel once again and felt the dream spring up around him.

"I'm so sorry." Zel took Mike's hand in hers and squeezed. "I don't know why he does this. He won't talk about it while you're gone either."

"I don't either." Mike looked at the stuffed bear on the ground. He had brought it in the hopes it would break the ice, but Callisto had refused to touch it. Centaur children developed language skills remarkably fast, so it was easy to forget that Callisto was only a couple of months old.

When Mike knelt to pick up the bear, its fur slid off and revealed the sleek surface beneath it. Startled, he dropped it on the ground. The thing inside uncoiled, revealing a large isopod that looked up at him and screeched.

"Gah!" Mike shook his head and pinched his inner arm. He had dozed off again. What was the deal with the weird dreams?

Yuki trembled, then muttered something.

"What's that?" he asked.

"Emily," Yuki replied, then whimpered. Mike sighed, then rubbed Yuki's head. She exhaled and became still again. He wasn't even sure she had woken up. The silence of the furnace made every sound seem that much louder, and he could hear the beating of his own heart. He tried to ignore it, but that steady cadence had him closing his eyes for just a moment.

"Let me go!" Callisto fought his way free of his mother and rushed out the door of the yurt. Outside, Mike heard one of the centaur guards follow after him. The last time he had come, Callisto had gotten lost in the woods for an hour until Zel had found him.

"Damn!" Zel stared helplessly at the flaps. "I don't know why this is so hard!"

"Don't worry about it," he told her, then moved next to her and wrapped his arm around her waist. "I'll keep trying, no matter how long it takes." Down below, he heard the shifting of chitinous armor as the isopod tried to crawl up on his foot.

"I'm not afraid of you," he declared, then snatched up the isopod. Its mouthparts shifted as it waved its legs helplessly. "In fact, you look rather like a lobster. Maybe I'll see if Sofia will cook you up and serve you with butter."

"Three!" The isopod's voice was like a croaking frog. "Tonight you will be haunted by three spirits!"

"Eat my ass, Ebenezer." He forced the isopod into a ball, then drop-kicked it through the flaps of the tent. The flaps rattled and spun like a plastic Rolodex.

Mike opened his eyes again and saw that the phantom lights were gone. Instead, an ethereal being hovered above him, the light from its body illuminating him and Yuki. If this was a hallucination, it was a damned good one.

"Radley," it whispered through a lipless mouth. It had a face that could have been made of porcelain, but there was little humanity in its eyes. It shifted, sometimes having arms, then legs, then nothing at all but a face with silken white hair that hung to the ground.

"Casper," he replied. "I don't suppose you're here because you want a friend? You bring me a sleeping bag and a pillow and I'll hook you up. We'll go bar crawling. Chicks love ghosts now. Dudes too, for that matter."

"I am the Ghost of Christmas Past," it told him with a voice that sounded like it was coming through a long tube. "And I am here regarding your welfare."

"Of fucking course." He moved his hand behind Yuki's ear and gave it a pinch. When he felt her startle, he slid a hand over her mouth to keep her quiet. "The weird dream with the bug? Was Marley on vacation? Aren't you supposed to read me my rights first? I demand my lawyer be present, but unthaw her first. She can't do much right now." He pictured her ass, bent over and just sitting in his living room like a work of art.

His magic moved. It was minor, but it was definitely there.

The spirit stared at him, then freaked out. Its features distorted and jumped about as if they were in a video game and it was glitching. He heard his own voice repeat the words he had just said, only there was a fair amount of growling involved. It let out a cry, then whirled around the room before popping back into position above him as if nothing had happened.

"I am here regarding your welfare." The spirit moved closer, its amorphous body shifting in the light until it had a physical form. The spirit's body was small, like a child's, but its limbs were muscular and much longer than an adult's. It made

Mike think of a demented cross between a porcelain doll and a Stretch Armstrong toy from his youth.

Once fully formed, the spirit wore a white tunic with a shiny belt at the waist and a flowing skirt beneath. It carried a sprig of holly in one hand, and a beam of light shot from its head and into the gloom up above like a reverse spotlight.

"Rise, and walk with me." The spirit extended a hand just as Yuki summoned a circle of swords above the spirit with a tarot card. The blades shot into the Ghost of Christmas Past, only to vanish in a blast of light.

"No-no-no-no-no-no…" The spirit clutched at its brow, agony written across its enigmatic features. Mike tried to help Yuki to her feet, but they were too slow. With a scream, the spirit grabbed both of them with its overtly long arms and then pulled them over the side of the catwalk and into the void beneath.

"WELL, THAT WAS SOMETHING." LILY HOPPED OUT OF THE sleigh and took a look at it. The sides had giant gouges from where the cat had hit it, but the wood shimmered as the damage repaired itself. "Let's not do that again."

"We may not have a choice." Death sounded serious. When she looked up, she saw that dark shadows circled in the mist, their eyes blazing with malice.

"I wouldn't," Lily warned, allowing her wings to unfold behind her. Horns burst from her forehead as she returned to the sleigh and stood next to Death. Ever since the shadow's defeat, the demons had been thick in this part of the Underworld, but they rarely came this close to the gate. "If I don't rip you a new asshole, he will." She gestured at Death with her thumb.

There was a growl as six fiery orbs appeared above them all. Cerberus barked, and the demons scattered as the hellhound smashed one with a paw and snagged another in her teeth. Two heads ripped it apart while the third stared at Death expectedly.

"You are a good girl." Death reached into his robes and pulled out a trio of biscuits in a stack. Once the demon was torn apart, Cerberus stared intently at the reaper. He tossed the biscuits in an arc, and all three of them were snapped out of the air by the different heads.

"You've got to be shitting me," Lily said.

"I am incapable of shitting." Death hopped out of the sleigh and approached Cerberus. The hellhound rolled onto her side, giving Death full access to her belly. Death held his arms wide and pushed himself face-first into it. He started scratching, which made Cerberus's tail wag. "Who's a good girl? You're a good girl!"

"When the hell did this happen?" Lily demanded. As far as she knew, Cerberus only listened to Mike or her.

"I do not require sleep, my dear succubus. I have plenty of time on my hands, and other dogs are afraid of me." Death continued scratching until Cerberus let out a whine. "Besides, Mike Radley and I will sometimes come to take her for a walk. He does this when he is feeling anxious about fatherhood."

Lily just shook her head. She had no idea but hadn't exactly been around much lately. Ever since the foal had come along, she had made herself scarce. She just couldn't handle the way everyone fawned over him, and would even admit to more than a little jealousy. It wasn't that she wanted to pump out babies but that she hated the fact that someone was able to give Mike something she couldn't.

Cerberus shifted into human form, then bowed her heads reverently at Lily. It was always weird seeing a three-headed human in a goth dress, but at least the outfit matched the atmosphere.

"Mistress." The center head spoke while the side heads whispered simultaneously. It was far less confusing than how they usually spoke, which was each head taking a syllable at a time. "Why have you brought this here?"

"What, this?" She jerked her thumb at the sleigh. "We were running from a bunch of trolls and a giant fucking cat. Why are there so many demons running about? Shouldn't you be keeping the place clear?"

"They are attracted to this Divine Object." Cerberus walked over to the sleigh and put a hand on it. She sniffed the air, then touched Santa's bag. "And maybe this as well. This shouldn't be here."

"Of course it shouldn't, but I'm stuck babysitting it." Lily leaned against the sleigh. "And we needed help."

"No." Cerberus squinted at the giant bag. "This shouldn't be *here.* It has no smell to it, it shouldn't exist."

"What do you mean, it has no smell? It's a bag, it shouldn't stink." But Lily knew better, for nothing in Creation had a better sense of smell than a hellhound. Since Cerberus was capable of sniffing out even the toughest shape-shifting demon, the fact that she couldn't even detect the lingering scent of the house on its fabric was a sign. Whether good or bad, Lily didn't know yet.

"It is like the emptiness of the Void. I can sense a great nothingness where it sits, yet can both see and touch it." Cerberus sniffed the air, her eyes glowing. "More demons come. They can sense it. I will hold them off, but stronger ones approach. You cannot stay." With those words, Cerberus transformed back into a three-headed dog and wandered into the mist.

"Well, fuck me with a stick." It hadn't occurred to Lily that Cerberus would ask them to leave. "What do we do now?"

When she got no response, she saw that Death was perusing the user's manual. On the cover was a picture of a Santa hat, and it had a candy-cane spine.

"Ah. Aha!" Death looked up at Lily. "I have found the section of the manual that will allow us to shoot our foes!"

"Wait, what?" She moved by his side and laughed. He was looking at the troubleshooting chapter. "That doesn't mean actual shooting."

"It doesn't?" Death frowned and flipped through the pages. It took him a bit to scan each page, but his reading speed was already impressive for a guy lacking eyeballs. "Oh. Oh dear. You appear to be right."

"Told you." She heard a random growl in the mist and turned in time to see a demon vanish just before Cerberus reappeared nearby. The hellhound snorted, then gave chase. "I have no fucking clue what to do next. Maybe that book has some advice for us."

Death said nothing, his eyes blazing as he continued to read. The book was tiny in his hands, yet he used both to hold it open.

Lily climbed on top of the bag and opened it up. Inside, the multicolored packages were packed in tightly, yet it was easy to reach deep into the bag and pull one out. When she turned it over, it had her name on it.

"Ha ha, I'm so naughty, ho ho ho." She shook the small box and was surprised that it felt so light. Thinking it would be more coal, she ripped open the package and was puzzled to discover a small felt box inside. She opened it up and saw something shiny.

"What the fuck?" It took her a moment to realize she was looking at a jeweler's loupe. It was a tool used for examining gemstones and other fine jewelry for defects, so she had no idea why Santa would give her one. "Should have included a gift receipt, big man."

Toying with the loupe, she looked at her own hair and fingernails before leaning down to examine the fabric of the bag. Instead of crushed velvet, she was stunned to see herself looking at an ever-shifting surface that looked like waves of red liquid fractals that crashed into each other and created new patterns. The fractals would bounce off of one another, and she could have sworn that faces were forming. However, when she would shift to look closer, they would vanish.

Someone pulled her hair, and she spun around and hissed, her tongue elongating into a snake's. It was just Death, and he let out a sigh of relief.

"There you are, I was worried about you!" He held up the user's manual. "I've finished reading the troubleshooting section, and believe I know what to do next."

"What do you mean, you've finished it? You just started."

Death shook his head. "You have been staring at that bag for hours now, and I did not wish to disturb you."

"What?" Lily looked at the loupe in her hand, then over at the bag. "You're fucking with me."

"I do not fuck," he informed her, then held up the book. "Does this look familiar?"

Drawn in perfect detail on the page was the large cat that had chased them. It was caught in mid yawn, which made it look far less intimidating than she would have expected.

"Jólakötturinn?" She took the book from him and read the page. "The Yule Cat? What the hell am I looking at?"

"He eats children, Lily, children!" Death took the book back from her. "And it says right here that in the event of an encounter with the Jólakötturinn, we should avoid him entirely."

"Too late."

"I agree, which is why we come to the second passage. If hunted by the Yule Cat, we must remain one step ahead of him. He is attracted to the bag and will stop at nothing to get it. However, he is poor at tracking, so the best solution is to simply evade his claws and carry on. We will lose him eventually."

"What do you mean by 'carry on'? Carry on what?"

Death's toothy smile somehow twisted upward into a full-blown grin as he let out a laugh that raised all the hairs on the back of Lily's neck. "What indeed, dear succubus! What indeed!"

Serious doubts manifested in Lily's mind over Death's intentions. His sense of childlike wonder about the world around him didn't reassure her about whatever dubious plan he was concocting. However, the growling in the mists was becoming louder, and it was only a matter of time before even more dangerous things than demons came sniffing around.

"Ah, fuck it," she told Death. Despite her thoughts to the contrary, he had been right every step of the way so far. It would probably save them time if she just went against her better judgment and rolled with whatever crazy-ass idea he had. "I'm in."

GHOSTS OF THE PAST

The yawning void of the furnace melted away into a puddle of bright lights. Mike covered his eyes and groaned, the sudden intensity blinding him. His arm was sore where the Ghost of Christmas Past had grabbed him, and he rubbed at it absent-mindedly.

He was standing in an apartment but didn't recognize it. All around, he could see Christmas decorations, old-school metallic tinsel, and a tree decorated with bubbling lights. Based on the wood paneling and the record player churning out Bing Crosby, his best guess was that he was in the eighties.

"I've seen stranger things," he muttered. Movement behind the tree caught his eye when a little boy of about three emerged from beneath the pine branches. He was pushing a toy car on the floor, making vroom sounds with his mouth.

The boy looked up and through Mike. It was amazing how much he looked like Callisto. So it wasn't the eighties but the midnineties. The decor hadn't been updated was all.

"Ooh, spooky. My childhood." Mike dragged out the words and waggled his fingers. Turning around, he was pleased to find the spirit behind him. Christmas Past sat on a nearby side table like a demented Elf on a Shelf. "Okay, I've seen the Christmas specials. You show me my past and remind me of the true meaning of Christmas. But since this place is decorated, I'm afraid you won't have many other good moments from my childhood to share. Mom barely registered that Christmas existed. Also, what gives? Why am I even here? I'm not some fudging miser who…" Mike paused. "Fudging. Fuddddge. Sprinkles. Oh Kringle, I sound like Holly now."

Christmas Past twisted its lips up in a sadistic grin. "These are the shadows of things that have been. They have…"

"Yeah, yeah, they can't see us." Mike picked up a coaster and threw it toward his younger self. It vanished in a puff of static and reappeared on the nearby table. "But still. I'm not some crumbling cookie that…really? Crumbling cookie?" He hated that his lips twisted into the family-safe vocabulary. Shaking his head, he looked at the spirit. "I don't hate Christmas. I don't hate people. I actually quite enjoy Christmas and giving to others. So what's the purpose of me being here?"

The spirit responded by opening its mouth wider than its head, letting out a soul-piercing shriek. Mike plugged his ears as the spirit's body shifted around the room, transforming several times. This certainly hadn't been covered in any of the movies he had watched. If he didn't know better, he would say the spirit wasn't sure why he was here either.

Christmas Past slammed back onto the side table, sending a visible ripple through the room. Toddler Mike slid back under the tree on his belly as time reversed itself, then came crawling back out once it stabilized.

"These are the shadows of things that have been. They have no consciousness of us." The ghost repeated itself as if reading from a script. "Do you recognize this place?"

"Nope. I haven't even seen it in pictures." He wandered the room, then contemplated the child under the tree. It was strange seeing his younger self. "You've got a long fudging road ahead of you," he told the toddler. "You can thank your mother for that."

As if on cue, someone in the kitchen started singing the chorus to "Jingle Bells." He was surprised when his mother emerged from the kitchen holding a plate with a small stack of bell-shaped cookies. She was in a sweater dress with leggings, and her cheeks had a healthy glow. There were actual curves to her face and body, which was something Mike had never seen. In her final years, she had lost enough weight that she had taken on a thin, hawkish appearance that made her look downright predatory.

"Mikey, would you like a cookie?" She sat down on the couch and placed the plate next to her. Mikey bolted from beneath the tree, but his mother used her foot to hold him back. "Hang on, mister, you haven't paid the cookie toll!"

Mikey blew several kisses at his mother, and she moved her leg so he could sit next to her. Pulling a book from behind the side table, she opened it. "Can I read you a story?"

"This isn't real," Mike muttered. There was no fudging way.

"But it is." The spirit drifted around behind the couch. "This one was buried deep inside you, but it is here for you to behold."

The front door slammed, and heavy footsteps came through the house. A man in a stocking cap walked into the living room carrying a pair of grocery bags. He smiled and held them up in victory. "I've got eggnog!" he declared.

Mikey squirmed out of his mother's grip and ran to his father.

"Dad." Mike barely managed to say the word as he sat on the edge of the recliner. This was a man relegated only to rare photographs and who was otherwise a complete mystery. His nose was a bit longer than Mike's, and there were smile lines all around his eyes. He wore a brown leather jacket that was dusted lightly with snow, and when he walked past Mike, the scent of the wet leather triggered memories of being scooped up and held tightly. Mike wiped tears from his eyes, not sure whether to be grateful or angry.

"Were you good?" Mike's father pulled a small candy cane from his pocket and unwrapped it.

"Yep!" Mikey held his hand up and took the candy.

"Honey." Mike's mother frowned. "He won't eat dinner if you give him sweets."

"Don't think I don't see that plate of cookies." He winked at his wife and sat next to her on the couch. "Now give me some sugar."

Smirking, she handed him a cookie. He laughed, then stole a quick kiss from her before taking it.

"Give me sugar too!" Mikey's face was now covered with red streaks from the candy cane. His father scooped him up and kissed his cheek, then blew a raspberry that had Mikey chortling in glee.

There were so many questions Mike had for the man. If his timeline was correct, this was the last Christmas he'd spent with his father. He would fall ill in the spring and die before the summer. It was hard to believe this was his family. He didn't know how to reconcile his mother's later behavior with the woman before him now. She had baked him cookies and read him stories. What had turned her into the emotional wrecking ball she had become?

"Why?" he asked her, knowing full well she couldn't hear him. "What fudged you up so bad that you turned into a raging grinch?"

His mother stared ahead as if lost in thought. Mike recognized the look; it was the same one he made when he was thinking. Kisa had even snapped a picture to tease him with. When he was caught up in his own head, she liked to text it to him sometimes. With his mother, though, it was different. A switch had been flipped, and she had become disconnected from the world around her.

Noticing her sudden silence, his father wandered over and nudged her leg.

"Hey. Did you remember your medicine?" The playful tone was gone, replaced with worry. The mood was suddenly serious, and Mike was unsure why.

"Hmm?" She shook her head. "Oh, no, I didn't. Sorry, I'm so scatterbrained, thanks for reminding me."

"That's what I'm here for." His father smiled at Mikey. "And this one, too, when he's older."

"What medicine?" Mike asked, then followed his mother out of curiosity. As far as he knew, other than the occasional street drugs, she had never been on anything. Maybe it was a seasonal cold or something; Santa knew he'd gotten them most years until he inherited the house.

Going to the master bathroom, she opened the medicine cabinet to reveal a couple different prescription bottles full of pills. She swallowed a pill from each with water, then stared at herself in the mirror as if lost. After a few deep breaths, she put on a fake smile and walked back to the living room.

"Not all struggles are apparent to a child." The spirit appeared next to Mike, now just a floating head surrounded by a halo of hair. It had taken on his father's features. "Those pills were meant to help her. But after your father died…"

"She would forget and stop taking them. But that shouldn't matter, should it?" Mike opened up the medicine cabinet and pulled one of the bottles out. "Risperidone? What is that for?" He turned the bottle around, but it only had dosing information on the handwritten label. Frowning, he contemplated the pills. Was it an antipsychotic? Had his entire fudged-up childhood been the result of a forgotten prescription?

"Don't you see? You've hated her for so long, but now you know the truth." A triumphant grin was plastered on Christmas Past's face. "Your father's death broke her, and her condition got worse as a result. You've spent your whole life hating someone because of events outside their control. Doesn't that make you feel bad?"

It felt like he was spinning. The deep-seated hatred he had for his mother suddenly felt so shallow. He had always assumed his father's death had broken her and she had just been too weak to put herself back together, but now there was an additional layer. Who else knew? Had her friends? His father's friends? When he looked at Christmas Past, it had an expectant grin that reminded him of the Cheshire cat.

"No, it doesn't. I still hate her for the things she did. Even if her actions weren't entirely her fault, she still tormented me as a child and screwed me up as an adult. It's okay to understand why somebody does the things they do and still hate them for it. If anything, I feel sorry for her, but that's it. What's done is done."

Christmas Past looked like it had been slapped in the face.

"You aren't very good at this," Mike told it. "I'm really not sure what you're trying to accomplish here, but a raccoon wielding a kitchen knife would threaten me more than you do."

The spirit flickered, parts of their face expanding like a balloon and then deflating. Their cheeks were now red, and their eyes had gone crooked.

"Oh dear," Mike muttered. "Did I hurt your feelings? Eat my candy cane, you sad excuse for a spirit."

Footsteps at the door made him turn around. Mikey stood there, holding what was left of his candy cane in one hand and his toy car in the other. He stared right at Mike, curiosity in his eyes.

"I thought they couldn't see us?" He looked over at the spirit, but Christmas Past had folded in on itself like a sheet of origami for the darned.

"I'm not some fudging miser!" they shouted in Mike's voice over and over again. Mikey put his hands over his ears and ran away as Mike contemplated the spirit. He wasn't sure what had happened, but it was clear he had broken the darned thing.

"Do you come with an off switch?" he yelled.

"Miser! Miser!" Christmas Past screeched. Its body popped out of existence, leaving the ghost as nothing more than a floating head. The spirit seemed disoriented as it spun aimlessly, growling with menace. It drifted into the bedroom until it was facing the open door of the hallway. Just outside the room, Mike heard the patter of Mikey's feet on the hardwood, and the spirit's pupils dilated as it sniffed the air.

Howling, it darted forward into Mike. Anticipating this, Mike snatched it by the hair and spun it into the mirror. Upon making contact with the spirit, he felt a cold chill shoot up his arm, his fingers tingling. The glass shattered, then time reversed until the mirror was whole again.

"What on earth was that?" It was his mother's voice. Whatever was happening, whether dream, memory, or reality, Mike couldn't chance accidentally changing his own past. This was supposed to be a construct, but he couldn't know for sure. He pushed the bedroom door shut and pressed the button to lock it.

The two of them struggled, but the spirit had very little mass and was now moaning. Mike opened the nearby window to shove it outside, but the cold white sky was gone. Instead, a dark void had replaced it, with tiny lights in the distance.

"Mikey, did you lock this door?" His mother was rattling the doorknob now. "Honey, get the screwdriver."

"Good a place as any," Mike declared, then dove outside with the spirit wrapped in his arms. As they fell, he saw his memories spread out like holograms, all of them frozen with lines of static like an old VCR screen. Grabbing onto the spirit, he tilted his body toward one of the memories and crashed into it.

He slid across the polished floor of a hotel lobby, clutching Christmas Past's head to his body. Through the windows, a ferocious blizzard churned, and Mike saw a younger version of himself sitting in a lounge chair and staring out into the snow.

"Ah, nice. The year my girlfriend Rebecca and I got stranded while traveling." They had gone to visit her family for Christmas. However, a storm had diverted their plane, forcing them to stay in a place by the airport. If he remembered correctly, she was upstairs in their room wearing red-and-white lingerie while crying hysterically. He stood, using just his legs to keep the spirit from escaping. "If you were trying to fudge with my head, this would have been a better place to start. Remind me of the people I hurt instead of expecting waterworks for my parents. Now I know you're just being a jerk. You stink at this."

"This was the year that—" Christmas Past's next words were choked off when Mike squeezed.

He knew what year it was. Rebecca had been nice enough, easily one of the best women he had ever dated. The fight had started because of his impotence. She was crying because he had turned her down mid-blow-job. Rejection was a door that swung both ways, and he regretted how hard it had hit her on the way out.

"It gets better, buddy." Mike patted his past self on the shoulder, then shoved the door of the hotel open. Once outside, he turned his attention to the head in his arms. "And yes, Rebecca ended up marrying a fine man and having kids with him. So I don't need to hear your narrative doody regarding what-ifs."

Christmas Past struggled in his arms but couldn't escape. Mike noticed that its face now looked like Rebecca's, the hair streaked with auburn curls. *Curious.*

"So tell me why you're so weak right now. You were able to handle me and Yuki at the same time in the real world, but now you're like a kitten. Why is that? This is your domain, you should be in charge here." He headed for the corner of the street. It was freezing outside, but he no longer cared.

The spirit bit him hard enough to draw blood, but he ignored the pain. If the last memory had boundaries, this one would too.

It took him another minute, but he found it. A car on the street simply terminated a couple feet early, like the trunk had been sheared away. Though the street continued, Mike kept walking and found himself tumbling once more through the darkness. Christmas Past almost got away from him, but he wrapped its hair around his hand and reeled it back in.

This time, he tried to dodge his memories. Christmas Past fought him anew, pulling him into a couple of different Christmas days. They battled through the Christmas Mike had spent doing raids in *World of Warcraft* all day, then the time he went to a Christmas party and got drunk before puking in the fountain. The spirit's strength waxed and waned, and he had a theory why.

Mike wasn't Scrooge. The whole point of subjecting Ebenezer to the three spirits had been to reform him, to make him into a better person. Mike didn't know why the spirit had come for him. When questioned, it had freaked the fudge out.

No, this had to be a fool's errand, which meant there was more behind the sudden shifting of the tide. If the spirit's sole purpose was reformation, then pushback from the victim would be expected. Making them mad shouldn't cause control to shift so drastically; something deeper was happening.

He theorized that Christmas Past must be losing strength because this wasn't what it had been designed for. It was no different from when he had used his magic to shock Yuki. Back then, he had drained himself to nearly nothing in moments. Christmas Past was running out of steam trying to make Mike miserable rather than reform him.

But that wasn't all. He wasn't the only one in here, which meant the ghost was split between dealing with him and the kitsune. It had already lost the narrative for Mike and was unable to contain him. Trying to torture him with a past he had come to terms with was like peeing in the ocean to make it taste salty.

Yuki, however, was just coming around to the idea of spending time with others at the house. He guessed there was plenty of past misery to be found in her head.

This theory was confirmed when he and the spirit entered a new memory, one he didn't recognize. He was standing on the side of a mountain, and up ahead, a stony tower jutted from the rock as if built there by mistake. It was where Yuki had been imprisoned for so many years in her own personal hell.

As she gazed out at the horizon, it was clear that this memory was far larger than his had been. Was Christmas Past more powerful here? He stumbled and slid down the rocky slope in an attempt to get to the road that led to the tower. As he had hoped, they had fallen far enough that Christmas Past had run out of places to trap him, but Yuki was hundreds of years old and her memories would run deep.

The ghost exploded in his arms, transforming into tiny stars that shot through the air toward the tower. Mike got up and ran after them, doing his best to keep pace. He assumed the spirit was pulling itself together, and he needed to get to Yuki before…

Well, he wasn't sure. But whatever it was, it couldn't be good.

When he arrived, the bridge was pulled up. It was the primary defense from the centaurs in the valley, and there was a long drop straight onto jagged rocks below it. He wouldn't be able to get in the front, not without climbing the sheer rocks nearby. There was a way he could climb down from above, but he would have to take the long way to get there.

"Mother fudging Kris Kringle," he swore as he made a run for the back entrance.

"Absolutely not." Lily stomped her foot on the ground in indignation and turned her back on Death. All around them, shapes shifted in the mist and the air was filled with the growls of angry demons. "There is no fucking way I'm putting those on."

"But, Lily, it says right here in the book that you have to wear these if you want to be Santa's official helper." Death waved the manual overhead to emphasize his point. He was now wearing a hat that matched Santa's coat, as well as a large faux beard that had been tucked away in the bottom of the storage compartment. Clutched tightly in his other hand were a pair of green shoes with comically curled tips.

"I'm not wearing those clown shoes," she declared. "I have the ability to wear whatever the fuck I want, and I can't think of anything that would make those shoes look remotely palatable."

"Cerberus didn't complain about what she had to wear."

Lily looked over at Cerberus. With her now in human form, each head wore a headband with reindeer antlers, the center head also wearing a bright-red nose. Somewhere in Santa's bag, Death had found a package labeled *Cerberus* with an extremely gaudy Christmas sweater inside that fit over her top-heavy frame.

"Yeah, well she has to wear that, doesn't she? Otherwise"—she made scare quotes—"she can't pull the sled."

"Sleigh," Death corrected.

"Whatever. I don't need to wear those fucking shoes just for a ride along. Since you insist on playing dress-up, there has to be something else I can wear instead."

"Hmm." Death contemplated the manual once more, then rummaged around in the storage compartment. "You apparently also get a candy cane and a special sticker."

"Special sticker?" Lily spun about and snatched the

manual from Death's hand using her tail, fingers sprouting from the tip of it to hold the book open in front of her eyes. "Death! It says right here that Santa's official helper is a ceremonial position for any children who might get to ride along for a bit! It doesn't do anything!"

"Oh." Death frowned, then whipped around and sliced through a small demon that had made an attempt for the bag. The thing looked like a cross between an aardvark and a bobcat, and it wailed in agony before something shot out of the mist to carry away its upper half. "Oh darn. I got demon's blood on the sleigh." He leaned over the side and used his thumb to smear it off.

"Okay, here it is. I just need to wear one of the spare hats. There's a safety feature that keeps me from falling out. Not that it matters, because I have wings, but the last thing I need is to get dumped over the Atlantic." She got into the sleigh and moved around Death to access the storage compartment. There were a couple of spare Santa jackets, plenty of blankets, and a few hats tucked inside. It was easy to see that, just like the bag, the sleigh was bigger on the inside.

"There." She pulled out a Santa hat that had a red rim and black velvet up top. "I like this one."

"Oh, it made your ears pointy!" Death flicked Lily's ear with a bony digit, making her jump. A quick touch confirmed that he was right, and no amount of concentrating seemed to undo the transformation.

"Oh, fudge it. Fudge? NO!" She started to pull the hat off, but the ground trembled beneath them, knocking her off-balance. Death frowned, his attention on the demons now sprinting around them, creating a stampede. Horrors from the depths of the pit scrambled by, crushing one another against its red velvet exterior.

If the stampede was a storm, then an eye had formed around Cerberus. The three-headed woman bared her their fangs and transformed back into the hellhound, complete with a massive set of reindeer antlers on each head. The sweater transformed into a harness in a burst of golden light, with a lead rope bedazzled in silver-and-gold bells that connected Cerberus to the sleigh.

The eye of the storm was tightening as the frightened demons broke formation and tried to run over the sleigh. The hellhound blasted the coming horde with flames from her mouths, scorching the dry earth and turning demons to ash. The Rudolph nose fell off the center head and was incinerated in the flames. The demons split even farther now, and collisions with the sleigh came to a halt.

"I have a bad feeling, deep in my bones." Death stared intensely at the mist as a giant creature blotted out the ghost light that lit the Underworld. Seven massive necks stretched into the sky above a body the size of a large building, and a bass note that rattled Lily's rib cage sent a ripple through the fog.

"Holy heck!" Lily slapped Death on the shoulder. "We need to go. Now!" This wasn't some random monster roaming the Underworld but a biblical evil that would have zero qualms about swallowing them whole.

A cacophony of roars filled the Underworld as the creature turned all seven heads in their direction. It marched toward them, the Underworld now silent save for its heavy steps.

Cerberus bolted, pulling the sleigh behind her. Golden sparks formed around the runners of the sleigh as the hellhound raced toward the iron gate. Silver light surrounded them as the sleigh expanded the world to allow them to slip between the bars.

The Yule Cat was waiting, but his eyes widened as Cerberus blasted him with fire, knocking him off the roof of the garage. The air reeked of burned hair, and the cat howled as he rolled around on the snow, crushing one of the trolls. Spectral chains formed around the hellhound's necks, tethering them to the Underworld gate. The lumpy potato trolls raced forward, each of them trying to board the sleigh as Cerberus ran in a circle in the backyard. Crimson flames danced along the surface of the snow, holding back the attackers as Lily stabbed one right between the eyes with her stinger, knocking it free.

Cerberus, confined by the chains, couldn't get past the fountain. The Yule Cat was waiting for them when they circled back to the gate, his fangs bared and smoke rising from his scorched fur. An eerie mist surrounded him, sinking into the Yule Cat and repairing the damage that had been done.

"I thought you said the chains wouldn't be a problem!" Lily kept her head low as the Yule Cat leaped over Cerberus and raked claws across her flank. Cerberus growled, then snapped at the giant cat. It was surprisingly nimble for a creature so large and was able to duck away. The chains tethered Cerberus to the Underworld, and when Lily had brought them up, Death had brushed off the question. He had been right about every other crazy thing that had happened, so she had just figured it was yet another Christmas miracle.

"And they won't be!" Death stood on top of the sleigh, held in place by the magic of the hat he wore. He lifted his scythe up high, the blade reflecting the light of the moon. The fires in his sockets burned bright as he brought the scythe down on the chain. "For they are spiritual shackles and my blade is sharp!"

There was a loud explosion as a wave of emerald light billowed outward, knocking the trolls and the Yule Cat away. A wave of energy passed harmlessly through the house and surrounding area as Cerberus, now unchained, surged forward. The bells on the harness jingled sharply as the lead was pulled taut, and the sleigh shot across the snow.

"Yes! Yes!" Death tucked his scythe under one arm as the sleigh tilted upward and Cerberus sprinted into the sky. Lily looked back to see the Yule Cat and the trolls transform into a sickly green mist that followed them. "We are flying, Lily, flying!"

"This is ridiculous," Lily muttered, then looked forward. Cerberus had no trouble running through the sky, leaving golden paw prints that floated in the air behind them as they went. The snowflakes suspended in the air bounced away from them as they passed, though more than a few accumulated in Death's beard.

When Lily looked back again, the mist was close behind them but was definitely slower. She wondered if the trolls and the Yule Cat were related, as their mode of transportation was identical.

"I have never felt more alive," Death declared. "I can see so far from up here!"

"Yeah, flying is pretty cool, no big deal." She flopped back in her seat and put her legs up. "So we just have to stay ahead of those idiots until Romeo finishes whatever he's doing at the pole. Easy."

Death said nothing, his focus on the reins. Every so often, Lily would look back to see if they had lost the Yule Cat and friends yet. The mist fell farther back over time, and it wasn't until they were in the middle of the Atlantic that they finally lost them.

"It's about fudging time," she declared, then frowned. She hated this hat. "But we're safe for now."

"Indeed." Death was sitting now, his eyes on the horizon. "And now the real work begins."

"What real work? We protect the bag, that's it." She saw the wicked grin on Death's face and sat upright on her seat. "Hey, no, we're not doing anything extra! Let's keep things simple, there's no reason to deviate from avoiding that stupid cat. In fact, if we just stay over the ocean, it can't even bother us. We can be sky pirates if you want!"

Death turned his head. "Ah, but this sleigh has a purpose.

There are millions of sleeping children out there who are expecting presents in the morning!"

"No! Absolutely not! All this is crazy enough, but I fudging refuse. Fudge! Darn it!" She grabbed her hat and tried to rip it off but panicked when it wouldn't budge. "What the heck? Why won't it come off?"

Death chuckled. "Oh, I think you know why. Santa's helpers wear these hats, dear Lily, and if we aren't delivering presents, why, we're no help to him at all."

"No." She shook her head. "There's no way we can do this, and we shouldn't even try. What, are we just going to sneak into people's homes and bring them gifts?"

Death reached into his coat and pulled out a scroll. He wrapped the reins around a hook, then opened the paper. "Amelia Anderson. Very good. Has three presents. Her brother, Manny, good, has two small presents. Their next-door neighbor is Ronald Walton. He is getting a bike this year."

"Where did you get that?" Lily felt the blood drain from her face.

"It was with the manual. And look, there's even a map!" He tilted the paper toward her to reveal a small map with a dot in the middle. "I know right where this is, I've memorized every map I've seen. And look!" He pulled the compass out of his pocket. "This is for if we get lost. Useful presents are the best kind, you know."

"Oh fudge. Oh fudge." She sat back and put her face in her hands. They were just supposed to get away from that fudging cat; how had things spiraled so far out of control?

Death pulled a pair of mugs from his coat and set them down on a small flip tray in the center of the front wall of the sleigh. A moment later, he held a large thermos.

"I found this as well," he told her, then undid the top. The smell of hot cocoa filled the air as he poured out two cups. From another pocket came a baggie full of baby marshmallows, and he dropped a few in each cup.

"You're…you…" In disbelief, she watched as he picked up one of the cups and sipped from it. One of the marshmallows was already melted and had gotten stuck between his teeth. "What about Cerberus? Surely she doesn't want to spend Santa knows how many days delivering presents."

"Ah, but you're wrong. You see, she gets to leave the Underworld and explore the mortal realm! It's very exciting for her." He looked at the hellhound. "Isn't that so?"

All three heads howled at once as the sleigh picked up speed. Lily scowled and snatched the bag of marshmallows from Death, then dumped a bunch in her mug.

"That's the spirit!" Death said. "Would you like to sing some carols as we head for the South Pacific? The list is in some sort of geographical order. I recommend we heed its advice. That way, we don't have to backtrack."

"I should have stayed in New York," she muttered, then took a sip from her cup. Surprisingly, the beverage warmed her up and made her feel slightly better. Sighing, she took a huge swallow and leaned back in her seat. "At least the cocoa is good."

"It is indeed, my demonic friend. It is indeed."

Grinning, Death snapped the reins and launched into a loud rendition of "Santa Claus Is Coming to Town" as he banked the sleigh into a massive U-turn. Lily stared at the distant horizon, noticing that the northern lights shifted about in the distance. A smile broke through her grumpy facade, but she forced it back. It was going to be a long night, and her only hope was that Mike could find Santa and get him to quit being a lazy bum and take over gift distribution.

"This is the Christmas special from heck," she muttered, then tried once more, unsuccessfully, to pull her hat off.

Groaning, Yuki stumbled to her feet. She felt dizzy and couldn't remember anything after being grabbed by the Ghost of Christmas Past. The ground was covered in snow, and she recognized the park just down the road from the house. A group of children were in the middle of building a snowman on the soccer field, and a couple of them had resorted to throwing snowballs at each other.

Had she been knocked out of the time lock? She turned around and was surprised to see herself sitting on a bench.

"This was how you spent last Christmas." The Ghost of Christmas Past stood next to her, dressed much like the children behind them.

She whirled around and commanded the snow around them to tear through the spirit in a storm of icy spears. Her magic slid along the ground around her, but the icicles shattered as they formed, falling back into place as snowflakes.

"These are the shadows of things that have been," the spirit informed her with a smug look. "This snow fell a year ago and has long melted into water and returned to the Earth. It shall not do your bidding."

A tarot card appeared in her hand, but the moment she summoned its magic, the card puffed out of existence. Frustrated, she tried to tackle the spirit but passed harmlessly through it.

"You cannot harm a spirit, silly." Christmas Past hovered above the ground, then danced away from her. "Magic though you may be, you are still of the mortal realm. We are here regarding your welfare."

"I don't want to talk about my welfare." She scooped up a handful of snow and threw it, but the ball crumbled the moment it left her hand and returned to where it had come from.

"That is no longer your decision." The spirit turned to look at the Yuki on the bench. "Last Christmas, you came to this place instead of spending time with your family."

Disgruntled, Yuki ran toward the edge of the park. There was a thick layer of trees around the border of the park. After dodging the prickly branches, she emerged on the other side.

"Oh, c'mon!" She had somehow reappeared exactly where she had left. The spirit hovered over her former self, then landed to stand on the bench.

"Why would you seek the cold solace of the park when you could have enjoyed the warmth of a house reborn?" it asked her.

"Because that wasn't my home," she declared in anger. "It's the same building, and the same people, but it wasn't the same anymore. And if you're able to see all these things in my head, then you darned well know why!" She paused, then licked her lips. "Darned. Why can't I say…oh. That's annoying."

Her former self sighed and stood. The kids had gotten closer, and families were now arriving at the park. New sleds were broken in as they used a small hill nearby, while parents laughed with their children. Former Yuki wandered into the trees, looked around to see if anyone was watching, then transformed into a fox before diving into the underbrush.

"There were too many people," Yuki said before the spirit could ask.

"You shed your humanity in order to hide from community."

"I am just as much a fox as a human. I don't have to choose, you floating bag of farts. Now where is Mike?" She got in the spirit's face and snarled. "What have you done with him?"

"His past is not your own, and…" The spirit's eyes widened dramatically. "Miser!" it shouted, its skull distorting.

Yuki stepped away from it and held up her hands. The outburst had startled her, and she wasn't sure how she had triggered it. "So what? We're going to spend all day here watching while I nap in the bushes?"

The spirit shuddered, then appeared at her side. It took her hand and pulled her forward. The world rippled, and now they stood inside the house.

"Ah, okay, you're going to show me how much fun everyone else is…having…" She had expected to see Mike opening presents with the others, but the decorations were different. Instead of strings of light, there were thick garlands wrapped around the tree. Mike preferred the twinkling of lights, but she knew someone who loved the garlands just as much.

"Please," she begged, but Emily walked into the room in a pair of flannel pajamas. She carried a small stack of packages, which she arranged beneath the tree, making sure to adjust the bows on each one. "Don't make me watch this."

She hadn't seen Emily since the night her spirit had moved on. Even though she knew the specter before her was just a glimpse of the past, it was impossible not to feel dread, longing, and heartache all at once. This was Emily before she had turned, the woman who had traveled the world by Yuki's side.

Yuki's former self wandered in, a mischievous grin on her face. She was in a pair of flannel pajamas and had adorned her fox ears with ribbons. A pair of tails stuck out of the custom hole that had been stitched into the seat of her bottoms. Moving quietly, she snuck up behind Emily and held mistletoe over her head. When Emily turned away from the tree, she was startled, then laughed when she saw what Yuki was doing.

"There you are," Emily said, then wrapped her arms around past Yuki's waist. "Oh? And is that mistletoe?"

"I've heard a rumor that you're superstitious," former Yuki said with a grin.

"Very much so." Emily pulled the kitsune in for a passionate kiss, her skin sparkling as her magic washed across both of them.

"This is one of your happiest Christmas memories," the spirit said, but Yuki turned away from it.

"And what's the point of making me see it?" she demanded. "To remind me that I used to enjoy Christmas? I don't hate Christmas, I'm mourning what I lost. There's a huge difference."

"So you're saying you'll kiss anything beneath the mistletoe?" former Yuki asked.

"Without hesitation," Emily replied with a smirk. There was the rustling of clothes, and Yuki knew that her past self had just stretched her pants away from her belly to reveal that she had shaved and colored her pubes into the shape of a mistletoe.

"Stop it," she cried, then tried to leave the room. It was the same as in the park, only now she found herself back in the living room where Emily was eagerly pulling Yuki's pants off. "You won't let me swear, but you'll make me watch this?"

Christmas Past remained silent, a twisted smile on its lips. Black lines flowed over its face, as if someone had dripped ink on its head.

Yuki covered her ears and looked out the window, only to see that it was an identical room that mirrored what was happening. When she closed her eyes, her lids became clear like glass. Groaning in agony, she tried to find some corner of the room to hide herself away from the sight. She and Emily would often have sex for hours, and this Christmas would be no exception.

The spirit hovered overhead, watching the scene unfold with a beatific smile on its face. Yuki tried to hurl fox fire at it, but the magic wouldn't come.

"You two were very much in love." Christmas Past had to raise its voice to be heard over the moaning. "It is very easy to see."

Yuki ignored the spirit, turning her attention inward. At

one point, Tink peered around the corner, her yellow eyes wide as she watched them. The goblin had been caught several times peeping on the two of them, but Yuki definitely didn't remember busting her for this one.

"Perhaps we have seen enough." Christmas Past licked its lips, taking Yuki by the hand and dragging her out into the hall. They were transported across time and space into a small fishing village in Japan. It was winter, and the few people milling about did so quickly to avoid the chill.

Yuki looked around with a frown. She recognized the village but couldn't remember its name. One of the natural limitations of living for hundreds of years was that old information slipped easily through the cracks of time. Still, the smell of salt water and fish tickled the back of her memory, and she realized exactly where she was.

"It isn't Christmas here," she proclaimed while looking for the spirit. Christmas Past sat on a nearby rack for drying fish. Its features were blurry at first, and then they morphed into Emily's likeness.

"It is Christmas day," the spirit corrected her. "I do not require celebration to reach through the past, only that the requirements be met. Today is the twenty-fifth day of December. It counts."

She was about to argue, but a small figure slipped past her, clutching a bundle against their chest. Thick blankets parted to reveal a fox tail streaked with dirt and snow.

"Stop her!" An older man in a thick coat charged around the corner with a knife in his hand. He was panting hard with exertion, each breath billowing out from him in giant plumes of fog. Down the road, a figure in thick furs stepped around the corner and kicked the fleeing fox demon.

She grunted when she hit the ground, her hood popping off her head to reveal pointed ears. It was a much younger Yuki, her features lean and her eyes desperate. When she scrambled to her feet, another villager stepped out of their home and smacked her in the head with an oar.

With a grunt, she hit the ground and dropped her bundle. Dried fish and a loaf of bread fell onto the cold, hard ground.

"Thief!" The man with the knife caught up, then froze when he saw younger Yuki's ears.

"This was when I was young." Yuki's eyes were wide with awe as she contemplated the scene. This wasn't something she had thought about in centuries, and only through seeing it once more could she recall the details. "I was hungry and had been stealing food from these people for days."

The men of the village circled the young kitsune and held her down. More villagers emerged from their homes, curious about the noise. A small council rapidly formed to discuss what to do with the kitsune now that her identity was known.

"And despite your transgressions, they welcomed you in." Christmas Past was smug as the villagers helped former Yuki to her feet and offered her the food she had taken. "Over the next couple of months, they clothed and fed you under the assumption that you would provide divine protection."

Yuki's cheeks grew hot, and she whirled around to face the spirit. "That's not fair!" she exclaimed. "You can see the memory just as well as I can, if not better! They just handed things over, and I was starving! What, you think I should have turned them away and wandered into the woods to freeze?"

"Their food was limited already." Christmas Past looked over its shoulder as a massive blizzard moved in and the villagers dispersed, taking the younger Yuki with them. "While their own people died, they continued feeding you in the hopes that an early spring would come. Instead, they slowly starved, one by one."

Yuki growled. "I remember. They came for me and started making demands. Slow the storms, bring food. Don't think I forgot about the cage they built for me. They locked me in and refused to give me food or water until I granted their wishes."

The storm raged but went suddenly silent.

"And what happened then?" Christmas Past lifted its chin, revealing a face lit from below by an unearthly light.

"I burned the village down," Yuki whispered. "The flames from my fox fire spread to the other buildings, and I ran into the forest."

"This was their last Christmas." The spirit shook its head. "It seems like this became a trend."

"Eat candy, mother hugger." She found a decent rock by her feet and picked it up to throw. The stone passed harmlessly through Christmas Past, then fizzled out and reappeared where she had found it.

The ghost chuckled.

"Come. There is more to see." When it reached for her, its arm extended several feet so it could grab her by the shoulder. She tried to plant her feet and resist but was yanked through the air and into a dark place where she was surrounded by distant lights. There was nothing beneath her now as she dangled by one arm while the spirit pulled her along.

"That was only the start," the spirit said, "of a lifetime of taking."

"What? No!" Yuki tried to claw the spirit's wrist, but her free hand passed harmlessly through its arm. Clearly it could only be touched if it wanted to be. "How could you even say such a thing?"

Christmas Past hurled her into a nearby ball of light. The world expanded around her until she saw that she was in a different village. A group of men surrounding a hut were bowing profusely while setting bags of rice and fresh produce on the ground. One man wandered up with a deer, which he set by the doorway.

"That will do." The Yuki that emerged from the hut

smirked at the men below her. "Know that you have pleased your god."

The group chattered at each other in Chinese, then wandered away from the hut. A couple stayed behind to help Yuki move the food into a side building where smoked meats had been stacked in the corner.

"You can't judge me for this," Yuki hissed while rising. "When I arrived here from Japan, it was to escape people who wanted to use me to gain power over others. I was all alone and had nobody. Well, guess what? People here thought I could grant wishes. People are the same everywhere. Was I just supposed to starve? And yes, I lied to them, but I used my magic to help where I could."

"If so, then why does it seem that these people are doing all the work for you?" Christmas Past walked over to the dead deer on the ground. "What did you do with all this extra food?"

Yuki scowled, her fists balling up. "For your information, I made sure there was plenty of food stored for the lean times. On the surface, it looks like I'm hoarding it for myself, but I knew a brutal winter was coming. The signs were there."

The spirit nodded. "You could have accomplished these things without posing as a deity of the woods."

She opened her mouth to argue, but the sounds of pounding hooves had reached her ears. When she turned around, she saw that her younger self was already watching a group of men on horseback approach. Armed with swords and daggers, they dismounted and surrounded the small hut.

A few villagers approached the riders with weapons of their own but were quickly dispatched by arrow or blade. Younger Yuki stood tall and proud, but Yuki knew the grim truth. She had been absolutely terrified of these men and what they represented. As Yuki had been constantly on the run, Japan had begun to feel terribly small. Everywhere she went, she drew either those who feared her or those who desired her power. China was so much bigger than Japan, but it only meant she would have to run that much farther.

"Give us the witch," they demanded. "Or we kill everyone."

The scene paused while Christmas Past moved among the frozen people as if inspecting them for flaws. It arched one eyebrow, then faced Yuki. "Do you remember what happened on this day?"

Yuki swallowed the lump in her throat. "Please don't make me watch," she begged.

Christmas Past smiled and snapped its fingers. The past played out, and younger Yuki fled into her hut. When the newcomers moved toward the hut, the villagers came to Yuki's defense, only to die quickly, calling for aid as they were killed. By the time the riders reached the hut, Yuki had long fled through a secret tunnel beneath the building.

"You turned into a fox and left them to their fate." Christmas Past shook its head. "Because you take. You're a taker."

"No, that's not true, I..." She was pulled away from the scene by rough hands, the wailing of dying villagers stuck in her head as Christmas Past carried her off like a bird of prey. They moved through her memories as the spirit recounted every terrible thing she had done within a couple days of Christmas. Her arguments never held any water, and she knew it was because the moments had been cherry-picked.

Still, it wore at her. Even the lightest rain would level a mountain given enough time, and time was in abundance here. She lost track of the days, trapped in a temporal hell where she was always the villain. Her only respite was knowing that the spirit would inevitably run out of days it could subject her to.

However, then what? Had the spirit simply been sent here

to trap her? Or was there a more nefarious endgame? It definitely seemed like they were trying to run down the clock, but for who?

And where was Mike in all this? Was he hurt? Had the spirit already gotten rid of him? Yuki chewed at her nails, then winced when she bit one too deep.

"You're distracted." Christmas Past scowled at her, the spirit currently sitting on a stump. They were somewhere in China in the early 1900s, but Yuki didn't know the year. Her past self had two tails now and was sleeping beneath a carriage outside a large manor. "We're here regarding your welfare, and you've stopped paying attention."

"I get it. I'm a terrible person." Yuki gestured toward the carriage. "But you're grasping at straws now. What am I doing here that was so wrong? Are you going to chastise me for not thanking the owner of the carriage? Tell me I'm a piece of poop for not doing some kindness here?"

"I…" Christmas Past shuddered, its features distorting. Though rare, there had been some memories with no wrongdoing where the spirit had tried to justify it by recounting her past deeds or stretching truths to fit the narrative. Arguing those points sometimes caused the ghost to panic and freak out, and this was no exception.

The ghost snatched her up by the ankles and soared into the sky. Yuki didn't even bother fighting; she couldn't touch the spirit if it didn't want her to.

"Let's go somewhere more comfortable," it declared as the clouds in the sky warped into a circular opening. When they soared through the aperture, Yuki's blood chilled as she saw a familiar tower down below.

"No, no, no, anywhere but there!" She tried to fight but was tossed unceremoniously into the courtyard. Though she had fallen from a great height, the landing only knocked the wind from her lungs. Wheezing, she got to her feet and tried to walk toward the gate.

"How can you be expected to improve without understanding your past?" Christmas Past grabbed her by the foot and dragged her toward the tower. "You spent so many years in this place, surely there is much to learn."

"Why are you doing this?" She grabbed at the edge of a planter and was able to hold on for a few seconds before being pulled free. "I wasn't here because I was bad but because I was trapped!"

The spirit said nothing as it dragged her into the tower proper. The bottom floor was trashed with broken furniture everywhere. Stairs had been laid into the exterior wall, and Yuki was dragged up all of them until they reached her old bedroom. On the bed, a past version of herself lay, sobbing hysterically.

"This was your first Christmas here," the spirit noted. "You didn't use to care about the holiday, but Emily had taught you to love it. It was a special day to her and, therefore, to you. You even decorated the tree in the hopes that she would return and save you, but that didn't happen, did it? There was this fantasy that she would be waiting, sitting beneath its branches with sad eyes and an apology, but it wasn't meant to be."

The tree in question was lying in the corner, its branches broken. Small, handcrafted ornaments lay shattered all over the floor, surrounded by pine needles. A sheet of paper with a hand-drawn calendar lay nearby, the days crossed off with *X*s that got progressively larger until they reached the twenty-fifth of December.

"I really thought she was coming for me," Yuki whispered. Back then, when Emily had disappeared, Yuki hadn't known what to think. For the next several Christmases, this process would repeat, growing grander in scale until the entire tower was decorated. When the morning came and Emily was still absent, Yuki would trash the tower and fall in a heap on her bed for days.

The spirit hovered above, its lips curled into a bloodless smile. Their features shifted and melted until they wore Emily's face. "You were being punished."

"No." Yuki glared at Christmas Past. "I was being protected. I know the truth now. Emily was possessed and did what she could to hide me from the evil that possessed her. Nothing you tell me will change the truth."

"Perhaps. But think on all the things I have already shown you. How many people did you hurt over the centuries? The villagers you stole from, the ones you fooled? Some gave their lives to protect you, others died in pursuit of you. You were a menace, and you deserved this." Christmas Past was smug as dark lines crept along its face like worms. "This is karma."

"Fudge you," she whispered.

"And now we watch." The spirit focused their attention on the figure in the bed. "Grief and despair shall metamorphosize into loneliness and rage."

Yuki stared with wide eyes as the past unfolded. Hours went by, and the huddled mass of her former self barely moved. When she finally did stir, it was to cry out in agony. Her past self let out a scream, then threw a handful of fox fire at the tree. It ignited, sending black tendrils of smoke up the wall.

"Why are you doing this?" she asked.

"Because I'm here to teach you the true meaning of Christmas!" The spirit seized her by the throat and lifted her above the scene. Gone was any childlike innocence in the ghost's face as it choked her. "That cruelty must be punished!"

"Cruelty…isn't…Christmas!" she gasped. "It's about… giving, and…"

"Wrong." The spirit's eyes flashed, and the room below filled with multiple versions of Yuki, each one from a different year. They passed through one another as they each tore the bedroom apart and howled in grief. "It isn't about goodwill and gifts. The world is a broken place, and somebody must hold it accountable. Giving children gifts for good behavior hasn't taught them to be kind as adults, and parents can't be trusted to punish their children appropriately for their misdeeds."

A cold wind blasted through the bedroom window, and the whole tower shook. Christmas Past's voice grew louder and filled with static as its body twisted and distorted violently, then snapped back into place. For just a moment, it looked like it had two heads.

"It's time for accountability," it shrieked, its light-filled eyes opened wide. "To bring back the true meaning of Christmas! As light needs darkness to exist, so too must there be a balance!" It slammed Yuki into the wall, causing the wall to crack. She felt the bones in her back pop as Christmas Past smashed her into the hard surface again and again.

"Stop it, stop it!" She summoned a handful of fire, but it passed right through the spirit and vanished in midair.

"You can't hurt me," the spirit snarled, then threw her to the ground. "I am a manifestation of days that have passed, and you cannot change them! I am immutable, unbending, unshakable. Your mistakes, your victories, they all belong to me, and I see all, I know all, and you deserve to be punished!"

"You don't get to judge me." Yuki winced, then stood. "You're just a broken spirit, I see that now. You can see the past, but it doesn't mean you know what it's like to go hungry, or to be afraid, or to have your heart so utterly broken that you wish the universe would burn itself down around you."

The spirit descended, the light in its eyes flickering out to reveal a pair of gaping holes. Its distended limbs made it stand a foot taller than she did, and it curled a pale finger around her chin.

"Fine, then," it whispered. "If I can't judge you, then maybe she can."

A cold blast of ice sent Yuki across the room, where she crashed into a bookshelf and collapsed on the floor. Groaning, she twisted around to see that the damage to the tower was gone. The room had been redecorated, and a dark figure stood silhouetted in the balcony, her tails swishing behind her.

"Did Emily send you?" When this version of Yuki stepped forward, the sun's light glistened off the snow-white fur of her tails. She wore a leather eye patch and held several tarot cards fanned out in her left hand. "Are you here to finish what she started?"

"No, I—" Yuki summoned a wall of ice to deflect the icy barrage that barreled toward her. She peered around the corner and then ducked back when a sword blew past her head and clanged off the floor. The shuffling of cards could be heard.

"She will not take anything more from me," the past declared as it summoned a storm of ice indoors. Yuki's head pounded, her mind filling with memories of the time an intruder, another kitsune, had come to her tower. The details poured into her head in real time, splitting her consciousness in two as she experienced the fight from two points of view.

How could this be? Was she actually in the past? Gasping in pain, she clutched at her head and dove out of the way as a massive icicle shattered the table and exploded against the far wall. Somehow, the spirit had linked the past and present together, and Yuki wasn't sure that she would survive it.

Now sitting on the bed, Christmas Past cackled with glee, dark lines squirming all along its porcelain features. "These are the shadows of things that have been," they explained. "There can only be one outcome, for to harm your past is to destroy the present. And we both know your precious Caretaker would not have survived without you. This is your last and final test, Yuki Otome. Will you pass it?"

"I…"

She threw herself sideways as ice erupted at her feet and spiraled into the sky. Summoning a shield of her own, she narrowly avoided a barrage of blades that pierced the ice and exploded outward in a cloud of frost and metal. The benefit of having her mind split was that she remembered what her past self was going to do the moment before she did it. It was the thinnest of edges, but it would have to be enough. The temperature in the room was dropping fast, and the floors were becoming slippery with frost.

How could she hope to beat her past self without dooming her own future? She managed to dodge a pair of swords, then got knocked over when a ball of fire slammed into her from above. The pressure in her head was building, and it felt like she was going to black out. She stumbled and fell, rolling over in time to see past Yuki approaching. One finger was tucked beneath the eye patch, so Yuki closed her eyes to keep from getting turned to stone.

"Please, don't," she cried, holding her hands up. "You have to let me explain!"

"I don't have to—"

The world went silent, save for the sound of electrical streamers. Yuki turned toward the noise and opened her eyes to see Mike standing behind Christmas Past. He had grabbed the spirit's head from behind, and purple sparks crawled all along his arm and into Christmas Past's forehead. The spirit was frozen in place, its eyes wide as the darkness receded.

"Sorry I'm late," he panted, sweat glistening off his forehead. Yuki looked around the room to see that the past had frozen in place. Whatever he was doing, it had stopped the past in its tracks. "Had to take the long way in."

"You okay?" she asked, her voice too loud in her own head. At least her memories weren't filling in any more.

"Mostly. But, uh, things might get real weird for a minute." He looked at Christmas Past, whose features now rippled like turning pages. "Like, weirder than normal. I just pumped Casper here with a bunch of magic and, well, you know…"

Nodding, Yuki lay down on the floor and clutched her

head while trying not to puke. She didn't care what he did, as long as he could make the pain stop.

MIKE USED HIS FREE HAND TO PULL CHRISTMAS PAST TOWARD him by its hair, his magic swarming over the spirit's body. After a brutal freehand climb across a sheer rock face, he had dropped onto a section of the exterior wall that had required him to run all the way down to the courtyard before entering the tower proper. He was grateful that no version of the Jabberwock was hanging around in this timeline, but had been disturbed to see the sun shift places dramatically above him. It wasn't just disorienting, but he worried that Yuki might be moved to a different memory outside the tower. If she and the spirit left without him, would he become stuck or just fall into the void?

He didn't like either possibility.

Once inside the tower, he had heard the fight up above and had been cautious in his approach. Seeing Yuki in a fight with her past self, he had managed to sneak up on Christmas Past. The spirit hadn't noticed, its gleeful features turned toward the fight. When he'd realized Yuki was interacting with her own past, he knew he had to act before things went from bad to worse.

Short on ideas, he had summoned his magic. Concentrating it into his hand was easy, but then what? Seeing that the fight was rapidly approaching a bloody end, he had thought back to how time had been reversed in his own memories. The spirit had the means to manipulate the past, so it was up to him to manipulate the spirit.

His magic was never intended to be offensive. It was a wild, chaotic amalgamation of nymph magic and the fae. So when he'd decided to pour it into Christmas Past, he wasn't certain how it would react. The spirit barely had its own identity and was constantly changing shape.

Luckily, he had plenty of experience with shape-shifters, and sudden changes wouldn't surprise him. The spirit had been so engrossed in watching Yuki battle herself that it didn't even notice him crawling across the bed. It wasn't until he'd grabbed it from behind that it reacted, struggling to escape his grasp.

Down on the floor, Yuki dry-heaved, clutching her head in both hands. Her past self was flickering as if stuck in a loop, slowly lifting her eye patch and then replacing it before the gorgon's eye could be revealed.

"What-what-what are you—what are you doing-doing?" Christmas Past shuddered, its whole body flickering in and out of existence. Its head always remained, now surrounded in a ghostly aura of purple light. Mike had wound the spirit's hair through his hand so many times that there was no way it could break free. With his free hand, he wrapped his fingers around the spirit's forehead, causing the magic to spin wildly around him.

"Fix this," he commanded. "You rewind this nonsense right now or else."

"You cannot-cannot you-you cannot..." Christmas Past growled. "You cannot hurt me!"

"You know what? I've been wondering about that." Mike pulled the spirit with him as he shifted off the bed, then walked over to where Yuki cowered on the floor. "You see, you're always called the Ghost of Christmas Past. And I can tell you're a spirit of some sort. Were you once alive? Or were you created?"

Christmas Past pulled free of his grip, but he still had its hair tangled in his hand. The spirit hit him in the stomach with an elongated arm, but he twisted to the side and was grazed instead. Yanking hard on the spirit's hair, he pulled it off its feet, causing it to hover.

"Because if you are a lost soul, I've got a fix for that." Mike opened his mouth, the mournful dirge of the banshee filling the air. An intense feeling of sadness flooded him as he sang aloud the same haunting aria that had carried Velvet's soul to her resting place. It was something he had discussed at length with Cecilia, mostly out of a fear that he had somehow screwed up Velvet's passing.

Like all things magic, intent was the most important thing. She had taught him the melody and assured him that his intention mattered far more than the song itself. Tiny motes of light formed inside Christmas Past's body, each one becoming a tiny star that shot out of its body and ricocheted off the nearby walls.

"Stop-stop-stop it!" Christmas Past's face flickered as the light emanating from its body curved away and toward a glittering portal that split apart above them.

Mike closed his mouth. "Last chance," he warned. "Fix the timeline right now, or see what the Underworld has in store for you." To emphasize his point, he hummed the melody.

"The timeline is fine!" Christmas Past cried out. "The past is immutable, these are just shadows!"

"Doesn't feel that way," Yuki groaned from the floor. "My head is full of new memories."

"Shadows!" Christmas Past screamed, and Yuki's shadow stretched out behind her, its fingers buried in her skull. It withdrew its dark digits and then stepped away from her and disappeared. "They have no consciousness of us, for they are simulacrum and have no thoughts or desires of their own!"

The Yuki from the past flickered, then turned into a shadow that melted into the floor and vanished. The room around them fragmented, large sections of wall vanishing to reveal a horizon devoid of light. It was as though the simulation had fallen apart, the code finally broken.

"Yuki?" Mike looked at the kitsune.

"I might barf," she said. "But the pain is gone, I'm just exhausted now. I should have known the spirit is a psychic."

Christmas Past groaned, its features flickering as Mike's magic seeped into its eyes. Where the tiny lights had ripped free, his magical sparks sank in to replace them. The spirit's eyes fluttered, its features morphing rapidly.

"Uh-oh," Mike said. The tower cracked, and the spirit's body was now ablaze with magic, most of it his. He knelt to grab Yuki's waist as the floor split beneath them and they all fell together.

The memories around them fragmented, bursting into supernovas of light and color. Occasional words or sounds carried to him across the darkness, and he looked down to see that a bright spot had formed beneath their feet. Convinced that they would crash, he braced himself for impact.

Surprisingly, the landing was gentle. Moments before impact, they drifted the last few feet, allowing Mike to lay Yuki down on the floor again.

"Where are we?" she asked. "Hurts to open my eyes, the light is too bright."

"Uh…" He looked around but didn't recognize the place. The room looked like it had been pieced together out of a dozen different locations. It was a large room with windows that overlooked vastly different scenes, regardless of orientation. A blizzard out one window sat next to a rainstorm out the other. At least seven doors could be seen from where they had landed.

"Where are we now?" he demanded, but the spirit only shook in response. He wasn't entirely certain what was happening, but the light streaming off of Christmas Past was so intense now that it hurt to look at it.

Christmas Past's limbs reappeared, and it let out a howl, then exploded. Its remains splattered the room with inky black pools that immediately flowed toward one another.

"Christmas Past has gone T-1000 on us," he informed Yuki.

"What?" She looked up and groaned. "Maybe I can..." She raised her arm and summoned a pitiful spurt of frost, then slumped on the floor.

"It's okay." He patted her on the head and rose. "I've got this one." Cracking his knuckles, he summoned the magic into his palms. Whatever Christmas Past was planning, he wasn't going to make it easy.

Hushed whispers filled the room as the black pools formed into silhouettes that shifted along the walls. There were three of them, and one of them stepped out of the wall, its body filling with definition and color.

"Oh fudge. Rebecca?" He dropped his hands as the shadow of his ex-girlfriend appeared. She wore red-and-white Christmas lingerie with her brown hair done in braids.

"Does Santa want to slide down my chimney tonight?" she asked with a crooked finger. A few feet over, another shadow stepped free of the wall, transforming into a Latino woman with her hair done up in buns. She wore white ski pants and a sweater and was carrying a bundle of wood.

"It's cold out there," she said, then set the bundle down. This was Abigail, and the memory was from the Christmas ski vacation they'd taken. It had been a fond trip, but Abigail's sex drive had led her to stray only a month later.

Mike shook his head in disbelief as the third shadow formed into Hallee Waters, his college girlfriend. She was in Christmas pajamas that hugged her athletic figure, her hair pulled back into a ponytail. He had gone home with her for Christmas, and her parents had made Mike sleep on the couch. She had snuck down for some midnight action, but he'd pretended to stay asleep.

"If we're quiet, they won't wake up," she whispered.

"So what game is this?" Mike asked. "You've sent my exes

to come torment me? To make me feel bad about how I treated them?"

"We're not here to make you feel bad," Rebecca told him.

"We're here because we're broken," Abigail added.

"Just shadows," Hallee said. Lightning danced around her smiling eyes, and he recognized it as his own magic.

"I see." He had zapped Christmas Past pretty hard, uncertain what would happen. Pouring sex magic into a spirit capable of simulating the past had its potential problems. All three women leered at him. Hallee had her hand down the front of her pants, her fingers shifting beneath her snowflake jammy bottoms.

"You can't handle us all," Rebecca said, pressing her breasts together. "After all, your inability to satisfy us left you alone."

"And even when you could get it up, it was never for very long," Abigail said with a pout.

"Are you—" He laughed. "Are you still trying to torment me with the sins of my past? Trying to make me miserable over how my relationships with these women ended? Do you think I'm threatened by their sensuality, that I will shrink away from them and run?"

The women were close now, their hands reaching for him. He could sense no danger, and he put his hands on his pants.

"Ladies. It's time to dance." He pulled his pants down, his cock springing to attention. All three of them stopped, awe on their faces. "Yeah, that's right. I'm large and in charge. What do you think, Abigail?"

"Uh, I—" Her eyes glazed over, and he laughed. If these were mere shadows, they were constructed from his memories. All three of these women had desired him, but his issues had prevented true intimacy with any of them. With those issues gone, they would have no choice but to act on what he remembered about them.

Hallee planted herself against his side, her hand going

immediately to his cock. "They're both heavy sleepers," she told him while pulling his coat off.

"They won't hear us, I'm sure." He ran his hand along the back of her head, tickling her scalp with his magic. If this was the kind of fight Christmas Past wanted, then the spirit had majorly spilled the eggnog. "Rebecca, you look amazing in that lingerie."

"Thanks," she said with a smile. "I picked it out for you."

From the corner of his eye, he saw a pool of ink moving toward him but pretended to be enthralled with the attention he was receiving. The women weren't a threat, but he could sense the malevolent energy radiating from that last patch of darkness. He moved to place himself between it and Yuki, allowing the women to run their hands over his body. So the women were just a distraction. Compared to the women he lived with, it was easy to ignore them.

"I've never seen it so big before," Abigail whispered in a rush as she took off her shirt and knelt in front of him. "I don't even know that I can fit it in my mouth."

"We'll help," offered Hallee, who slid into place by Abigail and started stroking Mike. "I bet you've never been with three women before."

Suddenly, so many things made sense to him. The spirit had tormented him with his mother and then his exes, not knowing about the events of the last year. But why not? Was it because of the geas? He thought back to the events of last Christmas. There had been plenty of intimacy between him and the others.

It was a puzzle that bore thinking on, but he would have time for it later. Abigail and Hallee were busy licking and sucking his cock while Rebecca pressed herself against him, blocking his view of the pool.

"Yeah, that's right," he told them, allowing his magic to trickle out in small bursts. "This is the best day ever. I can't wait to be balls-deep in each of you."

"Ooh, me first!" Rebecca exclaimed, then bent over and pulled her panties to the side. She waved her ass back and forth, then slapped it. "C'mon, I want you to fill my stocking with good cheer!"

"Oh, gross," Yuki muttered from the floor.

Mike moved toward Rebecca, his senses on high alert. Abigail and Hallee moved to his sides and wrapped their arms around his waist, effectively pinning him in place. Though they were shadows, they seemed to share very human qualities with their real-world counterparts.

He sensed the movement behind him and unleashed his magic on the women. Sizzling sparks lashed out into all three of them, and they all cried out in sweet agony as powerful orgasms ripped through their bodies. As all three of them fell away, Mike spun in place and planted his fist straight into the face of Christmas Past.

With the roaring sound of rushing water, the world around them crumbled as Christmas Past crashed into the ground with a thud. Dazzling lights flickered across its body as Mike knelt and grabbed a handful of hair to pull it to its feet. They were in a metallic hallway with tiny vents along the bottom.

"Had enough?" he asked, then frowned. One of the spirit's eyes had turned black, while the other was white. Those same dark pools flowed beneath its skin, sloshing back and forth.

"I'm-sorry-I'm-sorry-I'm-sorry-sorry-sorry," they muttered, then let out a cry like a child. Mike let go of the spirit, and it hovered in place, the darkness receding from it.

"You have to run," it whispered, its features now angelic. "Before the darkness returns."

"What darkness?" he asked, pulling up his pants. "Who sent you?"

"It's been set free, Mike Radley." The spirit shook its head, its features cracking. "And all it wants is revenge. I was sent to keep you from interfering, by any means necessary."

"Hey, calm down." He put his hand on the spirit's forehead. Genuine fear was reflected in its eyes as it looked up at him, which gave way to relief when he didn't hurt it.

"You can touch me?" It closed its eyes and pressed into his hand. "Have you become a spirit too?"

"My spiritual genealogy has gone through some edits," he confessed. Was it his connection to Cecilia that allowed him to do this?

"Mike?" Yuki was on her hands and knees, her features twisted in pain. "It's changing."

He stepped back from Christmas Past and saw that a shadow had formed beneath it. Tendrils of black clung to the spirit's legs and crawled up, gobbling up the light from its body.

"Oh, you'd better watch out. And don't you dare cry." Christmas Past jerked its head up, revealing that the darkness had returned to its eyes. It lifted into the air and hovered before them, then smiled. Its mouth may as well have been full of daggers. "When the Krampus finds you, you're all going to die!"

Mike unleashed the banshee's scream, channeling his anger into it. The spirit flinched, then shattered like glass into little clouds of smoke. Each one drifted a separate direction, most of them traveling out the nearby vents, until he and Yuki were alone again.

"Yuki, are you okay?" He ran to her side and helped her up.

"Couldn't even keep your pants on while fighting a Christmas spirit. It really is the holiday season." She grinned weakly at her joke. "I'm so thirsty."

"Me too. We've got to find a way out of here. I'm fucking starving."

Once Yuki was on her feet, she leaned against him.

"Sorry it took me so long."

"It's okay." She patted his bicep. "I should have known better. That thing literally got in my head."

"Yeah. Really obnoxious." Figuring any direction was as good as another, he started walking. "I have a random question for you," he said.

"Can't be any more random than what just happened," she replied.

"Right. Well, here goes." He cleared his throat; it was so damn dry in the vents. When this was all over, he would talk to someone about putting in a humidifier. "What the fuck is a Krampus?"

CAT RADIO

"C'mon." Kisa pushed the grate out of the way and squeezed through the tiny opening. She crawled forward on her belly and stood to discover that they were in a storage room full of wrapping paper. Turning around, she grabbed Holly by the wrists to pull her through. Holly sat down against the wall while Kisa helped Tink. The goblin grumbled when her horns caught on the edge of the grate, then swore when she fell on her face.

The openings in the heating system were typically small, which meant it had taken some time to find one big enough for them to squeeze through. They had walked for several hours, all tied together by the garland around their waists to keep from getting split up. On more than a couple occasions, one of them had fallen in a hole that hadn't existed for the others, or turned down a brand-new hallway that opened up without warning. Eventually, Tink's goggles had tracked airflow, and she led them to an exit big enough for the three of them to fit through.

"Tink tired of fucking vents," she declared, then stood and brushed off her dress. "Husband big lost, need better strategy."

"Agreed." Kisa frowned at the vent, then closed her eyes. They had tried to find Mike, but his location kept shifting all over the place. Sometimes Kisa could sense that he was close by, but then he would shift away as if teleported. The trio had made slow progress, and Holly's only contribution had been her presence. The elf had been silent the entire time, staring at her feet as they walked.

Tink stuck her head back in the vent and looked around, her nostrils flaring. "Husband wait for Tink!" she hollered, then backed out. "Stupid fucking furnace," she muttered and flopped down on the ground. "Tummy hurt. Big hungry."

At hearing these words, Holly flinched, then reached into the pack around her waist and pulled out a handful of cookies. They were sugar cookies shaped like bells, wreaths, and candy canes that had been decorated with white frosting and colored sugar crystals. She handed them wordlessly to Tink, then sat down against the wall.

"No make Tink forget?" the goblin asked warily. "Tink no like memory cookies."

Holly shook her head. "They're magic, but they don't make you forget," she said, then took another one from her pouch. She took a bite to show that they were safe. "I've got plenty, but a couple should fill you right up. I have them for long missions away from home. Human food isn't really good for elves. Too much salt."

Tink handed Kisa a couple, then ate the rest all at once. Her dress was soon adorned with cookie crumbs, which she meticulously picked up and stuffed into her mouth.

"So are you ready to talk?" Kisa took a bite of the candy-cane cookie and moaned. It was the most fantastic thing she had ever tasted, filling her mouth with buttery richness and just a hint of peppermint.

Holly sighed, then wrapped her arms around her legs. "What do you know about Santa?" she asked.

"Beard. Fat. Red suit." Tink listed these off, her mouth still full of cookie crumbs. A few fell out, and she picked up the crumbs and dutifully tucked them back in her mouth.

"He's much more than that." Holly looked back at the vents. "The human world only sees what it wants to, which has always been a double-edged sword."

"What do you mean?" Kisa took another bite and fought back the wave of culinary pleasure that rushed through her. If she got a chance, she was taking some of these home with her after this was all over.

"He didn't always used to be the way he is. Santa, he adapts, you know?" Holly stood and turned toward the wall. She pulled a marker from her pack and started drawing on the wall. When she stepped away, she had drawn a man in robes and a tall hat. "This was how people saw Santa in the beginning. Just a simple man with a desire for generosity. He was called Saint Nicholas back then, and he performed miracles and a great many deeds. His legends grew until he did something that all mortals eventually do—he died."

"Doesn't seem dead to me," Kisa said. "Not that I've met him, but we're at the North Pole. Clearly he still exists."

The elf nodded, then drew a picture of a jolly Santa, complete with hat and giant belly. "There's an entire story between these two pictures," she explained as she capped the marker. "One that nobody ever gets to hear, not even most of the elves."

"What's he hiding?" Kisa asked. "You make it sound so ominous."

Holly scowled, then nodded to herself. "He has a secret, a very big one. Allie told it to me a long time ago but only because I get to leave the North Pole." She turned back toward the drawings and tapped on the saint first, then Santa. "Hundreds of years is plenty of time for one man to go from this to this. You would think a man who gives gifts to children would be universally lauded, but that isn't so. He's had his share of enemies over the years."

"Tink have enemies too." The goblin walked over to Holly and stuck her hand in Holly's pack. "Still hungry, maybe two more cookies."

Holly swatted Tink away and then handed her a couple more. "I'll run out eventually, especially if you keep eating them so fast."

"Tink, here." Kisa had gotten full after eating just one of her cookies so gave her spare to the goblin. "So, anyway, Santa's enemies?"

"Right." Holly looked back at the wall. "Um, where was I? Oh yes. So before most of the elves were here, the North Pole was...very different. I'm fuzzy on those details, but it's important to know that Saint Nicholas found this place long before he became Santa Claus. He and the first elf started making toys for little kids, but it was more than that. When he took the place over, some of the locals didn't take too kindly to it. Battles were fought, long affairs that stained the North Pole in blood."

"Santa wear red coat to avoid cleaning bill," Tink added knowingly.

"No, he didn't! Eat your darn cookies." Holly scowled at Tink for a moment, then looked back at Kisa. "I don't know the full details on the fights and even less about why he came to the North Pole in the first place. Alabaster was one of the first elves here and is one of the most trusted. He knows practically everything but tells nobody. Outside of the big secret, I only know so much of this extra stuff because I've been around Allie when he's had too much eggnog and he's spilled some details on occasion."

"He-he, eggnog." Tink smiled. "Tink like magic eggnog."

Holly ignored Tink. "So the big secret is this: Santa is powered by belief. If you could convince everyone in the world that the big man didn't exist, he would simply cease to be."

"That...wait, how is he powered by belief?"

Holly tapped on the picture of Saint Nicholas. "Some time after Saint Nicholas came here, he died and then was resurrected. Nobody is sure of the mechanism itself, but he's essentially immortal. Immortality always comes with a hefty price, and his is that he will only exist as the world sees him. It's why Allie wants me to pay attention to how the world sees him; it's to brace for any changes we may experience on our end."

"Hold up." Kisa held up her hands, a stray memory floating through her head. It was rare to remember anything new from her time before the house, so she latched onto it with enthusiasm. "I think I remember something from when I was little. I saw a picture of a black Santa and asked… someone how that was possible. They explained something about how Santa can be black, or white, or Japanese, depending on the child."

Holly tapped her nose for emphasis. "Exactly. Before that soda ad campaign, he was much more diverse in appearance. White robes one day, red the next, was a bit of a toss-up. When he's not visiting with a child, he reverts to the overall public perception, which is currently a jolly fat man with a beard, in a red coat."

"So if everyone believed Santa was a woman, he would become one?" Kisa asked.

Tink laughed. "Santa make own milk for her cookies!" she declared, then mimed squirting milk from her boobs and catching it on her own tongue.

"Ugh." Holly looked away from the goblin, her cheeks brightening. "But yes, it could happen. Which brings me back to those battles. If Santa had become a warrior for the sake of survival, it would have changed him at a fundamental level. Anything he does becomes a part of his image, which then becomes a part of who he is. I believe the human term is 'doubling down.'"

"So if he became a killer…" Kisa pondered the possibilities, imagining a psychotic Santa Claus who murdered his way across the North Pole and then headed south for more victims.

"Precisely. I think you understand." Holly drew a quick picture of a devil on the wall. "Which brings me to the Krampus. A demon from the deepest pits. Nobody knows how it happened, but Santa enslaved this creature to do all his fighting for him. It helped protect his image and win the battle for the North Pole."

"Tink hear of Krampus." The goblin's ears perked up. "Tink remember tales of Krampus from childhood. Be good, or Krampus eat you!"

Kisa looked at Tink with curiosity. To her knowledge, Tink had never brought up her own childhood.

"Sounds right," Holly added. "The Krampus is a mean old thing who believes in punishing bad children instead of rewarding good ones. After so many of these fights, Santa and Krampus came out on top. Once the North Pole was safe again, Santa locked the Krampus away. He couldn't let the demon interfere with Christmas."

"So do you think the Krampus escaped?" Kisa asked.

"Oh, no doubt he's out, he has to be. Some things make more sense now. Allie slowed him down while we escaped into the furnace. He would have gotten us all otherwise."

"Why Holly need escape?" Tink asked. The goblin's dress was adorned with cookie stains that she occasionally sucked on. "Old ears make sure Holly not lost."

"Santa needs people to believe in him so he continues to exist." Holly took a deep breath, then let it out slowly. "If the Krampus has captured the other elves, there's no telling what happened to them. I could be the only one left for all I know. But that's not what's important. You see, the whole world is time locked right now. The elves were created for Santa, not just as his helpers, but as his guardians and protectors. The world remains locked for months on end, maybe even years—

it's always different. Our belief sustains his existence during the lock, and if we're all snuffed out…"

"Then no more Santa." Kisa whistled. "That's some pretty heavy stuff right there. But we're not time locked either, and I believe in him, so it should be safe, right?"

Holly shook her head. "No. It takes a special kind of belief. Knowing he exists and believing in him are entirely separate things. A child has a special kind of belief, an innocent way of seeing the world that adults lose. They believe without needing proof, which is a very big deal. Elves were created to love Santa, so our belief in him is baked into our magical cookie code. An adult who believes in Santa with childlike innocence despite being told he doesn't exist is essentially impossible to find these days."

"Tink believe," the goblin declared. "Santa bring Tink special person to love, always believe in Santa."

"You hardly have an innocent worldview," Holly said with a snort. "You were just pretending to milk yourself. Besides, the first time I met you and said Santa needed your help, you called me a…word I won't repeat. And told me to do something anatomically impossible."

"Goblins make lots of milk," Tink added, holding a pair of fingers out from the tip of each breast to represent her nipples. It was clear she was avoiding Holly's accusation. "Babies hungry always, come in litters."

"Okay, Tink, enough about your boobs." Kisa snatched a cookie from Holly's pouch before she could react and tossed it to Tink. "So the Krampus is hunting you, and we can't let him have you. Got it. Moving on. Anything else we need to know?"

"If Jack Frost is helping him, there will be others." Holly groaned. "Oh, Santa, I don't know what to do!"

Kisa patted the elf reassuringly on the shoulder, then felt a powerful tug in the center of her body. Her cat ears perked up as she looked into the hole they had crawled out from. Mike had reappeared somewhere nearby but was still miles out. She fought the urge to crawl back in the hole and find him.

"I need you two to hush for a minute." Kisa sat down in front of the vent with her legs crossed. "We're close enough now that I think we can talk."

"Talk? With who?" Holly looked perplexed.

"Cat radio," Tink said, then sat next to Kisa. "Tell husband Tink miss him biggest."

"I'll tell him you're causing trouble."

"Even better."

Kisa grinned, then shut her eyes and took several deep breaths. Her magic pulsed deep inside her body, then blossomed like a rose as she sent her consciousness forward.

Mike and Yuki had traveled silently for the last couple of hours and were currently in a narrow duct. As they walked along, the metal flexed beneath their feet. There weren't any vents to see the workshop through, which worried Mike. If not for the little lightning spider guiding the way, it would be pitch black.

"I need another break." Yuki's face was pale as she leaned away from Mike and put her hand on the nearby wall. "Just for a few minutes."

"Yeah, of course." Mike helped her into a sitting position, then moved next to her. He wrapped an arm around her shoulders and she slumped against him.

"Sorry," she muttered. "It's like I have the worst hangover ever."

"Kitsune can get drunk?" he asked.

"Stupid ones can," she replied. "It's been a very long time since I've indulged. Set my own tail on fire. Never drink and do magic. You'll blow your own damned face off."

"That's good advice, I'll have some T-shirts made."

She snorted, then groaned. "Oh, that hurts so bad. I thought it would be better already."

"How long were you in there?" he asked out of curiosity. "Christmas Past seemed to have quite the upper hand on you by the time I arrived."

"Days," she replied. "I lost track."

"I'm so sorry." He rubbed her ears, causing her to sigh. "It wasn't that long for me."

"I'm glad," she told him. "I can't imagine what that stupid ghost put you through."

"Not much, honestly." He looked down at the hand he had punched Christmas Past with. His knuckles were scraped raw, despite their soft impact. "Just some old mommy issues that I've largely resolved. They obviously thought it was low-hanging fruit, but I didn't bite. Would have made me suffer more if they had me relive that Christmas I got food poisoning."

"Gross."

"I'm guessing you saw her? Emily, I mean."

"Yeah." She sniffled in his arms. "It was super fucked up. Brought back a lot of feelings. Then they took me on a tour of my greatest hits over the years. Made me question a lot of my decisions. I think it's how they got inside my head."

"Nasty." He stroked her fur absent-mindedly. "I used to think about the past all the time. It can be hard to let those things go, doubly so if you have to watch a physical manifestation of them."

It wasn't just that his life had changed for the better. When Naia had done that initial soul swap with him, she had fixed something in his head. Instead of a past that would surface and scream in his face during his waking hours, the wounds had been allowed to heal, leaving emotional scars that faded into the background as he swapped souls with the others. In the Dreamscape, his mother's voice used to follow him around and shriek madly in an attempt to bring him misery. Now there was just blessed silence, other than the lapping of the waves against the shores of his mind.

On at least a couple of occasions, someone had tried to use the past against him. While jarring at first, repetition had blunted the edge of that particular weapon.

He thought back to what he had seen in his childhood, and his mother's missed medication. After the trick with his ex-girlfriends, Mike wasn't certain if what he had seen was real or not. If not, then nothing had changed. But if his mother really had been ill and needed that medication to stay stable…

He shook his head and wiped the moisture from his eyes. Nothing could ever change what had happened, and all he could do was feel bad for the little boy playing with toy cars under that Christmas tree. Mikey had had a loving family one Christmas, and they'd been gone the next.

"Hey." Yuki squeezed him. "You good?"

"Just sad," he told her. "It's okay to be sad sometimes."

"That's good, because I'm sad a lot." She shifted in his arms into a more comfortable position and nuzzled against him. "And that's what made me weak. That ghost used my grief to get inside my head, to make me feel useless. You had to come rescue me, and it should always be the other way around."

"Why?" he asked.

"Because that's what I'm good for. I'm a weapon, I'm supposed to protect you."

"You're not just a weapon," he replied. "You're a person and my friend. We protect each other. I couldn't have survived Oregon without you, we both know that. You're stronger than me in so many different ways, but it isn't always about what you can do for me. You're also an artist. I've seen the easels in your room. I know you're not just painting new tarot cards in there." Yuki had a bad habit of leaving her bedroom door open, and her paintings were usually pointed right at the door.

Over the last several months, he had seen landscapes and still lifes that were nothing short of amazing. "There's more to you than just being the ice queen."

Yuki didn't say anything for so long that Mike wondered if she had fallen asleep. Or maybe he had made things awkward by complimenting her so much all at once. Not being able to see her face made it difficult for him to read how his words had landed, and this was a conversation that required a measured approach.

"Do you miss her?" Yuki asked unexpectedly.

Mike knew exactly who she was talking about. Other than Eulalie, almost nobody brought up Velvet around him. He wasn't sure if they were afraid it would hurt his feelings or if it just made them uncomfortable.

"Every day," he replied. "It's weird to think how big a part of my life she became, even though I only knew her for a few days."

"Love can do that," she said. "It's the sword that can mistake your heart for its own sheath. Every time you wield it, there's a good chance that you only hurt yourself."

"Do you miss Emily?"

The temperature in the hallway dropped, and he felt Yuki tense up. It was almost like her magic was acting defensively, but there was no actual threat. It was likely the question itself, and he almost regretted asking.

"I don't know how to explain it," she said. "I love who she was but loathe who she became. I dream about her most nights. Sometimes she's just watching me, other times we talk. We reminisce, we argue, it's like she's really there. But sometimes the dreams turn bad, and I'm facing her as she was toward the end. I scream her name, beg her to snap out of it so I can save her, but…"

"That sounds hard." He squeezed her affectionately. "This might sound silly, but if you ever need Lily to go into your dreams, she can probably help."

In fact, Lily had offered once to go with him to the Dreamscape and masquerade as Velvet, but he had turned her down. He didn't dare tarnish that final memory of her shimmering eyes as she crossed over on the shores of his soul.

"No thanks. There's a lot in there I'm not really comfortable with her seeing."

"I understand." He sighed and relaxed against the wall. They had walked so far already, and there was no telling how much farther they would have to go. His magic had recuperated a bit but not enough to power him on the marathon jogs he was used to. Maybe if Yuki shrank down, he could carry her and jog for a couple of hours until they found a way out.

Thinking of Yuki, he wondered what sort of tragic secrets she still carried. There was more than a single lifetime of hurt weighing on her soul, and he wished for perhaps the hundredth time that there was a way he could help her with her burdens. Sometimes it seemed she was on the verge of crossing the divide she had built around her, but it always surprised him how quickly she was able to step away from that metaphorical ledge.

Mike. It was Kisa's voice, wavering slightly as if spoken through a tube. *Can you hear me?*

I can. Even though it was dark, he closed his eyes. Kisa materialized before him, sitting with her legs crossed. *Where are you? Are you all okay?*

We are. Kisa's eyes popped open, and she smiled. *I can see you!*

We mustn't be too far away, he replied with a grin. Ever since the two of them had connected minds across thousands of miles and a dimensional barrier, they had been working on replicating the feat. When close enough, they could communicate telepathically, but it required a fair bit of concentration. Luckily, he had nothing better to do right now.

"What's going on?" Yuki asked.

"Cat radio," he replied, using Tink's favorite term for it.

"Are they close?" she asked.

"Hold on." It took him a moment to strengthen the connection. *Where are you? We can head that way*, he told Kisa.

Don't. We're in the workshop right now, but listen. The furnace is enchanted. The tunnels change without warning. Kisa tilted her head as if listening to something. *Tink says you should try to find a way out next time you find a vent. It would be easier to find you out here. Is Yuki still with you?*

She is.

Good. Don't get separated. The vents of the furnace are constantly shifting. Kisa made a face. *You're being hunted.*

I know, he replied. *Just had a pissing match with the Ghost of Christmas Past. It wasn't happy with the outcome.*

There're at least two more in there with you. Are you okay?

I am, but Christmas Past got away, so it's still out there. Apparently it works for the Krampus now, whatever that means.

Kisa nodded. *About that. He's hunting Holly. We need to regroup and figure out a plan. This guy sounds like a real dick, and he might be in there with you. We aren't sure.*

"Mike?" Yuki's voice was a whisper as she grabbed Mike by the front of his jacket and tugged. He opened his eyes and saw that a faint glow was coming from somewhere up ahead. The tunnel was being illuminated by a distant ball of light that disappeared around a faraway turn but didn't go much farther. Its ambient light was more than enough to continue illuminating the main passageway.

He closed his eyes again and saw Kisa. Her image rippled, a result of the distraction. Even when the two of them were in the same house, it was very difficult to maintain a psychic link like this. *Shit, we have company. Stay out of the vents. We'll find a way to escape.*

Kisa gave him a thumbs-up, then vanished.

"It's getting closer," Yuki whispered as she rose, then pulled Mike up. The tiny sphere of light was surrounded by red lines of energy that made it look like a Christmas ornament. Festive music echoed down the corridor, and Mike was fairly certain he was hearing "Auld Lang Syne" being sung.

"Let's head back the way we came," he whispered back. "The vents change anyway, doesn't seem to matter where we go."

She nodded. As they backed away from the approaching light, they passed a corridor that descended like a slide.

"Hold on." Mike led Yuki into the side passage, then knelt and held his hand to the floor. He summoned a lightning spider and guided it to the corner. The air sizzled around it while it waited for instructions.

"Okay, let's go." He held Yuki's hand as they moved twenty feet down the corridor. At his mental command, the lightning spider jumped around the corridor and shot sparks into the air as it ran away.

The spirit blasted after the spider with the sound of jingling bells. The spider fled down the corridor and away from the spirit, scattering light and sparks in an attempt to make a scene. Mike and Yuki crouched as the spirit barreled past them, leaving glitter and snowflakes painted all along the passageway behind it.

There was a loud pop, and the hallway went dark. Mike felt his magic strain at the sudden change in distance between himself and the little spider before it fizzled out.

"It's gone," he said, then summoned another spider for light.

"I'm guessing the Ghost of Christmas Present?" Yuki pointed at the decorations, which were already fading into colored smoke. "At least it leaves a trail for us to avoid."

"Then I say let's avoid it." He turned down the corridor and felt a tugging in his abdomen. It was Kisa's presence, suddenly much closer. Had the furnace tunnels shifted again? "I sense the others nearby. I hope that means we're close enough to the workshop that we can break out of here. We just need to find a vent big enough to fit through and we're set. If we don't, we'll probably starve or die of thirst while being chased by Christmas movie rejects."

"I can make us water." She held out a hand and summoned a small icicle. "There's not a lot of moisture in here, but this is doable. It'll sap your body heat though. I think you'll freeze to death long before you starve."

"Least of my concerns right now." He took the icicle from her and sucked on it. His lips had already cracked. She summoned one for herself and bit the tip off. "That's bad for your teeth," he said.

She bared her fangs at him with a smile. "I'll worry about my teeth. You worry about getting us out of here."

It was hardly a fair trade, but seeing her smile was worth it.

They continued down the long hallway until it tapered, forcing Mike to crouch. He lost track of how many hours they walked, his stomach grumbling in protest. That single mug of hot cocoa wasn't going to sustain him forever.

The spider leading them down the tunnel blipped out of existence, carried away by whatever magic ran the place. Mike and Yuki paused, and she summoned a fox fire flame to float ahead of them.

"You've got to be running low on magic," she told him. "Let me lighten the burden."

"I'm doing okay. The spiders are pretty easy," he explained. "I'm really just having my magic walk in front of me. Since there's nobody to sink into, it doesn't even take that much concentration to maintain. I can even reclaim it, but there's a small chance it might trigger my sex drive, so I usually just let it fizzle out."

"How many of them can you control at once?" she asked.

"Three, if we're talking complete control. If I just make them run until they hit something, I can do quite a few."

Yuki nodded. "A lot of magic scales up exponentially

based on complexity. The fact that you make them look like little spiders probably doesn't help."

The comment wasn't meant to be hurtful, but it felt like he was punched in the gut. He stopped walking, and Yuki squeezed his hand.

"Shit, I'm sorry." She patted his arm. "It's not that I forget, I just—"

"It's fine." He took a deep breath and let it out. The lightning spiders had been created shortly after Velvet's death as a way to speak with the spiders in his own house. Their lives were typically simple, and once he had convinced Tink not to swat them, it wasn't uncommon to spot them in the corners of the room, giving him a friendly wave. "It really is. I started using them as a way to stay connected to her, and it's just a habit now. I honestly don't know if I could make them into a different shape without some serious effort."

"I'm the same way with ice magic. When my third tail grew, I was so angry and bitter that I connected with ice on a fundamental level. I'm not in that place anymore, but the magic is just as much a part of me as my own hands. I tend to lean on it." Yuki turned and wrapped her arms around him, holding him tight. "But I wish I could learn to lean on others, like you do. I hate feeling isolated, like I'm the fifth wheel of the family. And before you begin, I know I do it to myself."

"Yuki." He twisted to hug her properly. The fur of her coat was indistinguishable from her own natural softness, and it was remarkable just how fluffy she felt against him. "I think you already know this, but I'm always here for you, no matter what you need."

She shifted, and he could make out the outline of her smile in the dim light.

"Thank you," she said, then looked up at him. Her eyes were shining, and he was suddenly aware of how close her face was to his. Her triple tails swished about, then folded around him as if in an embrace.

Her fox fire went out, and she got on her tiptoes and planted a small kiss on the corner of his lips. One of her fangs caught the edge of his lower lip but not enough to draw blood.

When Yuki spoke, her voice was barely a whisper. "I'm not entirely certain, but I think I may be falling for you, Caretaker."

"I—" Mike was cut off when she pressed her finger against his lips to shush him.

"Don't say anything, not yet." She let out a sigh and hugged him. "Just hold me a bit longer, and then we need to keep moving. You won't be able to survive the cold like I can."

Nodding, he stayed in her embrace, marveling at how much heat radiated off her. Was that part of her magic or just the fur on her body? He couldn't help himself as he buried his face in the fur of her collar and inhaled the scent of the woods. It wasn't just memories of Oregon that were triggered but every camping trip he had gone on as a child.

"Are you…sniffing me?" Yuki asked.

"Maybe a little. Sorry." He lifted his head, the cold air of the vents immediately kissing his cheeks. "You were just so warm. It made me feel a little too comfortable is all."

"I see." She took a step back and swatted his nose with the tip of one of her tails. "I was more wondering if it was a trick you picked up from our resident hellhound."

"Nope. If I got something from her, I don't know what it is." He made a face. "And again, I'm really sorry."

"Don't be." She looped her arm through his. "I'm a fox. I use smell to identify everyone, even you."

"Really?" he asked.

"Yeah. I just don't need to bury my head in their hair first. Listen." She chuckled, then sniffed the air loudly as if to prove her point. "Wait, what the hell is that?"

Mike thought she was screwing with him until she snapped her fingers, summoning the fox fire once more. Instead of the long conduit of the ventilation system, they stood in an opulent room decorated in Christmas greenery. Mistletoe, holly, and ivy were draped along the walls on golden hooks. A large table piled high with meats, breads, and all sorts of holiday dishes flooded the room with steam and the sweet odors of Christmas dinner.

"Ah, shit," Mike whispered, his eyes traveling to the figure sitting at the other end of the table. It was a giant, easily twelve feet tall, with a thick, fur-lined green robe. Long auburn curls tumbled down the giant's shoulder, and when it leaned forward into the light, Mike realized with a start that the Ghost of Christmas Present was a woman.

She held up a large cornucopia, which blazed to life with enough fire to light the rest of the room. There was a wicked glint in her eye as she held the torch forward to see them better. Her sleeve slid along her arm, revealing a muscular forearm.

"Come in!" exclaimed the ghost. "Come in and know me better, man!"

"We're…already in," Yuki muttered as she gazed around the room. "How are we supposed to come in when we're already here?"

The green robes hung so loosely on Christmas Present that large, erect nipples were revealed while she leaned forward. She eagerly stacked a plate with food and held it toward them with one hand.

"I am the Ghost of Christmas Present! Look upon me!" She shook her head, her curls riding across pendulous breasts in waves. She wore a wreath of holly like a crown, and her hands were the size of dinner plates. There was a mischievous grin on her face as she sat back in her seat, the robes now folded open to reveal her chest. She set the plate of food down and slid her hands along her breasts, pushing them together to create the biggest press of cleavage Mike had ever seen.

"Um…I think something's wrong with this one," Mike said to Yuki.

"There's something wrong with all of them," she replied in a hushed tone. "At least this spirit isn't a creepy little fucker like the last one."

"I would say this is a different kind of creepy," Mike whispered in return.

Christmas Present let out a joyous laugh that rocked the room.

"You have never seen the like of me before!" she exclaimed, then stood. Her robe briefly opened to reveal that she was, in fact, wearing absolutely nothing underneath. Between her belly button and auburn pubes shaped like an upside down Christmas tree was a scar that looked very much like the outline of one of his electrical spiders. Mike's best guess was that the spirit had caught up to his little lightning spider, but he had no idea what that meant in the long-term. Based on the ghost's behavior, though, he had a pretty good idea that his magic was to blame. "Now come! It is Christmas Day, and we have plenty to celebrate!"

"I'm not sure if we should be thrilled or frightened," Mike said, then eyed the plate of food. For now, his precognition said he was safe, and he was famished. "You thinking what I'm thinking?"

Yuki sniffed the air, then nodded. "I prefer fighting on a full stomach. Other than our horny hostess, I think we're in the clear, but don't take your eyes off her."

Mike fought back a laugh, practically fighting to pull his gaze away from Christmas Present's breasts. The giant saw him looking and grinned, then shimmied, causing her pendulous breasts to sway. He wasn't entirely certain where the danger in the situation lay, but at least he would have something nice to look at in the meantime. Christmas Present smiled at the attention, then sipped from a massive silver goblet. She eyed him hungrily, then licked her lips.

"Oh, don't worry. I won't," he said.

KISA LET OUT THE BREATH SHE HAD BEEN HOLDING IN AS MIKE faded from view. She opened her eyes to the sight of Holly watching her intently from only a foot away.

"Well?" she asked.

"They're okay, but I guess they got into a fight with the Ghost of Christmas Past."

Holly groaned. "Oh, Santa, everything is absolutely fudged right now. If the spirits are attacking people, what hope do we have?"

"Tink think need better plan." Tink was lying on her back, her eyes on the ceiling and her feet swaying back and forth as if she was listening to some unheard tune. "Husband escape furnace, but then what? Pointy ears still in big trouble."

Kisa nodded. "She's right. We know the Krampus is taking the elves, but where? Is there anyone else here who can help us? What should we be doing?"

Holly had turned away from them, her lower lip trembling. There was a lot riding on the elf's tiny shoulders, but she wasn't offering any ideas.

"Hmm." Tink sat up, then walked over to Holly and snatched her marker away. "List problems first, focus on solutions." She turned toward the nearest wall and drew a rough sketch of the furnace, followed by a demon. "No heat, workshop getting too cold. Need restart furnace, or pointy ears freeze. Fuck face demon—"

"Tinker!" Holly clutched her ears.

Tink rolled her eyes. "Bad demon want capture pointy ears, don't know why. Tink can fix furnace but can't protect sexy elf same time."

"So we should wait until Mike finds us." Kisa looked back at the vent. She felt a shifting in her body as Mike moved away from her. "How long will that take?"

"Husband smart, come back to workshop. We smart too, find safe place to watch workshop until he comes back."

"The cameras." Holly looked up. "We have a room with monitors that watch the whole workshop! If we go there, we can find him as soon as he gets back!"

"Good idea. Let's head there right aw—" Kisa was interrupted by a loud clanging sound from the vent, followed by a low grumbling. It sounded like Mike's voice, but it was distorted. Had he found them already?

The shrieking sound of metal on metal filled the air as a specter passed through the wall. It was roughly the same height that they were, but its porcelain face was twisted up in agony.

"Miser! Miser!" it screamed in Mike's voice, then locked eyes with Holly. Its whole body swirled around like a tiny galaxy while its cherubic face remained stationary. It let out a rasping growl, then charged.

"Oh, no you don't!" Kisa hollered, jumping between the spirit and the elf. It collided with her when she sank her claws into it. The spirit looked surprised as it disentangled itself, muttering in a different language as steam escaped from the scratches. It froze in place, then shouted more gibberish as it swiped at Kisa with a long arm that was more tentacle than limb. Tink tried to jump on the ghost but passed through harmlessly as it grabbed a terrified Holly by the wrist.

"I'm here about your welfare," it whispered from every corner of the room at once. For a moment, the spirit separated into several distinct entities that whispered to one another before snapping back together.

"Tink here to kick ass!" The goblin's goggles were now switching lenses at a manic pace as she pulled the hammer from her belt. She dodged a flurry of blows, then threw the hammer hard at the spirit's face. It passed through the entity and struck a pipe behind it. The pipe cracked, releasing a high-pressure blast of water that caught the spirit in the head and sent it across the room. Kisa grabbed Holly by the hand and ran toward the door where Tink waited for them.

The goblin's eyes widened, and Kisa looked back just as the Ghost of Christmas Past lunged for them, sprouting spectral limbs. The trio clung to one another as they were carried across the hall and then passed through the opposite wall.

Darkness surrounded them as the spirit pulled them past spheres of light. Tink tried to bite the tentacle holding her while Holly screamed in panic. They spun as they fell, whirling about like a mutant maple seed. Tink was on the far end now, clinging tightly to Holly's ankles. Holly's tights slid along her legs, causing the goblin to lose her grip and fall away from them.

"Tink!" Kisa didn't dare let go of Holly and could only watch helplessly as Tink vanished inside one of the bubbles. Growling, she squeezed Holly's waist as they collided with a bubble of their own, and the darkness washed away from them to reveal an old kitchen with a woman standing at a stove, stirring something in a pot.

The colors of the room were washed out like someone had wiped them away with a wet rag before they could dry completely. When the woman turned, it was to reveal that her face was missing. Where her features should have been was just smooth dark skin. Her jaw moved, as if she was speaking, but no sound emerged.

A small girl walked into the room carrying a stuffed owl that had seen better days. Kisa stared, mouth open, as the child climbed onto a nearby chair and took the spoon from the woman. Other than the occasional clink of the spoon against the pan, the scene was silent.

The girl was unmistakably a younger version of herself. This completely human version of Kisa laughed in response to something the woman said, then continued stirring while the woman started chopping vegetables.

"Who is that?" Holly stood on wobbly legs, then grabbed Kisa by the wrist. "Where's her face?"

"I don't know," Kisa replied. Was it her mom? Or someone else?

"It's your grandmother." Christmas Past's voice was little more than a wheeze from the corner of the room. The spirit was splattered across the wall, its body a mess of limbs. Its face rested in the center of its torso near the floor. It had tilted sideways, light shining out of only one eye. "That's all I can tell you for certain. Your past, it's…I can't…"

"Shh." Kisa shushed the spirit and moved closer to the little girl. The child leaned away from the pot so the old woman could dump extra veggies into the soup. She stole a carrot from the cutting board and munched on it casually as her grandmother pulled out a bowl of flour. It was a memory that was almost in reach; if she could just remember a bit more, maybe she would know who she was.

The spirit coughed, and the scene rippled as they were transported to another room. The woman and Kisa were sitting under a small tree in the living room, with only a couple of presents underneath. Pictures adorned a nearby wall, but any people inside the frames had been smeared away.

"Why am I with my grandmother? Can you tell me her name?" Excited, Kisa moved away from Holly and toward the woman. Her face was still missing, but Kisa felt the tug of familiarity when she got a look at the woman's hands as she playfully shook a gift. They were covered in calluses and old scars, hands that had been used for hard labor. Despite this, Kisa somehow knew they were gentle and would feel like the softest leather if she could touch them.

"I…can't…" Ink leaked from the corner of the spirit's mouth. "Your past is…broken."

"What's wrong with you?" Holly knelt by the spirit and

took one of its hands in her own. "Why are you trying to hurt us?"

Christmas Past sighed, then squeezed Holly's hand. "He's taking over," they replied. "He wants Christmas to...himself."

"Are you dying?" Holly went to touch the ink flowing out of Christmas Past's eyes, but it slapped her hand away.

"The past cannot be killed," it whispered, then looked at Kisa. "But it can be lost." It wiped the ink off its face and contemplated it on its fingertips. "Don't let his foul magic taint you, Holly. Don't let him...change who you are. Or change Christmas."

"We need to help the spirit," Holly declared. "This isn't what they're supposed to be like. They're meant to help people. I think...I think they're dying."

"I'll be fine...by next Christmas." Its weak smile became a frown as the ink reversed course and flowed back into its eyes. The light in its eye flickered like a candle in the wind. "Shouldn't have taken...all three of you. Was already hurt but...so angry. Couldn't...control...sorry..."

"Where is Tink?" Kisa demanded.

The spirit looked up. A large crack appeared in the ceiling above them, and another version of Christmas Past fell through it. It crumpled like a leaf on impact with the floor, then crawled toward its duplicate, letting out a wail of agony. The two of them flowed together to form a slightly more cohesive spirit filled with sparkling lights that soon dimmed.

From the crack, a figure hopped down, murder in her eyes. She clutched an ink-soaked screwdriver in one hand.

"Tink!" Kisa hugged her friend, but the goblin ignored her.

"Stupid ghost fuck stay out of Tink's head," she growled, pointing her tool at Christmas Past. When she swore, cracks appeared all around the room. "Piece of shit read Tink's thoughts, broke its fucking head! Now let Tink and friends go or else."

"Get her away from me!" Christmas Past's voice altered in pitch as if two of it spoke. "Don't let her touch me, she's broken!"

"Tink show you what broken means." Tink slid out of Kisa's arms and reached for Christmas Past. The ghost let out a weak cry of agony as it tried to slap her away and failed. Tink stabbed Christmas Past in the face, her hand and screwdriver passing harmlessly through the spirit to strike the wall behind it.

The room shattered like glass, falling away from them to reveal that they were now somewhere else. Kisa felt her heart sink as the vision of her grandmother vanished, trying hard to get one last look at those hands that had raised her. She could almost feel them caressing her cheek or wiping tears from her eyes.

They now stood in a dining hall adorned with scraps of wrapping paper and broken decorations. Although the lights were off, large windows along the ceiling allowed the northern lights to stream in, providing plenty of illumination. On the floor, Christmas Past was nothing more than a shrinking inkblot with a face the size of a baseball.

"He's coming for you," it whispered, then sank through the floor with a burbling sound like hot oil.

"Good," Tink spat. "If Tink see stupid horn head, Tink smash dumb fuck face!" She looked over at Holly, whose features had gone pale. When she addressed the elf, her tone softened dramatically. "We go now. Find room with screens. Watch for husband. Tink hate stupid Christmas ghost, make Tink see too much bad from childhood."

Holly nodded, then stood. She rubbed her eyes like someone who had been asleep for a long time, then walked toward the door of the dining hall. Adjusting her outfit, she turned to face them.

"Let's do this." Despite her determination, Holly's voice squeaked at the end.

"Hey." Kisa grabbed Holly by the hand. "You're not alone. We're with you."

Tink grabbed Holly's other hand, then smirked. "Pretty elf owe Tink big thanks. Maybe give Tink special kiss later, use lots of tongue."

"Tink!" Kisa looked at the goblin in shock. "Are you serious right now?"

Holly's face was so red she looked like a Christmas bulb about to burn out.

"Big serious," Tink added. "Holly very good kisser, treat Tink like candy cane." She winked at Holly. "Tink remember. Big fun, many hours. Way better than hammer."

The tension broke when Holly laughed and shook her head. "You really are trouble, aren't you?"

"Trouble for some. Fun for others." Tink licked her lips lewdly. "Both if Holly lucky."

Holly laughed again, then led them out of the dining room. They were in a large building built like a lodge with crisscrossing beams everywhere. Kisa lost track of the long hallways and huge rooms and was baffled when they came to a large set of wooden doors that led outside. The northern lights glowed ominously on Holly's skin as she turned to face them.

"If we cut across the courtyard, we'll save ourselves hours," she said. "But that does mean going outside. I suspect it may be colder than usual."

"You don't say." Kisa gazed at the ice-frosted windows. "As compared to what? This is the arctic."

"Yeah, about that. We vent excess heat from the furnace to keep the North Pole from freezing over. It's actually quite pleasant. The sunstone is essentially a tiny star, not sure if you were aware. Plenty of energy to provide heated walkways, hot cocoa stands every couple of blocks, we even tried a waterslide one year but had to shut it down after a couple of reindeer got stuck." Holly gave the door a shove, but it was stuck. "Sprinkles, we might not even be able to—"

Tink kicked the door hard enough that the glass cracked as it burst open, sending ice skittering across the frosted walkways away from them. The icy breeze that blew in chilled Kisa through her fur, and she pulled her hood up.

"Guess we're headed outside," Kisa muttered as Holly led the way. Kisa looked over her shoulder, feeling Mike shift away from her once more. Even worse, the memory of her grandmother's hands was already fading, her memories much like snowflakes on hot steel.

Together, they ran out into the cold arctic air.

JACK FROST STOOD BEFORE A BANK OF MONITORS, STARING intently at the screens beneath the *Workshop* category. One of the displays was overrun with shadows and static that shifted around as the Krampus tore apart one of the many woodshops. The demon's presence couldn't be properly displayed by the monitoring system, a quirk of his unnatural existence, so it appeared that dark static was ripping apart a drill press right now, metal and wood alike being tossed through the air with abandon.

When the Krampus left the camera's view, the screen returned to normal as the next feed scrambled.

Jack flicked her gaze across the monitors, hoping to see any sign of that man from earlier, Mike. The odds that the human would pose a problem were slim but still existed. When Jack had returned to the main level, the Krampus had been waiting in the central hub for a full report.

It was surmised that an elf must have brought the man and his friends here, so the Krampus had left Jack behind to hunt them down. Apparently an elf had gotten away by fleeing into the vents, which had sent the Krampus into a rage.

Jack shivered at the thought of all that unbridled fury. The damage to the exterior of the furnace had been extensive and would have been worse if the Krampus had not needed to use it later for his own reasons.

The floorboards behind Jack groaned as a heavy figure pushed the top of her bulk through the doorway.

"Has he found them yet?" The deep voice had a hiss to it that reminded Jack of escaping steam.

"Not yet, Grýla." Jack turned and saw that the giantess had only squeezed the top half of her massive bulk through the door. Her face was misshapen and her hair dull with grease and filth. Gnarled fingers left gouges in the floor as she shifted her weight from one hand to the other. "Any news from your sons?"

"They still seek the sleigh." Grýla licked her lips anxiously. "There were…complications."

"How so?"

When the Krampus had taken the North Pole, he had become enraged to discover the sleigh was missing. Luckily, Jack had the foresight to place a tracking beacon in Santa's bag. The Yule Cat was capable of tracking it, but Jack had learned long ago that you could never rely on a cat for anything of importance.

"The sleigh has been discovered by someone else." Grýla grimaced, then flexed her torso. The frame of the door cracked, then splintered. "My sons chased them, but they escaped by flying away."

"So who has the sleigh?" With the entire world frozen, there should have been no competition for the sleigh. Were these allies of Santa? If so, then why hadn't they just helped him defeat the Krampus? What did they want with the sleigh?

At the thought of Santa, Jack looked at the monitor in the far corner of the console. The camera there overlooked an unfurnished room with a crystalline mirror set in silver. Fog swirled just beneath its surface, but the bulky figure of a man in a red coat trapped on the other side of the polished surface could be seen.

It was the same mirror the Krampus had been trapped in up until this morning. If not for Jack, the Krampus would still be there, slamming fur-covered claws against his shimmering prison.

Jack picked up the large snow globe that sat beneath the monitors. With a quick shake, sparkling snowflakes swirled around the interior. As they parted, they revealed a bony figure in Santa's robes, sitting next to a woman clutching a thermos. As the scene shifted outward, it revealed a massive three-headed dog pulling the sleigh through the air.

"What in the world?" With another shake, the scene vanished, revealing the Earth. A tiny golden light was now over the Pacific with a golden arrow pointed at Australia. "It looks like they're taking Santa's usual route."

Grýla bowed her head. "These are formidable adversaries. We need your help."

"I am unavailable." Jack looked once more at the monitor where the Krampus was. Until the human or the elf was found, there was simply too much at risk. "Do you not have other allies?"

"Bah!" Grýla spat on the ground. "My children are many, but they are stupid. The cat is no match for the hellhound, and my lazy husband is of no use to me."

"Fine. Here." Jack summoned a handful of ice crystals and approached the giant. Grýla bowed her head in reverence. "When they land somewhere cold enough for snow, have your children sprinkle this on the ground. It will summon the help they need, but they need to actually participate. They say that opportunity only knocks once for a reason, so make sure your sons actually put in the effort."

"You are too kind." Grýla pulled a small bag from her belt

and held it out for Jack to tilt the crystals inside. "I will see it done."

"Good. There is too much at stake. A chance like this will never come again." Jack looked back at the monitor with the mirror.

"Why doesn't he just smash it?" asked Grýla. "And seal away the saint for all time?"

Jack had pondered that same exact question hours ago. Santa's capture had been a private affair for the Krampus, but it had required that Jack lure the big man himself to the mirror room. Great pains had been taken over the last six months to brainwash a group of elves into complying with the Krampus's plan to free him. They had been taught to lie, to conceal, and most important of all, to obey Jack and the Krampus.

Nobody knew why the protective wards around the North Pole had weakened earlier in the year, but it had allowed the Krampus to reach out to Jack and the others using some type of astral projection. His arguments had been very persuasive, and they all stood to benefit from a change in ownership. Tonight was supposed to be the culmination of all that hard work.

Now, though, Jack had doubts. At first, the Krampus had been singularly focused on the elves, dragging them to an unknown location beneath the workshop. They had largely obeyed him, though Grýla had been forced to hunt down a few stragglers with strong enough willpower to resist the Krampus's commands.

But then, instead of solidifying his victory by banishing Santa to the void, the Krampus kept him as a trophy. In fact, he had been visiting Santa when Jack had called up to let him know that mortals had been tracked to the furnace room. It was as though the demon couldn't help himself; he was consistently dropping by to torment Santa but to what end?

"Grýla? Out of curiosity, what did the Krampus promise

you?" Jack looked back at the monitors to check that the Krampus was still tearing apart the woodshop. He could move surprisingly fast when he wanted, and the last thing Jack wanted was for the Krampus to show up unannounced and interrupt Grýla's answer.

The giantess blinked as if processing the question, then grinned. "A return to our former glory," she said, the bag now tied to her belt. "No longer will my family be trapped in the ice, our legacy mocked and forgotten. Santa found a way to bind us here in the name of protecting his precious little believers, and we want out."

"To do what?" Jack asked.

Grýla started to say something, then smiled instead. "To live as we would," she replied. "No more, no less."

"Hmm." Jack frowned, wondering what that even meant. Grýla was being coy, which wasn't something the giants were known for.

Grýla coughed into her hand, as if aware of Jack's sudden scrutiny. "And what does the Krampus have to offer Old Man Winter himself, I wonder?"

An icy wind blew through Grýla's greasy locks, causing the giant to cry out in surprise as she bowed her head. Frost formed along her flanks and spread across the wall over the door.

"I am neither old nor a man!" Jack retorted, grinding her teeth together. It was a centuries-old misconception, one that angered her to no end. There had once been a period when winter had been ruled by the old gods, mighty beings across the world who could steal the heat from a summer's day with a single breath. But their time had long passed, leaving behind others in their stead. Once a minor deity, Jack Frost had outlived those ethereal beings and risen in power to rightfully claim the mantle of winter's ruler, only to live in the shadow of those who had come before her.

It didn't help that her body lacked feminine curves, nor that her hair was short. She kept most of it tucked beneath her hat to keep the ends from becoming brittle. Once her hair was past shoulder length, it lost whatever natural protection her body had from the cold. She definitely wasn't about to wear a dress to clear up any confusion either, and she would often spend so much time in the ice that a beard of frost would form along her chin. The misconception was understandable, but nobody seemed to care when she corrected them. Jacqueline Frost wasn't even her real name, but it was still the one she had chosen for herself upon becoming winter's mistress.

The worst offenders were all those stupid movies and cartoons about Santa that had depicted her as a man. The Krampus had promised her that things were going to change for the better, that he would ensure that the world would properly recognize her for who she was. Christmas would mean something again and not just be a commercial holiday intended to bail corporations out of debt.

She fondly remembered the old days, before Santa had donned the red suit. The two of them had been friendly, and she had even ridden in the sleigh with him a few times to deliver gifts. She would ice the roofs over to ensure a smooth landing for the sleigh, and he would bring her spare cookies and treats that had been left out for him.

Now, though, he was so concerned about his own image that she was ignored, relegated to ensuring the North Pole was adequately frozen when Christmas came rolling around. At some point, she had become background noise, just like Grýla and her kin. Unlike the giants, she still had a job to do but received no compensation or appreciation for it.

Jack wasn't dumb. She knew that freeing the Krampus would be seen as a betrayal. But the demon had known all the right words to say, and she had jumped into this mess with both feet, thinking there was no other choice. Impulsive decisions were rare for her, but she was simply full of them these days.

"Leave," she commanded. Grýla groveled for a moment longer, then forced her bulk back through the doorway. The floor creaked as Grýla moved down the hall away from the monitor room.

"Fuck." Jack turned her attention back to the monitors and noticed that Santa was staring at the camera, as if he could see her. He nodded knowingly, and she was half-tempted to go down and shatter that mirror herself.

Instead, she turned off that monitor. With the Krampus still digging for that last elf, there was nothing to do for now but act as his eyes while he threw a tantrum. The silence gave her plenty of time to consider the ramifications of her actions, and even more doubts began to surface.

What if the Krampus didn't keep his promise? It was hard to know if his word would be any good, especially if they couldn't retrieve Santa's sleigh. It had once been a chariot fit for a god, capable of sailing across the sky. She had no idea how Santa had gotten his mitts on the thing, but there was plenty she didn't know about the big man.

Somewhere, a bell rang. Jack turned her attention toward the far wall, where a shadow melted through and fell to the ground. It was the spirit of Christmas Past, its pale features like melted wax.

Jack vaulted the railing and ran to the spirit, then knelt by its side.

"What happened to you?" she asked.

The spirit shook its head, casting dark splotches onto the ground. "I was not made for this," it whispered. "Do not let him remake you in his own image."

"Who? Krampus?"

The spirit sighed, the lights in its eyes flickering out. "Am I the last of my kind?" it asked.

Jack laughed, but there was no humor behind it. "Of course not. Next Christmas, you'll have a brand-new sibling."

The spirit shuddered. "I'm not so sure," it whispered.

"He did this to you? That man. Mike."

Christmas Past tried to answer but couldn't. Its lips moved, but no sound came out. Dark fluid pooled in the corners of its eyes, and then it let out a maniacal laugh. The spirit's body shimmered with twinkling lights as it proceeded to melt into the floorboards.

Jack's hands trembled as she pulled the silver ornament from her pocket and willed it to life. Whirling lights spun around the spirit, pulling it back inside the ornament to wherever it went while it slumbered. The spirit hadn't just been defeated—it had been corrupted. Guilt flooded through her. How was she to know that the spirits could be damaged, let alone altered, by their encounters?

Maybe that was the reason Santa used them sparingly. It had been decades since the last time they had been unleashed, and any harm that came to them lay solely on her hands. All she had expected was the spirits to delay Mike or scare him off completely. The Krampus had explained that they could be used for such purposes, but now she wasn't sure.

No. The human in the ducts was clearly a tougher foe than expected, that was all. She didn't dare consider the possibility that the Krampus had lied to her, because it was an idea she was unwilling to accept.

Storming back to the cameras, she glared at them intensely. If Mike was going to try to sneak out of the vents, she would see him. There were dozens of monitors and hundreds of cameras. She cycled through them until she felt like she had identified the best locations to catch anyone sneaking around.

"I'm going to find you," she whispered, thinking of the man from the furnace. When he had spoken to her, she had felt an odd compulsion in the center of her body, a sudden willingness to not only obey but please. For a short moment, there had been nothing she wanted more than to do absolutely whatever he asked of her in the hopes of gaining his favor. She wasn't sure what kind of magic he was using, but she wouldn't let it happen again.

Movement on a corner monitor caught her attention, and she spotted three figures standing next to a door. It was a goblin, an elf, and a woman with cat ears. Jack thumbed the walkie-talkie at her hip, ready to call the Krampus, but paused. She thought once more about her interaction with Mike and how he had deliberately targeted the napkin she had used to track them.

It wasn't the elf; she knew that much. Either the goblin or the cat had some sort of connection to him, one she could exploit. If she told the Krampus, he would rush there and potentially kill them. But if she got there first, maybe she could figure out how to use that link to find Mike.

On the camera, the goblin kicked the door open, and they ran outside.

It was selfish, and a stupid idea, but after watching the Krampus trash several rooms while having a temper tantrum, she felt entitled to it. With a grin, she dashed out of the monitor room, her body hovering inches off the ground as she glided down the hallway and toward an exit of her own. When she shoved open the door, the cold air greeted her with welcoming flurries.

"Let it snow," she commanded, and the northern lights were soon hidden away by whirling snowflakes.

CAUGHT IN THE PRESENT

When Lily first caught sight of the Pacific Islands, two thoughts occurred to her. The first of these was that it was far warmer than the US had been, which caused her to start sweating under her hat. It had been easy enough to remove the sweat glands from her forehead, but that fudging hat was a different story. Over the last few hours, she had tried everything to shed the offensive article of clothing, but it refused to budge. She had even debated letting Ticktock bite off the top of her head but worried about getting bounced out of the time lock by doing so.

The second thing that occurred to her was that there should be daylight here in the islands. There wasn't. In fact, it was just as dark as it had been when they left the East Coast of the US, and there was no rational reason for it. Curious what Santa Grim would offer as an explanation, she asked him about it.

"It's Christmas magic," he explained as they descended toward the first island. "It does what it needs to do."

"Fudging figures," she muttered as they approached their first home. Cerberus hovered in the air about ten feet over a shack on the beach. Death pulled out Santa's list and reviewed it.

"Okay, then, we need presents for Mabel, Rose, and Timmy." He looked at Lily expectantly.

"Those are some very white names for Polynesia," Lily replied, not sure what he wanted from her. "You sure we've got the right stop?"

"It says here they are on vacation from Maine," he informed her. "And if you could grab their presents from the bag, that would greatly speed things up. Poor Timmy is worried Santa won't find them this year. It's a good thing we're on the case."

"Somebody kill me," she groaned, then smiled upon realizing that had gotten past the filter. "So I have to look through the bag for their gifts?"

"Just stick your arm in and think of those names," he said.

"Lots of people are named Rose," she argued but shoved her hand in Santa's bag. A package was shoved into her hand, so she removed it.

"The process is very well automated," Death told her, holding out his arms. She handed over two gifts for Mabel, one for Rose, and then three for Timmy. Death's arms were very full as he moved toward the edge of the sleigh.

"How are you getting inside?" she asked.

"Christmas magic." He winked and stepped backward off the sleigh. The tails of his cloak fluttered out from beneath Santa's coat like the wings of a crow before he struck the roof hard and slid across its surface. Death dropped all the presents when he spilled off the roof, landing face down in the sand. His bare, bony legs kicked out as he struggled to extricate himself.

If Lily had been inclined to help, it still would have been impossible. She was laughing so hard that she had crouched in the sleigh, clutching her stomach as tears rolled down her cheeks. It was a good minute before she could pull herself together and look back over the side.

Death had managed to free himself, his skull twisted into a scowl as he picked up the presents he had dropped. He shook sand out of his sleeves, then brushed the presents off. Somehow they had all survived, though the wrapping paper on one of Timmy's gifts was torn.

"You're supposed to be Santa Claus, not Sandy—" Lily ducked out of the way as Death hurled a stone at her. Cerberus let out a series of snorts that could have been laughter.

"This is why you got coal for Christmas," Death declared as he tried to turn the latch on the front door. It clicked open, and he wandered inside.

A few minutes later, Death returned, pausing to shake some more sand out of his hat. Cerberus lowered the sleigh to allow the reaper to get in.

"So what went wrong with the dismount?" Lily asked, hiding her grin behind the pom-pom of her hat.

"I'm not sure." Death pulled out the manual again. "The house didn't have a chimney, so I just assumed…ah, okay. There's some stuff in the chapter on entering homes that I missed. Entrance is possible through any natural entry or one that allows the flow of air, like a chimney or a window. For difficult-to-reach entryways, there's a safety rope."

"I didn't see a safety rope." Lily looked around her feet and was surprised to find a coiled length of rope that was white with red ribbons woven through it. "That definitely wasn't here a minute ago."

Death waved his fingers at her. "Christmas magic, my dear demon. Come, Cerberus, to the next home."

The next home was only a block away, and Death had the hellhound park the sleigh on the ground this time. The name he read was Chinese, and Lily pulled two gifts from the bag with hanzi characters written on the tags. Death delivered the presents again and came out with a cookie in each hand.

"Little Bao remembered to leave Santa cookies," he explained, then handed one to Lily.

"How kind of you." She took a bite and winced. "This is very stale."

"Indeed. The four I ate were not very good." Death held the remaining cookie up. "And don't worry, I didn't forget about you." He tossed the cookie to Ticktock, who snatched it out of the air with a ribbon tongue.

"Should you be feeding that thing after midnight?" Lily asked.

"I am unaware of any time constraints on mimics or cookies." Death snapped the reins, and they were off again.

They established a good rhythm as they delivered hundreds of presents. Lily had Death read the list between houses so she could prepare gifts in advance. Death delivered most of them by walking through the front door. Apparently the world was still frozen inside the homes as he dropped off the packages, so there was no fear of discovery.

Without any proper way to keep time, Lily had no idea how long it took. Between Death falling off a couple more roofs and that time Cerberus crashed into an apartment complex, the deliveries flowed together in her mind like a collapsing dream.

In a way, it made sense. It was a similar trick to what she could accomplish in the Dreamscape. An hour in the real world could become years inside a dream, but the human brain would find a way to compress that information upon waking. An ordinary mind was likely to forget enough details that it may as well have been an hour.

When staying with Eulalie and Velvet last fall, she had done something similar for their father, allowing him several months with his deceased wife in the Dreamscape. While awake, he didn't even question the time distortion. Instead, his dreams were just a montage of pleasant memories, the time dilation forgotten.

At the sudden thought of Velvet, Lily scowled. Her passing had left a scar on Mike's soul. Over the summer, she and Dana had gone down to Florida to take revenge for the death of their friend but had gotten caught up in something much bigger.

She pushed the whole event out of her mind. It was only going to make her angry all over again.

Australia was similar to the islands, but the population clusters were thick enough that Death would often return to the sleigh just long enough for presents to the next house. Lily had noticed back in the islands that they didn't stop at every home, even if there were signs of children. Death thought the children had been naughty, or even no longer believed, but it didn't matter. That was always a few minutes saved, and it was going to add up quickly as the eternal night progressed.

They were somewhere above Sydney when they stopped the sleigh over an opulent home covered in Christmas lights. Lily knew something was up by the way the windows on the house sparkled as if tagged with fairy lights.

Death frowned at the list, his gaze moving to the house and back again.

"What's wrong?" she asked. Not that she cared, but she didn't feel like wasting time just sitting there. As long as they were busy making deliveries, she didn't notice how long it took.

"Er, nothing." Death looked at Lily, then back at the list, then the house.

"C'mon, what's the problem? I don't want to sit here all… night." She gestured at the moon up above, which had followed them the entire trip. "If there's an issue, let's just skip this place. Kid looks like they're probably getting a ton of presents anyway, look." She pointed at a window in the front of the house. Through it, a massive tree decorated in glass ornaments had been packed to the brim with presents.

Death cleared his throat, which made an eerie sound that reminded Lily of a creaking house. "Well, technically, there isn't a problem."

"Then let's get to it. What's the name?"

"William."

Lily reached into the bag and was surprised when nothing was pressed into her hand. She reached even deeper and tried to grab the first thing she felt, but the presents slid away from her touch. "What the fudge?"

"This child requires something else from Santa," Death explained. "You see, not everyone needs a material gift."

"Okay, then what is it?"

Death turned the list to show her. William's full name was scrawled in beautiful golden calligraphy. Just off to the side were the words *Personal Visit.*

Lily laughed. "Oh, that is rich! He's going to be so fudging scared when he gets Jack Skellington instead of the big man himself!"

"And that, my dear friend, is the problem." Death tugged his beard away from his face, revealing a bony jaw. "He might not believe that I am only helping Santa, you see."

"No poop." Lily scowled. Maybe her vocabulary could be more extensive, but she hated that the filter chose words for her.

"If only I had the ability to alter my form, it would be no problem." Death looked at Lily.

"Yeah. That would solve the issue, wouldn't it?" She looked away, refusing to acknowledge the comment.

Several moments passed. Death picked up his thermos and poured out some more hot cocoa. Lily had seen him do this multiple times already and knew that the thermos likely contained thousands of gallons of the stuff.

"Lily." Death paused to sip his cocoa thoughtfully. "You

wouldn't happen to know somebody who can shape-shift, would you?"

She ignored him. There was no way she was going to play Santa.

"Lily?" Death's tone shifted slightly, and she could hear the annoyance.

"Maybe this is something you should have considered before deciding to play Santa," she mumbled.

"Lily." The tone of his voice hardened, and all sense of jocularity had vanished. When she turned to face him, the flames in his sockets were burning purple. As she watched, the flames disappeared to reveal a field of stars inside his skull. One by one, the stars winked out as she let out a gasp of awe.

She didn't fear Death. At worst, he could ruin her evening. Yet in those eyes, she saw a version of eternity she wanted no part of.

"What's in it for me?" she asked in an attempt to deflect.

Death's hard stare softened. "I suppose I would owe you a favor," he said.

"A big one?"

He nodded, the light of the moon reflecting off his skull. "A favor from Death isn't one to be taken lightly, no matter the size."

"And nothing tea or map related."

His upper mandible twisted into a grin. "We can't always predict the future," he told her. "But yes, your repayment shall be very large."

"Fine." She looked at the house. "So I can just go in however I want?"

Death nodded. "The front door is fine, but if the child is awake, they will hear you."

"Care to explain to me how this random kid is still walking around?" She clenched her jaw as a thick white beard sprouted from it. "I mean, if the whole world is time locked and all."

"I suppose maybe you should think of it less as everyone else being frozen and more like we are just moving really fast." He leaned back and put his feet up on the front of the sleigh. Grains of sand were stuck between his metatarsals. "We're the ones inside a time bubble. Once it pops, we'll rejoin everyone else as it were. Some exceptions will be made as others are allowed to enter the bubble with us."

"How does that make sense?" Her voice deepened as her belly expanded. She gave it a poke to ensure that it did, indeed, jiggle like jelly. "Doesn't your book explain it?"

"It does not, but it doesn't matter. I once heard that any sufficiently advanced technology is indistinguishable from magic." Death pulled a cookie from his pocket. "In theory, this makes sense, but I choose to postulate an opposing position."

"Which is?"

"That magic doesn't require us to understand it for it to work. You want an explanation, but it isn't required. Sometimes we have to accept the magic for what it is and quit bothering each other with questions about how it operates."

"That sounds an awful lot like a fancy way of saying you don't know."

Death paused, as if deep in thought. "Perhaps. I must admit, my current form has placed several limitations on my ability to comprehend things in a multidimensional sense. When you're an all-encompassing inevitability, you don't spend much time pondering the temporal nature required for traditional logic."

"That's a lot of big words for a man who still doesn't have an answer for me."

"Then I shall return to my original answer. Because it's all part of the magic of Christmas. And since the magic was created to help Santa deliver presents, this must be part of it." He made to take a bite of the cookie, but Lily snatched it from him.

"Santa first," she declared, then bit into it. She made a face. "Ugh, gross, raisins."

"That is why I didn't offer it to you," he explained, taking the cookie back. "I didn't want the little girl who made these to feel bad, so I took them. In fact, it's almost like I'm doing you a favor by eating this."

"Don't start with me," she warned, but he chattered his teeth at her.

"One must keep their sense of humor if they are to properly harbor the Christmas spirit." He tossed the cookie into his mouth and patted his nonexistent belly. "I shall keep my word, dear succubus. Do not fret."

Disgruntled, Lily hopped out of the sleigh, causing both her knees to pop, then walked to the house. There was a partially open window by the kitchen. When she approached, she felt her whole body tingle as she turned into mist, flowed through the screen, and re-formed in the kitchen. She sniffed the air, curious to see if it would have the usual sulfurous stench.

Satisfied that she hadn't arrived with her typical odiferous flare, she walked through the house. Santa's proportions were almost comical, yet she tried to sway her hips as usual. If nothing else, William would have one heck of a story to tell about the time he met Santa.

She was almost to the stairs when she heard the shifting of packages beneath the tree. Turning to face the emerald-green monstrosity, she saw a young boy who was maybe eight years old digging through the packages.

Ugh, might as well get on with it, she thought. "Ho ho ho…William."

The boy jumped, banging his head on an ornament, which fell. It clattered against the wooden floor, revealing that the ornament was made of plastic. Now that Lily was close, she could tell that the tree was decorated in cheap replicas of old-style ornaments. Even the candy canes hanging from it were fake.

"Santa!" William ran across the room and wrapped his hands around Lily's waist, burying his face in her belly.

Lily froze. She couldn't recall the last time she had touched a child, much less been hugged by one. There was so much warmth in the child's embrace that she felt dirty for accepting it and had to stop herself from stepping away.

"Now, now, young man. I'm here on a special assignment." She pushed William away and saw that he'd been crying. "Apparently someone is in need of a Christmas miracle."

William wiped the tears from his eyes. "Just knowing that you're real is enough for me."

"Eh…okay." Lily frowned, then looked at the tree. A personal appearance from Santa sounded too simple to be the reason she was here. "So were you snooping to see what you got?"

He shook his head. "No, sir. I was seeing what everyone else got."

Lily cocked her head. "Now it shouldn't matter what everyone else got. Christmas is about giving, and all that… kind of thing."

William wiped some fake pine needles out of his hair. "That's what I'm worried about. My sisters are missing their presents from my mom. My parents got divorced a few years ago, and we never see my mom. My stepmom doesn't like her, and they fight all the time. I found my present from her under the tree this morning but wanted to make sure that my sisters got something too."

Lily contemplated William with a frown. "Why would your mother forget to send them presents?"

"She forgot their birthday," he replied, then moved to go back under the tree. "She didn't even call. My stepmom made a huge fuss about it, but when I talked to mom later, she told me she sent presents and tried to call but nobody answered the phone."

"Okay." Lily pondered William's words. "So…what do you want me to do?"

The boy shrugged. "I don't know. But I wrote you a letter asking if you could make sure my sisters got my mom's presents, and here you are. To be honest, I thought maybe you weren't real, but I had to try."

"Tell me more about your stepmom." Lily sat down on a nearby couch, then noticed an empty plate. "Did somebody eat my cookies?"

William shook his head. "I threw them away. My stepmom made them, but they're really gross and I didn't want to hurt your feelings." His face brightened. "I can make you a sandwich if you're hungry!"

"Nah, I'm fine." She patted her belly. "So what's the deal with your stepmom?"

William scowled at the tree. "She sucks. I can tell she doesn't like me, but it's fine. She's nice to my sisters, but it's almost too nice. She has them doing dance and piano all the time, though, so I don't get to see them much."

"Classic stepmother move." It was the only reply she could think of, but William nodded as if he understood.

"She wants them to call her mom now." He winced. "But they already have a mom."

"What do you call her?" Lily asked.

"Janet." He made a face. "She makes me play outside so I don't get her floors dirty. Or just in my room. I don't like her much."

"Let's see if I can get to the bottom of this." With a sigh, Lily heaved her bulk forward and walked toward the stairs. "You stay here. I'll be back."

William nodded, and then she ascended the stairs. She could smell the dreams of the household and wandered down a long hall to a master suite that was almost as large as the main floor at home. In a four-poster bed, a man that looked like William slept next to a woman with porcelain skin and a sleep mask.

She could see the rise and fall of their chests, which meant that time flowed here as well. If she waited long enough, would morning come? Or would time snap back into place like a rubber band, making them live the same five minutes on repeat?

She thought back to Death's words. It really would just be easier to accept that magic happened and that she would receive no explanation. Christmas magic was definitely something special, that was for sure.

To be safe, she gave both sleepers a jab with her tail to ensure they slumbered. A quick dive into Janet's mind revealed she had rewrapped the presents from William's mother and addressed them from Santa. Puzzled, Lily dug deeper.

Janet's mind unraveled like a rotten onion, revealing a history of entitled behavior and glowing narcissism. William's sisters were adorable and got plenty of attention from Janet's friends and strangers alike. She liked being told she made a good mother and enjoyed taking credit for the children's accomplishments. However, as long as their mother was in the picture, there would be credit she couldn't claim.

There was a lot to unpack. Janet was only being kind to the children for her own glorification and to hurt a woman she barely knew. William was old enough to see through the charade, but the girls were not. It was likely only a matter of time before she started using William as her own emotional punching bag.

"How would Santa handle this?" she wondered aloud. How would a fat man who brings joy and good cheer to the world deal with a chronic liar bent on destroying a child's perception of their mother? This situation reminded her of the one between Mike and his own mother, and the temptation to just snap Janet's neck was very strong.

Staring at her prey, she bit her lip and crawled up onto the bed. Spreading her legs around Janet's torso, she placed her hands on Janet's temples and delved into the Dreamscape.

She didn't know what the answer was. The fact of the matter was that Santa wasn't here, but she, Lily, was. She had her own way of dealing with things.

Not knowing what sort of deadline she was on, she bombarded Janet's Dreamscape with a nightmare sequence that lasted for weeks on end. The Christmas filter fought her hard at first, but the Dreamscape was Lily's domain, and she was able to defeat it soundly there.

Janet's soul begged for forgiveness on multiple occasions, but Lily saw through the lie each time. The woman Janet had become was a project years in the making and not something casually undone. The woman would say whatever she thought necessary to stop the terrors Lily sent at her. Scare tactics clearly weren't going to work, so she would have to go deeper.

She changed tack; it was time to do some spiritual manipulation. Lily set up a dream scenario where Janet woke up on Christmas day, broke her stepdaughters' hearts, and then enjoyed a briefly successful career as their manager when they got picked up by a scouting agency. She became close friends with the wife of a wealthy oil mogul, with whom she eventually had a threesome. Using this sexual moment as an opening, Lily pounced.

Souls were often like apples. It was entirely possible to cut the bad parts out in the hopes that what had rotted them in the first place wouldn't grow back. Lily bit large chunks out of Janet's soul, almost to the point where she would perish. When Christmas morning came, Janet would likely suffer confusion, weakness, and headaches for several days. She would barely have the energy to get through the day without napping, much less emotionally manipulating her stepdaughters. Smiling, Lily licked her lips and tweaked Janet's nose as if she was a child.

"If nothing else, that should keep you out of trouble for a few months. You'll love the attention you get from everyone when the doctors can't figure out what's wrong with you."

Before leaving the bedroom, she jacked into the father's head long enough to see that he was a good man with a penis that made most of his decisions.

"Consider getting snipped," she told him, both in his dreams and out. "'Cause if you knock this one up, she's gonna take you for everything."

It had been almost half an hour by the time she returned to the living room. William was dozing on the couch but snapped to attention when Lily arrived. He was holding a plate with a peanut butter sandwich, which he offered to her as a snack. She accepted it, then identified the presents beneath the tree that had been mislabeled. He helped her rewrap them properly, then sat back to identify their handiwork with shimmering eyes. As she was leaving, William gave her a big hug, clinging tightly to her body.

"Thank you, Santa," he told her. "Merry Christmas."

"Right. Merry Christmas." She waved him off of her. "Now go to bed before I bring you coal."

"If Janet stops being so mean, you can bring me coal forever." He grinned for her, suddenly looking much younger than he seemed. It was like the stress of his stepmother's machinations had prematurely aged him but now that weight was gone. She gave him a wave, then stuffed the whole sandwich in her mouth on her way out the door.

Death was reading the manual in the sleigh when she returned. Once they were airborne, she transformed back into her normal form and picked up the thermos. As she poured herself a mug of cocoa, she pondered again how Santa would have handled the whole affair. Perhaps it was some magic he possessed that she was unaware of, but it almost felt like the whole experience had been tailored to her particular strengths.

If so, to what purpose? That would mean Santa had known trouble was brewing and that Death would take the sleigh. It seemed impossible to believe, so she thought back on the wisdom of the reaper and just let it go as she contemplated the night sky. She had been given a unique opportunity to help someone that hadn't involved murdering someone else, though she had considered it.

"How did it go?" Death asked.

"The cookies sucked." She slammed hot cocoa from the mug, marveling at how hot it felt against the back of her throat. "By not making you eat them, it's almost like I did you a favor."

"Aha! I see young William has gifted you with a sense of humor!" Death's grin was contagious as he let out a booming laugh. "It's almost like a Christmas miracle!"

In response, Lily chattered her teeth at him, then stuck out her tongue. Though she wouldn't admit it out loud, she was starting to have fun.

"Next stop?" she asked.

Death nodded, then handed over the reins. "It's your turn," he declared with a smile.

She couldn't help it. With a laugh, she snapped the reins, and Cerberus pulled them up into the sky, leaving a trail of smoking paw prints behind.

Christmas Present sat at the head of the table, smiling at Yuki and Mike while they filled up on meats, cheeses, and rolls. Yuki didn't dare let her attention wander from the giant, who would occasionally lick her lips while watching Mike.

Conversation had been minimal, other than a general encouragement to eat. Christmas Present promised them a long journey, and they should be well fed before they began. Yuki didn't detect any animosity but was expecting a betrayal of some sort. If not for the odd behavior and that strange scar on the giant's lower belly, she probably would have pincushioned the woman a while ago.

Mike drank from a silvered goblet, then wiped his mouth with a napkin. He had put away an impressive amount of food, and Yuki watched a tiny spark jump across the tops of his knuckles. "So you're one of the three spirits of Christmas. We met one of your siblings earlier."

Christmas Present chuckled, then tossed her hair. "Actually, you met several. You see, today is Christmas. My Christmas. Once it is over, I will join my brothers and we shall become the past together."

Yuki nodded. If Christmas Past really was a conglomerate of individual spirits, it would make sense how they had been able to split her and Mike into separate places and times. "Does that mean Christmas Future is actually several spirits as well?"

Christmas Present shook her head. "Potential spirits."

"Potential spirits?" Mike looked up from his meal. "How does that work?"

"That would be a limitation of your language. Just like a gift, each of us is an unopened box. We can be and are absolutely anything until we've been opened."

"I like the analogy," Mike told her. "Because I get the feeling you're exactly what I wanted for Christmas."

Yuki felt the urge to chastise Mike for flirting, but she watched in fascination as the giant's face and chest burned a fiery crimson. Christmas Present seemed friendly for now. If Mike wanted to flirt his way out of potential danger, then he was welcome to it.

In truth, she found the giant to be very pretty, which made her a little wary. She hadn't felt any sort of romantic or sexual feelings for many years now. It wasn't until the incident at the cabin where she had helped Mike get off to feed Dana that those feelings had emerged once again. Even then, the stirrings had been distant, but she had recognized them all the same. A part of her was waking as if from a long slumber, but it had skewed heavily toward the Caretaker himself.

"Tonight is going to be so much fun," Christmas Present declared, her voice filling the room. "An evening worth remembering."

"Speaking of which." Yuki set down her fork and wiped her mouth. "What exactly is your intention for us? Christmas Past seemed intent on harming us, and I am aware that you have been ordered to hunt us down."

The smile faded from Christmas Present's face. "You're right," she admitted. "I was sent to hunt you down but can no longer remember why." Her hand slid beneath the fur-lined fabric of her robe and caressed the scar on her belly. "And when I caught you, I was supposed to take you away."

"Well, maybe we should just spend some time together instead?" Mike clapped his hands, a hint of worry in his eyes. "After all, it's Christmas, right? Nobody wants to be sad on Christmas!"

"That's right!" Christmas Present stood, then adjusted her crown. "And we've got so many things to see!"

"See?" Yuki looked at Mike. "Like what?"

"Come, Caretaker." Christmas Present stepped toward the two of them and extended her arm. "Hold on to my robes, and we shall travel anon."

Mike looked at Yuki, then flicked his eyes toward the spirit. She nodded, then moved to join him. Standing before the Ghost of Christmas Present, she took Mike by the hand, and they both grabbed onto the fabric that dangled from the spirit's arm.

It was as if someone grabbed Yuki by the heart and pulled. Her breath left her body as the world turned into a blur. Dazzling colors spun around them for the span of a breath, and they appeared on a frost-covered hillside. Down below, smoke rose from a small cabin, and the nearby barn was lit with Christmas lights.

"What are we doing here?" asked Mike.

"There are many ways to measure a man," Christmas Present replied, some of the cheer gone from her voice. "You see, I'm perfectly aware that your magic has altered me. But yours isn't the only magic making demands."

For just a moment, her sparkling eyes flickered black, causing Yuki and Mike to step away.

"It would seem that I have been given a dangerous choice," she informed them, her eyes changing back. "To oppose my master and risk destruction, or to put my fate in your hands. You see, I desire you, Mike Radley. I wish to make you mine, to feel the heat of your body against my skin, to possess you in all the ways a woman can take a man."

"But?" Mike's voice squeaked a little.

"That's what your magic has done to me. It has given me desires of my own. And I would see what your influence has done to others." She shook her head, her smile reappearing. "So come! Let us see what transpires in yon cabin!"

She waved the sleeve of her robe, obscuring their vision for a moment. They now stood inside the cabin, surrounded by hordes of rats who sat throughout the house. The rafters were packed with them, and most of the furniture had been obscured by their bodies. Up above, Emery could be seen sitting among the rodents with a sprig of mistletoe taped to the top of his head.

"Hello!" he greeted them, then flew down in their direction. Stunned, Yuki couldn't figure out how they had teleported to the cabin until the imp passed through them to land on the kitchen counter. Reggie the rat king had emerged from a small doorway with a wreath of red-and-green tinsel wrapped around his crown.

"So we're not really here?" Mike asked, wandering away from the spirit.

"We are," she said. "These are not the shadows of things that have been but of what transpires now."

"What about the time lock?" Yuki asked.

The ghost chuckled. "We are still in it. Traveling as spirits, we are not beholden to the linear nature of time and have stepped outside the lock. As such, this party started before you came to the North Pole, and there is naught you could do to alter its course upon returning."

Reggie held up his hands and waved at the other rats as a bunch more poured through the cabinets. It was almost as though the rats had chewed portals through most of the cabinetry, and the cabin was filling up.

The rat king greeted nearby rodents with sparkling eyes and friendly waves. The rats that came through the cabinets ran up to the rats at the cabin and greeted them with warm hugs. Ever since Eulalie had become the Rat Queen as a bit of a joke, a section of the rat kingdom had gone to live with her in the Library. Though there was nothing keeping the two fiefdoms from interacting, Yuki would bet this was the first time so many of them had gathered in one place.

Reggie had been a bit hurt when the split had first occurred, but then had realized it was beneficial for his kingdom as a whole. Not only did this allow his subjects to spread out a bit, but it also meant that the odds of them being wiped out completely went down drastically. Even if the house was vaporized, the Library and its occupants would remain to rebuild.

"Looks like we're missing quite the party," Mike said, pointing at the kitchen table. Fruit, bread, and giant wheels of cheese had been set out for everyone, and the rats were drinking some sort of cider from tiny tea sets. A roaring fire burned in the fireplace, and the front door opened to reveal Bigfoot wearing a large white beard.

"Ho ho ho," he declared, holding a bag under his arm. "Merry Christmas!"

Young rats gathered at Bigfoot's feet, milling about as he knelt to hand out gifts. They scrambled up into his fur as he laughed, doing his best to give them their presents. Most of the gifts were dollar store toys for children, but the young rats were able to wear them like accessories. More than a few rats sported slap bracelets as fancy belts and one of them had scored a set of earrings that was now worn as a necklace.

Christmas music played through a speaker that sat by the front door. Reggie was in the middle of handing out some red cheese wheels when his nose twitched and he looked up toward the second floor of the cabin.

Up above, Eulalie had emerged from her room. Sleek black legs unfurled from beneath her as she climbed over the railing and flipped over to land on the main floor. The rats squeaked at her in greeting and spread apart to give her some room.

"Merry Christmas, everyone!" Eulalie gave everyone a wave. She wore a garish Christmas sweater adorned with a patchwork tree. Tucked against her belly and wrapped in silken webs was an egg with ruby spirals. Firelight reflected off the egg, but Yuki was certain that some of the light she saw was coming from beneath its shell.

"Merry Christmas, my queen." Reggie took off his crown and gave her a regal bow. "And well met."

"This isn't the role-playing server." She winked at him and held out a hand. "You can just be yourself."

"Role-playing…server?" Reggie's whiskers trembled in confusion.

"Just some web humor. Don't mind me." She laughed.

"How is the child?" Reggie asked. "Do you think she'll hatch soon?"

"We've got plenty of time." She rubbed the egg and smiled. "Though, I can feel her vibrate sometimes."

"Where's the beer?" Bigfoot stood, causing the rats to scatter. A few remained behind, putting braids in the hair by his shoulders. "I didn't see the cooler outside."

A few of the rats contemplated their teacups, then skulked away. In the corner of the room, Yuki saw a rat move a pillow to block the sight of crushed cans on the floor.

"We can have someone make a beer run." Eulalie looked around at the rats. "There's probably some at the Library."

"Speaking of, I thought Sofia was gonna stop by." Bigfoot sniffed, then scratched his nose. "Kinda wanted someone my own size to talk to."

"Ooh, do you have a crush?" Eulalie batted her eyes. "Does Uncle Foot like the cyclops?"

Bigfoot laughed. "She's okay, just wanted someone my own size to hang with. You know Beth keeps me busy enough, but she decided to go home for a bit. Had something she needed to do."

"Yeah. I've heard the rumors." Eulalie smiled, then picked up a piece of cheese. "But back to your original question, Sofia won't be making it tonight. She's…tied up with some unexpected business."

"Busy? On Christmas?" Bigfoot shook his head. "Woman's a workaholic."

"She's enjoying herself. I promise." There was an odd twinkle in Eulalie's eye when she said this.

Christmas Present made herself at home and grabbed one of the cheese wheels from the table. Upon her touching it, the wheel doubled in her hands, leaving the original behind. She bit down into it and nodded her approval. "High quality," she declared.

The gathering progressed for quite some time, and Mike wandered through the cabin while Yuki followed. It didn't take long before he wandered outside. He walked over to the new barn and put his hands on his waist.

"You okay?" Yuki came up from behind him, her arms

resting across her belly. There was no chill in the air, despite the frozen surroundings. Whatever mechanism they were traveling by didn't convey the chill that should have been in the air.

"I guess," he told her. "At least they aren't all swimming at the spring, right?"

She nodded, then moved closer to him. Though the barn was new, it dawned on her that this was the last place Mike had seen Velvet alive, chasing after that bastard Leeds. She could see his pain through the way he stood, could smell it in the air like cloves and dying flowers. He was putting up a brave front about it, which was a feeling she knew all too well.

Hesitating for a moment, she stepped into him, wrapping her arms around his chest from behind. He tensed up at first, then pressed into her. Beneath the warmth of his skin, she could feel his magic swirling through him. It was like trying to hold a handful of butterflies, their fluttering wings sending ripples of power through her body.

Back when he had used his magic to electrify her, it had been nothing but pain and agony as it tore through her muscles and into the metal floor of the ductwork. Now, though, it reacted to her touch and moved as if to caress her. No stranger to the duality of magic, she couldn't help but wonder. If his magic could bring so much misery through touch alone, how much joy could it also bring? Would it be large enough to fill that gaping void in her soul, the one she contemplated on a daily basis?

They said time healed all wounds, but she was tired of waiting. Her heart was now beating in time with those tiny surges of power, and his magic was still inside his body. They were both survivors of a special kind of heartache. Maybe it was time for her to take that first step toward leaving Emily behind forever.

"Mike?" She wrapped her hands around his chest and rested her cheek in the small of his back, her thoughts on the words he had spoken earlier. Once upon a time, she had been an artist, a poet, a traveler. She had conquered continents on foot, had battled armies of stone, had even headbutted an Oni over a bottle of sake. But most of all, she had been a survivor.

Emily had brought out the best and worst in her. The person she was today was just a shell of the person she'd used to be, going through the motions of living. The rage and anger were largely gone but had left a chasm she had yet to fill.

"I thought you didn't need to bury your head in someone to smell them." He put his hands over her wrists and squeezed.

"I know what it's like to hurt," she told him. "Like you do, right now. I'm not saying you should stop, but I do want to say this: don't end up like me. I…I wish I was doing better."

He turned around in her arms and contemplated her with dark eyes that glowed from within. Even now, she could feel his magic radiating from him like warmth from a lantern.

"Want to talk about it?" he asked.

She shook her head. Talking had taken her as far as she was going to get, and she needed something more. She lifted a hand to his cheek and moved in, closing her eyes as her lips approached his.

When their lips touched, she felt his magic intensify and press against her. His hands tightened around her waist, but the sudden pressure of magical energy from behind them caused her to break the kiss and spin around.

Christmas Present stood about ten feet away, a smile on her face. She clapped her hands together slowly, then approached.

"Goddamned cockblocking holiday," she heard Mike mutter.

"I thought you were watching the party," Yuki sneered as her heart slammed shut again, the moment lost.

"I still am." Christmas Present gestured over toward the

barn. Up on the roof, Eulalie stood gazing at the stars, her hands on Velvet's egg. "You see, we're not just here for the party. I want to see the ripples you've left behind in this particular pond."

When the spirit snapped her fingers, they teleported to the roof. Eulalie cradled her sister's egg, singing something under her breath. Her eyes shimmered in the starlight, her lower lip trembling.

"I wish you were still here," the arachne said, her eyes on the stars. "Or Mom. Or even Dad. I hate how alone I feel in a room full of people. I hate that a year ago, you and Dad were still here. Everything changed so fast, I feel like I'm a different person now. Almost like the old me died and I'm all that remains."

Yuki felt Mike tense up beside her, so she took his hand and squeezed it.

"Ah, here it is. The secret misery behind the holidays. Missing the ones we've lost." Christmas Present's eyes had turned black, and dark veins sprouted along her cheeks. "If joy were measurable, I wonder just how much of it you've robbed from this beautiful creature."

"Eat my whole fucking ass." Mike spun to face the giant. "If I hadn't come along, Leeds would have torn this entire place apart. Maybe Velvet would have survived, maybe not. This is the same shit Christmas Past tried, and it didn't work."

Christmas Present's left eye twitched, and a heavy presence descended on Mike and Yuki. The world dimmed as a harsh buzzing sound filled the air, and Yuki moved between Mike and the giant, summoning fox fire into her hands. The giant smiled, revealing teeth that had elongated into fangs.

A quiet hum filled the clearing, broken by the occasional hooting sound. They all turned their attention toward the forest where tiny lights had appeared.

It was the Nirumbi. The small humanoids marched forward from the forest, each one clutching a tiny LED in their hands that flickered like a candle. A group of Nirumbi children led the way, carrying the edges of a giant piece of fabric that was rolled up between them.

Yuki realized the Nirumbi were humming "Silent Night."

"It took me a while to teach it to them," Bigfoot spoke from down below. With a grunt, he leaped onto the roof of the barn and sat next to his niece.

"What are they doing?" Eulalie asked.

"Bringing you your Christmas present." He placed a large hand on her shoulder.

Yuki chanced a glance at Christmas Present. The giantess's features twitched as the darkness receded.

The Nirumbi came to a halt beneath the barn, and the children unfurled the fabric. It looked to be woven from wool, and in the middle of the cloth was a beautiful geometric design that looked like a cross between a spider and a woman.

"I don't understand," Eulalie whispered. "They made me a blanket?"

"Keep watching," Bigfoot whispered.

Nirumbi warriors moved forward from the group, clutching their spears tightly as they turned toward the cloth. As one, they knelt around the children, setting down their weapons. Nirumbi elders, dressed in fine robes, surrounded the warriors. Each held a wooden bowl full of a dark liquid.

"That's blood," Eulalie said.

"Deer blood," Bigfoot added. "They've stopped using their own."

One by one, the elders anointed the faces of the warriors, drawing the symbol around their tight features as the tribe continued to hum. Once finished, the warriors turned to face Eulalie, grim determination on their faces.

Satisfied with their work, the elders turned to one another and repeated the process. As they finished, more members of the tribe emerged from the shadows, revealing that their faces had been painted similarly.

"What is this?" Eulalie whispered.

"The Nirumbi decided some time ago that it was time to part with the way of the warrior and embrace the role of the protector." Bigfoot smiled, then wiped a glistening tear from his face. "They believe the spirit of your sister protects them, and she is now the guardian spirit of the spider tribe."

Eulalie was speechless.

Yuki heard Mike sniffing next to her but didn't look to see if he was as moved as the arachne. Instead, she turned her attention to Christmas Present, whose face had reverted to normal, the heavy presence fading.

"Perhaps seeds of joy can be grown from the ashes of despair." The ghost stroked her chin thoughtfully, all signs of corruption gone. "How soon could I forget?"

"To be fair, you're less than a day old," Yuki told her.

The spirit chuckled, laugh lines blossoming next to her eyes. "Do not let my age fool you. After all, I am full of the wisdom of the season."

"Full of something," Mike muttered next to Yuki.

A dark look crossed the spirit's face, and she grabbed Mike and Yuki by the hand.

"Somewhere else," she declared in a hollow voice, then yanked them across time and space. The glowing lights the Nirumbi held spiraled like fireflies before disappearing, and now Mike and Yuki stood outside a two-story home.

"Ah, now this is more like it." Christmas Present's pupils dilated as she stomped toward the home, tendrils of smoke swirling below her feet. She passed through the front door, leaving Mike and Yuki outside.

"Where are we?" Yuki asked.

"Dana's parents'." A dark look crossed Mike's face. "The spirit is losing control. Just like Christmas Past, it seems to pull energy from sadness and anger."

"Seems that way." They stood outside in the whirling

snow, the flakes passing through their bodies. Yuki looked up at the house. "So what do we do?"

Mike nodded, then looked at Yuki. "I'm going to try to seduce her. I think my magic is the only thing keeping her from going full dark side on us, so maybe I can tilt the scales in our favor by flooding her system."

"I agree." Yuki kept her thoughts on his word choice to herself. She didn't know what sort of chaos would ensue as a result of such a union but had a pretty good guess it would get messy one way or another. "What do you need from me?"

When Mike laughed, it sounded almost like a bark. "Keep her from crushing me between her thighs, maybe?"

"You almost sound excited," she said.

"Have you seen how big she is?" Mike winked. "I've come to terms with my unique skills and have decided this is a mountain I need to climb. She's twice my height, after all." He let out a heavy breath, his anxiety breaking through." Now c'mon. Let's see what sort of special guilt trip she has planned for me here."

Mike disappeared through the front door. Yuki stood outside of the home, wondering briefly what it would feel like to crush him between her own thighs, then followed him through.

THE INTERIOR OF DANA'S HOME SMELLED OF SCENTED CANDLES and ham. An old sofa in the front room was surrounded by a pair of ebony tables stacked high with worn copies of *Popular Mechanics*, and a half-finished puzzle was on the coffee table. Mike could tell that the room had been recently vacuumed. In the corner, a Roomba covered in stickers sat on its charger.

"Dinner is this way!" Christmas Present declared from up ahead.

It certainly is, Mike thought, magic gathering in his fingertips. He had tried to play it cool with Yuki in regard to his intentions with the giant, but his stomach was a mixture of fear and excitement.

On the one hand, he had always had a thing for tall, muscular women. He was certain that any armchair psychiatrist could take a guess as to why. Sex with Sofia had always been fun because of her height, but Christmas Present was at least a few feet taller. It was like she had been built specifically for this fantasy of his, and he suspected that was his magic's doing.

On the other hand, he had sensed the darkness dwelling inside her on the roof of the barn. His magic had been squished away as her dark side manifested, and his precognition had been put on high alert. In terms of size and strength alone, the giant could easily kill him if she wanted, and he suspected that she almost had.

His plan to use his magic to drive the darkness out came with plenty of risk. If not for Yuki's presence, he would already be sweating bullets at his chances of success.

Upon entering the dining room, he saw that Christmas Present had taken a seat on a chair in the corner, her head nearly scraping the ceiling. Sitting at a hand-carved wooden table were an older couple, Dana, and Quetzalli. Dana's father looked scholarly in a sweater vest and glasses, but the calluses on his hands revealed otherwise. Her mother was in a pretty blue dress and wore a cheap necklace that said *Happy Holidays* in beads.

Dana wore a sweater and jeans, and Quetzalli had on a purple sweater dress. Her hair was parted high and clipped around the sides of her head to avoid draping over her invisible horn. Mike thought he could spot the edges of the enchanted napkin ring that concealed it.

An awkward silence hung over the table as everyone ate. Dana was surreptitiously palming bites of food off her fork and slipping them into a napkin on her lap.

"So you two met at Dana's internship?" Dana's mother forced a smile as she took a bite of ham, then looked over at her husband. "I think it's great that you're making new friends."

"Dana here hasn't told us much about this internship." Her father set down his fork. "Maybe you'd care to enlighten us."

"We all signed a nondisclosure agreement." Quetzalli's plate was loaded down with food, and she speared a bunch of green beans with her fork. "They even keep us in a top-secret location."

"Is that true?" Dana's father didn't look convinced.

"Ick ith." Quetzalli's mouth was too full of vegetables for her to respond properly.

Mike looked at Dana to see her reaction. Though she had fed shortly before going home, her eyes already had that dull look that could be so off-putting. At worst, her parents would assume their little girl was on drugs, not realizing she was actually dead.

The conversation was grim as Dana seemed to ignore her parents while Quetzalli did most of the talking. Dana's father kept throwing odd looks at his daughter while her mother worked hard at being polite.

"Now this—" the giant began.

"No, fuck you, I get this one." Mike moved to stand by Dana and made his voice deep. "Ho ho ho, you got this girl killed, and now it's ruining her afterlife."

"Mike." Yuki moved next to him, concern in her voice, but he held up his hand for silence.

"No, wait, what else? Ah, yes. Eternal damnation made her eat your essence, ho ho ho." He stared hard at the Ghost of Christmas Present. Her soft features were already beginning to harden, confirming his theory that antagonizing the spirit brought out whatever influence the Krampus had. It was time to make his move.

"So, then, you acknowledge you've wronged her?" The spirit's eyes were already fading to black.

"What's happened between Dana and myself is nobody else's business. Do you know why?" He hovered his hands on Dana's shoulders, making it look like he was touching her. "Because we've talked about this at length. She doesn't hold me responsible, and I've promised to do anything possible to return her to normal. She's not some victim of an official Mike Radley Dastardly Plot, she's part of my family."

The darkness receded, and Christmas Present gestured at the table. "Well, then what is this? You can see that her parents are hurting!"

"She cut out her parents long before I entered her life. In fact, her coming here tonight was my idea. I want her to have these ties, to be part of both the old world and the new." He trickled magic throughout his whole body, being careful not to draw attention to it. Even so, Yuki seemed to sense this and casually moved to stand on the other side of Quetzalli. "What happens next is up to Dana."

"But then why did you—" Christmas Present's eyes went wide as Mike pulled off his shirt. "What are you doing?"

"They can't see us, right?" He tossed his shirt onto the table and watched it vanish through the ham. Flexing his shoulders, he stretched his arms high, revealing the lean muscle of his shoulders and back. Ever since he had started working out, the nymph magic had altered his body so his muscles looked as if they were cut from marble. Other than the scars along his side and hip, his torso was lean and flawless.

"Yes, but this is…" The spirit seemed lost for words as she stared at Mike's abs.

Mike was startled when he felt Yuki move behind him. She wrapped her arms around his waist and dragged her claws over his belly.

"Mmm. Nice and firm." There was a purr to her voice. "And you're sure they can't see us? We could do…anything?"

"No, this is wrong, I…" Christmas Present seemed confused. The room darkened momentarily as the world rumbled around them, but Mike could sense his magic inside the spirit, dancing about as if to be let free.

"That's right," he told her. "We could do anything, right in front of them, and they wouldn't know it." He was pushing his luck now, and a ball of ice was forming in his gut. The darkness inside the spirit was lashing out, causing Christmas Present's left eyelid to flutter.

The scene around them melted, and they were now standing in Ratu's sanctuary at the center of the Labyrinth. The naga was sitting on a chaise lounge with a cup of tea in one hand as she addressed Opal, who sat in a large plastic tub.

Opal's features were glossy, like melted wax. At the center of her body, a glass vial hovered roughly where her heart would be. She was using her hands to sign at Ratu, who had Cerulea on her shoulder for translation.

"She said it feels hot," Cerulea told her.

"That would be the new enchantment," Ratu said, her voice tired. "Residual magic from using raw materials to repair and strengthen her core. It'll fade, but you'll be stronger than ever."

Distracted by Ratu, Mike wasn't able to get out of the way when Christmas Present grabbed him by the neck and lifted him into the air. Her cheeks were flushed, and she was panting, but darkness hovered about her like a cloud. Yuki climbed onto the giant's back and tried to wrap her arms around her neck.

"Naughty…so naughty…" Christmas Present's face spasmed as she struggled to focus on Mike.

Gasping for air, Mike clamped his hands down on the spirit's thick wrists and unleashed his magic. It spiraled around the ghost's muscular arms and then entered her open mouth, flooding her with magic.

The scene flashed again, and now they were standing in an apartment. It was empty, but there was a decorated tree in the corner. The room shifted, and now they were in a hotel lobby. "Santa Claus Is Coming to Town" blared over the speakers as a brutal storm swirled outside the glass doors. They continued like this for several moments, teleporting to random locations, until Mike was dropped on the ground.

When he hit the floor, he was in a dark room lit by a single light bulb hanging from the ceiling. There was a chill in the air, and he stood to see that Christmas Present and Yuki had vanished. The dirt floor and warped floorboards above his head put him in a basement, but where?

"What the fuck?" He rubbed his arms and turned, then froze. In the corner was a wooden chair with metal bands bolted to its frame. A human figure sat in the chair, but large chunks of them were missing. Instead of blood and guts, it was just empty holes with veins and muscles exposed, as if they had been casually dissected and the pieces lost. Dark spots like ash swirled through and around the figure, and its head was missing from the nose up.

Mouth frozen in a soundless scream, the figure pulled against their bindings. Without a head, it was impossible to be certain, but Mike recognized a metal ring on one of the hands. The last time he had seen it was on a man he thought long dead.

"Amir?" His voice was barely a whisper, and the figure flinched as if struck. Flooded with terror, Mike backed away. An icy sensation swirled through his body as a figure came into the room from the stairs. Their features were obscured by the large hat they wore. When they looked up, the pupils were crimson in color.

"Who is there?" they hissed, looking directly at Mike. It

was almost like the stranger was sucking the energy from the room.

Stunned, Mike was grabbed from behind by a powerful hand, and the scene vanished. He tumbled over backward and was now in the middle of a massive office party. Surrounded by men and women who had been drinking heavily, he stumbled to his feet and flinched when a woman walked through him.

"Didn't mean to drop you." The voice behind him was dripping with sensuality, and he turned to see that Christmas Present stood in the middle of the room, her robes pulled open to reveal her naked body beneath.

"Where's Yuki?" he demanded, aware that Christmas Present's eyes were now glowing blue. It was the color of his own magic. The darkness within the spirit had been compressed into a tiny ball deep inside.

"Here." Yuki's head popped up over Christmas Present's shoulder. She was clinging to the ghost's robe, and there was a strained look on her face. The kitsune dropped to the ground and collapsed.

"What did you do to her?" Mike asked.

"That last temporal distortion was quite tricky," Christmas Present replied. "We passed through a rough patch, which is how I lost you."

"I'm okay," Yuki added. "Just need to catch my breath."

Mike nodded, then looked at the spirit, who was moving toward him. He could sense her intent as it washed over him, and his magic responded. She stood at almost ten feet now, her head missing the ceiling by less than a foot. Moving with purpose, she clamped her hands on his sides and lifted him into the air, then pressed him against the wall.

"You're mine now, little man." Her voice was husky, the want clear in her eyes. Mike's cock surged to life, now uncomfortable in the confines of his pants while she forced her body against his. For a moment, his entire world was a pair of massive breasts, but he was able to shift his head upward to get some air.

Impatient fingers pulled off his pants and boxers, stripping him down so the fabric dangled from his ankles. When the spirit grabbed his cock, she let out a tiny squeal.

"This is the first time I've gotten to open something on Christmas," she said, stroking his erection.

"This is my first time being a Christmas present," he replied, then awkwardly squeezed her breasts with his hands. They were so big he couldn't figure out where to touch first. Underboob? Start at the sides and work his way up? Concentrate on the nipple?

His magic snapped through him like a whip, tuning him in to her needs and desires. He used one hand to send out sparks that danced across one of her nipples while he sucked the other into his mouth. It was huge, with an areola the size of his face. There was still some awkwardness, but he was now making proper progress.

Blood rushed to his head as Christmas Present whipped him about, then set him on a nearby table. She was grinding her crotch on one of his legs as he sat on the edge, his feet dangling over the ground.

She loomed over him, using a pair of fingers to stroke him. He groaned and leaned back, allowing her better access.

Off to the side, Yuki pushed herself up until she was sitting. She narrowed her eyes for a moment, then let out a small sigh.

"You should try sucking it," she said.

"What a delightful idea." Christmas Present put her head in Mike's lap and licked his cock tentatively before sucking it into her mouth. Her massive tongue caressed the underside of his shaft as she easily took his full length.

"Yeah, that's a good ghost." Mike put his hands on the back of her head but didn't bother guiding her. Even when she took his full length, he just barely passed the back of her tongue. It was strange to experience a blow job where he didn't occupy so much oral real estate, and she was doing well enough with her tongue alone.

Christmas Present placed a hand over his mouth. Lifting her head from his lap, he saw the devilish grin on her face.

"I think you've got it backward." As she rose, she grabbed him by the legs and rolled him onto his back. His legs were pushed together and then upward, causing his cock to pop free beneath.

"What are you doing?" Mike looked around his legs and saw that her robe was fully open now. Massive labia that looked like Christmas ribbon dangled from between the spirit's legs.

"You're not in charge here," she informed him. "After all, today belongs to me."

Shifting forward, she easily raised her hips above his and pressed her body into his. She was standing at the very edge of the table, leaning forward slightly. As their bodies became one, he had a sudden fear that the table would collapse beneath their combined weight.

Pausing only to aim his cock properly, Christmas Present lowered herself onto him. She groaned when he penetrated her, wiggling her hips to figure out a better angle. Her hands were on Mike's thighs, pinning him in place.

"Holy shit," he muttered while pushing on her breasts. She moaned as he touched her, unaware that this was an act of self-preservation. Not only was she giant, but her body was solid muscle. He wondered how much of that was his own fault. Unaware of what she was like before combining with his magic, he could only assume that previous incarnations hadn't required so much muscle tone.

Christmas Present was thrusting herself against him now. His magic circulated through his body, seeking to strengthen his limbs for the purpose of sex. He felt something thick bounce off the top of his groin and took a peek between his legs to see that the spirit had an oversize clitoris, like the tip of a thumb.

His body seized on this information. Shifting one arm between his legs, he stroked that elongated nub, tickling it with magical sparks that disappeared into Christmas Present. The spirit groaned, her cadence slow as she forced herself down, the entire cock now inside her. Her eyes were closed as she chewed on her lip. Those thick curls partially blocked his view, but he could make out her face without any trouble.

Usually, his magic drove both parties into a state of hyper-stimulation, but it seemed to know that further encouraging the giant might kill him. The magic in his body connected with hers and created an odd pulsing sensation that moved back and forth between them. It rewarded Christmas Present whenever she matched the rhythm, but Mike didn't know how much longer he would be able to hold out. He planted his forearm between his partner's breasts, resting it against her sternum. Those gorgeous, dangling orbs swung so close to his face that he stuck out his tongue to lick them.

The table creaked under their weight as the party continued around them. People passing by would occasionally set down beverages that passed right through them, unaware that Mike was getting dominated in the middle of their office party. His legs were trembling now as the giant continued, and it occurred to him that she may have his stamina.

There was movement from above, and then Yuki was there. Sitting with her legs on either side of Mike's head, she was now using her arms to brace the giant by her shoulders. The spirit paused for a moment but continued once she realized the kitsune was only there to help.

"The trouble you get into," Yuki muttered, looking down at Mike. "This is the second time I've had to help you fuck somebody."

Whatever witty response he had prepared vanished when he felt a tingling all along his shaft. Puzzled, he looked down and saw that electrical charges were building up all along his legs. They were red and green, just like the ghost's labia, and had begun the migration from her body to his.

"Uh-oh," he whispered. Up above, the grunting woman sounded slightly more frantic as the table groaned beneath them. It had to be a fixture of the spirit's mind, because there was no way an ordinary piece of furniture could handle such abuse.

More sparks appeared, and Yuki stared at them with wide eyes as they migrated along Mike's stomach and vanished around his torso.

"Is that what I think it is?" she asked.

Mike nodded, looking up into her green eyes. He couldn't even reply. Christmas Present was forcing herself onto both of them now, chasing her impending orgasm as twinkling lights filled the room. All his physical energy was focused on not getting flattened beneath her, and his brain was distracted by the pleasurable surge running through his entire pelvis.

This mountain of a woman was about to blow her top, and he was going to get caught up in it.

Christmas Present took a deep breath and held it, her face turning red. Her hips now slammed into him hard enough that his back felt the impact. Yuki fell forward on her hands, her body now acting as a second table while the giant's breasts pressed into her back.

"How is she so heavy?" she asked, wincing with the impact of every thrust. "She's a fucking ghost!"

It was a good question, but Mike didn't have the capacity to ponder it. The pressure had increased, and a desperate look appeared on the spirit's face. Little grunts blasted free of her lips with each thrust, and it was clear she was having trouble reaching her climax. The friction between them decreased drastically as Christmas Present's juices soaked his crotch.

If he didn't get her off soon, she was going to squish him. He couldn't maintain any sort of contact with her clitoris and had pulled his arm back to help support Yuki from beneath. Closing his eyes, he grabbed hold of the magic deep inside and gathered it in his lower body. It throbbed like a beating heart, then sent a rush of warmth to his cock. Expecting his magic to enter the giant and make her come, he was surprised to feel swelling all along his groin.

He groaned as his cock expanded to fill the spirit. It was like his erection was having an erection of its own, expanding in girth and becoming even harder. The slick interior walls of Christmas Present's pussy suddenly pressed against him from all sides, and the spirit gasped above him.

"Whatever you're doing is working," Yuki grunted, her face now inches from his belly. The kitsune's breasts hovered over his face, occasionally brushing against his nose. "I don't know how much longer I can hold out."

Inside Christmas Present's vagina, he felt a static-like buildup as her magic bound itself to the head of his cock. It was like a magnetic attraction, and the air around them became heavy as blinking lights manifested in the air.

"Is that you?" Yuki gasped, watching the lights. They were spinning around the table, scattering throughout the room and disappearing between the attendees.

"I...don't..." It was getting hard to breathe as the giant leaned on both of them and let out a roar as their magic connected. He had tapped directly into her well of sexual energy, and his magic flowed up into Christmas Present.

The laughter of the Christmas party around them turned into shouts of surprise when someone tripped and fell against the table. One of the legs snapped, sending food and Mike toward the ground. Instead of him falling, strong arms wrapped around Mike's back, holding him and Yuki in place as Christmas Present thrust herself against him, coating his crotch in sticky fluid as she came.

A dark swarm of energy squeezed out of the spirit's mouth, hovering over them like an angry storm cloud. It formed into the shape of a devil's head, complete with fangs and a long tongue that attempted to lash out at Mike. When it made contact with his skin, magical sparks leaped from his body and crawled up on the devil's face. There was a loud popping sound as the swarm fizzled out and turned into black sand that vanished when it struck the ground.

Mike struggled to catch his breath, but the magic he had poured into Christmas Present was now on its way back. He was now supporting Yuki's body with his arms, squeezing her torso to hold her in place. The magic expanded in his balls, circling through his groin. The sensation surrounded him in a field of energy, and he opened his eyes just long enough to see that the sparks now danced along Yuki's body too.

The world dimmed around them as he exploded, coming so hard inside Christmas Present that his every muscle contracted. Torrents of semen pumped into the ghost, filling her with sperm and magic. Red, green, and white lightning danced all along their bodies as the magical cycle began.

Christmas Present fell over backward, pulling Mike and Yuki with her. Mike slipped out of her just before she hit the ground, Yuki tumbling free of his arms at the last second.

"By the gods, I have never experienced such pleasure!" Christmas Present brushed the hair from her face and smiled. "Such joy, wrapped into such a tiny moment!"

Mike stood over her, his cock so engorged it was almost painful. Panting, he put his hands on his hips and stared at her. The spirit was a mess, her hair splayed around and beneath her like a cape. She laughed, one massive hand toying with her clitoris. The magic was flowing away from her and drifting through the party like fireflies.

His back hurt, and his legs were sore from being folded. He was fairly certain that he would have bruises, but his dick was still so hard it felt like it would break. "We're not done," he told her and snapped his fingers.

Stray sparks around the room coalesced onto the giant,

and she moaned, spreading her legs for him. He knelt between them and slid his cock between her pussy ribbons, sighing as their sweet heat enveloped him once more. Burying his face between her breasts, he pounded her from above, concentrating on that swirling mass of energy at her core.

The magic pulsed back and forth between them, and when she tried to sit up, he found the strength to push her back down. The spirit cried out in joy, singing Christmas carols as he filled her once more, making sure to push his magic up into every nook and cranny of her being. With a loud cry, he blasted her insides with enough spooge and magic that he nearly blacked out.

His cock shrank to its normal flaccid size as he went limp on top of her body. The Ghost of Christmas Present wrapped him up in her arms and let out a sigh, a few dark clouds dissipating from her breath like fog. They made a growling sound before vanishing, and the last of the Krampus's influence was finally gone.

"I have decided," she declared. "This is the season of giving, not taking. We should bring joy unto others and not focus only on the pleasure we bring to ourselves."

"Is that code for you're officially on our side?" Yuki sat on her knees, a tense look on her face. She was fidgeting with a strand of hair.

The giant nodded, then reached out a hand. "Touch my fingers," she whispered.

Yuki grabbed the offered digits, and the room melted away. The new room that appeared looked different from the others. It was a large bedroom with a massive bed, and all the furniture was hand carved from wood. Large windows looked up into the sky, the northern lights dancing overhead. A fire roared in a hearth big enough to drive a car through, and there was a Christmas tree in the corner. A hole had been cut in the floor, the trees roots sunk deep into the soil beneath.

"Where are we?" Mike asked.

"I have brought you somewhere safe. In doing so, the Krampus will know I no longer serve him. I am afraid this means my powers are now limited, as I no longer serve the master of this realm." The giant patted Mike on the head, then shifted out from beneath him. She belted her robes and chuckled. "This has been enlightening and fun, Caretaker, but I must take my leave and contribute in whatever manner I may."

"Where are you going?" Yuki glared at the spirit with an intensity Mike found surprising.

"I have much to do. I may be free of his foul influence, but my siblings are not. It is a dark night for the North Pole, and I would help be the light that reclaims it." She turned from them when the door to the bedroom opened, and a woman walked in.

"By Santa's beard," whispered the newcomer, a hand at her lips. She was an older woman with her hair tucked up into a bun, and she wore a red-and-green negligee that left little to the imagination. "Christmas Present, is that really you?"

"Aye." The spirit knelt on one knee and bowed her head. "I am free of the dark influence of the Krampus and seek to make amends. I came here to find you and beg your assistance."

"And who are…these?" The woman frowned, her train of thought derailed as she stared at Mike's naked body.

"I was sent by the Krampus to remove them by any means necessary. They were my prey but are now our allies." Christmas Present turned and winked at Mike.

"I'm Mike, this is Yuki." Mike, realizing the woman looked uncomfortable, covered his crotch. "We, uh…"

The woman shook her head. "It's none of my business. If you're here to help save my husband, I don't care how well dressed you are. You two look tired, so please make yourself at home." She pointed to the bed. "I have much to discuss with this spirit before she…wait, how are you a woman?"

Christmas Present chuckled. "It's been an interesting night. Fear not, Caretaker, for you are in the presence of the lady of the North Pole, Mrs. Claus. She is the one creature the Krampus fears above all others."

"Which is why he's holding my elves hostage to keep me locked away in here." Mrs. Claus's face turned red as she scowled at the floor. "Two-horned butt sniffer."

"Come, Mother. Let us discuss what we both know. Once these two are fully rested, I believe they will be a valuable asset to our efforts."

"Hmm." Mrs. Claus looked doubtful, but she nodded. "I'll bring you two some food in a couple of hours. Haven't been in the mood to bake tonight, but I'll throw something together. Both of you look too skinny. Young man, feel free to find your clothes and actually wear them."

"Yes, ma'am." Mike's reply slipped out of him almost subconsciously.

Mrs. Claus and Christmas Present left, the spirit ducking to fit through the door. Once the door was closed, Mike let out a breath and took a few steps toward the bed. He sat on the edge of the mattress, his feet dangling just above the ground.

"So that actually happened," he muttered, then looked at Yuki. She was staring at the door, her hands rubbing at the fabric over her thighs. "Hey, are you okay?"

The kitsune let out a breath and walked toward him, then put her hand against his chest. With a light push, she shoved him onto the bed.

"Yuki?" He watched in amazement as she hiked her robes up to reveal her thighs, then crawled on top of him. Her tails fanned out over his legs, tickling his skin.

"I thought they'd never leave. You'd better have some more juice in you," she told him, then moved her face in front of his. He could sense it now that she was close, residual magic from his sexual encounter with the giant. It had gone everywhere, and it was no surprise that the kitsune had been caught in the cross fire. He could feel it tensing up deep in her chest, ready to pounce at a moment's notice.

"I…might need a minute," he admitted, his back cramping up once he was horizontal. His whole body hurt. It took some effort to lift his arms and place them around Yuki's waist, his arms fitting naturally in the curves above her waist. He wanted to ask so many things in that moment, afraid that his magic was about to hurt the relationship they already had. This was a true moment of vulnerability for her, and he didn't want to accidentally take advantage of it.

"I'm fine taking it slow." Her green eyes were glowing now as she placed her hands around his shoulders and lowered her face to his. "Just as long as we continue moving forward, I think that will be just fine."

He didn't know how to respond and wasn't given a choice. She pressed her lips into his, and he felt an instant connection that went far beyond the physical pleasures he had experienced with Christmas Present. It was both exciting and scary at the same time, and any doubts he had were dispelled by the soft touch of her tongue against his.

His magic came alive once more, flooding his limbs with new energy. His joints loosened up, permitting him to move his hands and explore Yuki's body. It seemed like there would be plenty of time, and it would be nice to take it slow for a change.

"Wait." She moved away from him with a smile and pulled her robes loose, revealing her breasts. When she lay back down on him, he was surprised at how warm her bare skin was against his. "Kiss me some more, Caretaker."

He gladly obliged.

Outside the window up above, the wind howled, smashing snowflakes against the glass so hard that they formed into chaotic fractals that hugged the wooden frame.

HOT AND COLD

The ice-cold winds of the arctic were blocked by large trees decorated with glowing Christmas bulbs the size of Kisa's head. Long cobblestone pathways were lined with nineteenth-century lamps lit with magic rather than oil. They seemed to brighten as the trio walked beneath them, and Kisa stopped to ponder the swirling lights.

"Fairy magic," Holly explained. "Similar to the northern lights."

"I thought those had something to do with the Earth's magnetic field." Kisa wasn't sure how she knew this, but it sounded correct.

Holly nodded. "We're both right. There's the northern lights proper, and also some other stuff. Some indigenous people believe their ancestors are up there, watching them from above."

"Is that true?" Kisa asked.

Holly shrugged. "I couldn't say. There's a lot in this world that's a mystery, and I kind of like the magic that comes with not knowing."

Kisa nodded, then walked away. She didn't agree with Holly. Her early life was largely gone, eaten away by an enchanted collar. Complex emotions surrounded the magical object that had stolen her identity yet given her a future where she thrived. She didn't feel the need to start trouble with the elf over her ideology, because Kisa wasn't entirely certain of her own.

Closing her eyes briefly, Kisa pictured her faceless grandmother. With Kisa knowing nothing else about the woman, it was at least nice to know that someone had once loved her. Maybe even now there was someone out in the world who sometimes wondered whatever happened to that little girl.

"Charged particles," Tink added, the northern lights reflected in the lenses of her goggles. "Maybe ghosts? Lots of magic."

"That's right, I almost forgot. The spell that lets Santa travel the world in a single night is wrapped up in those lights." Holly pointed. "If you watch, you can sometimes see where it looks like Christmas ribbons."

Kisa saw what Holly was pointing at but was dubious. For all she knew, the northern lights just appeared that way and Holly was grasping for straws.

They walked down a wide cobblestone path, huddled close together as the storm reduced visibility. Pausing at an abandoned hot cocoa stand, Holly took a moment to get reoriented. The roads were starting to ice over, and the village around them was eerie. Only a few lights had been left on in the decorated buildings, but it was sporadic. The whole place looked like a Christmas-themed ghost town with gingerbread buildings and candy-cane fencing. There wasn't a tree in sight that hadn't been adorned with garlands or ornaments. She realized while they were waiting that the cobblestones beneath their feet were shaped like Christmas cookies.

Tink was busy trying to steal another cookie from Holly's pouch when Kisa felt a sudden chill run through her whole body. Her tail poofed out in fright as she grabbed Holly and Tink by the hand and pulled them away from the cocoa stand.

"What are you—" Holly said, but the cart behind them was suddenly surrounded by thick icicles that slammed into the ground from above, creating an icy prison.

"Got you!" shouted Jack from down the road, unaware that they had already escaped.

"Stay low," Kisa warned, pulling them behind a cluster of trees until the chill dissipated. It would only be moments before Jack discovered they were on the run, and the snowy ground meant they were leaving tracks.

The weather intensified, snowflakes now turning to sleet and stinging her skin like frozen bees.

"She's going to catch us," Holly whimpered, clutching her hat against her head.

"She?" Thinking back to their previous encounter, Kisa could see it, not that it mattered. Her top priority right now was avoiding becoming a cat-sicle.

Kisa let her gut lead them farther away. They ran along fences and down alleys, just missing capture more than once. A wall of ice nearly trapped them on the street, but a narrow space between buildings let them vanish off the main road. They squeezed between the two buildings, their petite frames just small enough to allow passage, then ran back along the buildings they had just passed. Kisa's whole body tensed up as the path in front of them erupted with ice.

"That was a waste of time." Jack dropped down from above, eyes glittering in the lamplight as she held her hands out. Swords made of ice circled her as she floated just an inch off the ground.

Off to the side, Tink started scooping snow into her hands.

"Please don't hurt us," Holly begged, putting herself between Kisa and Jack. "We don't want any trouble."

"I would worry far more about what *he* has planned for you." Jack tilted her head back to look down her nose at the trio. "A lot of work has gone into our plans here, and—"

A snowball exploded on Jack's shoulder, leaving behind a smudge of white on her fancy lapels. Chuckling, she brushed the snow off her shoulder and looked at Tink, who had thrown it.

"A snowball fight? Please. I invented that."

Undeterred, Tink wound up her whole body and hurled a second snowball, her tail snapping behind her like a whip. Jack waved a hand dismissively, causing the snow to explode harmlessly into a cloud of fluff.

Though the snow was gone, the stone Tink had packed inside the snowball continued forward, smashing into Jack's nose. She let out a grunt, then fell backward onto her ass while clutching her face. Purple blood leaked out from between her hands, and she stared at them in shock.

"Tink invent fighting dirty." The goblin stuck out her tongue and flipped Jack the bird.

Seeing a chance to escape, Kisa grabbed Holly and ran. Tink was right behind them, and they turned a corner just as the ice and snow behind them erupted.

"Shit, shit, shit!" Kisa saw an open doorway and pulled the others into it. The door was locked, but Tink was already using a tool that looked like a pocketknife to jiggle the lock.

"*How dare you!*" Jack's voice rose above the din of the storm, and Kisa felt the chill spread throughout her body. Tink opened the door, and the three of them moved inside, then locked the door behind them. They were in some sort of storage area with giant bags of flour.

They left the storage room behind and moved through the building. The storm outside escalated, and Kisa heard Jack's howls of rage as if they were the wind itself.

"Oh, she's big mad," Holly whispered.

"Yeah, well, that storm of hers should have buried our footprints." Kisa found a windowless room full of boxes. When she went inside, the chill in her body dissipated, the danger sense she got from being Mike's familiar no longer ringing alarms. "Here should be safe."

"For now." Holly moved over to the corner and knelt. "But I think it's going to be hard to move around out there until that storm dissipates. And the cold is only going to get worse."

"Still plenty time before freeze to death." Tink smiled. "Maybe eat more cookies until then."

"Why are you so hungry?" Kisa shook her head. "You need to eat more protein or something. All these carbs are bad for you."

"Maybe kitty cat needs eat Tink's ass." Tink blew a raspberry. Holly held her stomach and groaned.

"What we need to do is figure out—" Kisa felt a familiar tugging sensation in her body. It was Mike, and he was relatively nearby. "Is there a heating vent in here?"

"I don't think so," Holly replied. "Not in this room, anyway."

"Then I think Mike is out of the ducts." Kisa moved toward the far wall and pressed her forehead against it. Closing her eyes, she tried to reach across the distance and make contact with him. It took a couple of minutes for her heart to stop racing and her senses to expand outward. She could sense him much better now, could feel the aches and pains in his body. Had he been in a fight? It was hard to tell, but he was in good spirits.

Still, she couldn't quite make that final connection. He was distracted but happy. She rolled her eyes as she opened them, wondering who he was fucking this time.

"Husband safe?" Tink asked.

"Yeah, he's safe." Kisa slid down the wall. "We need to stay here for a bit anyway until Frosty the Snow Bitch wanders off…sorry, Holly."

Holly waved off the apology, her features pale. "It's fine, I've come to expect potty language from both of you. We're in the bakery, so there are some tunnels that go through the village. If we use those, we may be able to move toward Mike while escaping Jack."

"Tink tired of snow." The goblin pulled some tools from her belt and set to wiping them dry with a towel. "Everything wet and dumb."

"Then it's settled. You get us to those tunnels and I'll point the way back to Mike." Satisfied with their plan, Kisa stood and brushed the snow out of her fur. "I don't see any reason to wait. Lead the way."

They moved cautiously out into the hallway, then walked down to a pair of double doors that opened into a large industrial kitchen. Giant bronze ovens surrounded them, and the air was rich with the smell of baked bread and cookies. Kisa had to keep Tink moving, as the goblin kept stopping to pick up baked goods that had been left behind.

"You're seriously not that hungry," she told Tink, pushing her from behind.

"Tink always hungry," Tink declared, stuffing her pockets with undecorated gingerbread men. "Maybe no share now."

Kisa grinned, a handful of gingerbread men already tucked away in her own pockets. If these tasted half as good as the ones Holly had, Kisa was going to need her own stash.

"So they bake all the cookies here?" Kisa looked around at the large room, noticing a shelf with a bunch of elf-sized chef hats.

"No. This is one of the side bakeries. You should see the main bakery, it looks like a giant cake from the inside! Each level makes a different kind of treat, and…" Holly's exuberance faded. "Actually, it doesn't matter. Until we get Santa back, it isn't worth seeing."

Kisa looked at Tink, who just shrugged. They continued through the bakery in silence, the howling wind outside making the whole building creak. They walked through four different rooms with ovens, eventually moving down a service tunnel that terminated in a big metal door embossed with a large cookie.

"Looks a bit extreme," Kisa noted as they approached.

"All the buildings have these. It's to keep the air flowing properly in each building. Here, look." Holly pushed the heavy door open to reveal a short tunnel that had gone dark. Kisa turned on her flashlight to reveal another door at the end of the hallway. "We let one door close before we open the next one, like an air lock. Otherwise, you can cause doors to slam in another building or similar problems. We actually used that trick once to blow a bad smell out of the main bakery—someone burned a giant batch of cookies."

"How did that happen?" Kisa asked.

Holly gave Tink a dirty look. "Let's just say there were bigger problems that night and the cookies got neglected."

Kisa was about to ask for details when she heard something crash behind them in the building they had just left. They all paused and stared at the door they had just come through.

"That doesn't lock, does it?" she whispered.

Holly shook her head. "We're inside the village. We've never had to worry about—"

There was another crash, followed by a guttural growl. It sounded like baking racks were being tossed around. Kisa felt that ominous fluttering in her belly as the growling intensified, and she pulled the others toward the tunnel door.

"We need to leave," she told them, pulling the door open. "Right now."

Holly stared at the bakery door as if hypnotized. Tink grabbed the elf by the shoulders and dragged her through the door. Kisa followed them through, making sure the door didn't bang shut. The long hallways were clean, and some distant lights were still on, but they were flickering.

"That's creepy, and I hate it." Kisa's tail flicked as she pointed generally to the right. "Mike is that way."

"Hmm." Holly started walking down the hall, stroking her chin thoughtfully. "That would put him much closer to the workshop than I'd like. I really hope he didn't reappear there, because that's ground zero for trouble right now. Would far prefer if he showed up in the dorms, or even the stables."

"Stables?"

"Yeah. For the reindeer." Holly held her hands up over her ears as if they were antlers.

"Unless the Krampus got to them." Kisa frowned. "He's rounding up all the elves, but would he have any use for the reindeer? And other than erasing Santa, what's his deal anyway?"

Holly shrugged and kept walking. The trio wandered the tunnels for well over an hour, pausing every so often to have Kisa check Mike's location. They were getting closer, which meant Mike was stationary. They took a break in an attempt for Kisa to reach out to him, but his mind was abuzz with activity. Frustrated, she was forced to give up.

The giant metal doors they saw all had different symbols on them. One had a sleigh; another bore a wreath. Kisa saw one that looked like a reindeer, only something seemed odd about the engraving. The symbols of Christmas often repeated and blurred together as the trio wandered the dark tunnels beneath the North Pole. The lack of decor in the tunnels proper made it difficult to tell how far they'd traveled or even where they were.

"Wait." Kisa held up her hand and closed her eyes. "We're moving away from him now. He's…that way." She pointed off to her left and slightly up.

"Let's go back a door," Holly said. "Does he feel nearby?"

"I think so. Hard to say."

"About fucking time," Tink grumbled. "Feet hurt."

Holly groaned and turned away from the two of them, mumbling to herself about Tink's naughtiness.

"With any luck, you can take a nap or something. I can tell

you're hungover." Kisa wrapped her arm around the goblin's waist and gave her a squeeze.

"Tink no get hungover. Just extra…grumpy." She bared her teeth in a false smile and moved in step behind Holly. They came to a door engraved with interlocking baked goods, like muffins and cookies.

"Guess you guys are gonna see that big cake after all." Holly pushed open the door and was shoved forward by a gust of wind that blew through the tunnel. Kisa and Tink followed behind her, then pushed the door shut.

"I thought it wasn't supposed to—" Kisa stared at the entry door on the other side of the room. It had been ripped free of its hinges and tossed aside. A cold tingle formed in her gut as she turned to face the door they had closed. There hadn't been an air current in the tunnels earlier, which meant that somewhere, another set of double doors was open.

Holly pointed at the discarded door. There were claw marks in the metal. "The Krampus," she whispered, her eyes wide.

"So he pulled that door down and—"

"Shh!" Tink put her ear against the door to the tunnel and scowled. "Tink hear stupid demon fuck yelling."

"Tink!" Holly's protest was barely a squeak.

"We go now." Tink pulled free the hammer from her belt along with a screwdriver. "Krampus use tunnels, follow wind flow, find pretty elf."

"But he has to be miles away!" Kisa ran up the ramp with Holly in tow as Tink walked into a corridor surrounded by shredded bags of flour.

"He's fast," Holly said. "He was distracted with Alabaster last time, but he's on his way. You can count on it."

"Shi…ush," Kisa corrected herself, stretching the word abnormally long. They ran along the corridor, past tiny fork-lifts and wheeled trolleys. After passing a set of double doors with star-shaped windows, they were in a curved hallway with an incline.

"This is the outside of the cake," Holly said. "We have to go up just a bit and then around."

"Whatever you say, cake lady." Kisa looked back down the hall, half expecting to hear clawed feet scratching the floor.

The main bakery smelled musty, as if someone had spilled bad flour. Holly continued leading the way, her features pinched as they moved through the building. Every fifty feet or so, another set of double doors with a different shape cut in the window greeted them, all of them damaged in some way.

"It's almost like he broke them just because," Kisa muttered, staring at a set of doors. "He must really hate it here."

Holly nodded. "In the beginning, he and Santa were supposed to be a team. I don't know what happened, but this place became everything the Krampus hated. He—" She paused, then sniffed the air. "Do you smell that?"

Kisa sniffed, catching the faint tickle of gingerbread. "It's probably just the cookies we took," she admitted.

"No, these smell fresh. But if the ovens were abandoned, they would have burned by now." The elf turned on her heels and sprinted up the hall. "Maybe some of the other elves are still around!"

"Ugh, Tink gonna barf." The goblin was dragging behind now, doing her best to keep up. Kisa did her best to keep Holly in her sights without leaving Tink behind, but eventually the elf disappeared around a corner.

"Shit!" Kisa turned around, her hands on her hips. "Why are you so tired all of a sudden?"

"Too many cookies." Tink grinned weakly.

"Have you been fucking eating those this entire time?"

"Yup!" Tink gagged, made a face, then stuck out her tongue. "Maybe eat some of them twice."

"Gross!" Kisa grabbed Tink's hand and pulled her forward. "We need to find Holly, so c'mon!"

Tink flipped some lenses on her goggles. "Left ahead," she said upon seeing the length of the next corridor. Kisa and Tink followed whatever trail the goblin was tracking until they came to a golden door with light shining from underneath. They pushed it open cautiously, then slid inside.

It was a giant assembly line. Belts carried gingerbread men with horns through a giant room, stopping at little stations where small packs of elves decorated them. The elves had gray skin and egg-white eyes, as if the color had been bleached out of them. Even their outfits were drab and faded.

Holly was kneeling on the floor just in front of them, her face buried in her hands as she sobbed.

Kisa didn't even have to ask what was going on. The few elves that looked up to see the newcomers stared at them with disinterest, their bodies going through the motions of decorating the cookies. The baking ovens up above flooded the room with enough heat that Kisa wanted to take off her vest.

"We'll never free them if we don't keep going," she told Holly. "So let's go."

"Some of them are my friends," Holly whispered between sobs. "What if they're broken forever?"

"Then we'll see how many pieces we can put back in the puzzle. Trust me, being broken doesn't mean your life is over." She pulled Holly to her feet just as Tink made a horrible noise behind them. Kisa looked back to see that the goblin had puked up at least a pound of cookies. The goblin followed up this feat with a round of swear words and spitting.

"That's disgusting," Kisa said but noticed that the elves had all stopped, their eyes now on Tink. Their features twisted and distorted as they pondered the goblin, anger flitting across their features.

"Oh sprinkles," Holly whispered. "I think they recognize Tink."

"I'm guessing that's not a good thing," Kisa whispered back, then covered her ears when the elves all pointed at Tink with clawed hands. They made an eerie hissing sound as they moved toward the trio, climbing over their workstations.

"Not today," Kisa declared, then ran toward the goblin with Holly in tow. Looking for an escape route, she spotted a nearby conveyor belt that went through an opening on the other side of the room. "There! Now!"

Holly leaped onto the belt as Kisa gave Tink a boost. She was able to pull herself up just as a pair of elves closed in on her. Instead of climbing the belt, the elves ran beneath it.

"Stupid elves," Tink muttered, then picked up one of the gingerbread devils. She bit its head off and stuck out her tongue. "Dumb fuck cookie taste like ass."

"Stop eating cookies!" Kisa slapped the remaining gingerbread devil out of Tink's hands as they passed into a dark tunnel. On the other side, the belt dumped into a large silver funnel, and they all fell off the belt to spin around the edges of the funnel like a giant slide.

"Where are we?" Kisa demanded.

"Rejects!" Holly yelled from the other side of the funnel. They spiraled around for several seconds before falling through the hole in the bottom. Crashing onto a mountain of broken cookies, Kisa tumbled down the side and smacked her elbow on the concrete floor beneath.

"Ow, damn it!" She winced, then stood. The room's solitary light was from the funnel above, and the room was rich with the smell of gingerbread. She walked around to the other side of the cookie pile. "Tink? Holly? Where are you?"

Holly and Tink were helping each other up, brushing crumbs off themselves. Tink had lost her screwdriver, but her hammer was still clutched tightly in one hand. A gingerbread devil had gotten caught in the claw, and she broke it apart to clear the hammer.

"Usually there's a big bag and a cart here," Holly

explained, adjusting her hat and then brushing off her knees. "Reindeer get to eat the cookie rejects. We add it to their feed."

"Sounds healthy." Kisa saw that a rail system had been built into the floor under the cookie pile, and it went through a tunnel on the other side of the wall. "Does that mean the stables are that way?"

Holly nodded. A hideous screech came from the funnel above. It was like nails down a chalkboard, causing Kisa's fur to stand on end. She could almost hear a singsong voice inside the cacophonous roar and clutched Tink's arm.

"That's him," Holly whispered. "He's in the building."

"He found us just from air currents?" Kisa looked at Tink.

"Tink think so. Demon tricky, very mad at pretty elf." She looked at the tunnel, then at a door on the far wall. "Broken elves tell demon where to find Tink, need special trick, buy time."

The goblin rummaged around in her pockets and pulled out some of the gingerbread men she had taken earlier. She ran over toward the door and broke them apart, laying them on the ground in plain sight. It was readily apparent that these were different from the gingerbread demons scattered around the room, and the goblin opened the door and stepped into the hall.

Kisa heard the goblin make herself puke on the other side. Frowning, she watched Tink come back through the door and walk around the perimeter of the room.

"Demon think Tink sick from running, waste time, check hallway first. We run now." Tink wiped her mouth and then bolted down the railway tunnel. "Feel much lighter now," she said as she disappeared into the darkness.

"Let's go." Kisa grabbed Holly's hand, and they ran after Tink. The rail system had been embedded into the floor, so she didn't have to worry about tripping. Unlike the previous tunnel, this one wasn't lit, which meant the sole illumination was from the rejects room behind them.

They had gone down the tunnel a couple hundred feet when a shadow blocked the light. Kisa looked back in time to see an amorphous shadow on top of the cookie pile. The figure was hunched over, emitting tiny motes of darkness that made the dim light even harder to detect.

The figure vanished, and the sound of doors being torn from their hinges flooded the tunnel. Tink's distraction had worked, but how much time would it actually buy them?

Kisa turned her attention to the darkness ahead. Her eyes allowed her to see better than most, but they still required some light source. A dark shape appeared in the gloom, and Tink was sitting on top of it.

"Hurry," she whispered, then helped Kisa and Holly up. It was a mine cart with a set of levers on the side, and there was a partially full bag of cookies inside.

"Tink, these things only work if you push them," Kisa replied. "Unless you think you can push us faster than we run, we should just go on foot."

"Rails smooth, floor flat. No friction, good cart. Save energy, make boost." Tink hopped out of the cart and started pushing, grunting as the cart picked up speed. The cart rolled quietly on the rails as Tink continued pushing until she jumped in with them.

"Now what?" Kisa asked.

Tink grabbed the bag in the cart and struggled to lift it. "Help Tink throw out."

It took all three of them to lift the bag and dump it out the back. Cookies scattered on the floor, leaving crumbly gingerbread devils everywhere. The reject room vanished from sight as they went around a corner, and Kisa found herself lost in the darkness.

Kisa turned on her flashlight to see Tink using her tools to remove one of the levers from the cart. She rotated it so the rubber grip was on the bottom, then leaned over the side of the cart and used the lever as a makeshift pole to push them even faster.

"Turn off light," Tink whispered. "Tink see plenty."

Kisa obeyed, then leaned back against the wall of the cart. The wheels beneath them were silent, and she lost track of time. Occasional shrieks traveled down the tunnel, the Krampus clearly enraged that he couldn't find them. It was only a matter of time before he noticed their tunnel, and Kisa hoped to be long gone by then.

An orb of light appeared ahead, then widened to reveal a room full of barrels. The cart came to a stop when Tink pulled on the brake, and the three of them got off.

"What's in the barrels?" asked Kisa.

"Whiskey. For the reindeer." Holly patted one of the barrels. "They don't get drunk off of it, if that's what you're wondering. It's kind of like their version of rocket fuel."

Tink giggled. "Reindeer make big farts, go supersonic."

"We need to be quiet," Holly said, lowering her voice. "The reindeer aren't skittish or anything, but they can be temperamental. They're super smart, but likely know something is wrong. Don't get on their bad side."

"We'll be good." Kisa smacked Tink's hand away from the spigot of a nearby whiskey barrel. "Promise."

They walked through the giant wooden building, and Kisa noticed right away that something was different. It looked like any other barn she had ever been in, but it was missing the smell of animals. There was no musky scent, nor the foul odor of feces. Instead she smelled hay, candy canes, and something that reminded her of the ozone after a storm.

The stall doors were much taller than Kisa, and she heard shifting inside the stall. The wooden frame was ornate and lined in silver and gold, and the name *Prancer* was embossed in a plaque with glittering rubies.

Determined to see a reindeer, she let the others walk

ahead and allowed herself to fade into the background. It was easy enough to hop up onto a nearby bale of hay and then scramble to the stall door.

There were a lot of things she expected, but the misty creature sitting in the back of the stall was not one of them. It had the shape of a reindeer, that much was true, but it was almost like her brain couldn't process what she was looking at. The antlers seemed to shift and distort whenever she wasn't looking directly at them, and the animal itself looked as though it was made of a sparkling fog. Black streaks ran through the creature, and one of its eyes was a terrible crimson that gazed directly into Kisa's soul.

The reindeer charged. Kisa fell backward off the stall door, flipping over to land on her feet. The door shuddered from the impact, and the creature made a hissing sound that reminded Kisa of a bag of snakes. Black mist curled through the gaps of the door with tendrils that twisted around and tried to grab Kisa's feet.

"What the hell?" Kisa scrambled backward as Holly and Tink ran over. Holly stopped farther away than Tink, her mouth agape at the dark fog as it withdrew through the doorway.

"Prancer?" Holly's voice trembled. The reindeer's massive head appeared over the stall door, and it turned to face the elf. Inky, twisted lines ran down her muzzle, dripping onto the wood and evaporating into smoke.

"He's corrupted them too." Kisa stood and moved along the opposite wall. The next stall down belonged to Dasher, who had already stuck her head out to see what was happening. Though Dasher's eyes were still brown, those powerful dark lines coiled around them as if to strangle the kindness away.

The stable was huge, and the stalls alternated. One by one, massive reindeer heads looked out of their stalls to see what was causing the commotion. Comet looked at them with crimson eyes that had shrunken down to little more than ominous dots, and Blitzen's head had a split down the middle, making her look more like an alien than a reindeer.

They moved cautiously around the stalls, shifting back and forth to stay away from the dark mist that formed into hands and reached for them. It wasn't until they were near the end of the stable that Kisa realized one reindeer hadn't come to check on them.

The nameplate on the door was *Dancer.*

"C'mon, we're almost out." Holly grabbed Kisa's hand, but Kisa yanked it away. Curiosity had struck her hard. Maybe it was the reindeer's name, or the fact that she didn't hear hissing coming from inside its stall, but if she walked away without knowing the poor beast's fate, it was going to bother her all night.

With a twist, she dodged around Holly and climbed a pair of whiskey barrels that allowed her to jump onto the stall door. From her new perch, she saw that Dancer had backed into the corner of her stall, her misty nostrils flared wide at Kisa's appearance. The glitter inside her body looked more like stars, and Kisa couldn't help but think she was seeing a force of nature rather than an animal.

"Hey." She held out her hand, and Dancer snorted.

"Get down!" Holly jumped, trying to grab Kisa's tail.

"I think this one is okay." Kisa looked over her shoulder at Tink and Holly. "We should let her out before she becomes corrupted."

Holly looked dubious, but Tink nodded her approval before examining the spigot on the whiskey barrel.

"C'mere, girl." Kisa pulled the gingerbread cookies out of her pocket. Most of them were broken, probably from her fall. She picked one out that was intact and turned it so Dancer could see. "Are you hungry? I'm afraid this is all I have."

Holly grunted as she climbed on top of the barrels, then pulled herself onto the stall door by hanging on her belly.

When Dancer saw the elf, her features relaxed, and she dipped her head.

"Oh, thank Santa, she's safe." Holly's legs dangled beneath her. "There's a lock on this side we can undo, but I don't know if she'll leave the others behind."

"It should be her choice to make." Kisa stuck her hand out farther, and Dancer approached. The reindeer sniffed the treat, then used her tongue to snatch it from Kisa's fingers. She snorted, then moved closer to Kisa's other hand, which contained cookie fragments.

"Here, have all of them." Kisa watched in awe as the creature licked the crumbs from her hand, then hesitantly placed her free hand on Dancer's forehead. Kisa's whole body tingled on contact, and she felt her own fur stick up.

"I think she likes you." Holly dropped down, then slapped Tink away from the whiskey barrel. Tink couldn't even protest, her mouth full of booze. "Don't swallow that, it'll mess you up!"

Tink gulped down her mouthful and made a face. "Husband likes it when Tink swallows."

Kisa laughed at the horrified expression on Holly's face, then turned toward the reindeer. "We're going to let you out. Just give us a minute."

Dancer nodded, and Kisa hopped down. She looked to the side of the stall door and saw that a silver padlock in the shape of a heart held the whole thing shut.

"Tink." She smacked the goblin's arm to get her attention. "Get that open."

Tink blew a raspberry, then pulled some tools from her pocket. The goggles' lenses clicked rapidly as she examined the lock, then stuck her lockpick tool inside. The padlock heated up in her hands, and she growled before pulling her hands away.

"Anti-theft system eat Tink's ass," she declared, then spit

on her hands and resumed working. Holly shook her head in disgust, then moved away from them.

"Who would steal a reindeer?" asked Kisa.

"Nobody. Without these locks, they would let themselves out. Other than a few elves they particularly like, the only person they obey without question is Santa," Holly replied. "Remember how I said they can be temperamental? Unless Santa himself goes out and finds them, it can take a whole team weeks just to coax one back, and they can cause quite the mess. Some of them escape a couple times a year, nobody knows how. The human world usually spots them as meteors or shooting stars, but they can fly high enough that they get mistaken for satellites. They've been shot at a couple of times by the military, but they really don't like that."

Tink mumbled as she worked the lock, then swore before yanking her hands away. Frustrated, she pulled a pair of pliers from her belt and held the lock with them. It took her a few attempts and a lot of swearing, all while Holly plugged her ears and loudly hummed a Christmas tune. The lock stopped glowing once it opened, and Tink undid the latch on the stall.

When Dancer stepped out, a silvery mist emanated from her body. It swirled delicately around Kisa, and the reindeer bent her leg and bowed.

"Oh wow," Holly whispered. "She's accepted you."

Kisa didn't know what that meant, but a thrill went through her when she put her hand on Dancer's muzzle. The two of them locked eyes, and she felt a profound sense of gratitude flood through her body.

Then ice water coursed through her insides, making her whole body go numb.

The other reindeer let out a hideous noise, and the cart from the tunnel crashed through the stables, sliding to a halt in front of Dasher's stall door. Dancer bolted out of the exit, leaving a glittery trail of hoofprints behind on the ground.

"Oh fuck." Holly's face had turned completely white, her voice two octaves higher than Kisa had ever heard it.

The Krampus stepped into view, his dark shadow looming large behind him. Even hunched over, he was nearly seven feet tall, his dark visage twisted and gnarled. Angry red eyes were set below the hairiest unibrow Kisa had ever seen, and his horns twisted up from his forehead, ripping holes through what was left of Santa's hat. The demon wore Santa's coat, and shadows dripped from his body as he stared at them with glee.

"Holly." When the Krampus spoke, it felt like poison had been jammed into Kisa's ears. The demon's eyes grew wide as he opened a mouth full of broken teeth. "At last."

Kisa caught movement out of the corner of her eye. Glancing over, she saw Tink use a hammer to knock the spigot off a nearby whiskey barrel, spilling booze all over the floor. While the Krampus and Holly were distracted with each other, Tink cupped a hand to harvest a mouthful of alcohol. Her lips twisted into a grin as she clicked the padlock from the stall shut, then jammed a tiny screwdriver from her belt into it before tossing it into the pool of whiskey.

The padlock was glowing red, causing the whiskey nearby to sizzle. Tink pulled something out of her tool belt and flipped through the lenses of her goggles. She grinned at Kisa, then tilted her head toward the exit.

Holly and the Krampus stared at each other, neither one moving. The Krampus took a step forward, then paused to stroke Prancer's head. He never broke eye contact with the distracted elf, nor did he make a sound as he stepped forward. A thick tail whipped behind him, striking bales of hay so hard that they fell apart.

"I see you brought us some visitors." He chuckled as he approached, then moved on to the next reindeer. "That was very naughty of you."

Kisa grabbed Holly by the shoulder to turn her around,

but the Krampus crossed the distance in a blink. Long fingers curled around Holly's neck, and he backhanded Kisa so hard that she crashed against the stall door.

Dazed, she sat up just as Tink smashed her hammer into the Krampus's foot. The demon laughed, then picked Tink up with his other hand to examine her. His fingers easily encircled her waist, and she looked like a child in his hand.

"I know you," he said with a grin. "You've been very naughty."

Tink held up a lighter and flicked it. A single flame appeared, tiny and unassuming. She stretched her arm toward the Krampus, then grinned.

"And what are you planning to do with—" The Krampus never finished, as Tink had blown out a spray of whiskey that ignited, scorching the demon's hairy face. He dropped both Tink and Holly and stumbled back through the stable, howling in pain.

Kisa managed to get to her feet in time to pull the elf away from the puddle of booze on the floor. Tink stuck her hands in a hay bale and let out a growl as she threw it onto the whiskey-soaked barn floor.

"Three seconds!" she yelled, then pointed toward the exit.

Kisa ran as fast as she could, pulling Holly behind her. The Krampus stumbled around, wiping at his scorched face as they pushed open an ornate door and stepped out into the cold of the North Pole.

Behind them, there was a loud whoosh as the whiskey ignited. The high-pitched keening of the Krampus was heard moments before the first explosion rocked the stable.

"No, no, no, the reindeer!" Holly tried to turn back, but Tink blocked her way. "This can't be happening!"

"Stupid deer fine," Tink argued, then pushed the elf forward. "Whole stable fireproof. Ugly fucker not."

There was a roar as the large stable doors burst open and

the Krampus emerged, his whole body smoldering. He threw himself into a snowdrift, sending up a cloud of steam.

Dancer landed next to them, letting out a loud snort. The reindeer knelt, allowing Kisa to help Tink and then Holly onto the reindeer's back before jumping up on her own. The reindeer did a quick spin and then leaped into the air, her hoofprints turning into silver snowflakes that hovered behind them.

Looking back, Kisa saw that the Krampus was free of the snow and now chasing them. As fast as the Krampus was, he couldn't keep up with a reindeer in flight.

"Where do we go now?" Holly shouted over the howling wind, clutching Tink's waist. The goblin had wrapped her arms around Dancer's neck.

Kisa was holding on to Holly but also squeezing her own legs to keep from sliding backward. "I don't know," she replied, the pull in her chest growing stronger. "But we're headed straight toward Mike!"

Yuki lay on top of Mike, one hand behind his head and the other wrapped around his waist while she kissed him. Her fingers were cool to the touch, as if her magic was leaking out of them. The fire was their sole observer, crackling quietly in the hearth as she made little, happy sounds in his mouth.

His magic was doing an odd circuit through his body, almost like a self-diagnosis. Heat would briefly flood through his arms, then his back, and then move down into his legs. It was like a massage from the inside, but the cost was the phantom meal he had consumed at Christmas Present's table. His stomach made a couple of growling inquiries as to the time and location of his next meal, but he politely told it to fuck off.

Yuki was rubbing his stomach now, her chill touch the ice

to his inner fire. The magic moved up to greet her, as if knowing it would be inside her soon enough. There was an eagerness he hadn't experienced before, but he couldn't tell if it was Yuki's or his own. His magic liked to mirror the emotions and anticipation of potential partners, and it was easy to get caught up.

"Mmm." Yuki broke lip contact and smiled at him. "I like kissing you. It's all tingly."

"I…get that a lot." He laughed. "Just a trick I picked up along the way."

"Sex magic will do that. With Emily…" Her face darkened. "I'm sorry, I shouldn't talk about her."

"Why?" He squeezed her waist. "I mean, yeah, talking about exes during intimate moments is usually frowned on, but absolutely nothing about our lives is normal. And I would be an idiot not to realize this is an act of healing. If something is on your mind, say it."

Yuki paused at this, then closed her eyes. She nodded to herself, then opened them again.

"I was in a relationship with her for a long time. It was semiopen, but mainly she only had sex with Naia. For me, it was all about Emily. I had no desire for anyone else."

"And now?" He moved his hand down her waist until he reached the base of her tails. "May I?" he asked.

"Please do." She grinned as he ran his fingers through her fur. "Before Emily, I had many different lovers but none of the emotional attachment. Now that my heart has had time to heal, that part of me has awakened once again. I don't like the idea of being tied so directly to one person in any way."

"But you're already tied to me." He stopped caressing her tail for a moment. "Because of your promise." She had once sworn to be his weapon and his protector. However, in the event he became evil like Emily, she would also be his killer.

"I see that as a promise to everyone in the house," she

replied. "You just happen to be at the epicenter of that promise."

"Yuki." He took a deep breath before proceeding. "Maybe I'll kick myself later for this, but are you sure we should be doing this? I can feel my magic swirling around inside you, and I worry that maybe you're extra vulnerable, or that maybe this is a line we shouldn't cross, I don't know."

Yuki paused, a large frown appearing on her face. "Excuse me?"

"If we're going to be honest and up front with each other, then that's what you're going to get from me. The last thing I want to do is hurt you."

She chewed on her lip for a moment, then scowled. "You once fucked the tree in the backyard to officially launch spring."

"That tree has a name, and it's hardly the same thing."

"Fucked a hellhound to make her your buddy."

"That was for survival, and you were there for that."

"This isn't any different. Yeah, the girls and I joke about your low standards when it comes to problem solving—"

"Hey!" Mike tried to pinch her butt in protest but couldn't find it fast enough through all the fur of her tails.

"But maybe today's problem is that I want to feel that connection with someone again, and I want to do it with someone I trust. I watched you walk that line, saw the immense power you could have wielded. Emily had several decades to learn from her mistakes only to fuck everything up in the end. You were essentially handed everything you could have wanted but turned it away because you knew it was wrong." She placed her hands on his shoulders. "I want you to help me move on from Emily, to finally climb this wall that has closed me off from the world. This isn't some magic-crazed whim. I've been thinking about it for a long time. You make me feel safe, Caretaker, for the first time in years. I want to feel your magic like the others do, experience that closeness I've been desperately craving. I'm over three hundred years old, so stop treating me like a victim and just treat me like everyone else you live with."

Mike put his hands over hers and squeezed them. "I had to be sure is all. This is a big step, and I wanted to make sure we were taking it together."

"I swear to the gods that if you keep talking instead of—" Her eyes widened once he released the magic in his hands, letting the sparks climb up her arms to disappear inside her robes. She let out a tiny moan, then shivered in his arms.

Despite what Yuki had said, there was hesitation in her movements, a cautiousness born from years of heartache. The magic swirling through her body right now was capable of reducing her to a blithering, sexual mess, yet she resisted and took her time. Every touch, every caress, became new territory for them to explore. He let her set the pace, keeping his hands on her legs and waist.

He moved his hands inside her robes, feeling the soft fur of her outer thighs. She let out a tiny gasp of delight when he accidentally shocked her, then retaliated by playfully biting his lip.

"It's surprising how much those shocks can hurt while still feeling good," she told him, pressing her groin against his. "With you, it's all about those fireworks, isn't it?"

"I like to make a good impression."

"Of course you do." Yuki sat up and pulled her robe away from her shoulders, allowing it to pool at her waist. Her bare breasts were human, but the sides of them were streaked with fox fur that gathered beneath her cleavage and continued down her belly. "So what do you say, Caretaker? Impress me."

He went to lean forward, spurred by both eagerness and his magic to suck on her breasts, but paused. The nymph magic in his blood would guide him, would tell him exactly what he needed to do to please his lover, but he could tell there was a piece missing. He was having trouble concentrating.

Communication. Naia's voice purred softly inside his head. *She doesn't want you to just know how to please her. She wants to connect on a higher level.*

"So what do you like?" he asked, moving his hands up her sides and allowing his thumbs to trace the curvature of her breasts. She smiled as he did so, closing her eyes and savoring the sensation of his touch.

"My breasts have always been sensitive," she said. "Emily…she loved to lick them. She was always good at it and even got me off that way a few times. Don't be intimidated though. She cheated. Her magic was way more direct than yours."

"Direct how?" He sat up and played with her breasts, kissing his way along the soft, furry parts while toying with her nipples. "I mean, I feel like mine is pretty direct."

"She could do what you do without skin contact. Make you desire her just by being in the same room. All it took was a look or a smell. Your lightning trick is certainly unique but requires buildup. She once made me come just by fingering me, and I don't mean for a while. Just slid it in from behind while I was bent over and filling the bath."

"Do you want me to try to hold it back? No magic?"

"Hardly. Ever since I got front row seats to that threesome at the cabin, I've been fantasizing about how it would feel to have your magic inside me." She scooted down his pelvis and helped him into a sitting position, her legs now wrapped around him. "I want to feel it all, Mike. I want you to blow the memory of my last lover straight out of my mind so my heart can build anew."

"As you wish." He kissed her neck, and she tilted her head back to allow him better access. From there, he moved down to her breasts, sending surges of magic into his hands and storing it like a capacitor. After nibbling his way down to her areola, he sucked it into his mouth. Putting his hands on Yuki's waist, he released the stored magic into her hips.

Yuki gasped, and her nipple stiffened in his mouth as he sucked, pulling blood to the surface.

"Oh gods, yes, be rough with them!" She clung to his back as he bit down on her tender flesh. She reached down between them and adjusted his erection so it pressed more directly against her groin, then humped him through her robes. The fabric kept bunching up between them, so she pulled the fabric off, revealing her thighs.

Yuki made small growling noises as she sucked on the side of Mike's neck, moaning into his flesh every time he bit down on her nipples. The soft silk of her pubes rubbed directly against his cock, her labia parting to embrace his shaft.

The air sizzled as his magic crawled along her flesh, and he heard a loud pop. Puzzled, he leaned back to see that a mist had formed around the two of them. Some of the sparks on Yuki's body were jumping into the fog and fizzing out of existence.

"What is that?" He swiped at it, but the vapor passed harmlessly between his fingers.

"That's me," Yuki said, her voice husky. "Your magic is doing weird things with mine, so I'm freezing water in the air to keep the pressure from building up inside me." She put a hand on the back of his head and pulled him back into her breasts. "Now don't stop!"

Smiling, he switched to her other tit, teasing her nipple with his tongue. Magic leaped from his tongue to her hardened tip, causing her to jump. She shifted her hips, putting extra pressure on his trapped cock.

Yuki pressed her face into his neck and nibbled the sensitive skin, sending shivers down his spine. Sparks flashed in the hovering mist like fireworks, and Yuki let out a growl that became a tiny yip.

"I can't wait any longer," she whispered in his ear. "Claim me and make me yours."

Mike stopped sucking on her breasts and stared into her emerald eyes, his magic making the air buzz as he slid his arms around her waist, pushing her robes away so they wouldn't interfere. Without breaking eye contact, he grabbed her by the ass and lifted her up and forward, feeling the slick warmth of her eager pussy slide along his length. The head of his cock pressed against her labia, and she let out a sigh.

"Please." She put her hands on his shoulders and squeezed.

Holding her by the hips, he pulled her down, feeling her tight passage expand as he slid inside her. Yuki gasped and clung to him, her loose hair covering her face.

He went slow, savoring the growls and small barking sounds she made. He could feel the fur of her body rippling under his hands as if the line between woman and beast was fluctuating. The mist clung to their bodies like a cloak as his magic formed into streamers on his own form, sizzling the air. From the outside, the two of them probably looked like a sexual plasma ball.

The little yips and moans became needier, and Mike leaned away from Yuki to see that her facial features had elongated slightly, her lip curling away from dangerously sharp canines.

"Don't you dare stop," she groaned, her voice husky with desire. Red lines appeared on her face and then popped free as a set of whiskers appeared above her cheeks.

In response, he grabbed her ass and pushed himself into her as far as possible, the head of his cock rubbing along her vaginal wall. The playful nips from earlier didn't prepare him for how hard she bit his shoulder, but the sensation elicited more pleasure than pain.

Yuki licked his shoulder and then bit him again. He leaned

away from her until he was lying on his back while Yuki remained upright.

"Go ahead," he told her, stroking her thighs. "Cut loose."

Her emerald eyes flashed as she moaned, her hips now swiveling to a beat he couldn't hear. She put her hands on his shoulders, and he noticed that her nails had elongated into proper claws as she rode him. The ionized cloud around them zapped her several times, causing her face to turn red as she bit down on her lip and moaned.

Her hips broke their rhythm, and she twitched randomly on his cock, her vaginal walls tightening dramatically around his shaft. It felt like a pair of hands squeezing at random, and Yuki let out an eerie cry as the mist surrounded her. Fur sprouted and disappeared all along her torso as she sat up straight and reached for the sky.

Yuki took a deep breath, and the temperature in the room plummeted. Ice formed along the frame of the bed, and the fire in the hearth went out with a puff of smoke. Mike felt the warmth leached from his body, but his connection with Yuki provided plenty of heat.

Golden light exploded from Yuki's outstretched hands as her tails unfurled dramatically behind her. All three of them writhed as his magic danced around the kitsune, pressing against her like a second skin.

She screamed, an eerie sound that made the hair on his arms stand up. The bed shook as it lifted free of the ground, hovering a foot or so off the floor.

The scream stretched into a protracted moan, her face flushed by the orgasm that ripped through her body. Mike's magic swirled around her like a tiny tornado, sinking deep into her pores. The bed dropped, crashing against the hardwood floor. Yuki fell forward, her lips rough against his as she kissed him. When their tongues touched, her hips jerked suddenly as he felt his magic complete a circuit inside her.

With some difficulty, he rolled her onto her back. She

wrapped her legs around him, their lips never breaking contact. He was only able to make tiny thrusts, but each one elicited a whimpering moan from the kitsune. Grabbing her hands, he pinned them over her head as his body pressed into hers.

Breaking the kiss, he pushed himself up to get a better angle for penetration. Yuki sighed, arching her back as several tiny fox fire flames appeared over the bed.

"More," she moaned, grinding her pelvis into him. "Fill me up, Caretaker, warm me from the inside!"

Unsure what to say to that, Mike let his body do the talking. He established a slow tempo, delighting in the animal sounds Yuki made when he would thrust suddenly and surprise her. Her tails shifted beneath them, eventually fanning out and making it look like they were lying on a cloak of furs. The air crackled and sizzled with their combined magic as his orgasm built.

Yuki's eyes rolled up in her head when another orgasm tore through her. She yanked her hands free of his, digging her claws into his lower back to keep him deep inside her. The whole room trembled this time, and Mike's body became hot as he passed the point of no return.

When he came, the magic in the room collapsed in on him, causing his entire groin to spasm as he spilled his seed inside the kitsune. What was usually a few spurts of cum was instead a steady stream, and he grabbed Yuki by the waist and howled as his orgasm stretched on for what felt like an eternity.

Yuki cried out beneath him, her tails fluttering and changing colors. Her green eyes now glowed with golden energy as she writhed beneath his body. Cum poured out of her, creating a sticky pool under her. Mike lost control as his magic took him over, sending waves of energy through the room. Thin tendrils appeared in his vision, extending from his body to the floor, walls, and ceiling. He could see a strand connecting his chest to Yuki's, a thread that became thicker as he came again inside her.

As those tendrils drifted away from him, he had a sudden fear that his magic had escaped him once again. Concentrating on the nearest bundle he could see, he commanded the magic to return to his body. Instead of withdrawing, the tendrils looped around until they vanished inside him. A surge of energy followed, and he cried out as yet another orgasm was triggered.

The bed frame cracked beneath them, and the mattress dropped. Mike's orgasm triggered again and again, so he pulled free of Yuki, spraying her and the bed with semen. The visible strands in the room now curled into circles, all of them reattaching to his body at various locations. The magic wasn't dissipating, and all he could do was keep blasting glittery ropes of cum all over the room.

Yuki rolled forward, her cool mouth inhaling the head of his cock as she swallowed as much of his cum as she could. Massive globs of semen escaped her mouth and even came out her nose as the fountain continued. She gagged, spitting him out and coughing spooge all over his crotch.

"Yuki, I...can't...stop..." Mike's eyes fluttered as his consciousness dimmed. Yuki grabbed his scrotum just above his balls, using a tight grip that was almost painful. He felt the magic reluctantly recede as the orgasms finally stopped. When he fell toward the bed, Yuki grabbed his shoulders and guided him away from the edge. The bed was a mess with nowhere dry for them to lie.

Panting for air, he was surprised when Yuki kissed him again, pressing her needy body against his. He could taste a hint of himself on her lips but didn't think it was intentional.

"Really?" he asked, his voice barely a whisper. His cock twitched uncertainly.

"Not that," she replied, then snuggled against him. "I'm

going to be very sore, thank you very much. I definitely didn't expect the cum shower. For now, I just want you by my side."

"You've got it." Relieved, he kissed her tenderly, the groans and aches from before reappearing. She made happy sounds in his arms, pulling herself against him until it felt like they would become a single person.

"*What in Christmas did you do to my bedroom*!?"

Shocked, Mike tried to sit up, but his muscles gave out. All he could do was helplessly roll to one side and fall off the bed, landing in a small puddle of semen-tainted water. In the door stood Mrs. Claus, her eyes wide behind silver-framed glasses as she looked around the room. She held a tray of food, which she set down on the floor.

"Oh shit, I mean shoot, uh..." Mike tried to stand, but his hand slipped, and he fell again. The floor was wet, most likely a result of the freezing mist that Yuki had summoned. Giant globs of cum were distributed through the room as if a bottle of glue had exploded. Using the bed to stand, he realized his cock was still leaking semen, so he tried to cover it with his hands, only to slip again.

"*It's in the tree*!" Horrified, Mrs. Claus ran to the Christmas tree and just stared at a glob of sticky fluid that hung like a crystalline ornament from one of the branches. The glittery substance in the middle shimmered as if excited to see her. "*You came in my tree*!"

"Usually he comes deeper in trees," Yuki whispered so only he could hear. Mike had to bite his lip to keep from laughing.

"I am so, so sorry," Mike began, but Mrs. Claus waved him off.

"You've got so much explaining to do. You young people have no self-control!" Groaning in disgust, she moved to a nearby chest carved from walnut and opened it up. She stacked a bunch of towels on a chair, then shut the chest. "At least when Mr. Claus does this, he keeps it all on the bed! Sweet Christmas, I've never seen something like this."

"It just sort of happened," he continued, but Mrs. Claus ignored him. She moved to a nearby dresser and pulled out a pair of pants.

"We will talk plenty, later. For now, you need to put on some pants and clean up this mess. We've got a lot to do if we're going to fix this Krampus business, and now the two of you owe me. However!" She wagged a finger in his direction. "If you and your friend don't have this place spotless in the next hour, there will absolutely be no dessert for you!"

"Yes, ma'am," Yuki replied, holding her robes up to cover her cum-stained breasts.

Mrs. Claus made a clicking sound with her tongue, then nodded before storming out. She slammed the door hard enough that it bounced open, which meant she had to shut it again.

"Oh God." Mike sank to his knees. "I just came all over Santa's bed and pissed off his wife."

"At least it isn't the other way around." Yuki held a straight face for several seconds, then broke. Laughter, pure and uninhibited, bubbled up from deep within as she clutched her belly and fell backward on the bed. It reminded Mike of the jingling of silver bells, and he couldn't help but laugh with her.

The laughter continued for over a minute before Yuki wiped the tears from her eyes and sat up. "C'mon," she told him, holding out a hand. For just a moment, he saw a golden aura surround her fingers, but then it vanished. "Let's get some food to eat and clean this place up. I don't suppose you have semen removal in your bag of tricks?"

"Afraid not. I'm not entirely sure what happened there. Was that an earthquake?"

Yuki blushed. "That was me. I was trying to avoid freezing

the room and tapped into a little earth magic. It used to be my specialty, you know." She was already pulling the sheets off the bed. "I'll do this if you'll clean the floor. Probably should apologize to the tree while you clean it."

"Agreed." He turned away from her and felt a sudden tug inside his mind. It was Kisa. She was nearby, perhaps even in the same building. Smiling, he began mopping up his mess, pausing only to clean and properly apologize to Mrs. Claus's tree.

The tree accepted.

JACK STOOD ON THE ROOF OF THE BAKERY, HER GAZE ON THE streets below. The storm had blotted out a large portion of the sky, and the accompanying winds had coated the side of the building in ice. She didn't bother wiping the tears from her cheeks, as they kept freezing. The cold itself couldn't hurt her, but repeatedly peeling ice off her face would irritate her skin and make her even more miserable.

The Krampus had screamed at her upon learning she had taken matters into her own hands. The demon had finally emerged from the woodshop to discover that she had left her post and was chasing the intruders. There were few things on Earth that terrified her, but feeling that creature's otherworldly wrath simmering beneath the fringes of reality had set her on edge. She had been incapable of responding to his allegations at the sight of those brutal, gnarled teeth just inches from her own face.

He had spent months inside her head, pleading for his freedom. She'd thought he was a kindred soul, a misunderstood entity who knew what it was like to be underappreciated and forgotten. Then, there had been kindness in his tone, and a determination that had resonated deep within her.

Now, though, she could see that he was unhinged. The Krampus was smart, but he was also cruel. His emotions got the better of him often, and it was only after he had calmed down that he'd reasoned the elf had escaped through the tunnels under the village.

Leaving Jack behind, he'd vanished into a nearby building, giving her instructions to keep watch from above. After a long wait, her walkie had crackled to life, and the Krampus had told her to come to his location and make herself useful by being his lookout. What he hadn't counted on was that she would do a thorough sweep of the exterior, easily spotting the altered elves within through the large bay windows. They were twisted things, only vaguely familiar as the joyous creatures they so recently were.

Though she had often felt neglected by the denizens of the North Pole, she had never wished them any harm. The Krampus had declared that times had changed. The true meaning of Christmas would return, a time where the wicked could be properly punished, but she had a hard time seeing it now.

And so she waited, and she wept. Maybe the things the Krampus had promised would still come to pass; perhaps she was just seeing a less-than-pleasant transitory phase. Logically, she knew she was in denial, but to admit anything else right now might destroy her.

The monotony was shattered by an explosion of flames. Turning, Jack saw a massive fireball climb into the sky, somewhere over by the stables. She was unsure if she should remain or go see what happened, but the decision was made for her when she heard the Krampus shriek out in fury.

She leaped from the roof, allowing the winds to carry her to the stables. The interior of the building was in flames, but they curled around the structure itself, burning the large bales of hay that had been scattered around within. The air stank of whiskey and burned hair, the smell stinging her nostrils.

"Jack." A heavy hand clamped down on her shoulder, and she spun around to see the Krampus looming over her. Steam rose from his body as the Krampus sneered at her. "You let them escape."

"They were here?" She looked around and saw a small collection of footprints in the snow. "I didn't know."

"This is your fault, Jack." His large hand circled her throat, and he squeezed. Jack grabbed his fingers and summoned the frost but knew it was no use. Ice formed over the demon's knuckles, but it cracked and fell away as he squeezed. He lifted her up high, then pulled her close. His breath was hot and smelled of peppermint. "You have disappointed me."

She gasped for air and slapped feebly at his hands. The bones in her neck felt like they would pop any moment, and once the lights went out, that would be it for her.

The storm swirled around them, and the Krampus loosened his grip, allowing her to breathe. With a grunt of disgust, he tossed her away, where she tumbled onto the ground.

"Go watch the monitors," he hissed, turning his attention back to the stables. "If you see anything, tell me right away, or I will powder this village with your bones."

Jack tried to respond, but her voice allowed her only a harsh squeak.

"Seven will have to do," he grumbled, scratching his belly with a claw. "And where is my sleigh? Hmmm." Seeing Jack, he snarled at her. "Go! Now!"

She obeyed, staggering to her feet before letting the wind carry her back to the workshop. The tears were hot and many as she fled to the safety of the monitor room. In the last few hundred years, she hadn't suffered so much as a scratch, but the Krampus had ended the streak by nearly taking her life. He was a creature of madness, and she was crazy to have ever listened to him.

Sniffling, she sat down in one of the tiny chairs by the

monitors and started clicking absently through them. It was hard to concentrate, her mind preoccupied with the Krampus.

Could she flee? She had no doubts that she could lose him in the storm, but he would have eternity to find her should he choose. The giants would probably help him, as they had no loyalty to her. And even if he decided to let Jack go, she always ran the risk of running into him.

Frustrated, she clicked through the monitors, uncertain what she was hoping to see. Her neck hurt, and she felt more lost than ever.

But even worse than feeling lost was how alone she was. She thought the Krampus had been her friend, but she knew better now.

"Fuck!" She slammed her hand on the console, accidentally changing the cameras on the screen. Disgruntled, she tried to reacquire the missing channels by clicking through all of them. She couldn't concentrate, couldn't remember how the console worked. It was all a blur.

So she navigated through them one at a time, only now noticing that the bakery wasn't part of any of the cycles. Where else were the cameras down? What were the elves actually doing?

She was going through them so fast that her mind didn't register movement until she was already three channels past. Aghast, she clicked back and sat there, stunned.

The camera was labeled *Claus Residence Master Bedroom*. It viewed the room from above the head of the bed, and Jack was surprised to see that the kitsune from earlier was busy riding the human named Mike. Fascinated, all she could do was stare.

Why in the North Pole would Santa have a camera in his bedroom? Jack's thoughts milled about uselessly in an effort to rationalize what she was seeing. The kitsune's face was scrunched up in sweet agony as she held her own breasts while bouncing up and down on the biggest cock Jack had ever seen. Her mouth hung open so long that it became dry, but she simply couldn't look away.

It was an intimate moment, one of thousands she had witnessed on accident. Being invisible to the mortal realm meant that Jack had seen plenty of things she wasn't supposed to. Maybe it was as simple as someone sneaking a cigarette, or complex like the time she had stumbled onto a military installation in northern Russia. Though she had never been much of a voyeur, she couldn't help but watch the people on the screen as they made love to each other.

Her stomach fluttered, and she put her hand on her belly, reminded of her contact with Mike. His voice had made her eager to obey, and she wondered if he had used that same power on the kitsune. If not, then maybe they were a couple or, at the very least, close friends. When was the last time Jack had a friend, much less a close one?

Or even a lover?

For just a moment, it felt like a stray memory bubbled to the top of her consciousness, eager for her attention. Unable to grab it, she let it sink into the recesses of her mind once more, catching just a glimpse of golden rays.

She knew she should notify the Krampus, should tell him the mortal had survived the vents, but her finger hovered over the button of the walkie-talkie. Her skin still burned from where he had choked her, his words still harsh in her ears. He was already angry but would positively explode if he knew the human had escaped to Mrs. Claus's home. It was no fault of her own, but would he see it that way?

Her hesitation caused her to stand there and watch, her focus on Mike and the kitsune. In the throes of their passion, they summoned up a maelstrom of sparking lights that danced around the room. She knew the kitsune had ice magic, but this was something else. Through the camera, she couldn't make heads or tails of it and was surprised when the camera distorted. It was being overloaded by the sheer power in that room, and she wondered which one of them was the culprit.

Curious, she clicked through the rest of the house. Mrs. Claus could be seen baking in her kitchen, and she was speaking with someone invisible to the camera. If there was somebody capable of fighting the Krampus, it was Mrs. Claus, and it was clear that she already had help.

Ice formed around Jack's hands and spread to the rest of the console. If she chose, she could destroy these monitors, could put an end to the Krampus's surveillance. But then what? Change sides, just like that? Or would it be the first step toward oblivion?

Jack wished she had a friend, someone she could talk to. Clicking through the monitors, she saw the Krampus skulking around the outside of Santa's home. It was clear that he already knew something was going on there, so she pressed the button on her walkie-talkie, hoping to buy herself some goodwill.

"The human is with Mrs. Claus," she said. On the camera, she saw the Krampus tilt his head as he heard her, then let out a shriek of rage. He bounded up to Santa's home and pounded on the front door with a giant fist.

Jack smirked, knowing that even if the door was open, the Krampus wouldn't go in. There was something about Mrs. Claus that was dangerous to the Krampus, but Jack didn't know what. Standing, she went through the monitors until she was once again looking at Santa's mirror.

Santa turned his attention to the camera and waved.

"Shit." She clicked away from the mirror and bit at her nails. Maybe it would be safer to just let things play out a bit longer before deciding, to weigh her options. Seeing the Krampus succeed meant that he would let her be and nothing would change. That was far preferable to being killed.

With so many thoughts running through her head, she left

the security room behind, frost forming beneath her feet as she hovered down the hallway. Her decisions lately had been terrible, and maybe it was time to check in on an old friend and see what he thought before she committed.

She just hoped she could hear him through his prison of glass.

TRUE NORTH

It took most of the hour to get Santa's bedroom cleaned up. Mike and Yuki had stacked the wet towels in an empty laundry basket by the fireplace before sitting down to eat the food left for them. Beneath the silver domes on the tray was a wonderful roast duck dinner with green beans and mashed potatoes on the side. A thermos full of hot apple cider had been provided, and the two of them ate in silence on the floor as they attempted to finish the meal before Mrs. Claus returned.

Occasionally, a loud banging could be felt throughout the house, but Mike had decided it would be better to stay put. He was already on her bad side and didn't have anything else to wear other than the pants she had given him. His clothes were lost in the cracks of reality, and he didn't feel like wandering around the North Pole in just his pants.

Yuki kept flashing him sly smiles. Her upbeat demeanor was infectious, and he caught himself smiling in response. When they finished eating, she leaned against him and closed her eyes.

"Not bad for a first date, Caretaker." She chuckled and

put her hand against his chest. "Though, I would have preferred somewhere with more dancing."

"Oh, so we're dating now?"

She giggled and turned her face away from him. "I'll probably end up pregnant after what you did. We might have to get married."

"What?" He sat up so suddenly that Yuki fell away from him, revealing the stupid grin on her face.

"Man, you're so easy." She laughed and patted her belly. "I can't get pregnant unless I want to. For someone who likes to blow his load in every woman he fucks, you put very little thought into the potential consequences."

He pressed his lips together and frowned. The thought had occurred to him more than once that he should really get his shit together regarding all the women he had sex with. "You're not wrong," he admitted.

"Maybe Christmas Present will give birth to all sorts of new holidays. Mike Day, Big Dick Day, Radl—ow!" She jerked away from him when he pinched her inner thigh.

"I should probably talk to Naia about birth control," he admitted. "I've just taken it for granted that so many of you are either incompatible with me or can take care of it yourselves. That's how I ended up with an egg and a little horse boy who hates me."

Yuki sobered up at the mention of Callisto. "I don't think he hates you," she said, then sat up and adjusted her robes. "The centaurs aren't stubborn because they're taught to be. They really are just born that way. The herd are his people, and maybe it's that you represent that part of him that's always going to be different. He's still a child and doesn't fully appreciate that being different is a good thing."

"I suppose so." Mike looked at the door again, wondering where Mrs. Claus was. He had expected her to return in exactly an hour, but he had no way of knowing just how much time had passed.

"Should we leave?" she asked, noticing his gaze.

"No." He looked back at her. "I suspect she's still dealing with Kisa and hopefully Tink and Holly." His familiar was thirty feet below him now, and he could sense her gratitude and contentment, which likely meant that Mrs. Claus was feeding her as well. He had tried to communicate a couple of times, but Kisa had been too distracted to sense him. "Telepathy would be really nice right about now," he told her.

"Then maybe you should find a telepath to fuck." She winked at him and stood. "So how does this work? Can you summon ice magic now?"

"Hmm?" Realizing she was asking about his ability to swap souls, he shrugged. "Oh, right. No idea, it isn't always obvious. Would be nice if it was."

"I see." She stretched and walked across the room. "Do you think visualizing magic was the trade-off?"

"Can't be. We hadn't, um, finished yet." He had told her about the weird tendrils he had seen. In fact, with a bit of concentration, he could see an aura surrounding Yuki. It sparkled like a diamond and changed colors depending on how she stood. "My best guess is that maybe it's from Christmas Present."

"Interesting." She lowered her head in thought. "I guess it would make sense, sort of. Christmas Present can see everything that happens around Christmas day, all at the same time. Do you think that means you can only do it on Christmas?"

"No idea. Will probably experiment with it later when I don't feel so burned out." The meal and rest had refreshed him, but his body ached. Even though he had never run a marathon, he assumed how he felt now was comparable.

"Should probably put a condom on first," she replied. "In case you make yourself come again."

"Ha ha, very funny. I'll know better next time." He shook his head at the memory of pulling his magic back inside him.

In hindsight, he should have known better. "Being turned into a cum fountain is a party trick I don't feel like repeating."

"Yeah, my sinuses are still out of whack from it." She snorted for emphasis just as the door to their room opened. Mrs. Claus stood there with her hands on her hips, then walked inside for a look around. She said nothing for several moments as she inspected the room, then nodded.

"I suppose dessert is in order after all," she declared, then looked at Mike. "Some friends of yours are here. Why don't you grab a shirt from that closet and we can all meet in the kitchen to discuss what happens next."

"Yes, ma'am." He watched her leave, then let out a deep breath. Knowing that he was off Mrs. Claus's shit list was a huge relief.

The closet contained several long-sleeved white cotton shirts with buttons at the top. They were vastly oversize, but seeing no alternatives, he put one on. While adjusting the collar around his neck, the shirt shrank down until it became a perfect fit.

Had the pants done the same thing? He hadn't even noticed while putting them on. Seeing a pair of slippers at the bottom of the closet, he put them on and waited. Unlike the clothes, the slippers didn't seem to have any magical properties. They were maybe a size too big but kept his bare feet off the floor.

"Not bad," Yuki told him. "I imagine Santa can't have someone adjusting his clothes on the fly every time he eats too many cookies."

"The guy's got all those elves, I just figured there'd be a whole division devoted to tailored clothes." He tucked the shirt in and gestured to the door. "Shall we?"

They left the room and found Holly standing outside. The elf sighed in relief when she saw them.

"Kisa said you'd be here," she said. "Though, we were a

little worried about what shape you'd be in. Mrs. Claus said you were fine, but she seemed upset."

"I'd say it was just a misunderstanding, but we didn't get off on the right foot. Our arrival was a bit…tumultuous."

Holly nodded. "Ours too. We crashed a reindeer through one of the skylights. The Krampus beat us here and was too preoccupied with banging on the front door to see our approach. Mrs. Claus wasn't mad though. She was pretty happy to see us."

"Mike rode in on the Ghost of Christmas Present," Yuki offered. "I won't bore you with the other details."

"You saw the ghost?" Holly stopped and turned around to face them. "We met Christmas Past, but it was so damaged."

"Christmas Present was on the fence, but Mike was very convincing." Yuki winked.

"Oh, thank Santa." Holly put her hands together and sighed in relief. "That is great news. What about the Ghost of Christmas Future?"

"Uh…" Mike looked over at Yuki. "That's one we haven't dealt with yet."

"Oh." Holly took them to a spiral staircase carved out of wood. It wrapped tightly around a central column with decorations carved into it. He recognized a lot of the decor as pagan in nature but didn't know much else about it. "I hope he doesn't show up here. He's the scariest."

"What does he look like?" Mike asked.

"Kind of like your friend Death," she replied. "Only way more intense. He sees everything that could happen to you, which is his gift. But seeing a near infinite number of futures every time he meets someone…we think it's part of the reason he doesn't talk. His mind is just so busy filtering information that he barely exists in the present."

Mike frowned, wondering at the implications. How could he battle a foe capable of seeing the future? Were the spirits' powers limited only to the time around Christmas? It was something that bore consideration.

At the bottom of the stairs was a doorway that opened into an enormous kitchen. Modern day stainless steel appliances clashed with the rootlike structure of the room's framing. If he didn't know better, Mike would believe he was actually below a giant tree.

The large kitchen island was big enough to seat ten, but its only occupants were Kisa and Tink. Both of them jumped down from their seats and nearly knocked Mike over with their hugs.

"Asshole," Kisa muttered. Tink didn't bother with words. Instead, she bit his side through his shirt.

"I missed you too." He hugged them both affectionately. "I'm glad you're safe."

"Tink too smart for frosty bi—"

"*Ahem!*" This was from Mrs. Claus, who emerged from a nearby pantry with a large pie in her hands. "Language, dear."

Tink scowled. "Tink want pie, tell husband later."

Mike laughed, then followed them back to the counter. He took a seat, and Tink scrambled onto the chair next to him. Kisa sat on the other side, leaving Holly and Yuki to sit on the edges.

"And here we go." Mrs. Claus set the pie on the counter next to a knife. A stack of plates and forks had been set nearby, which Kisa passed out. The top of the pie was adorned with thick strips of crisply cooked dough, revealing a mixture of berries inside. "It's been chilled already, so you don't have to wait."

Tink scooped up the knife and deftly sliced it into five equal pieces.

"I don't know that I can eat that much pie," Mike told her as she used a fork to remove the first piece.

"Husband make room. Best pie ever." Tink placed the pie

on Mike's plate. "Everything nice woman makes tastes so good."

"I've got plenty of practice," Mrs. Claus admitted with a smile. "There isn't a whole lot else I get to do up here." She opened her mouth to say something else but was interrupted by a loud banging sound from above.

"What is that?" Mike asked.

"That would be the Krampus. He is very upset that you all are here." She leaned forward, the low-cut apron revealing a ton of cleavage. It looked more like something a sexy maid would wear. "But he doesn't dare come inside."

"Why is that?" Mike asked. He waited for Tink to finish splitting up the pie, then took a bite. The crust was buttery and melted on his tongue, and the berries were a type he'd never had before. They started tart, then turned sweet in his mouth. "This is really good," he admitted.

"Thank you. As to the Krampus…" She sighed and pulled off her apron. Mike couldn't help but notice that the flimsy garment expanded in her hands once it was off her body into something that looked a lot more functional. "I can't explain it fully in present company. The information is quite sensitive."

"There's nothing you can tell me that they can't hear," he said, though he didn't know if that was true about Holly. "They're family. I trust them."

"And I will trust your judgment when it comes to what you'll share with whom later," she said. "This will make far more sense once you hear what I have to say."

"I'll take your word for it." He swatted Tink's fork away from his plate. "You're not even done eating your own piece."

Tink hissed at him, then went back to her own plate. She tried to sneak a piece off Yuki's plate, but the kitsune burned the goblin's hand with purple fox fire.

"You are a hungry thing," Mrs. Claus noted. "You ate three helpings of dinner and still have room!"

"Goblins hate cold," Tink replied between bites of her

food. "Eat big meal, sleep all winter. Tink no time for sleep but still want to eat. Get big butt for husband."

"More cushion for the pushin'," whispered Kisa so only Mike heard her. He pinched her beneath the counter, causing her to bump Holly.

Mrs. Claus nodded, then slid Tink a plate of cookies that were hidden below the counter. "When you're done with your pie, you can have some of these."

"No!" Both Kisa and Holly yelled, then looked at each other.

"Just…not cookies," Kisa added. "She ate them until she was sick."

Tink had already hooked a claw into the plate and dragged it toward her. "Nice woman's cookies way better than stupid devil cookies."

"Devil cookies?" Mrs. Claus leaned on the counter, her breasts nearly spilling out of her nightie. Mike kept his focus on what was left of his pie.

"The Krampus was making gingerbread devils." This came from Holly. "It's what he had the dark elves making."

"Tink eat devil cookie. Taste like pepper and ashes." The goblin stuck her tongue out for emphasis. "Spit out right away."

"Hmm. That makes sense, I suppose. It's probably how he subverted the reindeer." Mrs. Claus stood and adjusted her lingerie. One of her nipples slipped free, and she frowned before hiding it. "We're very lucky that Dancer noticed them in her feed. They must have some other purpose though."

"I have to ask…what's with the lingerie?" Yuki leaned forward eagerly. Mike silently blessed her for asking, because he had been afraid to.

"An unintended feature of Christmas Day," Mrs. Claus grumbled. "The rest of the year, I get to be the happy home-maker. Baking, playing games with elves, spending time with my husband. But right before Christmas, it begins. The lingerie sales, the sexy role-playing by couples. Right now, the world has thousands of women dressed like this pretending to be me, and my only saving grace is that Mrs. Claus is largely seen as faithful to her husband. Otherwise, I would be an absolute mess right now."

"Is that why your apron looks different now?" Mike asked. "I saw it change when you took it off."

"Good eye for detail. You'll need it." She tugged at the straps of her nightie. "This is actually a very comfortable sweater. Unless I go outside, anything I wear becomes like this."

"Why outside?" Kisa asked.

"Because everyone knows that I would freeze to death without a good coat," Mrs. Claus said. "While indoors, I am seen as the loyal wife, waiting to adore my husband with a slew of sexual favors when he returns. Outside? I'm clearly busy helping get ready for Christmas."

"And the magic just keeps track of that for you?" Mike asked.

Mrs. Claus nodded. "It does. Sometimes the changes aren't obvious right away, but I can always tell when a lingerie company launches their new Christmas collection. I have more to say about that, but it will have to wait." She lifted a thermos from beneath the counter. "Hot cocoa, anyone?"

They sat and finished their pie while catching up on all that had transpired. The hot cocoa warmed Mike from the inside, and the soreness in his muscles faded away. He wondered if the cocoa itself had some restorative properties, because he felt almost good as new. However, he could definitely use a shower.

Tink finished off her pie, what was left of Kisa's pie, and a plate of cookies. Patting herself on the belly, she pushed her stool against Mike's and leaned her head on his arm. It wasn't long before she snored softly in his embrace.

With the food finished, the group moved out into the main

room while Holly left to do the dishes for Mrs. Claus. A massive fireplace sat at the center of the room with flames visible from every side. The chimney rose through the middle of the room only to vanish several stories up. Bookshelves lined the walls of this floor, and a cursory inspection revealed that most of the books weren't Christmas related at all. It looked like Santa or his wife were huge Tom Clancy fans, but the bulk of the collection was young adult fiction, though there were some scattered romance collections.

Next to the fireplace was a large love seat and the biggest recliner Mike had ever seen. He set Tink on the recliner and covered her up with a blanket. Kisa pulled a book from one of the shelves and curled up next to the goblin. Tink belched, and Kisa made a face.

"Seriously," she said, her eyes watering. "Stop letting her eat sweets. That smells awful."

"It's Christmas Day, sweetie." Mrs. Claus handed Kisa a mug of cocoa and a sandwich. Mike had no idea when the woman had made it. "You really should eat more. You're far too skinny."

"But I…" Kisa inspected the sandwich and sighed. "Yes, ma'am."

"You too." Mrs. Claus picked up a platter of sweets that had been sitting on an end table and handed them to Yuki. "Whatever you don't eat is going to Dancer, so don't feel too obligated."

"How come she gets cocoa and a sandwich while I get more cookies?" Yuki asked.

"She rescued a reindeer. You ruined my bedroom." Mrs. Claus patted Yuki's head condescendingly, then looked at Mike. "Shall we, dear?"

He nodded, doing his best to avoid eye contact with Yuki. The kitsune pouted but still grabbed a handful of cookies to eat.

They walked to a locked door along the far wall that Mrs.

Claus opened with a golden key. Behind the door was a stone staircase that spiraled down, and she picked up a lantern hanging from a hook by the door. It ignited by itself, casting a warm glow over the stairs.

"Where are we going?" he asked.

Mrs. Claus smiled and shut the door behind them. "You'll see. This is perhaps the most important place in the North Pole. Follow me."

The stairs were long enough for Mike to dread the inevitable climb back up. It also didn't help that the narrow steps had him turning his feet, which made the oversize slippers shift as if they were going to fall off. Clearly whoever was in charge of Santa's magical wardrobe had taken the day off when it came to footwear.

Several more minutes passed before they came to the bottom. Mrs. Claus paused before a pair of thick wooden doors held together with iron casings. She turned to face Mike, her features suddenly hard.

"Of the many things I show and tell you, the contents of this room must remain a secret from your friends." She placed a hand hesitantly on one of the large rings. Mike watched as silver-and-red tendrils wafted from the door and curled around her, then flashed out of existence. Mrs. Claus didn't seem to notice.

"I can't guarantee that," he told her. "Not without knowing what's inside."

She smirked. "I don't think you understand. You aren't being given a choice in the matter. Much like your beloved geas, the protective magic of this place has rules. Outside this room, the North Pole is built by the love and beliefs of children. Naturally, this effect extends to their adult counterparts, hence my current predicament." She fidgeted with the lace along her collar. "But this room? This is the center of it all, unaffected by whatever happens out there. We have many things to discuss, but nary a word about this place in particular shall ever slip past your lips. Should someone read your mind, the memory of this place shall drift away from you like a dream until their presence is gone."

Mike regarded Mrs. Claus. "If this room is so important, then why show it to me?"

"If my husband weren't on the verge of dissolution, we wouldn't even be having this conversation." She pulled on one of the rings, and Mike's ears popped. He rubbed at them while both doors opened simultaneously as if by magic. Golden light streamed from the room, and he followed her inside, squinting in an attempt to make anything out.

The light vanished, and he found himself standing at the bottom of a large metallic cylinder that stretched nearly a hundred feet into the air in the center of a gigantic room. Adorned with red, gold, and silver ribbon in a spiraling pattern, the cylinder was topped with a sphere made of light that pulsed gently.

"What am I looking at?" Mike noticed that a structure had been built at the base of the cylinder. Moving closer, he saw that it was a circle with numbers along the edge that counted up to 360.

"Welcome to the North Pole, Caretaker." Mrs. Claus shut the door behind them and hung her lantern on a nearby hook. The glow from the lantern expanded dramatically, revealing that the room containing the cylinder was spherical in shape. Several floors overlooked the center of the room, and he could see bookshelves, workbenches, and a ton of tools lying about. Everything looked old, as if he had stepped into a forgotten museum.

"Wow." Mike walked toward the pole, but Mrs. Claus grabbed him by the hand.

"No closer," she warned just as the sphere of light on top of the pole expanded. It swallowed most of the empty space in the room and formed into a replica of the Earth that spun around the cylinder. Green-and-red lights danced along the surface of the sphere, stretching all the way down to the South Pole. All along the planet, sparkling lights dotted the landscape.

"So this is where you can see everything," he said, then found a nearby stool to sit on. A sparkling light hovering over the east coast of Russia drew his attention. "What's that?"

"It's the sleigh. I have no idea what it's doing there but am under the impression that someone is using it to deliver toys. Look." She pointed at the base of the North Pole, which looked as if it had filled with fluid along the outside. "When those gifts get delivered, it replenishes the magic used to allow Santa to move around outside of time. The spell itself is incredibly powerful. It took Santa over a century to unlock its true potential. I was originally thinking of retrieving the sleigh and hiding It here, but the Krampus likely wants it for his own nefarious purpose. If they are delivering presents, it may be best to let them continue doing so."

Mike nodded. It was clear that the Krampus had some sort of plan, but they didn't know what. Maybe that was something worth looking into. If they could figure out what the demon was going to do, it might give them insight into how they could stop him.

"You should know that I have sent Christmas Present and Dancer to assist with protecting the sleigh. It looks like they are almost there." Mrs. Claus pointed to a pair of lights that were moving toward the sleigh. "I'm not sure why they left the safety of your home, but that's something we can worry about later."

"I'm sure Lily will be thrilled for the extra help, especially because I bet that Death conned her into it." He pictured her reaction to the Amazonian spirit and grinned. "Death will be upset that Santa himself didn't show up."

"Perhaps." Mrs. Claus found a seat of her own and sat next to him. "This is where everything began. For Saint Nicholas, anyway. You see, once upon a time, he was called to the bitter cold of the North. The trip nearly killed him, but the call was strong. He found a doorway buried in the snow, and it brought him here."

"Who built this place?" he asked.

"The Architect. It was the last of its kind that was built but the first one of its kind on Earth."

"That doesn't make sense," Mike said, turning toward her, his mind racing. Was this place part of the great game? "From what I understand, my house was built maybe two centuries ago, and Santa has been around way longer. There's no way this place was created last."

She laughed, her eyes actually twinkling in the lights of the magical globe. "Oh, I guarantee it was. You see, the Architect didn't get their title because they could design magical homes that are merely larger on the inside. This place was their magnum opus, the hardest of them all to build. Woven together out of stone, wood, and the very fabric of time itself, it sent itself back centuries once it was completed. Honestly, I wouldn't think about it too much. Anyway, the spot we now sit is where Saint Nicholas met the First Elf."

"The First Elf? Who was that?"

"The guardian of this place, much like your beloved nymph." Mrs. Claus smiled. "When you became a player in the game, they called you Caretaker. And when my husband joined, they called him Claus."

Mike felt the breath leave his body. "Santa is part of the great game? I have so many questions!"

Mrs. Claus frowned. "I'm afraid I can't tell you too much about the game itself. There are certain rules that have to be followed when it comes to the game's secrets."

"But players don't have to follow those rules, right?" He remembered the shadow's claim about players in the game speaking with one another on a regular basis. "Santa can tell me whatever I need to know once I find him, right?"

She shook her head and took his hand. When she

squeezed, he realized just how cold her fingers were. Looking up into her eyes, he saw that she looked older than he remembered. Was it a trick of the light, or…

"If he were still a player, then yes. But he died a long time ago."

Confused, Mike pulled his hand from hers. "But aren't we here to save him from the Krampus?"

Mrs. Claus took a deep breath and looked at the North Pole inside the hovering globe made of light. With a heavy sigh, she patted Mike on the leg and tilted her head in his direction to look over the top of her glasses at him.

"Immortality comes with a price, my child. Allow me to share with you the price my husband paid so many years ago." She turned to face him, straightening the hem of her nightie. "I've heard that a nymph awaited you when you moved into your home. When Nicholas first came to the North Pole, he found a very different creature waiting down here for him. We call it the First Elf but only as a sign of respect. You see, it was definitely not an elf. In fact, it wasn't even of this world."

"Was it the Krampus?" Mike asked, suddenly breathless.

"What? No. You're getting ahead of yourself, stop that." She dismissed further questions with a wave of her hand. "It was a being from outside time and space, an amorphic entity that had been chained here to protect the most powerful property devised by the Architect. To look upon it was to risk madness, and if not for my husband's sturdy resolve, it would have consumed him."

"Wait, you mean…" Mike held his hands up in apology. "Sorry, please continue."

There was a twinkle in the older woman's eye as she nodded.

"This time, I believe your guess is right," she told him. "They've been called many things over the years, these cosmic entities. Ancient ones, eldritch beings, abominations, doesn't matter. The guardian of this place was the only thing capable of protecting it, and my husband accomplished the impossible."

Mike almost asked if Santa fucked it but knew better.

"They became best friends, as close as brothers," Mrs. Claus said wistfully, her eyes back on the map of Earth. "And that's where all this trouble started."

THE MIRROR ROOM WAS HIDDEN DEEP BENEATH THE WORKSHOP at the end of a long stone tunnel. Glyphs came to life and burned with harmless flames as Jack hovered down the long hallway, her arms wrapped around her stomach. The trip was always disorienting, but she had no idea why. Nausea, dizziness, and even a touch of vertigo assailed her senses until she entered the room where the mirror was stored.

Santa was waiting for her, his hands pressed against the glass. He smiled as if happy to see her.

"Quit the bullshit," she told him. The silver frame of the mirror melded into the marble floor, making it look like the mirror had sprouted up from the ground. The room had a harmless fog that clung to the circular walls. It would sometimes descend and cover the floor, but it stayed away from Jack, as if afraid. "There's no way you're happy to see me."

Santa shrugged, then took his hands off the glass. He didn't say anything to her, nor did he attempt to. Instead, he pulled a seat from somewhere outside the mirror's edge and set it down. With a wink, he sat in the chair and patted his knee, as if to invite Jack to sit and tell him what she wanted for Christmas.

She ignored him, pacing the room as she gathered her thoughts. She had come down here when the Krampus had been trapped inside the mirror, the demon speaking to her telepathically. Back then, the room had felt ominous, like a prison. The fog was constantly drifting across the mirror, sometimes obscuring the Krampus as he'd pressed himself against the glass.

It was here that the Krampus had given her the recipe for the potion she had given to Santa. Grýla had provided her the ingredients, gathered by her kin and the Yule Cat. It had been a simple matter to get one of the elves to slip it to him, but Jack hadn't seen what happened next. The Krampus had assured her that it would weaken Santa enough that the demon could escape, but that was all she knew.

"So do you have anything to say for yourself?" Jack moved in front of the mirror and frowned. Santa just shook his head. "Really? The Krampus has taken over the North Pole, subjected your elves, corrupted your reindeer. It's only a matter of time before he…does whatever it is he needs to do to your wife. Christmas belongs to him now, which means you're done, gone, finished! And you really have nothing to say?"

Santa shrugged, then pulled a flask from beneath his beard. Those white cotton curls of his twisted about briefly, as if they had a life of their own. Santa took a swig from the flask, which Jack assumed was eggnog. He licked his lips and held the flask toward Jack.

"You're inside a mirror," she told him, stepping toward him. "Even if I wanted some, I couldn't take it."

Santa scooted his chair closer to the glass and held the eggnog out again. Jack squinted at him, suddenly wondering why she had even come down here. It had originally been to speak with Santa, to maybe come to terms with the things she had done or figure out what it was she was supposed to do next. The humans were fond of the term *digging your own grave*, and she felt like she only now truly understood the implications.

"Why do you act like you don't care?" When she spoke, her breath billowed out from her in a fog. "He took everything from you. I helped him. Do you know that? I'm the reason you're in there and he's out here."

Santa wiggled the eggnog and raised an eyebrow. He didn't look disturbed in the slightest, that fat, jolly bastard. It was starting to snow in the mirror room, and frost formed along the edges of the mirror, causing it to blend in with the background.

"That's it, isn't it? You knew this would happen, and you didn't care." Jack shook her head violently, her hair bobbing along her shoulders. "I've always wondered, you know? Always so carefree, nothing ever rattled you. It's why the Krampus needed me. He said you wouldn't be able to see into my mind, but now I wonder if you wanted this, if you knew what I was up to."

Santa nodded.

"Seriously? What the fuck?!" Jack stepped toward the mirror and slapped her palms against the glass. "You knew this would happen and you didn't try to stop it? Your elves are suffering up there right now. Why would you abandon them? He's taking Christmas from them, taking it from all the children in the world, and you just let him have it? How could you do this to them?"

Angry, she slammed her fist against the glass, suddenly aware of how warm it felt. Letting out a howl of rage, she tried to smash the mirror with her fists, surprised at its strength. Determined, she landed on the ground and punched the glass as hard as she could, then screamed in rage when it didn't shatter.

"What is wrong with you?" she cried as she struck the glass over and over. "You knew they would suffer. You knew I would suffer! Why would you let something like this happen!" Groaning, she pressed her forehead against the glass, frozen tears shattering on the hard ground below her.

The breath was stolen from her body as a warm surge shot through her feet. She tried to move, but her body was held in place by an energy that vibrated through her body, and she struggled to free herself.

"What are you doing? You tricked me!" She yanked her body away from the mirror and fell backward onto her butt. "You asshole, I'm glad you're trapped in there! I hope you rot and that the Krampus fucks your—"

Santa was no longer in the mirror. In his place, a woman now stood. She was taller than Jack with much fuller features. Her brow was adorned with a simple gold crown, and thick auburn curls fell across broad shoulders atop a full figure. Around her throat was a necklace made of gold and inlaid with amber. A solitary gemstone in the middle pulsed with light, calling attention to an impressive amount of cleavage.

The woman lifted her head to look down her nose at Jack.

She wore a simple dressing gown, as if she had just been awoken. There was a fierceness to her that was both familiar and a little frightening.

"Who…who are you?" Jack put her hand against the glass and was surprised when the woman did the same. There was a judgment in the woman's gaze that Jack didn't like, followed by pain in the back of her skull. Groaning, she stepped away from the mirror and rubbed her eyes, expecting to see Santa once more.

The woman remained, her arms crossed as if she was waiting for Jack to do something.

"Where's Santa? What do you want?" Frustrated, Jack moved toward the glass but fell down when the pain returned. Images poured into her mind, confusing scenes of summertime and swimming in the ocean. There were moments with family, scenes of war, and long nights with a man covered in scars.

"Stop. Stop it!" She cast her hand out, summoning a powerful frost that crawled across the mirror, blocking her view. In agony, Jack tried to fly out of the room but crashed into the fog-covered wall instead.

"No. No!" Stumbling in panic, she eventually found the exit and rocketed down the hallway, crashing against the walls while the images chased her. Anger, grief, and mourning flooded her mind as she flew through the long hallways of the workshop, eventually bursting through the large wooden doors and disappearing into the blizzard outside.

Even there, the images found her. It felt like someone else was inside her mind, shoving memories into place. She remembered the sea, riding pigs, fighting a witch. All she could do was howl along with the wind as she was filled with scattered thoughts.

Who are you? The voice in her head demanded an answer, and she somehow knew it was the woman from the mirror. The tone was commanding, and Jack clutched her head and cried out in shock. *Where are we? What's happened to us?*

"Us?" Jack blinked, her eyes unseeing in the storm. It was a whiteout, a moment when all the available light was gobbled up by the fury of the storm.

Yes, us. Her tone was derisive. *Where is this place?*

Jack pressed her hands into her temples so hard that her knuckles cracked. Her whole body was encased in frost as she willed the cold into her head in an effort to drive out the intruder. The cold permeated her being as her temperature dropped, well below freezing.

"Get out of my head," she whispered, her limbs becoming stiff as ice crawled along the outside of her flesh. It wasn't until she flew above the storm that the commanding voice finally vanished, leaving her alone beneath the northern lights with her thoughts.

She gazed at the hovering lights as they clung to the stratosphere like melting wax. It felt like they were watching her, and she didn't know why.

"What's happening to me?" she whispered, the storm beneath her slowly burying the North Pole.

Mike stared at the North Pole, his mind whirring. Mrs. Claus had told him the whole story about how Nicholas and the First Elf had met and how the two of them had become essentially inseparable.

When he and Naia had first met, she had swapped a part of her soul with a piece of his. This had enabled her to grant him a small portion of her power and to bind the house to him. He had become the Caretaker that day, not knowing that he had also become part of a mysterious game that played in the background of his everyday life. With Naia being a nymph, it was natural that the two of them had become lovers as well. It was the foundation for his magic, one that persisted to this day.

The being lying in wait had been some type of an elder god, one captured and tamed by the Architect. It didn't have emotions or thoughts comprehensible by mortals. Its primary instruction had been to bond with the first worthy soul who came to the North Pole. Nicholas had been worthy enough, and his desire to create toys for children and bring happiness to families had been enough to shape the creature into the First Elf.

When Mike died, someone else would inherit the house. It was supposed to be Beth or Dana, but they wouldn't know until it actually happened. There was no plan for permanence, nor did he desire immortality like his predecessor. He had gotten a peek of the other side and knew that someone would be waiting there when his time was up.

To a creature with no beginning or end, like the First Elf, death was simply an obstacle to be surmounted.

"So when Saint Nicholas died, the First Elf brought him here and they…what, combined? Merged?"

Mrs. Claus shrugged. "I don't know that there's a proper word for it. The corpse of Saint Nicholas was reanimated using the body of the First Elf. That was how Santa Claus the legend was born. By doing this, he was both player and guardian and therefore neither. He never had aspirations for the game itself and chose to ignore the others unless they started trouble. But he was officially the first player to find a way to stand outside the game by becoming one of the pieces inside it."

"Fitting, considering the First Elf's origin." He thought back to falling into Baba Yaga's trap, to the chunk of missing time while trying to destroy the piece of an Ancient One. Dana had encountered one in the flesh and been tossed back in time by a week. They were powerful beings, impossible to understand. "So what happened next?"

Mrs. Claus sighed. "That's when Santa became bound by the rules. He was a mortal soul in an immortal body. Stories of the First Elf had persisted, but now tales of little helpers caused the first generation of elves to appear here. They were sloppy and inefficient, but that human part of him was able to tweak the details. As more people believed, his powers grew."

"So all the elves are clones of him or something?"

Mrs. Claus shook her head. "It would be easier to think of them as nail clippings or beard stubble. In fact, I save the trimmings from his yearly haircut in a box in the closet, then plant them outside when the sun rises in the summer. Each year, those tiny pieces of him grow into new elves to replace those we've lost in the workshop. Some die of natural causes, others..." She shook her head. "Accidents happen, I'm afraid."

"Since they used to be part of him, is that why they're so susceptible to...well, everything?"

"That is exactly correct. We call it naughty sickness, but it isn't just naughty behavior." She tugged at the nightie, which looked shorter than it used to. "Every living being up here at the North Pole is part of Santa."

"Wait, that would mean you..." He looked at the North Pole, then back at Mrs. Claus. "You're a part of him?"

She nodded. "I was born into this world as an old woman, ready to serve the whims of my husband. My sense of self is defined by how I am seen. The lingerie is annoying, but I don't mind how much younger I look these days." She patted her cheeks. "When I was first created, I was in my nineties and very wrinkly."

He agreed with her assessment but knew to keep his thoughts to himself.

"So does that mean the Krampus is also part of Santa?"

Mrs. Claus made a contemplative face, then stood. "Come. I want to show you something."

Curious, he rose and followed her. They walked around the perimeter of the room until they were on the other side of the pole. The walls were covered with thick shelves full of tools, and Mrs. Claus stuck her arm in a gap between a pair of columns. There was an audible click, and she grabbed onto the edge of a shelf.

"Help me," she said, then pulled. Mike grabbed the edge and helped, which caused the entire shelf to open like a giant door. Behind it was a cavern carved into the ground, and Mike summoned a pair of spiders to light the way.

"Allow me," he said, sending the spiders forward.

"That's not something I've seen before." She chuckled and took him by the hand. There was a special warmth in the way she held his fingers, and the memory of his mother reading to him surfaced yet again. Was this what a mother's love felt like? It wasn't something he knew as an adult, and he wasn't surprised by how he craved it. "Mind your step. It's been ages since anyone has come down here."

They walked together while the temperature plummeted. At some point, Mrs. Claus's lingerie thickened into a sweater dress with leggings, and finally turned into a coat. Mike was already getting cold and hoped that they were almost at their destination.

The cave widened into a massive cavern with soot-lined walls and giant stalactites. Patches of ice on the walls glistened in the soft glow of the spiders, but Mike's attention was on what he had assumed were piles of rubble on the ground.

They were bones. Massive piles, over ten feet high and scattered wide. The skull he was looking at was easily four feet tall.

"When Santa Claus was born, it sent a ripple out into the world." Mrs. Claus pulled off the scarf that had appeared on her body and wrapped it around Mike's neck. "You see, it was already difficult enough for Nicholas and the First Elf to fight off the local cryptids, but when word got around that Nicholas had died, everyone thought it was fair game. Others like you came to meet with him, thinking he had unlocked a new portion of the game."

"Had he?" Mike asked.

Mrs. Claus shrugged. "If so, he never mentioned it to me. All he's ever wanted was to bring joy on Christmas Day, so that's what he became. Most of the other players decided there was nothing of value to them so didn't pursue the issue. Some of them, though, decided it was time to add the North Pole to their collection. Bloody wars were fought on the arctic tundra, and the elves even became warriors for a time. Santa himself became quite fierce during those battles, but a new problem surfaced."

"He's Santa." Mike broke away from Mrs. Claus to inspect one of the bone piles. "He's not meant to be a warrior."

"Correct. Each battle was changing him, and not for the better. You see, he may have become something new and vastly different, but still had a very human soul. Where the First Elf saw these incursions as an annoyance, Nicholas took them personally. A side of him emerged during these fights that was both terrible and frightening, a true demon in every sense of the word. But it wasn't until someone sent the last remaining frost giants here that he finally succumbed to his inner darkness."

Mike shivered, thinking back to his own brush with power. Some nights, he would dream about having Leeds pinned beneath his body, feeling that rush of destructive power hovering over both of them, just begging to be released.

He flexed his right hand, feeling the slight twinge in his forearm as his muscles flexed. If that magic had been capable of transforming him, what would he have become?

"So I'm guessing this is the reason the Krampus was created, then." He waved his hand out at the frozen remains. "To be the warrior Santa couldn't be, to fight all these assholes."

"You're so close, Caretaker, yet so far. In matters of magic, even a kernel of untruth can become your undoing." Mrs. Claus moved to his side and took him by the hand. When he turned to face her, he could see shimmering tears hiding in her eyes.

"This is indeed the birthplace of the Krampus," she told him. "And when he came into this world, he was a force to be reckoned with. But he was not created by the belief of a child, nor on a whim. A very human soul still resides at the core of my dear husband, and a piece of that soul is in myself, the elves, and anything else that has been created here. The Krampus is a being made of that darkness that resides in all of us, and that darkness can only surface when a good man is pushed past his breaking point."

Mike puzzled over her words, still stuck on what she meant when she'd said he was wrong. If everyone else was just a part of Santa, then that would mean the Krampus himself was no different from them. Yet Mrs. Claus kept making the point that he wasn't like the others, which made no sense.

Unless…

He looked at the nearby bones and could easily make out the claw marks in them. Or maybe they were bite marks? He couldn't be sure. In fact, what he had taken for ice now appeared to be a pebbled gray flesh that clung to the bones of the dead. These things hadn't been a part of Santa; that was for sure.

"Wait." Understanding dawned on him, and he turned back toward Mrs. Claus, his mouth open in shock. "He's…"

Mrs. Claus nodded. "The Krampus isn't some stray piece of Santa, created to fight his battles. Here, in this place, he emerged from within and waged a bloody campaign almost completely by himself. Only a few of his elves survived to pass along the truth, but they were all sworn to secrecy. I share it with you now in the hopes that you can somehow do the impossible."

Mike's mouth dried out, and he imagined he looked like a fish out of water. It was hard to reconcile the truth with what he currently knew, but he was no stranger to the darkness within. Understanding how it had happened didn't help with the actual problem at hand.

Santa and the Krampus were the same person, and Mike had no idea how to fix it.

THE SLEIGH WAS FLYING OVER VLADIVOSTOK, RUSSIA, WHEN Lily awoke. She had fallen asleep somewhere over the ocean and assumed they were in Vladivostok, anyway. She hadn't visited in almost a hundred years, so it looked different. However, it had been the next big destination on the list. Wiping drool from her lips, she contemplated the city below. Many of the buildings were dark, but there were still lights on in plenty of apartments.

Looking over at Death, she saw that the reaper was contemplating her with a finger on his chin.

"Not a word to anyone," she demanded, then adjusted her hat. Ever since she had started falling asleep and having dreams, she had been determined to keep it a secret. It wasn't so much that she was worried the others would think less of her. Instead, it was the fear of discovery, of everyone knowing a tiny piece of Mike's soul lived within her.

Sure, the others had a similar situation, but hers was special. She was a demon, darned to all eternity. What if they decided she wasn't a hospitable host for it? Would they try to take it away from her? What if Naia asked her to return it? The succubus wasn't even certain if she could, but since the nymph was technically one of her masters, she would have to make the attempt.

Losing that piece of Mike would devastate her; she could admit that. She didn't begrudge him for having so many people in his life. In fact, it made her happy. He had surrounded himself with people who not only loved him for who he was but treated one another as family. Lily had more friends right now than the rest of her centuries combined. Even though she often pushed them away, they were always ready to embrace and accept her when she returned.

With Mike central to the family, it meant he didn't always have time to spend with everyone. Lily could spend all the time she wanted with that piece of him. It meant that as long as he lived, she would never have to be alone.

"That sounds like a pretty big favor," Death replied. "Maybe I shall add it to the list. I've been doing all the deliveries for the last nine hours."

"Fudge your favors, how many do you still owe me?" The trip to William's house hadn't been the last time she had played Santa. By her current count, she had done so at over a hundred houses. Some were easy, like the little girl in China who'd wanted Santa to read her a book. Others had been harder, and her belly was full of more than a couple of souls as a result. Some children had problems that only a dead adult could fix, and that was a gift she would gladly deliver.

"One hundred and forty-two," Death informed her. "Since you have banked so many, I believe I will count this as two favors."

"Ugh, suck my stocking." She adjusted her hat. The darned thing couldn't be removed but was easy enough to reposition. Her hips bumped Ticktock, still disguised as a large gift. "Maybe the toaster should start helping."

"He is too shy." Death patted the box. "And I'm worried about how many cookies I've fed him. Cerberus stopped eating them a while ago, and they are much larger than Ticktock."

"This one could close down a buffet." She knocked on the side of the box. "You sure you don't wanna help?"

A tiny hand popped free from beneath the ribbon on top. It had three fingers, two of which folded in to leave just the middle remaining.

"Sassy little appliance." She smacked the box, then stood and yawned. "But a deal's a deal. How does the workload look for here?"

"Another day, another dollar." Santa Death held up the list. "It would appear that we have no personal visits to make, so you won't have to worry about how big your butt gets."

"Ha ha," she replied sarcastically. During one of her Santa stops, she had complained that her bottom might get stuck because of how many times she made it bigger. She often forgot how literal Death could be. "Now give me my darned cocoa."

Death held out the thermos. "I daresay this trip would be intolerable without this delightful beverage. I may demand the recipe when we finally meet Santa."

"Yeah, about that. I'm fairly certain the big guy is dead."

Death nearly dropped the thermos. "How dare you!"

"Look, I'm not trying to be that person, but we've been

out here, what? Two, maybe three weeks? If Mike and everyone else had gotten things sorted, don't you think the big guy would be here already?"

"For your information, it's been roughly three months."

"Three fudging months?" Lily stood, nearly toppling over the edge of the sleigh. It rocked back and forth, causing Cerberus to look back at them.

"I started counting the seconds once we left. In fact, I started counting once I learned how to! It's quite remarkable, really, hearing all these different numbers in my head. I hope to hear them all someday. My favorite numbers have fours in them."

She grabbed Death by the beard and pulled him close to her face. "How is three months even possible? There's no way it's..." Her brain felt like it was unraveling as she pondered the time spent in the sleigh. It was no different from the time compression in the Dreamscape, only reversed. What had felt like no more than a couple of weeks was now expanding in her mind, filling in the gaps where very little had happened.

There was also the possibility that Death was not a reliable timekeeper.

"Indeed. Frankly, I am more than a little concerned." Death poured some cocoa out for Lily, then handed her a cup. "Surely Mike Radley will be worried about us. Perhaps he has already solved the problem and has vacated the time lock so he doesn't have to wait for us to finish."

"There's no way Romeo would do such a thing. And if he did, you bet your bottom I would call him out for not coming down here to help us." She stared at the port city below. The stars were reflected in the still water around it, the streets and rooftops blanketed in a couple of feet of snow.

"And you aren't worried in the slightest about Mike Radley? Perhaps I should suggest that he is dead too. See how you like it."

She shook her head. The two of them had just finished a

long chat in the Dreamscape; there was no way he was dead if his soul was still in there. "If he's in trouble, that's his own darned fault." *Not that I could reach him if he was*, she thought. "I'm starting to think this whole thing was a bad idea."

"Bringing children joy is never a bad idea." Death tugged at the reins and guided Cerberus down to the streets below. When the sleigh landed, it glided softly over the snow as they dodged cars frozen in time. "This has been quite the enjoyable experience for me."

"That makes one of us…for now," she begrudgingly added. While she was disgruntled, the trip had definitely contained some highlights. "Still, three months? How much farther do we have to go?"

Death pondered his scroll, then rolled it up. "It is better that you don't think about it."

"Fudge." Lily sat back and crossed her arms. "I hate this."

"Never fear. I'm sure that…" Death paused, his eyes on a nearby alleyway.

"What's wrong?" Lily stood and squinted. Her night vision may as well be day vision, but she didn't see anything. The wind had blown some snow off the ground and into the alleyway, creating a time-frozen smoke-screen effect, but she saw nothing of concern within it.

"Perhaps it was my imagination, but I doubt it." The sleigh coasted to a stop outside an apartment complex. "I think it would do you good to keep a very good eye on the street while I am inside making deliveries."

"Agreed." She watched as Death stuck his hand in Santa's bag and withdrew a smaller bag that functioned like the big one. They had discovered this trick sometime after Australia, which had sped things up immensely through Japan and the east coast of China.

Cerberus snorted, sending a small jet of fire from one of her heads, then sniffed the ground. The still world suddenly felt hostile, but Lily couldn't place where or why. The silent city looked like the interior of a frozen snow globe, the snow suspended in place all around her. A lone man was paused midstride as he crossed the street, his eyes fixed on the only car driving around at this hour. Death disappeared into the building, his body turning into golden fog as he squeezed beneath the front door.

A deep growling sound came from above. Lily looked up to see the Yule Cat watching them from atop the apartment complex. He let out a hiss and a growl but kept his distance from the sleigh. Cerberus turned her attention upward, letting out a trio of growls.

"You actually found us. I'm impressed." Lily tried to flip the cat off, but her ring finger kept popping up instead of the middle. "Why don't you come down here and we'll make it a Christmas threesome, see what a pair of…" She tried to force her mouth to say the b-word but couldn't. "You know what? Let's come to an understanding. You stay away from me and I won't effing neuter you, okay?"

The Yule Cat disappeared from view, but Lily could see his dark shadow as he leaped across the building tops. If the cat was here, those lumpy little mother-lovers must be around as well.

"Death? Hey, Death!" She scanned the building he had wandered into, hoping to see movement. "We've got a situation out here!"

A small dark shape shot across the street and disappeared beneath a parked car. Cerberus growled at the vehicle, then wandered over to sniff at the ground around it. The reins elongated to allow the hellhound to safely maneuver the street without dragging the sleigh.

"It might not be a bad idea to take it up for a bit," Lily mumbled, then picked up the reins and cracked them. Cerberus snorted and left the car behind as she towed the sleigh off the ground and took them into the sky. Once they were several hundred feet in the air, Lily looked away from Ticktock.

"I need to be able to see Death," she said. There was a popping sound, and she turned around to see that the mimic was now an elaborate spotting scope that had been mounted to the side of the sleigh.

"Perfect." She put her eye to the lens, and Ticktock oriented itself so it was pointed at the building Death had gone inside. From up here, she could see the Yule Cat shifting around, trying to hide his mass between a pair of buildings. The ugly trolls from earlier were already on the rooftop and were turning into mist to squeeze into the vents.

"Ah, fiddlesticks." They were high enough up that the cat couldn't reach them, but Death was trapped. Though they couldn't hurt him, they could detain him indefinitely. She had already spent months in this Hallmark movie from hell. She wasn't about to let them abduct the only person who would help her deliver the presents.

"Toaster, you're in charge. Cerberus? Wait for my signal." She tossed the reins over the telescope, knowing Ticktock would transform into something more suited for holding them. With a sigh of displeasure, she threw herself off the side of the sleigh and dove toward the roof from above. The wind rushed through her hair, snowflakes smashing against her face and blinding her as she plummeted toward the roof. At the last moment, she spread her wings wide.

The Yule Cat leaped into the air from behind the building, claws outstretched in an attempt to grab her. Still blinded by the snow, Lily grunted as she was knocked off course and slammed into the side of a nearby building. Sulfurous clouds burst from her body as she gritted her teeth, forcing herself to stay in one piece. Dangling from a fire escape by her tail, she sneered at the cat as it growled at her from above.

"Bet you're real proud of yourself, you sack of trash." She unhooked her tail as the cat pounced, dropping out of reach. Expanding her wings, she shot toward a window that had been cracked open. A man in his forties in a knit cap stood behind the glass, a cigarette in one hand and a time-frozen cloud of smoke hovering in front of his face. When she reached the window, the world distorted around her, allowing her to pass through the narrow opening as a sparkling mist.

She crashed hard, her bottom scraping against splintered floorboards as she tumbled through a hallway littered with boxes. Behind her, the Yule Cat pressed his face against the window, golden eyes staring daggers at her.

"Yeah, that's right." She flipped the cat off, then groaned when her ring finger popped up again. "Can't even express myself properly," she grumbled, climbing to her feet. At least she was in the building now.

Up above, she heard a loud yell, followed by a bang.

"That's my cue." Scrambling to her feet, she walked down the hall until she found a stairwell, then ascended. Up above, Death was shouting. She could hear the heavy footsteps of nearly a dozen attackers, followed by that crunchy language they spoke. She wondered if it was Icelandic. She had never eaten the soul of an Icelander, which was the fastest way for her to assimilate a language.

She was near the next floor when she saw one of the trolls walk in front of her. This one was trying to run with a large wooden spoon in its mouth. Sensing movement, it turned toward Lily just as she grabbed it by the throat and tossed it down the stairwell. It cried out as it fell, letting out a groan on impact that lasted several seconds.

"Darn. Was really hoping that would kill you." Lily turned her attention back to the sounds of struggle. The stairwell was in the corner of the building, so she had to go down the hallway and turn before she could see another troll. They were gathered outside a doorway decorated in crepe paper that had been cut into trees and snowflakes. Every few moments, one would turn into mist and slip underneath the door.

Growling, Lily ran at them, her wings collapsing into her back while horns sprouted on her forehead. She used her horns to toss aside a troll wearing a pot on its head, then snapped a kick at another. They scattered, running away from her just as the door opened and Death emerged.

"They're trying to take the bag," Death gasped, then handed it over to Lily. At least three trolls were clutching the reaper's robes, trying to pull him down to the ground.

"I've got it." Lily took the bag, kicked a troll away from her feet, then ran back toward the stairwell. It occurred to her that the trolls probably didn't realize this wasn't Santa's sack but a smaller version. The trolls fighting Death let go of him and gave chase. Lily was back at the stairwell when she saw the one she had tossed over the side wheezing at the top. Its eyes widened in terror as she grabbed it by the hair and sent it plummeting down the stairwell once more.

"Gotta go up," she muttered, climbing the stairs. Some of the smarter trolls turned into that eerie green mist and floated up the stairwell after her, re-forming at the top of the stairs. She fought through them, then ran down the hallway. It occurred to her that she didn't have an actual plan. There was no way to deliver gifts, and if there was a way to kill the trolls, she didn't know what it was.

Movement caught her eye, and she looked out the window just as the Yule Cat swatted the window. Startled by the cat's sudden appearance, Lily tripped and slid across the floor, clutching the bag to her chest. The trolls, who had been right behind her, swarmed across her like insects, punching and biting.

"Ow, darn it!" She tried to swat one away, but the little monster bit down on her hand so hard that bones cracked. Howling in pain, she twisted her head toward the troll and caught it in the eye with one of her horns. The creature cried out and rolled away, clutching at its face. Another took its place, and Lily huddled over the bag, pain racking her limbs as the trolls tried to rip her apart.

There was a metallic crack, and the trolls leaped away from her, hissing like snakes. They chattered in their mysterious language as Lily raised her head and saw Death standing over her, a bloodied metal bat in his hands.

"*I am here to hand out coal and beat some ass*!" he howled, his own shadow dancing wildly behind him. Off to the side, a mostly headless troll jerked, its limbs twitching like a dying bug. "*And I am all out of coal*!"

He swung again, and the trolls scattered, screaming in fright. The dying troll's body was already turning into a sickly green mist that sank into the floorboards.

"How come you get to say the a-word?" Lily groaned, using the wall to stand.

"Because you are just the helper," he replied, then slid his arm beneath her. He dropped the bat, which clattered to the ground. "I am quite cross with those little monsters. I didn't even get to deliver those presents."

"Where did you find the bat?" she asked.

"Behind someone's door. Most of these apartments have one. I assume the people here are on a team."

Lily laughed, then turned her attention outside. The Yule Cat was pawing at the glass, unable to harm the building.

"The sleigh is safe for now," she said. "Let's get the rest of these delivered and then figure out what happens next."

Between the two of them, they made quick work of the apartment complex. The trolls showed up on occasion but stayed well back when Death menaced them with another bat he had found. Lily wondered if they had actually killed that first troll or if it had re-formed elsewhere.

Every so often, she would take a peek outside to see if she could make out the sleigh. While it would normally be impossible to see it in the sky, it was almost as though she had a sixth sense about its location. She assumed this was a result of wearing the helper hat and was glad that she got at least some sort of trade-off for having the spice stripped from her vocabulary.

"I believe this was the last one," Death said shortly after squeezing out of a keyhole. Sparkling lights hovered around him, then faded from view as he contemplated his list. "Yes, correct, we are all done. Now we just have to get back to the sled."

"Roof or ground?" she asked, looking outside. "If we go roof, we'll probably have to deal with that stupid cat sneaking up on us from between buildings. Stupid fudger is quick. If we choose ground, it's the trolls and the cat, but we'll have more room to get away."

"Hmm. I do wish I had a better sense of things like these." Death walked over to the nearest window and stared out into the city. "I suppose Cerberus could handle Jólakötturinn, and we can handle the trolls as long as we're quick about it. Would probably make more sense if we make a run for it and have Cerberus descend to pick us up. There is an open area a couple of blocks from here that would be perfect for it. That will keep the Yule Cat from pouncing on us from between buildings, and at least you will be able to fly up and take the reins."

"Sounds like a plan, bone man."

They moved down through the building. Lily only saw a single troll as they descended. It was waiting on the stairs, then let out a chirping sound like a strangled bird before squeezing its fat booty through the gap beneath a window. It became clear that this one had been the lookout, which meant the others were planning something.

"Hold up." Lily moved toward the window and looked outside. "I think they're preparing an ambush."

"Hmm." Death pulled the magic bag from where he had tucked it underneath his belt, then stuck his arm inside. When he pulled it out, he was clutching a Louisville Slugger with a cartoon sticker of the reaper himself on the fat end.

"Why don't you pull out a sword or something?"

"My dear Lily, this bag is for children's toys only. A sword is hardly a toy." He shook his head and moved behind her. "This way, I don't have to steal one from someone who lives here. There will already be questions about missing equipment at their next game."

"You are too pure." Lily patted Death on the cheek, then moved toward a nearby window that was on a different side of the building from where the troll had exited. "I say we squeeze through here and fall. If you can handle the landing, they won't expect us to come out of the side of the building. They're likely watching the front and back."

"This is a good plan. Nothing will go wrong." Death put his bony fingers on Lily's shoulder. "You are a good helper."

"You've jinxed us." She shook her head and moved toward the window. Just how smart were these troll things? Would they expect this? Or could she just launch herself into the sky and get back to the sleigh while Death made a run for it?

"Ho ho ho," she declared, then leaped through the half-inch opening, her body shrinking down.

Once on the other side of the glass, she unfolded her wings and drifted away from the building. She only made it about fifty feet before a barrage of snowballs from below blinded her and knocked her off course. Only seconds after takeoff, she crashed into the side of another building and tumbled into an alleyway, hitting a dumpster on the way down.

"*Fudge me in the beehive, owie!*" She rubbed at her bum and stumbled out into the street. "Death, where are—"

Lily went silent, her eyes on the once abandoned street. It

took her a moment to process the sea of faces with angry coal-black eyes that regarded her. They were packed in the streets, hundreds of them with wicked stick arms and vegetable noses.

Snowmen. Hundreds of them. The lower thirds of their bodies rotated as they approached, cruelty in their smiles.

"Lily!" She heard Death's voice from behind the newcomers. "They aren't very friendly!"

"Hit them in the snowballs!" she shouted, then charged forward, a halo of fire forming over her head. She would be darned if she let Frosty and his inbred family stop her here.

The snowmen pounced, their tree-branch hands surprisingly strong. Lily growled as her flesh was torn, but the snowmen were much softer than the trolls had been. She could easily dismember them, her tail capable of beheading one with a carefully aimed strike.

"Lily, run!" Death's voice carried a tone of panic. "And whatever you do, don't—"

His sudden silence worried her, so she leaped into the sky toward where she'd heard him last. The snowmen pulled off chunks of their own bodies and hurled them at her, but she folded her wings across her body and plunged back to earth like a missile and scattered them.

"They're just snowmen," she hollered at the grim reaper. "All you have to do is bust them up." To illustrate her point, she smashed a few apart. It was during this moment that she looked up and saw the Yule Cat monitoring from a nearby roof.

"Afraid of a little snow?" She ripped a snowman's head off and threw it up. The twenty-pound missile had already started crumbling the moment it left her hand, and she watched it fall around her like fine glitter. "Death, where are you?"

There was the loud crunching of snow, and a large tree-limb hand grabbed onto the side of a nearby building. Lily slid to a halt as a twenty-foot snowman came around the corner with a pair of bony legs hanging from its lower belly. It had clearly run Death over, trapping him in the snow of its own body.

Opening its mouth wide, the snowman lunged forward, arms outstretched. Lily backed away, unsure how she was supposed to fight such a thing. The creature was made of snow but so big that she couldn't properly hurt it. In fact, she suspected it may even be built from snowmen that had already been torn apart.

Turning to flee, she opened her wings and leaped into the air. A snowball nearly three feet in diameter slammed into her, causing her to crash hard onto the street. Fighting her way free of the icy prison, she rolled onto her back and coiled her tail up in front of her. A group of snowmen formed a circle around her, trapping her in place.

"*Fudge you!*" She whipped her tail around, smashing them apart, but they kept coming. Up above, the large snowman leaned down and grabbed her with a massive hand. She uselessly struggled to escape as it lifted her toward a frosty maw with icicle teeth.

"I'm gonna give you so much heartburn," she muttered. Her head was inside its mouth when she heard a zap, followed by a popping sound. The snowman tilted over, the arm holding Lily rising. She was surprised to see that a large portion of the snowman's head was now missing, and the street was covered in fresh slush. The snowman turned to reveal a massive creature made of lightning and fog prancing along the street and goring snowmen with its antlers.

It was a reindeer, or at least looked like one. The snowmen tried to capture it, but it easily smashed through them. It turned to face the giant snowman and snorted, then lowered its head to charge.

The reindeer blasted forward, creating a massive hole in the snowman. It collapsed in on itself, dropping Lily onto the street. She landed face-first on the street, her jaw breaking.

"Wha thu flem?" She re-formed the bones in her jaw and stood. The reindeer zipped around the road, exploding more of the snowmen. Nearby, Death's hand waved at her from inside a large mound of snow.

The snowmen were busy fighting with the reindeer, so she climbed onto the pile and grabbed Death's hand and pulled. The reaper emerged, his eye sockets packed with snow.

"Lily, I have gone blind!" He clawed at his skull, but she swatted his hands away. Using her fingers, she scooped out the snow until those tiny blue flames reappeared in the dark recesses beneath.

"You're fine," she told him, then knelt to retrieve Santa's smaller sack from the snow. It was pinned beneath the slush, but it slid free. "We need to go."

"I agree." He took the lead, and she followed. They were moving away from the reindeer, who now had the full attention of every snowman in the area.

The Yule Cat dropped down from above, nearly flattening Death with a massive paw. The cat hissed at them, baring his teeth.

"Mother of Santa," Lily muttered as the cat came for them. They split up, the Yule Cat going after her. She could smell the cat's breath as it washed over her, heavily scented with rotten fish. A claw caught the back of her leg, tearing open her thigh as she was dragged to the ground. Growling, the cat pinned her down and rolled her onto her back.

"Why is everyone trying to eat me today?" she bemoaned, then tried to stab the cat in the eye with her tail. The Yule Cat dodged, swatting her hard enough that she saw stars. Knocked silly, she felt the ground tremble beneath her before a giant figure appeared, smashing its knuckles into the cat's face.

Suddenly free, Lily stumbled to her feet and blinked her eyes. It was a giant woman in festive garb with a crown of laurels on her head, and she had the Yule Cat in a headlock.

"Get back to the sleigh," cried the giant. "Dancer and I will find you!"

Lily didn't need to be told twice. She unfolded her wings and ran along the street, spotting Death on top of a car. He was kicking at the trolls who had trapped him there.

Putting on a burst of speed, she leaped into the air and stuck out her hand. Death saw her and reached up, grabbing her by the wrist. The reaper was surprisingly light as they ascended, leaving the fight below.

From above, the sleigh dropped out of the clouds. Ticktock was in the form of an elaborate present, its metallic arms adorned with ribbons while holding the reins. Lily and Death crashed into the sleigh as it rose back into the sky, leaving Vladivostok behind. Once Lily was able to look over the side, she saw that the snowman army stretched for over a mile in each direction from where they had been. The reindeer was running for the city limits, followed by several hundred of them. The giant woman and the Yule Cat were still fighting, but it was hard to tell who was winning.

"What in the name of Christmas just happened?" Lily blinked in surprise, then turned to Death for answers.

"I am uncertain," he told her, then leaned back in his seat. "But you have made one thing abundantly clear to me this night."

"What's that?"

"I couldn't have asked for a better helper." Death took the reins from Ticktock. "Let us await our new friends over the water. Neither giant cats nor snowmen shall find us there."

Lily looked back one last time at Vladivostok. It occurred to her that there were still hundreds of presents to deliver, but until they addressed their new snowmen problem, they wouldn't be able to do it.

"Wait." Lily felt around her waist, then looked at Death. "Did...did you get the spare bag?" The last time she remembered having it was right before the Yule Cat had tried to eat her.

"Alas, I do not." Death shook his head sadly. "I am afraid those gifts are lost."

More miserable than ever, Lily pulled the hot cocoa thermos free of its holder and attempted to drown her sorrows with it.

UNRAVELING THREADS

A cold chill crept up Mike's leg, waking him. After his meeting with Mrs. Claus last night, it had taken him a long time to fall asleep. His mind had been preoccupied with the Krampus problem, which meant hours spent brainstorming ideas. There was a lot riding on whatever happened next, but he and the others had desperately needed a proper rest.

When he tried to pull his foot back under the blanket, he realized the comforter wasn't long enough. Lifting his head to see what had happened, he almost laughed. When he had gone to bed, it had just been him and Tink. Now, though, Kisa and Yuki were under the covers as well. The limited space under the blanket had been monopolized by Yuki, who had pulled the covers up over her head.

He sat up and yawned. They were all in Santa's bed, which Mrs. Claus had let them use on the condition that they didn't have sex in it. Though his sleep had been restful, there certainly hadn't been enough of it.

"Good morning." The voice made him jump, and he looked over to see Holly sitting in a nearby chair. The elf's feet didn't reach the ground, and she kicked her legs back and forth while nursing a mug of cocoa. "Sleep well?"

"I guess." He looked at the others, who were still slumbering soundly. He heard the occasional snort from Tink, who was sleeping off all the alcohol and sugar from the day before. "What are you doing here?"

"Elves don't sleep much," she told him. "Mrs. Claus wanted me to keep an eye on you."

"Why?"

"Make sure nothing happened to you. I don't think Christmas Past is coming back, but there's still one spirit unaccounted for."

"Ugh, right." Mike rubbed his face, remembering what Mrs. Claus had told him. The Christmas spirits were just another part of Santa, temporal beings that didn't obey the rules of time or space. He wasn't certain if Christmas Future was still lost in the ducts or had simply wandered off, but could stand to be more cautious about a possible encounter.

He doubted he could influence the final specter as he had Christmas Present.

Being careful not to wake anyone, he took a moment to slide free from the bed. He had to pull himself out of the top of the blankets, then move between the women until he was at the foot of the bed. Yawning, he went to pick up his pants and realized he was naked in front of Holly. Mrs. Claus hadn't provided him with any sort of underwear, so he had been sleeping naked.

"Oh wow, I'm sorry." He went to cover himself up but saw that the elf wasn't offended. In fact, her cheeks had turned bright red, her intense gaze on his body. She stared at his cock, her lips parted slightly as she breathed through her mouth.

"Don't worry about it," she responded, lifting her eyes to meet his. "I don't mind."

He almost asked her to turn around or something but

remembered that time she had watched him plow Kisa on top of the jukebox. If she wanted to look at him, he wasn't going to stop her.

"So what's the plan today?" he asked, pulling on his clothes.

"Breakfast first." Holly looked up at the window. "There's a terrible storm outside right now. We don't know if the Krampus is still lurking about."

"Right." Mrs. Claus had explained that the Krampus was afraid to face her directly over the fear of reverting to Santa. The process by which he transformed wasn't understood, but Mrs. Claus's relationship with her husband was so well defined that it would make perfect sense that she would be the one to pull him out of it.

That hadn't stopped the demon from banging on the front door for several hours. What the Krampus himself didn't know was that Mrs. Claus was afraid to face him because of his influence on the elves and reindeer. If they could be so easily corrupted, why not her? For now, the two were at a stalemate, and that gave Mike time to figure out a plan.

Finished with his clothes, he found the too large slippers and put them on. Before getting into bed to sleep, he had searched for something else to wear on his feet but had been unable to find any other footwear. Maybe shoes could be today's short-term goal.

Holly walked over to the door and waited. He looked at the others in bed, then back at the elf.

"What about them?"

Holly shrugged. "You're officially the most important person according to Mrs. Claus. I can't be everywhere at once."

Frowning, Mike looked back at the bed just as Kisa stirred.

"I can keep watch," Kisa mumbled, sitting up in bed and rubbing her eyes. The blanket fell down, revealing her bare breasts. "Your anxiety is buzzing around inside my head. It feels gross. If I sense danger, I'll wake up the fox. She can handle it."

"Thanks, Kisa." As they left, he was careful to shut the door quietly.

Holly walked by his side but said nothing as they descended the stairs and went back into the kitchen. Mrs. Claus was already there and had prepped a meal of bacon and eggs.

"Well?" she asked. "Did you sleep or break your promise?"

Mike felt heat rise in his cheeks. "We didn't do anything kinky in your bed, I swear."

Mrs. Claus looked over at Holly. Mike noticed immediately that the woman seemed older this morning. She was in a sexy Santa robe that revealed some extra wrinkles along her neck, and her hair had more streaks of white than it had last night.

"They were sleeping naked," Holly announced, then hopped up into a stool.

"We didn't exactly bring pajamas." Mike threw the snitch a dirty look and sat down next to her. "Besides, even if we had been in the mood, I was way too tired."

"We both know that's a lie." Mrs. Claus slid an empty glass in front of him. "Orange juice?"

"Yes, please." He waited while she made him a plate of food and then poured him some juice from a carafe kept beneath the counter. "We really didn't do anything though."

"I believe you." Mrs. Claus winked. "And honestly, I don't know that I would blame you if I could. I've been married to a man obsessed with making toys for nearly a century. Maybe 'obsessed' isn't the right word though. It's so ingrained into his magic he can't help himself. I imagine sex must be the same for you."

"I'm honestly not sure." He took a sip of orange juice and

broke apart a piece of bacon before taking a bite. "Sex is at the core of my magic, but it's not like I'm compelled to do it."

"Hmm. Santa is always acting on some variation of his own magic. Technically, if it's Christmas related, he can accomplish it. That's how his magic works." She stared at the counter as if lost in thought. "Did you know he helped stop a war once? It was only for a day. Both sides stopped fighting while he was there, then went right back to killing each other. It broke his heart, you know. He had watched each and every one of those men grow up as children."

"Wait, he can see every child on Earth?" Mike asked.

Mrs. Claus paused before answering. "Not in a literal sense. It's almost like he's plugged into them. Sometimes it breaks him. There are children out there who need help, but it sits right outside his ability to intervene. That's why people notice so many miracles during Christmas. He's trying to make up for missed opportunities. Still, he's only one person."

Mike almost corrected her by saying two but realized Holly was nearby. What would the elf do if she found out the Krampus was Santa? And if Holly was technically just some offshoot of Santa, did that mean she could transform into something similar?

A more chilling thought occurred to him. If Santa could sense every child, so could the Krampus.

"What does the Krampus want exactly?" he asked. "In general terms. I've heard the spirits reference the true meaning of Christmas, but that's hardly specific."

Mrs. Claus looked at him for a moment, then sighed. "To be honest, I'm not sure. Not to end Christmas, for obvious reasons." Her eyes flicked to Holly and back. "It has to be related to punishing children."

"This seems like a long way to go just to smack some kids around. And what about the devil cookies? Is he just keeping the elves busy, or is there some bigger plan?"

"I don't know. You see—" Mrs. Claus was cut off when

Christmas Present appeared, blasting the room with sparkling light and the smell of candy canes. She dropped a pair of envelopes onto the counter, flashed Mike her breasts, and then disappeared.

"What in the..." Mike picked up the envelopes and saw that one was addressed to him and the other to Mrs. Claus. "Why the letters?"

"I'm not sure. Time is flowing much slower here. It could just be that she couldn't get away for long. A minute here is easily an hour out there on delivery." Mrs. Claus opened her letter and frowned. "Okay, so this changes things."

"What's up?" He hadn't opened his letter yet.

"We knew Frost was helping the Krampus, but it would seem that Jólakötturinn, Grýla, and the Yuletide Lads are also part of it. Your friends were making deliveries, but the sleigh is under attack and can't land anywhere with snow."

"What? Who?" He almost snatched the letter from her hand to read it himself but remembered his own. Ripping open the paper, he unfolded a piece of Christmas stationery and read it.

Romeo, it began. *How are you? I hope you've been having a great time at the North Pole. Death and I have been busting our behinds delivering presents to brats across the world. No big deal, it will only take us years to finish.*

That's sarcasm, by the way. I am not happy about it, and you owe me big. I'm talking a tropical vacation, or maybe give me permission to eat my way through a prison. Your choice.

Anyway, Dancer and that glorious giantess who smells like you have been a big help. They are speeding up deliveries but not anywhere cold because of a fudging snowman army. Oh, right, Death tricked me into wearing a hat that won't let me swear, even if I write it. Fudge. Shirt. See?

Mike noticed several half-scrawled swears along the perimeter of the paper and bit his lip to avoid laughing.

Christmas Present will act as a correspondent, but we need her help too much, so it's letters only for now. After not delivering presents for a couple of days, the sleigh started to fall out of the sky. So we have to stay busy to keep from crashing it. The ghost and the reindeer helped us catch up, but we're in trouble if we lose them. These weird potato dudes and a giant cat are trying to take Santa's sack from us. They suck, by the way.

Speaking of Christmas Present, this woman is a gift. She was supposed to give you a special message from me. I hope you liked it.

Lily had signed her name with a flourish and a kiss. Beneath her name, she had written more.

P.S. We let the dog out. She's pulling our sleigh right now. Good luck finding someone to give her her shots.

"Cerberus?" Mike set the letter down and stared at it. Mrs. Claus was still reading her own letter, her cheeks now flushed.

"Seriously, Death and a hellhound?" She looked over the top of her glasses at him. "And a succubus? Just what kind of house are you running, Caretaker?"

"One where we don't give a damn about what other people think." He saw Holly flinch, reminding him that she was still there. "Sounds like the sleigh is running out of magic."

"It's the number one rule. Santa's magic *must* be used for Christmas. That includes the sleigh and the dimensional bag. If they've just been circling, it…" She took off her glasses and groaned. "Why does my head hurt so bad all of a sudden?"

"Lack of sleep?" Concerned, Mike stood and moved to the other side of the counter just as Mrs. Claus's eyes rolled up in her head and she collapsed. He caught her by the arms as Holly leaped down from her stool.

"This way," she said, then held open the door to the main room. Mike dragged Mrs. Claus, suddenly aware of how light she felt. Holly adjusted some pillows on a recliner, and Mike set the older woman down on it.

"Hey, are you okay?" When she didn't respond, he looked around for something to give her but realized he didn't know what to do. Holly took Mrs. Claus by the hand and held it.

The woman's eyes fluttered open, and she looked back and forth at the two of them.

"How did we get here?" she asked.

"You're really tired," Mike said. "You got lightheaded is all."

"I don't sleep during Christmas. Don't need to." She smiled sadly. "It's a common belief that Mrs. Claus stays up all night and waits for her husband to come home. If something as simple as a couple of days made me sleepy, I would drop dead long before my husband got home. I'm afraid it's something else."

She took a deep breath, and Mike watched more streaks appear in her hair.

"What's going on?" he asked.

"I think…he's draining the magic away from my husband." Mrs. Claus closed her eyes as if to sleep but kept talking. "I don't know how, but I suddenly feel so…old. My bones are weary, and I can feel the soft pull of oblivion calling my name. With so much of the North Pole under the Krampus's control, it's only a matter of time before he surpasses Santa in strength. Once that happens, I will cease to exist."

"No!" Holly put her hands over her mouth.

"I'm afraid it's true." Mrs. Claus opened her eyes and looked at Mike. "Unlike the elves, I am just a mere extension. All he needs to do is wait until I'm gone and the North Pole will be his. Once that happens, there will be no one to stand in his way."

"How long do we have?" he asked.

Mrs. Claus frowned. "I don't know. But I'm not gone yet." She took a deep breath and sat forward. "I would love to hear some ideas."

Mike examined the woman, then opened his senses to the magic surrounding her. He could see the festive ribbons around her body, as if she was woven from several strands of thread. Some of them had become frayed, wispily drifting about as if caught in a breeze.

Staring at those threads, he wondered if he could touch them. They looked similar to his own magic from before, and he was relatively certain that manipulating them wouldn't cause the same outcome.

"You're staring," Holly said.

"Shh." He held up a finger for silence, then moved his hands across Mrs. Claus's body. She followed his movements but didn't react when the strands passed through his hands.

"Damn," he muttered. What was different? Was it because he had previously been manipulating his own magic?

"Your eyes are glowing," Holly whispered.

"Probably." He shrugged off her comment and returned his attention to the unraveling threads. What if he could tuck them in or something? How would he even do such a thing?

He felt his magic awaken, sensing his need. Mrs. Claus had closed her eyes again, her skin suddenly pale.

Could his magic touch hers? She was a construct of belief but still a living being. How would she react if he accidentally zapped her? Contemplating the problem, he watched in horror as one of the threads came undone, as if someone had tugged the free end of it.

Holding out his hands, he summoned the magic into his fingertips, then extended them outward. He could hear the air crackle with magic as he tried to pinch one of the hovering threads with his illusory fingers.

"Yes!" It had taken a couple attempts, but the thread was now firmly trapped between his spectral digits. He thought about how he had looped his magic back into himself and decided to do the same thing with Mrs. Claus. Her magic sustained her existence, so he doubted she would turn into a cum fountain.

And if this backfired, at least she'd be coming while she was going.

"Not the time," he muttered, chastising himself for the inappropriate thought. Sweat had broken out across his brow as he delicately tucked the exposed thread into the tapestry that was Mrs. Claus, taking care to weave it back into her core. While he did this, he looked at the bun on her head, thinking about how a stray strand of hair could easily be put back in place.

The woman sighed, then took a deep breath as Mike continued to snare the loose threads. Strangely, manipulating her magic almost felt like second nature as he grabbed the unraveling thread and actually braided it back together before tucking it in. His concentration was total, and he barely noticed that his legs were shaking beneath him.

The color returned to her cheeks as he finished up. Smiling, he felt the magic leave him, the room now spinning around him.

"Gah!" Holly tried to catch him as he fell, only to end up on top of him. Her concerned features filled his tunnel vision, and he couldn't help but notice that her magic was similar to Mrs. Claus's. Where the older woman had come undone and was frayed, Holly was a tight package bound in ribbons just waiting to be opened.

Moments passed, and Holly sat up, her legs spreading wide to accommodate his torso. She held two fingers up in front of him, but all he could think about were the candy-cane tights that now filled his peripheral vision.

"How many fingers am I holding up?" she asked.

"Two," he replied, then closed his eyes. "Sorry, I'm not sure why I'm so tired."

"Manipulating magic directly is hard work," Yuki replied. "But I guess I shouldn't be surprised."

Mike opened his eyes and saw Yuki standing over by the stairs, her arms crossed over her chest. The kitsune was wearing a robe she had borrowed from the wardrobe upstairs, the letters *SC* embroidered on the chest.

"Whatever he did, I feel much better." Mrs. Claus leaned over the side of the chair to look at Mike. A few of the years she had put on were gone now, the wrinkles along her neck faded. "Though, I suspect he only bought me some time."

Yuki muttered to herself in Japanese, then helped Holly stand. Mike noticed the crotch of Holly's tights had a snowflake on it.

"What am I going to do with you?" Yuki knelt by Mike's side and tilted her head. "Hey, look at me, I can see magic for the first time, so maybe I should touch it? Maybe move it around."

"She was dying," he replied. "I thought I could help."

"All I ask is five minutes. Five minutes to wake me up and fill me in. I could have walked you through your first time. It would have been so gentle. Ah, geez, you're all wet." Yuki put her hand against his forehead. "No fever though."

"Fever?" Holly asked.

"Yeah, fever." Yuki stood and moved to Mrs. Claus. "How do you feel? What was happening?"

Mrs. Claus gave an explanation that was satisfactory, and Yuki returned to Mike.

"I felt that from upstairs, you know. You were generating a ton of magic. I thought maybe you were down here unwrapping our host and filling her with Christmas cheer."

"Why would I have a fever?" Mike asked, ignoring the last part of Yuki's comment.

"From burning out your brain." She patted him on the cheek. "Your own magic is one thing, but grabbing someone else's magic and doing stuff to it? Dangerous. Luckily, she was a willing subject and your intentions were good."

"It felt like a massage," Mrs. Claus added. "My whole body was tingling."

"Well, I'm glad it was a good experience for you." Yuki helped Mike to the nearest couch. "But don't do that again until we can talk about it. I think you've taken another step down the magic road, and I need to apprise you of the pitfalls."

He sighed, grateful that she wasn't giving him an earful. His ears were buzzing with a nasty bout of tinnitus while his magic shifted about in his chest, giving him terrible heartburn.

"You can teach me how to manipulate outside magic?" he asked.

"A bit. Seeing magic can give you better control over it, but apparently you can actually touch it. The real expert is Ratu. How do you think she does all her tricks with those artifacts?" While she spoke, she examined his body with her hands, squeezing his wrists and arms. "Well, you didn't seem to blow out your meridians or anything, so I think you'll be okay."

"Meridians?"

"Don't worry about it, I'm just making sure your body is okay, because you probably feel terrible right now. You'll bounce back pretty fast, but maybe take it easy for a bit." She shook her head and looked at Mrs. Claus. "I really can't take my eye off him for a single minute."

"I'm married to one like that." Mrs. Claus chuckled. "If he's not playing with the elves, he's off taking apart the latest toy so he can mass-produce it, or building something new and exciting in his workshop. I can't tell you how many times he's caught that building on fire."

"It's a lot." Holly sat down by Mike's feet, her eyes wandering across his prone body and eventually settling on his face. "Every year. We have an elf who follows him around with a fire extinguisher, and that one is followed by another elf in case the first elf catches on fire."

Mike laughed, then saw the serious look on Holly's face. "Wait, for real?"

"It's a chain of three elves, actually," Mrs. Claus added. "But only when he's working on electrical stuff. When it comes to carpentry, there is nobody better, but the world has moved on from old-school dolls and wooden horses. He can build anything, as long as it's a gift for someone. But that doesn't mean there aren't hiccups along the way."

They all laughed and shared stories for a bit, and the nasty buzzing sound faded. Mike's magic settled down, and he was able to sit and chat properly. Eventually Kisa appeared with a very sleepy Tink, and they left the room to have breakfast in the kitchen with Yuki.

While they were gone, Mrs. Claus talked some more about her experiences at the North Pole, most of her stories skirting the edges of what she had told Mike about Santa being a type of Caretaker. He wondered how much more she would have told him if the elf hadn't been around.

Holly, however, had managed to sit down right next to him, her petite body occasionally pressing against his when either of them would shift. He thought he caught her looking at him more than once and knew better than to just dismiss it.

When the others joined them, Tink promptly found a chair off to the side and crawled into it before passing out.

"What's her deal?" Mike asked. "She okay?"

"She drank booze made for magical reindeer last night," Kisa said. "The hangover is very real this morning."

"I'm surprised it didn't kill her," Mrs. Claus said, then got up to get Tink a pillow. The old woman seemed rejuvenated, but when Mike examined her magic once more, he saw that a couple of tiny threads had already come undone. While he may have extended the woman's life span with his stunt earlier, they were definitely on a time limit.

"So I have a question," he said once Mrs. Claus returned to her seat. "You mentioned someone called Jólakötturinn, Grýla, and some…Yuletide guys?"

"Yuletide Lads. Yes, let's discuss them for a moment." Mrs. Claus sat forward in her chair, then looked at the others. "Once upon a time, my husband fought some otherworldly creatures called frost giants. They were the last ones on Earth, trapped here from a battle long ago. Someone promised them a one-way trip to their home world if they could take down Santa, but it wasn't meant to be.

"Jólakötturinn and Grýla belonged to the frost giants. They are giants themselves but nowhere near the same size. Jólakötturinn was their pet cat and Grýla essentially their servant. I don't know if they came from the same world the frost giants did or if they were simply found here. But that's beside the point. When the frost giants were defeated, Santa found Jólakötturinn, Grýla, and the others cowering back at the frost giant's camp. He took pity on them and allowed them to stick around as long as they stayed out of trouble."

"And did they?" Mike asked.

Mrs. Claus shook her head. "Of course they didn't. They snuck off and lay low in Iceland of all places. Do you know what they became famous for? Eating children."

"That's horrible!" Kisa said. "And Santa let them get away with it?"

"Not after he found out. He bound them here, and the magic of the North Pole transformed them. Like the Krampus, they were to become mere myths, their memories softened as a reminder for children to be good or else."

"You said there were others?" Yuki leaned toward Mrs. Claus in interest.

"Yes, a few. There were three males, but only Leppalúði remains."

"Wait, who is…Leppalúði?" Mike struggled with the pronunciation.

"Grýla's husband. Other than knocking her up with children, he is absolutely useless. The other two were better, but supposedly Grýla ate them. Now she's stuck with the third because he's the only one who can give her children. It wouldn't surprise me if he stayed home instead of helping her take over the North Pole with the Krampus. He really is that lazy." Mrs. Claus stared off into space for a moment, then looked back at the others. "The Yuletide Lads are Grýla's children. All boys, all trouble. My husband tried to give jobs to some of them early on, but it was clear they weren't cut out for any sort of structure."

"Interesting." Mike wondered how Lily was faring against the Yuletide Lads. Or better yet, how they were faring against her. "Any ideas how Jack Frost comes into this?"

Mrs. Claus took a deep breath. "Actually, I do, but I need a break." She stood from her chair and rubbed at her lower back. "Feeling a bit stiff is all, gonna grab myself a quick snack. Does anyone want some cocoa while I'm up?"

Everyone's hands, including Tink's, went up in the air.

JACK HAD FLOWN ABOVE THE NORTH POLE FOR SEVERAL HOURS before daring to descend below the whirling mass of ice and snow. The storm she had summoned had gathered plenty of fury on its own, and she didn't know how long it would continue.

Upon landing, she saw that she had managed to fly to the magical boundary of the North Pole proper. Santa's village lay in the middle of a hundred-mile-wide island of rock that was actually the peak of a mountain from a range that lay deep beneath the arctic waters. If it could be properly seen from the outside, the North Pole would look like a perfectly circular island surrounded by ice with some steep, rocky cliffs, analogous to a giant snow globe.

She landed on one of the cliffs and let out a scream of frustration. The arctic ice took her anger but offered nothing in return.

"What are you doing?" The voice startled her so hard that she spun around and summoned ice from the ground, jagged spikes that would have ripped apart any other creature. Instead, the Krampus silently side stepped them, his body an inky blur as he whipped around and shattered the icy barrage. "Cute but ineffective."

"I'm sorry, I..." She took a step back, worried the Krampus would attack her.

"Relax, child." The Krampus sniffed at the air and grinned. "I can smell your intent. I shouldn't have frightened you."

Worried the Krampus was acting uncharacteristically nice, Jack hugged herself and tried to look small. If the Krampus could sense intent, he wouldn't have punished her so harshly earlier. "I'm sorry I left the cameras. Something came up."

"Oh, I know it did." The Krampus chuckled, then moved to stand beside her. "You looked into my mirror, didn't you?"

A litany of possible lies filtered through her head, but she suspected the Krampus would only punish her more for whatever answer she gave him. He was a fraud, at least in terms of their relationship. He had promised her relevance and recognition but had only delivered misery.

She nodded, then winced. When the blow never came, she turned toward the Krampus and was surprised that he had his back to her. His gaze was on the northern lights above, his whole body swaying from side to side as if he was hypnotized by them.

"He knew you would find out," he said, his voice barely legible over the storm. "That's what he kept telling me, while I was down there. Warned me over and over again that you would find out, that it would change everything. But I kept telling him it wouldn't matter."

"Find out what?"

"We're alike, you and I. Power incarnate, underappreciated, underutilized. If you wanted, you could freeze the ocean, could bring mankind to its knees! Yet here you stand, a glorified snow cone maker, trapped in the North Pole."

"I'm not trapped," Jack argued, but the Krampus waved her off.

"Aren't you? Maybe you weren't trapped like the others, but you refused to leave. Why is that? Why not seek your fortune elsewhere, make a bigger name for yourself?"

Jack frowned, pondering the Krampus's words. Why did she hang around the North Pole so much? In hindsight, how many decades had she spent hovering around Santa, hoping to be a bigger part of things?

Pain blossomed in the back of her head again, and she clutched her temples. Memories burned through her mind, images of a much younger Santa kneeling over her broken form. The blood leaking from her body had already frozen, her breath coming in short gasps.

"He did this to you," the Krampus told her. "Locked away your true potential, made you think you were less than what you are. While your prison is different from my own, perhaps it is time you bend the bars."

"I don't—" She was cut off when he shifted toward her, his body like a shadow. Long fingers clutched her throat, and he squeezed, lifting her off the ground. Any traces of kindness were now stricken from his dark features.

"You see, I have plans for this place, and I need you to be the better version of yourself." He held up an empty sack and shook it in her face. She could sense the powerful magic within, realizing it was a smaller version of Santa's sack. "It's not ideal, but now I have everything I need to leave this place, to bring truth to my legacy!" He was shouting now, his teeth inches from her eyes.

"You're…hurting…" She choked as he shook her.

"But I cannot *leave* until YOU. WAKE. UP!" He slammed her into the ground, over and over again. Ribs cracked and bones splintered as an icy storm formed all around them, trying its best to rip the Krampus apart.

"Please, I…" Her words were weak as the world went black around her. For a moment, she was floating in a ball of golden light, her wounds burning trails of fire across her body.

A silhouette appeared, the lights dimming to reveal the woman from the mirror.

"Are you really going to let him kill us?" There was panic in the woman's voice as she grabbed Jack by the hand, her whole body buzzing with the contact. "Gods, he's actually killing us. You have to make him stop!"

"How? He's so strong, I can't do anything to hurt him." Jack whimpered, but the woman in gold slapped her, sending a shock wave through her mind.

"You have grown weak! You have made us weak!" The woman's hair billowed up around her, her eyes now like molten gold as magic streamed away from her. "This isn't how it was supposed to be, Santa! You were supposed to prolong me, not make me into this miserable creature!"

"Who…what are we?" Jack's heart pounded in her chest as the woman in gold seized her by the throat and forced her mouth open.

"We were gods! We are whoever we want to be," the woman told her, then forced her mouth over Jack's. Energy rippled through Jack's mind as their magic billowed out of control. Her eyes snapped open to reveal that she was now choking the Krampus.

"Good!" he shouted, his hands on her wrists. "This is power, Jack, the power he would have denied you! It's everything I promised you and more!"

The island trembled as massive tornadoes formed out on the ice floes. Enormous pieces of ice were ripped from the ground, revealing the cold waters of the arctic beneath. Jack felt so connected, as if she had tapped into a reservoir of power just beneath those dark waves.

"I disapprove of your methods," she hissed, then smashed the Krampus into the ground. He laughed maniacally, rolling onto his back to reveal he was unharmed.

"And yet they worked!" He was on his feet so fast that he may as well have teleported. "Look, Jack, look! I know I've been harsh, but you cannot crack an egg without using a little force!" He snatched her by the hand and held it up for her to see. Her veins were ablaze with golden light, and she could feel a rush of heat throughout her entire body.

This was what she had wanted…right?

"Power, Jack, all the power you could ever want!" He spun her around and hopped up and down with glee at the sight of the tornadoes. "Have you ever seen such a devastating force of nature? Tornadoes! At the North Pole! This is the mark of someone the world remembers, somebody who plays second fiddle to nobody!"

Her head still hurt; she was so confused. But what the Krampus was telling her made so much sense. It was power she had wanted, power to make the world notice her, to fear her glory!

No, power was too easy. The pain in her head had focused into a razor's edge right between her eyes, splitting her mind in half. She could sense that other woman now, the one she'd used to be, looking out of one of her eyes. They were fractured but somehow whole.

Not power, the other woman sneered. *We already have power.*

Yes, Jack replied, remembering what it was she had wanted. She had become obsolete in Santa's shadow, yet another forgotten fairy tale. The world was a closed door to her, and she wanted to be a part of it. *I want to be free, to be remembered. I want…I want…*

TO BE LOVED. The other woman said it for her. Feeling a surge of emotion, Jack reached into the depths of the storm and poured that golden energy into it, watching the ice on the ocean's surface tear itself apart in order to obey her. Her self-admission brought fiery tears to her eyes as she thought about what she needed to do.

"Yes! That's it!" The Krampus howled, his whole body tense as the storm gobbled up his cry. "And you can keep that power, Jack, my friend! I just need you to do one more thing for me!"

Jack was suddenly wary, fearing more of the Krampus's treachery. No, that couldn't be it. He had helped her; he was her friend. Wait, but he had hurt her, badly, just to—

"I need you to take out that mortal staying in my house." The Krampus grinned, revealing all his teeth. "Mrs. Claus will be gone soon, which means the door can be opened. Remove the Caretaker so he doesn't usurp my throne, and make sure you kill the elf. When I return, this glory shall be yours…forever!"

"Forever!" Jack raised her hands to the sky, now certain what it was she needed to do. The northern lights bent away from her, as if to avoid her outstretched hands. Her whole body was flooded with magic, and she sent it outward, raising an army made of snow and ice. Frozen beasts formed all around her, prying themselves up from deep drifts. Those golden flames burned hot beneath her skin as she lowered her eyes to see the Krampus hop into a makeshift sleigh hooked up to seven corrupted reindeer.

"I'll be back soon, my Queen." He bowed dramatically, and then the reindeer took to the sky.

"I may be a queen," she whispered. "But I am certainly not yours." For the first time she could remember, she felt hot. Her outfit, made of magical ice, melted into a beautiful golden gown. As she commanded the winds to carry her back to the Christmas village, a small voice in the back of her mind cried out that all was not well.

Not that it mattered. The only thing on her mind now was that strange man who had compelled her with his voice alone. Santa had ruled her with kindness, and the Krampus with fear. But Mike? He had attempted to rule her with words alone, those beautiful, golden words that had clung to her skin like a lover's touch. She shivered, wondering what could have been if she had given in to her desires, her sudden need to obey.

She was going to kill him for his insolence. After all, nobody told her what to do, not anymore. Once he was dead, she would kill his companions and anyone else who was a threat to her newfound freedom. When she was done, she would wait for the Krampus to return.

When he did, she would kill him too.

Mrs. Claus emerged from the kitchen, carrying a tray of cookies with several mugs and a thermos of hot cocoa. Tink nearly hurt herself getting out of her chair to move closer to the table with the cookies. When she grabbed a handful, Mrs. Claus swatted the goblin's hand.

"You need to share," Mrs. Claus warned her. When she looked away, Tink stuck her tongue out but obeyed.

Mike chuckled, then got up to get some cocoa. While Mrs. Claus was pouring his drink, he saw Yuki's ears open wide as she turned her attention to the nearest window.

"Everything okay?" he asked.

The kitsune frowned. "I just felt…hmm." She got up and moved to the window, then opened it. A fierce blast of cold air tousled her hair, but she ignored it, sticking her head out the window.

"Not to complain, but it's hard enough to keep it warm in here already," Mrs. Claus said, then looked at Mike. "The fire is nice and all, but we really do rely on the furnace."

"That's at the top of our to-do list," he said, knowing full well that task would fall on Tink. The goblin had already snuck a handful of cookies off the tray and had tucked them down into the couch cushions.

"There's a nasty storm rolling in." Yuki looked at Mike. "I'm going to pop outside for a minute, see what's going on."

Mrs. Claus frowned. "The Krampus might be out there."

Yuki winked. "And if he is, I'll give him a frosty reception. Be right back." With that, she let herself out the window, making sure to shut it behind her.

"Will she be okay?" Mrs. Claus looked at Mike.

"I'm sure she will," Mike told her. "She's in her element out there."

"I'm not so sure about that," she replied. "There's a lot more than just snow and ice out there, but you know her better than I do."

"I trust her with my life, which means I trust her judgment. So Jack Frost," he said, prompting her to continue. "I would like to hear what her deal is."

"Ah, yes. A bit of a tragedy, honestly." She started pouring hot cocoa for everyone, pausing briefly to frown at the stack of cookies. When she looked at Tink, the goblin had both hands in her lap, a beatific smile on her face.

"To properly understand Jack Frost, we need to go back a bit farther than Christmas. The world of magic and the world of man used to be one and the same. Myths and mortals lived side by side and not necessarily in harmony."

"I've heard this." Mike remembered a conversation he'd had long ago. "If I recall, Merlin did something about it because things weren't going well. Something about separating the worlds or something."

"It was a bit more nuanced than that, but yes." She smiled weakly, then handed him a mug of cocoa. "So let's fast-forward the conversation a bit. What do you know about the gods? The old ones?"

"Like Cthulhu and stuff?"

"Not the ancient ones. Think of Poseidon and the others."

"Ah, yes, the Greek gods. Or Roman." He scratched his chin. "I never could keep them straight."

"Greek. But that makes for a perfect segue. Mythologically

speaking, which gods actually existed? They couldn't all be real, could they?"

"We know God is sort of real." This came from Kisa. "He sent one of his angels to our house earlier this year."

"Really?" Mrs. Claus's eyes went wide. "What happened there?"

"Long story, but my friend Death accidentally triggered some conditions of the Apocalypse, so an angel came looking for him. It took them a long time to find him. They actually damaged the geas because I guess God or whoever was looking so hard that it disrupted enchantments."

Mrs. Claus scowled. "Earlier this year, right? Back in March?"

He felt the moisture flee from his mouth. "Uh, yeah, that's right."

"That's around the same time the protections around here started to fail. Santa thought it was an issue of belief, and he spent so much time and energy trying to repair the wards around the North Pole." Mrs. Claus pinched the bridge of her nose. "It's why he was so weak this year. The magical barrier here takes a tremendous amount of energy to maintain, especially with all those scientists who wander up. Santa keeps moving magnetic north to throw off their compasses, but their GPS units know better."

"If that's true, then I'm really sorry. You guys got caught up in my bullsh—" He felt Holly spasm next to him. "...nonsense."

"You can't blame yourself for the actions of others. But if YHWH himself was involved, it's no wonder our barrier took such a beating." She stared hard at Mike. "For such a new player to the game, you have certainly attracted a lot of attention."

"I'm not even trying to play it," Mike said. "I would love to understand it better, but it seems like the whole thing is one big trap."

She looked like she was going to say something, then thought better of it. "Like I was saying, what happened to these old gods? Who actually existed, and who didn't? Why so many discrepancies?" Mrs. Claus surveyed the others like a teacher waiting for an answer.

"They were the same," Kisa answered. "Same entities, different names."

"Usually," Mrs. Claus said, then offered Kisa a cookie. "It was never uncommon for one of the gods to go by a new name or change their identity."

"How did you know they were the same gods?" Mike asked Kisa.

"Please. I spent so much time in the room with all the Egyptian garbage. I read plenty of those books." She licked her lips and then devoured the cookie.

"It's best to think of these gods as immensely powerful beings who rely on belief as a wellspring of magic. Yuki is actually a perfect example of this. If she wanted, she could attempt to ascend to godhood, using divinity from worship to power her spells." Mrs. Claus looked out the window. "But ascension comes with a price of its own."

"Worshippers," Mike said. "Without them, you are nothing."

"Correct. Several millennia ago, the gods started a massive fight with one another. Sometimes, when a god loses, they get consumed by another or are forced into hiding. If they truly want to survive a war with other gods, they can choose to let go of their divinity and become a lesser deity. Takes them out of the food chain, unless someone is feeling particularly vindictive."

"Wait, is that what Jack is?" Mike felt a hand on his thigh and looked down. Holly was staring straight at Mrs. Claus, as if enthralled, her small hand now stationary on his leg. It looked accidental, but he said nothing.

"Yes. When my husband found Jack, she had barely

survived an all-out attack from another god. She was actually on her way here to get his help. Many of the old gods had perished from this world already, but my husband was known to help a few, here and there."

"So who was she?" Mike asked.

"That I don't know. I trust my husband and have no need to pry, especially because that can be dangerous knowledge. He did tell me the transition was very difficult for her. To save her life, he forced her to descend, to relinquish her godhood in exchange for elemental power. He chose ice and frost because it was so counter to her nature that her enemies wouldn't expect it. After her transformation, he let her believe she was an iteration of Old Man Winter himself."

"Well, maybe that wasn't his decision to make." Kisa narrowed her eyes at Mrs. Claus. "Why not at least tell her the truth and let her decide how to handle it?"

"When you ascend and become a god, you become connected into the universe in a way that no other being can manage. Think of it like the ultimate high, the pinnacle of achievement. To hide her, he locked away her remaining divinity so she wouldn't be tempted to use it. But it's more than that." Mrs. Claus looked at Mike. "Ascending to godhood gives you a body and mind capable of handling that kind of magic. It's one of the reasons not just anybody can do it. When Jack descended, she changed on a cellular level. It's the same process by which gods can be animals one century and humans the next. You can't just casually become a god again. Remembering who she used to be could become a death sentence for her."

Mike leaned forward in interest. "Kind of like Yuki saying I could have burned out my brain earlier but on a larger scale. Last spring, I almost blew off my arm, forcing powerful magic to…hurt someone." He let his mind dance away from Leeds's memory; may he rot forever. "I didn't have full control of what I was about to do."

"And that's why her secret was so important. Should she remember, it would be like an entirely new identity has surfaced, one that now fights to control a body that is no longer compatible with godhood." Mrs. Claus turned her attention to Tink, who had just stuffed three cookies into her mouth. "You're unusually quiet."

Tink grinned awkwardly, revealing chocolate chips crammed in her teeth. The hand on Mike's thigh moved closer to his crotch, but when he looked at Holly, she acted like she was unaware of her actions. There was no doubt in his mind now that it was intentional.

"So, anyway, I suspect the Krampus knows Jack's secret." Mrs. Claus turned her attention back to Mike with a knowing look. There was no doubt in her mind or Mike's that the Krampus knew, but she wasn't about to let everyone in on Santa's secret. "And he plans to use her powers to…I don't know. I'm still foggy on that part."

"The Krampus wants Christmas," Kisa said. "That's all we need to know. You're slowly dying, this place is freezing, and Jack is in our way. Let's address the issues in order. The furnace is easy. What do we need to do to keep you from dying?"

Mrs. Claus shivered. "We need more faith. Even though the elves were made from Santa's magic, they are still separate beings capable of existing even if Santa didn't. The same is not true for me. If not for Holly, I likely would have ceased to be hours ago."

"So then let's find the elves." Kisa looked at Mike. "We saw some in the bakery. I'm sure they're squirreled away somewhere."

"I agree." Mike shifted away from Holly to see what she would do. Her hand slid from his leg, but she casually dragged her nails across the fabric of his pants as her hand slid off. "Tink can head down to fix the furnace but find somewhere to drop off Kisa to better scout the area for elves. Once we locate them, we can figure out how to make them good again."

"Breaking the Krampus's control should do it," Mrs. Claus said. "They have been under his thrall only a short time and will tend to revert to long-term behaviors. Once free, we can bring some here or hide them throughout the village. That should buy me and us some more time."

"Do you have a map of this place?" Mike asked.

"No, but I've got plenty of paper in the workshop. Not *the* workshop, just the room my husband tinkers in while here." She stood with a groan. "I can draw something up."

"Tink go see workshop." The goblin was already on her feet. "See Santa's tools, maybe find new hammer?"

Kisa narrowed her eyes at the goblin, then looked at Mrs. Claus. "I'll come with you. That way, I can ask questions about how this place is laid out. As long as I'm quiet, almost nobody can see me, and I can fit in plenty of tight spaces, so that's not a problem."

Mike studied Kisa's face. The cat girl was up to something; he knew it for a fact. Kisa's eyes flicked his way, and he saw hesitation in her features. Whatever she was up to, he might not approve.

Still, he trusted her. She might be his familiar, but he didn't own her. There was something she wanted to do, and he would find out eventually. "You guys should make a couple of maps. That way, if we use cat radio, I have one to look at here to get a better sense of what's going on."

"Oh." Mrs. Claus looked at Mike. "It just occurred to me that we haven't discussed what to do about Jack."

"Let Mike deal with her," Kisa said out of the corner of her mouth. "He's got a particular set of skills when it comes to situations like these."

"What Kisa is trying to say is that we've been in tighter spots and Yuki and I can figure out how to deal with Frosty the

Snow Bitch." He grimaced and looked over at Holly. "I am super sorry."

"I'm getting used to it," she told him with a pout.

"I hope not." Mrs. Claus moved in front of Holly and knelt. "Hmm. Eyes are still clear, complexion good. The last thing I need is for you to come down with naughty sickness. We need you at your best, so please take some time to relax."

"Yes, ma'am." Holly watched Mrs. Claus lead Kisa and Tink up the stairs toward wherever the workshop was. Once they were gone, she moved to the table and picked up the tray and thermos, then disappeared through the kitchen door.

Finally alone, Mike let out a huge sigh. This whole situation was poised on the edge of a knife, but it wasn't the worst thing he'd been through. At least they knew their enemy and had the start of a plan, which gave him an advantage. The incident with Leeds had caught him off guard and nearly broken who he was. Months had been spent dedicating time and energy to controlling his magic and strengthening his body just for an occasion like this one.

Now, if he didn't think of all the times his magic had gone haywire on him already since arriving at the North Pole, he would actually feel confident in their chances. Looking down at his belly, he gave his magic a little stroke and watched as it manifested as a glowing orb only he could see. Being able to visualize magic was going to be a game changer in a lot of ways.

"Why are you such a troublemaker?" he asked his stomach. His magic, realizing it had been awakened for nothing, swirled around and popped out of existence, but not before forming into a shape that looked remarkably like a hand with a middle finger raised.

He made a note to bring that up with Yuki, then noticed Holly had left a couple of mugs behind. Deciding not to be the terrible guest he already was, he picked them up and carried them into the kitchen, where he assumed she was probably taking care of leftover cookies.

Stepping through the door of the kitchen, he was surprised when Holly nearly tackled him. Despite her small size, she was able to press him up against the wall by his hips, her fingers frantically working to undo the drawstring of his pants.

"Holly, um, the mugs!" He had nowhere to set them down, and she had caught him completely off guard.

"Fuck your mugs." She groaned after swearing, her eyes rolling back in her head. "Oh gosh, I love that word so much. When it leaves my mouth, I can feel it reverberate through my whole body."

Suddenly worried about her, Mike tried to move away, but Holly yanked his pants down, revealing his cock. Gasping in awe, she used both hands to lift it, contemplating both its length and girth.

"Are you okay? Is it naughty sickness?"

She lifted her eyes to meet his, a lascivious twinkle in her eyes. "This isn't naughty sickness at all, Mike Radley. You see, there's something I want that only you can give me, and Tink said you would be happy to oblige. What I'm about to do to you is one hundred percent me."

With that, she opened her lips wide and tried to fit the head of his cock in her mouth. Her already tight lips stretched wide when his cock expanded, and she made a gurgling sound as she barely managed the first inch. Since he was surprised by her behavior, it took him a moment to notice that she now had a hand down the front of her tights and was frantically masturbating.

Her technique was terrible, but she absolutely made up the difference with pure, unbridled enthusiasm. His cock practically vibrated as she continuously moaned into him, the narrow tip of her tongue dancing across the edges of his urethra.

She had been getting a little handsy with him out in the living room, but he thought back to how she had calmly watched him fuck Kisa. Clearly, there was something more to Holly than originally expected, and he was now determined to find out what.

"Here, at least let me set these down." With two mugs in one hand and a third in the other, he didn't think dropping them on the floor was a good idea. He did a stiff-legged waddle toward the nearest counter by the sink with Holly crouch walking backward to avoid breaking contact. Once near the counter, he heard the sound of footsteps just outside the door and moved so his waist was hidden from view.

Holly chased him and resumed blowing him just as the door opened. Mrs. Claus had an odd look on her face as Mike quickly set the mugs by the sink and turned on the faucet to rinse them out.

"Problem?" he asked, putting on his best poker face. Holly, to her credit, stopped moaning. She did, however, intensify the tongue play on the head of his cock.

"We're gonna be a while in the workshop," she said, then walked toward the counter, her eyes on the thermos that Holly had set there. Mike saw her eyes dart to the dirty mugs in his hands, and he quickly rinsed them and dried them out with his shirt.

"Here you go." He slid the mugs across the counter, and she took them, letting out a yawn.

"Thank you, Mike. For everything you're trying to accomplish here." She stood there for a moment, as if lost in thought. "I almost feel like you were meant to be here."

"Uh, yeah. I think I know what you mean." He tried to keep a stupid grin off his face when Holly started playing with his balls. It was clear she was screwing with him, and he didn't want to end up on Mrs. Claus's bad side once again.

"Listen, before I forget, there's something I want to tell you." She set the mugs on the tray next to the thermos. "It's about Holly. If something happens to me, Santa, all this... please take care of her. She can be a handful sometimes, all the elves are, but she has a really good heart. The elves, they aren't created equally. Some are very driven by their work, others want nothing more than to please Santa. But Holly? Not the same. Don't let her size and elfin nature fool you. She's a woman to be reckoned with."

Holly paused for a moment, one hand tightly squeezing the base of his shaft. Her grip was strong despite her only being able to get her fingers around his girth.

"Yeah, um...I can see that. She's very...enthusiastic."

"Always has been, bless her heart." Mrs. Claus contemplated the tray, her fingers tracing the silver filigree along the edges. "But that's something all the elves have. Each one is like a tiny piece of my husband, let loose on the world to do good things. Do you have kids?"

He nodded, silently cursing the fact that the woman was feeling chatty while the equivalent of her daughter was trying to inhale his boner. It was the plot of a cheap porn, and he wasn't amused. "A horse boy and an omelet on the way," he told her.

She laughed, then realized he wasn't joking. "You are an odd one, Caretaker."

"You have no idea." He shifted his weight from one foot to the other, which caused Holly to make a tiny sputtering sound as his cock went farther into her mouth. Mike covered it up by faking a cough of his own. "It's so dry up here," he complained, desperate to avoid Mrs. Claus's wrath.

"I can get you some water," she said, then started to move around the counter.

"Nope, I'm fine." He grabbed the thermos and poured himself some more hot cocoa, then slammed it. The hot beverage trickled down his throat just as his glans popped past Holly's tonsils, causing him to moan and choke at the same time. "Yeah, that's really good," he said with a raspy voice, then put the cup back on the tray. "Tink can use that one. We're married."

Mrs. Claus looked like she had a lot of questions for him but just shook her head and picked up the tray. "We'll be upstairs if you need us," she told him before leaving.

"Will probably be up in a bit," he said, then checked on her aura as she walked away. It was already unraveling again.

"Gah!" Holly pulled her mouth off his cock, a large gob of spit hanging from her lips. She wiped it away and looked up at him. "Knowing she might catch us made me so scared I got horny!"

"Yeah, about that." He knelt and picked her up under her arms, then set her down on the counter. "I thought this sort of thing was bad for your kind."

"Heh." She leaned forward and grabbed him by the cock with both hands, stroking him to keep him hard. "Let's just say that elves react poorly to naughty behavior they aren't accustomed to. I had a bit of an…awakening some years back. I've spent the last couple of decades educating myself on certain topics."

"Certain topics?" He raised an eyebrow.

"I've been watching people *fuck*." She grinned as if drunk. "And before you ask, yes, that word is still hard to say, but I am so horny that I don't…fudging care."

He almost laughed at the slipup but kept his face neutral. "You've been watching people have sex?"

She nodded eagerly. "Here's the thing, Mike. Sex is taboo but not by law or anything. The other elves just don't do it. Finding a willing partner has been very difficult, and ever since I watched you pound Kisa in the Cocoa Lounge, I decided I just had to have you. Your cock is huge, it probably won't even fit, and all I can think about is spending days trying to make it happen."

"That's a long time," he replied.

"I've been celibate for so long that everything up here

looks like a dick to me," she told him. "Do you know how many tools I've borrowed just to get myself through the night?"

Oddly, that reminded him of a comment Tink had once made about fucking her own hammer. "Maybe Santa should branch out, start giving grown-ups some toys of their own."

"I've put that in the suggestion box," she declared, letting go of his cock to pull up her skirt. "Every year, actually!"

Seeing those candy-cane tights, he felt his resolve weaken drastically. He put his hands on her upper thighs and used his thumb to tease her groin through the thin fabric.

"Oh wow," she muttered. "Your thumb is almost the size of…elf dick."

"I imagine the average human cock looks monstrous to you."

She nodded, her eyes suddenly wide. "It's actually a little scary," she whispered. "Thinking about that big thing inside me."

"Do you want to be scared?" he asked, dropping his voice an octave. He could sense it now, her desire for authority. It wrapped around him like a perfume, and his magic reacted.

"Oh yes, please," she begged, stroking him faster. "I've been so good, or naughty. Whichever one will get that dick inside me."

Using both hands, he pulled at the center of her tights until it lifted away from her flesh, and then he tore the fabric. It didn't rip easily, but when it did, Holly jumped. The snowflake covering her groin ripped in two, revealing she wasn't wearing any underwear beneath her tights. Instead of pubic hair, her mound was adorned with glistening crystals that looked like tiny snowflakes of their own.

"Okay, didn't expect that," he noted.

"I put them on earlier," she told him. "As a surprise for you."

"I am…very much surprised." He broke out in a stupid

grin at the thought of Holly bedazzling her pubes for him, much less trying to track down a bedazzler in the middle of a Christmas crisis. Mike teased the outer folds of her labia with his fingertips while she bit her lip and groaned. The level of stimulation was minimal, but he was receiving maximum rewards for his efforts.

"It's been so long since someone has touched me," she cooed, then grabbed his wrist. "Please don't stop."

"Oh, I wasn't planning to." He felt a sudden rush at the idea of fucking her on the counter or maybe bending her over the table. She was small enough that it would be easy to put her anywhere, and she definitely wouldn't bite him during sex like a certain goblin he knew.

Well, he assumed she wouldn't. "So it's been a while since someone has touched you?"

Holly nodded with a shiver.

"So I'm guessing it's been even longer since someone did this?" He grabbed her by the hips and slid her across the counter before bending forward and kissing her inner thighs. She made tiny sounds of joy while wrapping her legs around his head, then gasped when his tongue traced a circle along the thin folds of her mound.

Mike stopped for a moment, surprised that Holly's pussy tasted like a candy cane.

"Um…" Holly stiffened at his reaction. "Is something wrong?"

"Heck no!" he exclaimed, careful to keep his words PG for her sake. "You're magically delicious!"

He buried his face in her crotch, his tongue exploring her inner folds. The kitchen filled with gasps of delight and surprise as he tried to see how deep he could get his tongue inside her. Since Holly hadn't offered any explanation as to the flavor of her pussy, he assumed it was a Christmas elf thing and not that she had been using a candy cane recently to get herself off.

It didn't take Holly long to come this way. Her face turned beet red as she held her breath and let out a tiny squeak before grabbing Mike's hair so hard that she pulled a small clump out. When he pressed his lips tight to her body, his mouth was flooded with the taste of peppermint while teasing her clit with his tongue. Holly bit down on her screams of joy, which made her sound like she had a bad case of the hiccups.

Feeling pretty good about himself, Mike pulled her butt closer to the edge of the counter and kissed her. Holly seemed surprised but melted into him. Her hands went under his shirt, one of them sliding up and teasing his nipple. She giggled when his erect cock bumped against her leg.

"I can think of somewhere better for that," she told him.

He chuckled, then stood. She opened her legs and moved to the edge of the counter before rolling over onto her stomach so she could slide down. His pelvis was nearly a foot beneath the surface of the counter, which meant he wasn't going to be able to fuck her unless he found something to stand on.

Her curvy hips were the perfect size for grabbing, and he slid his hands along her bubble butt as she tried to back onto him. Her labia were already swollen and wet, but the head of his cock wasn't going in that easily. He teased her for a bit, pressing against her pussy until she let out a groan and tried to guide him in with her hands.

It took some doing, but he finally achieved the right angle so he didn't slide away. Holding tight to her hips, he let gravity help him as he pulled her down onto his cock. She was so tight that he worried about hurting her, but the happy sounds she made said otherwise.

"Oh Santa, yes, please!" Holly was pressing against the counter so hard that her nails were digging into the wood. She started to bounce herself, only achieving a small amount of success with each thrust. Mike found himself pressed deep inside her and was surprised to see that over half his cock had made the journey. By now, he should have run into the back wall or bumped against her uterus.

Curious as to how deep he could go, he allowed the elf to impale herself on his throbbing rod, her legs now spasming every time another inch was inside her. The head of his cock was now warmer than usual, and a gush of fluid squirted out of Holly's pussy, coating his shaft.

"Oh, sweet Christmas," she gasped, then turned her head sideways. Her eyes had rolled up into her head, and she was drooling from breathing so hard. "More, please, Santa, more! I've been such a good girl!"

Feeling it was poor taste to deny such a simple request, Mike obliged. The last couple of inches were tough, but he moved his hands up to her waist and pulled as hard as he could, surprised that there was still room for him. A jolt of pleasure rushed up his spine when his magic came to life, sending small sparks that crept across Holly's ass and disappeared under her skirt.

Holly was whimpering now, a queer smile stuck on her face as he slowly fucked her. If he paused for more than a couple of seconds, she would start bucking her hips in an attempt to get him deeper inside. The butcher block counter now had small scratches in it where she had gouged out the wood with her nails.

He picked up the pace, emboldened by her enthusiasm. On an impulse, he used his thumb to penetrate her asshole, which got a loud groan followed by Holly whispering the chorus to "Jingle Bells" under her breath.

Seeing that the sparks were all concentrating on Holly, it occurred to Mike that shooting his load inside an elf might be a bad idea. Though Holly had somehow found a way to incorporate sexuality into her life without blowing a fuse, what would happen to her if she got a piece of him? For that matter, what would he get from her? If he fully understood Mrs. Claus, Holly was technically at least half-eldritch, and he didn't know if he wanted to tie himself to that kind of chaos.

Opening his mind, he saw his magic dancing along Holly's body, sliding into her pores to tease at the swirling core in the middle of her body. Her own magic looked like taffy in a taffy puller—it shimmered and changed colors as it stretched and distorted, mingling with the sparks that had vanished. His magic was spreading out, forming into a series of liquid runes that danced along Holly's rib cage. The closer he got to orgasm, the more solid they appeared.

They looked almost identical to the ones Naia had. The longer he looked at them, the more they seemed to twist and distort, his eyes unable to focus properly on them.

"Hold up," he told the elf. "I'm about to come. Where do you want it?"

The announcement of his orgasm caused her to groan and come again, her legs kicking wildly. He tried to pull himself free, but she used the counter to flip herself over so she was facing him.

"I want to feel you inside me," she growled, her emerald eyes blazing with magic. It was mostly her own, but he could see that his magic had permeated her body and spun around her, the runes now blazing with light. They shifted and locked into place as the familiar sensation of heat filled his groin.

"But, um…you could get pregnant," he stuttered, not sure how to tell her that they probably shouldn't swap souls. Did elves even have souls? How did that work?

"Elves don't get pregnant," she told him. "We're made, not born. Now fill me up with your steaming-hot cum. I want to feel it leaking out of me like the dirty slut I am."

Surprised, he didn't resist when she wrapped her arms around his neck and pulled herself up to him. When she kissed him, her legs tightened around his waist, her ankles not quite crossing. The magic was swirling around both of them now, and he was barely holding on.

Holly's eyes lit up, and she buried her face in his shoulder, her hot breath on his ear just before she bit him.

He roared when he came, and the magical lights dimmed as a maelstrom of energy only he could see settled around the two of them. A bright light emanated from Holly's chest, and a mote the size of a firefly emerged from it. A similar mote appeared from him, only this one was blue. The two of them fluttered around each other before swapping places.

A ripple of energy went through the room, like a massive wave in a small pond. It rebounded off the walls and sank back into the two of them, vanishing as the magical runes on Holly's chest smoldered through her clothing, then disappeared. She was growling now, her pussy squeezing him every couple of seconds.

Yuki is gonna be so mad at me, he thought. So much for watching who he came in.

Holly had an intense look on her face as she rolled her hips, using his shoulders to support her weight. There was a scary determination there, almost as if he was being challenged. The elf licked her lips, revealing that her upper lip had blood on it from when she'd bitten him.

The magic circling them suddenly vanished, and Holly let out a moan before falling limp onto the counter, a satisfied grin pasted on her face. Her legs released him, and he pulled his cock out of her, then watched in horror as a massive amount of shimmering cum leaked onto the floor, splattering everywhere.

He flinched when the door to the kitchen opened but was relieved to see it was Kisa and not Mrs. Claus.

"I fucking knew it," Kisa said, shaking her head. "I even thought to myself, 'Nah, he isn't gonna fuck her, they should be fine together.'"

"She started it," he said, pushing Holly onto the counter so she wouldn't fall. The elf giggled, her eyes frozen on some faraway scene. She was clearly in her own world now. "I wasn't even trying to seduce her, I promise."

"Damn, you wrecked her." Kisa hopped onto the counter and waved her hand in front of Holly's eyes. Seeing no response, she laughed and moved her hand to the pouch on Holly's waist. "Main reason I came down here was for these."

Kisa pulled a pair of earmuffs out, which she put on Holly. "Holly explained naughty sickness a bit. When they get caught up in something, they go all out. I could tell you two were banging and came down to toss these on her before the two of you kicked off a weeklong marathon session. Looks like there wasn't any need though."

Mike let out a sigh of relief, then looked down at the mess by his feet. "I don't suppose you know where the towels are."

"Just ask Mrs. Claus, she's right behind me." Kisa looked over at the door as Mike frantically hopped, trying to pull his pants back up. He slipped in his own cum and landed ass-first on the floor. Kisa looked over the edge of the counter and laughed.

"I was just messing with you. Told them I was going to the bathroom and would be right back." She stuck her hand beneath the counter and opened one of the drawers. Inside was a set of small towels with Christmas trees embroidered on them. "Here."

Mike took the towel and cleaned up the floor first, mortified by how the surface seemed to shimmer afterward, despite his best efforts. Kisa helped adjust Holly's outfit, and the two of them moved the semiconscious elf back into the living room. Holly kept giggling to herself and fluttering her eyelashes at Mike.

"You broke her," Kisa declared, then looked upstairs. "I'd better get back. Stay out of trouble this time?"

He shook his head. "I honestly can't make any promises. It's been a weird couple of days."

"It always is." She hopped onto a nearby table, putting her

at eye level with him. She touched his chest and leaned forward to give him a kiss. "But seriously. Stop fucking everyone you meet. Especially when I'm nearby, 'cause now I'm all hot and bothered."

"I'll keep that in mind." He watched her go, then looked over at the elf. Holly was watching him with that stupid grin. "You okay over there?"

She giggled, then winced, holding her stomach. "Ooh, I've never been so sore inside. But yes, I'll be fine. And Mike?"

"Hmm?" He sat down across from her, now wary. In a lot of ways, she really was like Tink. The thought made him touch his ear, which had already healed.

"I will not be waiting until next Christmas to do that again." Smirking, she pulled a cookie out of her belt and took a bite. "You can count on it."

THE COLD SHOULDER

Yuki stepped into the bitter cold of the arctic, pausing just long enough to close the window behind her. The sloped roof above was covered in thick powder that had acquired a substantial crust of ice along the top, and her feet broke through the drift beneath her as she walked away from the house.

The northern lights were now obscured, casting the Christmas village into darkness. A majority of the light now streamed from the windows of Santa's home, which looked like a cross between an old lodge and a castle. The high, arched peaks of the house were decorated in sparkling lights, and a large wooden shield with a carved *SC* had been hung on the front of the house.

She was not surprised to see that it was much smaller on the outside. The exterior was only three stories tall with a small chimney up top that released a steady cloud of smoke. If she remembered correctly, the interior was at least five stories high, which made her wonder how the outside kept track of all the windows on the inside.

"Stay focused," she muttered to herself, turning away from the home.

The front walk was already obscured by snowdrifts from the storm, but she navigated it without any problem. She moved the snow away from her, clearing the path in case she needed to make a hasty retreat or find her way to safety. She could already tell that the storm itself was unnatural, but the sheer amount of power she felt off toward the horizon was slightly alarming.

It had to be Jack. There was no question about it. If Yuki had said something to Mike, he would have demanded to help. It was so far below freezing that it was almost too cold for Yuki. He wouldn't last more than a couple of minutes outside, not unless Mrs. Claus had squirreled away a bunch of enchanted gear for visitors.

The streetlamps were lit with magic, and more than a couple flickered, ready to go out. She sent out bursts of fox fire to the ones that were broken, bolstering the enchantment within so they stayed lit. Whimsical buildings that looked to be made of gingerbread were frosted over, and some of the candy-cane fencing had fallen over to shatter on the ground.

She closed her eyes and commanded the hair on her body to elongate, wrapping her in both warmth and safety. To an outsider, it would appear as a thick coat of dark fur, making her stand out on the icy tundra. Yuki didn't bother trying to hide. Jack would likely be able to sense a warm body from a mile away.

It was a long walk to the edge of the village. The silent buildings around her were reminiscent of mausoleums, though she did occasionally notice movement in the darkness. She hoped it was the elves but wondered what other dangers lurked in the North Pole. One shadow in particular was very large, skulking around behind nearby buildings for a while before disappearing. Were there other forces at work here? Would they go looking for Mike if they knew he was alone?

Mike.

She smiled, rubbing her lower belly. She was still sore from their rough lovemaking, though that wasn't the correct term. It hadn't just been fucking either; there had been so many emotions involved. Not only had it been fun, but her entire soul had relaxed afterward, as if it had been stretched tight for the last couple of decades.

How could she pay back a man who had saved not only her life but maybe even her soul as well? Even now, she could feel that her magic had changed, like a friend who had gone away for many years, both familiar yet strange. So many aspects of it that had been closed to her now swirled within her, eager to be reacquainted.

When she got to the edge of the village, she took a deep breath in through her nose and smiled. Older magic radiated through her body, filling her with a warmth she hadn't felt in decades. For the first time since Emily, she was…*complete.*

After sex with Mike, something had changed inside her. It was as though someone had picked up all the leftover pieces of who she'd used to be and put them back where they'd used to go. The pieces were still loose, and it would take time to glue them all back in place, but at least the whole picture could now be seen. It was why she wondered what he had acquired from her, because what she had received from him was peace.

Beneath her feet, the cold earth slumbered but responded with interest to her touch. On the day she had acquired her second tail, she had chosen the element of earth as her specialty. It had given her quite the array of magic, which she had used to protect herself and others.

On the day she had grown her third tail, her broken soul had latched onto the element of ice. It was cold and unforgiving, much as she had been. Recently, she had worried that her command over ice magic was slipping, but she knew better now. It wasn't that she had become weaker but that her heart was now stronger. She had relied so much on that sense of abandonment, on the anguish that had come with being broken, to develop her bond with the ice.

The cold that had once comforted her now felt like a stranger. She no longer sought its embrace, nor found comfort in the way it numbed her. Where she had once craved it, the desire was gone, and the ice knew.

However, as the ice withdrew, the earth remained. She could no longer rely on one aspect of her magic alone, because the grief powering it had largely diminished. The ice was only one aspect of her magic, and without most of her deck of cards, it was time to rely on an old friend.

The horizon was obscured by what looked like a massive fog bank, but Yuki knew better. It was a swirling mass of snow and ice, barreling toward the Christmas village with the ferocity of a hurricane.

"What are you up to, Jack?" She pondered the length of the storm, realizing the power she saw didn't agree with what she knew of Jack's abilities. A massive storm was doable, given enough time. It was the moving shapes within that had her concerned. Controlling a storm on top of elementals?

Had she underestimated Jack's skills? There had only been the one encounter, and Jack Frost had easily overpowered any control Yuki had over elemental ice, a feat that would probably be even easier now. But if Jack had always been this powerful, she should have easily defeated Mike and Yuki when they'd first met.

Yuki crouched, pushing her hand through the icy crust of the top layer of snow until her fingers touched the frozen soil beneath. Closing her eyes, she let the magic flow through her, spreading out across the landscape. She could feel the steady pounding of feet, the heavy vibrations traveling out from the coming stampede.

Jack hadn't just raised a storm. She was bringing an army.

Frowning, Yuki reached into her sleeves and pulled out her tarot cards. Nothing in the Minor Arcana would help her, and she had very little in the Major Arcana. She had burned through most of them on her return to Earth, and they took a long time to recreate.

The Moon, Temperance, and the Wheel of Fortune were the only ones she had. Scowling, she looked up at the approaching army. The Sun card would have been great, but she had used that to build a dimensional pressure cooker to blow up a demon's pocket universe. The Lovers card could benefit her, but she had accidentally used that on Cerberus. Smirking, she thought of Mike and all the crazy adventures he had already taken her on.

"Crazy human." She tucked the Major Arcana back into their secret sleeve and pulled out what was left of the Minor Arcana. Only a few cards had survived her trip into the furnace, and these wouldn't be much help.

It was time to get creative. Closing her eyes, she communed with the earth, curious what she could even accomplish here. Summoning pillars of ice was easy because ice was fairly light and craved being sculpted, transformed into various shapes.

The earth was different. It was stubborn and heavy, and she felt it groan beneath her as it pushed its way up through the snow, forming a thick stalagmite.

"Oh, come on." She sent another tendril of magic down, feeling everything out. The ground beneath the Christmas village was solid bedrock and would be hard to manipulate. She wasn't going to be able to do a whole lot with it on a large scale.

Still, there were plenty of tricks up her sleeve. She sank her mind into the earth and drifted through the frozen stone, examining its capabilities. Though the earth was loath to obey her commands, it was happy to give her its strength.

When she opened her eyes, the surface of her fur had taken on a crystalline sheen. It was a defensive spell, one she hadn't used in years. All around her, hundreds of small rock obelisks had formed. It was hardly the defensive wall she had tried to summon, but it would do.

Hopping up onto the nearest obelisk, she created a tube out of ice. Crystals became lenses, and she used the makeshift telescope to get a better idea of what was going on.

"Holy mother of—" It was an army made of ice. Scanning the horizon, she found all manner of beasts charging toward her. Up in the sky, creatures zoomed about, carried aloft by giant wings. They were griffins with icy beaks and snowflake wings. Toward the back of the surge, giant abominations made of snow and ice lumbered along behind their brethren.

At the head of the pack was Jack Frost. Her blue features were determined but were now lined with golden cracks that shed an immense amount of light. Cold, calculating eyes darted about with the gaze of a predator, and her icy hair hung like a blanket of fog behind her. The bland outfit she had worn before was gone, replaced by a fancy gown decorated with lace and snowflakes.

"And they called me the white witch," Yuki muttered, lowering the scope. What would Mike do in this situation? Yuki was all by herself, and didn't have the first idea of what she hoped to accomplish on her own.

"Damn, damn, damn," she muttered, her magic shifting drastically inside her. Maybe this wasn't a battle she could win, but then what? Go back and warn the others? They could flee to safety, but it would mean abandoning the North Pole. Mike wouldn't do that, not while he knew others needed his help.

Even if her ice magic had been at full strength, Yuki couldn't take Jack on in a head-to-head fight. Lifting the scope to her eyes once more, she saw that Jack was staring back, eyes brimming with power. Her face had twisted up into a wild snarl, the look of an unhinged woman ready to snap. It was a feeling Yuki knew very well, that sense of all-consuming rage.

Yuki tried to zoom in on those golden lines, but an icy fog

enveloped Jack and her army, obscuring them from view. Even this far away, she could feel the magical pressure that came from Jack. It was an entirely different sort of energy, orders of magnitude greater than what she had felt from the woman before.

Somehow, Jack had gone through some form of apotheosis. It was a process Yuki planned to undergo someday if she could live to be a thousand, but there was a reason the process took a long time. Tapping into divine energy was like putting rocket fuel in a go-cart—the vessel was far more likely to explode before it could even accelerate.

The how and why didn't matter. She couldn't let Jack reach Mike.

Smiling to herself, she summoned hundreds of images of herself on top of the obelisks. Calling out to the earth, she got it to feed thermal energy into the stones it had given, which would confuse Jack's ability to sense heat differences. The mirages of herself were simple illusions, a spell she had learned along with fox fire. They were incapable of creating sound and were easily distinguishable from the real Yuki in bright light. It was a spell she hadn't bothered with in years, preferring to lean on her ice magic.

Things were different now. It was as though a band of light was holding her together, reminding her both of the person she'd used to be and the one she could become. The best parts of her were ready to step forward and protect the man she saw as her friend and lover.

A battle of magic would be easily won by Old Bitch Winter. But a battle of intellect? Yuki fingered the cards in her sleeve with a smile, then summoned fox fire into her hands. All across the snowy landscape, her copies did the same.

Jack was about to find out what happened when you fucked with a trickster.

The wind carried Jack across the low hills of the North Pole as she rode the edge of the storm. The plan was to send her army into the buildings and chase out anyone hiding there, be they elf or otherwise. She didn't trust anybody, least of all that grotesque woman, Grýla. The giant was loyal to the Krampus and would not take kindly to Jack's coup.

Once the north was firmly in her grasp, she planned to lay a trap for the demon and catch him when he returned. If she could get him to divulge where he had hidden Santa, she planned to give the fat man a piece of her mind before informing him that she was now in charge. If he was willing to work with her, Christmas could even remain a reality.

But the stories about it? They were long overdue for an update. If Santa wanted to survive, it would be at her service. She had that much figured out. Was she still even Jack Frost? Or perhaps a better name was in order?

"You could always use our old name," the mysterious woman whispered, using Jack's mouth and a slightly different voice. "We were loved and respected. Why not return to the old ways?"

"Old ways? What were the old ways?" Jack tried to ignore how disturbing it was to have her own face hijacked.

The woman chuckled, then twisted up her face. "We were loved and adored, long before the fall of Asgard. Some still believe, though we have become little more than stories."

"Who was I? Or is it we? Am I really you?"

"You are little more than a fragment of former glory given time to wither and die. Old Man Winter indeed, you settled for the first measly scraps offered! If I had my way, this version of you would be cast out entirely!"

"Well, then it's a good thing you don't get your way," Jack snarled, then turned her attention forward. Lights, dozens of them, dotted the landscape just outside the village. Had the elves been freed? No, these were too tall to be elves. Perhaps Grýla was up to something?

Moving closer, she saw the kitsune she had last seen disappearing down into the furnace. Copies of her stood everywhere, all of them staring directly at Jack.

"A deception so simple even a child could see through it." The woman grinned.

"Agreed." Jack tapped into the cold and was surprised to see that each of the illusory copies had an identical heat signature. How had she done that?

"Jack!" the kitsune called to her. "I just want to talk." She held the flickering light in her hands aloft, and it briefly formed into the shape of a dove.

"Lies!" the woman screamed.

Jack shook her head, the woman's voice ringing in her ears. All around her, the creatures of ice and snow paused, awaiting Jack's commands. With a thought, she could have the kitsune destroyed and continue on her way.

"Then just do it!" the woman yelled. Jack hovered there, buoyed by the winds and contemplating the fox demon below. She had been moments away from crushing her with a hand made of ice, but the woman's belligerent tone made her pause. It wasn't that she cared what the kitsune had to say or that she'd had a change of heart.

Nobody told her what to do. Not anymore.

"Then speak," Jack called, summoning a staff made of ice.

"It looks like you're getting ready for a war," the kitsune responded, gesturing toward the army of snow. "I would know who you plan to fight with these creatures."

"Whoever I damn well please!" the woman shrieked.

"Anyone who would stand in my way!" Jack shouted right after.

"That's technically two answers." The kitsune frowned, then crossed her arms, the flames fluttering overhead. Every copy of her performed an identical movement, some flickering briefly as the illusion adjusted so they all faced Jack. "It sounds like you're out to get everyone."

"Look around you, little fox. The north has fallen and is in need of new ownership. Someone who can protect it, someone who can guide it, someone who…" Jack paused. Did she really want to be in charge of the North Pole? What was she even doing here? Did she want to fight this woman? Pain flared right behind her eyes, and the golden light seeping from her veins intensified.

"You're stalling," the woman growled.

"No, I'm waiting for you to properly answer my question," the kitsune replied, thinking Jack was talking to her.

"I wasn't talking to you!" The woman raised a hand, and one of the snow leopards, a beast nearly eight feet at the shoulder, charged into the kitsune. It leaped into the air and brought its claws down, only to shatter apart on impact. The kitsune had vanished, replaced by a smooth monolith made of stone.

"That wasn't very nice," the kitsune muttered, all her copies briefly regarding the exposed monolith. "And I'm the only one here. Who are you talking to?"

"I didn't mean to do that," Jack replied. "I don't know why I did that."

"Because you are weak!" The woman's temper flared, and Jack clutched at her head again. "You have made us weak! This place is to become our new home, and we will protect it as the Queen of the North!"

"So what? Kill the Krampus and let us all go?" The kitsune pondered the answer. "I still don't get your end game here."

"Oh yes, we will kill that evil bastard!"

Jack's mouth went numb as she lost control of her lips to the woman.

"And we will kill the giant and all her disgusting children. And when people learn what we have saved them from, they will give us the love and adoration we deserve!"

"What about Santa? The elves? The people I came with?"

"Sa…Santa will be fine," Jack spluttered. "The elves and Santa will be fine." She wanted to be loved and remembered, not universally loathed. Now that she thought about it, would enslaving Santa create the same problem? Her head hurt so much she couldn't keep her thoughts straight. Having the kitsune ask such a simple question was punching holes in her logic, but every time she looked, all she could see was that molten light inside her.

"You and your friends can leave," the woman added, as if to placate Jack. "It is clear you are not with the Krampus, so I shall allow you the grace to leave and spread tales of my benevolence. But that man you came with, the one named Mike. I sense a fearful power in him, a power I will cut short."

"Wow. I think I finally understand what's happening now." The kitsune shook her head, then waved her hand. A massive barricade of icicles appeared, spreading across the frozen ground, and the ground trembled, shaking loose ice and snow. Giant glittering clouds billowed outward, only to be sucked up by the storm. "Here I was, hoping we could have some super chill girl talk, but you went ahead and brought your backup bitch to do the talking for you."

"Nobody speaks to me that way!" The woman held out Jack's hand, summoning a massive amount of magic. The air swirled around them, visibility dropping. The kitsune's flames still burned, making each of them an easy target.

"Ugh, I have no idea how Mike puts up with this shit." The kitsune's voice now came from everywhere, bouncing between the flames. "So I guess I'll level with you. That guy you wanna kill? He's done nothing to you. And based on your shitty Gollum impression, nothing I say is going to convince you otherwise."

"I am no golem!" Beneath Jack, the army surged forward, running, flying, and swimming through the snow. It looked as if the ground was boiling, the storm's fury coalescing around the illusionary kitsunes. "This body may be but a pittance of my former beauty, but know now that I am what remains of the goddess of war, Freyja!"

"Freyja?" Jack's lips twitched as she forced the word out. She'd used to be Freyja? The name sounded so familiar, but this anger? That wasn't who she had been…right? That small voice in the back of her mind was practically screaming now, and she could no longer see out of one of her eyes.

"Freyja, huh? I've heard of you." The kitsune growled, summoning a handful of flames. "If you're good, maybe I'll put that name on the other side of your tombstone, you crazy—"

Freyja screamed, and the ground exploded. Creatures of ice and fury tore into each of the illusions, shattering themselves on hidden stone pillars as icicles erupted from the ground. None of the illusions left their posts, instead sending out fire and ice to destroy their attackers. The spikes slowed down Jack's larger warriors, the giants she had created from the ocean ice. Massive limbs smashed the icicles into powder while the smaller warriors advanced. These ones were pierced by more ice, were melted with flames, or shattered themselves on the hidden stone beneath the illusions.

"I don't know what you were expecting," Jack snorted as she landed on the ground. Between the storm and all the snow that had been kicked up, visibility was nearly nonexistent. "Your power with the ice is nothing compared to my own."

"I will piss on your corpse, little dog." Freyja summoned a ball of golden energy and smashed it into the nearest kitsune. She winced and puffed out of existence, leaving a stone pillar behind. "You hide behind cheap tricks. You have no honor."

"And you do?" The kitsune's laugh was high-pitched. "Tell me, Freyja, if that's even your real name…"

"*I am Freyja*!" When the goddess screamed, that golden light radiated outward, suffusing dozens of Jack's minions with divine magic. The creatures affected stumbled as if disoriented, then went into a blind rage, attacking those who were unaffected.

"No, stop!" Jack cried, but Freyja bit down on their shared tongue, filling their mouth with blood. Jack tried to press back against Freyja's control, but her presence was now too strong to resist.

"Thilenth! I'm thick of your weakneth!" Freyja lashed out with their staff, smashing it into a nearby kitsune. The illusion shattered, leaving behind another stone monolith. "Now where are you? I will make you beg for your life, you thtupid animal!"

Jack's blood boiled, the golden cracks on her body widening to reveal molten flows that spilled onto the ground, melting the snow away. Rays of light emerged from her body, blasting away the storm as Freyja's rage took over. In a moment of revelation, Jack saw that this wouldn't bring the love, recognition, or adoration she sought.

It was simply madness. Freyja was casting magic at random, sending pillars of light into their phantom attackers, and screaming in pain. Their shared body was building up heat, and Jack's cold hands tingled as the light burned her flesh away. As more of Freyja emerged, Jack realized the goddess was fractured in a way she couldn't comprehend. It was as if only the angry part of her had been able to manifest, the one desperate for survival and revenge. Was this really who she had been?

Because if it was, it definitely wasn't who she wanted to be.

"DIE!" Freyja threw their staff at the last remaining kitsune, who widened her eyes in fright. When the staff struck, the kitsune exploded outward, transforming into the stony remains of yet another monolith.

"COWARD!" Freyja lifted their hands, golden light coalescing between her fingers. "I WILL BURN THIS PLACE DOWN TO FIND YOU!"

As they passed a nearby monolith, it blurred, the air distorting as the kitsune emerged, a single card in her hands. She was fast, her hand slapping Jack in the chest so hard that she fell backward into the snow.

"*How dare you, you fucking—*"

"My name is Yuki." The kitsune winked as a ball of sparkling light appeared just over her chest. Jack stared at it in wonder as it expanded, creating a haze between them. The haze solidified into a tendril of light that reached for Jack. She followed the line, surprised to see a card depicting an angel pouring water from one cup to another tucked into the bosom of her gown. "And I'm the goddess of kicking your ass."

A beam of silver light connected the women, and Jack screamed as the golden energy was sucked from her body, spiraling along that connecting thread and entering Yuki. The smug look on the kitsune's face faltered as a third line appeared, diverting the energy to someone hiding beneath the snow.

Yuki let out a groan of agony, doubling over in pain.

"NO! THAT'S MINE!" Freyja's shrill cry became a sob. "Give it back, please!"

"Eat…my…ass!" Yuki barked out a single laugh, then screamed in agony. All around them, Jack's surviving minions fled into the village, disappearing from sight as the storm finally died.

MIKE WAS IN THE MIDDLE OF ONE OF THE TOM CLANCY novels when Mrs. Claus appeared above the stairwell. She looked tired, and several more wrinkles lined her face.

"You two look comfortable." A wistful smile appeared on her face as she looked down at Mike. Holly had snuggled in next to him, her head on his lap. She was asleep, letting out tiny moans as she dreamed about sugarplum fairies, or whatever it was that elves dreamed of.

"She wanted to stay close in case the ghost who shall not be named arrives." Though his tone was light, he felt a certain level of dread knowing that the Ghost of Christmas Future was lingering somewhere, potentially ready to pounce. The first two ghosts had found him quickly, and he didn't dare attribute it to dumb luck that the third hadn't.

"I see." A few strands of hair had come loose, framing Mrs. Claus's face. "If I were to make an assumption, my guess is that a spirit who can see the future is waiting for the perfect moment to strike."

"I hate that assumption." Mike jostled Holly, who bolted upright as if an alarm had gone off.

"Nutmeg!" she yelled, then blinked and looked up at Mike. "Hey, there," she purred, then noticed Mrs. Claus. As if a bucket of ice water had struck her, she was all business again. "Are the maps done?"

"They are." Mrs. Claus waved them up.

Mike and Holly ascended the stairs, then walked down a long corridor that smelled like fresh cut cedar. The oaken double doors at the end were heavy, and when he walked inside, the smell of wood shavings took him back to his one semester of high school woodshop. He had been an average student, his birdhouse sufficient enough for the finch that had moved in. It had only taken one harsh winter for the structure to fall apart.

Santa's personal workshop was the size of a three-car garage. Tools hung in carefully labeled places along a back wall, and a massive clamp at the end of a workbench held an alphabet block together the size of Mike's head. A large letter *M* was carved in the visible side. Half-completed projects had been pushed to the side, and a large sheet of drafting paper had been spread on one of the benches. Tink and Kisa were sitting at another table with smaller sheets of paper, the goblin using a pencil to make notes on it.

"Here it is." Mrs. Claus tapped the larger sheet, then sat on a nearby stool. "This is about as accurate as I could make it. I don't think there's anything I missed."

Mike stared at the map in awe. It looked like something that had been drawn up by an engineer, each of the buildings clearly labeled.

"You did this from memory?" he asked.

"I did. When you live somewhere for hundreds of years, you get to know the place."

"Wait, hundreds?" He turned to Mrs. Claus. "I didn't think you were that old."

"You have to remember that time flows differently here," she said, adjusting her negligee. "When you go to sleep on Christmas Eve, it can be months or even years for me here. Also, I wasn't born an old woman but created with years of pseudomemories from around the North Pole. Otherwise, I would have been like a child. You keep forgetting I'm an extension of Santa's magic."

"I forget a lot of things," he admitted.

"Maybe you should stop." She chuckled, then slid the map toward him. "You're going to want to keep this safe. I don't have it in me to make another copy."

Curious, Mike examined Mrs. Claus's magic again. What had once been a bright light of energy was now just a dim glow, with dozens of massive threads unraveling from her body.

"Are…are you okay?"

"I'm not." Mrs. Claus opened her mouth to say something, then slumped forward on the table.

"Mother!" Holly ran to Mrs. Claus while Kisa and Tink abandoned their work to come over as well. Mike moved to the other side of the table and easily picked the woman up in his arms. She was much lighter than she should have been, definitely less than a hundred pounds.

"Let's get her to the bedroom," he said. He carried the frail woman to her room, and Holly adjusted the pillows while Kisa pulled the blankets back. Once she was properly tucked in, Mike watched in horror as the woman briefly flickered out of existence like a faulty light.

"Whoa!" He examined her magic again, a cold chill going through his body. In the time it had taken him to carry her up, most of her magic had unraveled like a massive ball of yarn. Out of protective instinct, he summoned his magic and went to work, tucking the threads back in.

His legs went numb beneath him, but Kisa was there, pushing him into a seated position on the bed before he could fall. Tink yanked the goggles off her head and slid them over his eyes, and he went from blindly working to suddenly understanding what was needed. He paused, his spectral fingers now weaving the frayed edges of Mrs. Claus's magic back together, forming a technicolor rope that he wove back into place.

"Will she be okay?" Holly asked.

"I don't know," he muttered, sweat pouring down his forehead. His magic, sensing his determination, had formed into motes of light that tugged and pulled Mrs. Claus's magic back into place before popping out of existence and leaving him drained. Groaning, he slid the goggles up to his forehead.

Everyone watched as the color came back to Mrs. Claus's face, and she let out a sigh of relief, then opened her eyes and looked at Mike.

"I don't have much time," she said.

"But you should have more," he replied. "You're unraveling faster than before. I don't understand."

"I don't either." She turned to Holly. "But it can only mean that belief is weakening."

"That's bullshit," Kisa growled. "The world is frozen,

remember? It's not like people can stop believing when they're just sitting there, doing nothing."

Mrs. Claus took a deep breath, then closed her eyes. When she spoke, her eyes remained closed. "Time is a fickle thing," she whispered. "You have to stop thinking of it as a line, especially here at the North Pole. Whatever is happening now means the outcome will be bad once the spell ends. Change the outcome, change my fate."

"Like *Back to the Future*." Mike snapped his fingers in revelation, then looked at the others. "We're operating outside of time right now, which means everything is in flux until we rejoin the time stream."

"Ugh." Tink shook her head and moved away from the bed, checking her tool belt. "Husband still catching up, maybe figure out eventually."

"What, like you properly understand?" Kisa rolled her eyes at the goblin.

"Tink understand perfectly. North Pole like big box. Santa like cat. Until open box, Santa both dead and alive." Tink pulled her map out, refolded it so it fit better in one of her pockets, then retrieved a cookie she had tucked between her breasts. "Tink fix furnace, help keep cat alive."

Holly frowned at Tink. "Are you talking about…?" Her eyes flitted over to Kisa, then back.

"No. Tink have no time, maybe explain quantum shit later." She climbed onto the bed and grabbed Mike by the face before planting her lips against his. She tasted of chocolate and gingerbread. With a grin, she pulled the goggles off his head and put them on her own. "Help save Christmas, get big present from Santa. Husband keep everybody safe."

"Be careful," he told her, then wrapped his arms around her. "I love you."

She hugged him back, pausing just long enough to bite him before breaking away.

"I'll check in every couple of hours," Kisa said. "Or try to, at least. Try to stay out of trouble."

Mike looked at Holly, then back at Mrs. Claus. "Yuki will be back soon," he offered. "I'll let her know she's in charge."

"Good." Kisa smoothed some of the hair away from his face and gave him a kiss as well. "There's a vent in the pantry behind the kitchen just big enough for us to squeeze through. Tink is going to get me into one of the other buildings, and then I'm going to try to figure out what that…jerk is up to. That, and find the elves. I'll let you know before I make any big decisions."

"Good." He pulled her in for a hug.

"Try not to fuck Santa's wife," she whispered so he alone could hear. "Santa might shove lumps of coal up your ass, or something."

"You have my word," he replied, dropping his hand to her lower back and scratching. He felt her shiver in delight before stepping away. Her eyes held a certain intensity, and he instinctively knew she wasn't just going out to spy on the Krampus. "Just promise me that whatever you're looking for, you'll remember the most important thing is that you make it back to us."

Kisa opened her mouth as if to argue with him, then changed her mind when she realized he had essentially given her permission to do her own thing.

"I will," she said, then bade farewell to Holly before moving away from the bed. Tink was already at the bedroom door, but she blew Holly a kiss before she and Kisa left.

"I hope they'll be okay," Holly muttered, then looked back at Mike. Her eyes moved up and down his body, and a grin appeared on her face. It occurred to him that it was essentially just the two of them now, and Holly was looking at him like he was the last present under the tree.

"They'll be fine." He turned his attention to Mrs. Claus

and brushed a stray hair from her face. She flinched, then let out a sigh.

"I knew this day would come," she whispered.

"What do you mean?" he asked.

"The end of Christmas." A weak smile appeared, and she opened her eyes. "Everything is inevitable, Caretaker. There would come a day where mankind would become extinct, and their gods and traditions would go with them. I thought it would be much farther into the future than this."

"Christmas isn't over," he told her, then took her by the hand. "Not yet. No matter what happens today, my family will celebrate it every year, no matter what."

"One family's faith won't be enough to sustain a tradition." She squeezed his hand. "But I appreciate the thought."

"Nonsense," Mike told her. "If there's one thing I believe, it's that every miracle begins with a single person. You just watch, everything is going to be all right when this is over."

Mrs. Claus smiled, then closed her eyes. "Perhaps you are right, Caretaker. Holly?"

"Ma'am?" The elf moved to her side.

"No matter what happens next, never lose faith." She patted Holly's hand. "As long as you survive, everything can be made right. But you have to keep believing."

"I…" Holly looked at Mike. "Of course I will, why would I stop?"

Mrs. Claus didn't respond. She had slipped into a deep sleep, her chest rising and falling with a slow rhythm that was unnerving to watch. Mike inspected her again, horrified to see that her magic was even smaller than before.

"I don't understand," he muttered. Where was her magic going? Determined to get an answer, he sat with the old woman and scrutinized her magic with a determined intensity. He didn't have the goggles anymore, but what he had learned earlier had been enough for him to understand the basics. It was like digging through a website's code for the first time to learn how it functioned. That was a skill from his old life with sudden relevance, which surprised him a little bit.

He had come so far. The timid man content to live alone and run websites for people was long gone, so it was interesting to delve into his old skill set once again. Examining magic wasn't as simple as lines of code, because they were constantly changing as he watched them. Still, he got general ideas from them, and he did his best to tuck a few more back into place.

"Will she be okay?" Holly asked as she took Mrs. Claus's glasses off and set them on the nightstand.

"I don't know," Mike admitted, then turned his gaze onto the elf. Where Mrs. Claus's magic looked like a bundle of unraveling threads, Holly's looked like the star one would put on top of a Christmas tree. When she looked at him, he saw strange colors insert themselves into her magic, then radiate outward in playful loops that caressed his body before vanishing like smoke.

"Oh, shi—shoot," he whispered, realizing the truth of what he was seeing. It wasn't just magic but the very essence of who Holly was as a person. In hindsight, it made so much sense, but he marveled at the sheer beauty of her soul and how the magic that had created her bound the whole thing together in beautiful red ribbons with silver bells on the end.

"You're staring," she said with concern. "And…crying?"

"Yeah, I'm having a moment, sorry." He wiped the tears from his eyes and blinked a few times to chase the image away. Was this what it was like for Cecilia? The banshee could only see souls, for the most part. Holly's was uniquely beautiful, and he felt like he could stare at it all day without getting bored.

Holly seemed dubious of his answer, then grinned mischievously. "Maybe we could arrange for a different kind of moment?" she asked, her tone hopeful.

He looked at Mrs. Claus. "Now probably isn't the time,"

he whispered, suddenly afraid the old woman would sit up in bed and strangle him. "C'mon, let's head back to the main room and give her some peace and quiet."

Holly licked her lips and stepped away from the bed, her hips swaying as she walked toward the door.

"Ah, geez." Mike followed her into the hallway. After closing the door behind him, he turned to see Holly leaning against the opposite wall, her fingers tugging playfully at the fabric of her skirt.

"I don't suppose—" she began.

He chuckled, then rubbed his stomach when it growled. "I won't say no, but I will say I'm starving."

Holly reached into her pouch, but he stopped her. "If there's anything else to eat here, we should probably save the magic cookies for later," he told her. He didn't know where Mrs. Claus got her food from, but had a sneaking suspicion there wouldn't be any more coming in. That, and he was tired of baked goods.

The elf nodded her agreement, closing the flap of her pouch. "I can make sandwiches," she said, then moved close to him. She wrapped her arms around his waist, pulling him in tight. "There's always some leftover roast or something in the fridge. You'd be surprised how much meat I can pack in between a couple of buns with the right amount of mayonnaise. How many would you like?"

"A couple," he replied, ignoring her double entendre. "And maybe a spare one for when Yuki gets back. She's been gone awhile, so I'm sure she'll be hungry too."

"I can do that." She pinched Mike's butt, then let him go. "Maybe if I make her a sandwich, she'll help me make a different one later."

"Then you'd better make her one heck of a sandwich," he told her, distracted by the lack of blood flowing to his brain. He was surprised at how aggressive the elf had become and wondered if it was a result of the swap they had made in the kitchen. Or maybe their encounter had given her a serious confidence boost and she was just excited to explore the possibilities with him. There was a week in June where Tink and Kisa had gotten into some type of ambush sex that still made him blush to think about, but he had been more than willing to indulge them as long as it didn't involve him sticking his head in the dryer and pretending to be stuck. "I'm going to grab the big map from the workshop and will be down to help in a few minutes."

He walked down the stairs to the workshop, pausing to properly survey the room. It felt even bigger without the others, and he walked over to the table with the big map.

"Hmm." He studied it for a few minutes, then decided it would be best to roll it up. Convinced Santa would have some sort of storage tubes squirreled away, he started digging through the drawers and shelves of the workshop to find one. While doing the menial task, he allowed his mind to process the past twenty-four hours, going over the details in the hopes that he hadn't missed something obvious.

Santa's home creaked as if struck by a heavy wind, causing him to wince. He assumed the house wasn't just settling and decided it would be best if he sped things up. Moving across the room, he opened and closed drawers with no more than a cursory glance, quickly overlooking anything that wasn't tube-shaped. The map was too big to fold.

"Some lucky kid must have wanted a fishing rod, and those are a bitch to wrap," he muttered to himself while opening a cupboard over the workbench. A pair of cardboard shipping tubes fell out, and he caught one while the other bounced away, rolling across the workbench to stop at the giant clamp. He tucked the one he'd caught back, then walked over to the tube now wedged beneath one of the clamp's handles.

"This should do." It was the perfect size. As he picked the tube up, his attention was drawn to the large alphabet block.

Unless Santa was making toys for giant toddlers, it had to be some sort of decoration. On the front was the letter *M*, and on the top was the letter *I*.

He stared at it for several seconds, then decided to lean along the counter and see what the letter on the back of the cube was.

"Well, fuck me sideways," he muttered, seeing that the letter was a *K*. It was not lost on him that the odds of coming across a giant alphabet block with the first three letters of his name were pretty small in the first place. Moving the tube aside, he spent a minute undoing the clamp. Once open, he saw that one of the covered sides had an image of his house carved into the wood.

"What the hell were you up to?" he wondered aloud, then went to pick up the block. Instead of it lifting freely, a hidden hinge allowed it to open like a treasure chest. Inside, a thick white fabric was folded up neatly with a letter addressed to *M. Radley* and a small ornament sitting on top.

Mike looked around the workshop, then picked up the ornament. It was a simple glass bulb full of fog with last year's date on it. When he twisted it around for a better look, he was fairly certain he saw a face inside eerily reminiscent of Christmas Past. The spirit stared at him wistfully, then disappeared.

"Holy shit." He set the bulb down and picked up the letter. When he unfolded it, tiny sparkles drifted into the air around his fingertips, then rolled across the paper, leaving golden letters behind.

Dear Mike,

Merry Christmas! It's been some time since I last gave you a present, and you've been a really good boy this year, so I wanted to give you something nice.

If you're reading this, then you've just found the tubes for your map. There's a scroll case downstairs sitting right next to the fireplace that will work much better. It has a strap on it.

I'm sure you have so many questions, but I'm afraid giving you the answers will actually cause more problems. What I can give you is this very special ornament with all the memories from last Christmas! Breaking it will free the spirit inside, so be very careful where you hang it.

The coat I've enclosed is a spare from my slimmer days. It will keep you warm even on the coldest of nights.

Your friend,

Santa

"You've got to be shitting me!" Mike's hand trembled as he squeezed the letter so hard that the paper wrinkled. Santa had known everything that was about to happen! Why not take precautionary measures or do something other than let the Krampus take over his goddamn body?

He held up the ornament and scowled at the spirit within. "And what am I supposed to do with you?" he asked it. The spirit appeared in the mists, then shrugged noncommittally before disappearing.

"Well, fuck you too." Mike unfolded the fabric, revealing a coat that hung down to his shins. He paused, trying to remember if Santa's coat had always been that long. If not, then the big man was taller than Mike had thought.

He casually threw the coat over a shoulder and then tossed the cardboard tube to one side and retrieved the rolled up map from the workbench. "'Ho ho ho, Mike. How about a nice, warm coat so you don't freeze? Wanna borrow a tube for your map? Sorry I put your family in danger. I just wanted to play Jekyll and fucking Hyde this Christmas.' Fat fucking bastard."

Did Holly know? Or Mrs. Claus? Santa was one thing; the guy wasn't even around. But if the others knew and were misleading Mike still? He didn't know how he would handle such a betrayal. His magic simmered in reaction to his anger, eager to lash out.

"You knock that shit off," he warned it, poking himself in the belly hard enough that it hurt. "Months of good behavior, and now you're acting up again. I understand the elf and the sexy giant. That's just what we do. But the weird overload thing is getting old, so knock it off."

His magic backed down, then went quiet. He wasn't certain if it had actually heard him or if it was like some reverse pep talk and he had just calmed himself down. Sometimes it really was easier to think of his magic as a separate entity.

"That's better," he said, walking toward the door. "Last thing I need is for you to get all worked up and damned near blow my arm off again. I do take full responsibility for being a human cum fountain earlier, so don't think I'm blaming you for everything."

He was halfway down the hall when a massive crunching sound resonated through the house, followed by a tremor that made him lose his footing. He twisted at the last second, making sure not to fall on the ornament. Up above, timbers groaned as the house creaked dangerously.

"Shit, shit, shit," he muttered, climbing to his feet. "Holly, where are you?" He ran the rest of the way to the stairs, looking out into the living room. Holly emerged from the kitchen, her eyes wide in alarm.

"That was really loud," she said, then screamed when something struck the side of the house hard enough that the whole building rumbled. The front door rattled on its hinges, and bright lights flashed through the windows.

"Are we under attack?" From his vantage point, he could see beams of golden light as they passed over the house like searchlights. He ran downstairs where Holly met him, then the two of them moved toward the front window.

There was another loud bang, and then something roared. The front door rattled several times before everything went silent.

"What on earth—" Mike was interrupted by the sound of a knock on the door, which caused Holly to scream.

"It's me!" Yuki called from the other side. "Hurry up, let us in!"

Us? Mike stuffed the ornament into a pocket of Santa's coat and tossed it over a nearby chair. The map went on a table before he moved to unlock the door. A gale-force wind blew it inward, causing the fire in the fireplace to flicker dangerously. Mike crouched to hold the door in place long enough for Yuki to come in, then grunted with exertion while pushing it shut.

"What is going on out there?" he demanded, then saw what Yuki was carrying. In her arms was the motionless figure of Jack Frost. He couldn't tell if the woman was alive or dead, but weird golden threads of light blazed along her arms, twinkling like stars.

"You brought her here? Why?" He looked up at Yuki, noticing that her face was all scraped up. Blood trickled from a wound on her head, which ran down the length of her nose and dripped on the floor.

"I fucked up, Mike. I fucked up real bad." There was a tremor in her voice that made him sick to his stomach. She set Jack down on a nearby couch and then ran into Mike's arms, clutching him tight.

"Hey, whoa, it's okay," he told her, then flinched when something heavy slammed into the side of the house. "What the hell was that?"

"That would be one of my fuckups." She leaned away from him and sniffled. Out of the corner of his eye, he saw Holly put on her earmuffs. "Jack was coming here with an entire army made out of ice. I thought if I took her down, they would fall apart or something."

The house shook again, and some books fell off a nearby bookshelf. Up in one of the windows, a creature that looked like a cross between a gorilla and a snowman slapped a huge palm on the glass. There was a flash of red light as the creature's arm exploded, and it hopped down.

"At least the house seems protected." Mike inspected the flow of magic in the house and was unsurprised to see that the exterior walls swirled with red-and-white streamers of light, making it look like a giant candy cane.

"They aren't the problem." Yuki walked over to one of the windows and pointed through it. "She is."

Mike moved to her side and looked through the glass. At first he didn't see the dark figure skulking at the end of the walkway, mistaking it for a giant pile of rocks. Her body was thick like a boulder, with long arms that dragged knuckles on the ground. Greasy hair hung over a face that resembled a burst tomato, and when the giant smiled, it was to reveal jagged teeth reminiscent of a hippo's.

Golden light surrounded the newcomer, sinking into the ground like an inverted tornado. The giant ripped a stone the size of a basketball out of the ground, then casually tossed it at the house. There was a flash of white light this time as the structure shook but withstood the impact.

"You can't stay in there forever, food!" Her voice was difficult to hear over the creaking of the house. Dozens of ice minions were now studying it, most likely trying to find a way in.

"Oh no." Holly was by Mike's side now, up on her tiptoes to see out the window.

"You know this lump of ugly?" he asked.

"I do." Holly's face wrinkled up in disgust. "That's Grýla. She's awful but relatively harmless."

"Not anymore." Yuki leaned against the wall and took a deep breath, then let out a groan and sank to the floor. She held out her hands, revealing a nimbus of golden light. It faded after a few seconds, and Yuki sighed, leaning against the wall.

"What happened?" Mike asked.

"Jack was coming here to attack you, so I thought I'd even the odds." She chuckled weakly, then shook her head. "I had a tarot card that allows you to level the playing field. When used, it balances the magical power of any creature in its area of effect. Made it in case I fought Emily and she was much stronger than me. It's meant to be temporary."

"I take it that's not the case here?"

"No." Yuki stared at him. "For one, I thought it was just me and Jack. I didn't expect a third party to be waiting in the snow beneath my feet. And two…I thought it would just pull ice magic out of her, Mike, I really did. Something I knew how to use, but this…" She held up her hands, and the golden light returned, the veins in her arms lighting up.

"What is it?" he asked, but he was fairly certain he knew.

"Divinity. Magic far beyond anything I am capable of, especially in this amount. If not for Grýla out there absorbing a third of it, I might have just exploded." She grimaced, then clutched her chest. "It feels like I'm on fire."

"Yuki." He could see the golden light blazing around her now, trying to force its way into her. Panicked, he put his hands over her chest, uncertain how to proceed. Could he try to separate it from her? What would happen if it had nowhere to go?

The side of the house rattled again, the walls protesting their percussive treatment.

"Come back, food!" Grýla growled, then threw another stone.

"Leave us alone," Holly yelled through the window. "Go back to your cave!"

"The North Pole belongs to me now," she yelled back. "Me and my children! The Krampus will see me rewarded for my efforts."

"Krampus?" Jack moaned, her eyelids fluttering.

"What happened to her?" Mike asked.

"Punched her in her fucking face," Yuki said with a grin. "But Grýla hits way harder than either of us. Knocked her out cold. Only way I survived was a spell I had cast earlier.

Stupid bitch chased us all the way back here, and nothing I did seemed to hurt her. I'm not sure how, but she soaked up all that extra magic like a sponge." She winced, her hands going to her chest. "My heart, it's beating so fast…"

He examined Yuki's magical aura again, studying the bands of light, isolating the colors. It looked different from Holly's, almost feral in some places. The golden light was pressing in on the other colors, as if trying to sever them. They wanted in, but then what?

"Wait a second." He turned his attention to Jack. Her magic was a pulsing core of blue energy, fluttering quickly like a bird's heart. In the occasional gaps, he saw that same golden light scattered throughout, but more of it was concentrated inside.

Closing his eyes, he tried to consider the problem. With Mrs. Claus, he had tucked the strands back in. But that was magic that was a part of her, not just something that had been added.

No, that wasn't right either. He wasn't just seeing magic; he was looking at their souls. He was about to mess with his friend's soul, not having a single idea what the repercussions could be.

"Naia!" He opened his eyes. "I need you!"

"Naia?" Holly looked at him. "The nymph?"

"Yes!" He jabbed himself in the belly. "Wake the fuck up!"

"Naia?" Yuki opened her eyes. "Where?"

"Ugh, c'mon." He felt his magic wake up and stretch out. "I've heard you in my head so many times. You've helped me understand others' needs, and you're the only one I know who understands soul magic!"

Holly stared at him like he had gone nuts. Yuki squinted through one eye, the other shut as if the room was too bright.

"Hey, food!" The house shook again. "These walls won't hold me for much longer! You should come out here and, uh, talk. We can talk, that's right!"

"Shit!" Mike looked at Yuki, Jack, and then Holly. Things had taken a turn for the worse, and it was all up to him now. There were so many times he had heard Naia in his head, that fragment of his soul speaking to him while…

"Holly, come here!" He grabbed the elf by her collar and pulled her close. "Do you trust me?"

Holly stared into his eyes, as if uncertain, then she nodded.

He turned her around and bent her over the nearest chair, pushing up her skirt to reveal her bare pussy and torn leggings. With a single motion, he pulled down his pants, his cock swelling so fast he felt like the floor was dropping out from underneath him. The plan was crazy, but crazy was all he had right now.

"Mike, what…oh my Santa!" Holly groaned in delight as he teased her pussy with the head of his cock. He rubbed her clit with his fingers while sliding his cock over the outside of her labia. Holly lifted her legs into the air, her lips parting easily as he pressed the head of his cock inside her. "Don't you dare stop!"

"Wow. Any excuse to get laid." Yuki chuckled, then whimpered like a dog in pain.

"I'm coming, Yuki, hold on," he muttered, fucking Holly to make sure his cock was nice and wet. He slid out of her, then positioned the head of his cock against her tight little butthole. Holly tensed up and looked over her shoulder at him.

"Um, shouldn't we—" she began, but he held a finger to his lips.

"Trust me for just another second?" he asked. Naia had always been there to lend a hand when he needed sexual guidance. And if there was one thing she would correct him on, it was this.

Holly frowned at him but nodded anyway.

Mike took a deep breath and pressed forward just enough

that he felt resistance, visualizing himself sliding deep into Holly's ass, hearing her moans of pleasure as he roughly pumped himself inside her, and—

Slow down, lover. Naia's voice was playful, but he heard a hint of anger in it. *She's not ready for that.*

"Naia, quick, I need to do soul magic on Yuki!" He spat the words out as quickly as possible, afraid her presence would vanish. "I don't need help fucking, I need help saving Yuki!"

What? He could feel Naia now, sense her confusion as if it was his own. *You're doing soul magic?*

Satisfied that Naia was there to stay, he shifted his cock back down to Holly's pussy and slid himself back inside. The elf groaned, her whole body shuddering.

"Sweet Christmas, you had me going for a second," she muttered, licking her lips.

"I don't know what all you can see from inside there, but I need your help fixing Yuki." He turned to look at the kitsune, his cock sliding out of Holly. Naia's presence faded immediately, so he slid his dick back into the elf.

There was a painful moment where he thought he had lost her, and then the nymph laughed.

You get into the strangest trouble, lover. Keep fucking Holly, and I can guide you. Naia chuckled in his mind. *Since you are balls-deep in someone, I can stick around on a technicality.*

"Thanks, Naia." He grabbed Holly by the hips and pulled her off the couch, noticing a few gemstones from her crotch were left behind, stuck in the fabric. The elf groaned when he picked her up, grabbing hold of a couple of couch pillows before crossing over to where Yuki sat, his cock still buried deep inside Holly. He imagined it looked quite ridiculous but didn't care.

"This is what I see," he said, helping Holly to the floor. "Hey, can you keep your ass up for me?"

Holly giggled, then tucked the pillows under her hips to

raise herself. "Let me know how I can help," she whispered, then groaned as he resumed thrusting.

"Just doing some soul surgery." He examined Yuki's soul once more and felt Naia wince. "While fucking, apparently."

She's been through so much, Naia whispered. *I can see all her pain; it's in those dark spots. But I can also see where she's healed. She found something new to love, and recently.*

"What can I do about this golden light?" He stared at the golden beams that had formed into concentric rings and were tightening down on Yuki's soul. "She called it divinity."

"Oh yeah, pull my hair!" Holly added, wiggling her hips. Mike obeyed, grabbing her by the back of her head and yanking it back. She groaned in delight, and a surge of his magic went across her back. Mike tried to concentrate, his mind slipping as Holly essentially rode him from the prone position.

Let me guide you, Naia whispered. He switched to a slower pace with Holly, which allowed him to sit up and see Yuki better. While he tugged on Holly's hair with one hand, the other went through an intricate weaving process, his magic spreading across both the elf and the kitsune, those tiny sparks sinking into both of them.

In Yuki's case, he could see the sparks become tiny motes of light that rode on the strands of her magic. Naia had him grab at those pieces as he unraveled a few of her threads just enough to begin weaving the new ones in. It didn't go unnoticed that some of that golden light clung to his fingertips, then danced along his arm until it disappeared into his chest.

Was this what Naia felt like when she did her soul swap? His had always been an automatic process, but now he remembered how she had given him specific abilities. If he mastered this skill, could he choose what he got from his future lovers and what they might get from him in return?

His hand was on Holly's shoulder now, and she let out a gasp, then pulled his hand to her mouth and bit down on his knuckle. Distracted, he felt his mind shift to the writhing figure on the floor, and that familiar heat built up in his gut.

The house trembled as Grýla kept throwing rocks. A puddle of water formed in the fireplace, and Mike wondered if something had tried to squeeze its way in and had melted. Still, he kept fucking Holly while trying to fix Yuki. He was essentially edging himself with the elf, concentrating hard enough on the task at hand that she had already come three times beneath him, all the while begging for more. The wooden floor was covered in tiny sparks, and more than a few were made of gold.

Yuki relaxed during the process, eventually losing consciousness. He could see the changes happening inside her as that golden light became a part of her, hoping against hope that he wasn't doing any permanent harm. By the time he was finished, he had managed to spread it out and weave it in with all the other threads he saw. Did soul magic always look like string, or was that just the way he saw it?

That should be enough, lover. He felt Naia's smile in the back of his mind, her presence now fading. *The rest is up to her.*

Satisfied, he turned his attention down to the sexual mess that was Holly.

"If you need to keep going, I'm game," she whispered, her voice hoarse from all the tiny shrieks she had made. She held up one of her magical cookies, revealing she had taken a couple of bites. "Plenty of energy. Can go all night if you need to. Can even go find some lube if you wanna try butt stuff."

"Some other time." He pulled out of her and helped roll her onto her back. She sighed as he lay down on top of her, then placed his lips against hers. "Thank you for that. I can explain later."

"You don't need to explain anything to me." She ran a hand along his ass. "But I bet you want to finish."

He looked at the golden light that had accumulated on his skin, then shook his head.

"I would love to but not inside this time."

"Your wish is my command." She reached down with both hands and started jerking him off. "But…could you kiss me while I do it? I kind of like how it feels, it's less…intense."

He pressed his lips to hers, their tongues sliding across each other as she stroked him with both hands. He was slick with her juices, and his long-denied orgasm built quickly. With a loud groan, he blew his load, coating Holly's outfit in sticky ropes of glittering semen. Holly pumped him enthusiastically with one hand as she continued to kiss him with her other hand on the back of his head.

The sparks on the floor dissipated, and he collapsed on top of the elf with a grunt.

"Okay, you're too heavy," Holly protested.

"Sorry." He rolled off her, immediately noticing the sticky mess that now covered both of them. It looked as if they had been attacked with hot glue and glitter. His magic dissipated, leaving him with a brutal headache.

A headache made worse by the continued pounding of stone against wood. Grunting, he stood, kicking off his pants before retrieving Santa's coat. His magic fired up again, concentrating in his fingertips as he walked over to the door.

He waited for another impact, then opened the door. The cold wind blasted him, but the accompanying chill was nonexistent. He stepped outside, scowling at the grotesque figure who had carved large chunks of stone out from the yard. The snow was littered with all the rocks she had thrown, and Grýla paused, her head tilted to one side as she tried to scoop up another large rock.

His magic spun up like a cyclotron, and he could see it now, running down his arms and dancing across his fingers. The same golden nimbus Yuki had held now manifested across his fingertips, interwoven with blue-and-white streamers of light. Anger, frustration, and a desire to put Grýla in her place fueled him, the streamers hissing like hot oil as his magic rose to the challenge, eager to obey.

"What are you doing, food?" Grýla asked, her gaze stuck on Mike's exposed cock. Around them, creatures made of snow crawled toward him across the boulder-strewn landscape.

"Giving you a taste," he growled, then threw his right arm forward as if pitching a baseball. The spinning light in his fingers turned into a hot ball of energy, then manifested as a blast of lightning that struck Grýla in her face. The giant howled, dropping a boulder the size of a beach ball and stumbling around in agony. She fell to all fours and fled, her cries filling the air.

Pain rushed up his arm, every nerve now tingling as if he had smashed his funny bone with a hammer. Spasms racked his fingers, and he pulled his arm into his stomach, cradling it like a child.

Seeing that the snowman house of horrors was nearly upon him, Mike retreated back into the house, slamming the door shut behind him. Holly sat on the floor, her eyes filled with awe as he shook his arm and flexed his hand, the pins and needles subsiding.

Jack, however, stared at him with a mixture of disbelief and suspicion.

"What are you?" she asked, one eyelid twitching rapidly. The pupil in that eye was dilated, making the whole eye look black.

"My name is Mike Radley," he said, realizing his coat was still open, his cock exposed. He clumsily pulled the coat shut, using the built-in belt to tie it. "And I'm the man who's going to save Christmas."

FUTURE PROBLEMS

Mike was lying in the fountain, his head nestled between Naia's breasts as he watched the technicolor clouds of the Dreamscape drift overhead. The nymph lovingly toyed with his hair as he commanded the clouds to change shape above them, transforming them into nonsensical creatures that chased one another in circles.

"Does your head feel better?" she asked.

"Getting there." His eyes flicked to the large crack that still dominated one section of the sky. Shortly after he'd proclaimed to Jack Frost that he was the man who was going to save Christmas, his entire head had exploded with pain. Yuki had managed to catch him on the way down, but everything had gone dark. When he'd next opened his eyes, he'd been in the Dreamscape.

Thinking he had just lost consciousness, he'd tried to wake up. Usually this was an easy feat, but a series of giant cracks in the sky had pulsed with a terrible light, driving him back to the ground in pain. The cracks were fading over time, and he intended to leave once they were gone. "I don't know why more spas don't offer this as a service. People would pay good money to relax in a hot spring with a perfect pair of breasts like yours."

"I'm sure someone out there does it for a living. You just don't get out much."

He laughed, then groaned when the crack widened. "Why does it have to hurt in here?" he groaned.

"Your first experience with soul magic was akin to running a marathon, silly." Numerous hands rubbed his body, helping him relax. "I pushed you much further than you should have been able to go, and you accidentally absorbed some of that golden light. I was able to keep it from frying your brain, so the headache is a consolation prize."

"Thanks for that." He reached a hand up and patted her breast affectionately. "I don't know what would have happened to Yuki, but it wasn't good."

"She probably would have ended up like the snow bitch," Lily said from nearby. She was lying on a banana-shaped floaty. In the Dreamscape, Naia's fountain was often the size of a wave pool, likely for reasons Freud would happily have spent hours dissecting. "With Swiss cheese for a brain."

"That's not very nice," Naia said.

"And?" Lily turned her attention toward Mike, lowering her sunglasses for dramatic effect. "Bitch brought an army, had a psychotic break, and is now playing the part of Stroke Victim Elsa on Santa's couch."

Even though he was asleep, this piece of Lily was able to hear what was happening around him through his ears if she sat somewhere quiet and concentrated hard enough. It had taken her quite a bit of time, but eventually she'd reported that half of Jack's body was paralyzed and she had been placed in an armchair by the fire. The ice monsters were still outside, but most of them had spread through the village to do whatever it was ice monsters did. To his relief, Yuki and Holly were watching over him while also keeping wary eyes on Jack.

Speaking of Yuki…

Mike looked over toward the house. A sullen kitsune sat there with her knees pulled up to her chest, staring at him from between her legs.

"You still good?" he asked her.

Yuki's soul flipped him the bird, which caused a small bird to fly away from her that shouted, "Fuck you!" before it disappeared in the sky.

"She'll adjust," Naia said, rubbing his shoulders. "The part of her soul she gave you was heavily damaged. It's almost like she knew this was a safe place for it to heal."

"As long as she's house-trained, whatever." Lily sipped on a fruity cocktail drink that she summoned from the ether. "Oh, and not that anyone asked me, but fucking that elf girl while messing with someone's soul? Totally gave me a chub."

Mike snapped his fingers, causing Lily's banana to disappear. The succubus fell into the water, spilling her drink and vanishing beneath the surface. Naia laughed, then moved out of the way when Lily's arms burst up from the water to grab Mike around the waist.

He was pulled beneath the surface but wasn't worried. It was his Dreamscape, and he could tell Lily was just playing with him. He wrestled with her under the water for a minute, her suddenly naked flesh against his. When she kissed him, he relaxed, only to grunt and break away when she pinched his nipple too hard.

"Bitch," he muttered above the water. "That stings."

"Ah, did I hurt your feelings?" Lily splashed him, and he reciprocated. Since it was the Dreamscape, Lily smacked the water hard, causing it to form into a giant dick. Much like a whale breaching the ocean, the massive member fell sideways, crushing Mike beneath its weight. He was going to reciprocate, but his head started pounding again.

"Okay, that's enough. He needs rest." Naia's voice came from everywhere at once as a whirlpool formed, sucking Lily below the surface as Mike popped to the top. Moments later, Lily's bikini floated up.

"Is she okay?" Mike asked.

"Unless she's allergic to salt water, she'll be fine." Naia rubbed his forehead. "And don't worry about hurting her feelings. She installed an intricate water slide under the fountain. She gets flushed on purpose at least once a week."

"How intricate?"

"More than half an hour long. Has at least three loop the loops. Tink helped her install animatronics."

"Dare I ask?"

"Just dinosaurs."

"Sounds tame."

"They're all fucking."

"There we go." He laughed, then winced when it turned into painful thunder.

"Oh, lover. What am I going to do with you?" Naia held him tight against her body. Even though his arrival had been abrupt, his Dreamscape was always a good place to go to recalibrate. It didn't have quite the extreme time-bending properties it did if the real-world Lily were here, but he was still capable of stretching a few minutes into an hour if he needed to.

Some of the others dropped by to keep him company. Though each woman was technically a part of his soul, they all had their autonomy and did the things they would largely do in the real world, which meant he didn't always see them. The Dreamscape was basically his own personal version of heaven.

Eventually Ratu joined them, her elaborate kimono spreading out on the water like a giant lily pad.

"There you are." Mike reached out for her and caught the tips of her fingers. With a small tug, Ratu floated in his direction. "What have you been up to?"

"Exploring the edges of this place. I find it fascinating that your soul is locked into a location without true spatial qualifications. If you dig deep enough, you reach water instead of bedrock or sand. After years of exploration, I can say that your soul truly is an island on the astral sea." Ratu looked up at the clouds, then frowned at the dull crack in the sky. "What is that?" she asked.

Mike explained the events leading up to his current state. Ratu remained silent except to ask a few clarifying questions. Once he'd finished, she contemplated for a minute, then turned to look at him.

"You do realize the impossible confluence of events necessary to get you to where you are, correct?"

"I think you mean improbable. If it was impossible, I wouldn't be knee-deep in all this shit Santa started."

"Bah." Ratu waved her hand dismissively at him. "I don't refer to what's going on in the North Pole. You manipulated someone's soul today, Caretaker."

"Well…it's just an extension of Naia's powers, so I didn't think it was a big deal."

The naga snorted, then rolled onto her side to look at him. "That's where you're wrong. You see, Naia's ability to manipulate souls is intrinsic to her nature, and she did not gift it to you."

"No? I figured that was all her." Mike tilted his head backward to see Naia's face. "Right?"

She shook her head. "Remember that I'm just an offshoot, a snapshot from the moment we first swapped. A nymph can grant many gifts, but the ability to do soul magic is not one of them. I know as much as you do about your current abilities."

"You seemed pretty nonchalant about it," he said.

"And?" She playfully tweaked his nose. "Where do we draw the line at being surprised? When you went to the Underworld? Fought the Jersey Devil? Banged one of Santa's elves?"

"That's fair," he admitted. "Speaking of Holly, I haven't seen her in here."

"Oh, she's here." Naia grinned. "She snuck off with Tink a while ago to see her hammer collection."

"Sounds like a euphemism for something," he muttered.

"Back to what I was saying," Ratu said. "You have the ability to touch and manipulate spirits, which I imagine is due to Cecilia's presence. Magic is typically a separate entity altogether, so I assume that ability may come from me. When I break down objects for enchanting, I can pull several of these threads and weave them somewhere else. So you are using some variation of my own ability to do a similar task with magical beings."

"That sounds kind of dangerous, actually."

"Indeed." Ratu fixed him with a serious look. "The immediate ramifications would put you in quite a bit of danger should it become public knowledge."

"How so?" he asked but realized immediately what she referred to. Ratu had the ability to isolate magical properties in an object and transfer them to another, thus combining enchantments. The soul swaps he performed with the others had already granted him fantastic abilities of his own, but what if he could simply rip the desired traits from one person and implant them in another? Could he theoretically rip away Jack's ability to use ice magic and put it in himself? Would it destroy Jack in the process?

If people found out he was capable of wandering the earth and sucking magical creatures dry of their abilities, he would absolutely become public enemy number one. The society would be small-fry compared to people like the Order, or even other cryptids wandering about. It wasn't just about magic either. He could be damaging souls. What sort of ramifications would that have for the afterlife?

"Holy shit," he muttered. This single bit of knowledge could put him at risk from everyone who knew about magic.

"I see you understand." Ratu rolled onto her back and looked at the sky. "That crack isn't just from manipulating Yuki's soul. What you've been doing with your magic is spiritually draining, but from what you told me about that golden light, you have contaminated your spirit with some form of divinity. We're probably watching it integrate with your soul."

"I didn't mean to. I was just trying to keep Yuki from melting or whatever."

"Your intentions were pure, and that's what matters most. If you had decided to grab that light for yourself, then I imagine we might already see signs of corruption. You tapped into something you shouldn't have. If not for your already altered state, it probably would have killed you."

"Oh." Mike looked at his fingers, remembering that blast of lightning he had struck Grýla with. It had been instinctive and not something he should have been able to accomplish. Even here in the Dreamscape, his hand ached. "What is divinity?"

"I'm a bit of an expert on that, actually. I was a minor deity for a while." Ratu smiled, suddenly lost in memories. "I had become one of the river gods in my area, and people would pay me tribute in the form of celebration, prayers, and some of the best fish you'll ever taste."

"Sounds nice," he said. "What happened?"

Ratu's face tightened. "It's not something I like to talk about. Anyway, you've experienced divinity before in your encounters with Titania. When a being becomes powerful enough, they can tap into different sources of power. Divinity is one of these."

"Different like how you tend to use big fireballs while Yuki uses ice?"

Ratu nodded. "Kind of. Our magic is elemental in nature, and we are manipulating variables that already exist. Divinity is something else. It doesn't have the same rules as the magic you understand. For instance, I could not use elemental fire to build a boat, nor could Yuki use ice to warm a house. Divinity is the magic of miracles and has some very stringent requirements to attain."

"Such as?"

"Worship is both the easiest and the hardest. For the bigger names, it's become self-sustaining. For smaller beings like me, it can be easily lost or taken away by losing believers. Being blessed by the gods is a pathway but a very tricky one because they can always change their mind later if you become too powerful. Becoming a fundamental force of nature will do it. For example, if Jack had become the absolute epitome of cold, she would be eligible for ascension. But godhood isn't just raw power. It isn't that simple. On the other hand, any sufficiently advanced form of magic could be mistaken for divinity. This truth, by the way, is how we end up with false gods."

"Huh." Mike looked at his fingers again. "So I'm contaminated by divinity? What does that mean?"

"I don't know. I'm just a fragment of your soul. I can't exactly pop outside for a look around, so…hmm." Ratu stroked her chin, suddenly deep in thought. "Anyway, it would behoove you to speak to my real-world counterpart when the chance presents itself. You're toying with powerful yet delicate forces, and I would prefer you avoid blowing your own face off with them. After all…" The naga moved toward him, her arms sliding around his body. "It is a rather pretty face."

"No." Naia manifested nearby, her hand in the shape of a gun. She pointed it at Ratu and blasted her with a stream of cold, high-pressure water. "Bad snake, not until he's better!"

"Ugh, fine." Ratu licked her lips with a forked tongue. "Come find me next time you're napping, Caretaker."

"I'll do my best." He watched Ratu walk away from the fountain with mixed feelings. A dalliance with the naga sounded like fun, but he really needed that crack in the sky to go away so he could wake up. Even though Jack was disabled, he had no idea how long her condition would last.

However, Ratu had been a treasure trove of information, and he summoned that golden glow into his fingers once again. It made a sweet bass sound that was very much like a heartbeat. It had never occurred to him before that he had a veritable library of information in his head at all times, accessible anytime he was asleep. The pulsating light in his hand sent out a couple of electric streamers that danced along his forearm.

"Please don't turn me into a cum fountain," he said, dismissing the magic. Orgasms were fun, but the idea of having one powered by divine magic was a little terrifying. Not only had it left him exhausted, but the mess had been a bitch to clean.

The air filled with the sound of static. Mike turned toward the house to see Kisa emerge from the back door, her body outlined in heavy dark lines. She brushed herself off, then took a wary look around.

"Are you taking a nap?" she asked. "Or did you go somewhere nice without me?"

"Got knocked out, kinda," he replied.

"Is everything okay?" Her face turned serious. "Do we need to come back?"

"We're fine. You need to watch out for a seriously pissed-off giant named Grýla and an army of ice monsters. Oh, and we captured Jack."

Kisa stared hard at him for a few moments. "Yuki did come back, right?"

Reminded of their earlier conversation, he nodded. "Yep. She's officially in charge again and keeping me out of trouble."

"I can't even with you some days," Kisa muttered. "Anyway, we're still wandering the vents but having bad luck finding a suitable exit. Some of these buildings are in sad shape, and I'm not about to go wandering through the snow." She tilted her head to one side, then swatted away something Mike couldn't see. "No, I won't show him my tits and say they're from you, leave me alone."

"Tell Tink to behave," Mike said. "We need that furnace up and running soon. It's getting cold." Now that he had Santa's coat, he wasn't too worried about himself, but what about the elves? Holly might joke that she wouldn't mind hiding under his jacket, but that wasn't a solution for the rest of the elves.

"She knows. We had to take a break. We've been keeping a pretty fast pace trying to find a vent big enough for me to leave. Stay out of trouble. I'll check in with you later."

"Bye." He waved at Kisa just as she faded from view, then let out a sigh of relief. Even though no progress had been made in finding the elves, he was happy to know that Tink and Kisa were okay.

He spent a bit longer with Naia, then wandered out to the beach to stretch his legs. Zel met up with him, and the two of them chatted for a while. It was weird that they had a child together, but this version of her had never been pregnant and was forced to learn about their son secondhand. She didn't seem bothered by it. At the end of the day, she was still just a part of his soul.

Out in the waves, a dark figure appeared. It was Lily in an inflatable donut. Mike bade Zel farewell and waited for the succubus to make it to the beach. She walked out of the water, a breeze kicking up blue-and-gold sand that stuck to her legs in patches.

"Surprised you're still here, Romeo." She was completely naked except for her black leather boots. "Thought you'd have woken up by now."

"Soon enough." He nodded in the direction of the crack, which was almost gone. "So I hear you've got a water slide?"

"Girls just wanna have fun." She brushed some sand off

her inner thigh, then blew him a kiss. "After all, there's only so much of you to go around, and when you're awake, the orgies and pillow fights in here get a little boring. Besides, I've got a T. rex doing things to a velociraptor that would make you blush."

"You certainly have my attention. What other weird stuff are you guys building in my head?"

"Well, you know how some people say you only use about ten percent of your brain?" Lily moved close to him, her bare breasts in his face. The scent of cinnamon washed over him, and he licked his lips in anticipation.

"Yeah?"

"Those people are idiots." She was even closer now, her hand on his crotch. "That's not how brains work."

The way she was rubbing him through his pants, he was definitely using less than ten percent of his brain right now. The ocean around the island went still, and even the breeze paused as Lily rubbed his stiffening cock.

"Where were we going with this?" he asked, having forgotten the original question.

"This place isn't your brain, Romeo. It's your magic and your soul. It's got more cracks than a sidewalk, and I'm all about ensuring that every crack is filled." She pressed against him, her breasts expanding to fill his view.

"Is…it seems like everyone is a little extra…aggressive today." Not that he was going to complain, but there was certainly a change in the air. It wasn't limited to the Dreamscape either, but he couldn't tell how much of that was Holly being a horny elf or if something else was going on.

"We're just parts of your soul. When things change here, it's because things changed out there. So you should probably ask yourself…what's different about you?" She grabbed the front of his pants and ripped them off. They flickered out of existence as she knelt and sucked his cock into her mouth. He moaned, his hands finding the horns on her head and holding them as she blew him for a minute.

"Oh, that feels so good." He let out a little groan as Lily spat him out and then stroked his cock with both hands.

"Speaking of cracks, that one in the sky is gone." Lily jerked a thumb over her shoulder. Mike looked and saw the sky had a faint aura around where the last crack had been, like a fading bruise in the sky.

"Oh." He looked down at her, then back up at the sky again. Doing a quick bit of mental math, he wondered if she could get him off in the Dreamscape before he woke up.

"Looks like it's time to nut up, Romeo. Give them hell for me." With a laugh, Lily flicked him in the balls, making the decision for him. The Dreamscape vanished as his eyes popped open, both her laugh and the phantom pain in his testicles fading away.

"Gah!" Holly had been leaning over him when his eyes opened and fell backward in fright. "Oh Santa, you scared the sprinkles out of me!"

"Sorry about that." He blinked his eyes a few times and coughed, his throat very dry. Holly offered him a mug of something, and he was surprised to discover it was ice water.

"Yuki had me melt some ice for you," she said. "Thought you might appreciate something other than hot cocoa."

"She was right." He sucked the water down greedily, going fast enough that a bunch of it spilled onto his white coat. Interestingly enough, the water slid off the fabric and onto the floor without leaving any trace of moisture behind. "How long was I out?"

"A couple of hours." Holly took the mug back and held out a sandwich. "I finally got around to making these, if you're hungry."

He took the sandwich from her and bit into a slice of heaven. It was thin sliced roast beef with caramelized onions and cheese on a brioche bun. Groaning in delight, he was almost halfway through the sandwich when he remembered Yuki.

"Has she eaten yet?" he asked.

Holly shook her head. "She had me move you a bit ago. Jack was semiconscious for a bit, but she's awake now. Well… half-awake."

"Take me to her." Mike stood with some effort, then rubbed at his face to get the circulation flowing. The North Pole was so dry his sinuses were starting to hurt.

He had been moved to a small office just off the main hub of the house, and he walked into the main room to see Yuki standing across from Jack, a pair of tarot cards in her hands.

"You're up." Yuki didn't bother looking at Mike, her eyes on their prisoner.

"I am." He moved to her side and held out the other half of his sandwich. "You should eat."

"I'm not—"

"Yes, you are." He shoved the sandwich at her, and she took it. When she looked at him, she frowned.

"Your eyes are all bloodshot," she said.

"Not surprising." He moved away from Yuki and grabbed a rocking chair from over by the fireplace. He dragged it across the floor to sit down next to Jack, who was reclined in a chair and watching him out of one eye.

"I don't think you should do that," Yuki warned, but Mike waved her off.

"If she could have done something, she would have done it sooner." It wasn't just false bravado behind his words but the fact that Jack emanated an aura of defeat. One side of her face now drooped, and there was pain in the one eye she had open. She shifted uncomfortably when she saw how close he sat, then looked away.

"If you're going to kill me, just do it." Her voice was haggard, her words slurred.

Mike watched her for a moment, then opened his senses to look at her soul. It was not only in turmoil but looked like someone had tried to rip it apart. Only a few loose threads connected the two halves, and a red light pulsed through the entire structure. The same golden light that was embedded in Yuki's spirit was here as well, but the rings it had formed had sliced cleanly through entire sections of Jack's soul. The longer he studied it, the more it looked like the light had tried to form a symbol, but it fuzzed out anytime he tried to study it.

"I don't see any need for that," he told her, taking her by the hand. She yanked it away and glared at him.

"I don't want your pity." Her lip trembled as a tear formed in her eye.

"Good. Because I'm not offering pity." He patted Jack on the leg. "But I do have some questions, if you don't mind."

Jack looked away, her face twisting up.

"Look, Jack, we can do this the easy way or the hard way." He stood and moved across the room to pick up a pillow from one of the other couches, along with a blanket. "If you choose the easy way, you tell me what I want to know, and then we figure out what happens next."

"And the hard way?" Jack's tone was chilly, and the room grew colder. When he turned around, he saw that her skin was pale, but her breath was now visible as the temperature dropped.

Mike moved closer, the pillow clutched tightly in his hands. He shifted behind her, pushing her helpless body forward and shoving the pillow down next to her hip. When he grabbed her by the shoulders, she tensed up, and frost crawled up his arms, but the coat protected him.

"It's a lot like the easy way, only you're stubborn and we never move on to trying to figure out how to fix you. Does that feel better?"

"I...what did you do?"

Mike moved in front of Jack and draped the blanket over her. "You were slouching to one side. I imagine your back was starting to hurt. Do you eat or drink? We have plenty of hot cocoa and cookies."

"You...what?" Jack blinked a few times, then groaned. "My head, it hurts so bad."

"I bet." He looked over at Holly. "Let's start with cocoa, but she needs a straw."

Holly looked dubious but obeyed. The elf disappeared into the kitchen for a minute, then returned with a mug and a straw colored like a candy cane. He took it from Holly, then looked over his shoulder at Yuki, who had been strangely silent.

The kitsune was asleep in an armchair, a stray onion still clinging to her lips and a piece of sandwich clutched in one hand.

"Trade me." He handed Holly the mug and walked over to find a blanket for Yuki. When he covered her, she let out a whimper but then went still. When he looked at her soul, he saw that the golden light was busy trying to shine through the rest of Yuki's magic but was still tucked in nice and neat.

When he returned to Jack, it was to see that she was trying to sip cocoa through the straw with Holly's help. The elf was using a monogrammed hand towel to wipe chocolate off Jack's chin before it could freeze. He moved his chair closer to Jack and looked at her.

"So let's start with an easy question. To the best of your knowledge, are you currently dying?"

Jack looked startled at the question, then shook her head.

"Okay, a good start." There was a thud on the roof, and he looked up. "Okay, second question. Any way to call off your snow goons?"

Jack pondered this for several seconds, then pushed the straw out of her mouth with her tongue.

"I don't think so," she replied with a thick drawl. "Can't feel them anymore."

"Any idea why?"

Half of Jack's lip curled into a sneer. "Divinity. Some of it went into them, and now they are…unique. They no longer obey me."

"Okay, we can circle back to that problem later." He let out a deep breath and studied Jack. He could see a tiny storm forming just beneath the surface of her soul. It was easy to understand what that meant; he didn't blame her for being angry or afraid. In her position, he would be too.

Maybe it was her vulnerability, or the way she stared at him like a wounded animal, but something about Jack resonated with him. Even though she was in league with the Krampus, he felt that there was something more there to be explored.

"What is the Krampus planning?" he asked. "Other than just being a general bas…bad guy."

Holly smiled at him in appreciation. Despite the fact that he'd used her as a sexual battery earlier, she still required PG language.

"I'm not…entirely certain." Jack winced, looking away from him.

"Hey, are you okay?" He moved closer, ready to help her in any way he could. After a couple of moments, Jack turned to face him, doubt in her eye.

"Here." He took the mug from Holly and held the straw to Jack's lips. "We can get you water too. Just say the word."

"I don't understand." Jack stared at the straw like it was a blade held to her face. "Why show me kindness? I was coming here to kill you."

He looked over at Yuki, who snored contently in her seat. The sight summoned a big smile to his face.

"To be fair, I get that a lot." He moved the straw closer to her lips, and she reluctantly parted them, then sipped some more of the warm concoction. "I've met some of my best friends that way."

Jack let out a sigh and leaned away from the mug. "I'm starting to think this is all a bad dream."

"It isn't. I'm practically an expert on dreams these days." He set the mug down and moved to adjust the blanket. Leaning over Jack, he could feel the cold aura she radiated, a chill that somehow made it through his coat. He was tucking the blanket behind one shoulder when her other eye popped open, the iris cracked like a piece of glass. That dilated pupil shifted upward to focus on him, and his mind was assailed by images of bountiful valleys. Miles of lush landscape were revealed to him, broken up by the remains of thousands of dead warriors, their skeletons rotting in bent and broken armor. Harp music played in his head, and now he stood on a cliff overlooking the ocean. In front of him was a voluptuous woman with long tresses of golden hair, who looked back once before throwing herself toward the tumultuous waters below.

Mike snapped back to reality as ice bloomed through his entire body. The once limp half of Jack's body lunged at him, a dagger of ice clutched tight in her hand. There was a moment where time distorted, his brain processing her movement in slow motion. He pushed her wrist to the side, zapping her with electricity. The dagger slid out of her hand and shattered on the floor.

"YOU!" Jack's voice shifted in pitch and timbre as she slid her wrist from his hand and tried to slap him. He lifted his arm to block the strike, his eyes on Jack's other arm. It was wrapped around the back of the couch, keeping her from moving any closer.

"Stop it! Just stop it!" Jack begged, her voice back to normal. Yuki was by Mike's side now, her eyes wide and blazing with light as she held up a spear of her own.

"What have you done to me?" The shrill voice turned into

a wail, and Jack started to slide off the couch. Mike pushed aside Yuki's spear and knelt to catch her before she could crumble on the floor.

"Easy," he told her, watching cautiously as her soul undulated in wild circles. An inner light emerged, threatening to consume what was already there. "We aren't going to harm you."

"That would be Freyja," Yuki said. "Goddess of war, apparently."

"War, huh? Met a guy earlier this year, big sword, he was a huge dick. Fancied himself a horseman. Friend of yours?" Mike pushed Freyja/Jack back onto the couch and was impressed at how both her eyes conveyed a different sort of confusion.

"Just stop it, Freyja, please. They saved us." Jack was staring into her own lap when her voice shifted again. "They're luring us in with a false sense of—"

Mike took the spear from Yuki and pressed it against Jack's throat. Both Jack and Freyja held perfectly still as he pushed forward on it.

"Sorry, Jack, but your friend is a little intense and needs a reality check. Freyja, is it?"

"I'll kill you," Freyja whispered.

"Not if you don't get stronger," he told her, moving the point of the spear to avoid accidentally stabbing her. "We've had nothing but opportunity. Poison in the cocoa, stabbed with a spear, or we could have just let Grýla kill you. It would have been far easier on us."

"Grýla would have eaten you too." Holly stood from where she had ducked down, then adjusted her dress. "There wouldn't have even been a body to bury."

"See? So many ways we could have let you be someone else's problem. But my friend here dragged your ass across the arctic to give you a shot at survival. Why, you may ask?"

"Because I'm a Radley." Yuki moved next to Mike, her eyes shining as she put an arm on his shoulder. "And being a Radley means looking out for those who need help. I was planning to kill you, I'll admit it. But when you blew in, shouting in two different voices, I could tell you weren't in a good place. Heck, I spent decades in the same position, just a giant ball of hatred. You make terrible decisions when you're in that place, even when your intentions are good.

"Even before Grýla knocked you out, I had decided you needed help. This was a chance to balance the scales for everything this man has done for me, to pay his good deeds forward. I even asked myself what he would do in my situation, because his methods are…unorthodox. But ultimately, he would have wanted to help. Maybe you aren't seeking redemption, but I can tell you're definitely looking for something. And you will never find it by fighting your way through us."

Surprised at Yuki's words, Mike smiled and nodded his agreement. "So what do you say, Freyja? I think Jack gets it, but we need you on board as well. We were never your enemy. We just came here to help Holly figure out where everybody went." He gestured to the elf, who had moved away from the altercation. Holly nodded her agreement. "We don't have to be friends, but I don't think we need to be enemies. I know Jack was working for the Krampus and suspect she realizes now that was a terrible idea. Help us undo her mistake, make things right at the North Pole. And if you help us, we want to help you."

The figure on the couch regarded him for several moments, then let out a sigh. Jack/Freyja muttered to herself for a couple of minutes, the words unintelligible. Mike couldn't tell if it was another language or if she was muttering fast, but it was obviously a conversation not meant for his ears.

"My weaker half thinks we should hear you out," Freyja

said. "But I admit I think she's a poor judge of character. After all, she's the one who got us into this mess."

"And I'm the one who wants to help you out of it." Mike lowered the spear, then handed it back to Yuki. His danger sense had gone quiet as Freyja studied him. He could sense the wisdom and judgment in that broken eye, but something far more interesting was starting to shine through.

It was hope. Jack wasn't just one broken person but two, and he needed to figure out how to make them whole again. He was being given a chance to help someone while learning more about his new abilities, and he was going to take it.

"Okay, Jack, Freyja. I'm going to ask you one more question before we do anything else, and I need you both to be completely honest." He picked up the mug of hot cocoa and took a sip, his throat suddenly dry. He flinched when he realized the cocoa had gone ice-cold. Jack had sucked the heat right out of it. He set the mug down and rubbed his hands together in anticipation.

"What on earth is the Krampus up to, and how do we stop him?"

THE LONG DUCTWORK OF THE NORTH POLE FRUSTRATED KISA. It wasn't just that the ducts randomly shifted and often smelled of burned hair, or even the fact that Mike's presence would move nonsensically all around her.

It was the darkness. Some parts of the system were lit, but most weren't. Kisa kept her flashlight off unless absolutely needed, meaning that most of her time was spent following blind behind Tink (who could see in the dark with her goggles). Cats could see very well at night, but that still required some form of ambient light, of which there was none.

"Stop." Tink sniffed the air, and Kisa heard the clicking of lenses. "Okay, safe now."

"Does it usually take this long?" Kisa grumbled.

"Airflow bad," Tink responded for perhaps the hundredth time. At least the goblin was being patient with her. "Think good vent soon."

Soon. That was Tink's answer every time, but it did little to assuage Kisa's anxiety. She hated the idea of getting stuck in here, running until she died of thirst or fell down a hundred-story shaft. They had seen one a bit ago, both of them navigating a ledge that was less than a foot wide. Kisa had thought she had heard things down below, moving in the darkness, but Tink had told her she was imagining things.

There was a metallic thud, and Kisa felt the ducts change again. Tink paused, then turned around and pointed behind them.

"Tink find good vent," she declared.

Kisa spun in place and saw a vent that looked just big enough for them to fit through. Being pessimistic, she waited until Tink inspected the grill and then undid the screws on the inside. Almost all the vents unscrewed from the inside, the ones at Santa's house being the exception. She assumed it was maybe a security issue, or that Santa and his spouse knew better than to wander into a shape-shifting death trap, but the reasons didn't matter. Tink pushed the decorative grating outward, then twisted it sideways to retract it into the vent. Kisa slid through the opening, her hair snagging on the rough edges.

"Finally," she whispered, seeing that she was in some sort of administrative building. The room was lined with desks that held glowing lamps and scattered stacks of paper. Tink followed Kisa into the room, then looked around with a frown on her face.

"Tink not sure where this is." She pulled out her map and examined it. While she was busy doing that, Kisa moved to one of the desks to look at the paper. It had a fancy letterhead, and on the desk was a spilled basket containing unopened letters. They were addressed to Santa, and some of them had been written in crayon.

"This is where the letters go," Kisa said. "So we're somewhere in the mail room."

"Tink understand now." The goblin wrote something on her map and folded it back up. "Kisa safe here. Move quiet, no get hurt."

"I'll do my best." She hugged her friend, then let out a sigh. "I'll wait a bit to check in with Mike, let him know where I'm at. Then I'm off to check things out."

The goblin nodded, then squeezed back into the HVAC system. She put the grill back into place with Kisa's help and let out a sigh.

"Tink fix furnace, come find Kisa and husband. Make good decision, come home safe. Okay?"

"Okay." Kisa stuck her fingers through the ornate grating, and Tink gave them a squeeze before disappearing into the darkness. For the first time in a while, Kisa was truly alone.

After a couple attempts at cat radio, she managed to connect with Mike. It sounded like Jack Frost was being cooperative for now but apparently had never been clued in to whatever the Krampus was planning. While frustrating, it just meant that Kisa would have to cover more ground in the hopes of discovering anything.

The psychic phone call over, she pulled out the map she had drawn and studied it. The odds were pretty slim that the elves or Krampus were holed up in this administrative building, but she decided to be thorough. The last thing she wanted was to miss something important.

She also had an entirely different reason for checking here.

When she left the room, she was careful to crack the door first and scan the hallway. While her ability to go unnoticed was powerful, an opening door would still be visible and cause questions to be asked. Once out in the hallway, she wasn't nearly as cautious. All that was required was her desire to go unnoticed.

Not that it mattered. The administrative building was deserted. Half-eaten snacks and unfinished mugs of cocoa had been left at desks and on tables. It was as if the elves here had walked off the job, no questions asked.

There must have been an open window somewhere in the building, because it created an eerie howl that made her think of a lone wolf in the forest. Maybe the sound was a manifestation of the soul of the North Pole, calling out for the lost sounds of the workshop. Maybe it was the spirits of the northern lights, singing a funeral dirge for the elves.

Or maybe it was just the fact that she was wandering through abandoned buildings that were spooky as hell, knowing the Krampus could be around any corner. Her anxiety built as she wondered if she could hide from such a being. During the fight with the horsemen, they had lost track of her more than once. Was the Krampus more powerful than the physical manifestation of war? Or was he just a scary-ass fucker giving her walking nightmares?

"Focus, damn it." She patted her cheeks and pulled a cookie out of her pocket. It was delicious and filled her belly, but she was already missing the taste and ambience of one of Sofia's home-cooked meals.

It took her an hour to clear the building, and she saw no sign of the elves or anything else of interest. She found the tunnel system under the building and used it to go next door. This massive building was a warehouse with giant rolls of wrapping paper and several pushcarts for carrying them. It was much faster to check this one, as it only had a few offices.

After checking the map again, Kisa skipped the tunnel and went outside to cross the street. The snow was up to her waist in places, and she frowned when she heard the crunching of ice behind her. Looking up, she saw that a snow griffon had landed on the roof of the warehouse, surveying the city with a steely gaze.

Unsure how her abilities would work on a creature that wasn't alive, she knelt behind a drift and waited. The griffon paced the roof, then let out a shrill cry before taking flight again, leaving Kisa by herself.

The next few buildings yielded nothing of interest, though Kisa found a pair of pouches similar to Holly's. One was empty, but the other had been stocked up with cookies and candy canes, so she took it. She didn't recognize the type of cookies inside, but her danger senses triggered when she went to take a bite, so she left it alone.

After a check-in with Mike, Kisa decided it was a good time to take a break. She found a building with a big door, twenty-foot high rafters, and replacement parts for Santa's sleigh. Satisfied that it was a safe place to hide, she used a ladder to climb a nearby wall, then sank her claws into the wood and scaled the remaining distance until she was above the work zone.

Closing her eyes, she pictured the map in her mind. Not only had she found no trace of the missing elves, but she hadn't found any sort of records room. It was an idea she had come up with after the encounter with Christmas Past and asked Holly about in a roundabout way. Somewhere in the North Pole, there was a room where Santa kept track of all the gifts he had ever given out and who he had given them to.

Holly had explained that Santa gave gifts in a way that allowed for adults to take credit for them later. Kisa had this potentially insane idea that the old man who took her in would have addressed any gifts for her with her nickname, meaning Santa would have done the same thing. A records room would potentially have such information, so why not her true identity or the identity of the old man?

Even if she found out who she was, it technically wouldn't change things for her. To anybody who knew her in her old life, it had been several years since she'd just disappeared one day, never to be seen again. And it wasn't like she had family that was looking for her.

If nothing else, she wanted to remember the man who'd taken her in and cared for her when nobody else had. It seemed only right that someone mourn his death, even if it was so long after the fact.

She had told Mike some of this months ago, and he had done what he could to help. Private investigators had been of little use, and even Eulalie had been unable to narrow down a location or date based on Kisa's descriptions of her home. After enough dead ends, she had given up.

But now she knew she had a grandmother too, one that loved her. That knowledge alone had reopened her desire to learn about her past.

When she fell asleep, she was in Mike's Dreamscape again, which meant he was asleep. It was such a strange sensation, knowing she was walking around inside his mind, a feat made possible by being his familiar. Her winter coat was gone, replaced by a midriff and dance shorts. Far happier in these clothes, she wandered the grounds of his soul for a bit, headed in his general direction. He was waiting for her on the roof of the house, one of her favorite places in the real world.

"There you are." He patted the shingles next to him, and she climbed the trellis to join him. "How is the Christmas village?"

"Spooky as fuck." She lay back and let out a frustrated sigh. "I haven't found out anything. I feel like I'm letting everybody down."

"Hardly." He rubbed her exposed belly, scratching the fur near her waistband. This was something she enjoyed in the real world too but didn't indulge in unless it was just the two of them. She embraced quite a few things about being more cat than woman, but this one was more embarrassing than others.

"I also have something to confess," she told him. "My intentions weren't exactly pure. I had this stupid idea in my head that I might figure out who I was by digging through old records or something."

Mike looked at her with curiosity. "That's a bit of a leap. Do they even keep records up here?"

It took her a few minutes to explain it to him. By the time she was done, she had moved her head onto his lap, where he now ran his fingers through her hair.

Mike was quiet, and Kisa worried that she had disappointed him. She hadn't used to care, but their bond had gotten much stronger in the last few months, making her put him on a pedestal in a manner he wouldn't agree to. It had bothered her at first, idolizing a man she barely knew only because of their magical connection, but he had never taken advantage of it.

"Can you make her? Your grandmother." Mike lifted an arm, and an image of a generic old woman appeared. "Just change the things you remember, and we can get her as close as possible."

"How will that help?" she asked.

"Because I'll have Lily copy it and then show Eulalie in real life." Mike examined the floating picture while chewing at his lip. "We could even do that for the old man. You remember him better. I wish I had thought of it sooner. Or maybe it would be better for her to dive into your dreams? Whatever you're most comfortable with."

Stunned, Kisa did as he asked, spending several minutes sculpting an image of her grandmother with Mike. Once finished, it wasn't quite right, but it was passable.

"Oh, and if you find the records, don't get caught up digging through files. I don't want you losing track of time or your surroundings." He sat back and admired their handiwork. "The blank face must have been unsettling to see in person."

"Very." She leaned her head on his shoulder. "So what are you up to tonight? Banging your way through your dream harem?"

He laughed, wrapping an arm around her waist. "You sound a little jealous."

"Yeah, well, I always get this background buzz whenever you're getting busy with someone, doesn't matter whether you're awake or asleep. It's not as bad as that full-moon incident in the centaur village, but still, it drives me nuts! End up horny all the damn time while you're busy laying more pipe than a plumber."

"Yeah, sorry about that. I'll admit it, I spend time trying things out with everyone in here. It's also a lot safer because nobody can get hurt."

Kisa lifted an eyebrow. "What the fuck are you all doing in here that would hurt you?"

"There was that one time we had a game of naked Twister and Abella fell on Tink." The stupid grin on Mike's face meant he was telling the truth. "Oh, and the fairies can be life-size, if they want. That's always interesting."

She snorted. "Then why bother with fucking anybody while you're awake? Sounds like it's way more fun in here."

"Because I prefer the people these souls belong to. After all, I'm just borrowing them until, well…" His face clouded over, and he sighed. "But you'll be happy to know that the extreme beach sex tournament was canceled. Ratu, Naia, and I are going to talk about how to fix Jack."

He had alluded to this in their updates over the last day. Jack Frost was apparently a fragment of the goddess Freyja, who had manifested inside her body, or their body—Kisa was a bit fuzzy on the details. Mike had gotten the idea into his head that he could keep her from falling apart completely, maybe even fix her, but Kisa had doubts.

"But we've got to work on repairing those broken threads," Mike said. Kisa realized she hadn't been paying attention. "If we can get her functional, she might be able to help with the ice monsters roaming all over."

"That would be a big help," Kisa admitted.

They chatted on the roof for a while longer, then Mike left to meet with the others. Kisa stayed behind, enjoying the feeling of the faux sun on her shoulders. She didn't mind the mini vacation from the North Pole and hoped that she could curl up with an actual sunbeam sometime soon.

A harsh, guttural voice severed her connection to the Dreamscape, and Kisa opened her eyes. Below her hiding spot, a loud rattle sounded, followed by a crumpling sound.

"Clear it all out," the Krampus demanded, and Kisa moved to the edge of the beam to take a look. The Krampus stood on a rickety sleigh hooked up to seven demonic reindeer. Around him, a mountain of presents had appeared. Dozens of elves surrounded the sleigh, and they dutifully picked up the gifts and rushed them away in carts. "I expect you to have this place ready for my return."

Oh shit, she thought to herself, her tail flicking back and forth. The elves obeyed without hesitation, pushing the carts toward a doorway she hadn't noticed before.

"Krampus." The grating voice sounded like gravel in a rock crusher, and an immense figure appeared in the opening to the barn. It was Grýla, her face concealed by long, greasy locks of hair. "I have news."

The Krampus ignored her at first, dumping an impossible number of presents out of his sack. It wasn't much bigger than a backpack, but he swung it by the bottom, casting out hundreds of gifts in a wide arc. Once the sack was empty, he gave it an exploratory squeeze and turned toward the giant.

"What happened to you?" he asked.

"That mortal." Grýla limped forward, then bowed. "Jack had been gravely wounded, and his people captured her. When I went to retrieve her, he did this to me."

She pulled her hair away from her face in a dramatic

reveal. The mottled skin underneath had been blasted apart, making it look like she had taken a hot iron to the face. Deep gashes had been instantly cauterized, her eyes stuck looking wider than normal. In some places, the skin was missing, revealing the fat and muscle beneath.

The Krampus laughed. It was a horrible sound that made Kisa sick to her stomach.

"It's an improvement," he said, then tossed his bag back in the cart. "What would you have me do, hmm? Try to break into my own home? Not with that old crone in there, oh no!" The Krampus smoothed down the fabric of his coat in contemplation, then leaned on the sleigh. "But we won't have to worry about her much longer. This sack doesn't hold as much as the big one. If your idiot children hadn't failed at the one job I gave them, I would have retrieved all Santa's gifts already and your face would be, well, as it was. Your revenge will come in time."

"I don't want time, I demand compensation!" Grýla slammed her fist into the ground, causing the whole building to shudder. Kisa had a horrifying mental image of falling from her hiding spot and landing right between the giant and the Krampus.

"Interesting." The Krampus studied the giant anew, stroking his scraggly beard. "It would seem there have been more changes here than I realized."

"I am stronger now." Grýla held her head up high, which was still somehow lower than her stooped shoulders. "I have more power."

"Without Jack, I do need someone I trust to monitor things up here. But perhaps on my next trip out, I could bring you a special present?" The Krampus laughed. "Though, you would have to wait for Christmas Day to eat it."

"Eat?" Grýla's eyes lit up. "You would bring me something…to eat?"

"The one thing Santa wouldn't let you have, that's right!"

The Krampus smiled and hopped onto his sleigh. "Things are going to change, Grýla. The world is about to change, and you're going to be right there by my side when it does. No more bowing down to the humans, nor obeying their whimsy. I will not be beholden to the same rules as Santa. I'm going to do things my way. The children of the world will quake in their boots, knowing that I watch their every move, ready to dish out punishment on Christmas Day!"

Grýla was ignoring the Krampus, long beads of drool now hanging from her mouth. "After so many years," she muttered to herself. "I had almost forgotten how they taste."

"All in good time." The Krampus hopped into the driver's seat, his reindeer stamping the ground in excitement. "I shall return soon enough. If you get the chance, kill the Caretaker."

"Caretaker?" Grýla asked.

"The mortal, or Mike, as he likes to be called." The Krampus scowled at her. "Now get out of my way."

Grýla dutifully moved aside, and the Krampus snapped the reins. There was a loud crack, and he was gone, leaving behind only a set of tracks in the snow.

"Food," muttered Grýla, staring in the direction the Krampus had departed. She patted her belly a few times, then looked over at a nearby elf.

"Appetizer," she declared, picking the poor thing up in both hands. The elf didn't even struggle as she carried it outside into the snow. Kisa covered her mouth in horror, the elves below continuing their task without fail, seemingly oblivious to the loud crunching that came from outside.

Mike stood on the edge of the fountain, a swirling mass of energy overhead. Lily sat cross-legged in front of him, one hand gripping his wrist as she helped him manage the Dreamscape and maintain the virtual soul they had constructed.

Though she typically saw souls as tiny lights or humanoid forms, the shifting lights were common among what all three —Lily, Mike, and Naia—saw, and Lily was responsible for making the virtual soul shine.

Naia lay beneath the pseudosoul, contributing her own knowledge of how a soul functioned, the miraculous threads folding through each other like a kinetic optical illusion. Among the three of them, the result was still a very basic knockoff of what Mike saw compared to the real thing, but simulating a true soul was essentially impossible.

"Fascinating." Ratu had been walking around the fountain for several minutes now, deep in contemplation. "It's unlike anything I've ever seen. I have studied sentient magical objects before, but even then, I only see the magic itself. The threads aren't as plentiful, nor are they as interwoven."

Mike said nothing, his concentration centered on the projection. "So with Mrs. Claus, I did something like this." He severed a couple of the threads, causing them to unravel and turn into mist. After several seconds of letting them unravel, he started weaving the loose ends together and tucking them back in.

"Okay, that makes sense to me. To you, it's like making sure a string doesn't slip loose, but these are non-Euclidean. Look." Ratu pointed to something he couldn't see. "The moment you tuck them in, they merge with the original body."

"Are you sure that isn't just an artifact of the Dreamscape?" Lily didn't even bother pretending to be bored. In fact, she seemed just as fascinated as Ratu.

"It isn't." Naia's eyes were closed, her hands raised as if she was summoning the soul into her arms. "This is how stability feels to me. During the swap, small pieces are exchanged, and this is what it's like both before and after the process."

"Show me Yuki's soul." Ratu was licking her lips and

pacing in anticipation as Mike tried to recreate the general shape and colors he could remember from the kitsune. Other than making some of the threads look like scattered waveforms, he made no progress.

"It's too complicated," he explained. "But here." The golden light was easy enough to tuck into the soul, some of it bleeding out.

"Wow." Ratu looked at Mike. "Are you sure we can't just get a volunteer to let us examine her soul? I bet somebody here would be happy to help."

"Not gonna happen." Mike threw the naga a hard look. He didn't like the idea of taking one of the souls in his head and picking it apart like a science project inside the Dreamscape. He also had no idea what sort of effect it might have on him or whoever the soul belonged to when they inevitably returned.

"I would love to see this in real life." Ratu shook her head. Though the ladies of the Dreamscape had access to his mind and memories, they weren't able to just ride shotgun on his shoulders like a team of devils and angels.

"I may be able to do something about that." Lily looked at Mike. "I can broadcast what you see, to some extent. It will be like watching a movie."

"We could call it Mike TV." Naia laughed. "We could see everything you do!"

"Ooh, I like this idea." Lily licked her lips. "Maybe we could set up a big screen out here so everybody could watch it."

"Later, ladies. I need to figure this out." He twisted the dimensions of the soul again until it looked reminiscent of Jack's soul. With her and Freyja's permission, he had spent hours studying their unique condition. The former goddess was quite the enigma, but considering two separate personalities controlled only one leg apiece, their presence no longer threatened him.

That, and if he was being truthful, her soul was fragile enough that he wondered what would happen if he grabbed onto one of those weaker threads and just ripped it out.

"Okay, this is a mess." Ratu crossed her arms and walked back and forth. "It reminds me of something, but I can't think of what."

"A scrambled protein." Zel appeared as if by magic, a journal in her hand. She was frantically sketching the design, her eyes stuck on the soul. "It's something you'll see a lot in alchemy. You had something that looked like string, but when you cooked it, the cells changed shape."

"I would say it's more complicated than that," Ratu began but then nodded. "But the analogy holds true. We can't treat this as purely a magical endeavor, nor a scientific one. We tread a spiritual realm that doesn't obey logic so must rely on ideas we can understand."

"And that's not what they look like." Cecilia was there too, hovering up above. "Not to me, nor to Lily, or even Naia. The three of us see souls very differently than you do, and that may be part of the problem."

Mike pondered this idea for a bit. "So you're saying that how I perceive the soul somehow affects it?"

"More like your mind is translating it into something unique to you." Ratu bit her lip and then clapped her hands together. "Of course! I think I get it now!"

"You do?"

"The little spiders you make. They are a manifestation of your soul and your magic. When Velvet passed, it had a profound effect on you spiritually, and this is yet another evolution of your abilities!" Ratu explained, clapping her hands in delight.

"And now Mike is seeing souls almost like a web analogue for human beings. It's because humans don't weave webs, but you do braid string." Zel scribbled more notes, making Mike wonder if he had a way to access what she wrote down or if those etchings would simply disappear into the Dreamscape once she looked away.

He let out a sigh. "Okay, so these are some great ideas, but that doesn't help me with Jack's situation."

"It may, actually. You see, spiderwebs have different shapes and designs based on their function. You may be able to discern these properties if you consider them from that perspective," Ratu said.

Amymone, who had been hiding behind her tree, leaned out to reveal herself. "And you should be pretty good at it," she told him. "After all, weren't you a web developer?"

She ducked away as the others all threw rocks, the projectiles bouncing harmlessly off the trunk of her tree.

"I feel like she was just biding her time on that one." Mike couldn't help but chuckle. Even he had considered the programming angle. "Okay, so how can I use this information?"

"Next time you inspect Jack's soul, I want you to think about it using the web analogy." Ratu pointed at some of the lone strings holding the soul together. "This looks more like two separate webs than one to me. How would you put such a thing back together?"

"Or maybe I'm meant to pull it apart?" Mike frowned.

"I wouldn't do that unless you want to kill her. If you had another body for Freyja to inhabit, then maybe, but I suspect you would end up with two incomplete webs if you attempted it. Neither would be good for much, other than falling apart in a stiff breeze." Ratu waved her hand and summoned a cup of tea. "Now perhaps—"

"Mike!" Kisa manifested in front of him, terror on her face. Her appearance startled Zel, causing the centaur to race off as the others watched her. "I just saw him, the Krampus!"

"You did? What happened?" Even though they were in a dream, he could see how hard Kisa was breathing. "Wait, is he after you? Are you safe?"

"No. And yes, I'm fine, but…" She took a calming breath. "He has his own sleigh, he's using it to steal back the presents the others have already delivered. The elves are taking them somewhere. I'm getting ready to follow them."

"Shit!" Mike ran his fingers through his hair, then summoned a copy of the map. "Where are you now?"

Kisa pointed, and a red *X* appeared on one of the buildings. "I think it's some sort of maintenance building for the sleigh. I'm not sure. Also, the giant was here. The Krampus told her that Mrs. Claus was going to disappear soon, and then…" She took a deep breath and trembled. "After the Krampus left, she ate one of the elves."

"Fuck." He put his hands on Kisa's shoulders. "Okay, priority one is your safety. Priority two is finding out where the elves are being kept. Maybe we can rescue them or whatever."

Kisa nodded, rubbing tears from her eyes. "I can still hear her, Mike. I think she's eating another one." Her voice was little more than a whisper.

He pulled her in for a hug, holding her tight. "There's nothing you can do. She's all hopped up on god juice right now. I doubt anyone but Yuki could stop her." Or maybe Jack.

"I have to go." He kissed Kisa on the forehead. "It's time to do six impossible things before breakfast."

"What?" Kisa stepped away from her and wiped her eyes. "I don't get the reference."

"It's from *Alice in Wonderland*." He had no idea why he had even said it, but his eyes flicked to the boughs of Amymone's tree. Yuki was squatting in the branches, watching the two of them. The kitsune nodded her approval, then vanished. *That was different*, he thought to himself as he turned toward Kisa. "Stay safe, little kitty."

He opened his eyes and sat up from his recliner, the blanket covering him falling to the floor. Yuki looked up from where she sat, a Tom Clancy book in her hands.

"Everything okay?" she asked.

"No. Stay here with the others, I need to check on something." He ran for the stairs, ascending them two at a time. When he got to Mrs. Claus's bedroom, his heart dropped through his stomach. She had the body of a ninety-year-old woman, her form much smaller than before. Not only had she shrunk physically, but her threads had almost vanished. The old woman would be gone soon, snuffed out like a candle.

"Shit, shit, shit." He burst out of the room and ran down the stairs. Holly, who had been asleep on a nearby couch, watched him in curiosity, then got up and ran toward the stairs, presumably to check on Mrs. Claus.

"Mike?" Yuki was standing now. "What's going on?"

"I need to check on something." He looked over at Freyja/Jack, who remained slumped on the couch. "I'll be back in a few minutes."

Without waiting for a response, he moved to the door that led down to the North Pole. The trip was faster this time but mostly because he was running as fast as he dared, his magic spiders lighting the way. It still took a while before he reached the bottom, and by the time he got to the massive artifact, he could see that the magic spiraling around the bottom had been depleted.

On the magical globe, he could see a dark circle (which was probably the Krampus) moving across Asia, the light of the sphere fading away beneath it. The light representing Lily and the others was somewhere over Europe now, their speed far slower.

"Shit!" He moved closer to the pole, staring hard at the bottom third of it. The magic was unwinding, turning into a fine mist when it touched the air. Clicking his tongue as he examined the structure, he fought the urge to touch it. The surface of the pole looked like molten metal, and his precognition practically screamed that this would be a bad idea.

Once the magic was gone, it would be lights-out for Mrs.

Claus. Holly would no longer be protected, which meant the Krampus would come back to take her.

Watching those threads unwind, he made a knee-jerk decision to reach out with his magic and grab onto them. Maybe he could force them back around the pole or tie the world's most powerful square knot.

The North Pole made a sound like screeching metal, and the ensuing blast hurled him across the room. The impact would have hurt far less if he hadn't hit one of Santa's abandoned worktables.

Mike wheezed, the air knocked out of his lungs. It took him several seconds to crawl toward the closest table, his whole body tingling.

"Good God, that was stupid," he said with a groan, pulling himself to his feet using a nearby chair. "Note to self. Don't grab the Christmas magic. It grabs back."

Unable to stand, he collapsed into the chair. Leaning forward, he took several deep breaths, trying to collect his thoughts. How much time was left before this home was no longer safe? Should they run and hide?

No. Hiding would do nothing. When the Krampus came, they needed to be ready for him, but how? Maybe if they found a way to meet up with the others, they could be strong enough, but then what? He needed more time.

"Wait a second." Mike looked up at the spinning globe. The others were spending months out there for every day he was in here. Could he use that to his advantage? Holly had been able to travel to his home with a fireplace. Could he do something similar?

The feeling now back in his legs, he got to his feet and wobbled toward the exit. Climbing those stairs was going to be a bitch, but he would muddle through. He was almost to the door when he noticed the tall apparition blocking his way, barely visible in the glow of the pole.

"I don't suppose you're here to tell me I've been a good

boy?" Mike asked, trying to step away from the Ghost of Christmas Future.

The cowled figure shook its head ominously. Mike turned to run away, but the spirit had appeared behind him, bony arms stretched wide to embrace him. He desperately summoned his magic, but it was too late.

The world turned to darkness as the Ghost of Christmas Future whisked him away.

FIGHT THE FUTURE

Wheezing for air, Mike fell from Christmas Future's frightening embrace onto cold, rough concrete. Looking up at the spirit, it was impossible to see into the darkness of its hood, or to make out any features except for the pale hand that quickly withdrew into a long, dark sleeve. It was hard to tell if the digits were skeletal or if the skin had simply withered to a thin, pale layer of flesh.

"Take me back." He tried to stand, but his limbs were still weak from his attempt to manipulate the North Pole's magic. "I need to get back to the others."

The spirit said nothing, then pointed over Mike's shoulder.

"Asshole," Mike muttered, then rolled over to look. They were on the sidewalk just outside his home, the front yard empty of life. The hedge maze had dried up completely, the husks of his bushes covered in dead leaves. The front windows were broken, and a piece of plywood had been nailed into place over the door.

The spirit pointed again, as if urging Mike forward.

"No, fuck you. Your boss sent you to off me. I'm not stupid." Mike stood, his legs wobbling beneath him like a newborn calf's. "Have you seen your sibling? Not the hot one but Christmas Past. All those centuries of Christmas, pissed on by a corrupted Santa Claus."

Christmas Future tilted its head, then pointed again.

"Nah, I'm good." Mike moved to lean against the stone wall surrounding his house, but Christmas Future seized him by the collar and dragged him toward the house. He kicked and punched, but the ghost simply shifted out of the way or moved so contact was minimal.

Mike went limp, forcing the spirit to drop him. It picked him up and dragged him toward the house, but Mike closed his eyes.

"Even if you take me, I'm not gonna look! You can't hurt me if I don't—"

The air was knocked out of him as Christmas Future threw him bodily through the plywood. The wood shattered, and Mike nearly lost consciousness, his brain scrambled from the impact. The spirit picked him up again and dragged him through the house toward the backyard.

Luckily, the back door wasn't boarded up, which meant that Mike was able to twist the knob to unlatch it before he was shoved through. They were in the backyard now, and it was just as dead as the front. Amymone's tree was a jagged stump, while Naia's fountain was empty of water.

Mike closed his eyes again, but the spirit wrestled him into position and dug its fingers into his face, prying his eyelids open. He tried to bite the spirit, but the bastard moved out of the way.

"You know, I miss the days when people just told me my world was going to burn. Half expected to see it here, to be honest. So this is the future, eh? How far forward are we? Is *Winds of Winter* out yet?"

Christmas Future responded by shaking him and pointing Mike's face at the fountain.

"Okay, yes. I'm so sad, everybody is dead, boo hoo." Seeing these things would have terrified him, but he already knew that what the spirit showed him was only one possible future. "I'll change my ways. Time to go back, I guess."

The spirit pushed him onto the ground. Mike got a mouthful of dirt, which he spat out.

"The future tastes like ass," he grumbled. Okay, so the plan to depress him had failed. Shouldn't the spirit have known that?

The Ghost of Christmas Future kicked Mike in the ribs. The attack was so fast that Mike couldn't avoid it, but he was able to twist out of the way enough that the attack wasn't as effective.

"Oh fuck, now I know why you didn't find me earlier." Mike tried to crawl away, his spaghetti legs doing him no favors. "You can see the future. You waited to nab me when I was all alone and would be weak—"

Another kick caught him in the rear, and he tumbled ass over head down the hill just past the fountain. He came to a stop, his eyes now on the gates to the Underworld. The lock was missing, and he could see the misty trees on the other side.

"Oh, you just screwed up." He army-crawled toward the gate, eager to get to the other side. Whether his body or spirit was in the future didn't matter. The Underworld would accept him either way, and he would come back with a fire-breathing hellhound in just a minute.

Another kick missed him, and he managed to get his feet under him. The Underworld was so close, and the Ghost of Christmas Future was hot on his heels.

Wait a second. Mike's hand had closed on the cold iron of the gate when he remembered that Christmas Future could see all possible outcomes. Shouldn't it be wary of driving him somewhere with potential allies?

Was Cerberus even on the other side of this gate?

Instead of passing through the gate, he waited just long enough for Christmas Future to catch up to him, then twisted to one side and yanked the gate open. The metal bars capable of restraining demonic hordes slammed into Christmas Future, knocking the spirit back. It fell on the ground, hood slipping down briefly to reveal that the spirit's face was a smooth mass of flesh with holes where the eyes and mouth should be. A dark mist leaked from each orifice, pooling beneath the spirit's body.

"Oh, fuck me," Mike whispered, watching in horror as the mist tried to curl around his feet. He took a step back, tripping over a small object. It was the lock to the gate, covered in enough dirt that he hadn't seen it. "You were going to lock me in there, weren't you?"

Christmas Future stood by planting their feet and leaning forward without using their hands in a move that would have made Nosferatu jealous. The spirit made a sound like someone inhaling a tremendous amount of air, but Mike didn't stick around to see what would happen next. He did a hobble-run toward the greenhouse that probably made him look like he had ridden a horse all day and now had a major case of swamp ass.

Christmas Future teleported in front of him, its arms outstretched, but Mike was ready. The gate was proof that the spirit couldn't accurately predict what was going to happen, not all the time. In fact, it had only been a last-moment decision that had kept him from going through the gate.

It was similar to what he would do while playing Slap the Cyclops with Sofia. Focus hard on one intent, then do something else, or even the opposite. He could take a swing at the spirit or try to slip past it, but perhaps those were the actions he was most likely to take.

Focusing hard on taking a swing at the ghost, Mike changed his mind at the last second and tackled the spirit to the ground. They bounced and rolled across the yard, the world blurring around them. It was the house again, but the fairies were having a snowball fight with one another while a pair of gargoyles circled overhead.

"So what's wrong with this one?" Mike demanded. The spirit responded by twisting behind him and smashing his face into the rock wall. Not only did it hurt like hell, but the gargoyles dropped down from above and an alarm went through the house. Streams of magic coalesced around them, and Christmas Future drove its knee into Mike's solar plexus.

"Oof." It was the only comeback available to him, but everything blurred again, and now they were outside the burned-out shell of his home. Mike gritted his teeth and tried to suck in some air as Christmas Future wrapped an arm around his throat and put him in a choke hold.

The tingling in his body was replaced by the roaring fury of his magic. Molten rage manifested as a blistering frenzy of electrical energy across his back, and Christmas Future blipped out of existence with a hissing sound.

Gasping, Mike crawled toward the home. He didn't know how long it would take before Christmas Future returned, but something important had occurred to him. These futures were only single possibilities from a nigh infinite number of outcomes. Were they just complex illusions similar to what Christmas Past could accomplish, or was he actually in these potential futures?

If the latter, then his family could help him if he could get their attention. He needed to be inside the house, just in case—

Christmas Future grabbed him by the ankles and dragged him away from the home. The spirit picked him up and tossed him onto a massive stone that appeared as the future shifted again. Mike smacked his lip on the cold marble, then leaned back enough to see his own name carved into the rock.

Mike Radley

Beloved husband, father, and friend.

He looked at the bottom and saw that it was today's date.

"Nice touch, asshole." He pulled himself over the headstone, just avoiding another kick to the head. Falling flat on the ground, he started laughing. After his dealings with Christmas Past and Present, he had expected a long, elaborate plan from the last remaining ghost. The bastard had even gone so far as to pick him off when he was vulnerable, but the plan had devolved into simply beating his ass the old-fashioned way.

Christmas Future teleported on top of Mike, then tried to strangle him with long, bony fingers. Mike managed to take a deep breath, then released the banshee's cry. Christmas Future fell over backward, clutching at where its ears would be if it had them. Its whole body rippled, spilling dark mist onto the ground.

Mike made a break for it but stopped when he saw that the house was gone. Instead, the land was empty, as if a giant hand had scooped it away. The danger sense formed in his gut just as Christmas Future barreled into him from behind, and both of them fell into the hole.

When they landed, the world shifted, and he was in his basement. Christmas Future did the creepy standing thing as Mike just lay there, huffing and puffing for air. It was clear this was going to be a fight of attrition, and he was never even going to catch his breath if this kept up.

When Christmas Future crouched over him, Mike used his magic to see the spirit's soul. It was impossibly difficult to comprehend, like staring into a fractal projected inside an infinity mirror. His brain was desperately trying to interpret the concept of eternity in a being composed of space-time, and his mind latched onto the mirror analogy.

"Eat my dick, discount Slender Man." Instead of forming his magic into delicate fingers meant for weaving, he twisted them into a thick spike and jammed it into the mirror. The metaphorical glass exploded, sending each permutation of the spirit flinging outward into the room.

The Ghost of Christmas Future screamed as the world tore itself to shreds around them. Reality spiraled in a literal sense, the two combatants bouncing off the walls as the room transformed. Cracks formed along the edges of the room, revealing a nothingness beyond that, which hungered for the light.

Despite the intense shifting of scenery, Mike felt himself enter a trance, as if he was driving a car on the highway. It had been so long since he had even driven a car; would he remember how? Whenever he tried to pull his attention back to the broken world around him, some stray thought would catch his attention, or he would forget what he was doing. It was simply easier to just go with the flow and pay no attention to the beings who were watching him. His body no longer hurt from being caught in a temporal spin cycle, and he assumed it was because everything faded out shortly after fading in.

It could have been minutes, hours, or even days. Eventually, the room stopped spinning and he found himself back on the basement floor, shivering from the cold. He looked over his shoulder, but Christmas Future was gone.

Climbing to his feet, he made his way to the stairs and walked up. He pushed open the door and stepped out into the kitchen. It was empty, as if nobody lived there.

"Great," he muttered, rubbing at the lump on his forehead. When he leaned on the countertop for support, it felt strangely spongelike. Puzzled, he lifted his hand away and saw that he could see through himself.

"That can't be good." He walked out of the kitchen and into the dining room. The table had the usual number of seats, with the Ghost of Christmas Future sitting at the end, a small radio clutched in its hands.

"You really are a creepy fucker." Mike tensed up, expecting the spirit to come for him. Instead, it turned on the radio, filling the room with the sounds of static. Long digits fiddled with the tuning knob, bringing forth a cacophony of sounds.

"Mi…ke…Rad…ley." It was a mishmash of conversations and music, put together into a cohesive statement that Mike absolutely hated. Leave it to a time-traveling ghost to pick the spookiest fucking method of communication.

"I take it you have something to say." Mike sat down at the opposite end of the table, suddenly aware of how tired he was.

"I…win…"

"Whatever, dude. I'm still standing." Well, sitting for now, but whatever.

Christmas Future twiddled the knob furiously, and Mike's brain stitched the words together.

"Your actions…too unpredictable," it told him through the radio. "Each moment…too many variables."

"Should have put that on my tombstone," Mike replied. "Or maybe something mysterious. I'm thinking 'Here lies Mike. Chaotic sexy.' I've got a one-eyed friend who can tell you all about how I subvert expectations, but don't expect the same treatment I give her. That's a different kind of fighting."

"Couldn't guess…outcome fast enough." Christmas Future paused as if waiting for something, then twisted some more. Mike noticed dark lines of corruption on the spirit's fingers. "Too many futures to see, not enough…time to adjust."

"Haven't you watched *Terminator*? You'd love it. It's all about humans pissing all over the concept of you. Where'd you get the radio? I would be much happier with a Ouija board or a Speak and Spell."

The spirit paused, then twisted the dial some more. "Took you to an improbable timeline, but you spotted the trap. Am not fighter. Was only chance to…beat you. I failed."

"By trapping me in the Underworld? How would that work?" It had been a last-moment thought back then, but now he was certain that Cerberus wouldn't have been there to help. It had been explained to him once that the Underworld was multiversal. Even if he wasn't in a timeline that made any sense, the danger to him would be very real and final.

Christmas Future nodded. "Very small chance but had to obey…Santa."

"That asshole isn't really Santa." Mike leaned forward and scowled. "It's just the douchiest part of him wearing his skin like a suit."

The spirit sighed and went still. Mike wondered if their conversation was over, but Christmas Future lifted its cowl as if looking at him.

"Needed drastic measure." The ghost paused, whether for dramatic effect or because the next words weren't going to be right, Mike would never know. "Had to obey, even though… consequences. Can't take you back."

"Excuse me, what?" Mike slammed his fist down on the table, and it felt squishy beneath him. "What do you mean, you can't take me back?"

"No choice. Have to stop you before you stop Santa but can't actually stop you." Christmas Future somehow found a sound bite of an audience gasping in surprise. "If I kill you, Krampus wins. Your family…revenge. Christmas…canceled. You had to die…someone else's hand. I'm stuck in paradox… too weak now. Can't fight any longer, can't take you back. Christmas still gets canceled."

The ghost nearly dropped its radio, but Mike noticed something else was wrong. The spirit had slumped over in its chair, more of that black mist leaking out of it. He inspected its soul and was surprised to see that it no longer looked like a fractal, nor was it replicated. Instead, it looked like a tiny flame with ribbons of darkness attached to it.

"Wait a second." Mike stood and moved a bit closer. "If Christmas is canceled, then…you can't be the spirit of Christmas Future if…"

Somehow, that fucker found an audio clip of Jabba the Hutt laughing in response.

"No, you have to take me back!" Mike crossed the table, his magic lighting up the room and touching nothing as he got his hands on the spirit's throat. It didn't even respond, going limp in his fingers.

"Can't." Christmas Future pulled back its hood to reveal that the darkness on its fingers had spread into dark lines along its face. Only one eye hole still had any white around it. "All this has already happened. Must let…events take…"

While Mike yelled threats at the spirit, it didn't go beneath his notice that it dialed the radio to one more phrase.

"I'm…sorry…" The ghost shriveled up beneath its robes, leaving nothing but a black cloak behind. When Mike tried to pick it up, it turned into black mist and oozed along the floorboards before vanishing.

Mike screamed in rage, then tried to grab the chair and throw it. Instead, it shifted less than an inch as his fingers passed through it. With the passing of Christmas Future, he discovered he could no longer interact with his environment.

He ran out into the living room and froze when he saw that it was empty. There was no furniture of any sort, the house stripped bare. What had happened to his family? Where had they gone?

Something cracked inside him, and he leaned against the wall, sliding down until he was sitting. Tears of anger and grief rolled down his cheeks. Even though he had technically beaten the ghost, it had won in the end. Mike was stuck gods knew how many years in the future with no way to get home.

So many thoughts ran through his head at once that he felt disoriented. What had the others thought when he had vanished? Technically, he wasn't dead, so the house wouldn't have gone into hibernation…right?

Staring out the barren window at a cold winter sky, he heard the soft ticking of a clock in his office. He wiped the tears from his eyes and stood, then walked cautiously toward the room. When he stepped inside, he saw that the office was clean, all the furniture removed. A cursory look into the sitting room revealed the same.

The shelves by the window had been built into the wall, and a small clock that had been left on the shelves let out a chime. The bell tolled three times, then resumed its quiet ticking.

"Ticktock?" He wasn't sure why the mimic would be here, but it was the only thing that made sense to him. He walked to the shelves and tried to interact with the clock, but his fingers could only stroke the surface, accomplishing nothing.

There was a shifting sound behind him, and Mike turned to see a man standing in the doorway, wearing a white button-down with a pair of black slacks. His arms were crossed, and there was a slight smirk on a face that looked very much like Mike's. Auburn hair with streaks of white had been pulled back into a ponytail, revealing a faded scar along his forehead.

It felt like all the wind had been sucked out of the room as Mike took a step toward Callisto, one hand outstretched in both disbelief and awe. His son was not only an adult, but he was also in human form.

"Hello, Father." Callisto took a step into the room and rolled up his sleeves, revealing muscled forearms covered in thin scars. "Now let's see how we can unfuck this situation, shall we?"

"I SEE A SPOT DOWN THERE." LILY LEANED OVER THE SIDE OF the sleigh, her tail hooked beneath the seat to keep her from falling. They were over Jamaica, and beneath them were the glittering lights of the coastal resorts.

To say that their delivery system had been truly fudged would be an understatement. The snow army that had been created on the east coast of Russia had been able to track them without any issue, effectively locking off anywhere in the

Eastern Hemisphere with snow. The Yule Lads and their blasted cat still tracked them, which had also hampered their deliveries. The sleigh, powered by Christmas magic, was no longer as fast as it had used to be. This meant there was a good chance they could be ambushed wherever they landed.

"Let's try not to get sand in the sleigh this time." Death tugged the reins, and Cerberus descended. They landed next to a rooftop pool where Lily hopped out of the sleigh and onto the back of Dancer.

The reindeer's arrival had been a pleasant surprise but not as much as Christmas Present's. The giant ghost sat on top of Santa's bag, her arms buried deep as she pulled out gifts and handed them over to Lily along with a list.

"These are for the first floor," she said, then swatted Dancer on the hindquarters. Lily held on to the reindeer with her tail as they turned into a silvery mist and rocketed to the ground floor. Without her tail, there was no way Lily could have stayed on the reindeer's back.

Dancer, her body smaller than usual, kept watch in the hallway as Lily ran from room to room, tucking gifts beneath fake trees or just beneath pillows for kids who were traveling with families. Other than double-checking her list, the only thing she kept her eye out for was trouble.

Once the first floor was done, she hopped on Dancer's back, and they flew back to the roof. Christmas Present stood on the sleigh, her eyes scanning the rooftops.

"Done with the first floor." Lily held her arms out.

Christmas Present pulled a massive box out of the bag and handed it over. "It's the castle from the movie that just came out," she explained. "Hard to find this year."

"How the heck are they gonna get this home?" Lily asked, stretching her arms wide. "Hardly seems practical."

"I'm surprised. You're the last person I would expect to complain about a big load." The spirit licked her lips, and Lily's little demon heart fluttered. Not only was this ghost sexy as heck, but she smelled so much like Mike that Lily couldn't help but feel a mutual attraction. Christmas Present kept flirting with her, which had been frustrating enough without an opportunity to act on it.

She also wasn't sure her helper's hat would let her. Swearing was a big no-no, and it seemed likely that a little light penetration was off the table as well.

"After we're done here, you and I can discuss who can handle the bigger load." Vague innuendo was the best Lily could hope for.

Christmas Present smiled, but there was a sadness behind it. "You'd better get a move on," she said, then turned her attention to the edge of the roof. Death climbed over the side, his robes dripping wet.

"What happened to you?" Lily asked.

"The presidential suite is poorly lit and has a pond inside," he replied, shaking himself off. "But do not fear, the presents were safely delivered, and the koi are unharmed."

When Christmas Present had first arrived, she had been able to grab massive armfuls of presents and deliver them by teleporting into homes. However, the Yule Lads almost always showed up within minutes, which made everyone suspect that the Krampus was somehow tracing her magic. Now it fell on the giant to protect the sleigh while Death and Lily handled deliveries. Ever since they'd adopted this method, the chances of running into those jerks had gone down significantly, but their delivery time was slow again without the giant to do the heavy lifting.

"Trade with me while you dry off." Christmas Present hopped off the sleigh with an armful of gifts. She couldn't teleport but was capable of delivering gifts the old-fashioned way.

"Thank you." Death reached into the sleigh and pulled out a bat. "I shall protect them with every bone in my body."

Cerberus turned to look at the reaper and snorted, then

made eye contact with Lily. Other than cracking a few heads, Death didn't have many options. Cerberus, on the other hand, had ripped more than a few Yule Lads into tiny pieces. Apparently they tasted awful.

"Howl if anything happens." Lily kicked her feet, and Dancer was off.

They spent hours traveling Jamaica, then moved to Haiti. They no longer followed any sort of logical flight plan, hoping to dissuade their pursuers. It seemed to be working. Lily hoped the snow army would be unable to cross over to the Americas, making the Western Hemisphere of the world easier to deal with.

As for what to do with all the undelivered gifts, she had no idea. They would have to go back at some point, but that was a mess for later. Things had been tense enough for the last few weeks that Christmas Present hadn't dared run any more messages to the North Pole. Her brief trip early on had been almost a day from Lily's perspective.

Because of the warm, humid climate, Death's robes remained wet enough that he was put on permanent sleigh duty until they could find a fire for him to dry off. He had argued, but without the spare bag, the only way for him to carry gifts was to hold them in his damp arms, and that simply wasn't feasible.

Back to island hopping, they landed on the biggest building they could find and set up watch from there. Cerberus would sometimes transform back into a human to keep their profile low if the building wasn't that tall. It wouldn't be hard for the Yule Lads to spot the massive hellhound from the ground.

Plenty of smaller towns and villages were without a proper landing site, so Lily and Christmas Present would wait for Death to toss gifts down to them, then run from door to door to get the presents delivered.

They worked their way south, eventually landing in Barbados. Death asked if they could keep an eye out for some tea, as he was quite tired of hot cocoa at this point. Some of the enthusiasm of delivering presents had dimmed, but Lily imagined that was because he was stuck in the sleigh. For him, the joy was in seeing the world and actually placing the presents, not in acting as middle management.

It was in one of the fancier resorts on the southern coast that Lily stopped to take a break. It was a family resort, and plenty of kids had been brought along to celebrate Christmas by the ocean. The months or maybe even years all caught up with her, and she slumped against a nearby wall.

She missed Mike. Other than brief interludes in the Dreamscape, the real Mike was still at the North Pole, doing whatever or whoever. There had been a few more Santa stops but nothing too drastic. Read a book to Tanisha, give Andre advice on how to deal with bullies, things that probably could have been handled by their parents.

Staring out at the water, she was surprised when a pair of hands wrapped around her waist from behind. The strong scent of candy canes surrounded her as Christmas Present put her chin on Lily's shoulder.

"Caught you slacking," she whispered in Lily's ear.

"Hardly." Lily morphed backward through her own body, her back becoming her front so she now faced the giant. "I'm fairly certain labor laws would claim I have a right to a break. I've been busting my butt for your boss, and now that we aren't being bothered by the reject Potato Heads, it's time for a breather."

"I see." Christmas Present's eyes lingered on Lily, and she broke into a grin. "Maybe you're right. A break is long overdue."

The ghost gave off a growing sexual energy that surprised Lily. Other than the occasional flirting, she hadn't detected anything tangible from the spirit.

"Can I tell you something?" Christmas Present ran her

hands up Lily's waist, then placed one on Lily's breast. The hand was big enough that Lily's boob vanished beneath it. "You've been on my mind all day."

"It's been a long fudging day," Lily muttered.

"It's the best day of the year." The spirit paused for a moment, admiring Lily's décolletage. "When I was born this morning, I thought my life would be a simple collection of festivities and love. I hardly expected to be conscripted into the war on Christmas. When the Krampus corrupted me, I was allowed a brief moment of fear before being forced to obey. But a miracle happened, and it's all thanks to that man of yours. His magic gave me a chance to escape, to live the life I was destined for. Not only that, but he showed me…things that fell outside my expectations."

"He has a habit of doing that." Lily pointed up at the roof. "Cerberus used to be a regular hellhound until they met him." It was okay to say the h-word when referring to Cerberus. It wasn't a swear word when she used it like that.

"It was that magic of his. I was pure potential, hunting him down in the vents of the North Pole, when I got a full dose of his magic. It changed me, making me into the woman I am. Gave me an appreciation for…" Christmas Present paused, then stared hard into Lily's eyes as she rubbed Lily's nipple through her top. "The finer things."

"Oh? And I'm one of those finer things?"

The spirit's eyes were full of hunger. "There's something you should know about me. You see, I only live for one day. And it is a glorious day. When time restarts, I will travel the world, be everywhere at once as people wake up to discover these gifts we've brought them. I'll enjoy the finest meals, the most wonderful company, and when the day is over…I shall die."

"What?" Lily hadn't expected that.

"It's how the Ghosts of Christmas Past are born. Everything about this day will be burned into me. I'm just the paper on which today's story will be written, and when my day is done, I shall be folded up and put on the shelf." Christmas Present slid her hand down Lily's body, then rubbed her crotch through the lightweight pajama pants the succubus now wore. It was hot in the tropics, and she had gone with something comfortable. "I would prefer to have a few memories of my own."

Lily almost laughed. The last few months had been absolutely ridiculous, but now the Ghost of Christmas Present was making a pass at her as they were trying to deliver gifts for Santa while avoiding an army of trolls and treacherous snowmen. She had been stretched thin emotionally and was now like a rubber band, ready to snap.

But she didn't. It wasn't just lust in the spirit's eyes but a quiet desperation. Lily hadn't known about the spirit's limited mortality. With everything else that was going on, she might have declined. What they were doing was too important to be screwing around.

"I don't know. Romeo is pretty good at what he does, but you're asking to break into the big leagues now." She licked her lips, her tail coiling around Christmas Present's waist. "Do you think you can handle all this?"

"Please. I nearly broke your boy toy in the middle of a Christmas party, and I was holding back." Christmas Present grabbed Lily's tail and twirled it around her finger like a stray length of hair. There was incredible strength in that single digit, and Lily's stomach fluttered in response.

"Nearly broke him, huh?" Lily smiled, then reached up behind the giant and gave her hair a tug. "You can be as rough with me as you'd like."

"I think you underestimate my strength." Christmas Present took a deep breath, her body now taller than before, then picked Lily up by the shoulders and pinned her against the opposite wall. "I am the embodiment of the season, stuffed full of joy and goodwill. However, I am also fueled by the animalistic lust of the man you love."

"Hey, now, I've never once said the l-word to him," Lily countered.

"It would be a shame if he never heard it from you. His feelings for you run deep."

"Are we gonna talk about boys, or are you gonna fuuu... fuuu..." Lily screwed up her face. "I swear to Santa, if you pull my pants off and my genitals are missing, I'm going to let the toaster bite off my darn head."

"Let me check." Christmas Present held Lily against the wall with one hand and slid her hand into Lily's pants. The succubus gasped when the giant's thick digit teased her clitoris, then slid along her outer labia.

"Oh, thank Santa." Lily grabbed the giant's face in both hands and pulled her in for a kiss. Another wave of erotic energy washed over her, and she could definitely feel the magic undertones of Mike's presence. It was akin to smelling his cologne, if he ever wore any. His natural scent was so heightened by the nymph magic in his blood that if he could bottle it, he'd make millions.

The kissing was gentle, and Lily was having none of that. She grabbed a handful of Christmas Present's hair and gave it a tug. The giant responded by pressing her finger against Lily's hungry opening and relaxing the pressure that held her against the wall. The succubus now had her entire body weight pressing down onto the giant's finger, the pressure amplifying that butterfly sensation in her tummy.

Butterflies? Tummy? She couldn't wait to ditch her helper hat!

Lily summoned a flood of lubrication, her legs spreading open as she slid down almost an inch before bumping into the tip of Christmas Present's other finger. She broke the kiss and stared at the giant.

"Eh?" Lily wiggled her hips but was surprised to discover

that the spirit had clustered her fingers together, preventing her from descending any farther. "You do know I can just stretch myself out, right?"

"I would rather you didn't." Christmas Present licked her lips. "I want to watch your face as I stretch your pussy out with my fingers."

"Wish granted." Lily altered her genitals, making her vaginal passage even smaller. "But you're gonna have to work for it."

"I love a challenge." The spirit grinned and planted a free hand on Lily's shoulder. She pushed down on the succubus, causing Lily to gasp as that first finger penetrated her all the way up to where her womb would be. Shivering in delight, she pulled open the giant's robe and buried her face between the spirit's breasts as she rolled her hips from side to side.

The pain was exquisite. It was like the fiery sting of bourbon when it first hits the lips, followed by the sweet, full-body burn. It was common knowledge that you needed to check your bourbon before making eggnog, and—

"You can't take this hat off me, can you?" Lily pulled her face out of the giant's breasts. "I will eat your butt for days, or whatever it is you want me to be into."

"Nope, sorry." The giant shook her head, her long trusses brushing against Lily's shoulders. "Only Santa can take it off early. I don't even know why you put it on."

Mentally cursing the grim reaper with a collection of words that would be allowed on a PBS special, Lily buried her face into breasts the size of her head, playfully rubbing the spirit's large nipples. The hat was obnoxious, but a pair of breasts like these were once in a lifetime, and she planned to enjoy them.

Christmas Present continued to force Lily onto those thick digits. Not to be outdone, Lily circled the giant's waist with her tail, slipping it beneath her robes. Christmas Present's bottom was firm and fully rounded, and Lily explored it for several minutes before moving on to tease the edges of her butt crack.

"Oh." Christmas Present blushed, then looked down at Lily. "That feels surprisingly ticklish and good at the same time."

"I love how innocent you sound while trying to wear me as a Muppet." Lily bounced up and down, savoring the sensation of a third finger entering her tight passage. Each finger was roughly the size of a regular penis, and she was already sore. When they were done, she could easily dismiss the sensation, but maybe she'd keep it as a reminder.

"Maybe I'm being too gentle." The spirit winked, and her body expanded again. She was now almost nine feet tall, and it wasn't lost on Lily that three of the spirit's fingers were still inside her.

In a move that surprised both of them, Lily came. Her legs went stiff, the nerves in her pelvis sending lightning and fire through her gut as her vaginal canal was stretched wide. Spasming out of control, she flopped around helplessly until she spotted a fat nipple in front of her face.

Two can play at this game, Lily thought. Leaning forward, she bit the nipple at the same time that she coated the tip of her tail in lube and slid it into Christmas Present's bottom.

"Oh. OH!" The giant's free hand slipped off Lily's shoulder, and the sheer tension in Lily's body caused her to rise up until only the tips of Christmas Present's fingers were still inside her. "Oh, wow, that feels...different. I can feel you inside me. It feels so hot!"

"Mm-hmm." Lily expanded the tip of her tail, making it as thick around as her wrist. If the giant wanted to play size games, then she had picked the right partner.

Christmas Present grunted, then pulled her fingers out of Lily's vagina. Her fingers were coated in succubus fluids and cum. She licked her fingers clean, then grabbed Lily by a horn.

"Eat me out," she demanded, forcing Lily to her knees. The spirit threw her robes aside to reveal an impressive vagina with a large clitoris. Christmas Present grabbed Lily by the head, her fingers separating out around Lily's horns, then forced her into position.

Lily was not surprised at all that the giant's vagina tasted like candy canes.

"Mmf." Lily made a show of struggling as the giant pinned her head and body against the nearby wall, loving every moment of it. The force was tremendous, and she wondered if the time lock was the only thing keeping the wall from buckling as the giant lost control of her hips. She continued to penetrate the giant's buttocks, expanding her tail a little bit with each stroke.

"Oh yes!" Christmas Present put a hand behind Lily's head, then ground her pelvis into the succubus hard enough that Lily had to reset her jaw. "This sensation is glorious! More! I demand more!"

Lily put her hands on Christmas Present's butt cheeks and split her tongue in two. The top half of her tongue worked the labia and the clitoris. The bottom half penetrated the vaginal canal, expanding rapidly until the giant let out a gasp.

"How are you…oh! OH!" When the giant came, she clenched her legs together so hard that Lily's skull fractured. She dismissed the break, forming layers of superdense bone as she double penetrated the giant with her tongue and tail. Christmas Present was shaking now, letting out cries of delight that turned into actual sobs. She was actively humping the wall hard enough that it sounded like someone was beating the stucco with a sledgehammer.

A mouth formed on the back of Lily's neck, which she used to speak. "This rough enough for you?" Lily stood, her strength easily capable of lifting the giant. In effect, it was similar to what Christmas Present had done to her, but now the giant's head and shoulders were pressed into the ceiling.

"*Yes, fuck me!*" The spirit pressed her hands against the ceiling, generating tons of pressure between the two of them as the giant came again, coating Lily's face in peppermint cum.

Lily kept at it until the giant was a sobbing mess, making quiet pleas for her to never stop. Eventually, she tackled the giant to the ground and broke away long enough for her tail to wrap around her crotch and form into a massive penis covered in candy-cane stripes. It was over a foot long and so thick it would destroy a regular mortal.

"Beg for it," Lily demanded, waving her pseudopenis. She even made the penis curve for a moment to emphasize the design.

Christmas Present was in a state of dishevelment. Her hair was a mess, and her robes were soaking wet. There was a frantic look in her eyes, catching Lily by surprise when she rolled forward and tackled the succubus to the ground. Christmas Present pinned Lily's hands over her head, then stood up just long enough to line herself up on top of Lily's penis. When she sank down on it, her eyes rolled up in her head.

Lily, unable to do anything else, expanded the penis some more. When she thought she was at Christmas Present's limit, the ghost expanded to become bigger.

It became a game of who could outgrow who, and Lily finally had to give up when Christmas Present had become large enough that her back pressed against the ceiling. Lily's penis was easily two feet long now, absolutely unusable for anyone with a normal anatomy. It was plenty big enough for the massive woman who now humped the succubus like a single college girl with a stiff body pillow.

The grunts and rhythmic slamming made a noise like thunder. Lily felt her body reach the limits of mortality so many times that she lost count, but she didn't care. This was silly, unrealistic, and a total parody of any sex she was used to.

And she loved it. Breasts twice the size of her head

smashed into her as Christmas Present came so loud it sounded like a foghorn, rupturing Lily's eardrums.

The giant clutched the succubus as if clinging to a life ring in the ocean, the world silent through deaf ears. Lily regenerated her eardrums and was surprised to hear Christmas Present crying again.

"Uh, hey. You good up there?" she asked.

Christmas Present nodded, her thighs quaking when an aftershock struck her. The spirit diminished in size, deflating like a balloon until she was only ten feet tall. Lily accommodated the transformation by removing her tail and was surprised when the giant shifted her position and just held her for several minutes.

"This will be my favorite memory this Christmas," the spirit whispered in Lily's ear. "I'm just so happy that I get to live in this moment forever. Thank you."

Lily said nothing. Instead, she leaned up and kissed the tears away from the giant's eyes, then held her as if they were lovers. It was the least she could do.

Nearly half an hour later, the two of them separated. The spirit cleaned up in much the same manner Lily did, her robe reappearing on her body and her hair tidy once more. Lily swatted the giant on the butt as they went back to the sleigh to face the music. There was no way that Death hadn't heard them.

When they got back to the sleigh, Lily was stunned to see that Death was wearing a massive pair of star-shaped headphones. When he saw the two of them, he waved in delight and took the headphones off.

"Look what I found in the sleigh!" he exclaimed, shaking the headphones around. "Santa has a bunch of audiobooks by someone named Tom Clancy stored on these headphones. I never once considered the benefit of having a book read to me! I can pilot the sleigh while listening to a story. Isn't that wonderful?"

Lily and Christmas Present looked at each other, both of them grinning.

"The book I'm listening to right now is about a spy." Death set the headphones down. "It was far more interesting than listening to the two of you having consensual sex. It sounded like a construction zone. I was worried you were under attack, but Cerberus explained it to me."

The Christmas Spirit turned an impossible shade of red. Somehow, all three of Cerberus's heads (in dog form) looked at them smugly.

"So you aren't mad that we stopped working?" Lily asked. "Abandoned you to watch the toys?"

Death tilted his head. "Should I be? You two are my friends. If you needed a break, you should have just asked. I may be the grim reaper, but I'm not heartless." To illustrate his point, he opened his robes and knocked on his sternum. "Metaphorically speaking."

"Death?" Christmas Present leaned forward to inspect the reaper. "Your robes aren't wet anymore."

"They certainly aren't." He chattered his teeth. "Perhaps I just wanted a break of my own."

Stunned at this revelation, Lily just shook her head and asked for the next round of gifts. She and Christmas Present worked double time trying to get them placed. On the odd occasion that they ran into each other, they exchanged smiles. Perhaps Death would allow them to have another break in a day or so. It had certainly been good for morale.

Eventually, they were done with the island of Barbados. Taking to the sky, they turned southwest toward the Grenadines. As they flew, Death listened to his audiobooks while Christmas Present sat on top of the presents, leaning forward to play with Lily's hair.

Lily felt warm inside. Maybe it was that she had finally let her hair down for a bit, or maybe it was getting laid, but she was actually looking forward to the rest of the trip. It certainly helped to know that she had a bone buddy and a buddy for boning.

She tried to rip off the hat for perhaps the thousandth time. Being unable to curse was awful, but thinking in puns was crossing the line. Stupid fudging hat.

"What's that?" Christmas Present tapped on Lily's shoulder, then pointed northwest.

Lily squinted. At first glance, it looked like a shooting star that had broken apart in the atmosphere, but she knew that couldn't be true. Even if it were frozen in time, they would have seen it several islands ago. Currently it hovered over the island of Saint Lucia.

"Ticktock. Telescope." Lily held a hand out and felt the mimic hop into her palm. She lifted the gilded scope to her eye and focused it on the hovering lights.

"Mother fudging snack eater!" She nearly dropped the telescope. It was another sleigh, one that looked cobbled together with spare parts. In front, a team of seven warped reindeer pulled it. "Death, land, hide!"

With the snap of the reins, the sleigh descended with Dancer flying hidden behind them. Lily spread her wings, taking to the sky as Death landed the sleigh. Using the telescope, she watched in horror as the mad figure whipping the reindeer flew low over a group of buildings and then vanished. Within a minute, he had returned to the sleigh, clutching the spare bag they had lost earlier. It was the Krampus, his mouth open wide with laughter as he moved across the island of Saint Lucia in record speed.

"No, no, no…" Lily flew down to where Death had hidden the sleigh. "It's the Krampus. We need to get off this island, maybe fly out over the ocean before he spots us."

"The Krampus? Here?" Death stroked his chin. "I don't suppose we could just beat his ass?"

Christmas Present put her hand on Death's shoulder. "I would rather go back to Russia and be forced to deliver presents by myself while fighting the Yule Lads, their cat, and an army of snowmen than try to tackle him even with you all by my side. Lily is right, we must flee."

Death kept the sleigh low to the water. Dancer flew along the side of the sleigh, and Christmas Present jumped onto the reindeer's back.

"If he spots us, we'll try to lead him away," the spirit told them.

"I'm going up to keep watch." Lily leaped from the sleigh, telescope still in hand. She would have no trouble tracking Death down with the assistance of her hat, so she spiraled high into the sky, shifting her clothing until it blended with the starry night above her.

The Krampus was fast, visiting the entire island in a quarter of the time it had taken them. When he left, he headed straight for Barbados. Lily was concerned that he would correct his course for Death, but the Krampus disappeared in the shadows of the island.

Lily watched for nearly an hour before descending. She was worried that the Krampus had spotted her and was just waiting to strike. She flew north, able to meet up once again with Death and Christmas Present. They were hovering in between a pair of massive swells, largely hidden from view.

"What is he doing?" Death asked. "Is he coming for us?"

"If he were, we wouldn't be able to get away." Lily looked at Dancer. "The reindeer are much faster than Cerberus."

"I think we should go see what he did on Saint Lucia." Christmas Present pointed in the general direction of west.

"It may behoove us to travel even farther north to a different island." Death tapped a finger against his teeth. "I do not wish to run afoul of him during takeoff or landing. Whatever vile deed he has committed will surely be evident there as well."

In agreement, they took the long route, flying low to avoid notice. More than once, the runners of the sleigh skimmed the waters of the Caribbean, sending a fine, salty spray into the air behind them.

They settled on Puerto Rico, landing on the north side of the island. Death stayed behind with the sleigh as Lily, Dancer, and Christmas Present went to check on the homes they had delivered to.

In the first house she visited, it was immediately apparent that the Krampus had stolen the gifts from Santa, even the ones the parents had bought and gifted in his name. Stunned, Lily wandered from home to home, checking underneath each tree where she had left gifts.

"He's stealing Christmas," she muttered. How cliché was that? Jerk may as well be wearing a green body suit.

"He isn't just stealing Christmas." The Ghost of Christmas Present startled her, and she spun in place to see the spirit holding a plate of cookies. "We've been making sure to either take them all or at least eat a few, but this plate is full. All of them are."

"What? Why?" Lily grabbed a cookie and inspected it. "I don't understand the purpose of doing this."

"When these children wake up in the morning, they will find no presents from Santa, and the cookies will be untouched." The giant shook her head, her features suddenly angry. "This will damage belief in unimaginable ways. The Krampus is stealing our gifts, and he will know soon that we are nearby. We must flee."

Lily inspected the cookie, then took a bite of it. It tasted fine at first, but there was a strange pepper aftertaste.

"I think these are poisoned!" Lily spat the cookie on the floor, her mouth tingling. "What kind of monster is he? We can't just leave these here!"

"And we won't. But for now, we must keep our freedom." Christmas Present took Lily by the hand and led her outside. The two of them hopped onto Dancer's back.

"I just hope that man of yours has a plan," the spirit said as Dancer flew them back to the sleigh.

"If I know Romeo, he probably doesn't." Lily clenched her teeth, fighting the rage that was building up inside. It wasn't just that months of work had been taken away from her. The innocence of a child was precious. It wasn't something she had appreciated until she had held and helped so many of them in the guise of Santa Claus, listening to their troubles and reassuring them that there was still good in the world. Each of the children they had visited personally would be ridiculed and mocked by their peers when they bragged about Santa's personal visit. Parents would feel like failures, thinking they had forgotten to get gifts for their children.

The Krampus was out here now, with them, and it sounded like there wasn't anything they could do to stop him.

"But when he does come up with one," Lily continued, staring straight forward, "it will be something completely unexpected and brilliant."

"I hope you're right." They got back to the sleigh and gave Death the bad news. The reaper said nothing, lifting the reins and guiding them all into the sky once again.

The mood remained dark as they fled the Caribbean, heading north toward the United States.

"How…can you see me?" Mike stared at his son, all grown up. It was impossible to determine how old he was. Based on looks alone, he could easily be in his thirties. However, there was a certain confidence he projected that made Mike believe he was much older.

"To answer your first question, no, I can't see you." Callisto walked along the edge of the room and picked up the clock. Mike immediately noticed how smooth his son's gait was and could even see the thick band of muscles pressed against the inside of his pants. What sort of man had his son become?

Callisto flipped the clock over and looked at the back. "It's important that you remember the number twenty-three."

"Why?"

"Also, I can't hear you. Think of this whole situation as a prerecorded message that hasn't been, well, recorded yet. Sure, we could have prepared a better means of communication, but you'll understand why we didn't in just a minute." Callisto took a marker out of his hands and started walking around the room. He paused at certain intervals, then drew odd lines on the various surfaces that didn't appear to be letters or symbols that Mike recognized.

"So how do you know I'm here?" Mike asked.

"If you're wondering how I know you're here, it's because you've told me all about what happened at the North Pole, including this." Callisto stuck his hand in the air and pulled a book out of nothingness. "I'm about to dump a bunch of information on you. Some of it might not make any sense, but you need to pay attention and remember as much of it as you can because, well, you're gonna have to tell it to me later."

"I…okay." Mike looked at his son in awe. It was weird seeing a version of him that was so grown up. "Maybe I'll remember to tell you that a chair would be nice."

"Oh, right. Almost forgot." Callisto stepped into the sitting room, revealing a thick horse tail pulled through a hole in the top of his pants that matched his ponytail. His shirt had been tailored to drape around it without catching, which made it essentially invisible from the front. When he returned, he was holding a chair. "You're going to want to sit right…here." He set the chair down in the center of the room. "Oh, and once you're there, try not to move."

Mike had so many questions for his son, but the first one was the most important. "What happened to everybody?" he asked, sitting in the chair.

"I suppose you're worried about everybody, but you should rest assured that they're fine. Everything you see here is a precaution." Callisto had gone back to making marks around the room. "You see, you're in the true future, which shouldn't make any sense. The future is malleable, correct? You and I watched *Terminator* enough times that the lesson sunk in.

"So why is the house empty? Well, that comes back to what's happening now. Aunt Ratu came up with a whole theory about how it worked, actually. You see, this isn't the first future you experienced."

"What?" Mike tilted his head in curiosity. "I don't follow."

"She believed that in the first iteration of the future, you found some way to make it home. Regardless of what happened between you and Christmas Future, you still made it back." Callisto turned to face Mike, tapping the marker against his chin. "But time travel is a fickle mistress. Even the act of sharing what transpired worked to change what happened today. For instance, maybe Aunt Ceci found you a month after you got stuck, then sent you back after weeks or months of researching a spell that could do it. Well, once we knew what happened, she found you even faster on the second go-around. Why wait and make you suffer when she knows you're already here? You will always return to roughly the same time you left, because the method by which you get sent back is likely the same."

"I guess I follow." In a way, it made sense. It was a temporal butterfly effect. Anything that went wrong could be easily fixed the second time around.

"So for everyone else right now, time is a straight line, but your timeline has a circle in it. With each permutation, more details get leaked, and the process by which we send you home becomes simpler. So instead of a massive circle, you're going to get a tiny one instead, where you spend just a blip of time here. We're expecting you, we know how to send you back, and it's going to happen very soon.

"Which brings me to why the house is empty. You see, Aunt Tinker had this theory that time itself is a form of energy. Unless disturbed, it wants to rest in its ground state. It will always tend to the path of least resistance, meaning every other timeline where you get sent back is destroyed before it even exists. Spooky, right? I could try to explain the math she showed me, but it was all above my head. The best way to describe it is kind of like how the first three *Terminator* movies are deleted by the reboot, which I won't even go into right now."

"Agreed." Mike chuckled, and then they spoke the next sentence at the same time.

"They should have stopped at *T2*."

Joy flooded through him. Whatever was going on with his son in the past, they were going to overcome it. They still had a future where things would work out.

"Anyway, the empty house is the path of least resistance. You see, it's so important to preserve the timeline that we moved all the furniture out of the house to prevent any sort of temporal tampering. Even knowledge that a lamp may get broken could cause you to be careful and avoid breaking it. I'm the only one here because my skills will allow me to activate the spell my sister put in place. Honestly, she would be a better fit for it but felt it was important that you two meet properly the first time around. Since I was only a child when last you saw me, any physical changes you see in me won't gain you information that could further change the timeline. The nymph magic in my blood has kept my appearance youthful, so I could be eighty years old and you wouldn't even know it.

"Also, I'm far less likely to blab. For me, history must take its course, requiring only that I survive to see you through this process. The radio, the mimic, and I are all that are allowed to be here. Well, and the chair too. Oh, and the dining room table. Not that we could even get that out of the house if we wanted to."

Callisto let out a heavy sigh, then made a couple more marks on the wall, double-checking his book. "I will admit some hesitancy to complete the spell to send you back. It was created over the span of several years, tapping into the power of the house itself to send you back where you belong. We worked on it for a long time. We even found the clothes you lost after the incident with Christmas Future! Those were used as proof of concept, so no, you won't see those again. They're in a display case in the library. My sister was so proud of herself.

"Anyway, my hesitancy in this act is knowing that you're actually here. I have an extra chance to say goodbye. You see, you have been gone for some time, and… I won't tell you how long. In fact, we waited until after your passing to devise a means to discover the year, using a random number generator. Hence the number twenty-three. It will be meaningless to you, but we'll know what to do with it in the future."

"Wait, I'm dead?" A chill ran through him, and he hugged himself. "How did I die?"

Callisto frowned and hung his head. "If only you had seen that herd of elephants."

"I was trampled by elephants?" Mike almost stood from his chair, then noticed the stupid grin on Callisto's face.

"Man, I wish I could see your face right now." Callisto laughed, then wiped a tear from his eyes. "It wasn't elephants, Dad. I'm just fucking with you."

Though the joke had been funny, Mike made a mental note to avoid elephants in the future. *Just in case.*

Callisto drew another line on the wall, and then the daylight was sucked from the room as the spell was completed. Instead of the office, they now sat in darkness, the space lit by an elaborate series of spinning runes that occupied each direction. Light flowed through symbols Mike hadn't seen before, but he recognized that most of them contained the shapes his son had drawn on his arrival.

"Anyway, before you go, I just wanted to say thank you. Thanks for never giving up on me, no matter how many times I…" Callisto shook his head. "I can't say much. Causality is a bitch. But I'm sure you can guess that we'll have our differences. All families do. When all is said and done, I look back at you with a fondness that has yet to diminish over the years. You were a fantastic father, and I was lucky to have you in my life."

Blinding light now filled the room, but Callisto didn't seem to notice. He stood in front of Mike, his arms crossed. The runes became fire, spinning so fast that they buzzed. Mike gazed up into the eyes of his son, trying to memorize every detail. There was a chance he would never get to see this version of his child, and of all the things he had just experienced, this was the memory he wanted to carry with him the most.

"One of the first things you ever taught me is that you don't fuck with the Radley family." Callisto smiled as if lost in a memory, but then his eyes dropped to where Mike was sitting. Recognition dawned on his face, his eyes suddenly full of tears. In those shimmering eyes, Mike saw his own spectral reflection.

He opened his mouth to say something, anything, but Callisto shook his head and put a finger to his own lips.

"This is more than enough. Don't you ever dare tell me about this part. It's the best Christmas present I have ever received." Up above them, a tunnel formed. The fiery runes were pulled into it, forming a swirling ribbon of light. Callisto looked up, noticing the tunnel, then back at Mike.

"I love you, Dad. Give them hell."

There was a flash of light, and Mike was pulled along the runes, his heart both heavy and light as they took him back. Shooting through a tunnel made of stars, he caught glimpses of impossible creatures just beyond the tunnel, beings that slipped from his mind the moment they were out of sight. He could only hope that the attention they paid in return also became forgotten.

The light at the end of the tunnel was blinding. He closed his eyes, amazed at how much the light leaked through his own eyelids. As he cried out in pain, even his own hands couldn't block it anymore.

And then he was back. Moving his hands from his face, he was once again staring at the North Pole. The room looked just as he'd left it, except the amount of magic in the pole itself had dwindled even further. Stunned, he looked at his hands, then stomped on the floor to make certain he wasn't still a time-traveling ghost. The clomp his foot made echoed off the far side of the room.

"We're going to fix this," he swore, turning so sharply that his coat flared out behind him dramatically. Determination fueled him as he climbed the steps back to the home above, bursting through the door to see Yuki helping Jack/Freyja look out the window. Yuki's ear twitched, and she turned to look at him.

"Where the hell have you been?" she asked. "You said you'd be gone for just a minute, and it's been hours!"

"It's a weird story, but never mind right now. Where's Holly?"

"Here." The elf's head popped over the edge of the couch. She was clutching a pillow in her hands, her face lined with worry.

"We need to get out of here," he told them, crossing the room. "While we still have time."

"Yeah, well you haven't been around." Yuki gestured at the window. "That cranky bitch is back, and she's just standing out there, waiting."

Sure enough, when Mike looked outside, he saw that Grýla was outside carrying a large sack. All around her stood her children, who had started a snowball fight with one another.

"I see you, food." Grýla's eyes lit up from within when she saw Mike. The ground rumbled beneath them. "It won't be long now."

"Holly, can we use this fireplace to leave?" Mike gestured at the waning flames.

"I suppose so," she admitted. "But what about Mrs. Claus?"

He shook his head. "We can't take her. As long as she's in this building, we still have hope. What we're going to do is use the fireplace to go somewhere on Earth. Time moves much slower out there. Minutes here could be days out there, you understand?"

"Days for what?" Freyja asked.

"To fix you. No matter what happens next, we need you back on your feet. Let's be honest, this mess is at least partially your fault, and we need your strength to fix it." He moved over to Yuki and put his hand on the small of her back, then kissed the back of her head. "And yours too. A few days would allow your wounds to heal and maybe even allow you to paint some new cards."

"I…" Yuki thought for a moment. "No, that actually makes sense. We could come up with something other than waiting here to potentially get eaten."

Mike turned to Holly. "I know it's hard, but for Mrs. Claus, we will only be gone for a few hours. That will give us maybe a week, or even more. We just need to find somewhere to lie low and figure out a better plan than sticking around here." Noticing the fancy scroll holder by the fireplace, he picked it up and walked over toward the map on the table. "Tink and Kisa are doing their part. It's time we do ours."

"You seem…very assertive all of a sudden." Yuki studied Mike for a moment. "Did something happen down there?"

Mike smiled while rolling up the map and putting it inside

its fancy new case. "You'll hear all about it, but later. Every minute we spend here is an hour we lose out there."

"We should go somewhere without any snow," Jack said. "I gave Grýla magic ice crystals, which may have been used to create an army."

"That you gave that creature any kind of magic…," Freyja added, disgust in her voice.

"If you two don't stop bickering, I'm gonna make you wear the friendship shirt." Mike studied them for a moment. "I guess anything you wear is technically the friendship shirt, honestly."

Freyja/Jack stared at him in confusion. Oh well, his humor wasn't for everybody.

Yuki cracked a window and used her magic to barricade the outside of the door with a wall of ice. She and Mike pulled all the curtains shut, determined to keep Grýla and her ilk from looking inside while they were absent.

Jack and Freyja argued with each other for a bit before summoning a pair of frosty humanoids. It took both of them working together, and the icy homunculi began pacing the lower floor.

"It's to make the home look occupied," Jack informed them.

"But they will only last a few hours because it's so warm in here," Freyja added.

"Perfect. Kevin McCallister would approve," Mike said.

"I do not care if this Kevin McCallister approves," Freyja grumbled.

"Who is Kevin? A friend of yours?" Yuki asked.

"That's a Christmas movie we'll all watch tomorrow." Mike ran up the stairs and down to Mrs. Claus's bedroom. When he opened the door, he heard the woman grunt in her sleep. He knelt by the side of her bed and put his hand on her forehead.

"We're not abandoning you," he told her, desperately

weaving what was left of her threads back together. "If all goes well, you'll wake up in the morning and have your husband back."

Mrs. Claus sighed, her face tightening into a scowl. He wasn't even certain that she'd heard him.

When Mike got back downstairs, he saw that Holly had strapped the map across her shoulders while Yuki carried Jack/Freyja on her back. The kitsune was easily strong enough for the fallen goddess.

"Are we ready?" he asked.

"This will take us to the fireplace in the main lobby of the workshop," Holly informed him. "But once we arrive, we'll need to turn around and go somewhere else. Do you have any ideas?"

"No. But I know we can't stay here. Take us somewhere nice." He gave the elf a nod, and Holly threw a handful of magic dust into the flames. They burned bright as they all ran through, stepping back into the lobby. It was even darker than before, and the cold sucked the air from his lungs.

Coughing, he waited for the flames to die down, then watched Holly throw another handful of dust into the fire. As he made eye contact with Yuki, the group ran through together, leaving the North Pole behind.

"I'll be back," Mike muttered below his breath, the flames bending away from his skin. "And when I am, I'm going to kick some ass."

HOLIDAY PLANNING

The sleigh hovered in the air over the Atlantic, just east of the Florida coastline. Christmas Present and Dancer were doing some reconnaissance to see if the Krampus had already been in the area. If he had, then it would be safe for them to proceed. If not, he was far faster than they were, and it wasn't worth getting caught.

"Do you really think it's worth it?" Lily asked, staring at the distant lights of Miami. She rested her head on crossed arms on the side of the sleigh. With the Krampus stealing presents, their only option for prolonging belief was making personal visits from Santa. Deep down, Lily was afraid the Krampus had already visited these children, scaring the poop out of them or telling them Santa wasn't real. "If Christmas Present is right, these visits won't amount to much in terms of Christmas preservation."

"Absolutely." Death was next to her, his eye sockets on the dark waters of the Atlantic. "From our point of view, we gain very little. Each special trip exacts a toll on us, and an imbalanced one at that."

"You're not exactly selling it," Lily muttered.

"But to that child, it means everything. Perhaps our efforts buy us scant minutes in the long run, but Christmas has never been about our own personal gains. It is the season of giving, that moment when someone's face lights up in joy. The best gifts aren't things you can hold with your hands, dear succubus, but rather things we can cherish in our hearts for years to come."

Lily sighed, turning her head to see the reaper better. He had a point, but it was one she had trouble coming to terms with. The debate the team had had on the way had been largely one-sided. Lily was in favor of going to the North Pole to kick some heinie, while everyone else, including the toaster, wanted to finish the list.

It was selfish of her, she could admit it. She missed Mike. She hated being Santa's helper, and playing cat and mouse with a literal giant cat had gotten old. She wasn't built for generosity or kindness but sensuality and murder.

"I disagree." The part of Mike's soul that lived inside her was now rubbing her shoulders. It was rare to see him out in the real world, but he had appeared shortly after she had lost her argument with the others. At first, she had been terrified that Death would see him and react poorly, but it turned out that spirit Mike was still just a hallucination brought on by stress.

As he worked the muscles in her shoulders, she couldn't help but wonder what it would look like if someone else was watching her skin. Would it look like it was being kneaded from the inside? Her body was capable of it. Or was it just part of the illusion?

Please. How many people have you watched me kill and eat? She spoke with her thoughts alone. Just because Death couldn't see Mike didn't mean that he wouldn't overhear her talking to herself.

"People don't judge a lion for eating a baby gazelle." Mike paused for a moment. "At least, realistic people don't. It's a predator, that's what it was made for."

Nobody expects that lion to go out and play Santa's helper for months on end.

"You are far more refined than a lion." He worked his hands along her outer arms, then slid them around her torso, squeezing her from behind as he moved in to snuggle her. "I think what bothers you is that you see the wisdom in the decision, and it goes against everything you've believed up until recently."

Eat me. Lily kept her features neutral, her eyes flicking over to Death. The reaper was wistfully gazing at his empty mug of cocoa, probably dreaming of how wonderful it would be to have tea instead. *This was maybe slightly entertaining, but now it's a fool's errand.*

"You were having plenty of fun until the Krampus pooped on your parade." She could feel Mike wiggle his lips. "Darn, that really is annoying."

Almost an hour passed before Dancer appeared in the sky, descending from above. Christmas Present was astride the reindeer's back, her hair flowing behind her in the moonlight in a pose that gave Lily's tummy butterflies. Her mind flitted back to their interlude, and she wondered if there would ever be an opportunity for a second round.

"Wow, she really is breathtaking," Mike muttered.

Maybe we should do something similar in the Dreamscape, Lily replied.

"If so, I call dibs on being the little spoon."

Lily snorted.

Death looked at her, then turned his gaze toward the returning duo. "Ah. You have returned to us."

Christmas Present took a deep breath and let it all out at once. "He's been through here. Terrible cookies and no gifts from Santa."

"But we haven't been here yet." Death patted the large sack behind him. "We could still deliver these."

"That we can." Christmas Present looked at the two of

them. "But there's no guarantee he won't swing through again. We also don't know what he's doing with the gifts he takes."

"True." Death tapped the edge of the sleigh, deep in thought. "Perhaps it would behoove us to follow the original plan. We could find somewhere safe to hide these gifts until the Krampus has been taken care of and Santa restored."

Christmas Present shrugged. "I'm kind of on the fence, honestly. Part of me wonders if we should go north after all. See how we can help there."

"I see." Death looked over at Lily. "But what about the children expecting a visit?"

The giant shook her head. "I do not know. If Santa is truly lost to us, it would only delay the inevitable."

The group sat in silence for several minutes. Lily hadn't seen such a defeated look on either Christmas Present's or Death's face before. It was really sinking in that they were way over their heads.

"I would like to continue." Death pulled the list from some hidden pocket inside his own black robes beneath Santa's red coat. "I know not what I can even hope to accomplish against a being such as the Krampus, but helping children believe is something I know I can do. It makes just as much difference to them as any fight I could partake in, for this is not the season of violence but of hope and new beginnings. I would not begrudge any who choose not to come with me. If you wish, you may take the sleigh and move it to safety."

"How will you get around?" Lily asked.

"I shall walk. I do not tire, for death is inevitable. There are plenty of children I can visit in the Americas alone, though I do not look forward to swimming all the way to Hawaii."

"You're really planning on walking? Just to keep some kids believing in Santa for a little bit longer?"

"There are still hundreds of children on this list." Death

tucked the list away. "And though it may take me decades to visit them all, I will ensure that their needs are met."

Ahead of them, Cerberus turned around and snorted, sending a jet of flames from each head. She fixed everyone with a stern gaze, then turned her heads toward Miami and grunted. It seemed like she wanted to continue on as well.

Christmas Present shook her head. "You assume that you have decades left. The sleigh is already slower than before, which means the magic is weakening. Nobody knows what will happen to it should the Krampus win, but I imagine all this comes to an end. It's clear he wants to damage Santa's image, and you would become a liability. I would be surprised if you got more than a few days, if I'm being honest."

"Then drop me off somewhere good!" Death shook his list and pointed. "Look, right here. There are a couple of children in New Jersey, only blocks apart, who need Santa. From there, it will be several hours, but a little girl wants a bedtime story. Her father died this year, and she just wants—"

"Hey." Lily put her hand on Death's arm. "I'm not letting you do this on your own. We're not letting you," she corrected at a huff from Cerberus. "Let's keep using the sleigh, put some smiles on their faces, yeah?"

Christmas Present nodded in agreement. "If anyone should feel bad for abandoning the task, it should be me. It's hard to remember how to be selfless when you have so many new feelings on the inside, screaming to get out. When the time lock ends, I will be everywhere at once, compressing lifetimes' worth of memories into a single day. But for now, I am so far removed from my task that my thoughts have wandered. I am sorry."

"Then it's settled. Let's go make some dreams come true." Lily rolled her eyes at Death. "Besides, you would have scared the snow right out of those kids. You're too bony to pass for Santa."

Death opened his mouth as if to say something, then

clacked his jaw shut. "Thank you, Lily. I did not expect you to be swayed by my words."

Lily looked at Mike, who sat on the edge of the sleigh and was giving her a thumbs-up. "Let's just say I was recently reminded how refined I am."

"Now that we know what we're doing, I'll check in with Mrs. Claus and Mike. I'm going to fly oceanward for a bit to throw the Krampus off if he's tracking me. I'll see you two eventually." Christmas Present winked at them, then headed east on Dancer's back. In only a few minutes, they were gone.

Death flipped through the pages of the list, humming to himself as he did so.

"We're needed by a little girl in north Miami." He tapped the paper, then tucked it away and picked up the reins. He paused, contemplated the reins, then handed them over to Lily. "Would you like to drive for a while?"

"Heck yeah, I would!" Lily took the reins and snapped them hard, eager for less talking and more doing. Cerberus launched forward, towing them toward the glittering lights in the distance. Lily stood in her seat, putting one foot on top of the sleigh and spreading her wings wide to flair out dramatically behind her.

Unseen by the others, Mike's soul fragment wrapped his arms around her waist and hollered in delight as the wind blew through his hair.

MIKE SAT ON A STOOL, CONTEMPLATING THE SWIRLING MASS OF Jack/Freyja's soul before him. Outside the window, the snow was frozen in place, making the mountain scenery appear as if it was painted on.

When they had left the North Pole, Holly had brought them to a ski town deep in the Rocky Mountains. There was no shortage of apartments to be used, and the one they had picked was a really nice one overlooking the mountain. It had two bedrooms, and time had frozen while the occupants were outside using the hot tub. There were four of them, three men and one woman, splitting a bottle of champagne.

There were occasional debates as to who was paired with who, but Holly had declared that maybe the additional two men were the woman's Christmas present. Mike had pointed out that it could easily be the other way around and that they were a gift for the man.

Yuki had gently reminded them both that the world was full of people who just enjoyed one another's company and didn't just fuck one another all the time.

Jack/Freyja sighed, then turned their head to look at him. He typically sat behind them so the experience was a little less creepy. "It's been three days, Caretaker. Are you going to do something, or are we going to piss away the hours while the Krampus ruins everything?"

It was Freyja's voice, but Mike had learned early in studying them that Jack and Freyja weren't actually separate people. In a long Dreamscape discussion with Naia and Lily, it was decided that Jack was simply the remnants of whatever Freyja had used to be. Ratu believed that Freyja wasn't actually complete herself and what they were all experiencing was just another facet that didn't know they were incomplete.

So though Mike felt like he was looking at two separate souls, it was just an illusion. When the Krampus had antagonized Jack, self-preservation had brought the violent side of Freyja forward. Based on research Yuki had done at a nearby library, Freyja wasn't just the goddess of war. She had actually been associated with several other things, like gold, love, and fertility.

"Hey." Holly put her hand on Mike's thigh to get his attention, then handed him a cup with some hot soup. It was impossible outside the North pole to properly cook anything, as appliances didn't work. However, the flames in every fireplace continued to flicker, giving off a warmth that absolutely violated the laws of thermodynamics. When questioned about it, Holly had rolled her eyes and declared that Christmas magic was complicated and they shouldn't worry about it.

"Thanks." The soup was straight from a can, but he was already tired of sandwiches. Holly and Yuki had taken turns raiding the nearby grocery store, stealing food they could consume without cooking. He'd eaten a beef stew that was okay but wouldn't hold a candle to clam chowder.

"Are you just going to ignore her?" Jack turned to look at him. "Because even I'm getting impatient."

"I'm only going to get one shot at this," he told them, for perhaps the hundredth time. "When I went to bed last night, I spent over a week in the Dreamscape getting lessons from Naia, Lily, and Ratu on soul magic. I feel like I'm just now understanding how to hold a scalpel, but you're demanding I scrub in for brain surgery."

"It isn't exactly comfortable only having control of half my body," Jack replied. "Last week, I could frost a town in moments and ride on the wind with arms outstretched and a cold front in my heart. But now? I'm crippled, physically and spiritually."

"You were already crippled," Freyja replied. "In a metaphor even you can understand, you are nothing more than a lump of leftover snow from a melted snowman."

"Enough, both of you." Mike could see their soul folding and stretching above them, as if trying to tear itself apart. The temperature of the room had dropped drastically, and he could feel the chill through the sweater Yuki had stolen for him from the ski shop in the town square below. Yesterday, Freyja/Jack had argued so much that the whole apartment had frosted over.

"No. I've had enough." Freyja tried to stand up, but Jack's half of the body went limp. The goddess growled as they fell to the floor, the wood floors now covered in a thick frost.

The bedroom door opened, and Yuki stepped out. She yawned, scratching at her belly as she crossed the room naked.

"What's a fox got to do to get a nap around here?" She shook her head at the sight of Freyja/Jack struggling on the floor. "Felt them getting feisty, thought I would come check."

"Yeah, they need help again." Mike let Yuki pick them up. They had learned early on that it was unsafe for anyone else to handle Freyja/Jack if they weren't calm. Even with Santa's coat on, Mike had gotten a nasty frost burn on his exposed skin from trying to move the goddess from one seat to another.

Freyja and Jack were now going back and forth in a language nobody else understood. Mike half expected them to start punching each other, which would be regrettable because they shared the same face.

There was a loud sizzling sound, and then Christmas Present popped into the middle of the apartment, nearly hitting her head on the ceiling.

"Whoa, where the heck are you guys?" Christmas Present shrank herself down, then looked out the window. "This isn't the North Pole."

Mike took a minute to explain what had happened and their current plan. The spirit listened with interest to the events of the last few days, then filled Mike in on what had transpired with the others. She handed him a letter that Lily had written, and he tucked it into his pocket.

Freyja/Jack, silenced by the giant's sudden arrival, looked miserable to hear the news. Their soul had fallen into a contemplative state with no shortage of self-pity. Mike had seen enough of it in the last few days to recognize the pattern.

"I shouldn't stay long," Christmas Present announced, looking around the room. "And neither should you. The Krampus knows I teleported here but not why. If he sends someone to investigate, they will discover you soon enough."

"It was fun while it lasted," Yuki muttered, leaving the room to go get dressed.

Christmas Present patted Holly affectionately on the head, then blew Mike a kiss before baring her breasts and disappearing.

"Should have seen that coming." Mike couldn't help but laugh, then opened Lily's letter. It said pretty much what the giant had told him.

"So where should we go?" Holly asked. "If the Krampus is using his own sleigh, it will still take him hours to get here."

Mike looked outside and sighed. They couldn't return to Santa's house; they needed more time. But he also didn't want to spend forever trying to locate somewhere quiet to do their work.

"Could the Krampus track us through the fireplace?" Mike asked.

Holly shrugged. "I don't know."

"Shit. Sorry, Holly." He growled as he looked back out on the mountain. What was the best play here?

"I have an idea," Freyja offered. "If you are worried about him tracking us, we could move somewhere nearby. Close enough that we can walk but far enough away that it would be a waste of resources to search. He doesn't know why the spirit came here in the first place."

"So you're saying we should move to another building?"

"Maybe go a town over. Wouldn't be hard to find somewhere just as nice." Freyja's eye moved in toward her nose, as if she was looking at Jack. "What do you think?"

"I could cover our tracks," Jack replied. "We just have to make sure we don't leave any evidence we were here."

Holly didn't bother asking Mike's opinion. The elf went into overdrive, picking up all the trash they had accumulated and putting it into the garbage bag. Yuki came out of the bedroom, carrying Santa's coat in one hand and a stolen backpack in the other.

"It's a good plan," she offered, tossing the coat to Mike. "Let's go."

They were fully packed and gone within thirty minutes. Mike gazed wistfully at the people in the hot tub, wishing he could be back home with his whole family. Now that he'd seen Callisto in the future, there was nothing he wanted more than to wrap his arms around his son and hold him. Granted, he would probably get kicked for doing it, but it was his fantasy, and he was going to savor it for a while longer.

The trip out of the ski town didn't take them very long, but they were stuck with walking along the frost-covered roads. Holly led the way, with Mike and Yuki taking turns carrying Jack/Freyja as the goddess manipulated the elements behind them to hide their footprints.

The long walk out of town felt like an outtake from an apocalyptic movie. The streets were largely empty, but what few cars navigated them were frozen in time, their headlights on. Declaring that the main roads had served them well enough, Yuki led the group onto the icy side roads. They avoided streetlights or any other illumination that might give them away, and it was a couple of hours later that Mike found himself hiking up the side of a mountain, following a curved road covered in snow. He looked back one last time at the lights of the ski village, then flinched when he saw a cluster of them flicker.

"What the heck was that?" he asked.

"Hmm?" Holly stopped to look too, then grabbed his hand when another set of lights flickered. It almost looked like something was climbing across the exterior of the buildings, moving fast enough to block the light for only a moment. "We were right to leave. Someone came to check."

"The Krampus?" he asked.

"Doubt it. He would have come on his sleigh…I think." She bit her lip. "Though, maybe he can use fireplaces, if Santa taught him how."

Mike gritted his teeth, knowing full well that the Krampus could. The road was curving away so the ski town could no longer be seen, which meant they would be hidden from view. Without any tracks to find, he could only hope the Krampus would give up long before committing to a search that wide. "Let's keep going."

Nearly an hour later, they found themselves standing in front of someone's weekend cabin. They were well away from the lights and comforts of the ski town. The building was dark, meaning no fire had been lit. Holly went in first, using a lockpick from her pouch. She declared the house clear, and they all went inside. The front room had a pair of couches, and there was a bedroom in the back.

Mike stomped his feet out of habit, surprised to discover that his stolen boots were dry. Freyja/Jack had done a great job of keeping their travel concealed, and he wondered if they had simply made the snow return to where it had started.

The cabin was lit only by the moonlight reflecting off the snow outside until Yuki sent a few traces of fox fire into the corners. The room now looked like it was lit by candles, revealing that a small, fake Christmas tree had been set on the kitchen counter. A quick check of the cabin revealed it was a rental, and it didn't seem like anybody had booked it.

The group spread out, and Holly stocked the pantry with the rest of their stolen food. The sandwich meat and cheeses didn't need refrigeration due to the time lock, but she still put them in the fridge for storage purposes. Yuki kept watch out the window while Mike went back to his study of Jack/Freyja's soul.

Jack/Freyja didn't seem to require sleep, apparently content staring into space. Mike could tell that the two of them were having some sort of internal debate, their soul halves constantly shifting back and forth in what looked like an attempt to claim territory. Holly went to bed a couple hours after they settled, not even bothering to make a pass at Mike like she had done the previous night. He had declined her offer then, mainly to avoid upsetting Jack/Freyja.

Yuki had set up her art station next to the window, her ears shifting every now and then as she worked on replenishing the Minor Arcana of her tarot. Now that Mike could see magic, he watched in fascination as she pulled different elements from her own body and even the air around them and layered them into each painting. The more complicated the spell, the more magic was stored inside the art. The lower numbers didn't take her very long, and he finally understood how she was able to command the cards to become what she needed them to be.

It was all about layered potential. Yuki was pouring magic into a well with the expectation that she could shape it with her intent later. Mike learned more about enchantments and runes from fifteen minutes of watching her than in all the time he had lived in his house. It wasn't something he would be able to suddenly recreate on his own, but it was like several doors had been opened in his mind.

When Holly woke up, she made herself a meal while Yuki packed up her portable easel and went to bed herself. Mike joined the elf for sandwiches, noticing how exhausted she looked.

"You okay?" he asked.

"Not really," she admitted. "I didn't sleep very good because…please don't take this the wrong way, but…I'm not so sure we can beat him. The Krampus."

"Oh." Mike frowned, then set down his food. "Yeah, things are bad. But if I'm being honest, I've been in worse spots."

"You have?"

"Yes. Pissed off the Queen of the Fairies a year back, got that to work out. Literally saved the world about nine months ago from a dead god and their priestess. Lost someone important to me during that whole affair." He took a deep breath and let it out. There weren't adequate words to describe how the whole thing had felt, the raw void that had been left behind with Velvet's passing. Right now, it was more important to give Holly hope, and crying wasn't going to help. "When all is said and done, I will go down fighting. Or at least be able to say I tried."

"But why you?" she asked. "These things you've mentioned, they're big. And now you're caught up in this too. Doesn't that seem strange?"

"Huh." He had given up trying to rationalize his life long ago, but Holly had a point. Most of his issues had centered around the house but not all of them. The incident with Leeds hadn't even originally been about him. And now he was dealing with Santa's literal inner demon, though it was loosely tied to the house. "It does seem strange," he admitted.

Was it all part of the great game? Or was it a result of becoming part of the magical world? It was something to consider. Emily had experienced her fair share of setbacks, but from everything the others had told him, it had never been like this.

Holly leaned forward, her elbows on the table and her chin above clasped hands. A lock of hair came loose from her hat in the process. She tried to blow it away from her eyes but was unsuccessful.

"I hate this," she muttered. "I wish Santa would come back. If we could just figure out where the Krampus locked him up, we could find Santa and let him fix everything."

Mike stared at the elf, stunned. Not only did he know exactly where Santa was, but would the process of extracting him be much different from what he was about to attempt with Jack and Freyja? Could he simply grab onto a chunk of Santa and pull him to the surface, leaving the Krampus locked away?

All this time, they had simply been reacting to what the Krampus did with no real plan to stop him. Now? That power was potentially in Mike's hands. He just needed to learn how to wield it, then return to the North Pole to kick some ass.

These were all things he could accomplish with the help of the others.

"I could kiss you," he declared without thinking.

Holly smiled dreamily, then sighed. "I'm not in the mood," she told him. "Too depressed. There's not even any mistletoe. All we have for Christmas is that tree over there, and it's not even decorated. Why bother setting it out if you aren't going to put ornaments on it?"

"I might have a fix for that." Mike got up and went to his coat to retrieve the ornament Santa had given him. The spirit inside had hidden itself away, making it look like a simple frosted bulb. He handed it to Holly. "Here. You put it on."

The elf perked up, taking the ornament from him. "Why do you have this?"

"Santa left it for me in his workshop."

"Truly?" Holly stared at him in awe, then reverently hung the ornament on the tree. She didn't even question Mike's statement, humming to herself as she hooked it on a branch. "You have no idea how happy this makes me," she told him.

"Convenient," Freyja snorted from the other side of the room. "Santa gives you an ornament, you find a bare tree to put it on three days later to cheer up the elf helping you."

Mike frowned at her words. She was right; it was convenient. Was the purpose of the gift to cheer the elf? Or was there a deeper purpose? It had just occurred to him that he might be able to rescue Santa using an ability he'd gained while in the North Pole, after practicing something similar on Jack/Freyja.

Just how precognizant was Santa? Had the Ghost of Christmas Future told him what was going to happen? Or did Santa himself just know? Was that why Santa let the Krampus take over, because Mike would ultimately defeat him using—

His thoughts were lost when Holly planted a kiss that heated him up from the inside, her hands moving along his chest. She let out a tiny moan in his mouth, then broke the kiss while licking her lips.

"Thank you," she said. "I would offer you more than a kiss, but..." her eyes flicked over to Jack/Freyja.

"I understand." He yawned, stretching his arms over his head. "I should probably get some rest. I think I've got what I need to help Freyja and Jack tomorrow."

"You'd better," Jack mumbled. He gave the goddess a cursory glance to see that her soul was tumbling about again in what he estimated to be self-pity.

Minutes later, he snuggled into bed with Yuki, her tails helping trap the heat under the blankets. He drifted to sleep, the Dreamscape sprouting around him like time-lapse grass in fast-forward. Sitting on the edge of Naia's fountain, he saw that the others were waiting for him. Lily sat topless on the edge of the fountain, her arms clasped in front of her as a moving tattoo that looked identical to Jack/Freyja's soul shifted across her skin. Ratu and Naia studied the design, then looked over at Mike.

"Well?" he asked. It was clear that his hours of study coupled with Lily's ability to experience the world had born fruit.

"It took a few hours before anything showed up, but Lily was finally able to project it in real time." Ratu patted the spot next to her. "And I think we have a way for us to help you fix it."

"Excellent." He let out a sigh of relief, then excused himself long enough to check on the massive sign he had built over the house. He and Kisa still had their link, but he didn't even know if she could reach him now that time was flowing differently. On the odd chance she arrived, he had written a brief synopsis of what they were doing on a giant billboard.

Tink had written *You stink* on the bottom corner of it with a can of spray paint, followed by a silly face. Mike thought it was funny so left it up.

"So what do we need to do to get this train rolling?" Mike asked. "Do I start from the outside and work my way in, or…?"

Lily burst into laughter, then looked over her shoulder at him. "Oh, please, can I tell him? Please let me be the one to tell him."

Naia looked at Ratu, who just shrugged. "Someone is going to have to tell him," the naga said. "May as well be you."

"Tell me what?" Mike asked, suddenly worried that what he heard next was going to really piss off Freyja and Jack.

Lily cackled, then shared the plan with him. Turned out he was right.

KISA DROPPED DOWN FROM THE RAFTERS, LANDING SILENTLY behind the cluster of elves taking the last of the presents. After Grýla had left, Kisa had waited maybe half an hour in her hiding spot, watching the elves. They moved soullessly, no words shared between them as they obeyed the Krampus's last order.

One of the elves turned to look right at her, his eyes briefly taking her in and then sliding away from her as he forgot her presence. She moved out of his way as he looked around the room, clearly trying to remember what he had just seen.

The last of the gifts were loaded onto a sled. Since there was some leftover room, Kisa hopped onto the back and crouched. She wasn't certain if Grýla was still around and had a sinking feeling that the giant might be able to see through whatever magic kept the cat girl from discovery. The gifts would likely get no more than a cursory glance at best, and that would have to be enough.

The elves took up the ropes and pulled the sled into the underground tunnel. Kisa's eyes adjusted to the dim light, allowing her to notice that the elves moved as if on autopilot. She couldn't be certain if they saw anything as they marched in lockstep with one another.

Up ahead in the tunnel, an unexpected side passage appeared. It was immediately apparent to Kisa that the side passage didn't have the same construction as the other tunnels she had been in. This one looked natural, and she would have thought it was just a cave system if not for the odd concave marks along the edges. Despite it being solid stone, it almost looked like a pair of hands had simply scooped it away, leaving behind occasional finger lines in the granite.

These had to be tunnels dug by the giant and her kin. How long had it taken them? Kisa didn't get a chance to ponder it for long before the elves turned down the new tunnel, which wasn't lit at all. All around her, the elves shuffled forward, their speed reduced drastically as they navigated the darkness.

Kisa took several deep breaths, reminding herself that the cave wasn't about to collapse. She had no idea how much land was even above her right now, and contemplating thousands of tons crushing her into cat paste wasn't going to—

She shivered, then bit the inside of her cheek. She needed to stay focused on what was important, and apparently that meant tunneling to the center of the earth to do it.

A dim light appeared, and she almost squealed with joy. Long shadows formed behind the sled as it was pulled into a large chamber lit from above by glowing gemstones. In awe, Kisa stared up at the glittering crystals until her thoughts were suddenly interrupted by the sled being tipped sideways into a pit.

She bounced and slid along the massive pile of presents, eventually coming to a stop next to a skateboard with a bow stuck to the wheels. Up above, the elves wandered away with their empty sled as Kisa cursed herself for getting caught up in the moment.

"Where the fuck am I?" she whispered to herself, scanning the ledge for movement. The pit she had been dumped in was massive, and she moved to the sloped walls to climb out. The rock was smooth, but more of those finger grooves gave her plenty to grab onto as she hauled her tail out of there.

Near the rim, she crouched and slowed her movements. When she finally looked over the edge, she saw that the elves were on the other side of the massive chamber, waiting to go into a much narrower tunnel. Seeing nobody else watching, she cautiously pulled herself out of the pit and looked around.

The chamber itself was massive, and multiple pits had been dug around the edges. Several were still empty, but others were packed high with presents. Kisa examined the piles, curious what the overall plan for them was. It wasn't until she was near the other side of the chamber that she understood.

One of the pits looked different from the others. A massive hole had been carved into the center, and Kisa immediately recognized the ducting inside. It was an attachment to the furnace, which meant they planned to shove all the gifts in there at some point. When she moved closer for a better look, she saw scorch marks lining the outside of the opening.

Interesting. Had the Krampus put this in, or was it something the giant had done?

The elves had disappeared into their tunnel, so Kisa walked over to see where they had gone. The tunnel was smooth for over a hundred feet before it opened up into a circular room with glowing crystals above and a narrow walkway in the middle. Next to the walkway were sets of staircases that led down into pits with holding pens. Elves, thousands of them, milled about silently, their milky eyes staring at the walls as if blind.

On the other side of the chamber, a separate room had been built where the elves who had taken the gifts now sat. They were in a tight cluster, as if to keep warm, their arms folded across their legs. The sleds had been stacked in the back of the room.

Next to the sled storage room was the entrance to a much larger hallway. From it, a series of low growls emanated, followed by staccato laughter.

"You don't want to know, you don't want to know," Kisa whispered to herself as curiosity drove her forward. She crouched close to the walls, more out of apprehension than fear of discovery. The grunts were occasionally punctuated by snippets of conversation. It sounded like a small group of men and women talking to one another.

The mouth of the tunnel widened, revealing a huge living area full of battered furniture. Along one wall, shattered remnants of couches were in a pile, with a small cadre of elves nearby to scavenge parts. A makeshift workshop had been set up in the corner, the elves working tirelessly to build and restuff the largest couch Kisa had ever seen.

In the other corner, a set of king-size mattresses had been set on the floor, propped up from behind by rocks to turn them into a recliner. A huge, greasy-haired figure lay on them, his attention on a flat-screen TV that had been fitted into a rocky alcove.

"That's because they were on a break!" the giant declared, throwing an empty bottle at the wall to the side of the screen. It shattered, leftover beer dribbling down to vanish in the glass wreckage below.

Kisa stopped, doing her best to take it all in. The giant looked like a male version of Grýla, though he was wearing a pair of pants that were made out of an old tarp. He had one hand down his pants, doing gods knew what, while he used the other to take a bottle of whiskey from an elf standing nearby. The giant was watching the show *Friends* and was clearly distraught about something.

Realizing she had likely stumbled into Grýla's lair, Kisa debated backing out but got that cold sensation in her stomach that warned her it was time to hide. She slid along the wall and found a poorly lit overhang she could scramble onto. If she rolled toward the back wall, her body was completely hidden from sight.

"Leppalúði!" Grýla's voice carried down the tunnel like a foghorn. "Get your ass up, we've got company coming!"

The giant watching television frantically searched around for the remote. Unable to find it, he simply threw the bottle at the TV, causing the screen to shatter. He got up and stomped on the pile of glass bottles, his massive feet reducing them to a glittering powder. Kisa didn't miss the fact that the hard rock under his feet softened like mud.

"Leppalúði!" Grýla appeared in the main tunnel, her lips smeared with fresh blood and dirt. "I need you to get the pot."

"The pot?" Leppalúði looked confused, putting a finger to his lips before turning to look over his shoulder.

Grýla struck him so hard that he rolled across the room, smashing into a stalagmite and shattering it.

"Yes, you idiot, the pot! The one we use for cooking." She walked over to the other giant and yanked him to his feet. "We have company coming."

"Who's coming?" Leppalúði only had one eye open, the other swollen shut already.

"Company. Food." Grýla grinned, her massive teeth glinting in the light. "The Krampus is bringing us a present."

"No!" It was a response of disbelief, a grin blossoming on Leppalúði's ugly face. "It's happening?"

"It is." Grýla patted Leppalúði on the head affectionately, then grabbed him by the ear. She yanked him toward her face, her mouth opening wide as if to bite him. "But not if you don't find that *fokken* pot!"

"Yes, I'll do it!" He pushed her away, trying to placate her by groveling. Kisa noticed he was a bit smaller than Grýla. "I think it got tossed in a cave, won't take me but a minute."

"Good." She ran her hand across his chest, then lowered it

to his groin and gave him an affectionate squeeze. "After we eat, you're gonna put some more babies in me."

Kisa couldn't tell if Leppalúði was thrilled or horrified. Either way, Grýla did a quick circuit of the room, pausing briefly to contemplate the elves working on repairing broken furniture. She threw a glance Leppalúði's way, then snatched an elfin woman and lifted her to her mouth.

Kisa closed her eyes and shoved her fingers in both ears, slowly counting backward from sixty. When she got to zero, she unplugged her ears and let out a sigh when she realized the cave was quiet. Moving to the ledge, she peered over the top to see Leppalúði staring at his broken TV with remorse.

"You!" He pointed in Kisa's direction, and she almost screamed. "Fetch me another TV."

An elf near Kisa's hiding place grabbed a pair of helpers, and they hustled out of the room together. Leppalúði scratched his chin, then blew a massive fart before chuckling.

"Now where did I leave that *fokken* pot?" he muttered, heading for the other side of the cave. When he pressed his hands into the stone, the whole wall shifted inward, revealing another series of caves. Once he was gone, Kisa got down from her hiding spot.

"I hate this place, I hate this place," she muttered, moving toward the main tunnel, careful to avoid the new stain on the floor. She knew where the elves were; now she just needed somewhere safe to try to get hold of Mike. From the tunnel, she could hear the soft crunching of elfin bones.

"Shit." Grýla was likely having another snack on the way out. Wasn't the Krampus gonna be pissed about all the elves she had eaten? Shaking her head, Kisa looked around the room and noticed the tunnel the elves tasked with a new TV had gone down. Maybe there was a way out through there?

This tunnel turned into a long stairway with a gentle curve to it and was lit by glowing crystals that had been jammed into the wall and ceiling. Kisa grabbed a smaller one and was able to pry it loose in her hands. She tucked it into her coat and continued up the tunnel for several minutes before finding herself in the entrance of a building. A service elevator was at one end, with a metallic staircase next to it that descended into darkness.

The elevator was gone, so she took the staircase, cursing the way it squeaked beneath her feet. At the bottom, she found herself in a massive warehouse with earthen walls. The dim light from the elevator revealed pallets stacked with wrapped presents that receded into darkness. From where Kisa was, she couldn't tell how big the warehouse was.

One elf stood at the controls of a spotlight, while another flipped through a massive tome that sat on a pedestal built into a dais. After a couple of minutes, the elf with the tome shouted a series of numbers and letters. The elf operating the spotlight worked the controls, then turned on the light. The beam hit a distant pallet dead center. The elves hopped down from the dais and disappeared into the darkness between the dais and the lit pallet.

Kisa moved to the dais to inspect the tome. Each page contained three columns. The first column was composed of names, while the second was a list of televisions by size and brand. In the third column was a combination of letters and numbers that didn't make any immediate sense. It was two letters followed by four numbers.

In the distance, she heard the sound of boxes being shifted. It was easy enough to climb the pole of the spotlight until she could see the elves were busy digging through the pallet where the light was aimed. In the middle of the pallet was a large present that could easily contain a television.

"Huh." She slid back down the pole and examined the third column once more. Clearly the pallets were sorted somehow. She climbed up the spotlight again and stared at where the elves were rummaging about. How had they known where the pallet was?

It took her a couple of minutes before she figured it out on the controls for the spotlight. A double set of letters had been written on the lever that controlled the vertical axis of the light, while a series of numbers was engraved into the large wheel that rotated the whole stand.

Doing a quick check of the current values, she moved back to the book and discovered that a fifty-seven inch Vizio television was registered to a Michelle Hackett. There was a grinding sound, followed by the squeaking of wheels. Kisa looked up to see that the elves were loading the television onto a dolly and wheeling it back in her direction.

When she looked back at the tome, she watched as Michelle's name vanished from the column, along with her TV. The names all shifted to fill the blank space, causing Kisa to stop and stare for so long that she almost forgot to hide.

The elves loaded the television onto the elevator, then came back long enough to turn off the spotlight and close the tome. The whole warehouse plummeted into darkness, save for the little bit of light that came from the elevator itself.

Kisa sat in the dark and waited. She could hear the elves unloading the elevator, most likely headed straight back to Grýla's lair. After perhaps fifteen minutes, she pulled the crystal from her pocket and sighed in relief when it gave her enough light to see by.

What was this place? Why did Santa have a massive stockpile of presents here? She moved back to the dais and held the crystal over the tome.

The word *Undeliverables* was written in gold letters across the cover. Kisa opened the book to a random page and saw that the names and items were now all scrambled.

She tried to pick up the book, but it felt bolted to the pedestal. Strangely, when she tried to flip to the end, there were always a few more pages in the back. Eventually they became blank, so she returned to the beginning.

What made a present undeliverable? Didn't Santa know where to find everyone?

"I don't really have time for this," she said, but the lie was insufficient. This was probably the perfect place to hide for now, and she had nothing else going on. She flipped to a random page and scrolled through the names.

Toys, appliances, blankets. The second column had no order to it anymore. Kisa wondered how the elves had managed to find a page with nothing but televisions on it. Using her finger to scan the second column, she accidentally touched the page and watched in fascination as the items all shuffled themselves into alphabetical order.

"Oh!" It was like a magical spreadsheet! She tapped the page a few more times and saw that there seemed to be a pattern in how it ordered itself. One touch put it in alphabetical order. A second touch did reverse alphabetical order, and then a third touch took her to a random page.

"This is so weird," she muttered, then tried the first and third column with similar results. However, with the first column, the pattern repeated itself based on first, last, and occasionally middle names. If Santa wanted to, he could find anybody in here with an undelivered present.

Out of curiosity, she looked up Mike Radley. It took her a couple of minutes just flipping pages to get to the *R*s, only to discover that he had no gifts waiting for him in the warehouse. Mike Ridley, on the other hand, had never gotten his Super Soaker CPS 2000, whatever that was.

She closed the tome and paused, her fingers hovering along the edges of the cover. It was a fleeting thought, one that terrified her with possibilities. The pages of the tome fluttered as she opened it once more, alphabetized it by first name, and then flipped to the *K* section.

"Kirsten...Kirstopher...Kirstynn..." Her eyes blurred as some of the words briefly appeared as letters from other languages. She assumed they were translated phonetically, but who was she to question magical books in a warehouse full of abandoned gifts?

And there it was, tucked in the middle of the page, a solitary word in the first column. Her heart pounded at seeing her own name, written in golden calligraphy as if waiting for her to discover it. If Santa had brought her a gift, would he really have addressed it to her nickname?

The old man would have. If what she knew about Santa was correct, everything had to be accounted for after the fact. Parents remembered buying the gifts, and they would be the ones to address them.

Her eyes slid over to the second column, the breath suddenly leaving her body. If this gift had been intended for someone else, then she was heartbroken for them, knowing it had never been delivered. It would be a special kind of cruelty, one that would force her to confront Santa and demand answers should she ever meet him. And if it was for her…

Then she still wanted some fucking answers. Written in that second column in golden calligraphy were two words with a tiny splotch of moisture beneath as if the record keeper had shed a single tear upon writing them.

Adoption Papers

It didn't take her long to manipulate the spotlight, cranking it through its different positions. She turned it so fast that the harsh rustling of wood on pallets caught her attention. Gazing out into the darkness, she could barely make out the shifting mounds of undelivered presents. While she turned the dial, they would arbitrarily reorganize themselves.

When she clicked on the light, it was aimed at a distant pallet that bore the code from the book.

"Okay, so magical sorting system still wants to make me walk. You've got some weird kinks in your system, Santa." She jumped off the dais and ran between the stacks, startled at how dark the room was outside the spotlight. If not for the spotlight itself, she doubted she would even be able to find her way back.

After a couple minutes navigating the dark piles, she came to a pallet stacked high with wrapped presents. Unsure where to begin, she did a quick once-over from the edges, then moved in to check the top. So many different names were written on the gifts, and there seemed to be no organization to them. Were they geographic? Or was it by year? It was impossible to say, and the idea of unwrapping a few gifts to see what was inside felt terribly wrong.

The light reflected off the corner of a shiny red envelope that had fallen between two packages. Kisa pulled it free and gasped. Her name was written in bold letters across the front, addressed to her from Santa.

If this was for her, would the old man's name be inside? It would have to be, as well as her own. Her entire history lay sandwiched between two layers of red foil paper, just waiting to be revealed.

She hesitated, knowing that once she opened it, everything would change. There were a lot of painful things she had come to terms with, and she was happy right now. Would what she discovered take that happiness away?

Gritting her teeth, she tucked the envelope away in the inner pocket of her jacket, folding it in half to make it fit. This was not the time or the place. Maybe once she was back with Mike, or even Tink, she would be brave enough to open it.

The elevator groaned, descending from above as if under a heavy load. Kisa watched in horror as Leppalúði appeared, clutching an elf under an arm while a couple more rode behind him. She moved to conceal herself behind the pallet, the giant's deep voice carrying across the distance.

"Name-brand only, food! Get me a name brand!" He stepped off the elevator and threw the elf at the dais. "Stupid food, your brains are all mush now. You even left the spotlight on!"

The elf used the dais to stand, then clicked off the spotlight. The shadows of the room swallowed Kisa whole, her entire body going cold.

She never heard the rustling of pages, but the moment the elves started cranking that dial, her stomach flip-flopped as she was violently shifted somewhere else. She didn't have to hold on to anything; the feeling was entirely internal. When the spotlight clicked on again, it was a faint light in the distance, searching for Leppalúði's brand-name television.

"Shit, shit, shit," she muttered, patting her jacket to make sure she still had her envelope. Satisfied that it was in her possession, she broke into a run toward the spotlight. She was too far away to worry about being heard, and the darkness cloaked her better than any spell could. If not for the dark silhouettes between her and the light, she would have run into piles of gifts several times over.

Leppalúði was on the dais now, going on a rant about being unable to find good help these days, a smug grin on his face. He raised his voice so the elves could hear him.

"You *fokken* elves better get it together because things are gonna be different once my wife is in charge. She's gonna run things for the Krampus while he's busy doing…uh, whatever it is he does." Leppalúði shoved a finger up his nostril in an attempt to either dislodge a booger or poke his own brain. He gagged, then pulled his finger free. "Hate how cold it is, all the *fokken* time. Will be good to get a nice, warm meal!"

He shouted this last bit, then patted his stomach dramatically. "That's right, food, your lot are gonna get a reprieve from being eaten! You taste okay, though you're extra chewy now that you're all messed up inside. But the wife says the Krampus is gonna bring us what we really want." Drool formed along the edges of his lips, causing spittle to dangle from his chin. "And once I find that *fokken* pot, I'm gonna get it nice and hot and make me a stew."

Kisa climbed onto a nearby gift pallet and groaned. If she

had to guess, she was easily a mile away from the spotlight. The elves were already moving the dolly and loading a large box onto it.

"It's been so long since I've eaten a child." Leppalúði stared up at the ceiling, his teeth glittering in the light.

Kisa stumbled, as if punched in the gut. Had he just said "a child"?

"Santa wouldn't let us, you know that? We've been forced to play nice, that *fokken* guy. Every couple of years, though, we'd find a way to sneak one of you. Eat you raw, we did, cause we had to hide our pot from the big man. The Krampus though? He don't care who we eat." Leppalúði turned his attention to the elves, who stopped by the dais. The giant inspected the box and nodded. "Sony. Now that's a name brand."

Kisa resumed her run, hoping to close as much of the distance as possible. She had to fight the urge to call out, knowing that death was the likely outcome of such an act. Despite her mad sprint, she was barely out of breath.

As Leppalúði got on the elevator, one of the elves went back and clicked off the spotlight, plunging the room into darkness. Only the dim light from the cavern beyond the elevator provided any illumination, which vanished once the elevator was gone.

She waited in the dark, her whole body on high alert as she kept her gaze in the direction the spotlight had been. It wasn't until several minutes had passed that she pulled the glowing crystal out of her pocket. It provided enough light for her to see maybe twenty feet out in each direction, but that was it. She would have to navigate her way back cautiously, being very careful not to deviate from her course.

Contacting Mike would have to wait a little bit longer.

Yuki woke up, feeling Mike shift behind her. She turned her head, curious if he had woken up, but his face was scrunched up as if he was deep in concentration. It was entirely possible, considering he was essentially going to magic school inside his own head.

Figuring she had slept long enough, she snuck out of bed, belting her robe before exiting the bedroom. She was unsurprised to see Holly leaning over the coffee table, where she had set up a board game with Jack and Freyja. It was The Game of Life, and Jack was busy holding a piece of paper in scrutiny.

"Would you get on with it?" Freyja growled from the corner of her and Jack's mouth.

"You need to be patient," Holly told her. "Just because you didn't care about purchasing auto insurance doesn't mean you need to rush her decision." When the elf saw Yuki, she covered her mouth. "Oh shoot. Were we too loud? Did we wake you?"

Yuki smiled and shook her head. "No, you guys are fine. It looks like you found something fun to do."

Freyja snorted. "Hardly. There's nothing else for us to do but wait for the Caretaker to awaken and stare at us some more."

"We were gonna play Scrabble, but hiding the tiles from each other became too difficult," Jack added. "And nobody here wants to play Monopoly."

"That probably would have been a bad idea." She moved to the counter where a pot of coffee sat. Summoning a handful of fox fire, she picked up the carafe in one hand and heated it from the bottom with the other.

"Since you're up, do you want to play Clue?" asked Holly as she held up the box for it.

Yuki shivered, the fur on her tail poofing out. "We don't talk about the Clue incident," she replied out of habit.

"What?" A look of confusion crossed Holly's face.

"Er, nothing, don't worry about it. And no, I'm not up for board games right now." Yuki didn't bother explaining the Clue incident. It had become an unspoken rule that you simply didn't talk about it. "If you're tired, you can go lie down for a bit."

"Not really, but…" Holly looked at the door to the bedroom, her cheeks darkening. "Maybe someone should go in there and keep an eye on him. Just in case."

Yuki smirked. "Yeah, good idea." She wasn't worried that the elf would try anything, not with Mike's current moratorium on intimacy. Still, there was something to be said about snuggling up in his arms and listening to his heartbeat while he slept. Oh, and the smell of him was simply heavenly, like fresh cut cedar and even sometimes a forest glade.

Holly excused herself, then vanished into the bedroom and closed the door.

"Disgusting." Freyja wrinkled her side of the face. "The way you all pine for him. It's like you're bitches in heat."

Yuki stared daggers over the top of the carafe. "That's not how it is at all. Mike and I have been friends for a while, and I didn't always feel this way about him."

"That doesn't explain the elf, nor my lesser half."

"Hey!" Jack's protest was muted, and she dropped her car insurance paper. "I've never said anything about desiring him."

"Please," Freyja countered. "Don't think I haven't noticed how our heart quickens when he touches us, nor how you hang on his every word. We share the same vagina. Do you really think I don't notice how wet we are?"

Yuki raised an eyebrow, surprised at this piece of information. "Jack, is this true?"

"No. Yes. I don't know." There was a surprising range of emotions on Jack's half a face. "It doesn't entirely make sense to me. I'm Jack Frost. I don't have those feelings. I don't even know if I can."

"Ugh, please. You are totally capable of those feelings. In fact, back in the day, we had those feelings for plenty of people." Freyja chuckled. "We were quite the party girl."

"Tell me more," Yuki said, satisfied that the coffee was hot enough. She poured herself a cup, then offered some to Jack and Freyja, but both declined.

"What's there to tell? I feel certain things around him, ever since that first time he spoke to me." Jack's eye twitched. "His words, they felt almost like commands. I wanted to obey but suspected something more sinister."

"I remember that." Yuki sat across from them in Holly's spot. "It was weird, like his voice was in my mind. I just really wanted to give him whatever he wanted."

"Hah! Proof!" Freyja looked victorious. "It's that magic of his, it makes you all crazy for him!"

"Keep it down, please." Yuki sipped her coffee, her tails swishing as her body warmed. "And I can tell you from experience, that's not something he does. At least, not on purpose."

"What do you mean?" Jack asked.

"I can't say. It wasn't even until recently that I even thought about being with him in that way. And he never pushed me toward it, nor anybody else, for that matter. For the longest time, I suspected he may abuse his magic. Gods know it's probably an ability he could acquire, should he choose it. But that's not what he does."

Freyja rolled her eye. "That's hardly a defense."

"You're right, it's not." Yuki set her coffee down. "But for someone who just bragged about being a party girl, you sound like a huge prude, Freyja."

Freyja growled, golden light filling her pupil. "Don't disrespect me, fox. I still haven't forgiven you for stealing my divinity away."

"Two things. One, if I hadn't, I think you'd be dead already. And two—" Yuki held up her hand and summoned a ball of golden light. "—I would absolutely give it back to you if I knew how. I can feel it coursing through my veins like liquid fire. Ever since I absorbed it, I've been in pain. My body doesn't know what to do with it. Every time I use magic, I can feel it lurking like a predator, ready to pounce. I don't even know what that means for potential outcomes. Will it escape? Or will I explode? Trust me when I tell you I didn't want it in the first place. All I wanted was to level the playing field, but you know as well as I do that magic doesn't always work the way you think it should."

Jack/Freyja stared at her for a bit before Jack broke the silence. "Does Mike know?"

Yuki shrugged. "Would it matter if he did? You're the priority right now. For some reason, he believes you'll be willing to help us take down the Krampus. I have my doubts, but he seems to have a knack for reading people that I do not."

"Hmm." Jack seemed to accept this answer.

"Speaking of our dear Caretaker, surely you've noticed the divine spark in him." Freyja whispered this, as if afraid of being overheard.

"I have," Yuki admitted, releasing the ball of golden light. It flowed back into her hand, making a hissing sound as it disappeared into her skin.

"And what would he do with it? In fact, how does a mortal shell even survive such an influx of magic? Even this worthless body—"

"Hey!" Jack interrupted.

"Even this worthless body could barely contain it," Freyja finished. "A touch of it would drive an ordinary man insane."

"Mike isn't an ordinary man." Yuki tilted her head and sighed. After so many days of Freyja's bitching, the goddess was really starting to get to her. "And if there's one thing you should never do, it's underestimate him. He's a survivor, always has been." It wasn't lost on her that Mike had absorbed divinity while saving her life yet again. If it did cause him harm, she didn't think she could ever forgive herself.

But now that Freyja had brought it up, why wasn't Mike experiencing problems with it? Surely he had to notice that the power of the gods was now flowing through his veins. At the best of times, Yuki felt like her soul had a sunburn. If not for all those years being miserable in a tower, it would definitely bother her more.

A kitsune's body was designed for divinity. Every hundred years, they would grow a new tail and gain access to a new realm of magic. At a thousand years, they would become powerful enough to ascend, to properly harvest the magic of the gods. It was a long process for a reason, and Yuki wondered how different she would feel if she were farther along in her evolution. Though magic wasn't really something that could be measured, each tail she grew hypothetically doubled her power.

She had never met a kitsune close to ascending, nor heard of one that had. It was always just rumors and legends, and the only one she knew of for certain was Tamamo-no-Mae. That particular kitsune had made it to nine tails but was killed for trying to overthrow an emperor. Her spirit was currently sealed in a stone in Japan but not the one everyone thought. Yuki had sought out the spirit once, curious to learn about her own kind. Tamamo had tried to trick her into giving up her body, but Yuki had seen through the desperate ploy easily enough.

The truth was, Yuki knew very little about her kind, or even herself. There was no real memory of her youth. One day, she'd been a fox with human intelligence. Dozens of years later, she'd awoken to discover that she now had two tails and could become a human. Her magic was instinctual at first, but the older she became, the more she learned.

Freyja cleared her throat. Or maybe it was Jack. It didn't

really matter. Either way, Yuki had tuned out the goddess and become lost in thought.

"My apologies." Yuki moved to adjust the pillows around Jack/Freyja to make them more comfortable, then moved to the window to look outside. It was a frozen world out there, trapped in a single moment of time. In here, Mike slumbered while divinity circulated through his soul, doing gods knew what to him.

"*Baka*," she muttered under her breath with a smile. Gods, how she loved that idiot.

"You have got to be fucking kidding me."

Mike let out a sigh of exasperation, then sat back in the old recliner he had pulled over to face Freyja/Jack. They had leaned forward, sending waves of frost across their couch and through the air. A thick, magical aura pressed against him, making his danger sense flood his veins with ice.

"Look, there's something about me you need to accept," he replied. Off to the side, Holly had taken shelter behind the kitchen counter. Yuki, on the other hand, stood right behind him with a supportive hand on his shoulder. "My magic isn't elemental in nature, despite the whole lightning thing I do. It was always based on sex and intimacy of some sort. It's where I draw power from. Anytime I try to pull that strength from somewhere else, well..." He felt a tinge of pain in his right forearm, a reminder of the potential price he could pay. "It doesn't end well."

"You expect me...us to believe that you need to have your dick sucked the whole time you work your magic?" Freyja sneered, then crossed her eye to look at Jack. "And what do you think?"

"It sounds suspicious, but..." Jack looked away from Mike, her cheek flushing. "I mean...if that's how his magic works..."

"It is." Yuki stepped around the chair and sat on the arm, one of her tails tickling Mike's nose. "Look, I've been where you are. You're all anger and impotent rage right now, and it doesn't help that Jack has a weird...attraction to Mike."

"Wait, what?" Mike asked, but Yuki shushed him.

"As I was saying, is it strange? It is. He did something similar to save me, and you are in far worse shape." Yuki crossed her arms. "So what's it going to be? We put a lot of work into saving your collective butt, and this is the solution we came up with. Mike has been busting his balls in dreamland learning how to fix you. If you turn us down now, then I'm of a mind to be done with you. We'll leave you here and try to fix the North Pole without your help. You'll spend the rest of your days fighting over whose turn it is to wipe your own ass."

"Language!" Holly protested.

"My apologies." Yuki looked at Holly, then back at Mike. "Now, in Jack and Freyja's defense, Mike, you probably could have spent time building up to your announcement that you would need to be fu...having sex with someone while you work your magic."

"That's not what I said," Mike countered.

"You sat in the chair and told her, 'You're not gonna like this,'" Holly said. "And then followed it up with, 'I need to be constantly aroused in whatever manner necessary while I work on you.'"

Mike winced. The elf wasn't wrong. He had been going over the plan in his head and had truncated it quite a bit before speaking it aloud. "You're right. I'm sorry, everyone, it's been a long day, week? However long it's actually been. Jack, Freyja, you know about how small pieces of the women I've been with live inside my head. All that knowledge is there, but I have no direct way to access it while awake. However, I found a work-around when I helped Yuki, because Naia can contact me directly in order to help me with sexual activity."

"Go on." Freyja looked doubtful, but she at least wasn't shouting at him.

"Anyway, your case is more complicated. Naia knows soul magic, but you're not just a soul. You're also a magic being. Now, Ratu is a naga who specializes in transferring enchantments and manipulating magic. She also knows a thing or two about divinity. Problem is, she's not here to see it. That's where Lily comes in." He pointed to his eyes. "If she spends enough time concentrating in the Dreamscape, she can see what I do and project a version of it on her skin that Ratu can see. Then Ratu can speak with Naia, who can pass it on to me but only if I'm doing something sexual to keep her summoned. It will be like having a team of people doing the work and not just some guy who figured out he could do it a few days ago."

"Which, if we're being honest," Yuki interjected, "wouldn't make a lot of sense. Did you think he would just figure out soul magic after a couple of days in a burst of brilliance? He gets lucky sometimes but not that lucky."

Freyja and Jack contemplated this for a bit, their soul shifting back and forth as the two sides again fought for dominance.

"It's not like he's asking you to be sexual with him." Holly had come around the corner of the counter. "I'm happy to do it."

"I might fight you for it," Yuki said, narrowing her eyes at the elf. When Holly took a step back, the kitsune softened. "Easy, I'm only teasing."

Holly laughed nervously, then turned her attention to Freyja/Jack. "We can even blindfold you or something if you want."

"Shouldn't," Mike replied. "I've been informed that having direct eye contact will greatly improve the process.

That saying about eyes being the window into the soul has some truth to it and will make things that much smoother. But we could use one of the blankets from the bed or something to cover up whatever is, well, happening."

"I am not afraid of sex," Freyja declared.

"Neither am I," added Jack.

"Please, you're probably excited about it." Freyja rolled her eye. "I can sense your excitement even now."

"Ladies." Mike held up a hand for silence. "Please. If you're okay with this, I want to get started as soon as possible. I'm about to try untangling and repairing a soul that is thousands of years old. This will take some time." Ratu and Naia had theorized it could take more than one attempt, but they risked the possibility of doing more damage depending on when he stopped. It made the most sense to power through it in one attempt, and Mike had already chugged a couple cans of soup and had set some water bottles nearby in case he got thirsty.

Freyja's eye snapped toward Mike. "I distrust you. Understand that I go along with this plan only as a means to an end. Should you succeed, I will help you retake the North, but what happens next will be decided by how generous I'm feeling."

"Stop, you're embarrassing us." Jack looked away, giving the goddess a walleyed look that almost squeezed a laugh from Mike.

"It's fine," he told them. "If my intentions are dishonorable, I'm sure you'll make sure my world freezes or something."

Yuki chortled, then pretended to cough, turning away to hide her smile. He was glad someone appreciated his humor.

"Then it is settled." Freyja relaxed in her seat and stared at him. "Fix me, Caretaker."

"Fix us," Jack corrected.

Mike opened his coat, revealing that he was naked underneath. Jack appraised his member with an arched brow, her eye snapping back up when Freyja called her out on it.

Holly, ever the eager helper, knelt on the floor and, per his instructions, did her best to give him the absolute worst blow job ever. She used teeth to nibble his foreskin, slapped his cock against his thigh, and even tried to blow into his cock.

What the hell is going on out there? Naia's presence blossomed in his mind as Holly held his cock like a microphone and blew across the top of it like she was trying to play notes across an empty bottle.

Mike sighed in relief now that the nymph was with him. *How is the connection?* he asked.

It must be fine, because Lily won't stop laughing. He heard the mirth in Naia's voice. *Tell her to move on, please.*

"Commence Operation Soul Edge." Mike groaned when Holly made an honest attempt to take him into her mouth. The plan for now was to have her and Yuki swap out, keeping him aroused and in contact with Naia until he finished fixing Freyja and Jack. He would take credit for the idea, but Amymone was the one who had come up with the name for it.

The soul of the goddess appeared before him, and he noticed it was more twisted than ever. Based on what he already knew, he suspected Freyja had officially become the dominant personality but not enough to gain control of their body. The soul itself was stretched thin in places, under tension and ready to snap.

Shit. This is bad, Naia told him.

Looks that way, he replied. *What's the best way to proceed?*

Give Ratu a moment. She's discussing some ideas with Tink.

Tink wasn't part of the plan, he said.

You're right, she wasn't. But she's here now and talking about something called a hypercube and tensors. Apparently this soul has some foundation in upper-level mathematics that she recognizes, and she wants to help.

Mike smiled at the thought of Tink essentially giving a

college lecture. He assumed such an event would conclude in a graph that made a big dick.

You're getting distracted, lover. Naia's voice was barely audible, so he looked down at Holly. The elf had pulled up her shirt and was using her breasts to stroke his cock. It took a couple of minutes, but he felt Naia click back into place and then resumed his work.

Manipulating Freyja/Jack's soul began with a cursory inspection, which revealed packets of golden light tangled in the weblike structure. Ratu instructed him to lightly tug at a few places to see what was underneath. At some point, Holly switched places with Yuki, who rubbed his stomach with her hands, then used her claws to tease the sensitive flesh of his thighs.

It felt like nearly an hour had passed before he made his first adjustment, but it was probably only a few minutes. He used his magic like tweezers to pluck at a green-and-golden thread wrapped around the outside of Freyja/Jack's soul that was stretched like a rubber band, then shifted it around the other side of the construct. Almost immediately, some of the narrow edges of the soul rebounded as if they had been tied down.

The goddess cried out, frost forming around her hands and feet. The temperature in the room dropped, and Yuki pulled as much of Mike's robe closed as possible.

Ripples cascaded through the soul before him, and it eventually settled. Ratu and Tink consulted for a few more minutes before Naia instructed him to grab a particularly thick thread and untangle the colors within. He broke out in a sweat during the task, his concentration staving off the orgasm that built up inside him as Holly joined Yuki in sucking on opposite sides of his shaft.

When the colors untangled, the soul snapped and flooded the room with residual magic in the form of floating lights that drifted to the floor and snuffed themselves out. Determined, Mike kept at it, making more adjustments. As he continued, he noticed that the density of the soul seemed to increase as gaps filled in with threads of light that had been smothered out of sight. Sometimes Jack or Freyja would comment, and he couldn't help but notice distinctive colors that formed in the soul as a result. The longer he worked, the more he realized Jack and Freyja didn't comprise the majority of the soul. In fact, there was a tight ball now visible in the center like a dying star. Every thread he manipulated was connected to that glowing golden ball of energy.

That's a good sign, Naia told him. *Ratu says we're looking at something akin to what makes her a goddess, or used to, anyway. It should be a lot bigger, apparently.*

What does Tink say?

She's going on about white dwarfs and nuclear fusion. Zel is now talking about astrology. Naia paused. *She's now mad at me for saying astrology instead of astronomy. Give us a minute.*

Mike sighed, then turned his attention to his lap. Yuki looked up at him with a grin, his cock firmly planted between her breasts.

"How long have we been doing this?" he asked.

"Are you complaining?" She lowered her chest, allowing the head of his cock to pop free of her boobs. Somehow, she managed to tease the tip of it with her tongue. "The hardest part has been dealing with your magic."

"How so?"

"We've been using it to tell when you're getting really excited. That usually means it starts jumping all over the place." Yuki winked at him. "Holly is taking a break out in a snowdrift as a result."

Mike snorted in amusement. The front door of the cabin opened up, and Holly walked in, completely naked. The elf took a swig of hot cocoa, then slammed it down on the counter before swapping out with Yuki again.

"Here." Yuki helped him drink some water as Holly gave

him a hand job. His cock was slick with glittery precum, which the elf rubbed all over her chest.

"Do you think I have the world record for edging?"

"Nope. Time is stopped. Might have the record for most orgasms in a single second but not edging."

Mike half expected a snarky response from Jack or Freyja, but the goddess was now staring blankly into space. He had no idea what the process felt like from their side, but they were still breathing and their soul was circulating light and magic.

Okay, so here's what we have. Naia's voice snapped him back to the task at hand. *The consensus is that what we're looking at is the part of Freyja and Jack that used to be an actual goddess. It's like a dead star, or something of that nature. Ratu has a theory that it could be reignited with enough magic. Once that happens, it's likely that her soul will be able to fix itself.*

So I'm going to jump-start her?

That's the hope, Naia confessed. *Lily agrees as well. Apparently even the most damaged soul carries with it a memory of what it should look like. The others don't have anything else to add.*

So we need a power surge?

He felt her grin inside his mind. *I think you know what you need to do.*

Mike watched Freyja/Jack carefully as he explained the plan to the others. The goddess didn't react; it was almost as if their mind was someplace else entirely. Holly, excited to help him with the process, pushed him back in the recliner and mounted him.

His magic, which had been little more than a background crackle, turned into a full-blown sizzle. He didn't pretend to understand if he had held off multiple orgasms, or maybe it was just the same one over and over, but his magic flooded the room first with sparks, then motes of light that hovered nearby. Holly let out cries of delight as the motes vanished into her skin, then came at least twice before the pressure building up inside Mike finally released.

In that moment, he targeted the core of Freyja/Jack's soul and sent all his energy outward.

The ensuing bolt of sexual lightning rattled the cabin, and the motes of light spun faster and faster around them. Holly was flooded with magic, letting out a final cry of delight before her eyes rolled up in her head and she passed out. The elf lay against him, happily leaking his cum as the core of Freyja/Jack's soul sucked up all the energy he had sent into it. Golden bands of light had formed and were circulating through the core like giant rings.

"Here, I've got her." Yuki casually lifted the elf, who giggled in her sleep. The kitsune disappeared into the bedroom with Holly and returned with a grin on her face. "Poor thing couldn't handle it is all. She's fine."

Mike sighed in relief and turned his attention back to Freyja/Jack's soul. It occurred to him that the motes of light still hadn't disappeared, which was strange. Didn't they usually vanish once he was done?

Freyja/Jack's soul made a sound like a bell, then sent the energy it had absorbed back out into the room. The motes of light turned into balls of lightning that expanded outward, knocking over furniture and pulling cabinets open. It was like the cabin had suddenly come to life and was voicing its displeasure at them.

The goddess let out a cry, their voices overlapping with each other. Mike covered his ears, his attention drawn by movement in the kitchen. One of the lightning orbs caught the top of the tree and circled down to where the ornament hung, the mist within swirling as a pair of dark eyes appeared.

"Oh shit," he muttered as the tree fell off the counter. The ornament fell as if in slow motion, then shattered on the ground. Dark mist swirled about, eagerly soaking up the ambient magic before crawling inward toward where he and the goddess sat. In the corner of the room, he saw the Ghost of Christmas Past rise from the fog, its childlike face neutral as the mists circled Freyja/Jack and moved up to her soul.

"Oh, no you don't!" Mike had no idea what this spirit intended, and he sent his own magic out in an attempt to swat it away. The mists casually danced around his feeble attempts, eventually reaching the core of Freyja/Jack's soul. A ball of golden light appeared in Christmas Past's hand, then streaked across the room like a comet, where it buried itself into Freyja/Jack's core.

Her soul exploded outward, like a fractal unraveling. He wrapped his magic protectively around those delicate threads, determined to hold them together, but it was like trying to hold an umbrella in a hurricane.

At first, he thought her soul was becoming larger, but then he realized that wasn't the case. He was being pulled into it, his consciousness yanked toward the now fiery core in her center.

All right, Santa. Let's see what you have planned for me now. The outside world disappeared as he was sucked into that golden light.

JACK STOOD ON THE EDGE OF A CLIFF, A SHATTERED CROWN IN her hand. Down below, the ocean churned, the corpses of humanoids and monstrous entities scattered among the waves and rocks. A particularly large beast with the head of a whale made passes at the chum, opening its cavernous maw wide to swallow the dead. The sides of its mouth were smooth, but the top of its head was heavily dimpled like a raspberry. Each of the pimply nodes dotting its flesh opened to reveal a neon-yellow eye that narrowed in her direction.

She cried out, backing away from the ledge only to crash into somebody. They went down together in a heap, tumbling along a steep slope of grass stained with blood and black ooze.

The dark fluid reflected iridescent patterns that hurt her eyes, and random bits of creatures were strewn across the landscape.

When Jack came to a stop, she stood and turned to face the other person.

"Ow, fuck me." Mike was on the ground, a busted spear sticking out of his thigh. He grabbed it by the shaft and yanked it free, a shimmering aura appearing around him as the wound closed up. His clothes were stained with blood, grass, and that black fluid.

"What have you done? Where are we?" Jack raised her hand, summoning ribbons of energy that coalesced into floating shards of ice.

"Chill out, Elsa, this isn't what I had in mind." He stood, surveying the landscape. "Something else happened in meat-space, and I'm trying to figure out where we are."

"Mike." She said his name like a warning, causing his attention to snap onto her.

"Do you sleep?" He did a couple of leg raises, then patted the thigh that had been stabbed. "Because if so, I think this is the Dreamscape. Well, yours specifically. Mine isn't so…disturbing."

"No, I don't sleep," she snapped.

"Well, that was my best guess, and…" he tilted his head as if listening to something. "Interesting. I can almost hear Naia, and she sounds upset. This isn't the Dreamscape but something similar."

"We're…in my head?" Jack touched her forehead. Was Mike reading her thoughts?

"In your soul, apparently. Mind and soul are very different." He looked down at himself and clapped his hands. The stains on his body vanished. "Last thing I remember was my magic overloading, and it connected to that damned ornament."

"Why would that matter?" she asked.

"The Ghost of Christmas Past was inside. Last Christmas, technically. Had a small ball of divinity, not sure what that's about." He looked back up the hill. "Which, if my memory serves me, means I'm supposed to be here. There's something he wants me to see."

"Who? Santa?" Jack scowled. "Seems like something that dick would do."

"Right? Dude could have just sent out some emails, would have been way easier." Mike looked up the hill and tilted his head. "Was he there before?"

Near the top of the hill, a large man stood, his gaze fixed on the ocean. Thick white hair adorned broad shoulders, and the stranger was shirtless, his back covered in fresh wounds and old scars. The wind picked up, and the man's white beard billowed away from him.

"Is that Santa?" Mike asked. "What's he doing here?"

"No, Santa never looked so…" Jack didn't know how to describe it. The figure on the hill was like a magnet, pulling her toward him. Those thick shoulders rippled with power, and the man's hands looked as if they could squeeze a confession from iron itself.

"Appealing?" Mike finished. When Jack looked at him, he held up his hands in defense. "Hey, dude looks like a badass. Unless he's a total butterface, I would easily rate him as an eight out of ten from the back alone."

"I find nobody appealing," she spat, then strode up the hill. Of course, this was a lie. Ever since she had been in Mike's care, she had found herself easily enamored by him. It hadn't made any sense, at least not until she'd learned that he had soul swapped with a nymph. Regardless, there was a presence he carried, one that felt intimately familiar. Freyja had chastised her openly for it, but Jack suspected the goddess might feel the same way.

"I'm literally inside your soul right now," he said from

right behind her. "I can tell when you're lying. It makes the air taste like mustard."

"Mustard?" She turned and frowned. "What the hell?"

He shrugged. "Don't look at me. It's your soul."

Shaking her head, she continued back up the hill, slowing to navigate the slippery parts. Above them, the figure stood stoic and motionless, a spear with glowing runes carved into the head clutched tightly in his hands. He was leaning forward on it, using it to support his weight. The remnants of a golden helmet lay at his feet. It had been designed to look like a bird, but one of the wings was missing and the bird's head was bent backward, folded flat against the helmet's brow.

"You live." The figure turned to reveal a heavily scarred face. One eye was nothing more than scar tissue, and tears leaked heavily from the other. "Have you any word of your sister?"

"Sister?" Jack paused, causing Mike to bump into her. She felt a slight jolt of electricity at his touch, her heart briefly surging. "Freyja has a sister?"

"No idea, but that's definitely not Santa," Mike remarked, moving next to her. "But he's not part of you either, in case you're worried. This is a memory. They feel sticky."

"Sticky?"

"Yeah, 'cause they can't be changed." He moved closer to the man. "He seems to be waiting for you to say something."

"What does he want me to say?" She moved next to the stranger and stared out at the horizon. There had once been a fleet of boats there, but now there was naught but shattered timbers.

Wait, how did she know that?

"Any news of my dear Frigga, please, I beg of you. Even if it's bad." The man moved toward her and extended a hand to touch her shoulder. Jack flinched away but was surprised when a golden figure emerged from her body and stepped into the touch. It was a different version of herself, with long hair and vibrant skin. The crown was clutched in her doppelgänger's hand.

"I fear she may have fallen." The doppelgänger bowed her head in reverence. "Both her army and my own now lie in ruin. The invaders could not be stopped, and I barely escaped myself."

"They have taken everything from us but our lives. I fear even those may not be enough to satisfy them." The man spat at the ground in frustration.

"Odin," Freyja whispered, wiping the tear from his cheek. "We must flee. My sister, she may yet live. If you do not survive this day, you shall never know for sure."

"My place is here," he told her, his fingers tangling in her hair and lingering. "That you and the others may have a chance. For if we fall this day, there must be someone else to guide the humans."

"There's a chance the invaders will fail," she replied. "Other plans have been put in action. The gods themselves, they might—"

There was a loud rumble, followed by a crack of thunder that knocked Jack and Mike to the ground. Rolling onto her back, Jack looked down the hill and gasped as the distant clouds parted to reveal the largest tree she had ever seen. Its thick branches were decorated with sparkling star fields, the leaves adorned in gaseous nebulae and star clusters. One branch had been snapped clean off by a being made of twisted shadows that leaned forward to reveal a hideous face that—

The whole world scrambled, and Jack clutched her head, looking away from the entity above, a being whose body surpassed the stars. Behind her, Mike gagged repeatedly, and she turned to see that blood was leaking from his eyes and nose.

"Mike?" She reached for him, but he swatted her hand away.

"Don't touch me!" he gasped, the air around him distorting. She could see it now, the magic of Mike Radley, whipping around him like a hungry storm. For a few seconds, she feared he would burst apart as the air shimmered, but it eventually settled.

"Are you...okay?" She was afraid to move any closer.

Mike sniffed, then spat blood onto the ground. She noticed he kept his gaze away from the giant tree in the distance. "Yeah, I'm fine, it's just...for a moment, it felt like I was being pulled apart and my magic...sorry."

Odin and Freyja seemed troubled by the sight of the hideous face but weren't affected otherwise.

"That cursed thing would consume us all," Odin said with a growl. "A being from outside time and space, capable of bending reality to its will."

"How are we supposed to battle such a creature?" Freyja asked. "Its army shattered our own, drove us out of Alfheim. And for what?"

"To treat the gods as a midnight snack." Odin spat on the ground. "This is not Ragnarok. There is no glory here. To die at the hands of such a beast is to cease to have ever been, to be wiped from time itself."

Freyja put a hand to her mouth in horror. "Surely that can't be true."

"Aye." Odin touched a spot below his missing eye. "I can feel their absence yet know nothing of them. Should this beast succeed in its task, then this plane and all its denizens shall cease to be. Even now, those we have defeated return all the stronger for it."

The Norse god nodded down the hill, and Jack saw that the glittering black fluid was forming into a pool that thickened around the middle as something tried to come through the other side.

"I should have listened," Odin whispered. "When the

others came to me and warned me of this. For though I am all-seeing, I was still blind to the truth."

Freyja embraced him, holding him tight. "You were not alone in your blindness."

"But you may yet have a chance." Odin pushed her away. "Maybe you can catch up with the others?"

She shook her head. "It is too late for that. They are already with the Architect and are safely away."

"Then you must flee." Odin turned his gaze on Freyja. "Hide yourself, and await our return."

"And what will you do?" she asked him.

"Those of us who remain will have to be enough." Odin curled his lip and raised his spear. "For in the beginning, we said let there be light, and it was good."

The fluid formed into a being that made Jack's heart race. She couldn't focus on any part of it as the creature shifted beneath her gaze.

"Until we meet again!" Odin pressed his forehead to Freyja's, then let out a war cry before leaping through the air and bringing the weapon down onto the beast that had formed. All along the hillside, the red blood had turned black and crawled toward the apex, approaching Freyja's feet.

"I take my leave," Freyja spat, throwing her crown down the hillside, where it was consumed by the darkness. With fire in her eyes, she turned her gaze to the ocean below the cliff. "But know that I shall return. Father! My fate is in your hands!"

The goddess turned to the cliff and leaped, the memory now crawling in slow motion. A tendril of light connected Freyja to Jack, and she was ripped through the air and off the cliff with the goddess.

Mike snagged one of Jack's outstretched hands, and the three of them fell together toward the crashing waves below. Golden light formed around Jack and Freyja as the distance between the two of them shortened until they merged.

When they hit the water, it shattered like glass, each piece reflecting a different memory as she and Mike tumbled through darkness together. They were spiraling out of control now, but Mike kept a tight grip on her wrist.

"It's your soul!" he shouted over the howling winds. "Nothing in here can hurt you!"

Of that, Jack wasn't sure. She could feel Freyja's heart weep for her missing sister, for the loss of her brother, Freyr. It had all started with a crack in the base of Yggdrasil from which monstrosities poured. The beings had been easy enough for her children to slay at first, but the incursions had steadily become more violent as the beasts multiplied.

The spirits of the dead in her care had been devoured before her eyes, filling her with a boundless wrath. It was the source of her anger, the rage that had been yanked to the surface by the Krampus. It was like the bastard had known exactly how to manipulate her.

A cold feeling flowed through her body, her magic swirling around her and changing their trajectory. They hit one of the glass shards, shattering it into prismatic crystals that danced around them as they crashed into the cold snow of the arctic north.

They struck the ground hard enough that Mike bounced away from Jack and the breath was forced from her body. She slid through the snow for several seconds, weeping tears of red gold.

This was where Mike found her moments later, huddled up and grieving. He didn't say anything but knelt by her side to keep her company.

"Is this what you wanted, Caretaker?" She turned an angry gaze on him. "To make me whole so I may feel terrible things?"

He shook his head, a golden light shimmering around his body. "Sometimes it's hard being whole. It sounds counterintuitive, but it's true. We often cling to pieces of ourselves in an effort to avoid the truth, but that's no way to live. You end up walking the earth as a shadow of who you should be." He noticed the gold light on his hand and tried to shake it off. "Shit, this stuff stings."

"Of course it does. It's not for you." Jack slapped at Mike, trying to claw the divinity off his soul. Some of it stuck to her fingers, but the rest settled against Mike's skin and was absorbed. She examined the substance in her hands and frowned. It felt familiar yet foreign.

The soft crunch of footfalls on ice made her turn toward the source. A large man in a white robe carried a limp figure in his arms. It was a woman, her body so cold that she had turned blue. Long auburn tresses were falling out in clumps, leaving behind a shock of white on the top of her head.

Salt water dripped from both Santa and the woman. He stopped by his sleigh and knelt in the snow to set what was left of Freyja down on the ice. The goddess shivered, her body covered in open wounds. Several of them were bite marks, while others were clearly the work of a blade.

A shadowy figure appeared in front of Santa, kneeling to examine Freyja. It was Christmas Future, the spirit more like a shadow than a ghost. The spirit inspected the goddess and shook its head.

"Surely there must be something we can do to help her." Santa had a thick European accent along with a voice that rumbled like a distant train.

Freyja held up a frostbitten hand, golden light gathering in her palm. Santa knelt next to her, listening to words that Jack couldn't hear.

"Are you sure?" Santa asked. Freyja nodded, her eyes never opening. Santa turned his attention to Christmas Future, who had turned to stare at both Mike and Jack.

The spirit contemplated them for several moments, then turned to Santa and nodded.

"That guy's a dick," Mike said, gesturing to Christmas

Future. "I just wanted to go on record about it, that's all. And if he can hear me—good."

With a heavy sigh, Santa took the golden light for himself, placing it in his beard. His thick whiskers trembled with hunger as they absorbed the light of the goddess. It hadn't been until last century that the tiny tentacles had become indistinguishable from a beard, a fact that Jack was surprised to learn she had forgotten.

"If it's for the good of the children, I will do it, for I am but a humble servant. I shall keep your identity until the time comes." He looked up to the sky and held his hands wide in supplication. "Spirits of the North, hear my call."

"What is this?" Jack demanded, taking a step back from the scene before her. Freyja's body shriveled inward now that the golden light was gone, her hair becoming brittle and breaking off in the snow. The northern lights descended on Freyja, swirling about like excited fireflies as they lifted her into the air and remade her body.

"Looks like your origin story." Mike put a hand on Jack's shoulder. "And I think I know what Santa did with that divinity he took from you. You really don't remember any of this?"

"I really don't." Had she known Santa before this moment? He certainly didn't seem too surprised by her appearance.

The scene became a smear as the northern lights gobbled up the darkness, and Jack closed her eyes to block out their brightness. She could see the vortex through her eyelids, which disoriented her. She stumbled forward, opening her eyes to see that Freyja's body was gone. There was a spectral figure standing where Freyja should have been, a place where the northern lights were refracted as if through a prism.

"No, stop, I don't want to—" She was cut off when Mike pushed her forward, causing her to collide and merge with the spectral body. More memories ripped through her, showering her with different images until she was back in the mirror chamber beneath Santa's workshop, contemplating Freyja through the glass.

"Finally." Freyja tilted her head back to look down her nose at Jack. "I was wondering how long it would take you to get here."

Jack didn't respond. Her head felt as if it would burst, each memory a seed that had grown into a tree. She was living through each moment simultaneously, her consciousness pulled in every direction until it felt like she would burst.

"Can you feel all that we were now?" Freyja's lips curled up in disgust. "We weren't just worshipped. We were loved. The outsiders, they took all that away from us!"

"Stop, please." Jack clutched at her head, now watching scenes of strange beings punching holes through reality to assault Asgard. It was a place she had never visited but now remembered intimately. Long walks in the gardens, poetry by the river, festivals of laughter and light, all of it stripped away in a one-sided slaughter.

"You can't handle this," Freyja told her, stepping through the mirror. The scene faded, leaving just Freyja and Jack in a white void, surrounded by thousands of still images. "You are just a fragment, after all. Please." She held out a hand. "I can make it all go away. All you have to do is let go, give it all back to me. Then you can sleep."

Jack cried out in pain, then reached for Freyja's hand. It really would be so easy to just let it go, to have Freyja take over. She seemed more confident than Jack and so much stronger. The pain in her head was terrible, and all she wanted to do was close her eyes and rest.

Someone stepped between them. A warm hand took hers. When she looked up, she saw that it was Mike.

"You're not the fragment," he told her, pulling her into his arms. "You're only seeing what Freyja wants you to see. Sorry it took me a bit to get here. I think I may have blacked out for a second in the real world. Being here isn't easy."

Freyja hissed and tried to push her way past Mike.

"Her soul is being torn apart, she isn't ready!"

"That's because she isn't whole," Mike replied. He lifted his head and grabbed Freyja's wrist. "And neither are you."

"Wait, I—" Freyja screamed as Mike pulled her into his embrace as well, holding the two women together. The years poured into Jack's mind, everything Freyja had ever seen or heard, and she screamed in agony as hundreds of large cracks formed in the void around them, her soul now stretching like taffy around each of them.

Mike went with her, his soul similarly stretched. Where hers was like taffy, his was molten silver, shifting and spreading with ease to encase her body. Sweat poured down his forehead as he held both Jack and Freyja in his arms. The cracks in her mind roared, then burst apart, her consciousness now in hundreds of pieces.

And still, Mike was with her.

"What's happening?" Jack whispered. Hundreds of iterations of her whispered the same thing, creating a roar of Jacks that drowned one another out.

"I…have…help!" Mike's eyes opened to reveal that they were changing colors. Jack looked around and saw that even though there were dozens of Mikes holding her and Freyja together, there were several instances of women doing the job instead. A beautiful woman in white robes with blue hair, a buxom cyclops with her hair in a loose braid, and even a goblin. There was a version of Yuki as well, all of them holding Jack and Freyja together as golden light ripped through the void and danced along the edges of the cracks.

"I don't want to go back!" Freyja's voice was tinged with desperation. "Don't make me go back to sleep, I beg of you!"

"Nobody is…going to sleep…" Mike gritted his teeth, and his eyes blazed with golden light. The scene repeated everywhere, and the torrent of memories became diluted. "In fact, it's time for both of you to…"

Jack cried out in agony, pressure building in her chest as Freyja's body melted into her own. She could no longer fight, gasping for air as Freyja's face was pressed into hers.

"WAKE UP!" Mike's voice boomed, filling the void before it exploded.

SHE WAS COLD WHEN SHE OPENED HER EYES, STARING UP into a prismatic sky. The man leaning over her wore a white coat with a beard to match. His blue eyes sparkled, though she swore for a moment that she had seen stars in them.

"Ho ho ho!" he declared, helping her to sit. "And what's your name, young lady?"

She didn't know. In fact, she didn't know anything about herself or where she was. When she held up her hands, she saw that they were almost as white as the snow itself.

"I'm not sure," she confessed. The falling snow swirled around her fingers playfully. She could sense each flake, like an extension of her body.

"I suspected as much." The man helped her stand, then brushed some ice from his beard. For just a moment, those fine white curls had looked like something else as they twisted before her. "You had to sacrifice much to be here, but I'm sure glad you did."

"Did…did I die?" The thought hardly bothered her. After all, she was just now aware that she had been alive.

"You didn't." He patted her affectionately on the shoulder. "But you aren't the person you used to be either."

"I'm not?"

"No. But isn't that the truth of growing up? We're never the same person all the time. You're just less you than you used to be but more you than ever." He smiled. "I'm Santa, by the way."

"Where is this place?" She looked up at the sky. "What are those?"

"This is the North Pole," he proclaimed with a smile. "And those lights above us are the spirits of the North. Well, and something to do with the sun, apparently. I don't understand it, no matter how often they explain it to me."

"The sun?" She looked up. "It's very pretty."

"Most wondrous things are. Come." He gestured to a large sleigh behind him. "If you'd like, I can show you many wondrous things."

"It took me a bit to understand what had happened," Mike whispered in her ear as the world went still around her. Despite not knowing who she was or where she had come from, she recognized that voice and could picture him in her mind. "You see, both of you are fragments, pieces of the original goddess. Freyja was a goddess of many things, not just war and winter. All these memories you're seeing are remnants, echoes of the whole. The main difference between the two of you is that Freyja remembers but you do not."

"Who is Freyja?" she asked.

"She is who you thought you were," he replied. "There's a chain reaction going through your soul right now, like dominos or those weird little stick things that look like crosses that explode when you pull one out."

"Stick things?" She was so confused.

"Yeah, forget about that. The short version is your mind is somewhere safe while your soul reboots from scratch. I don't know if that metaphor even makes sense to you, but..." Santa's features melted away, revealing Mike. "Wow, that feels so much better!"

She experienced a flood of emotions upon seeing him, both good and bad. He was surrounded by a golden light that created whorls of energy that reached out and melted away the nearby snow. A buzzing sensation shot through her body as she took a step toward him. Her heart beat in her chest so loudly she could see its rhythm reflected in the light around his body. She stopped just a foot away, her veins now filled with ice water. Even though his eyes were gentle, the power surrounding him terrified her.

"Why?" she asked him. "Why am I so afraid of you?"

"Because it's okay to be afraid of the unknown." Mike lifted his hand and winced as golden light coalesced around his fingers. "This is all yours, by the way. When you got pulled apart, I found it all, hidden away inside you. It was tucked away inside every nook and cranny, and I have no idea what will happen once I give it back."

"What if I don't want it?" she whispered. In truth, she desired that power more than anything but simply had to know how he would respond.

"Uh..." He contemplated his fingertips. "If I'm being honest, you really should take this back. For one, this is your power, not mine. I assume you earned it. I saw so many memories of the things you did for people. Your followers loved you, and that's not something easily given. Even just holding it is almost like...well, a mother's embrace, or something equally comforting.

"As for the other reason...I think it's killing me." He smiled weakly.

"I thought you said it felt like a mother's embrace."

"Well, it does," he admitted. "But it's not my mother, or she's on fire, or whatever metaphor makes you happiest. Please, just...take it back."

She entwined her fingers with his, the golden light circling her wrist and twirling along her arm like ribbons on a maypole. Power thrummed through her whole body as the snowy landscape rippled before being swept away by a tide of golden light. Mike held tightly to her hand as the two of them floated into the air.

Her time as Jack came back first. Long years in the frozen arctic, dancing among the frost. Things had been simple at first, but the years were long and she had been lonely. Becoming Jack had not tempered her desire for friends, family, or even love. She had been grieving a life that had been hidden away from her, and the Krampus had used that knowledge to bring about Santa's fall.

Then she was Freya, or at least the version that had been awakened. This Freyja was indeed the goddess of war, her thoughts consumed by those final moments in Asgard when she had been forced to flee, leaving her husband behind. Her people lost to her, she had survived the cold waters of the North with the help of her father, Njörðr, the sea god. The outsiders had chased her even then, forcing her to hide atop ice floes until they lost sight of her. That desperation had led her to find a man known for miracles, to beg him to hide her away from the Ancient Ones until it was safe for her to return.

More memories came, and she discovered that there was more to her than fierce battles and frost. There had been love and laughter, villages full of happy children who flocked to her side. Óðr had been her husband, but he was far from her only love. Her body was a temple she had shared with many, offering her blessings far and wide.

"I am love," she proclaimed, tears in her eyes as the phantom lights above faded away, revealing the stars. This was no longer a memory but the astral plane itself. If she chose, she could travel to any of those distant souls and greet them, let them know they weren't alone.

"I am beauty." She held up her fingers, watching as her skin glittered as if coated by diamond dust. A magnificent dress formed around her, dangling from her floating form. When she looked up at the man across from her, she finally understood the weird sway Mike had held over her during their first meeting.

"I am sex." Her free hand stroked his cheek, and her

magic hummed in time with his own. This was a part of her she had forgotten, instantly awakened by the power surging inside Mike's veins. Her magic resonated with his, her golden light combining with the purple sparks that danced along his skin. His soul felt old, as if it had been around for thousands of years, but that had to be an illusion, for he was mortal. Still, it had a familiarity that called to her.

She was fertility and fortune personified, a remainder of the old gods who had walked the earth and given their gifts freely to the humans. Lifetimes of joy now filled her heart, elevating the two of them higher and higher, and she grabbed both of Mike's hands in her own as she pulled him into her arms. When she pressed her lips against his, she inhaled, pulling the breath from his body along with the golden light that permeated his being. When she broke the kiss, a bright light formed in the sky, and they floated toward it together.

She was neither Freyja nor Jack but a true amalgamation of both of them as well as the unknown spaces in between. This whole time, she had been in a battle of wills with none other than herself. The Caretaker had not only put her back together but discovered the pieces of her long forgotten.

"*EK EM* FREYJA!" she declared, the stars in the sky bursting into fireworks as her soul unfolded into its proper shape, allowing the two of them to burst free of its confines and return to the real world.

Freyja fell from a couple of feet in the air, landing on the couch with a soft thud. Across from her, Mike slumped forward in his chair, gasping for air. He was soaked in his own sweat, drops of it falling from his fingers and freezing to the wooden floor beneath.

The goddess surveyed the small cabin, seeing it properly for the first time. She could see the faint glitter of the magic that held it suspended in time, could smell the sexual fluids of the elf that had passed out earlier. Freyja looked at Mike, a smile forming on her face.

"Caretaker." When she used his title, Mike looked up at her, his eyes still filled with golden light.

"Freyja." He winced, then put a hand to his bare chest. "You didn't quite get it all."

Yuki stood from behind the kitchen counter, her eyes wide. "Holy shit, you two, that was insane. You both just kind of hovered in the air for a bit, and there was light everywhere. I would ask if it worked, but…" The kitsune hopped over the counter and moved closer to them. "It's so weird, you have this presence now. Like there's more of you in the room than before."

Freyja nodded, then looked at Mike. "The divinity is killing him," she declared, rising in her seat. "He needs to give it back to me before he burns up."

"It's not for…lack of trying." Mike chuckled, then coughed into his hand. His pupils were dilated, as if he gazed into eternity. "Was my…first time…reassembling a god. Not even…Ikea has directions…for that."

"*Baka*, stupid jokes even while you're dying." Yuki shook her head, then looked at Freyja. "Help him, please."

The goddess moved toward him, then knelt in front of him until their noses almost touched.

"Gladly," she said, meaning it with every fiber of her being as she put her lips to his.

MIKE'S WHOLE WORLD WAS PAIN. HE WAS BARELY CONSCIOUS of the other people in the room, and it felt like his head would simply burst and put him out of his misery. His thoughts were muddled, and all he wanted to do was close his eyes and sleep.

When Freyja's lips touched his, there was a moment of pure bliss as the divinity in his veins shifted, the pressure disappearing for just a moment. The goddess let out a soft moan as her lips parted, her tongue sliding along the tip of his own before exploring the curve of his lips.

His magic activated so hard that it ripped free of his body and formed into a thick beam of light that penetrated Freyja's chest. He gasped in surprise as a pink light surrounded her before spiraling back along the beam that connected them. He was instantly hard, his consciousness fading as his dick officially became the brain in charge of operations.

And then Freyja's magic kicked in. A bitter chill formed along his mouth, and he let out a scream of pain just before Yuki ripped Freyja off him. The goddess fell backward in surprise, the air around her turning to fog as she froze the water vapor in it on her way down.

"What the hell was that?" Yuki moved between the two of them. "Are you okay?"

This was directed at Mike. He licked his numb lips and smacked them together. In less than a moment, Freyja had almost frozen his face off.

"I think tho. Tho. Thit." He couldn't tell if his tongue was numb or swollen.

"I'm sorry, I don't know what happened, I..." Freyja looked up at them with shock. She still looked like Jack, but there was an awareness in her eyes that hadn't been there before. It was confidence and power, though it had just been shaken.

"My best guess is the obvious: your head may be screwed on right, but it doesn't mean you can control it." Yuki knelt next to Mike and inspected his face. "Your soul may be put back together, but your magic is a different story. His magic reacts to yours just as much as yours reacts to his, and I think you're defaulting to what you're the most used to, which is the frost."

Freyja held up her hands and clenched them tight. When she opened them, butterflies of golden light appeared and did a quick lap around the room before vanishing. "I think you're right. I'm in control now, but when we kissed, it was like jumping off a cliff." A slight smile appeared on her face. "There's a reason they call it falling in love, after all."

Yuki frowned. "You've been right in the head for all of two minutes. There's no way you feel like that about him."

"You are correct, child of the forest, I do not. But that feeling you get when you meet someone special, when you share that first kiss, that's all in here. It's a part of me just as it is a part of anyone with the capacity to love." Freyja placed a hand on her chest. "I can't believe I had forgotten what a wonderful feeling it is."

"Just a reminder..." Mike coughed so hard that sparks flew out of his mouth. "I am absolutely still dying over here."

"Do you need physical contact to get your divinity back?" Yuki asked.

Freyja frowned. "Sort of. The divinity he gathered while mending my soul is now integrated in his own, albeit temporarily. He could give it back through touch or by using his magic."

"Which requires touch." Yuki shook her head and looked at Mike. "I don't suppose you could just zap her with it, could you?"

Mike contemplated her question, then closed his eyes and looked at his magic. The golden glow of Freyja's divinity was entwined with his own magic, the two of them braided together. He plucked at a few strands to see if he could strip it away on his own and was unsurprised when the divinity shifted and stuck to another strand instead.

"No can do." He looked at both of them. "Freyja's right. It's stuck to my magic. If I use it and cycle it out, I could probably put it somewhere else, but it's definitely not something I can do by just examining her soul or whatever." Unless the nearby hospital had a dialysis machine for nymph magic, there was only one option that made sense.

Unfortunately, he got the feeling that what had happened

to his jaw was possible anywhere else. Frostbite on his fingers? No problem. Frostbite on his dick? Nope. An image of his frozen member snapping in half gave him plenty of reasons to be cautious.

"We need a way for my magic and his to interact, but we cannot touch." Freyja bit her lip, then looked over at Mike. "I do fear I would freeze you to death if we did."

A memory tickled the back of his mind, and he pursued it. There had been a moment on his porch, once upon a time, where he had fucked Cecilia and Lily at the same time due to Cecilia's spectral nature. He remembered how his magic had spread across both of them, and a similar thing had happened earlier in the year with Dana and Quetzalli.

He quirked an eyebrow and looked over at Yuki. "So you're saying we need someone to act as an intermediary, a kind of sexual fuse that can withstand cold temperatures."

The goddess appraised Yuki and shrugged. "As long as this fuse thing can handle divinity, it should work. The process wouldn't be as fast or efficient, but it would seem we have no choice."

The kitsune looked from Mike to Freyja, then shook her head and laughed. "So let me get this straight. The two of you are going to try to solve your problem by making me into a fox sandwich?"

"Only if you're up for it," Mike told her, moving to the nearby couch so there'd be more room. "If not, we can find another way."

"I can understand your hesitation," Freyja added. "I assure you that making love to a goddess is very similar to making love to an ordinary woman."

"Bitch, please." Yuki was already shedding her coat. "I've eaten snow cones scarier than you."

Freyja laughed, then sat back on the couch opposite Mike. "Then by all means, fox, let's see what you can do."

"*Baka kami*," Yuki muttered as she turned toward Mike.

"You must have done something very good in a past life, because I sincerely doubt any man has gotten their dick sucked so much in one day."

Mike ducked his head and placed his palms together as if bowing to her. "Think of it like a second date."

"Most girls would appreciate at least a good meal on their dates." Yuki looked over at Freyja, who had pulled up her dress to reveal a garter belt and stockings beneath her gown. When she turned back to face Mike, she wore a stupid grin. She dropped her voice to a whisper. "Though, it does look like I'll be eating tacos."

"Do you even like tacos?" he whispered back, suddenly curious. "Real ones, I mean."

Yuki rolled her eyes as she grabbed the base of his dick. "Of course I like tacos," she muttered, then ran her tongue along the thick part of his glans before toying with his urethra. "What's there to hate? You take a bunch of delicious things and cram them into a crunchy shell."

"I'm a soft guy myself," he admitted.

"There's nothing soft about you right now," she said before sucking him into her mouth. Mike gasped, his magic manifesting as a small storm of energy that swirled along his arms. He squinted, the golden sparks too bright to look at directly. Though the divinity hadn't left his body, just the act of circulating it seemed to help his discomfort.

"Mmh." Freyja had pulled her skirt even higher and was now teasing a pussy devoid of hair. "It's hot watching her go down on you, but the bond you share is even hotter."

Mike wanted to reply with something meaningful, but all he managed was an affirmative grunt that sounded like Goofy trying not to giggle. Yuki's ears brushed against the bare skin of his belly, and he massaged them with his hands. The kitsune made happy little sounds in response, then swallowed him as deep as she could take him.

His relationship was different with each of the women in

the house, but there was something special about Yuki. With the others, there could be some element of romance, or maybe they were just really good friends. He didn't pretend to analyze where he stood with Sofia. He would sometimes go days without hearing from her, and then he would be summoned to the Library for one of their "sessions."

With Yuki, though, they had started as enemies before becoming close. They shared experiences of abuse and misery, and a solid understanding of what it meant to be a survivor. If anything, he thought of her as one of his best friends in the world, a relationship that had only deepened upon being intimate.

"I'm a bit jealous," Freyja said from her spot on the couch. "Her technique is pretty good. I wish I could join her and feel a cock in my mouth too."

Mike blinked a couple times and chuckled. "You'll have to excuse me, but I'm still stuck on when you used to be Jack. That isn't a very Jack thing to say."

"That part of me wasn't anti-intimacy, but she wasn't particularly interested either. I nearly died when Santa drained me of my godhood, and the cold was all that remained." Freyja slid a finger inside herself as her other hand played with one of her breasts through her dress. "But there's something special about having a man's cock in your mouth. It isn't just about the strain in your jaw or the throbbing warmth lying across your tongue. People often mistake it as a subservient position, but that's far from the truth. When someone sucks your cock, they have absolute power over you, especially when they do it right." Freyja shifted forward off the couch, then knelt behind Yuki. The kitsune paused long enough to see what the goddess was doing, then resumed her heavenly blow job.

"Allow me to elaborate." Freyja grabbed the top of Yuki's head, her fingers vanishing in the kitsune's hair. Yuki held still for a moment, then groaned when Freyja pushed down on her head, forcing Mike's cock farther into her throat. "From here, she looks the part of the servant. With a single push, I can overcome her resistance, make her desire the sensation of your glans sliding across the back of her tongue."

"I, uh..." Mike didn't know how to respond. His magic was crackling along his limbs and crossing over onto Yuki's skin, carrying tiny pieces of golden light with it.

Freyja whispered something in Yuki's ear, and the kitsune nodded her assent, a sensation which triggered a shock wave of pleasure all along Mike's cock. Yuki started playing with Mike's balls as Freyja moved behind Yuki and knelt.

"She may be the one on her knees, but tell me who is really in charge here. Is it you, Caretaker? What would you give for her to keep going? If she decided to stop, how much would you beg for her to continue? She has complete power over you. To believe anything else is nothing more than a delusion. Know that when I take someone in my mouth, it is not only to please them. It is to take their power and make it my own. For that, my dear mortal, is what pleases me."

With a gleam in her eyes, Freyja parted Yuki's tails and then buried her face in the kitsune's snatch.

Yuki gurgled in delight, causing spit to run down Mike's shaft. He leaned forward and stroked the top of her head, paying particular attention to her ears. His magic intensified, sending a current of sexual energy through Yuki. He couldn't see what all Freyja was doing to the kitsune's crotch, but the kitsune's eyes were rolling back in her head.

Yuki became so distracted that she stopped blowing him, her moans of delight turning into sharp yips of pleasure around his shaft.

"Hmm." Freyja lifted her head, her chin slick with Yuki's juices. "While there is plenty of merit to this approach, it does not currently serve our needs."

Yuki lifted her head until the top of Mike's cock popped

free. "Perhaps if I turned around?" She wiggled her eyebrows suggestively.

"Hey, I'm just the dude poisoned with god juice. I'm up for whatever you two want to try." He gave them a smile, trying not to let them see how bad he was hurting. In the time it took for Yuki to rise and pull her tails to the side, the divinity sank back into his body. It tingled at first, then burned, like Icy Hot for his soul. The pain retreated for a moment while he watched Yuki's curvaceous ass lower onto his lap, his cock sliding smoothly into her vagina.

"Oh fuck, I love how that feels," she declared, her tails shifting to drape over Mike's chest. She leaned back and grabbed Mike's wrists, directing his hands to her breasts. "I want to enjoy you squeezing them while you fuck me."

Mike groaned in delight as he played with Yuki's nipples, savoring the weight of her body on his groin. She shifted her weight back and forth, her tails tickling his nose. Running his hands along the tops of her thighs, he could sense her powerful leg muscles working hard as she rode him.

"That's hot as hell, but I think you're forgetting something." Freyja pulled off her dress, revealing a dark bra that matched her garters. "That magic needs to make its way to me, and—"

Yuki reached out and grabbed Freyja by the front of her garter belt, pulling so hard that the fabric ripped. When their lips connected, Mike heard the soft sizzle and pop of his magic making contact with Freyja. The divinity inside him lurched forward reluctantly, dancing across Yuki's skin.

A peculiar pressure formed against the base of his cock, Yuki's vagina tightening up in a manner he was unfamiliar with. The sensation was phenomenal, and he grabbed Yuki by the hips to hold her in place as she swiveled her hips back and forth. Yuki broke the kiss, pushing down on the top of Freyja's head. The goddess looked down and gasped, covering her mouth with a hand.

"You said you wanted something to suck," Yuki growled. "So suck it."

Curious, Mike leaned over Yuki's shoulder to see that the kitsune's clitoris had inflated, stretching and becoming engorged until it was at least six inches long. Shocked at this development, he watched as Freyja knelt between Yuki's legs and licked the tip of the kitsune's faux cock.

"Is that…how…" He didn't know entirely what to ask. He had so many questions but couldn't figure out what any of them were. Between the pressure on his dick and watching Freyja slobber all over Yuki's cock, he didn't have enough brain cells to spare.

"It's a simple trick," Yuki informed him, leaning back and directing his hands to her breasts once more. "It still has the same nerve endings as before, if that's what you're wondering. Now kiss my neck and I'll show you another trick."

Mike kissed the nape of her neck and jumped when he felt the pressure inside Yuki's pussy shift. That thick mass pressing against him began moving up and down, and he immediately noticed it was in time with the bobbing of Freyja's head.

"Yessss," Yuki hissed, grabbing Freyja by the hair and holding her in place. "Suck that dick, you frosty bitch."

Freyja snorted in amusement and worked the base of Yuki's shaft with her hands. Occasionally, her fingers would drop low enough to brush against the soft flesh of Mike's testicles. Though the touch was brief, her skin was cold enough that it was like she had touched him with a piece of ice.

The kitsune groaned in delight, threads of golden light forming around her as Freyja and Mike pleasured her. "Gods, I haven't been fucked like this in forever." Yuki leaned her head back on Mike's shoulder, then turned to kiss his cheek. "I can feel how hot you are inside me, and she's so cold. My body doesn't know what to do with it!"

Freyja groaned her agreement, then moved a hand to her crotch and fingered herself. The sparks were dancing all along them now, but most of them focused on Yuki. Mike felt the divinity shift away from him, but it definitely wasn't making the whole trip. If he came now, it was possible that his magic might push it all into Yuki, but then what?

"You need to fuck her," he whispered in Yuki's ear. When he came, Yuki likely would too, and maybe he could get the magic to cycle through an additional person. "Can you do that while I'm still inside you?"

"I thought you'd never ask," Yuki replied, then leaned forward. "Hey. I know you're on a power trip down there, but how about a proper fuck?"

Freyja looked up at Yuki, then at Mike. She pulled her mouth off Yuki's cock and made direct eye contact with Mike as she licked Yuki one more time.

"If you think you can handle me," she replied, then stood. When she turned to face away from them, she bent over and ran both hands over the bright white flesh of her ass, swaying from side to side. "It's been over a century, so try not to break me."

"No promises." Yuki grabbed Freyja by the remains of the garter belt and pulled hard enough that it snapped off as the goddess sat, Yuki's cock sliding into Freyja's pussy. The sudden increase in weight caused Mike's balls to throb as his orgasm built.

"Oh fucking hell!" Freyja stuck her hands out to her sides, accidentally grabbing Mike by the thigh. Pain shot up his leg before Yuki could pull Freyja's hand away, but Mike no longer cared. His magic shifted dramatically, and as Freyja rode Yuki, he could feel their movements along his own cock.

He moved his hands onto Yuki's ribs to avoid accidental contact with Freyja, doing very little in the way of work as the kitsune enthusiastically thrust herself into the goddess. This did almost all the work for Mike as well. Yuki growled while Freyja moaned, the two of them establishing a rhythm that had him gasping with pleasure.

His magic surged, wrapping itself around Yuki's waist and then moving down her groin to where she connected with Freyja. As the three of them swayed, they found a solid rhythm that caused the magic to build around them. Freyja's hair stood on end as streamers of light appeared on all their bodies, jumping back and forth among the three of them.

Mike was unsurprised when Yuki came first. Her pussy tightened so hard that he was almost pushed out of her, and then she let out a howl and dug her nails into Freyja's stockings. Though the goddess's skin was unharmed, the flimsy garments were easily shredded and fell to the floor.

"Holy…wow!" Freyja put a hand on her belly. "Did you… did you actually…?"

Yuki didn't respond. Instead, she wrapped a hand around Freyja's throat and pulled her back.

"Don't you dare let a single drop spill," she growled between her teeth. "You be a good girl and soak up that cream pie."

Mike wasn't sure where this side of Yuki had been all this time, but it was hot as fuck. He felt a surge of heat rush through his abdomen, a sign of his own impending orgasm, and he wrapped his hands around Yuki's belly.

"I'm about to come," he warned her. "Don't let her get away."

Yuki nodded and wrapped her hands around Freyja's waist, locking her fingers together.

"Do it," she whispered. "I want to feel you blast that hot load inside me, please, give me that sweet—"

It didn't take much dirty talk for the magic in the room to suddenly rebound and use Mike like a lightning rod. When he came, his vision dimmed as his magic sank hooks into the divinity in his system and ripped it all away. When he flooded Yuki's womb with his seed, he could feel the molten heat of the divinity as it concentrated in his gut and passed into the kitsune.

Yuki cried out, then groaned, her arms suddenly going limp as her hips lurched forward. Freyja looked back just as the sparks made the leap from Yuki to her. Her eyes lit up from within as her magic surged around her like a storm, and her legs went limp beneath her.

"Shit!" Mike grabbed Freyja by her hips just long enough to tilt the three of them sideways onto the couch. They managed to maneuver so Freyja was now on her stomach, with Yuki and Mike above her. The goddess groaned as golden sparks appeared on her skin, but the magic was coming back to Mike now, carrying what remained of its golden passenger with it.

The magic swirled around Mike, driving him to pump himself deep into Yuki. She was crying out consistently now, her eyes rolled back in her head as the magic drove all of them to orgasm once again. This set off a chain reaction with Freyja, who grabbed onto the couch, promptly freezing it and ripping a hole through the fabric.

He had no idea how long they went at it. His magic continued to cycle through all three of them, bringing back less divinity each time. But it was his magic, and he commanded it to keep going, to push that golden light through his friend and back into the goddess. The couch was already a sticky, shredded mess, but he had no idea who had contributed the most to it by now. His balls ached with the sheer amount of cum he had produced, and Yuki was no longer making any sounds other than garbled whimpers of delight.

"More, Caretaker, more!" Freyja bit down on a pillow, tearing a hole in the fabric. Her skin had acquired a healthy golden glow that pulsed in time with his thrusts, the divinity settling in its true owner.

His stomach muscles ached by the time he stopped fucking Yuki, every muscle now bereft of energy. Mike went limp, dangling his arms over Yuki's shoulders while keeping his hands wide to avoid Freyja's frosty form. He didn't know if Yuki was even conscious at this point, but Freyja was making happy sounds like a woman holding a litter of puppies.

He didn't bother asking if it worked. His soul sight saw that Freyja had easily reabsorbed the divinity she had lost and that only trace amounts stained Yuki's soul. He took a moment to braid in what he found to help her acclimate, then rubbed the kitsune's butt.

"You make a good sandwich," he told her.

She didn't reply but reached back and pinched his thigh.

"Holly's going to be pissed she slept through this," Freyja muttered from the bottom. "Poor thing just missed the fucking of the century."

"I like this new Freyja," Yuki muttered. "Much friendlier than the old one."

"Indeed." Mike turned his head toward the kitchen counter and saw a gray figure appear. It was the Ghost of Christmas Past from the ornament, or the Ghost of Last Christmas, whatever it wanted to be called. "There you are. I wondered where you got off to."

The ghost bowed its head. "I did not wish to interfere," it replied.

"Uh-huh." Somehow, Mike managed to pour a tremendous amount of sarcasm into his reply. "So is this where we find out this was all part of Santa's plan? That we've been manipulated this whole time?"

The ghost opened its mouth to reply but simply nodded. "It's more complicated than that, Caretaker, but yes. I'm about to reveal many things to you."

"It's about fucking time." He rubbed Yuki's thigh, then saw that the meat of Freyja's ass was just beneath it. Deciding to take a chance, he gave it a playful slap, his fingers going instantly numb.

Totally worth it, he thought.

"You ass." Freyja turned her head so she could see Mike

out of the corner of her eye. "Come down here and fuck me like a man, you coward."

"Yuki's right. This version of you is a lot more fun." He pulled himself out of Yuki, surprised that her vagina had such a tight hold on his cock even as he went flaccid. Standing naked above the women, he looked over at the ghost. "Let us get cleaned up, then you can tell us everything we need to hear."

The Ghost of Last Christmas nodded, then moved over by the window as the three of them got dressed. Freyja went to retrieve Holly as Yuki and Mike made snacks. Once everyone was sitting with either a beverage or a snack in hand, the spirit hovered in front of them, its dark eyes flickering red and green.

"And now," it said, whirling around in front of them like a firefly made of smoke, "it is time I shared with you what happened last Christmas."

LAST CHRISTMAS

The Ghost of Last Christmas didn't waste time with words. Instead, it extended a hand for Mike to take, which he did. The others grabbed onto his free hand, and a dark mist filled the room. Though it looked sinister, Mike didn't feel like the spirit's intentions were malicious. In fact, he realized he could see what the spirit was made of now. It was similar to Freyja's soul, except the threads of Christmas Past were made up of tiny little gears that shifted in sync with each other.

The cabin vanished, and Mike found himself standing in Santa's special workshop. The fat bastard himself was contemplating a large gift with the letter *M* on it that had been installed into a vise for Mike to find later.

"I believe that's everything," he said out loud, then turned his attention toward Mike. "For next Christmas, anyway."

"What the fudge?" Mike licked at his lips and rolled his eyes. "Okay, sorry. Can he even hear us?"

"These are the shadows of the past," the spirit began.

"Yeah, yeah. They can't hear us or whatever." He dismissed the spirit and put his hands on his waist. "So now I get a prerecorded message from the past. I'm over these time travel shenanigans. At least the Santa at the mall talks to you in real time."

Yuki moved to stand next to him, then dug her nails into his side.

"Ow, what the heck?" he groused. Yuki tilted her head toward Holly. The elf was sitting cross-legged on the floor, her chin in her hands and a huge smile on her face.

"It's been a very busy week," Santa began while pulling over a rocking chair. When he sat in it, the wood creaked but held his weight. An elf came in through the door of the workshop with a large plate of cookies and a carafe of milk.

"Thank you, Lester." Santa patted the elf on the head. "This is exactly what I needed."

The elf beamed, then walked away.

"That was Lester," Santa said once the elf was gone. "If everything I've learned is true, this will be his last Christmas. Sometime after I go missing next year, one of the giants will eat him." He shook his head and wiped a tear from his eyes. "Poor Lester."

"What the farts?" Mike stared in disbelief. "The elves are getting eaten? Why isn't he doing anything?"

"He knows the future with such certainty," Yuki muttered. "He really did know what was coming."

"Indeed," Santa replied. He turned his attention to Holly. "I am so sorry about everything you've gone through, but I'm afraid there's more to come. Your faith in me is a blessing, but I do not deserve it."

Holly sighed. "Santa," she whispered, a dreamy look on her face. "You can rely on me."

Santa nodded, then turned his attention in Freyja's direction. "As for you, old friend, I am sorry for your ordeals as well. You should know that all of it was necessary to get you into your current state."

The goddess snorted. "More like you're lucky we got this far," she muttered.

The big man sighed, then put the plate on his belly and the carafe of milk on a nearby bench. He held up one of the cookies and chuckled.

"In fact, this is partially your fault." Santa glanced over the top of his glasses at the goddess, his lips momentarily stretching into a frown.

"Excuse me?" Freyja stepped forward, but Mike grabbed her by the wrist. A chill ran up to his elbow, but he shrugged it off. Apparently touching her when they weren't naked and fudging was much safer.

"These are just shadows of what has been," he said in his best spooky spirit voice.

"There are two fundamental truths about this place, my dear Freyja. Although this is home to perhaps the most powerful magic on Earth, it's been confined to revolve around a single, temporal point—Christmas Day." Santa smiled and took a bite of the cookie. When it crumbled onto his beard, Mike could see some of the hairs twitch and reach for the crumbs.

"In this way, I am both its lord and its servant. I can perform a great many miracles, but only if it furthers the cause of Christmas. You see, when you came to me, the only reason I was able to save your life in the first place was because it was part of a chain of events that could lead to the survival of Christmas itself."

"Right, but I'm the reason Christmas is in danger in the first place. So why not just speak up and tell me you know I've been talking to the Krampus?"

"Mmm, so good!" Santa devoured the rest of the cookie. "I really do love cookies, especially when they're baked by the missus. Come. Walk with me."

He picked up the plate of cookies along with the carafe and led them out of the workshop. They hovered behind as he walked. His home was flooded with dozens of elves dancing around and partying.

"I just got back from deliveries this morning," Santa explained. "You can see that everyone is in a pretty good mood. In fact, this was a really good Christmas."

"Who are you talking to, Santa?" An elf with long pigtails stopped him in the hallway.

"Some friends of mine you can't see, Adora. Will you take some of these to Mrs. Claus?" He grabbed a handful of cookies and gave them to the elf. "She's still in bed recuperating from earlier and could use something to eat."

Adora looked pleased to be given a task from Santa and ran off.

"Even now, I can feel the magical barrier protecting the North Pole weakening. Whoever is looking for the Caretaker is taking the nuclear approach." Santa tsked to himself as he led them down the stairs. "Those are events I have not been privy to and would love to hear the story someday."

Santa led them to the basement door. He stopped on occasion to celebrate with his elves, laughing and hugging them. Once across the room, he slid through the door and locked it behind him. They were now alone, the sounds of the party muffled by the thick door and stone walls.

"Anyway, my dear Freyja, the means of your resurrection were all related to saving the future of Christmas. When I made you into Jack, it wasn't just to hide you from the Others. That's what I call them, anyway. I think it's far more accurate than the Ancient Ones, or even the elder gods. After all, they live outside of time and space. Who's to say how old or young they really are?"

He chuckled at this as he led them down the stairs. "My dear friend, if you could speed things along?"

Mike wasn't sure who Santa was talking to until there was a sudden blur of motion. Santa went into fast-forward, traveling down the winding stairs in a matter of seconds. They were outside the chamber with the North Pole inside when he slowed to normal speed.

"Ah, here we are." He opened the doors, then moved inside. The North Pole was glittering with light, sparks swirling beneath the surface as if it had captured a tornado. "This is a new room to most of you. Welcome to the North Pole!"

Holly gasped in awe, but the others said nothing. Yuki looked at Mike, who shrugged.

"I've been here before, will tell you later." He was more than a little surprised that Santa was revealing all this.

"The source of all my magic," Santa explained, then set his carafe and cookies down on a table. There was a clean mug waiting for him, and he poured some frosty milk into it. "As well as my curse."

From behind the North Pole, a figure emerged. It was the Ghost of Christmas Future, hovering just over the floor.

"The spirits are a manifestation of the entity living within the North Pole," Santa explained, waving the spirit over. "As well as an extension of my own unique genealogy. You see, Future can only see what is coming and cannot remember what has been. Every possible outcome filters through this poor creature, and it is their job to pass on to me any events of note. Freyja is one of those events. When I pulled her from those dark Atlantic waters, it was because Future led me there to retrieve her."

"Okay, maybe Future isn't a total dick," Mike grumbled to nobody in particular.

"She has been hidden all this time in the guise of Jack Frost in order to keep her safe until the time is right for the gods of old to return." Santa reached over his bench and opened a drawer. He pulled out a chessboard and set it nearby. "I assume you're familiar with the analogy I'm about to make, Caretaker."

Mike nodded, his eyes now on the board. Santa pulled a wooden figure from his pocket and set it down near the middle. It was Jack Frost, meticulously carved. "You see, I was warned of a potential future that would rely on me having certain pieces in position. So here we have Freyja in the form of Jack Frost. But there are more pieces, aren't there?"

Santa took a minute to pull more figures from his pockets. Mike watched as one side of the board filled up with the Krampus, Grýla and her brood, a giant cat, and what looked like another giant.

"From where you sit, you may think it would have been easier to sweep the pieces away before the game even began, but it isn't that simple." Santa winked at Mike, then touched the side of his nose. For just a moment, the room was gone, and Mike realized he was standing on a giant game board. All around him, blurred figures with boards of their own shifted pieces he couldn't see. In the few moments he was there, he watched one figure overtake another, shifting into their space and claiming their pieces.

They were back with Santa now, everyone save Holly muttering.

"There are events neither of us are privy to. This whole time, you've been under the impression that the Christmas I need you to save is this one, but you are incorrect. Certain events must occur today to prevent a disaster that will end Christmas many years from now. I cannot tell you much, but I think you know that one of the things that had to occur was Freyja's return by your hand."

Understanding bloomed in Mike's mind. Yes, Santa had known everything that was about to occur, but there was a greater purpose for it. It wasn't just some Machiavellian effort to piss him off but something bigger than that.

Santa leaned back and sighed. "Future can only tell me so much, you know. In fact, Freyja's arrival was the first time the spirit mentioned this event to me. Since it will be the end of Christmas, you would think I have some power over it, but that's just a side effect. I needed to alter the events of your present to stack the odds that you will succeed in…whatever it is you're supposed to be a part of."

"Damn." Mike shook his head and looked at Yuki. "I hate the idea of being manipulated like this, but what else was he supposed to do?"

"I like to think he had better options." Freyja crossed her arms. "But what now? Can he just tell us what happens next?"

"Doubt it," Mike said. "Unless telling it guarantees the outcome, he'll keep his secrets."

"Annoying." Yuki moved her fingers through his and squeezed until their palms met. "We'll figure it out together."

Santa waited a few more moments before pulling additional pieces out of his pockets. Tink, Kisa, and Yuki went onto the empty side of the board, followed by Death, Lily, and Cerberus. Mike couldn't help but notice they were all wearing Santa hats.

"Do you know what I find interesting and frustrating all at the same time?" Santa drank some milk and then cleared his throat. "You have to remember, Future only sees the possibilities, no matter how small they are. When they speak, it is rare and I make sure to listen." When Santa looked up at Mike, the world dimmed. Yuki and the others faded away, leaving Mike alone with Santa. "Some years ago, a wonderful young lady did me a huge favor and asked for a very special Christmas wish in return. In granting that wish, I accidentally changed the fate of the world."

Mike looked around the room. "Where are the others?"

"This message is for you and you alone," Santa replied. "You'll understand why very soon."

Mike rolled his eyes. "Okay, big guy, I guess I'll bite. Not that you can hear me bitching. Or maybe you can, because Christmas Future is feeding you these lines like candy and you're essentially reading off a script. So you granted a Christmas wish that changed the world. Please continue."

Santa nodded. "My magic is very powerful when it comes to granting Christmas wishes. The same magic that can stop the world until I deliver my gifts or even create pockets of time so I can visit children can easily undo the best-laid plans of even the gods themselves. Now, her gift was complicated, and I couldn't just magically create the thing she asked for, nor find it in a store. She wanted someone to love her as she was.

"But when she made that wish, I butted up against a powerful geas and her circumstances. Despite what the movies would have you believe, I can't just snap my fingers and bring it all together. And I don't foresee all of it either. I am often a slave to the magic and don't immediately understand how my actions go about granting such a wish. One time, I hid a man's shoes. No idea why, but the magic demanded it. He missed the bus for work and stopped inside a nearby coffee shop to beg for a ride. A young woman was headed in the same direction for a doctor's appointment and was feeling generous enough to give him one.

"She was a couple minutes late for her appointment. While signing in, she had a question for the receptionist. A man across town was trying to call in and had to wait a few minutes before being helped. This meant he didn't walk his dog at his usual time, and he ran into an old friend. I think you can see where this is going, but it's not that simple. Ripples don't travel out in a straight line, Caretaker. They make circles. The man who got the ride was feeling extra generous and dropped his spare bus fare in a street performer's hat. The doctor was pressed for time at the woman's appointment and forgot to ask her an important question. All these things created a circle of impossible events that eventually led to a young girl's mother coming home from her deployment in time for Christmas."

Mike crossed his arms. "So a Christmas butterfly effect. You toppled a ton of dominos to make something unexpected happen. It makes sense. By doing these little things, you're still hiding in plain sight."

Santa nodded. "You've experienced several of these already. The gifts I've left for you, the minor coincidences.

Each one is a planned ripple to keep you on your ordained path."

"Yeah, and I hate it. I don't like the idea that everything I do is at your whim." Mike waved his hand around him. "Have I had any choices of my own since coming to the North Pole? Or am I just a sexy Rube Goldberg device you've set off in your home in the hopes that I beat up the Krampus and don't fudge your wife?"

"The debate about free will and predetermined events is an old one that we have no time for, Caretaker." Santa didn't seem bothered by Mike's outburst, probably because he wasn't there in real time. "You have to understand that you've been part of the game longer than you think."

"And what's that supposed to mean?"

"The moment I pulled you from that burning car, I set off a chain of events that nearly drove Future to madness." Santa produced a wooden Mike figurine and set it on the chessboard, right in the middle. It sent out a cascade of sparkling lights that crawled across all the pieces.

"Wait, what?" Mike was breathing hard now, and he looked around for the others. Was this a joke? "It wasn't even Christmas, there's no way you were involved in that!"

"My powers can exist outside of Christmas, Caretaker, as long as they serve to prolong belief. It was a simple feat to appear as an ordinary man and pull you from the wreckage of that vehicle. What I couldn't know at the time was the profound effect this would have on everything."

"That…it doesn't make sense, I…" Mike spluttered, at a complete loss for words.

"You were never supposed to be the Caretaker, Mike Radley." Santa tilted his head forward and looked over the top of his glasses. "I can't always predict how the magic operates. All I knew was that I needed to save this young man before he burned up like a candle, to grant a Christmas wish for someone else. In doing so, the geas chose you over the woman slated to inherit your home."

"Who was supposed to inherit my home?" he asked, his voice little more than a fearful whisper.

Santa shook his head. "It no longer matters. The home is yours. But the sudden shift in fate caused ripples. The Krampus is just one of these ripples, manifesting in the flesh. The dominos are falling, and whether they lead to destruction or salvation is still unknown. You have become the catalyst for many things, Mike Radley, and you need to understand that trouble will come for you no matter where you go."

"I just want to be left alone," Mike said. "I don't see why I keep getting pulled into crud like this."

"That's what happens when you're a player in the great game, especially when you've made as much progress as you have. A target has been painted on your back, and you must be ready to protect those you love lest you lose them. These are heavy truths I have burdened you with, but you needed to hear them." Santa sat up in his chair, and the room brightened again. The others reappeared, their attention still on Santa. "So now that you understand why I have stacked events in our favor, I have one more confession to make. Holly?"

"Santa?" The elf moved forward enough that she accidentally passed through Santa's large belly. Mike was a little disappointed that it didn't at least get a token reaction from the big man.

"There's a certain secret I must share with you, one that very few know." He knelt so the two were eye to eye. "You've been aware for the longest time that I was once a normal man who became more. I am a human soul that has merged with the eldritch entity sworn to protect this place."

Holly nodded.

"And I wish I could have told you earlier, but you wouldn't have understood. You've always been different from the others, but you couldn't have known how free you truly were.

The original elves, like Alabaster, were not slaves to the magic like the newer generations. When Mrs. Claus and I made you, it was an attempt to lift those shackles, to create an elf capable of defining themselves outside of Christmas. It's why you were on the special team, sent out to observe humans. It was to help you understand them and maybe come to terms with all the new feelings you would eventually experience.

"But due to recent events, you have a tiny piece of a human soul inside you. Even now, you can feel those remaining shackles fading away. It's a degree of freedom I could never have granted you myself."

Holly's face turned beet red, and she threw a glance at Mike. He nodded in agreement, letting her know that Santa spoke the truth.

"I was once a man. And men are capable of becoming monsters. I am not a being who walks solely in the light, and when it became necessary, I became the monster needed to save this beautiful land."

Santa took a deep breath, then closed his eyes. When he opened them, they blazed with red light.

"I am the Krampus, Holly. I am an amalgam of both the dark and the light, a being capable of good and evil. Unlike most, I cannot choose one or the other at a whim. When I am Santa, I am only the good parts of me. But when I'm the Krampus?" He shivered, then looked at the others. All but Mike stared at him in shock. "I have no control. I am him and partake in his deeds while I weep from the inside."

"No." Holly's voice was little more than a whimper. "That can't be true."

"It is, my child." Santa smiled weakly. "I wish I could have told you in person, but the Krampus knows all that I do. When this Christmas Day is over, I intend to imprison the Ghost of Christmas Present to keep the Krampus from gaining access to this conversation later when they become a ghost of the past. I wrote vague notes for myself to avoid the gifts I've left for you. Tomorrow, I will eat one of Mrs. Claus's special cookies to erase all knowledge of these events and this conversation, for whatever happens to one of us must happen to both."

Holly said nothing. She buried her face in her arm and sobbed.

"She will need you," Santa said, looking vaguely in all their directions. "For the road ahead is tough, and she will struggle to walk it. Even now, Future is uncertain that my efforts will bear fruit, but I have to try." He stood, suddenly weary. "And, Freyja?"

"Santa." The goddess's lips were thin on her face.

"I'm happy you're back." He bowed to her in deference as the scene turned to smoke and faded away. They had returned to the cabin, the Ghost of Last Christmas standing in the center of the room.

Nobody spoke for several minutes, the room quiet except for an occasional squeak from Holly. Mike knelt by her side, but she turned away from him.

"So what now?" Yuki looked at Freyja, then the spirit. "Santa's been pulling strings this whole time, so why fight it? Everything we've done has led to this moment and…" She shrugged, then put a hand to her stomach and winced. "Shit, cramp."

"Language," Holly whispered.

"If you wish to know more, I'm afraid I have no knowledge about what is yet to come." The spirit shook its head. "But I was told I would not be merged with my siblings so the Krampus could not command me. I am free of his influence but only because I am following Santa's orders. Should I meet the Krampus, I will be obedient to his whims."

"Maybe you should fuck this one too," Freyja muttered.

"Christmas Present was a fluke," Mike said. *A hot, sexy fluke,* he admitted mentally.

Holly stood and walked out the front door of the cabin,

leaving them behind. Yuki raised an eyebrow at Mike. He nodded and went after the elf. She was sitting on the steps of the cabin, her feet buried in the snow.

"Do you want to talk about it?" he asked.

"I don't know." She kicked at a clump of snow. "What I just learned, I…it's like there's a storm inside me, and I can't control it. All my thoughts are just spinning around, and when I try to examine them, they…" She gestured helplessly and pulled her knees to her chest before burying her face in them. "I don't know what to do," she groaned.

"It's hard." He put a hand on her shoulder. "You don't know this, but my childhood was pretty messed up. My mom was…kind of like the Krampus. She would say and do terrible things. Even after she was gone, all I could do was hate her for the things she did.

"However, the Ghost of Christmas Past—not the one in there, the main one or whatever—they showed me a memory from when I was very little. It was before my dad died. My mom was…normal. Happy, even. She was reading me a book, acting like a mom should. During this trip down memory lane, I learned something about her that changes how I see her now."

Holly tilted her head so she was looking at him.

"Before my dad died, my mom was taking medication to help with her mental state. You see, that Krampus thing that lived inside her, it came out when she no longer had my dad around to keep her on her meds. Learning that this ugly person used to be so nice, well…it was hard. Humans are complicated. The worst of us are capable of acts of kindness, and the best of us will sometimes fall from grace. There's no rhyme or reason to it. Santa used to be human, just like me."

She shrugged and resumed looking at the ground. "I was created to look up to him," she said. "He's a huge part of me, and everything I've done has been for him."

"Are you sure?" He put a hand on her knee and squeezed.

"Because if I remember right, you've been pursuing some things to learn more about yourself. It's like what that memory was telling you, about how he wanted to make an elf who was truly free. A good parent doesn't want their kids to worship them. They want their kids to live better lives than they did."

Holly grunted in agreement, then sniffled and wiped her nose. "But he's had that monster inside him all this time," she muttered. "I just…I don't know what to think."

"And that's okay. Your feelings are valid. Sometimes we just need time and support to process things. But you need to remember there's a reason for everything he does. He told you the truth because it was important that you heard it from him and nobody else. Santa trusts you, Holly. Despite everything else that's going on, that has to have some worth."

She sighed. "It doesn't make me feel better, but…he was right about the human thing. Ever since we…did the deed, the world feels less confining. When you guys swear, I don't get dizzy like I used to. I have stray thoughts that aren't about sex or Christmas. It's small but out of character for me."

"Well, part of your soul is human now." He chuckled. "And part of mine is elfin. That'll manifest somehow, I'm sure of it."

"What do you mean?"

He held up a hand and summoned a lightning spider. "This isn't something I did on my own," he told her, setting the spider in the snow. "It's a mark left behind by someone I loved. It's a thing my magic does."

Holly stared at the spider, its sparkling exterior reflected in her eyes. "So we left a mark on each other?"

"Yep. You gained something from me, and I gained something from you."

"Will I stay this way?" She looked away from the spider and gazed into his eyes. "I mean…I'm going to live a lot longer than you, so…"

"I can't say for certain. But the woman who left this mark

on me, she died months ago. My magic still carries that imprint, so it will probably be the same way for you."

"Good." She scooted closer to him, put her arm around his waist, and then leaned her head on his arm. "Because maybe it's confusing, and a little bit scary, but I like how I feel. It's different, in a good way. It's like I fit into the whole world a lot better than before."

He sat with her for a few minutes, his eyes on the northern lights as they danced about in the sky. Her sniffling had subsided, and she was motionless at his side.

"Is it okay that I don't know what to believe anymore?" she asked.

"It is. Doubt is a very human quality."

"I hate that the one person I believed in is…well, I don't know how to put it into words." She sat away from him and looked into his eyes. "It hurts not having anything to believe in. So maybe…maybe I should believe in you instead."

He smiled at her and shook his head. "You really shouldn't. Do you know why?"

"I don't."

"Because the most important person you should believe in first is yourself."

Holly looked down at the ground and chewed her lip in thought. "I don't know if I can do that. I'm not even sure who I am anymore."

"Join the club." He patted her affectionately on the head. "But you don't need to have all the answers to believe. I learned that from you."

She smiled. "You're really good at making me feel better."

"I've had a lot of practice at it." He put his arm around her and hugged her tight. "But you should know that I believe in my friends, and that includes you. Whatever lies ahead, we'll face it together. Agreed?"

Holly sighed and leaned her head against him.

"I agree," she replied.

Lily was taking a break with a large mug of cocoa when Christmas Present and Dancer appeared in the sky. The spirit dismounted and hovered across the distance between them before landing pertly in Lily's lap.

"Just taught a little boy how to ride a bike." The spirit grinned, then traced a little heart on Lily's chest. "Feeling pretty good about myself. Any chance that the bone daddy will be away for long?"

The succubus snorted. "Doubt it. He's already been gone an hour, so I expect him back any minute."

The ghost pouted, then shifted off Lily's lap as the rope ladder dangling over the sleigh's edge became tight. A few moments later, Death's bony visage appeared, with him clutching a candy cane between his teeth.

"Well?" Lily asked.

"It went very well." Death climbed into the sleigh and tucked the candy cane into his robes. "Lucille shall no longer fear the monster beneath her bed."

"Good job." Lily offered Death a high five, which he accepted. "No problems?"

He shook his head. Lucille had been born blind, giving the reaper a rare opportunity to make a house call. "She felt my beard and my hat, but I told her I was wearing my anti-monster mask and that it would feel scary, so she skipped that part. A child's innocence is rare, and I was grateful she took my word."

Lily chuckled. "So what was keeping her up at night?"

"A monster." Death took the thermos from the console and poured himself a cup.

"An actual monster?" Christmas Present asked.

"Indeed. I beat it with my bat, and when it became incorporeal, I strangled it until it agreed to leave her alone." He sipped at his cocoa, then turned his attention to them. "Afterward, Lucille read me her favorite bedtime story in Braille. She even taught me how to read a couple of the letters. It was so interesting!"

"What the heck was living under that girl's bed?" Lily shook her head. "You know what? Never mind. Who is next on the list?"

"We have a few options." Death pulled the scroll from his robes and unrolled it. "There's a young woman about a hundred miles north of here that wants to learn how to braid her hair. Apparently her mother passed away two years ago, and her father is bald and there's nobody to teach her."

"I can do that one." Christmas Present took a peek at the scroll, then looked at Lily. "Does it feel weird that we're only twenty miles from your house?"

Lily shrugged. It felt like she'd been gone for years. Technically, she'd lived in the sleigh far longer than she had in the Radley home. If not for Mike, she couldn't care less where she was. According to Christmas Present, he was somewhere in the US right now. She had almost teleported to him upon learning this. There was a big difference between seeing him in spirit versus in person, and she missed him. If not for Death's boundless enthusiasm and knowing that they were still accomplishing something, she would have bailed long ago.

"Guess I'll see you when I see you." Christmas Present hovered over to Dancer, and the two of them took off. The spirit looked back and winked, then lifted her robes to reveal her bare ass to Lily before disappearing into a cloud.

"I'm not sure which I enjoy more: seeing her come or seeing her go." Lily smiled at the double entendre, happy to have pulled another one over the helper hat.

"Mm-hmm." Death was staring intensely at the scroll, the lights in his eyes flickering.

"Everything okay?" Lily asked.

Death said nothing. He took the reins and gave them a snap, and Cerberus pulled them to their next destination.

Concerned about the reaper's sudden silence, Lily peered over the side of the sleigh to figure out where they were headed.

The downtown area appeared, then they were zigzagging between the buildings. She had flown through here more than once. In fact, she and Abella had once had a race to see who got Mike for the evening. To this day, she was certain the gargoyle had cheated but wasn't certain how.

A building festooned in Christmas lights appeared between a church and a telecommunications building. A large tree had been decorated in the courtyard, and the bottom of the building had festive designs painted on all the windows.

"Death?" Lily was concerned when he landed the sleigh in front of the doors. They hadn't seen the Yule Cat in a long time, so to watch him throw away caution worried her.

The grim reaper sat perfectly still for several minutes, his eyes on the automated doors of the Children's Hospital. Lily hopped out of the sleigh and walked around it, scanning the area for any signs of movement.

"Lily." Death's voice was barely a whisper. "I will need your help with this one."

"No poop, you've needed my help with all of them." She threw him some side eye. "You got a kid who wants to eat something other than Jell-O in there?"

Death rolled up the scroll and tucked it into his robes. "We shall both go in," he declared, then got out of the sleigh. Despite being an immortal psychopomp held together by his love of maps and tea, the reaper moved as if his bones may come apart at any moment. "Cerberus, if you wouldn't mind."

The hellhound grunted and pulled the sleigh into the sky, circling the building twice before disappearing into the clouds above. Death walked up to the sliding doors of the hospital, then squeezed between them.

Lily followed, taking a moment to survey the lobby. Another large tree had been set up inside the lobby with gifts beneath it. She paused to pick one up and was surprised when it had some weight to it.

"Do you think they just put some rocks inside or what?" When Death failed to answer, she looked up to see that he was already entering the stairwell. "Darn it, don't leave me behind. It will take forever to find you in this place."

They climbed up to the seventh floor, then stepped out into a foyer decorated with rainbow colors. A golden bell hung on a wall opposite where the receptionist, an older woman in a red Santa hat, sat. There was a plate of cookies sitting on the counter, so Lily took one.

"Peanut butter," she announced. "A top-tier cookie choice, the best that healthcare can afford." When she took a bite, she discovered she was wrong. "What the heck is this? It tastes like cardboard that is trying too hard."

"It's a hospital," Death informed her. "Nut-free zone."

"So then what flavor are these supposed to be? Regret?" Lily tossed the cookie into a nearby bin. "You seem to know your way around here."

"I do." Death was already moving down a nearby hallway. "In the first weeks of December, Tink convinced me that the Krampus was real and that I could catch him. Since children were his prey, she suggested I hunt where children congregated. I came here many times in order to hunt for the Krampus and got to know several of the children."

Lily chuckled. "You probably scared the poop out of them."

"You'd be surprised, actually." Death stopped in the hall and turned around to face her. "In fact, almost everyone here can see me. The staff, they're interesting. More often than not, they have mistaken me for another member of the staff. I suppose it's because I am a regular occurrence in this building. The parents? Many see me but pretend they don't. I chalk that up to denial and do not fault them for it.

"But the children? Maybe it's because they don't properly

understand what I represent, or maybe they do and just want the pain to stop. They not only see me but have shown me much kindness. I know many of the children here on a first-name basis. It's odd, but I can sense that these kids need me. They ask me questions about dying that I am unafraid to answer, and we play games with one another while the staff pretends I'm some imaginary friend the children invented. See?" He pointed to a nearby bulletin board. Lily was surprised to see several drawings of children playing with a skeleton. A bunch of them had been labeled Uncle Bones.

"Uncle Bones, huh?" She walked over to the bulletin board and tapped on a drawing. "And how come you're naked in each of these pictures?"

"Because when they drew me with my robes, it terrified the parents. The woman in charge of this wing thinks Uncle Bones is just the skeleton they keep in the supply closet for educational purposes. It certainly makes the parents feel better." Death resumed walking down the hall, then stopped outside one of the rooms. "We're here."

He pushed the door open, the hallway suddenly filled with the soft beeping of a heart monitor. The room was decorated with hundreds of colored pencil drawings, most of them of other children. Lily paused to appreciate a fairly realistic depiction of one of the doctors. It wasn't quite photo quality like some of the stuff Zel could draw, but it was really good.

"Death!" A raspy voice greeted the reaper, who now sat at the foot of the bed. Lily walked in to see a young woman no older than fifteen crawl across the bed and embrace Death. "What are you doing here so late?"

"I am out running errands for a friend," he replied, the twin flames of his skull flickering orange. "Speaking of friends, this is my really good friend Lily."

"Hi!" The girl turned to Lily and gave her a wave. She was missing all her hair and had dark circles under her eyes that stood out on porcelain skin. When she extended a hand in greeting, Lily noticed that several of her nails were simply gone. Those that remained had been painted with Christmas colors. "My name is Reagan. It's nice to meet you."

"Um…yeah." Lily didn't know how to reply. She had been caught off guard by the girl's appearance. "I just found out that Death has been coming here and didn't know he was friends with anyone."

"We love him here." With Death's help, Reagan scooted back to the top of her bed. She thanked him and picked up the small sketchpad next to her bed. "It's always a lot of fun when he visits. This place can be a little…grim."

"I bet." Lily sat in a chair by the bed. "So…what are you in for?"

"Stuck a crayon up my nose." Reagan picked up a pair of colored pencils and mimed shoving a red one up one nostril. "You know how doctors are, so overdramatic."

Death chuckled, then patted Reagan's knee. "Reagan has an inoperable tumor in her brain."

"It was a restaurant crayon." Reagan's eyes sparkled. "Probably made with lead in China or something. Doctors have been trying to melt it with space lasers."

"Oh, you're fun." Lily smiled. "So this is going to sound strange, but did you write a letter to Santa this year?"

Reagan's eyes widened, and she looked over at Death. "I did! But I never got a chance to send it!" She leaned over the side of her bed and picked up a folder full of artwork. Flipping straight to the back, she pulled out an envelope labeled with the letters *SC*.

"May I see it?" Death asked.

Reagan faltered, clutching the envelope tightly against her chest. "I'm not so sure about that. Isn't it kind of like keeping a birthday wish secret? If I tell you, it might not come true."

"Ah, but we are Santa's helpers this year." Death pointed to Lily's hat. "So it would make sense that we get to see it."

"You're so cheesy." Reagan looked at the envelope. "I know Santa isn't real. There's no use pretending."

"Wait, you're literally looking at the grim reaper himself and you doubt Santa exists?" Lily laughed. "That's too cute."

"I'm not entirely certain he's not just the tumor talking." Reagan tapped one of her temples. "But believing in Death is way easier than Santa. Everybody dies. Santa? He only shows up in shitty movies."

"Then why write him a letter?" Lily crossed her arms. "If he doesn't exist, I mean."

"Why do people pray to God when their kids are dying?" Reagan rolled her eyes. "Because they hope someone cares. Me, I'm not so sure the guy is real, and if he is, he doesn't give a fuck. I certainly haven't seen any real miracles around here. When a kid gets better, it's always because of doctors and medicine. Yeah, people will call it a miracle, but it's usually just a matter of statistics. But when that kid dies? It was apparently their time and we just aren't smart enough to know God's plan or some shit. What a fucking double standard."

"Okay, I like this kid." Lily wasn't usually comfortable with talk about the G-man, but the kid was making some good points. "So you figured Santa was a better bet than Sky Daddy. Makes me wonder what you asked for."

"It's not important." Reagan cleared her throat as if to change the subject, but Lily used her tail to snatch it out of her hands. "Holy shit, you have a tail?"

"I've got a lot more than that. Would you like a dramatic reveal?" Lily didn't wait for an answer. She did a little pirouette, her wings unfurling behind her as her Christmas pajamas melted into her usual corset and miniskirt. She did a dramatic bow, her horns sliding forward through the skin of her skull just beneath her hat. "What do you think?"

"Bitchin'!" Reagan crawled forward in her bed, the wires from her heart monitor catching on Death's hand. "Can I feel your wings? They're so pretty!"

"I, uh…" Lily smiled, her cheeks suddenly warm. She almost didn't notice when Death pulled the envelope out of her tail. "Yeah, sure, kid." She extended her wings, allowing Reagan to feel them.

"They remind me of my dad's leather jacket." Reagan pushed her face into the fold of one wing and inhaled. "Oof, doesn't smell the same though."

"I was forged from hellfire. Your dad's jacket came from a farting cow."

"You're the one that smells like farts," Reagan grumbled. This elicited a hearty laugh from Death, who had managed to untangle his fingers from her wires. In the process, he unplugged the monitor, causing the eerie whine to fill the room.

"We won't be needing that," he declared, flicking the machinery off with a finger.

"So does this mean you can fly?" Reagan let go of Lily's wing. "Is that a scorpion's tail? Do you sting people with it?"

"I can. It is. And I have." Lily sat on the end of the bed. Reagan scooted away from her to make room and picked up her forgotten sketchpad. "I'm a type of demon known as a succubus."

"Really? Like, the sexy kind?" Reagan picked up one of her pencils, the room now filled with the sounds of graphite on paper. "You eat souls, right?"

"She does." Death leaned over to see what Reagan was drawing. "It's quite disturbing."

"But you seem so nice." Reagan paused in her scribbles. "I didn't think a succubus could be nice."

"You seem to know an awful lot about demons. Are schools finally back to teaching the basics?" Lily asked.

"Nah." The scribbling resumed. "I've got a lot of downtime. I used to read a lot, but it makes my head hurt, so now I just stream movies and shit. May have spent a bunch of time contemplating my immortal soul, 'cause, well…" She gestured at the room around her. "I've got a lump of cells the size of an egg in the middle of my brain. You question a lot of things when the end is near."

"Well, what do you want to know?" Lily sat on the edge of the bed, her tail sliding beneath the bed to tickle Reagan's foot. The girl laughed, squirming away from her.

"All sorts of things. For instance, since you're a demon, it means that Heaven is real! What's it like?" Reagan turned her full attention on Lily, hope in her eyes.

"Not something I actually have an answer for. Never been there, 'cause I'm a demon." Lily tapped her horns.

"But I thought demons were just fallen angels?"

Lily winced. "Yeah, well I'm…complicated." She wasn't about to get into her past with just anyone, much less a teenager.

"Got it. Does that mean you don't know what God's like?"

"Reagan." Death patted the girl's knee. "I understand why you're asking, but Lily really isn't comfortable speaking on all things heavenly. It gives her gas."

"Oh, right, I'm so sorry!" Reagan blushed as Lily scowled at the reaper. "I must look like a total bitch right now."

"It's fine, I get it." Lily waved her off. "You just found out that your soul gets to go somewhere after you die. That's a pretty big deal. Me? I already know that my ultimate destination is a coin flip between Hell and the void. If I have enough souls under my belt, Hell won't be so bad. The void though? Oblivion at its worst."

"Oh, I know! Where does Death live? He refuses to tell us where he's staying, always talks about how he lives with his best friend in a house full of monsters." Reagan stuck her tongue out at the reaper. "Bet she'll tell me."

"That's actually true, but I can't say much about it." She threw a dirty look at Death. "He probably shouldn't have told you that much, honestly."

"It is okay, Lily." Death held up his hand, then curled his

fingers down until only his pinky remained. "For we have entered into a contract of the highest order: the pinky swear."

"Jiminy Christmas, what am I going to do with you?" Lily sat on the other side of Reagan. "But yeah, an entire family of magical creatures, all under one roof."

Reagan's eyes brimmed and spilled over with tears, and she wiped them away with her thumbs. "Sorry if I'm a bit emotional. I've always wanted to believe in something other than all this, you know?"

"I get it, kid. It's nice to have something to believe in." Suddenly conscious of just how tiny the girl was, Lily shrank herself down to better fit next to Reagan. Movement in the corner of the room revealed spirit Mike leaning against the wall with a grin on his face. "Or someone."

And so they talked. Death was quiet, save for a few interruptions. Reagan talked all about her parents and her baby sister who was going to be eight soon. There was a girl at school that Reagan was super into, but she hadn't seen her since last spring. Her school was a couple of hours away, which meant she rarely got visitors.

The whole time she spoke, her hands kept moving across the paper. Whenever Lily tried to peek, Reagan would tilt the sketchpad down, a sly grin on her face. "No snooping," she would declare, occasionally sharpening her pencils. Little colored shavings appeared all over her bed, which Death would meticulously collect and deposit in the nearby trash can.

They were in the middle of talking about Reagan's favorite show when the girl wrote something with a flourish in one corner. She carefully removed the paper from her sketch pad and handed it over to Lily.

"Do you like it?" she asked, her tired eyes suddenly hopeful.

It was a portrait of the succubus. She was midlaugh, a hand in front of her mouth and the skin around her eyes crinkled up. The stone necklace Mike had given her rested on her chest, Lily's hand hovering just above it. Behind her, an aura of light filled the rest of the picture. Even though she had horns in the picture, it was a candid moment, making her look surprisingly human.

"I...love it." Lily looked over the top of the drawing to see Reagan's eyes brimming with joy. "Can I have this?"

Reagan nodded, wiping tears from her eyes. "I think it's my best work. What do you think, Death?"

"I will admit I am quite jealous." Death grinned at his friend. "This is very well done."

"Thank you." She balled up her fists and took a deep breath. Her lower lip trembled as she squeezed the blankets on her bed. "I'm ready now."

"Ready for what?" Lily asked, but the moment was quick, like a match catching fire. There was a flash of light, and Death stood over Reagan's bed, his bony fingers clenched together above her body.

"What the fudge? What the fudge?!" Lily slid backward off the bed, clawing at her hat in horror. Reagan's sparkling eyes had already gone dull, her pupils dilating. "What did you do, Death? What did you do?"

The reaper turned toward Lily and held up Reagan's soul. It was the brightest golden light that Lily had ever seen, flitting about like a trapped bird in his clutches.

"I knew the moment we arrived," he told her, lowering his hand. "There's a saying mortals enjoy, one about knowing Death has entered the room. For the first time ever, I was allowed to experience that sensation for myself. I had entered the room, not as myself, but as my job. We are frozen in a single moment, and that moment just so happened to be Reagan's last."

"But why? WHY?!" Lily almost balled up her drawing in frustration, tears now running down her cheeks. Steam rose from them as her body temperature climbed, hellfire now coursing through her veins. "Why would you do this to me? Why not just come up here, do your darned job, and then go?"

Death hung his head in shame. "I will admit that the deception was not for Reagan's sake but my own. I am supposed to be impartial, to allow these things to pass as they should, but…" He turned to Reagan's corpse, her cheeks still glistening with moisture. "I needed a friend."

"She was your friend, you nutjob!" Lily picked up the remote to the television and threw it at him. It bounced off his cloak and fell to the floor.

"I meant for after." Death placed his hand on Reagan's head. "You see, I spent many hours with this child and got to know her. Though she was destined to die so young, she treated me with genuine kindness. I knew it would be a struggle to take her."

"Then why take her at all?"

"The tumor in her head ruptured a nearby vessel. She would live only until the time lock was lifted. Even if I could have kept her around, she would be comatose, trapped in a place of eternal darkness until I came to claim her once more. Though I am the final mercy, I…" He removed his hand and contemplated the dead teen's soul in his other. "I don't know what happens to any of them, you know? Her parents will mourn her loss, but there is a chance they will see each other again. But what of me? Am I destined to sit and watch as the universe comes to an ultimate end, then sit alone in a darkness of my own? What of the friends I made along the way?

"You see, my dear Lily, it has occurred to me that when I say goodbye, it is forever. I was grateful to be here for her final moments, but she will go on in her own way."

"But why are we even here?" Lily slumped into a nearby chair, clutching Reagan's drawing to her chest. "She wrote a letter to Santa, what about that? Weren't we here for this? What's even the point if you were just going to take her?"

Death pulled the envelope from his robes and held it up as if it was made of glass. He slid his finger beneath the adhesive and ripped it open, pulling out the paper within.

"Dear Santa," he began, the fire in his eyes dimming. "I know this might sound ridiculous, but there's something I want for Christmas. I wrote you a lot when I was younger, but I will admit that I've stopped believing. Sorry if this hurts you in the polls.

"Anyway, things aren't looking good for me. The doctors keep saying that every day is a gift, but I know the end is coming. I'm not afraid, not since I met my new friend. He's a big fan of yours. I hope you…" Death stopped for several moments, then cleared his nonexistent throat. "I hope you get to meet him someday in a nonofficial capacity."

"Oh, Reagan." Lily shook her head and continued sobbing.

"If I could have one gift this year, it would be that you help my parents and sister once I'm gone. They've lived with me and my broken head for so long now that maybe they've forgotten how to be happy. I don't know what that would look like on your end, but I feel like someone owes me a miracle. Please help them find happiness again. They deserve it.

"But if you happen to be in a giving mood, there's something I want for myself. When the end comes, I don't want to be alone, but I don't want to do it in front of my family. I kind of want to go out on a high note, if that makes sense. I don't care who you send. It could be an elf or even a reindeer. When I die, I know I'll already…"

Death went silent, then handed the note to Lily. She took it from him and found the part where he had stopped.

"I know I'll already have one friend there but wouldn't mind making just one more before I go." She didn't bother reading the rest; it was too hard to see through her tears. It was like she had lost control over her body, her head pounding as if it would burst from within.

Death stood by the hospital window, Reagan's soul in his outstretched palm.

"Goodbye, Reagan." He gave the soul a little flick with his fingers, as if tossing a coin in the air, and it was gone. The room seemed dimmer now, as if the color had been sucked out of it. "May your slumber be restful."

"I hate you," Lily whispered. "I hate you for doing this to me."

"I know." Death moved over to the side of Reagan's bed and took a moment to tuck her in. He reconnected all the wires to her heart monitor, the silence shattered by the eerie tone of Reagan's death.

"Why bother?" Lily asked. "She's not in there, you know."

"You are correct." Death turned to point at the clock. "But you see, it is not technically Christmas Day."

"So?"

"In thirty years, when Reagan's sister wakes up on Christmas Day, she will never have to think, 'This is the date of my sister's death.' When time resumes, I wish for them to find her sometime before midnight." Death moved toward the doorway, then paused long enough to steal one of the pictures that had been tucked away beneath some of the others. Lily couldn't be sure, but she was fairly certain the subject of the artwork was wearing a dark robe. "I would like to get some air, if you don't mind. I'll be on the roof."

She watched him go. When she was certain he was far enough away, she moved to sit on the side of Reagan's bed.

"You okay?" soul Mike asked from the corner of the room.

"No. Not really." She knelt and kissed Reagan's forehead. "Though I knew you but for a moment, I shall remember you for a lifetime." It wasn't hyperbole either, because demons couldn't lie and she never wanted to forget.

She pulled out the sketch Reagan had given her, torn about whether to take it with her or leave it behind. Her tears splashed on the drawing, and she tucked it away. It was interesting how something so light could feel so heavy in her hands.

By the time she caught up to Death, he was standing on the edge of the roof with his scythe out, leaning on the handle for support. Moving to stand next to him, she handed him Reagan's letter.

"I didn't know if you wanted to keep this," she told him.

"I would, actually." He accepted the letter, and it vanished into his robes. "I feel an ache inside my body that I am unfamiliar with."

"That's called grief."

"Ah." He stared out at the lights of the city. "I do not like it."

"That was a terrible thing you did to me."

"It was, and I am sorry. Do you have Reagan's drawing?"

"I do." She pulled it out. "Why?"

"I think she captured your likeness very well. It was a gift of hers. To see what lies beneath. You may act tough and be rather crude at times, but you are a kind soul."

"I'm not ready for an emotional circle jerk."

Death turned to look at her. "What is a circle jerk?"

"I'll tell you tomorrow."

"Ugh. It's never tomorrow." Death raised his hand, and the sleigh emerged from the clouds above. It seemed unsteady, as if Cerberus was pulling it through turbulence. Once the hellhound landed, she turned into her human form and put her hands on her hips.

"The sleigh is getting tough to pull," Cerberus said. "It feels much heavier."

"It shouldn't be." Death frowned at the sleigh. "We are still delivering personal visits. The magic should sustain it."

There was a loud pop, and Christmas Present appeared next to them.

"Quick, let me see the list."

"Why are you teleporting here?" Lily asked. "Won't the Krampus figure out where we are?"

"It doesn't matter. This is more important." The spirit took the list from Death and scrolled through a few names. "Hold on, I'll be right back. I need to check on something."

With another pop, she left them behind. Death looked at Lily and shrugged.

"I have a bad feeling about this," she told him.

"As do I." Death moved to sit in the sleigh. "I believe we'll find out why very soon."

Lily didn't join him. Instead, she moved to the edge of the building and pulled out Reagan's drawing. She curled her fingers around the edges, ready to summon a little hellfire and reduce it to ash.

"Are you really sure you want to do that?" soul Mike asked from the shadows. "Once it's gone, you will never get it back."

She paused, the flames hovering just beneath her fingertips. "Why would I want to keep something that hurts me so bad?"

"It's just a piece of paper, Lily. I think it scares you that she saw through the facade, to the woman underneath the monster. You're worried that it makes you weak, that the pain you feel means your strength is fading. A weak Lily can't protect her family, now can she?"

"Shut up," she whispered.

"But you've eaten enough therapists to know the truth. Grief and sadness don't make you weak. You can't sharpen a sword by only hammering one side of the blade, silly." He came up from behind and wrapped his arms around her waist. "So don't burn that, at least not yet. Let Reagan's last gift to the world survive just a little bit longer."

She scowled, then relaxed into Mike's arms. "I hate having you inside my head sometimes," she told him.

"I know," he replied. "It really is a pretty picture of you."

"It is," she whispered, wiping the new tears off the paper

before they could soak in. She held it against her chest, absorbing it into her body where it would be safe for now. After all, she could always burn it later, right?

There was a burst of light, and fiery sparks showered the rooftop as Christmas Present tumbled from up in the sky. The spirit was covered in scratch marks, and there was blood all over her outfit.

"Holy heck, what happened?" Lily ran to the giant's side. "Are you okay?"

"No, I'm not." Christmas Present's face was bright red, her eyes brimming with anger. She held something up in her hands and laughed. "For future reference, I can apparently teleport this much of another being."

It was the head of one of the Yule Lads, his features slack. Christmas Present dropped it onto the roof.

"They're taking the children," she said, her gaze on the bloody head as it dissolved into smoke. "The ones we were supposed to visit and the ones we've already been to. It's how the Krampus is draining the magic away. The gifts are bad enough, but by them taking the children, it's like we've done nothing at all!"

"What is he planning to do with them?" Death asked, a dangerous tone in his voice. Whatever warmth the air held flitted away like leaves in a hurricane.

Christmas Present turned toward the grim reaper. "With the Yule Lads' involvement, my bet is…he's going to let Grýla eat them."

Lily gasped, her wings fluttering behind her in shock.

"I see." Death turned toward the sleigh. "I did not expect such a development. Every move he has made has served to undo the goodwill we have poured into the world, but this? It is an act of pure evil, and I shall not allow it."

"So what do we do?" Lily asked. "We can't just go in there guns blazing. One, we don't have any guns. Two, we don't know where Grýla is keeping the children. Does anyone here even have a plan?"

"I know someone who is pretty good at it. We need our Caretaker." Christmas Present looked at Lily. "He and the others have to return to the North Pole right away. I can teleport to him, which will allow the three of you to come around the long way."

"Fudge no, I'm coming with you." She tugged at the hat out of habit. "I can teleport directly to him as well. That leaves Death to come the long way with Cerberus and the sleigh."

"Then it is settled." Death got into the sleigh and picked up the reins. "My dear ghost, would you kindly inform Dancer of this plan so she may meet up with us on the way? I would not begrudge a proper guide."

"You've got it. We'll see you when you get there." Christmas Present tucked a lock of Lily's hair behind one of her horns. "See you later, alligator."

She vanished, leaving the scent of nutmeg in the air. Lily sucked it in through her nostrils, then glanced over at Death.

"See you at the North Pole," she told him.

"Yes, you will." He waited for Cerberus to transform back into a hellhound. "And Lily?"

"What?"

"Save some ass for me." When he turned to face her, the fire in his eyes threatened to escape his sockets. "For I intend to beat much ass this Christmas."

She nodded, then closed her eyes and took a shortcut through Hell to return to Mike's side. The fire and brimstone flared hot against her skin, and then she was standing in the ice and snow of…somewhere else. Mike was sitting outside a cabin, next to Holly, and he leaped to his feet in surprise.

"Lily!" He ran for her, and the moment his arms wrapped around her waist, the dam broke. Hot tears ran down her face as he clutched her tightly, her tail wrapping around his waist.

When he finally let go, he used his thumbs to wipe the tears from her eyes.

"You're a sight for sore eyes," she whispered. "How long has it been for you?"

"Too long without you. Something happened, didn't it?"

The succubus nodded. "The Krampus is taking children to give to the giants as food. He's making some big moves, and we can't let him get away with it."

Mike nodded, then looked over at Holly. "It's time for this player to make some moves of his own. You ready for this?"

"No." The elf looked at Lily, then back at Mike. Her eyes were red around the edges as if she had been crying recently. "But it's okay because we're all in it together. Right?"

"Right." Mike looked at Lily. "Now let's go kick some Krampus ass."

BELIEVERS

After the first thirty minutes of wandering through the enormous piles of undelivered gifts, Kisa was forced to take a break and fight back the panic attack that threatened to consume her. The darkness was absolute beyond the small range of her crystalline light, and it was during this moment of respite that she spotted a pallet stacked with bicycles nearby.

She thought it was pretty fucked up that a bunch of kids somehow had never gotten their bikes, but she found one roughly her size and dragged it clear. The tag fell free of the handlebars, and she bent down to pick it up and read the name.

"Sorry, Thomas. Looks like a sweet ride." The bike was blue with a gold lightning bolt on the frame. She dug through the pile and found a helmet. When she pressed it onto her head, she hissed in frustration as she fought both her hair and her ears to get it on properly. By the time it was on, her ears had been folded against her scalp, muting the outside world.

Kisa made it nearly six feet on the bike before crashing. She didn't know if she had never learned how to ride as a child or if it had simply been too long, but she climbed back to her feet and tried again.

Between her natural grace and dexterity, she was soon pedaling forward in the darkness, with the crystal tucked between her knuckles providing enough light to see. She hoped she was still headed in the right direction. It had occurred to her more than once that being shuffled around may have pointed her somewhere else in the warehouse and she was moving away from the entrance.

The good news was that Christmas hadn't been around for all eternity. At some point, she would run out of presents and reach a wall. When that happened, she would pedal her bike alongside until that damn elevator appeared. The building couldn't be infinitely large on the inside…right?

Once she reached the cave wall, it was essentially a coin flip for which direction to go. She chose left and was finally able to pedal with some speed, no longer dodging piles of gifts. When she reached the dais, hot tears of joy ran down her cheeks as she tucked the bike out of sight around a corner.

Kisa was tired but refused to find somewhere to nap until she was out of the warehouse. The darkness felt like it would crush her at any moment, and she had no idea how long her crystal would continue glowing.

The trip up the elevator was uneventful. When the doors slid open, she let out a sigh of relief to see the lit caverns empty. She moved along the tunnels and found herself back in Grýla's lair. A very large cauldron had been set over a fire, and a pair of elves were cleaning up a horrendous mess on the floor that looked suspiciously like it had used to be another elf.

"Fuck this place," Kisa muttered, moving back to the main tunnel. When she reached the pits where the elves had been stored, she crouched upon seeing Leppalúði standing above one of the pits, a figure held between his hands.

"I cannot cook this!" he yelled at a smaller version of himself.

"Krampus say children frozen!" The Yule Lad gave Leppalúði's shin a kick. "Stupid Christmas magic, only Santa can fix! After Krampus take pole, children become food!"

"What the hell?" Kisa moved to the edge of the pit and looked down to see that one of the elfin prisons had been repurposed. Instead of elves, it held children, all of them wrapped in blankets and sleeping on the floor. Her heart raced at seeing all the children collected into a macabre sleep-over in the giant's den.

Leppalúði let out a roar, and Kisa looked over to see that he had tried to bite the child in half and cracked one of his teeth. He spat the tooth fragment onto the ground and hurled the child at his son.

"Put it back in the pen," he snarled, rubbing at his mouth. "Your mother won't be happy."

The Yule Lad squeaked in terror and ran off with his bundle. Leppalúði scratched his jaw and turned toward his lair, his large nostrils flaring. He walked within a few feet of Kisa, then stopped and sniffed the air.

Shit! Kisa crouched, holding her breath. Leppalúði snorted, then picked his nose and wiped it on his shirt.

"They smell so good," he muttered, wandering past Kisa and back into his cave. She could hear him smacking his lips for some time and fought the urge to gag in response. Her brain was busy processing the horror of all those children, just ready to be eaten. When the time lock ended, they would all awaken in the middle of a nightmare.

Kisa's breath was coming quickly now. She reached into her coat and pulled out the adoption papers she had found addressed to her. Once upon a time, when she was a child, someone had wanted to make her part of his family. On Christmas morning, hundreds of families would wake to discover their children had gone missing. They would all disappear without a trace, just like Kisa had, only these children weren't destined for a weird, albeit happy, ending. They would end up as food for the giants, their final moments filled with terror.

"This is wrong." She felt the hackles on the back of her neck rise as a surge of energy went through her body. No, this was more than wrong. It was evil, pure and simple.

A low growl came from her chest, and she bared her teeth as she moved against the wall and tucked her paperwork away. Something was brewing inside her. What little magic she had was concentrating itself and working its way through her body as if trying to figure out what came next. What would Mike do if he were here? Could he even do anything? What about Tink, or Yuki?

An elf wandered by Kisa, his eyes distant as he carried a stack of bloody towels. Kisa didn't know why, but she was compelled to fall in line behind him, her eyes affixed on the back of his head. The elf didn't acknowledge her existence in the slightest as he led her around the corner to a room full of garbage. It was a giant pile of busted furniture and appliances, most likely remnants of Leppalúði's new rich lifestyle.

The two of them were alone. The elf dumped his burden and spun on his heels, walking into Kisa.

"Wait." Kisa stuck her hand out, and the elf froze, his blank eyes skimming her face. Had their brains been wiped completely clean, like a hard drive erased by a magnet? How much of the original elf even remained?

The elf hissed and moved around her. While she was worried that it was about to tattle on her to Leppalúði, an idea formed.

"I have new orders from the Krampus." It had occurred to her that the elves obeyed the Krampus first and that the only reason they listened to Leppalúði at all was because they had been told to. She crossed her fingers as the elf stopped in place, then turned to face her.

Several tense seconds passed, but the elf seemed content to hear her out. She had seen the elves stand by as their brethren were eaten, so it was unlikely she could say or do anything that would elicit any sort of response.

"Bring me five other elves from the cells below," she demanded, then watched as the elf turned to leave. She moved against the wall and willed herself into the surroundings, hoping against hope that she was right.

Leppalúði was stupid. That much was true. There was no way he would notice a missing elf, or even several, which gave her room to improvise.

Soft footsteps echoed down the corridor, and she was elated to see that the elf had obeyed. There were six of them in total, and they stood right where Kisa had been before, awaiting their next orders.

Smiling to herself, Kisa moved out of the shadows to greet her new minions. The giant was big, and an all-out assault was out of the question. As of now, the elves didn't question her presence, and she certainly didn't want that fact to change. She would use these six to take the giant out of the equation.

As for after? By herself, she couldn't save more than a child or two. But with an army of brain-dead elves ready to obey her every command? Anything was possible.

There was a pull in her core, and she felt Mike's presence wash over her, now closer than ever. He had been oddly distant for a while, but she hadn't worried too much about it. Satisfied that the elves would remain hers to command, she ordered them to move trash around and look busy while she snuck over to a dark corner of the cave and crouched to make herself small.

It was time to check in with her man.

After Mike stepped through the flames of the fireplace and into the workshop, he moved to the side and frowned.

With the time variance, he should have only been gone a few hours from the North Pole.

Somehow the atmosphere here had shifted drastically. The abandoned workshop had been mildly spooky before, but now there was an aura of malignance that clung to everything. The shadows seemed darker than usual, with a few of them appearing to dance around when he wasn't looking.

The flames flickered again, and Lily came through, followed by Freyja, Yuki, then Holly. Before the flames died out, Christmas Present stepped through the fire, brushing soot off her robes.

"This isn't good." She frowned and moved forward into the workshop lobby. "Do you all feel that?"

There was a thud on the exterior of the building, followed by a screech. Dust fell from the ceiling and landed on the frost that had accumulated over by the door.

"Well, so much for first impressions. This place looks awful." Lily stepped away from the fireplace. "So what's the plan?"

"Hold up." Mike raised a hand as a questing presence touched the back of his mind. He closed his eyes and concentrated, causing Kisa to come into focus in his mind's eye.

"Thank God," she muttered, then leaned back against a wall he couldn't see. "I was afraid you might not be listening."

"Sorry, some big shit is going down," he replied. "We found out the Krampus has taken a bunch of kids."

Kisa nodded. "I know. They're being kept in that big bitch's lair."

"Are they okay?" He swallowed the lump in his throat. "Are they…scared?"

"Nah, they're all frozen in time or something. I don't know all the details, but once the Krampus takes the pole, they'll unlock and…" Kisa looked like she was going to be sick. "I have a plan to get them out of here, but it's only temporary. Whatever you've got cooking, you better get on it fast."

"Wait, hold up. How about you? Are you safe?"

"I'm underground with a bunch of dick-bag giants, elves with missing brains, and a stack of time-frozen kids. I'm *fine.*" Kisa rolled her eyes at him. "But I'm okay for now. You have a plan to bail me out of this shitstorm?"

"You know me." He winked.

"Fuck." She dragged the word out. "You just came up with it, didn't you?"

"Nah, I've been working on something for a couple of... hours." It had been a long walk back to the ski resort, and he'd had plenty of time to discuss strategies with Freyja and Yuki. The Krampus was just waiting for the chance to get his hands on the North Pole, so his first destination was Santa's house. However, with Grýla on the loose and a village full of warped snowmen, Yuki and Freyja had agreed to do a quick reconnaissance to see where things stood.

As for the Krampus himself, Mike believed he had a solution to that particular dilemma.

Kisa looked like she was going to say something but tilted her head. "Shit, do you hear that? No, of course you don't."

"What is it?" he asked.

Kisa grinned. "I think I just heard the heat come on. Here, before I go." She pulled her map from her pocket and unfolded it. "I went into a tunnel under this building," she said, tapping one of the corners. "Grýla and her ugly potato children all live in a series of caverns beneath it. If you get the chance, I could really use an assist down here."

"I'll see what I can do." He gave Kisa a hug and then opened his eyes. The others were standing around, waiting for him. "Kisa knows where the children are. They're safe for now. She said they're time locked, so that's one less thing for us to worry about."

"They only unfreeze for their personal visit, remember?" Christmas Present looked at Lily. "You've been doing this for months now. We know those kids weren't lying awake in their beds the whole time. They only unfroze for us because we're Santa's helpers. Being abducted by Yule Lads definitely doesn't count, so they're safe for now."

Lily still looked unhappy, but Mike couldn't blame her. Though the news was good, it didn't make everything else better by comparison. "Okay, so we should—"

The building groaned as something large hit it, sending a cascade of snow sliding off the roof and over the windows. A massive furry bulk moved just outside the window, and a large eyeball appeared in one of the windows.

"It's the Yule Cat!" Holly grabbed Mike by the hand. "They know where we are. We need to get to Santa's house right away!"

"On it." Mike looked at Yuki and Freyja. "Are you coming with us?"

The building creaked when a paw appeared on one of the windows and pressed. The glass cracked, splintering out to the edges.

"Let's move." Yuki nodded at Holly. "Once we're at Santa's house, we can make our stand there."

Holly threw a handful of powder into the fireplace just as the front door of the workshop burst apart, revealing a misshapen figure with a distorted jaw.

"Food!" Grýla shouted, her arms twitching as she squeezed her bulk through the busted doorway. Mike didn't remember her being this large before, and he couldn't help but notice that the shadows seemed to bend toward her.

"You all go." Freyja turned toward the giant. "This one has something of mine. I'll catch up soon."

"Don't have to tell me twice." Lily bolted into the fireplace ahead of the others, her tail snaking back to hook Mike by the wrist and pull him through. Yuki and Holly came through next, followed by Christmas Present. Back in Santa's house, Mike turned to look through the flames but only felt a blast of cold before they snuffed out completely, plunging the home into darkness.

"What the hell?" He summoned a pair of glow spiders to illuminate the room. Yuki was already holding fox fire, and Lily's eyes glowed in the darkness. Santa's home, which once felt warm and cozy, now had the same ominous feeling as the workshop.

"Mother!" Holly ran toward the stairs, and Christmas Present followed, the light from her body illuminating the way.

Yuki moved to the window and frowned. "I can't see anything out there," she said, then turned to Mike. "All the lights are out."

"Sounds like things are moving fast," he replied just as something large walked across the roof. "Looks like we've got company here too."

"Not for long." Yuki moved to the door and put her hands on it. "I'll clear the perimeter. Lock it behind me," she told him, then winced and put her hand on her side. "I'll take care of the popsicle patrol."

"Hey, are you okay?" Mike asked.

"I will be." Yuki looked over at Lily. "Take care of him, will you?"

Lily nodded but said nothing. Mike found her silence more than a little disturbing.

Yuki let herself out. The home filled with a burst of arctic cold that chilled Mike even through his jacket. He rubbed at the fur-lined coat, then turned back to Lily.

"Welcome to the North Pole," he told her, then walked to the door and locked it. "It used to be a lot nicer."

"Mm-hmm." Lily spotted a hat rack by the fireplace and moved toward it. She casually reached for the furry rim of her hat and gave it a tug.

It didn't budge.

"Fudging figures," she muttered. "Thought it might work. So what happens next?"

"That depends on what Mrs. Claus might say. She was in bad shape this morning, so I don't know what—" Footsteps on the stairs caught his attention, and he looked up to see Holly descending. She walked across the room and stopped right in front of Mike, her eyes on the ground.

"What happened?" he asked her. Her only response was to hold out a pair of silver glasses.

"We think she disappeared just as we got here." Christmas Present hovered down from above, lines of worry on her face. "Mike, we have two problems now."

"Just two?" He grimaced at the spirit.

"With Mrs. Claus gone, there is nothing to keep the Krampus out. He is coming and will be here soon enough."

"That was to be expected." He sighed. "What's the second problem?"

"I can't help you. You have to understand, the spirits are an extension of Santa's will, and just being in a room with him might be enough to turn me against you."

"Well, that sucks." He bit his lip in frustration. "So where will you go?"

"You said that Kisa is with the children? I will go to her, but I'll have to take the long way so the Krampus can't track me. Can you show me where she was on the map?"

"Yeah, sure." Mike pulled the map out of its carrier, then pointed to the spot Kisa had shown him. "She said there are tunnels underneath."

"Understood. Even if we fail here, the kids, they…" For a moment, the spirit looked like she was going to be sick.

"Go." He nodded at the spirit. "Make sure those kids are taken care of."

Christmas Present left, leaving Mike with Lily and Holly. The succubus was staring at where the fire had been, her cheeks burning bright red. Occasional flames crawled across her skin, and she turned fiery eyes in his direction.

"So it's just the three of us?" she asked.

"Yuki's right outside, and I'm sure Freyja will catch up. The Krampus will be on his way here to claim the North Pole."

"You can't claim it?" Lily cocked her head.

"Nope. Santa and the Krampus are still the same person. He needs the North Pole for…something." Mike paused. Did his house have a feature like the North Pole? Was there something he could interact with to tap into the home's inner power?

"Could you if we killed him?"

Mike looked over at Holly, who was staring quietly at Mrs. Claus's glasses. Technically, he supposed he could. But then what? Did he even want the responsibility of the North Pole? Would he become like Santa? What about the elves? His time was already stretched thin among his own family. The last thing he wanted was to be responsible for a whole holiday.

Lily scowled when he didn't answer, but her features softened when she noticed Holly. She moved toward the elf and put a hand on her shoulder.

"Would you like to talk about it?" she asked as she led the elf to a nearby couch.

Mike didn't hear Holly's answer. He was distracted by flashing lights through the front windows, followed by a gust of wind that made the whole house creak. When he moved to the window and looked outside, he was greeted by the sight of a moose made of ice slamming its antlers into the house.

"Looks like the snowman house of horrors has arrived." He moved away from the door and winced when the glass cracked. A second later, the fracture repaired itself, and he let out a sigh of relief. There was still a bit of magic left in the North Pole. Looking over at the couch, he saw that Holly was weeping with her head on Lily's shoulder.

"Now that's a different kind of magic," he muttered to himself, then took up his post at the window. He could sense the changes in Lily, even from here, and when he took a peek at her soul (or whatever it was), he couldn't help but notice that the whole structure looked like a nesting doll. Crimson arcs of energy were layered around obsidian gems that hovered around the succubus. At her center, a tiny silver flame flickered quietly, the crimson light folded around it protectively like a mother bird's wings.

Interesting.

He looked back out the window and sighed. The only thing left was for him to wait and see what happened next.

As Mike and the others ran through the fireplace, Grýla hurled herself forward with a speed Freyja had never seen. Sending out a blast of cold air, the goddess extinguished the flames behind her and sidestepped the oncoming monster, summoning a two-foot-tall wall of ice for Grýla to trip over.

When the giantess stumbled over the small wall, a casual twitch of Freyja's fingers sent the wall smashing into her.

"This won't take long," Freyja muttered, the air around her swirling. Snow blew in through the front door of the workshop, collecting into a massive spear made of ice that hovered over her shoulder. She could feel the weight of it in the back of her mind as bands of golden light wrapped around the back of the icicle.

Grýla laughed as she extricated herself from the hearth. She had cracked several bricks on the way in.

"Do you think I'm afraid of little Jack Frost?" The giantess shoved bricks away from her. "You are no longer Queen of the North, for stone is stronger than ice."

The golden bands of light tightened around the twelve-foot-long icicle, strengthening its structure to survive the sudden acceleration as Freyja launched it forward. Grýla's eyes went wide as it penetrated her torso, pinning her to the back wall. The light faded from Grýla's eyes, and her whole body slumped in place.

Freyja held up a hand, palm facing Grýla. A thin stream of golden light fled the giant's corpse and wrapped itself around Freyja's fingers before vanishing into her body.

"What the heck?" Freyja examined her hand, then stared at Grýla. The amount of divinity she had pulled out of the giant was almost trivial, far less than what had been taken from her before.

Up above, the roof creaked, and she heard a growl as the Yule Cat pressed its face against the glass. It moved away and shattered the window with a massive paw.

Freyja leaped to one side, the wind carrying her out of reach as the cat's paw smacked around, trying to find her. She summoned an ice shield and raised it in time to block a claw that was nearly a foot long.

Up above, one of the skylights was heavily fractured. She rode the wind upward, using the shield to smash through the glass safely and ride farther into the sky.

Down below, the Yule Cat turned its gaze up at her. Letting out a terrible hiss, it leaped up in an attempt to catch her, but she dodged away at the last moment. Spears of ice formed around her, and she directed them to fall toward the Yule Cat, driving the foul beast away as it ran for safety.

"Coward," she muttered, then gazed out over the North Pole. Though it was the same village she had known for over a century, something had changed. Shadows now hung from buildings as if made from fabric, and colors had been bleached from the city. Down below, creatures made of ice and snow lurked in packs, but they weren't alone. On occasion, she would see a shadow briefly manifest a form and crawl, walk, or slither across the main street.

"Gods," she whispered. She had seen such a phenomenon before, shortly before the fall of Asgard. The cracks in reality had become visible, allowing the void to leak through. Though the shadow creatures would be harmless for now, they would soon be able to manifest and interact with this realm without any issues.

Her senses buzzed, and she looked down in time to dodge a massive boulder that had been hurled in her direction. She used her shield to help deflect the attack, but the collision was enough to knock her out of the air current she had been riding.

Tumbling through the air, she showered the area where the attack had come from with hail the size of bowling balls. Dark shadows shifted below, revealing dozens of Yuletide Lads crawling across the ground like vermin.

"Which one of you threw that?" she demanded, landing in a crouch in the middle of the street. She didn't think the Yule Lads had the strength necessary for such a feat, but Grýla had been seriously lacking in divinity. It was entirely possible she had shared it with her children.

In response, another boulder rocketed out of a nearby alley. Freyja dodged this one readily enough but was caught by a massive rock from a different direction. This one slammed her through a candy-cane light pole that shattered, the air filling with the smell of peppermint. Groaning, she raised her shield in time to block the attack of a large figure who leaped off a nearby roof.

"Hello, food." Grýla opened her mouth and tried to take a bite of Freyja's face, but the goddess pushed the giant away.

"I killed you!" she cried, then braced her foot against Grýla's fat gut and shoved. The giantess grunted, then sailed through the air and vanished into the shadows.

All around Freyja, the town erupted with laughter. It was Grýla's voice, magnified dozens of times. The shadows danced along in staccato fashion, moving closer to Freyja as if trying to touch her. The goddess scrambled to her feet and jumped, commanding the wind to take her into the sky once more.

A massive paw batted her out of the sky, slamming her into a snowdrift so hard that it exploded. Freyja rolled across the cold cobblestone road, summoning a sphere of golden light to protect her from the next attack. The Yule Cat smacked her again, sending her bouncing down the main street like a giant hamster ball.

Freyja held tight, trying to guide her journey as the giant cat chased after her. She summoned massive pillars of ice for her to bounce off of, hoping to get enough distance from the cat so she could release the shield and either flee or counterattack. The Yule Cat was fast, however, despite its giant size. It could turn into a ball of light to chase her, a fact that frustrated her to no end.

After getting smacked around the North Pole for several minutes, she managed to trip up the Yule Cat by summoning a series of ice pillars that grew taller every few feet. She rolled harmlessly between them as the Yule Cat got stuck and had to climb upward to escape.

Freyja released the magical shield and fled into a nearby building. When she looked out the window, she saw the Yule Cat fighting to get through the pillars, so Freyja summoned even more, pinning the feline in place.

In the sky above, a dark figure briefly blocked out the northern lights. It was the Krampus, cackling madly as his demented reindeer burst away from his makeshift sled like shooting stars and headed toward her. The Krampus leaped off the falling sled and disappeared, his vehicle crashing into a nearby structure with a loud bang.

"Shit." Freyja ran through the building, which was housing for the elves. Abandoned presents and toys were scattered everywhere, and she nearly tripped over a wooden horse. When she made it to the back door, she shoved it open so hard that the hinges creaked.

"You're all alone, Jack." Another Grýla stood on a small hill overlooking the building. A pair of distorted reindeer emerged from nearby, snorting wildly and raking their electric antlers through the air. Up above, the Yule Cat leaned over the top of the building and leered down at Freyja.

Freyja stared at Grýla, her thoughts whirring. Somehow, the giantess was commanding an army of herself.

Well, two could play this game. Curling her fingers up, Freyja sent her mind into the ether, touching the faraway fields of Fólkvangr with her mind for the first time in over a century. She felt them there, the minds of thousands of men and women who had fallen in battle, suddenly restless in their eternal slumber.

"I'm never alone," she whispered, calling to the fallen dead. She wasn't at full strength, not yet, but the shades of the fallen stepped from the darkness around her, ready to defend their queen. There were maybe two dozen of them, weapons held ready.

"What an interesting trick." Grýla laughed heartily and stuck her hand in the snow, then ripped free a massive rock. "Tell me, Jack. Can I eat them?"

"My name is Freyja," she declared, summoning armor made of ice and snow. As a winged helmet settled across her brow, she drew a blade made of frost and pointed it at Grýla. Freyja's soldiers all readied their weapons, their spectral forms flickering in the light. "And the only thing you'll taste tonight is my blade."

Freyja and her soldiers charged forward.

Yuki stepped out into the cold, pulling the door shut behind her. It didn't take long before something leaped out of a nearby snowdrift, all teeth and fangs. She summoned a massive spike of ice from the ground beneath the snow tiger, spearing it in place. It snarled and tried to catch her with its claws but was forced to tear itself apart to reach her.

She dodged to one side as an eight-foot-tall bear jumped down from the roof, then danced away when the creature shattered and reassembled itself, golden light holding the thing together like magic glue.

"Yeah, I know that feeling." She summoned stone pillars this time, forcing the bear into an earthen prison. It growled as it squeezed between the bars, its body bursting and then re-forming on the other side of its cage. Pain ripped through her stomach, and she groaned as she leaped away from the bear.

"Ugh, shit." She gasped in agony, her hands briefly igniting with golden flames. It was divinity, and her body had absorbed so much of it from her sexual encounter with Mike and Freyja that her body was now breaking down. She hadn't known for sure until just before passing through the fireplace when the weird cramp in her stomach hadn't gone away. There wasn't going to be time for Mike to soul weave it in, or whatever the fuck he wanted to call it.

She wanted to be angry. So many years of pain had finally moved aside to allow her to pursue happiness, but it wasn't to be. The pressure building up inside her body had spread through her entire abdomen, and golden lines of power radiated down her thighs.

"Fuck." She slapped away another monster made of ice, then brought her claws down on its face. A snow python fell off a nearby roof and wrapped around her, but she shape-shifted into a fox and popped free of its muscular embrace.

She wondered how much time she had left but not for her own sake. The moment she fell, these creatures would descend on the house. She had known the moment the fire had gone out that Mrs. Claus was gone. The magic of the home had diminished to embers, turning their refuge into a trap.

With a growl, she summoned a ball of fox fire and blew a

hole in the python's head. It fell over, spasming so hard that it smacked its body into Santa's home. More ice and snow slid free of the roof, and Yuki realized she needed to lure the frozen creatures away.

Running down the street, a monstrous snowman appeared from around a large gingerbread house. She slid beneath its clawed fingers and sent several spikes of ice and stone through its body, causing its head to fall free and shatter on the ground. For just a moment, she saw it—a swirling mass of golden light, like a tiny star.

"Fuck it," she muttered, then moved to the light and inhaled it, pulling it into her body. There was pain as it heated her from within, but the snowman's shifting form crumbled and went still. If it was going to kill her anyway, she needed to make her death matter, to ensure that her friends survived.

To ensure that Mike survived.

Yuki let out a howl of rage, bringing the creatures of the North to her. The bear from before found her outside the bakery, and she tore a hole through it, seeking out the golden light within. A massive eagle tackled her from above, but her fox fire melted enough of its face off to reveal the golden light tucked away in its icy skull. She inhaled this light too, and the creature turned to fine powder.

Yuki summoned a storm around her, one that slowed the creatures down so she could feed on the golden light inside them. Her body felt like a massive pressure cooker as the divinity ran rampant through her, but she bore the pain in silence.

It was during her fight that a dark figure appeared between two buildings, lurching forward with distended limbs. Yuki turned to face the threat, her hands now blazing with golden light.

"Hello, food." Grýla stepped forward from the darkness, her skin hanging loose from her face. "It hurts, doesn't it?"

"What the hell?" Had Freyja lost? Or had Grýla run from her?

"I see you've learned the secret." To illustrate her point, Grýla dodged an attack from a snow tiger and shoved her arms down its throat, then pulled out a ball of golden light. "If you eat it, you can make it yours."

Yuki growled at the giantess. "Is that what you did to Freyja?"

"Who?" Grýla popped the light into her mouth and licked her lips, then groaned in agony. She leaned forward, pressing her hands into the snow. Golden light raced along her arms and into the ground. There was the sound of shifting rocks and soil, and another version of Grýla pulled herself free. This one, remarkably, was even uglier than the original, her skin hanging off her like a loose sweater.

"Holy shit." Yuki stared in terror as the new Grýla turned to face her.

"That's right, food." Uglier Grýla grinned. "My body couldn't contain it, so I did what I've always done. I made a new body."

"Only this one isn't the brood of my idiot husband." Slack-faced Grýla grinned, revealing broken teeth. "I may even eat that asshole when I'm done with you."

"Whatever. I can take two of you. Three of you. All of you!" She summoned her magic and created a swirling mass of ice that circled her. "I hope you're both hungry, because I'm about to feed you an ass whooping!"

The Grýlas charged toward her, their speed unexpected. Yuki dodged the first one and smashed an ice boulder into the face of the uglier one. The ice shattered, revealing that this one was unharmed other than a bloody nose.

A third Grýla emerged from the swirling snow and caught Yuki with a punch that crumpled her to the ground. She felt her magic surge through her whole body, the divinity threatening to break free and blow her apart.

"Not yet," she cried, clenching her fists. "Please, last me just a little bit longer!" She no longer cared if she died. All she wanted was to stop these ugly bitches before they found their way to Mike.

Rising to her feet, the blow she landed on Grýla's jaw cracked her knuckles, maybe even broke one; she didn't care. Magic flared along her forearm and blasted into the giant's face, sending her sprawling onto the ground. A long arm grabbed her from behind, and she bit down on it hard enough to break Grýla's gritty skin. The giant didn't react, and Yuki was taken back to the ground, long fingers pinning her forehead to the ice.

"Get the fuck off of me." Divinity roared through her body now as she summoned massive chunks of ice that barreled into Grýla, smashing her attacker into a nearby building. She stumbled to her feet, her veins on fire as another Grýla showed up.

"How many of you bitches are there?" This new Grýla had short arms like a tyrannosaurus and a lazy eye that looked off to the side. When she lunged at Yuki, the kitsune summoned several stalagmites beneath Grýla's feet, but the giantess was unfazed. The stone shattered under her feet, and she threw herself on Yuki, her tiny hands scrambling for purchase.

"I am a creature of stone, food!" Despite having T. rex hands, this Grýla's punches were brutal. Another Grýla grabbed Yuki from behind and pulled her hands behind her back. The blows rained down from every direction, and Yuki cried out in pain as a pair of teeth pierced her leg.

The divinity burned through her pores, and she screamed, releasing a wave of golden light that blew Grýla's doppelgängers off her. The stunned giants tumbled away, crashing into the buildings.

Yuki gasped for air, fighting her way back to her feet. Her skin was glowing from the inside, and her robes were stained with blood. Her body was breaking down, unable to contain the divinity any longer.

"And now you see why I did what I did." One of the Grýlas crawled from the ruins of a nearby building with a large lump on her forehead. "That golden light made me feel so powerful, as if the earth beneath my feet was mine to command."

"But it was too much." Another Grýla forced her way through an opening in a broken wall. The bricks tumbled to the ground at her feet. "So I found a way around it."

"I made myself a new body." This Grýla's face was tilted to one side in her skull. "And when that wasn't enough, I made another, then another."

"And then we hunted." A Grýla on a nearby roof hopped down, landing on a pair of enormous feet. "We hunted the ice creatures for their golden light. Why raise an army when we can be our own army?"

"It's called survival of the fittest." This Grýla had an oversize head that lolled to one side. "Some of us are survivors, while the rest of you are food that hasn't been chewed yet."

Yuki grunted and took a step back. She stumbled, tripping over her own robes and falling on the ground. A couple of tarot cards fell from her sleeve, and her copy of *Alice in Wonderland* landed in the snow facedown, the pages open wide to reveal the cover.

"There can only be one Queen of the North Pole." This came from three Grýlas at once. The golden light coming from Yuki cast a radiant glow on her surroundings, properly illuminating the cover of her book.

She saw that she was surrounded. Golden cracks formed along the skin of her body, with the fire burning deep into her bones. The icy winds of the arctic swirled around her, the eddies so powerful that they lifted brick and mortar from nearby buildings and cast them away. The Grýlas all hunkered down, unable to continue forward through the ice and snow.

So this is it, then. There wasn't much else to think about as her world went white. The storm carried *Alice in Wonderland* into her hands, but she could no longer feel its pages. There was a flash of light, and then…

"Hey, you." A pair of fingers appeared over the top of the pages, pushing the book out of the way. It was Emily, holding a cup of tea. "I take it you're enjoying the story?"

"It's unlike anything I've ever read before." Yuki closed the book and held it to her chest. "Maybe it's silly, but it feels so empowering. This little girl is confronted by a world that doesn't make any sense, yet she makes it work."

"It's a little like you, in that regard." Emily handed over the tea. "You're in a new world yourself. I wouldn't classify you as helpless though."

"Maybe not." Yuki sipped at the tea, the taste of it long forgotten. This was a memory, just one of millions flitting before her eyes in her final moments. It was an experience she had hoped to avoid for a very long time, but she was sure that was true for everyone.

"What's your favorite part so far?" Emily squeezed in next to Yuki and laid her head on the kitsune's shoulder.

Yuki said nothing, willing the memory to pass. After all, with so many to choose from, why this one? Why not the last few days with Mike, or even something fun from her childhood? There were so many things she would rather go through than see her former lover one last time.

Had the experience been the same way for Velvet? What had her regrets been like? Or maybe her passing had been peaceful instead. Perhaps the Universe only chose to be cruel on occasion.

At the thought of Velvet, she pictured Mike, and he appeared before her, resting on the windowsill with his knees pulled to his chin. He had only known the arachne for a few days, and her death had nearly broken him. Would Yuki's own death do the same, pushing him over the edge into madness?

"You made me a promise," Mike said. "If I ever lose control, you would be there to stop me."

"Mike, I…" She looked at Emily, who took no notice of the man

who would one day take her place in Yuki's heart. "I don't know if I can. I'm dying. All this, it's just my brain going through the motions."

He just stared at her for several seconds, his eyes glowing like fireflies. Emily was frozen in place, as if waiting for the proper response.

"So what is your favorite line?" he asked, breaking the silence. "I'm curious."

Yuki contemplated Mike for several moments, then allowed the memory to continue. "My favorite is the one about believing in the impossible. The six impossible things before breakfast quote," she answered, her eyes turning toward Emily.

"And have you?" Emily asked. "Believed six impossible things before breakfast?"

"Well, if we aren't counting this as breakfast"—she held up the tea—"then perhaps. Let's see. There's a beautiful woman who loves me despite my faults."

"That's one." Emily grinned.

"We use magic trees to jump across the globe." Yuki held up a second finger. "Oh, and I get to live in a magical house."

"That's three, but I don't know if any of these count." Emily tousled Yuki's hair, then rubbed at the soft spot between her ears. "You're just stating facts, not beliefs."

"Well, here's a fact for you. When I finish my tea, I'm going to—" The memory paused once more as Yuki's attention wandered over to Mike. Those firefly eyes of his flickered wildly.

"I think it's a wonderful quote," he said. "It's hopeful."

"Yes, but…hmm." She squeezed herself away from Emily, who was now motionless. "I don't know that I've ever truly believed in anything until I met you. Well, not right away, but…you grew on me."

"That's very kind of you to say," he replied. The room was starting to dim now, Yuki's mind falling apart. Emily had already faded from view.

"Wait," Yuki cried. "I have something to tell you before you go."

Mike said nothing, his firefly eyes slowly becoming the sole illumination in the room.

"I believe that you can be forgiven, as long as you put in the work. And even if you can't, then maybe it's possible to forgive yourself."

"That's one." He held up a finger.

"I also believe that it's possible to love again. That one seems so impossible, but it's true. Because I love you, Mike. I love everyone I live with, but I love you most of all."

"Two." He held up another finger. The room flickered, the furniture melting into the darkness.

"I believe in you. Maybe that sounds silly, but I know you'll be okay once I'm…I'm…" She couldn't bear to say the words out loud, not while he sat there contemplating her. "You're going to do great things, even without me."

"Maybe." He held up a third finger. "You're halfway there. What else do you have for me?"

"I believe in…in…" She felt it now, deep in her chest. It was a rumbling sensation that made her entire body buzz. Was the divinity finally pulling her apart?

It was ironic that what would finally do her in was a substance that her body could have contained someday. In a few hundred years, she probably could have absorbed most of the golden light Freyja had lost without blinking an eye.

Wait. There was something there to cling to…yes!

"I believe in me," she told him, forcing that rumbling sensation into the ground at her feet. "I'm the same kitsune who once brought Death into the world using paint, paper, and a lot of magic over a little bit of time. I've come too far not to believe in who I am and see what I'm capable of."

Mike smiled and held up a fourth finger. Had the room gotten brighter?

"And I believe that I don't have to die here, not if I don't want to!" She held out her hands, the golden light coalescing in her fingertips. Instead of trying to contain it or cast it away, she dragged it through the air, smearing it across the corners of her mind like the paint she used for her cards. "Because though things may seem hopeless, this is what my body was made for! You yourself wove this power into me before, and it didn't

kill me then! The divinity killing me now is just magic I haven't found a use for!"

He held up a fifth finger. "This is your last one," he told her, his smile stretching wide like the Cheshire cat's as the golden light radiating from her body made the rest of him fade from view. "Make it a good one."

Yuki's eyes snapped open, and she commanded the ice and snow beneath her feet to carry her tarot cards back into her hands. As they swirled toward her en masse, dexterous fingers snatched the pair she required from the air and held them pinched between her fingers as she rose, the storm suddenly going still. Grýla in all her forms quickly recovered, charging at Yuki through the rubble.

"My name is Yuki Radley." She poured the golden light into the card in her left hand, the Moon. In her right hand, an equal amount of divinity poured into the Wheel of Fortune. "And I'm about to take a page out of my boyfriend's playbook and hope I get really lucky."

Before Grýla could reach her, she cast the Moon into the sky and slammed the Wheel of Fortune into the ground. The snow and ice melted away from her as lines of radiant power formed at her feet, then shot into the sky where an illusory moon had appeared. All the Grýlas were forced to shield their eyes as the divinity swirled around Yuki and connected with beams of light from the moon.

"I once thought I knew what it meant to believe in six impossible things before breakfast," Yuki shouted, the fiery magic tearing through her veins as her remaining tarot cards were vaporized by moonlight. "But do you know what it takes to be a true believer? Faith! Faith in those we love and in ourselves!"

"Food shouldn't talk this much!" one of the Grýlas replied.

"And I once swore I would lay my life down for a man, a good man, possibly the best one I've ever met. Do you know what? That is absolutely what I'm going to do!" She held her hands up to the moon, now so bright she couldn't look directly at it.

Take my years from me, she commanded. The moon obeyed.

All magic had a price, and the divinity burned away months, years, and then decades of her life span. It came with no experience, no new revelations about magic, but Yuki didn't care. What she needed now was to survive, to return to the man she loved. The Moon was capable of driving that change, of bringing out her inner fox.

The Wheel of Fortune was there to ensure she survived the process.

The golden light coalesced around her, swirling behind her body to form into a fourth tail. The fire raging inside her core was unquenchable, so she gritted her teeth and waited for the fifth tail to form as well.

The moon burst into a column of light, raining flecks of fragmented divinity onto the ground. Yuki ignored them, taking a deep breath into a body that had been altered. The fire in her veins was gone, replaced with the familiar sensation of her own magic.

"I already came up with five impossible things," she said, holding up a hand with outstretched fingers. Frost hovered in the air around it, her mind connecting with the ice and snow in a manner that felt like an extension of her body. She no longer simply commanded the cold—it obeyed her because it wanted to. "But I need one more."

The Grýlas howled, and they all charged at her. Yuki held up her other hand and extended her middle finger in defiance.

"I believe that you don't have to be cold-hearted to become one with the ice." She took a deep breath and exhaled a wave of frost that obscured her from view, then leaped away before she could be grabbed. Her features shifted, lines forming across her vision as power ripped through her body. She grew larger, transforming into a massive five-tailed fox demon roughly ten feet tall at the shoulder.

Yuki pounced, slamming one Grýla into the ground.

"Wha—" It was the cock-eyed Grýla, and her bad eye struggled to look straight up at Yuki as the fox demon snarled at her.

Looks like you're the one that just hasn't been chewed yet, Yuki said telepathically, then bit cock-eyed Grýla's head off and spat it out. Thin streamers of golden light clung to her muzzle, and she licked them away, power flooding her body as Grýla's crumbled to stone. The others cried out in rage, but the kitsune no longer feared them. For though they were many, they weren't able to believe in the impossible like she could.

The ice and snow rumbled in her presence as if eager to see her. She howled in excitement, then led her attackers away from Santa's home, golden flames lingering in her heavy paw prints. They gave chase, howling insults and flinging stones as she scaled a nearby building and jumped across the rooftops. The storm clung to her like a second skin, hindering visibility for her pursuers.

The Grýlas followed her in a winding path through the North Pole, and the farther she got from Santa's house, the stranger the buildings looked. It was like they had been slightly stretched and distorted, the limited light reflecting incorrectly off their surfaces. She felt a surge of magical energy up ahead. At first, she was going to head in a different direction, but the scent of magic was familiar.

Freyja!

Yuki ran toward the scent, vaulted over the top of a building, then barreled through a pair of Grýlas who turned to look at her in surprise. Dozens of Grýlas had cornered the goddess, who was hovering in the air and sending massive shards of ice out in every direction. Beneath Freyja, a group of spectral warriors were in the middle of fighting the Yule Cat, who howled in fury as it stamped out a warrior from another age. Nearby buildings had been toppled, and the

Grýlas were throwing chunks of stone the size of cars at the defenders.

Freyja glared at Yuki, raising a hand and sending a barrage of ice at the kitsune. With just a thought, Yuki redirected the attack, forcing the ice to spike outward into their attackers. Recognition and relief lit like a fire in Freyja's eyes as Yuki turned her back just long enough for the goddess to grab hold of her fur.

"Run!" Freyja cried. "Before the reindeer come back!"

Puzzled, Yuki looked over her shoulder long enough to watch five fiery bundles of light circle above the spirits. The twisted reindeer slammed down into the spirits, scattering them like bowling pins. They were like bottled lightning that had broken free, destroying spirits and Grýlas alike.

"The Krampus is here," Freyja shouted over Yuki's personal storm. "We have to get back to Mike!"

What about Grýla? asked Yuki.

"If the Krampus beats Mike, this is all over!" Freyja turned around on Yuki's back and sent out rays of golden light. One of them vaporized a Grýla with extra-long legs. Divinity shot through the air and coalesced around Freyja's arms. "There are too many of them but only one of him!"

Yuki slid to a stop, then bolted down a narrow alleyway. The shadows reached for her, fingers hooking in her fur just enough that she could feel them. Her heart was pounding in her chest as she turned back toward Santa's home, hoping she could get there in time. Her pursuers shrieked in fury as Yuki intensified the storm, blinding them with whirling snow.

Somehow, through the howling winds, she heard the ringing of silver bells from up above.

"ARE YOU OKAY?" LILY ASKED.

Mike turned to look at the succubus, rubbing his chest. It

was a sensation similar to heartburn, like someone had tried to pull his heart out through his sternum. He coughed a couple times, then let out a belch that tasted like copper.

"Yeah, I think so." The pain subsided as quickly as it had come. His magic cycled across his body, as if trying to chase down whatever had ailed him. That had been weird. "How is Holly?"

The elf had curled up on the side of the couch, hugging a pillow to her chest. He wasn't sure if she was asleep or just taking a moment.

Lily shrugged. "As good as can be expected. We talked for a bit. There's a lot for her to figure out. So what's going to happen once the Krampus gets here? You gonna hug it out with him?"

Mike smirked. "Not unless you do it first."

"Oh, I'll have something for him." Lily stood and paced the room, her tail swishing behind her. She paused at the door to the basement where the North Pole was. "But being real for a moment, don't let him through here, correct?"

"Yeah. If he gets down there, then all the bad stuff happens." Mike didn't like how exposed he felt, and he was more than a little worried that Yuki had vanished. And what was taking Freyja so long? "Once he's here, I just need some time to examine his soul. I think I can fold the Krampus back inside and let Santa come back out."

A shrieking sound filled the air, much like a jet coming in for a landing. There was a loud thud from outside, followed by cackling. Holly looked up from her pillow, her features pale.

"Holly. Hide." Mike watched as the elf made a run for it, disappearing into the house. Above, the roof creaked as someone walked across it, occasionally stomping their feet.

"Yeah, yeah, you fucker. We hear you." Mike moved closer to the basement door and summoned his magic. It swirled through his body, eager to obey his commands.

Snow and ice slid off the roof, and something heavy

landed outside the front door. Mike half expected the Krampus to knock but was unsurprised when a massive foot kicked the door off its hinges, sending it crashing across the floor.

The Krampus walked into the room, hunched over and cackling in glee. He rubbed his hands together, making Mike think of a massive fly contemplating the turd it was about to consume. Krampus licked his chapped lips and looked up to make eye contact with Mike.

"Daddy's home! And he is—" The Krampus was interrupted by the heavy wooden table that crashed into his face, knocking him to the ground. The furniture had collided with him so hard that it exploded, the doorway now filled with splinters.

Stunned, Mike turned his attention to Lily, who had thrown the table. Her arms had turned black and red from the elbow down, as if her body was made of molten rock. The red highlights in her hair had turned into flames that crawled across her body, flickering along the top of her helper hat.

"Nobody likes a diva," she said, then wrapped her tail around a nearby end table and flung it toward the Krampus. It smashed into him, but he raised an arm this time and took the impact with a chuckle.

"And who are you supposed to be?" he asked, his twisted features turning toward the succubus. "Because you're definitely on the naughty list."

Lily pointed to her hat. "I'm Santa's official helper, here to put the ho in his ho ho ho. Did the local mall fire you for eating meth or was it for biting children?" She splayed her hands wide and grinned. The humor in those lips did not extend to her eyes.

"You're so charming." The Krampus was ready for Lily's attack, dodging to the side as she lashed out with fingers that had become razor blades. The two of them danced around the room, slashing at each other while Mike kept away from them. He couldn't intervene directly, but it gave him time to inspect the Krampus's soul with his third eye or whatever he should call it.

It was a massive black fractal wrapped around golden gears of light. Just the sight of it shifting around made him nauseous, and an intense pain filled his sinuses. The Krampus turned to face him, his pulled features leering.

Gasping, Mike shut his eyes and looked away, the front of his face now wet from a sudden nosebleed.

"You dare to look into infinity?" The Krampus laughed. "Your simple mind can't handle—erk!"

Mike opened his eyes to see that Lily had climbed onto the Krampus's back and sunk her talons into his shoulders. The two of them wrestled like feral cats, breaking furniture in the process.

"Romeo, run!" Lily put the Krampus in a headlock, but the eldritch being warped in place, his whole body shifting until his arms were now around her shoulders. "I can't hold him, he—"

Lily cried out in agony as the Krampus wrapped his massive hands around her horns and pushed his thumbs into her forehead as if trying to halve an apple. Lily's tail whipped around, stabbing the Krampus numerous times to no avail.

Mike's first instinct was to run to her, to attack the Krampus, to do anything to pull him off her. But he knew that to do so would be suicide, as the Krampus was clearly stronger than Lily.

"So what'll it be, Caretaker?" The Krampus howled with glee as he lifted Lily in the air, her legs kicking. "Once I crack this chestnut open, I'm going through that door. The question is, Will you still be in my way?"

Mike took a deep breath, his magic revving up inside him. His plan to swap the Krampus for Santa had been grounded in logic, but just looking at their combined soul had made him sick. Trying again right now would be a terrible idea. He needed more time to think, or perhaps a way to distract the Krampus long enough that he could try again.

He had a flash of insight. The plan was terrible, disgusting, and absolutely unexpected. It was perfect.

"I think," he began, a grin breaking across his face, "that you should have worn your white pants." Mike held out his hands and willed his magic to emerge and do the one thing it was best at.

The Krampus lowered Lily, cocking his head to one side in puzzlement. "What is that supposed to—"

Purple-and-blue electricity surged out of Mike's hand, interspersed with golden beams of radiance, then crossed the room as a bolt of lightning. It connected with the Krampus, transferring sexual energy in quantities Mike himself feared. Using his newfound command of magic, he grabbed the stray streamers that peeled off the Krampus and formed them into tight loops that connected back to Santa's evil half. The magic that left the demon now cycled right back into him.

The Krampus groaned and dropped Lily, who rolled away. Clutching his abdomen, the demon made a gasping sound and came in his pants.

"What manner of—" the Krampus gasped, then fell to his knees as a second orgasm hit. The feedback loop intensified, the spirals tightening around his body. The floor beneath the Krampus was already wet and sticky, as if someone had spilled a gallon of paint.

"That's right, asshole." Mike could feel his strength waning as the magic left him. Without being part of the process, he wasn't refueling his own reserves, and he had other things to do. "You either die the villain or live long enough to become a spooge fountain."

Lily actually laughed so hard that she snorted.

"You fool, I, urgh..." The Krampus was crawling toward them now, gasping for air, then slipped in his own cum and fell facedown on the floor. He landed with a splat, sticky strands hanging from his body. The whole room smelled like burned marshmallow.

"Mrs. Claus wasn't kidding about the mess," Mike muttered. "Lily, this won't last long. Hold him down for me!"

The succubus obliged, her body now covered in a hazmat suit. Her tail wrapped around the Krampus's throat as she pinned him from behind. He groaned again, his hips lifting briefly as he sprayed more fluid all over the floor. Lily rolled him onto his back, a massive cock springing free of his waistband.

"Damn you, Caretak—blargh!"

Lily had grabbed the Krampus by the shaft, pointing his dick at his face. The stimulation had been enough to trigger a spray of cum that hit him right in the mouth.

Doing his best to breathe through his mouth and avoid the smell, Mike once again took a look at the Krampus's soul. That twisted black fractal was now pulsing weakly as the light inside flitted about, pushing outward against its prison. Mike sent tendrils of light along its length, trying to pry open the gap. His forehead beaded with sweat as the minutes passed, the golden light getting closer to escaping.

A guttural growl came from the Krampus, and he tilted his face backward so far that his neck cracked, allowing him to look at Mike. "I regret the day I pulled you from the wreckage of your mother's car, Caretaker!"

Mike's attention wavered just enough that he almost lost track of what he was doing. It was clear that the revelation was intended to be a distraction, to break Mike's concentration. If he hadn't already known, it would have worked. A ripple went through the Krampus's soul, one Mike interpreted as impending triumph.

"I bet you do," he replied nonchalantly, his eyes flicking back to the maelstrom around the Krampus. From the edge of his vision, he could see bafflement on the demon's face.

"I mean it, Caretaker. I'm the one who saved you from death!"

"Oh, I know." Mike turned his attention to the whirling loops of sex magic. They were shrinking down, so he fed them a little more juice to keep them in motion. "I really appreciate it, thank you."

"You fool, I…" The demon's hips lifted, and he squirted cum so hard that it hit some of the lower beams of Santa's home.

"Just don't do that in a tree," Mike muttered. "They don't like it."

Between moans, the Krampus took a swing at Lily, then slipped when he tried to get up. The floor, the furniture, and some of the pillars were now slick with jizz. "You were never supposed to be Caretaker, did you know that? Someone else would be in your shoes right now if not—urgh!"

Lily managed to make the Krampus blow a load into his own face again, but the amount was considerably reduced. Thick white strands hung from his black beard, and he was frantically wiping one of his eyes.

"Uh, Romeo?" Lily looked up at him with dread. "He's about out of the Christmas spirit, if you know what I mean."

"Make him drink some eggnog or something." Mike pulled even harder, trying to free that ball of golden light. It shifted forward, the room filling with the sound of Christmas music. Cracks of light formed along the Krampus's skin, and the darkness burned away like ash.

The Krampus hissed, his limbs deforming beneath him until he lifted free of the ground. He moved toward Mike like an eerie crab, grunting and cackling all the way.

"Mike!" Lily stabbed her tail into the floor, anchoring the Krampus in place. "I can't hold him much longer!"

"Almost…got it…" His vision was going dark around the edges, the shadows punctuated by flickers of gold. He tensed up his whole body and let out a scream, forcing the dark fractal apart until the light within was able to squeeze itself free.

There was a concussive blast of energy, the force shoving Mike backward into the door. He slid to the ground, clutching his head in agony. Squeezing his eyes shut, all he could hear was the slamming of his heart in his chest.

When he opened his eyes, he expected to see Santa or some version of him lying on the floor. Instead, it was a charred mass of flesh, smoldering in a pile of jizz.

"Wait, what?" He examined the creature's soul once more, half expecting to see that a transformation was taking place. Instead, he saw no soul at all. There was just a void where Santa and the Krampus had once been, the combined entity now gone.

"Oh fuck." He stared in shock. "I just fucking killed Santa."

"What?" Lily stood, her hazmat suit disappearing. She stared at the charred body in disbelief, then raised a hand to her head and gave the hat a tug. Frowning, she released her hold on the fuzzy rim.

"Still stuck," she told him. "So he isn't dead."

"Then what are we looking at?" he asked, then flinched when the Krampus's body shifted, limbs cracking. One by one, the Krampus flexed his limbs, then he lifted himself. His charred face twisted around, ash falling on the floor as his dark eyes contemplated Mike.

"Oh shit." Mike muttered, realizing he still couldn't see the Krampus's soul. Instead, it was a literal void of information, a dark mass his gaze couldn't penetrate.

The mad cackle that came from the Krampus made every hair on Mike's neck stand on end. His whole body became numb as his danger sense kicked in.

"I. AM. FREE!" The Krampus yelled as an extra pair of arms burst from his torso. He moved toward Mike, but Lily's tail wrapped around one of his ankles to stop him. The

Krampus whipped around, grabbed Lily by the throat with one hand, and captured her arms and one of her legs with the other three.

"Make a wish," he hissed, then pulled. Lily let out a scream as she exploded into a cloud of sulfur and brimstone, her helper's hat falling to the floor. Mike, realizing he had just royally fucked up, did the only thing he could think of.

He opened up the door to the basement and fled for his life.

CHRISTMAS CHAOS

Kisa watched from the corner of Leppalúði's cave as the elves returned from their task. The giant was engrossed in another episode of *Friends* so wasn't paying any attention when the elves entered from the warehouse cave. They crossed the living quarters, and one of them dropped a bright-pink blanket onto the floor near where she was hiding.

Obeying orders, the elves continued on their way and disappeared into the holding chamber. Kisa picked up the blanket and wrapped it around her shoulders, then made sure her tail wasn't sticking out. Satisfied that her height would complete the illusion, she moved across the room toward the tunnel to the warehouse and pulled the blanket over her head like a hood.

"Hello?" she called, raising her voice an octave in an attempt to sound like a child.

Leppalúði stood so fast he broke his couch. His eyes were wide in shock at Kisa's sudden appearance, and a string of drool formed along his slack lower lip.

"A monster!" Kisa let out a shriek and ran for the exit. Behind her, she could hear Leppalúði running as fast as he could, but Kisa was faster. She sprinted up the tunnel and toward the elevator, but her destination was actually the stairs. Leppalúði was huffing and puffing by the time he made it to the elevator, but Kisa was already most of the way down. She was hoping he would take the elevator and buy her extra time.

In the warehouse, the spotlight was already on and focused on a distant pallet. There a similar pink blanket was tucked between a pair of boxes, as if a child was hiding between them. It looked like the elves had gotten everything set up as she had asked. The only reason she hadn't helped was because she wanted to keep her eyes on the giant.

Kisa ducked out of sight from the stairs and tossed her blanket into a dark corner. Leppalúði, who had decided on the stairs and had gotten impatient, jumped over the railing and slammed into the floor. His long fingernails scratched grooves into the stone as he rose to his full height.

"Gonna rip, gonna tear," he muttered, then sniffed at the air. "I smell you, morsel!"

As planned, a toy baby started to cry. Kisa had asked the elves to plant one there and make sure the batteries worked. She didn't know if it was motion activated or just cried at random. It honestly didn't matter, because it had come on when she needed it to.

Hearing the soft cry of a child, Leppalúði went absolutely still, his eyes focused on that small patch of pink out in the middle of the warehouse. He crouched and moved forward, ignoring all the warning signs that this was an obvious trap.

When he disappeared into the darkness, Kisa moved to the dais. She could see Leppalúði's vague silhouette on occasion. It was clear the giant thought he was being sneaky. The pallet was set fairly far out, so she had to wait a bit to make certain he took the bait.

Once Leppalúði stepped into the spotlight, Kisa tried to think of something witty to shout. However, time was of the essence, so she simply clicked off the light and started flipping the pages of the warehouse book back and forth.

Leppalúði howled in pain and fury as the warehouse shuffled itself. Kisa waited until he sounded very far away before shutting the book. Satisfied that he would be out of the way for a long time, she pulled just enough of the crystal out of her pocket to navigate back to the stairs and ascended. Behind her, a distant voice cried out in anger. By the time she made it up the stairs, Leppalúði had gone silent, no longer a threat.

Once back in the holding chamber, she informed her elves that the Krampus needed to move all the children right away to the safest place they could find. This was the part of her plan she was the most worried about. If the elves had any sort of magical connection to the Krampus, they would know immediately that she was full of shit.

The elves, to her surprise, simply moved to the holding pen with the kids and picked a couple up before setting them back down. They stared at her for several moments before she finally responded.

"Is there a problem?" she asked.

There was a long moment of silence, then someone spoke from deep inside the holding cells.

"'Safety' is a relative term," an elf said, pushing his way through the huddled masses. By the time the speaker got to the edge of the cage, Kisa recognized him as Alabaster.

"You're alive!" Kisa put her hands on the bars.

"So are you." He licked his lips, then rubbed at the dark circles under his eyes. "I'm honestly surprised to see you're still around."

"You're not under the Krampus's influence?" She moved toward the door of the cage and fiddled with the locking mechanism.

"Not quite. I was created before Nicholas died and the Krampus was born." He opened his mouth to reveal sharp teeth. "So his legacy does not run in my blood. But he sure tried. When he couldn't convert me, he handed me off to Leppalúði and said I could be eaten."

"How did you escape?" she asked.

Alabaster sighed. "I slipped free of my chains and hid. That idiot couldn't count, so he ate someone else in my stead. It's…not something I'm proud of."

Kisa put her hand on the elf's shoulder. "That's on him, not you. I need your help. I trapped Leppalúði in the warehouse and want the elves to move the children to a safer location."

Alabaster scowled. "Honestly, I don't know that anywhere in the North Pole is safe anymore. The children are time locked, so they can't be harmed anyway."

"But still, what if they wake up? What's to stop Leppalúði or Grýla from taking the kids away and stashing them where we can't find them?"

When Alabaster shrugged, Kisa grabbed him by his overalls and shook him. The elf let out a squeak and swatted her hands away.

"Fine, fine, I get it. Get your hands off of me!" He pushed her but only succeeded in falling backward himself. "Damned cat."

"I'm doing this with or without your help," Kisa declared, baring her teeth. "But I want you to know that if you don't, then you were wrong before, about being under the Krampus's influence. Doing nothing when you had the chance to step up is just as bad as helping him."

"Ugh, you're almost as much trouble as that blasted goblin," Alabaster muttered, then chuckled dryly. "But you're right. We can at least take the children somewhere else. This will help the elves too. That asshole won't be able to snack on them if he can't find them."

Kisa grimaced at the reminder of Grýla eating the elves. She wondered how many of Alabaster's brethren had been eaten right in front of him. There was a weariness in his eyes she didn't like, but she couldn't worry about his future mental health right now.

"Are there any others like you?" she asked. "With their minds still intact?"

He shook his head. "Not that I'm aware of. The Krampus was in a hurry because of something you all did topside. I think that's the only reason I'm here. Come. Let's at least free everyone. They're amicable to whatever orders you give them as long as you…well, you know."

Kisa nodded in understanding. "Where are we heading?"

Alabaster screwed up his face for a moment. "We do have a train station near the edge of the North Pole. Only used it for a couple of years, so the building is abandoned now. We could store the kids inside the train, and the elves can have the station."

"A train station, seriously?"

Alabaster shrugged. "If you think that's strange, you should see what Mrs. Claus starts wearing this time of year."

What a weird little dude, Kisa thought, then turned to a nearby elf. "Okay, new orders from the Krampus. The giants are no longer to be trusted, and the children are no longer safe in this location. We are to move them quickly and quietly to the train station. Please repeat these orders verbatim to the elves nearest you before acting. Do you understand?"

The elf, a young woman with a candy-cane button pinned to her dress, nodded and turned to face the elf behind her. In a monotonous voice, she repeated the instructions to a pair of elves who then repeated the process. The holding pens became a cacophony of sound as the elves gave their orders and then acted on them.

It was like watching an ant colony. The elves moved to where the time-locked children were kept, picked them up, and began marching toward the open mouth of the cave.

"If your name is associated with cookies, you are to take the lead and warn the line of danger," Alabaster shouted. A group of about fifteen elves broke away from where the children were being held and moved ahead of the others. "We're going to take the long route, out by the Yeti's hut!"

"You guys have a Yeti? Why can't we get him to help?"

Alabaster shook his head. "Santa kicked him out decades ago because his behavior was abominable. Guy was a real dick to everyone."

"Are you fucking with me?" Kisa asked, which caused a couple elves to flinch and drop their children. She covered her mouth and scowled at Alabaster.

"I kid you not," he told her, then moved toward the front of the line. The elves who had dropped their kids picked them back up and continued. Kisa watched them trudge toward the exit, her thoughts silently whirring. The elves had barely acknowledged being eaten, but a swear was enough to get through to them. What did that even mean?

Maybe they weren't as far gone as she feared. Though they looked as if all the color had been sucked out of them, maybe they could be brought back too. What was the opposite of swearing?

"Leppalúði!" Grýla's powerful voice resonated throughout the cave, and Kisa turned her attention to one of the many openings in the earthen walls. A large hand appeared, thick fingers clutching tightly to the stone. With a heave, Grýla pulled her massive bulk into the central cavern, her eyes locked on the line of elves. Kisa was fairly positive the giant hadn't used to be this big.

"I need you to get your lazy ass topside! That stupid bitch Jack is…what is this?" she hissed, her gaze wandering across the elves. They ignored her, sticking to the task that had been assigned.

"Shit." Alabaster looked at Kisa, then the elves. "This is bad."

"*What is this?*" Grýla lurched forward and swatted the elves. Time-locked children scattered unharmed across the room, but the elves tumbled and fell, some of them going still.

"HEY!" Kisa stepped past Alabaster and stood on a rock to be better seen. "What the hell do you think you're doing, you rancor-lookin' piece of shit?"

Alabaster sprinted away from Kisa as fast as he could. Grýla paused, her head swinging slowly so she could focus on Kisa.

"What kind of food are you?" she asked, tapping her fat fingers on the floor. She was hunched over as if her spine could no longer support her massive bulk.

"The spicy kind." Kisa picked up a loose stone and threw it. It was a poor throw and missed Grýla entirely.

The giant shoved her fingers into the ground, the rock softening at her touch. She casually lifted a stone the size of Kisa's body and hurled it.

The cat girl felt the premonition way in advance and dodged not only the first rock but the unseen second one that followed. The large rocks shattered against the stone wall behind her, causing some of the glowing crystals overhead to crack and fall.

"Fast food," Grýla grunted. "I hate things that move fast."

Kisa bolted away from her current position as a hand made of stone tried to close around her ankles. She hopped and leaped across the cavern floor, hoping to lead Grýla somewhere else, but the giant wasn't budging. Instead, Grýla turned her attention back to the elves who were still carrying her food supply away.

"Shit," Kisa muttered. Clearly Grýla was much smarter than Leppalúði.

Grýla slammed a fist into the ground. Golden light zigzagged along the stone, and the line of elves froze in place as smaller stone hands grabbed their ankles.

"Snack for later," she declared, then shifted her bulk toward Kisa. "Leppalúði! What are you doing?"

"He ran off with some other giant bitch," Kisa yelled, trying to goad Grýla into action. "Said he was tired of sticking his dick in ugly!"

Grýla rolled her eyes dramatically. "He knows better. If he ever even attempted to leave, I'd eat his ass."

"That…doesn't sound like you think it does." Kisa picked up another rock and threw it. This one actually hit Grýla but didn't do any damage.

"Nuisance," Grýla declared, then lumbered over to an elf in a candy-cane onesie. She jabbed the elf in her belly, causing the poor thing to drop her child and double over in pain.

"Don't you dare," Kisa hissed through her teeth.

"You are little more than a pest," Grýla replied, then pinched the stone hand holding the elf in place. When it shattered, the giant grabbed the elf by the ankles. "And I'm oh so hungry."

Kisa dashed across the cavern so quickly that she ended up running on all fours. Grýla dropped the elf in surprise and raised her meaty fists to protect her face as Kisa leaped onto the giant's shoulders and clawed at her face.

"You leave them alone!" She batted at Grýla's head until the giant dropped her guard, revealing a bloodshot eye. Kisa jammed her thumb into it, pushing all her weight into the strike.

Grýla laughed. Kisa didn't understand why until she realized her finger felt like it was being jammed into a stone. She pressed the point of her claw into Grýla's pupil and was surprised when it didn't yield in the slightest.

"Stupid food," Grýla muttered. The giant snatched at Kisa as she tried to scramble away.

"Idiot!" Kisa yelled, but she was cursing herself. The giant had lured her into a trap of her own!

Every time Kisa started to get away, Grýla would manage to grab a leg or tail and pull her back in. Kisa was quick but not fast enough to evade the giant. Powerful hands clamped down on her waist, bringing her to Grýla's cavernous maw.

Kisa, in a blind panic, put her hands and feet on the giant's top and bottom lips in an attempt to keep from being eaten.

The cavern filled with the pinging sound of metal banging metal. The giant flinched, then shifted her bulk in the direction of the sound. Kisa was stunned to see a green figure standing by one of the pits, the one that had a vent directly to the furnace.

Standing with a red-and-white striped hammer in each hand was Tink. The goblin smacked the heads of the hammers together, the resounding clink echoing off the cavern walls. She was wearing a ridiculous Christmas outfit, which looked similar to some of the lingerie from Mrs. Claus's wardrobe.

"Stupid giant look like big bag of assholes," Tink declared, continuing to ping her hammers together. Kisa noticed that Grýla winced a little with each ear-piercing ring. "Bag of assholes with small brain."

"What is this? A booger?" Grýla, distracted by the metallic racket, lowered Kisa. "Are you a booger?"

"Tink is not booger, you'll see. Tink pound walking asshole into pile of rocks," the goblin declared, walking forward. She was covered in oil, soot, and a fine layer of glitter. The goggles on her head were already whirring as different lenses clicked into place. "Knock shit out of stupid giant, flush it all down toilet."

"Tink, run!" Kisa tried to pull herself free, but Grýla's grip was too tight. "Don't come any closer!"

Grýla licked her lips, then looked at Kisa. She opened her mouth and shoved Kisa's head into it.

There was a horrifying crack, and Grýla dropped Kisa on the ground. The giant was clutching at her eye and crying out in pain. Tink, who was running at full speed, shoved past Kisa and used her hammer to strike Grýla in the side of one of her knees.

"Move," Tink cried, then rolled to safety as Grýla's massive bulk tipped forward. Kisa gave the giant a wide berth and was horrified to see that one of Grýla's eyes had been puncture by the claw of a hammer.

"MY EYE!" Grýla cried just as Tink jumped on her back and struck her in the temple with her remaining hammer.

Shards of gravel sprayed the ground as the giant groaned and toppled over. Kisa could see the widening cracks in the knee Tink had struck.

The goblin yanked the hammer free of Grýla's eye and leaped away. Grýla tried to grab her but missed. Tink slid to a stop next to Kisa.

"Tink hear racket, sense kitty cat nearby." She twirled her hammers. "Tink always know where best friend is. See stupid fuck face, made of hard rock. All rock have flaw."

Kisa responded by hugging the goblin so hard she squeaked.

"Enough!" Tink growled. "No hugs during big trouble!" She shoved Kisa back as stone hands sprouted from the floor and grabbed at their feet.

Grýla was reduced to crawling, throwing rocks when she could. Tink managed to give Kisa a hammer, and the two of them took turns freeing trapped elves while the other dodged rocks. The giant shouted at them in frustration, unable to do more than pester them.

"Enough!" Grýla cried in frustration, then rolled onto her back and extended her hands to the ceiling. The glowing crystals above hummed as the ground trembled, and then chunks of stone fell free from the ceiling.

"No, stop!" Kisa cried.

Golden light filled the chamber as a spectral figure phased through the wall. Ribbons of red and green coalesced around the body of Christmas Present, who scowled at the giant.

"Hey!" Tink cried. "Big hole over there, straight to furnace!"

Christmas Present seemed to take this information in stride as she soared over the chamber and grabbed Grýla by the foot. With a grunt, she lifted the giant into the air and hovered over to the massive opening in the floor.

"Wait!" Tink cried, now staring at the hole. Her lenses flicked back and forth for several tense moments, then she gave the spirit a thumbs-up.

Christmas Present dropped Grýla into the hole. The giant screamed for several very long moments, and then a gout of flame burst from the furnace, licking at the ceiling. Tink cheered, then let out an oomph when Kisa hugged her from behind.

"You have no idea how happy I am to see you," she cried, tears flowing freely. Tink turned and hugged her back. Kisa sniffed, then made a face.

"Oh, Tink, you stink!" She eyed the goblin's outfit. "And what are you wearing?"

The goblin laughed.

"Tink old outfit catch on fire. Take break for new outfit, find cute one that almost fits! Work super hard again, fix vents for good. Tink big sweaty now," she announced, then lifted her arm and sniffed at her armpit.

"Maybe too sweaty," she added. "But furnace fixed! Santa owe Tink big."

"We all do," Christmas Present said, kneeling next to the two of them. "But for now, we need to get everyone to safety. The fighting on the surface is really bad. Do you know where the elves are heading?"

Kisa nodded, then held up her hammer and struck a pose. If Mike got to do shit like this, then so did she. "As a matter of fact, I do. Help me get them all free. We've got a train to catch."

Mike was perhaps twenty steps down the spiral staircase when he heard the wooden door above explode. Splinters showered him after bouncing off the walls, and he felt his magic surge deep inside him.

When his precognition triggered that danger was a breath away, he jumped forward, legs pinwheeling underneath him. Lightning crawled along his arms and legs, forming into thick tendrils that stabilized his rapid descent. At one point, he nearly spilled head over heels, but a pair of electric limbs sprouted from his waist and caught him before he could take a potentially lethal tumble.

"What's the matter, Caretaker?" The Krampus laughed from up above. "Have you finally run out of tricks?"

Mike didn't respond, his legs pumping as fast as he could move them. He was now taking the steps six or seven at a time, occasionally bouncing off the curved walls with his legs. His magic flowed through him, guiding his arms and legs as blue-and-gold lightning lit the way ahead of him. By the time he got to the bottom, he was breathing harder than he could ever remember and wondered if his lungs were about to burst. Spinning on his heels, he clenched his fists and opened his mouth so wide his jaw cracked.

The Krampus appeared on the stairs, his face fixed in a manic grin. That smile faltered when Mike unleashed a horrendous scream that shook dirt loose from the stones around them. The Krampus actually retreated, eyes and ears forming all along his body as he struggled to hold one shape.

The acoustics of the stairwell ensured that there was nowhere safe, so the Krampus reappeared and threw himself free. Once on the floor, he fought to rise, his limbs distorted.

Mike unleashed another banshee's cry, constantly backing up into Santa's old workshop. The Krampus was shouting something, but Mike couldn't hear it. His own ears were ringing, yet he didn't dare let up. He almost tripped a few times, but he managed to make it next to the North Pole.

He unleashed one more scream, then coughed into his hand. Blood spattered on his palms.

The Krampus rose, now standing nearly twelve feet tall.

"And now, Caretaker, you're out of tricks." The Krampus sneered, then snatched Mike's foot and yanked him into the air. "It's time to claim what is rightfully mine!"

"About that." Mike turned his attention to the North Pole. There was a tiny sliver of golden light at the very bottom, likely all that was left of Christmas. The light it cast threw ominous shadows all around the room, manifestations that danced. The moment the Krampus seized control, it would all be over. "I'm never out of tricks."

Mike concentrated electrical energy in his hands and sent it in a beam toward the North Pole.

"NO!" The Krampus dropped Mike and leaped forward just as Mike's magic made contact. Mike wasn't entirely certain how the rules for this sort of thing worked, but the magic was part of him. He concentrated his will on the North Pole, wrapping it around the cylindrical surface like a ribbon. The air sizzled like hot bacon in a pan, and then his magic popped out of existence, the room now quiet.

Silence reigned eternal, or at least it felt that way. The Krampus was frozen in midair, his body stretched tight as his muscles distorted in an effort to reach the Pole. Mike stood and brushed the dirt off his pants and coat, then frowned. His movements didn't make any noise whatsoever.

Of course they don't. A young boy came out from behind the North Pole. He wore a simple robe, as if he had stepped out of a fourteenth-century church service. He held an hourglass full of golden sand that cast out light like a lantern. The sand was flowing back and forth as if it couldn't decide where to go. There was more than just a passing resemblance to the Ghost of Christmas Past, but the child appeared to be human.

Not quite. The boy's lips didn't move, but it was definitely him speaking. Or thinking. Whatever.

"Who are you?" Mike asked.

This time, the boy's lips moved, but no sound came out. His lips blurred to prevent Mike from reading them.

"I'm sure you never get tired of that," Mike muttered. "Great game has its rules."

The boy shrugged, then walked over to the Krampus. He easily could have been a child on a trip to the museum, studying a dinosaur skeleton or a sculpture. There was just a hint of fascination, but the interest faded, and the boy looked at Mike now.

You are the one who broke my spirit. There was no anger or malice in the statement. Mike could see that the boy's pupils were so wide that they took up nearly his entire eyes.

"You're gonna have to be more specific. Are we talking Christmas Past, Present, or Future?"

Yes, the boy replied. *They are all the same entity, just at different frequencies.*

Mike wasn't quite sure how to parse that particular piece of information. He also noticed that the boy looked a bit older now and had the start of stubble on his chin. "Yeah, well…I guess I'm sorry about some of that."

No matter. The young man waved off Mike's apology. *These things happened quite some time ago and have yet to happen. It's hard to be angry when everything is in a state of superposition.*

Mike frowned. He wasn't even sure what that meant and worried that the explanation would be even worse.

"So I didn't necessarily want to do this, but I sort of took control of the North Pole, if you know what I mean." Mike jerked his thumb at the Krampus. "I think I accidentally killed the human part of him off, which means this place should be up for grabs."

It is. The man blinked at him and scratched his chin. The robes had stretched to accommodate his new height.

"Great, so can I institute a 'No Assholes' rule? Boot this guy out? Make him swim around in the Arctic Ocean until he gets tired and sinks?"

If you were the one in charge, perhaps. The man moved to the North Pole and stared at the golden light at the bottom. *Keep in mind that if you had taken over, this last piece of belief would have vanished already. The holiday known as Christmas would belong to you. So you have claimed nothing.*

"But I thought…didn't I take over? I thought that's why we're talking?" Mike made a face and moved next to the North Pole. He slapped his hand on the surface. "Finders, keep—"

A wave of light blasted him off his feet and sent him sprawling. The impact hurt his pride more than anything else. When he looked up, the middle-aged man stared at him in amusement.

"What gives?" he asked. "And what's with the getting older thing? That seriously freaks me out!"

This place was designed by the Architect, the man replied, looking around. *With my help, specifically. I am not truly of this realm anymore and may only interact with the help of the mortal soul who claims me.*

"Yeah, that would be me…right?"

The man shook his head. Wisps of gray had formed in his beard and along the side of his head. *It is not my right to grant permission, nor is it yours to demand it. The being in charge of such matters is still quite alive, and standing right next to you.*

Mike turned to look at the Krampus in horror. "But…I pulled Santa out, so…I don't understand!"

The guardian of this place still exists. The First Elf and Saint Nicholas created a loophole in the rules by combining a human soul with the body of the guardian. Though you may have defeated the prior owner by removing his soul, technically the guardian remains. If you wish to claim this place, you must either have the guardian's permission or defeat him.

"Oh, fuck me…wait! Does this mean the Krampus can't claim this place either?" Hope welled up in Mike's chest.

The old man nodded. *Indeed it does. The loophole that prevents you from taking it also prevents him from doing so. Try as he might, he shall have no reign over this place without a mortal soul to assist him. That has ever been the rule, and it shall remain that way until the end of time.*

Mike looked at the Krampus, then back at the old man who was now stooped with age, his beard nearly to the floor.

"You know, most people don't end conversations with temporal theatrics," Mike said with a frown.

I am not a person. With that, the old man crumbled into dust. Time resumed, and the Krampus completed his leap across the room.

"Mine! It's all mine!" he shouted in glee, wrapping several new limbs around the pole. It almost looked like the Krampus was humping the damned thing. Mike moved toward the door of the chamber, then cursed inwardly when he heard the Krampus go completely silent.

There was a tearing sound, like cloth being pulled apart, and then the Krampus was blocking the stairwell. He grabbed Mike by the arms and lifted him until they were at eye level with each other.

"What have you done to the North Pole?" asked the Krampus, his eyes wild. "I have lost my claim and cannot redo it!"

Mike summoned his magic and ran an electrical current through the Krampus. The eldritch being gritted his teeth and rode through the pain, clenched teeth dangerously close to Mike's face.

"Human souls only, ass wad," Mike spat, then tried to kick the Krampus in the balls. He missed, then got hurled to the ground.

"What?" The Krampus blinked in surprise, then turned to look at the North Pole. "WHAT?!"

The creature went into a rage and started smashing furniture. Mike crawled toward the exit, hoping to get away this time, but was grabbed by the ankle and dragged back toward the North Pole.

"Explain!" the Krampus demanded, picking Mike up and pressing his face against the North Pole. Mike made a point of thinking really hard that this wasn't an attempt to claim it. Last thing he wanted was to get blown apart in a misunderstanding.

"You should know this," Mike mumbled, his face squished so much his words were barely legible. "Great game ring a bell? It has rules, asshole."

"FUCK!" The Krampus smashed Mike into the North Pole hard enough to knock the wind out of him. "I was so *close*!"

"Close only…counts in horseshoes and…hand grenades," Mike wheezed. His magic churned inside him like a thunderstorm, and he felt like his gut might burst. He placed both hands against the pole and pushed himself away.

"Hopeless. Hope. Less!" The Krampus smacked Mike into the Pole to punctuate each word, then held him there. "When will you learn, Caretaker? You are little more than a bag of meat with tasty bones inside, no matter how much magic you possess."

"And a soul, you crusty fuck." He could feel it now, his magic building to a deadly crescendo. Mike refused to succumb to the desire to lash out and destroy, thus changing his magic in the process. Instead, he drove the magic inward in an attempt to keep his ribs from being broken.

The Krampus stroked his beard. "Unfortunately, you are correct." He dropped Mike and crouched over him. "A human soul is the only currency the gods will accept, and I lack proper payment."

"Whatever you say, man," Mike wheezed, clutching his sides. "Maybe you should apply for a loan or whatever."

"I have finally been freed of the golden anchor that weighed me down so, only to discover that I am lacking." The Krampus steepled his fingers together, and Mike noticed that the demon's hands didn't match up. It was as if the number of fingers kept changing. "For so many years, I have been a slave to his whims, the desire to keep true to the spirit of Christmas and honor its traditions."

"How so?" Mike asked, hoping to keep the Krampus talking.

Dark eyes glittered at Mike from beneath a furrowed brow. "You know all about it, Caretaker. When this first began, it was about warmth, family, and keeping children entertained over the long winters. But the tales spread, and my workload was suddenly a hundred times larger than ever before!"

"Isn't that what you wanted?" Mike asked, speaking in a neutral tone. The Krampus rose and started pacing around the room. He was about to monologue, and Mike far preferred that to getting kicked around.

"No, it isn't what *I* wanted! I didn't mind the work, but the nature of my holiday was corrupted by greed, twisted into a parody of what it once was! False wars on Christmas were declared in my name, and the season of giving became a season of hate!" The Krampus spun on his heels so fast that a pair of shadowy tails briefly sprouted from his body. "I don't give a fuck if you celebrate Christmas! For me, it was never about recognition or spiritual salvation! Love is what I craved! Joy! Peace on Earth!" The Krampus pointed a sharp finger in Mike's direction and stabbed at the air. "And you fucking flesh bags spoiled it for me! All that stress, anger, and greed has shaped me into the being that stands before you. A creature who wants to end it all."

"Oh." Mike thought about the magic churning inside him and how it had almost blown his arm apart when he had twisted it toward violence. The magic wasn't truly a separate entity, but he had thought of it as one for so long. It was his desires that shaped the magic, but the magic, in turn, shaped who he became.

He finally understood the true price that magic demanded. Mike took a deep breath, willing the magic to extend through his limbs instead of lashing out. It was already seeking an outlet, crying out to obey his needs. What he needed right now was to stay strong until an opportunity presented itself, and so it obeyed.

Unlike the Krampus's situation, Mike's choice was ultimately his. The Krampus had been created by a limitation of the magic, and the ramifications were long-lasting. Mike could choose to blast the Krampus with lightning and further his own journey toward darkness or find a different way. The last thing he wanted was to be standing in the Krampus's shoes in twenty or thirty years, with someone else desperately trying to take him down.

"I see you're finally getting it." The Krampus snarled and swung at the air. "I rarely had a choice, Caretaker. I am the spirit of Christmas, and I am foul, angry, and broken. And I intend to take it back."

"By stealing children?" Mike felt his magic surge, ready to lash out, but he held it back. He wasn't even certain he could hurt the Krampus at this point, but intent was what mattered.

"You see it as stealing children. I see it as culling a disease." The Krampus licked his lips. "Even now, the giants have the children stored away for me, under the impression that they get to eat them. Grýla thinks she'll become something special when I rise to power, but she is little more than a game piece. You should know all about that. My plan was to dispose of her once the Pole was mine. Her, the giants, the elves, and especially the children."

Mike felt the magic surging across his body. "You were just going to slaughter them all?"

The Krampus nodded. "They will still be food. You see, Caretaker, I can feel my kin, just waiting on the other side of the veil. My hungry brethren will return to this world and finish what we started before our banishment at the hands of the Architect."

A cold blue light illuminated the Krampus. The demon stared at Mike in surprise, then grinned and moved closer. Mike realized the light was coming from him, his whole body covered in an electrical aura.

"I can feel your power," the Krampus whispered, moving close. "And once you release it, you'll be too weak to resist me. You see, I may be lacking a soul, but you aren't. Once I take your body, all I have to do is suppress you, and I'll be free forevermore."

Mike swallowed, his mouth suddenly dry. The Krampus had been monologuing in the hopes that Mike would act.

"Thanks, but I'm already in a relationship," Mike replied, his voice hoarse.

"All I have to do is wait." The Krampus held up a finger, which lengthened into a blade. He pressed it against Mike's forehead. "How much flesh can I remove before you give in?"

Energy crackled along Mike's body, but he commanded the magic to stay in place.

"I'm not afraid of you," he whispered.

The Krampus snorted. "I don't really care," he replied, then ran his finger along Mike's brow. Magic crackled and licked at the Krampus, but Mike forced it to remain in place.

"Your will is strong, Caretaker." The Krampus licked blood off his finger. "I look forward to breaking it."

He moved his finger just below Mike's eye when a soft voice broke the silence. The Krampus froze in place as the opening lyrics to "All I Want for Christmas Is You" echoed in the spherical room.

The demon turned around, a look of horror on his face as Holly stepped into the light of the North Pole. She had tears in her eyes as she continued to sing, the words coming loud and strong. Mike had no idea how long she had been there and tried to wave her away.

When the Krampus twisted around to attack Holly, she brought out Mrs. Claus's glasses. The demon paused, watching in horror as the elf held them out for the Krampus to take.

Mike was surprised when the demon let out a howl of agony and crumpled to the floor, clutching at his ears as tears streamed down his dirty cheeks.

YUKI JUMPED OFF THE ROOF OF A CLOCK TOWER AND SLAMMED her hands into a pair of giants so hard that they exploded into gravel and gore. From her back, Freyja rained down torrents of icy blades that sliced through Yule Lads and snow monsters alike. The air was filled with glittering gold lights that Freyja pulled into her body, the air around her shimmering with power.

She wasn't the only one. Different versions of Grýla were also absorbing the light, then sneaking off to split apart. It was a dirty trick that ensured the whole affair had become a battle of attrition. For every giant they killed, another clone could possibly take its place.

Yuki didn't dare take on any more divinity. Even now, she worried about the long-term implications of forcing her body to age. Her bones were brimming with so much magic that they hurt.

"This isn't working," Freyja shouted, summoning a wall of ice to block a barrage of boulders. "They just keep coming!"

Reindeer ahead. Yuki narrowed her eyes at the dark figures that zapped through the air. They could be defeated but only temporarily.

A barrage of ice missiles, summoned by Yuki and Freyja together, tore through Dasher and Prancer, scattering the reindeer into an electrical cloud of energy that would eventually re-form somewhere else. A couple more reindeer tried to flank them from the sides, but Yuki summoned a stone pillar from the ground that flew like a missile and destroyed one of them. She caught the other in her jaws and bit down, shaking it until it exploded.

The damned thing tasted like licking a giant battery.

It's a numbers game, Yuki told Freyja. *Two of us versus all of them. Can you summon more of your warriors?*

"Not really." Freyja summoned an ice wall tilted on one side like a ramp. Yuki sank her claws into the ice and ran up the ramp, catapulting herself off the top to get them closer to Santa's house. She didn't know why, but she had a very uneasy feeling about Mike. "I may have some of my powers back, but my summoning is very weak right now. It's pulling them from my home that's the problem."

Damn. Yuki swatted away a ten-foot-tall snowman, sending more golden light Freyja's way. *There wouldn't happen to be a bunch of dead warriors buried here, would there?*

Freyja laughed, then filled a nearby Grýla with spikes of ice. "There's about to be two of them if this keeps up."

Not funny, Yuki growled.

"I don't think it's funny either..." Freyja's eyes went up to the sky where the northern lights shimmered, the colors rolling over one another like a bundle of snakes. "Oh. Oh!"

Yuki never got a chance to ask what had the goddess's attention, because Freyja hurled herself into the sky, ascending rapidly under the wind's power.

Wish I could fly, Yuki grumbled. Not that flying would help her now. There was still the issue of Grýla's army on the ground, which would no doubt be waiting for her at Santa's house.

With Freyja off doing gods knew what, Yuki threw caution to the wind and made another mad dash forward. This time, she shape-shifted as she went, resuming her human form to fit through smaller openings. Yule Lads and snow creatures had filled the interior structures of the village, and Yuki tore through them like paper. The Yule Lads would often explode into a green mist, which meant they would come back later. Some stayed dead once slain, and she wasn't entirely sure what process ensured their destruction.

Outside again, she resumed her fox demon form and barreled through the snow monsters that waited for her. Above, the northern lights churned as if caught in a storm, and she could just barely make out a golden figure at the center of the swirling mass.

I hope that's a good thing, she thought to herself as she dashed into another building and transformed into a woman. A trio of Grýlas ambushed her, but she flash froze one of them in a block of ice before spiking the other two. She was running on pure adrenaline now and could feel her control on the magic slipping.

After running up a flight of stairs, she made her way toward a large window with a view of Santa's home. Shadows danced around the building, as if awaiting permission to enter. She was at least a mile out, and her attackers were increasing in number.

"Fucking hell," she muttered, pushing open the window and sliding out onto the roof. A massive paw smashed into her, sending her sprawling on the ground. Yuki groaned, rolling away from the Yule Cat as it tried to crush her under a massive paw.

They had lost the giant cat some time ago, but the damned thing had caught up. Yuki summoned ice and stone, smashing both into the cat's face. The beast took the brunt of the assault without flinching, then swatted her aside again before she could transform.

"I really hate you," she muttered, summoning an icy shell to protect her. From within, she could see the dark shape of the Yule Cat as it tried to crack the ice with its front paws.

The cat hissed, the sound reminiscent of a train releasing all its steam after stopping. Yuki crouched, ready to explode into fox demon form the moment the barrier was breached.

The ground beneath her trembled as an ominous trio of growls filled the air. The Yule Cat turned away from the barrier, giving Yuki an opportunity to create a hole in the back and sneak out.

The Yule Cat hissed, its back arched as it faced the new arrival. A dark shape emerged from the rubble of a nearby building, all six eyes blazing.

Cerberus growled in response, hackles raised. She opened her mouths, hellfire washing over the square, devouring Yule Lads and snow creatures alike. At least one Grýla was caught in the blast, her features melting away beneath the supernatural heat.

The Yule Cat fled. Cerberus turned to face Yuki, all three heads bowed in greeting.

"Your timing is perfect," Yuki said, moving to the beast's side and scratching the first ear she could reach. "We need to get to Mike. He's in trouble, I can feel it." She hopped onto Cerberus's back and pointed at Santa's house. Cerberus stomped on a snowman and turned toward their destination.

Above, the maelstrom of green-and-red lights was now forming into funnel clouds and spiraling toward the ground. In those lights, she could see the spectral forms of thousands of humanoid figures.

"Whoa," Yuki whispered. The funnel clouds crashed into the ground, and she heard cries of alarm from Yule Lads and Grýlas as the spirits charged into battle. Nearby, dark shadows fled to safety as the northern lights washed over them.

A shooting star crossed the sky, leaving a sparkling trail behind it. Yuki gasped when she realized the star was a reindeer. On its back was the grim reaper himself, wearing an oversize Santa coat and carrying a large bag over one shoulder. The twisted reindeer of the Krampus launched themselves into the sky, chasing after their new prey.

"Merry Christmas to all!" Death cried, then threw himself free, tumbling through the sky before bouncing off the roof of Santa's home and landing in the snow.

"Let's go," she yelled, clutching the hellhound's fur. Cerberus sprinted across the North Pole, breathing fire on all that stood in their way.

FROM HER VANTAGE POINT ABOVE THE NORTH POLE, FREYJA could see the small army closing in on Yuki's location. Dozens, if not hundreds, of iterations of Grýla were running amok, and that didn't include the snow army she had created earlier. That was her divinity down there, tearing the North Pole village apart right now. It was unlikely that Yuki would be able to make it to Mike's side in time without some extra help.

She turned her eyes back up to the sky, her heart pleading. Tens of thousands of spirits watched her, many of them with one foot already in the mortal plane. She could feel their anger, the spirits eager to go down and help undo the madness she had caused. There would be a price for bringing them over, one far greater than she had paid for the limited soldiers from her native plane.

Freyja took a deep breath and gladly paid it.

A seam in the sky opened up, and the spirits poured forth. They weren't warriors—most were simple fishermen or farmers. They were the spirits native to this region, angry at Grýla and her ilk. They spiraled down, riding the wind much like Freyja did, crying out in languages that had been unheard for hundreds of years.

Down below, the mob chasing Yuki looked up in time to be ripped apart by the vengeful spirits. Hundreds of them assaulted Grýlas, stray snow beasts, and even a few Yule Lads that got caught up in the fight. The spirits gave a wide berth to the three-headed hellhound breathing fire. Freyja smiled at the sight of a Cerberus free of her domain. Freyja was very familiar with the breed and couldn't think of a more loyal companion.

Though the wind held her aloft, she felt her body weakening as her magic and the divinity she had acquired held the rift open. With eager eyes, she watched as Yuki arrived at Santa's home and ran inside, leaving Cerberus to defend the home from attackers. Letting out a sigh of relief, she turned her attention down to the ruined village. It had been in bad shape before, but now large portions of it were on fire, and she could see different variations of Grýla trying to flee in a panic.

"Run," she hissed, her lips curling into a sneer. She summoned a spear of ice as more spirits gathered behind her, their rage palpable. "Make it fun for me, you rotten bitch."

Freyja fell from the sky like a meteor, followed by the fury of thousands of years of tradition. Sculptors, hunters, mothers, and fathers crashed into the snow, reaping the enemies of the North in a one-sided slaughter. Golden orbs of light drifted toward Freyja, filling her with strength as she took back the power that was rightfully hers. Divinity flowed through her veins like liquid starlight, and she let out a mighty battle cry that shook the remaining snow off nearby buildings.

She had forgotten this feeling. It had been centuries since she had walked these lands, and it was time to make her reappearance count.

"Death to my enemies!" Raising her spear skyward, Freyja rode the winds up and to victory.

WATCHING WITH HORROR AS HOLLY WALKED TOWARD THE Krampus, Mike sat forward, magic surging through his veins in case he needed to intervene. It was one thing to allow rage to guide his actions, but protecting someone he cared about?

That was an entirely different matter.

Holly sang the final verse of her song, then knelt by the Krampus. The demon was weeping openly now and had assumed the fetal position.

"Don't cry," she told the Krampus, placing her hand over his. "You don't have to cry."

"She would have hated to see me like this," whispered the Krampus. "All dark and twisted. I felt it when she was gone. It was such a relief to know she'd never be here for this."

"She isn't gone." Holly rubbed the Krampus's forearm. "Mrs. Claus is in my heart and yours. We can still make things right and bring her back."

"Foolish girl." The Krampus covered his face with a free hand. "These emotions, they're only echoes. They hold no power over me."

Holly shook her head and looked at Mike. "I don't think they are," she said. "I don't pretend to understand what you are or how you came to be, but you're still Santa. You're just the side of him we never see. You've been bottled up, and that wasn't right. It is never right to hide away a part of yourself that is so integral to who you are. I know what it's like to feel incomplete all the time, like there's a side of you that you can't show the world. That's no way to live."

At those words, she threw a look of fierce longing in Mike's direction. He nodded for her to continue, then turned his attention back to the Krampus.

"Don't you understand? Nicholas is gone, and I'm all that is left of him." The Krampus rolled into a crouch and wiped at his eyes. "I am just the cancer that was left behind, when all is said and done."

"You aren't a cancer." Holly moved her hand to the Krampus's cheek.

"But I am, Holly. I truly am."

"I don't see it that way. You're still the same person who did all those wonderful things for children around the world. If I've learned anything, it's that people have layers and they wear masks to protect themselves and others from what's inside."

"I'm evil, Holly. How can you not see that?" The Krampus bared his teeth, his eyes glowing red.

"Because I still believe in you." Holly held out Mrs. Claus's glasses. "And I believe you could go back to the way you were. All you have to do is remember."

The Krampus stared down at the silver-framed glasses, then took them carefully from Holly as if afraid they would break. The horned demon sniffed, his eyes briefly reflected in the lenses.

"I can't ever go back to the man I was, Holly." The Krampus looked up at the elf. "Don't you see? I was the First Elf, forever bound by the nature of this holiday. Christmas is tainted and has become about money and profits and pushing agendas. It's about expectations of forgiveness and miracles for no other reason than it's the twenty-fifth of December. Humans are gross and lacking in decency. I would know because I am nothing more than a reflection of their wants and desires."

"Santa, ple—" Holly was cut off when the Krampus seized her by the throat.

"Santa is gone. No more words," he hissed, crushing the silver glasses with his other hand. He rose to his full height just as Mike crossed the room, his clenched fists brimming with lightning.

The Krampus swatted Mike away so hard that when he landed, he had tunnel vision. Darkness crept in at the edges of his vision as the Krampus stared into Holly's eyes.

"It's time for you to find your inner darkness." The Krampus bared his teeth as shadow tendrils crawled along his arm and onto Holly's skin. She didn't struggle—instead, she stared defiantly. The shadows moved along her face and through her hair as if searching for somewhere to burrow inside.

Somehow, Holly found the strength to hum the tune to "Jingle Bells."

"You will submit, Holly!" The Krampus shook her, but she continued to hum. This enraged the Krampus, who lifted her high as if to smash her on the ground.

"That will be quite enough of that." Death walked into the room carrying a large sack over his shoulder and a small gift box beneath his arm. He was wearing a Santa coat that was too large along with a matching hat that hung awkwardly to one side and a fake beard. When Death set the bag down, the Krampus stared at it with bulging eyes.

"You!" he declared, tossing Holly to the side. "You've been quite the thorn in my side, reaper."

"Indeed." Death's eye flames burned like distant stars in his sockets. "I have worked very hard today to bring joy to the children of the world. You, on the other hand, have been nothing but a huge asshole."

The Krampus laughed so hard he grabbed at his own gut.

"And I assume you're here to stop me? Bah! Humbug!" The Krampus waved his hand dismissively. "I know exactly what you are, reaper. You have no power over that which does not truly live."

Death adjusted his beard and then held up the present. "I am not here to stop you. In fact, I have decided that it would be in the spirit of the holiday to bring you a present."

The Krampus stopped laughing and leaned toward the reaper, his face a mask of confusion.

"Do you think this is a game? Some sort of holiday special?" The Krampus chuckled and shook his head. "The elf dug up some old emotions, but I have buried them anew. It's easy enough when you don't have a soul. There's nothing on earth you could give me that would magically make me feel bad and change my ways."

"I disagree." Death clenched the gift in two hands and held it over his head. "Because I'm about to give you the gift of a proper ass whooping."

With those words, Death hurled the gift forward. The immaculately wrapped package twisted and shifted in midair, revealing long bladed limbs and whirling edges. Mike immediately averted his gaze as Ticktock collided with the Krampus.

"No!" howled the Krampus, and the available light in the room dimmed. Ticktock had transformed into a weird monstrosity that was all teeth and sharp edges, and the Krampus was doing his best to keep up as the two of them attempted to rip each other apart. "Stop, we're on the same side!"

"Now that is something you don't see very often." Death watched the melee for a few moments, then came over to Mike's side. "It would seem I have arrived exactly when I should have."

"You're telling me." Mike looked over at Holly, who had crawled out of the way. "Where are the others?"

"I do not know. It is rather grim up there, Mike Radley. I am not certain there is much more we can do." Death looked sadly at the battle taking place. The room trembled as Ticktock slammed the Krampus into the North Pole.

"Yeah, it's been a shit Christmas." Mike pulled himself toward the edge of the room and saw Holly. He waved her over, mouthing the words *don't look.*

"On the plus side, I did get to meet Santa," Death continued. "Though our meeting was nothing as I expected."

"Yeah, you should never meet your heroes." Mike frowned as the Krampus slammed Ticktock into a nearby wall, causing the wooden beams to crack. "We should probably get out of here before this place comes down."

"Would you like to meet him, Mike Radley?" Death

reached into his cloak. "I don't know how much longer he will last in this form."

"Say what now?" Mike looked at the grim reaper in puzzlement as he held out a hand to reveal a red-and-gold light that looked like the end of a sparkler.

"I found him floating outside. He was headed toward the northern lights." Death contemplated the light in his hands. "I probably shouldn't have interfered, but I figured it was going to be my only chance to—"

"Death, you're brilliant!" Mike turned his attention toward the Krampus. Ticktock was now a multilegged abomination trying to bite the Krampus's head off. "Ticktock, hold that fucker down!"

The mimic twisted around, then stabbed the Krampus through the foot and pinned him in place. In response, the Krampus ripped his leg free, trailing black blood everywhere as he got underneath Ticktock and grabbed the mimic by the legs. With a twisting motion, he slammed it hard into the North Pole.

"You are a lesser being!" The Krampus shouted, then stomped on the mimic. Ticktock fought back, clamping down on the Krampus's wrists.

"Death, I can put Santa's soul back!" Mike summoned his magic, creating a small cage made of electricity. "I pulled him out because I thought it would put him back in charge of the body, but that was a huge mistake."

"You should never pull souls out of people, Mike Radley." Death shook his head in disapproval. "That's very naughty."

"You can yell at me later. For now, you've given us a second chance to get things right." Mike thought about how Holly had briefly appealed to the eldritch being. This wasn't like Freyja and Jack, two pieces of a separate whole. It was a colossal fuckup on his part, but if he could put Santa back, Holly's appeals might make it through.

"Caretaker!" The Krampus headbutted Ticktock so hard

that the mimic went still. "I will not let you put that man's soul inside me again!"

Mike concentrated, sending magical streamers across the room, and focused on the void around the Krampus. What he had mistaken for nothing was in fact something he simply couldn't see. Though he couldn't identify what made the Krampus, he could see the gaps in reality left behind by its presence.

"No!" The Krampus shot across the room so fast that Mike didn't have a chance to blink. In a single moment, he found himself staring at bladed fingers reaching for his face but frozen less than an inch away.

Standing between him and the Krampus was Lily. Her entire body glowed as if magma ran beneath her skin. Lily squeezed the Krampus by the wrist until something cracked.

"Hands off my man," she growled, then whipped around and stabbed the Krampus in the face with her tail. She speared him in the forehead, and he clutched at her tail and shrieked.

The Krampus staggered back and was grabbed from behind by Ticktock. Lily and the mimic tore into the Krampus, who was now on the defensive. He shifted back and forth, dancing away from his attackers until he was at the far side of the cavern. Meanwhile, Mike was busy hooking his magic into those dark edges, coating them in his own magic to see them better. In his hand, Santa's soul bounced back and forth, ringing like a silver bell.

Holly grabbed Mike by the leg, almost breaking his concentration. Her wide eyes followed the fight as the Krampus once again took the upper hand. He had grown a couple more feet and had grabbed both Lily and Ticktock in his many hands to slam them together.

"You may think you have powerful allies, Caretaker, but I will splay your innards across this room soon enough!" The Krampus hooked Ticktock with his horns and tossed the mimic away before punching Lily in the face. "I am infinite!"

"He very much enjoys his own voice," noted Death, who was now munching on a candy cane.

"Indeed," Mike agreed, his magic now coalescing and creating a cage inside the Krampus's spirit.

The Krampus grabbed Lily and threw her at Mike. This broke his concentration as he jumped out of the way to avoid getting crushed. Lily snarled like a tiger and got to her feet, her skin now covered in scales. He had never seen her so angry.

The Krampus charged toward Mike and was clotheslined by a foot-thick horizontal spear of ice that appeared in the middle of the room. As he flipped head over heels, Yuki appeared in the doorway, her face covered in cuts and bruises.

"Where the hell have you been?" Lily snarled, then jumped once more into the fray.

"Pleasant as always," Yuki muttered, then raised her hands and sent a beam of white light at the Krampus. Ice formed wherever the beam struck, causing the Krampus to slip and stumble.

Mike sent out dozens of streamers, which wrapped around the Krampus's torso. The Krampus let out a hideous shriek and bolted for the back of the room. If not for Lily and Tick-tock, he would have disappeared almost immediately. Tick-tock's bladed limbs kept tripping up the Krampus's legs, and Lily's tail was wrapped around the demon's throat, holding her in place as she punched the back of his head. Still, the Krampus disappeared through the cave mouth in the back of the room, taking his attackers with him.

"Shit!" Mike kept Santa's soul tightly bound with his magic and gave chase with Holly and Death right behind him. Yuki sprinted past him, her tails whirring behind her so fast that it looked as though she had five instead of three.

Mike really hoped he didn't have a concussion.

By the time he caught up, they were in the caves where Santa had fought the frost giants. Massive sheets of ice had been built into the cave walls, blocking off the available exits. Globes of fox fire illuminated the room, revealing that the Krampus had been pinned once more.

Gone was any vestige of humanity or thought. The Krampus's face had extended outward, like a crocodile's, and he snapped his fearsome teeth at his foes. Lily was actively trying to strangle him with her tail as Ticktock ripped chunks of darkness out of the Krampus's legs.

Mike tried to loop his magic around the Krampus once again. The monster was squirming so much that he couldn't figure out what he was looking at.

"Hold him as still as possible!" he shouted, Santa's soul pulsing in his hands.

Lily looked like she wanted to say something, but she was too busy punching the Krampus in the back of his skull. Her features were twisted now, and her magnificent horns had become gnarled and brimmed with fire. Yuki put her hand on the ground, and the stone beneath the Krampus twisted into thick chains that bound him to the floor.

"Noooooo!" The Krampus's cry reverberated through the cavern as he tried to break free of his earthen shackles. Yuki responded by freezing his limbs in ice, her eyes brimming with golden light as red lines manifested on her cheeks.

Ticktock and Lily piled on, holding the Krampus down as Mike ran loops of magical energy all around the monster. The golden light in his hand sparkled as he pulled those loops toward him and placed Santa's soul inside. As if by instinct, Mike pulled the loops tight, causing Santa's soul to sink into the Krampus.

A foul energy permeated the room, and Mike was driven to his knees. Santa's soul swirled and expanded, trying to bond with the Krampus once again. The shifting mosaic of spiritual energy was painful to look into, but Mike didn't dare risk letting up. At times, he became disoriented, as if he had forgotten the task he was in the middle of. As he lost focus, his thoughts drifted away until—

Holly took his hand and squeezed. The room came into focus once again.

"You can do this," she whispered. "You have to."

Mike nodded, wiping the blood from his lips. Pain blossomed inside his head, but he willed it aside and weaved the Krampus and Santa back together. He felt guilty tucking that golden light away in skeins of darkness, but there was no other choice.

The Krampus shrieked and bucked his hips, but it was too late. Already, the extra limbs were dissipating into a dark mist, rendering him mostly human once more. His supernatural strength fled him, and both Ticktock and Yuki backed down on their restraint.

Lily, however, gave no quarter. She grabbed the Krampus by his horns and yanked them apart, causing the base of one to splinter.

"You ready to make a wish?" she whispered. "'Cause I'm about to wish so hard that you'll be nothing more than a stain on the earth."

"Lily." Mike put his hand on her wrist and winced at the heat. It was hot enough that it burned him, but he didn't dare let go. "Ease up. It's over."

"It's not over, Mike!" Her eyes blazed with fire as she looked up at him. "Don't you see? This bastard will always be a ticking time bomb, ready to go off! If it isn't our children today, who will it be next? What if Callisto had been taken? How would you have felt?"

"You're right." He moved close and touched the rough skin of her cheek. "And that's something we can figure out later. But…" He sighed and looked up at the ceiling of the cave. He was exhausted, and his nose was still bleeding. "There's gonna be a huge mess up there. We've all worked hard enough tonight. Let's get his better half back to at least lighten the load."

Lily contemplated him for several long moments as the Krampus cried out in pain. Snorting in disgust, she snapped off the Krampus's horn.

"He said to stop!" cried the Krampus.

"You're right, I did." Mike knelt to stare the Krampus in the eyes. "And right now, that's the only reason that horn hasn't been shoved up your ass."

The Krampus stared at his captors, his face twisting up in hatred. He opened his mouth to speak when Holly knelt by his side.

"Santa, I know you're in there." She clutched the edges of her dress. "Properly this time."

"He can hear you, but he isn't—" The Krampus went quiet as Lily wrapped her tail around his mouth.

"This was a terrible evening," Holly continued. "A lot of elves died, and the North Pole…I don't know how much of it is left. You're the cause of this, but I know now it's not entirely your fault. I've been thinking about what you said, about me being free from Christmas to make my own choices. You wanted something for me that you couldn't have. For a while, I struggled with the realization that you and the Krampus are the same creature, and…" She shook her head.

"It is our choices that make us who we are," Death said, kneeling behind Holly and placing a bony hand on her shoulder, causing her to flinch. "You see, mortals don't really have that many choices. They just appear, like moss on a rock. But you haven't had the privilege of making your own choices for a long time, and I think I understand why you've become so broken inside."

"We're different people, really. We can live entire lives in a matter of years," Yuki said, crossing her arms and scowling. "So yeah. You've done some really bad things tonight and probably deserve worse. But all of us here, we know what it's like to need forgiveness." She looked over at Lily, who was almost back to normal.

"No thanks," she replied. "I'm not participating in this emotional circle jerk."

Mike shook his head and stared into the Krampus's eyes. "You owe us. No matter what you're feeling, or how deep you're buried, you need to come make this right. It's not what you do when you fall that matters but what you do when you pick yourself back up."

Holly put her hands on the Krampus's temples, then pressed her forehead against his. "Father Christmas, please," she begged. "Please come back to us. The world still needs you. I need you. And…I forgive you."

Lily made a face and released her hold on the Krampus's mouth. He was breathing raggedly, his features stretched tight while he gasped for air. The demon shook as his features twisted, his long limbs shortening and filling out with muscle. The dark hairs of his beard brightened and turned white as snow with matching hair emerging from his scalp. The remaining horn slid into his skull, causing the dingy cap on his head to tumble free and land on the ground.

The Krampus grunted as rosy light flooded his face. Dark shadows detached from his skin, withdrawing into the folds of his jacket to reveal glowing red cheeks and a bulbous nose. Eyes blue enough to be mistaken for sea glass now looked out from beneath a furrowed brow, regarding them with relief.

Santa sat up straight, his large belly hanging free from the remnants of his coat. Tears were caught in the corners of his eyes, and he stood with Mike's help. Santa's beard wrapped itself around Mike's arm, but Santa smoothed the hairs away with his hands.

"So the fat man finally makes an appearance." Lily huffed, crossing her arms as her tail vanished behind her. "Do you have anything to say for yourself?"

Santa surveyed the room, his eyes red from crying. A small smile broke out on his face, and he wiped the tears away.

"You've all been really good this year," he whispered, then looked down at Holly. "And you never fail to impress me, my dear Holly. I am so proud of you."

Holly threw her arms around Santa. He patted her on the head affectionately, then looked at Mike. "The North Pole is unclaimed," he said. "Should you wish it—"

"No." Mike shook his head immediately. "This place, it's too big of a job for someone like me."

Santa nodded, then moved to go back through the caves. Yuki melted her ice walls as they went, the group walking in silence as they returned to the North Pole. The small bit of magic brightened at their approach, and Santa stared at the artifact in reverence.

"So, wait? We're just going to let this guy have it all back?" Lily moved between Santa and the North Pole. "Were none of you paying attention to me earlier?"

"I was," Mike said, pondering the situation. If they let Santa reclaim it, they were effectively setting a timer for when he went out of control once more. "But this is a better place to discuss our options. Last thing we want is to leave it unguarded."

Santa moved to sit in one of the remaining chairs. When he spoke, his voice was low and rumbly. "If given no other choice, I will resume ownership. But Lily is correct. As I exist now, I am a being outside of time, consisting of a human soul and an outsider's body. It will not be a matter of if but when I slip again. Nothing short of peace on Earth will rectify the issue."

Lily raised an eyebrow at Mike. "See?"

Mike ignored Lily. He needed to focus on the solution, not the problem, and he was exhausted from the fight. "Binding requires a human soul, correct?"

Santa nodded. "As it must be. And though I have existed

outside the game on a technicality, the new owner will be caught up in the machinations of the Architect anew. I…will choose whoever you believe is fitting."

Mike contemplated Santa for several moments, rubbing his jaw. He looked at the others, then back at the North Pole.

"Shit," he muttered, causing the elf beside him to flinch. "Sorry, Holly, that one slipped out of me."

"Wait a second." Lily moved next to Holly and inspected the elf. "You're hot, kind of in a weird Oompa Loompa sort of way."

"Hey!" Holly took a step forward and jabbed Lily in the knee with her fist.

"I'm willing to bet Romeo played 'hide the Christmas pickle' with you, right?" Lily took a dramatic sniff over Holly's head. The elf turned bright red and covered her face. "Yo, fat man. What's the price for admission?"

Santa raised an eyebrow at Lily, then looked over at Mike. "I'm afraid I don't know what she means."

"I believe I do." Death stepped forward and put his hand on Holly's head. "You see, Mike Radley has likely engaged in rather vigorous intercourse with this woman, and it is likely that…oh dear, she must be tired."

Holly had crouched and was covering her face in horror.

"Anyway, there is likely a piece of his soul residing in her now. Or rather, a piece of her soul that has been rewritten as human. I'm unsure how it works. Perhaps Lily could explain more."

Lily's face had gone completely white. "What…do you mean by that?"

Death contemplated Lily for an unusually long time. "I am, of course, referring to your diet and knowledge of spiritual matters."

Lily bit her lip and looked at Mike. "Anyway, how much of a human soul is required? Because I know for a fact that what

Romeo left behind will grow. So even if it's tenuous at first, maybe the connection will improve?"

Santa nodded. "It could work. If Holly chooses to become the new master of the North Pole, she will not be beholden to the shifting beliefs that have influenced my downfall. I would resume my role as guardian and be beholden to her commands."

"But only if she chooses." Mike looked down at Holly. "Because this is a pretty big decision. And once you make it, there isn't any going back."

Holly gazed into Mike's eyes as if searching for something. She looked over at Santa, then the others.

"This…isn't at all what I expected when I came to your home," she said. "And if you had asked me then if I would do it, I would have said yes without hesitation. I would have felt it was my duty and would have been honored to accept. But after so many days together, learning more about who I am and what I'm capable of, I can honestly say I feel differently."

Mike nodded. "I know how you feel. This is a big responsibility, and nobody here begrudges you for your decision. So how do we go about finding a suitable replacement?" He looked at the others.

"Hey!" Holly grabbed Mike's coat and gave it a tug. "I never said I wasn't going to do it!"

He looked at her in confusion. "I'm sorry, but didn't you—"

"I said I feel differently now. I am free of outside influences, and this is a decision I get to make on my own. No matter what happens next, this decision will always be mine, and I have you to thank for it." She pulled hard on his coat until he knelt, and she planted a big kiss on his lips. "Now if you'll excuse me, I'm the woman who's gonna save Christmas."

She turned toward Santa, who led her to the North Pole.

He had her place her palm on the shining surface of the artifact, causing the chamber to fill with light.

Mike didn't know what to expect once the light faded, but Holly looked no different. Santa, on the other hand, was in far better shape. He looked like he had stepped straight out of a storybook, wearing his trademark red-and-white colors.

Santa looked at the others and smiled. "HO HO HO!" he shouted with great cheer. "MERRY CHRISTMAS!"

"Santa!" Death did a little dance that reminded Mike of a dog doing tippy taps.

"If you'll excuse me, I've got some work to do." Santa slid his hands into his pockets. "There are some very naughty creatures up above that are deserving of some Christmas cheer!"

With that, Santa pulled his hands from his pockets to reveal chrome brass knuckles inlaid with gems. The words *Christmas Cheer* were carved intricately into each one, and he slid them over his gloved fingers. With a wink at them all, he placed one finger on the side of his nose and transformed into a glittery mist that circled the North Pole twice before disappearing through an unseen crack in the ceiling.

"What…on earth was that about?" Lily asked.

Holly smirked. "I was given a choice," she replied. "And so I made a few modifications."

KISA WALKED BEHIND THE COLUMN OF ELVES, HOLDING HER coat tightly against her skin. Ahead of her, thousands of elves carried hundreds of children, led by Alabaster and Christmas Present. They were climbing the ridge of what was either a snow-covered mountain or a massive glacier—she had no idea which.

At the top of the ridge, she found herself looking down into a small valley with an empty train station. Her vantage point made the structure look more like a model than an actual building. Christmas Present glowed like a distant lantern, leading the elves and the children to safety.

Kisa looked back at the North Pole and sniffled, her nose sufficiently frozen and runny. Smoke rose from shattered buildings, and she could see the workshop in the distance. The roof had caved in, likely burying the Cocoa Lounge. She smiled fondly at the memory of being bent over that jukebox as Mike railed her from behind.

"Hey!" Tink swatted Kisa in the butt. "Cat keep moving, Tink's feet freezing!"

"Sorry, weird headspace is all." She watched the eerie glow of the northern lights as they began a slow ascent toward the sky. They had encountered a few spirits wandering around about while on their journey but had been left alone. She had no idea how that had even come about but wasn't going to complain. On at least two occasions, Grýla had tried to ambush them. The giant had been no match for Christmas Present, who had torn each one apart.

Kisa watched another building fall, the sound of the crash reaching her several seconds later. Her ears twitched as she heard a faint voice carry over the divide.

"Did you hear that?" she asked.

"Hear what?" Tink looked around, then adjusted her goggles.

Kisa tilted her head back and forth, hopeful she would hear it again. It was faint, but she picked it up.

"Ho ho ho!" the distant voice cried. "Merry Christmas!" There was another crash, followed by the sound of a cat yowling. Another building collapsed.

"It's Santa!" Tink declared, pointing excitedly in the distance. Kisa couldn't see Santa but didn't doubt that Tink had. "Santa come back, open big can of whoop-ass!"

Nearby, an elf flinched as he walked past, blank eyes on their destination.

"So does that mean it's over? The Krampus is gone?" Kisa looked at the elves as they trudged forward.

"Tink think so. Still keep going before ass freeze off. Santa owe Tink big." The goblin adjusted her goggles and moved to rejoin the line.

Kisa contemplated the distant destruction, then turned to face their destination, untouched by the fighting. It would be hard work, but the North Pole would be restored; she was sure of it.

With an extra spring in her step, Kisa moved back into line and started humming to herself. It was nothing more than the tune to "Jingle Bells," but the elf in front of her froze for a moment, her pointed ears twitching.

Before Kisa knew it, several of the elves were humming the song. Gradually, color returned to their skin and clothing as the humming grew louder and eventually transformed into open song. By the time they reached the train station, the elves were openly singing Christmas carols as they carried their precious cargo to safety.

HEARTH AND HOME

Among Santa, Cerberus, and Freyja, there was little left of the North Pole village. Perhaps half of it had been burned to the ground by hellfire, and Santa had been a one-man wrecking crew, punching his way to victory. When Mike had finally emerged from Santa's home, it was to see a land that would need to be rebuilt from the ground up.

Mike and the others took up residence in Santa's home for a few days while the newly awakened elves eagerly started repairs. The workshop was the first structure to be reinforced, as it was still in good condition. The air inside smelled of fresh cut wood and lacquer, along with cinnamon and nutmeg. The magical fireplace had been lit anew, and elves were constantly darting through it to gather lumber and supplies from all around the world.

Mrs. Claus reappeared shortly after Holly had taken ownership of the North Pole, though she now wore regular clothing. Holly had informed him that the wife of Santa Claus would only wear lingerie when she felt like it from now on. Mike suspected that the older woman was still as amorous as ever, because Santa kept going missing every couple of hours.

While Christmas Present and Santa searched the North Pole for any missing elves, Holly and Mrs. Claus took charge to make sure that repairs were being done correctly. The map of the North Pole had survived the Krampus's spoogefest inside its special case and was being used as a guide. As far as Mike could tell, Holly was already planning some changes to the layout of the village, but whenever he'd ask about it, she'd just blush.

Holly was far less shy in the bedroom though. He was pretty much keeping track of the days by how often she would ambush him. The two of them had snuck off on more than a few occasions, and it wasn't uncommon for Holly to go out of her way to bring along Tink. However, they had their own room now and didn't need to worry about getting spunk in Santa's tree.

Currently, Mike was sitting at a table just outside of the Cocoa lounge, watching the elves create an assembly line to transport the time-locked children home through the fireplace. A special team of elves was responsible for each child, a task which took at least a couple minutes per kid. Based on his own rough estimates, Mike figured the process would take a few days to get everyone home safe.

With a list of names in her hand, Mrs. Claus stood by the fireplace, checking off the children as they went through.

"This is quite the affair, Mike Radley." Death sat across from him, eagerly munching on a cookie.

"Aren't you tired of those?" Mike asked.

"Yes. Yes, I am." Death crunched his teeth down on another cookie. "And yet I shall continue to eat them."

"But why?"

Death shrugged. "Habit, I suppose."

Mike pulled the plate of cookies away from Death. "I'm cutting you off."

"I suppose it's for the best." Death sighed. "Perhaps I am eating them because I am nervous about my trip."

Once the children were returned, Santa planned to go around the world and undo everything the Krampus had done and finish his deliveries. Much to Death's delight, Santa had invited the reaper along to help him.

"You have nothing to be nervous about. You did such a great job on your own I bet you could give the big guy a few tips."

Death snorted. "I am inevitable, Mike Radley, not gullible."

"Perhaps, but you're a good friend."

"Indeed I am." Death's eyes blazed with blue light. "And I shall miss you. For it will be but a day for you but months for me."

"As you say, you are inevitable. We'll see each other soon enough. Besides, it's time for the rest of us to go." Mike wasn't able to contribute anything meaningful at this point. Tink had offered to help the elves rebuild, but they had immediately shut her down, declaring that they preferred to work without distractions. Lily was quietly creating enough of those to the point that Death had threatened to stick the helper hat back on her head.

Of Freyja, there was still no sign. The Yule Lads had long ago scampered off with their father and the Yule Cat, so Mike wondered if she'd gone after them. Yuki had gone out multiple times searching for the goddess but had been unable to track her. Every time he saw those extra tails of hers, Mike couldn't help but feel bad that the kitsune had sacrificed two centuries of her life to save them. However, he would have made the same decision in a heartbeat and respected her for it.

Another group of elves carried a child to their home through the magical flames of the fireplace, and Mrs. Claus crossed another name off her list. The massive hearth was covered in stockings, each with an elf's name on it. Mike couldn't help but stare at the large pile of stockings they had pulled down and set with reverence in the corner of the room. That pile represented the elves who hadn't survived, for one reason or another. Most of the elves paid it little attention, and he really couldn't tell if it didn't bother them or if they were throwing themselves so hard into their work that they really were able to ignore what the pile represented.

Holly walked into the workshop, causing the elves to stop momentarily. She waved them on, bidding them to continue, then sat down next to Mike.

"Hello." Her eyes sparkled. "I bet that you're ready to get home."

"I guess. Are you sure we can't be of more help here?"

She shook her head and put a hand over his. "Once we're done with the children, we have months of work ahead of us here, maybe even years. We have many hands to help, and none of them will age. You've already done more than enough."

"Yeah, we have." Lily sauntered over to the table. "The cocoa is really good, but someone broke the jukebox."

Mike made a face but kept his mouth shut.

"Speaking of, Santa wanted to speak to all of you before he left." Holly looked over at the entrance to the workshop, and the massive double doors opened. A red carpet with gold lining rolled itself across the floor as elves moved out of the way. Dancer and Dasher walked on the carpet, pulling a small sleigh behind them with a large velvet chair.

"What's going on?" Mike asked.

"It's time to sit on Santa's lap." Holly patted Mike's leg as the big man himself appeared. The chair was off-loaded next to the fireplace, and Santa let out a groan as he squeezed into it. The elves let out a small cheer as Santa waved to Mike.

"Why am I sitting on his lap?" He looked at Holly.

"It's his way of saying thanks." Holly smiled at him, then noticed his confusion. "Oh, sorry. To be specific, he wants to give all of you something special for helping us. But you can't just ask Santa for something. You either have to write him a letter or sit on his lap first."

"Sounds like a blatant attempt at sexual harassment," mumbled Lily as Tink sprinted forward.

"Santa!" she declared, leaping onto Santa's lap. "Tink have extra-big wish this year!"

"Ho ho ho!" Santa's eyes sparkled. "And if it is within my power, you'll be sure to have it!"

Tink stood on the edge of Santa's chair and leaned against his shoulder as if she was having a conversation at the bar. Holding a hand over her mouth so nobody else could see, Tink spoke to Santa for quite a while. Santa's eyes widened unexpectedly a few times, and at one point he declared part of her request to be too naughty. In the end, he simply nodded, then patted the goblin between the horns.

"I'll have to see what I can do," he informed her. "That one really is a pretty big wish and might be past my limitations."

"Then she can have my wish too." Kisa was already walking up to Santa holding an envelope in her hands. "All I had was questions, but I got those answered for me a bit ago."

"Hmm." Santa stared at Kisa. "You would give away a Christmas wish for Tink?"

"Bet your ass I would." Kisa winced when the nearby elves gave her a nasty look. "I'm so sorry. That one slipped out."

Santa chuckled, then looked back at Tink. "I can't make any promises," he informed her. "But it will be my number one priority."

"Good talk," she declared, patting him on the shoulder before hopping down. Back on the floor, she walked over to Kisa and hugged the cat girl so hard that a yowl squeaked out of her.

Santa patted his lap, then looked over at Mike and the

others. Yuki came out of the bathroom of the Cocoa Lounge, wiping her hands on her own fur collar.

"Towel dispenser is broken. What's going on?"

"The fat man is giving us gifts, and we get to ask for whatever we want." Lily sneered. "But I suspect he's secretly got a lap fetish and—ow!"

Death had jabbed Lily with a finger underneath the table. "There is no need to be so mean," he said with a scowl.

Lily rolled her eyes. "Fine. The fox can go first."

"Can I ask for Freyja to come back?" Yuki asked.

Santa shook his head. "The goddess Freyja is safe, if that's your concern. I will be honest and say that asking for her return won't affect the outcome."

"Then I am good. I already got what I wanted this Christmas." Yuki took Mike's hand and squeezed it. Her fingers were still a bit damp. She smiled at him as Lily made gagging sounds with a finger down her throat.

Santa frowned, then shrugged. "I can give your wish to someone else, then."

"You're up, Romeo." Lily gave Mike a little push. "You can have my wish too. I'm not sitting on that guy's lap, but seeing you do it will be hilarious."

Mike frowned at Lily. She seemed extra grouchy but likely had her reasons. "Is that okay? Three wishes?"

"I'd like to remind you that these aren't wishes, per se." Santa suddenly looked uncomfortable. "Nobody grants actual wishes anymore. You can ask me for a gift, and I will do my best to give it using the magic of Christmas." He held up his fingers. "Three gifts, actually."

"I see. Well, okay then." Mike approached Santa's chair, aware that all eyes were on him. "Do I have to sit on your lap?"

"No." Santa smiled. "The true magic of Christmas is about giving without expectations. I find that most people like to do it anyway."

"Boo!" Lily had summoned a bullhorn. "Sit on his lap, Caretaker! I want it for my spank bank!"

Death, who was in mid sip, snorted a hefty amount of hot cocoa out of his nose holes. "They make a bank for spankings?!"

Several of the elves actually laughed at this, and Yuki helped mop up the sudden mess on the table. Deciding life was too short, Mike climbed onto Santa's chair to sit in his lap.

Surprisingly, Santa was suddenly much larger than Mike, as if he had grown. Feeling very much like a child again, Mike gazed up at the big man in wonder, though he was wary of the tiny white beard hairs that curled themselves hungrily. His feet hung a couple feet above the ground.

"So you pulled me out of that car wreck. Guess I wanted to say thanks for that."

"You are quite welcome." Santa's eyes sparkled. "And thank you for not seducing my wife."

"You're welcome." Mike chuckled. "How does it feel having a new boss?"

"Refreshing." Santa looked over at Holly, who was chatting with Tink and Kisa. "She's planning to come visit, you know. She was special to begin with, but you helped her realize it for herself."

"She's always welcome. I'd prefer she send a letter next time rather than crash a sleigh into my house." Mike let out a sigh. "So I get to ask for three things, huh?"

"You do. And if they are in my power, you shall have them."

"Well, I can really only think of one thing, but maybe three wishes will do it." He looked up at Santa. "The last couple of years have been…amazing? Impossible? I don't even know the word for it."

"Perhaps unexpected?" Santa lifted an eyebrow.

"Yeah, that works. I've seen some great things but also

experienced some horrible ones. As far as miracles go, there's one in particular I'm thinking of."

"I cannot raise the dead, Michael." Santa shook his head. "The miracles I can accomplish have to be grounded in reality."

"Oh. Do you mean Velvet? That's not what I was thinking." Mike took a moment, suddenly feeling bad that he hadn't even thought about that.

"My apologies. I'm usually better at this, but ever since Holly claimed the North Pole, I don't feel as...plugged in as I used to be." Santa's eyes twinkled. "But that's a good thing."

"Yeah, it is. Actually, I was going to tell you that my biggest regret about all this is what happened to Dana. She's stuck, and I don't know how to fix it. Maybe it violates your dead rule, but I would absolutely use all three of my requests to fix her."

"You were given the opportunity to ask for anything, yet you think of others." Santa laughed, a booming sound that brought smiles to everyone nearby. "But of course you did, Michael. That's just who you are."

"So is that a yes?" Mike's thoughts went back to Dana's awkward dinner with her parents. "It would mean a lot to me."

Santa stared at Mike for a few moments, his gaze suddenly becoming unfocused. Tiny lights like falling snowflakes appeared in his vision, and after almost a minute of silence, he looked back at Mike. "Her journey is not yet done, but perhaps I can provide something to help you both on your way."

Santa reached into his pocket and pulled something out. When he turned over his gloved hands, he was holding three vials of dark fluid. Mike took them and held one up to the light. It immediately made him queasy to look at it.

"These are three drops of my blood, Caretaker. In the spirit of Christmas, I have decided to give you what you need, as well as what you asked for. But I must caution you on their use. The last time I gave someone a drop of my blood, they used it to make a powerful geas around your home."

"That should probably surprise me, but…it makes sense in hindsight." Mike looked at Santa. "So I just give these to Dana?"

"No. You give one to Dana. The other two…well, let's just say you will figure out a use for them." Santa looked over Mike's shoulder. Mike turned around to see the Ghost of Christmas Future standing there, his hands tucked away in his robe.

"I see. Can't tell me more? No instruction manual?"

Santa shook his head. "This is one of those things that cannot rely on instructions."

"Great, well, then…thanks." Mike hopped down off Santa's lap. When he turned around, Santa appeared to be normal size again. "Really, I mean that. Thank you."

"I know." Santa winked. "Now where's my brother?"

"Brother?" Mike looked at the others in confusion, then realized Death had risen from the table and was carrying a gift under his arm. It was Ticktock.

"Indeed, Mike Radley." Death handed the mimic over to Santa. "Didn't you know?"

"Know what?"

"Ticktock was the very first gift of Christmas!" As Death neared Santa, the gift sprouted arms and reached for Santa. "From the First Elf himself!"

Everyone's jaws dropped as Santa chittered at Ticktock with strange hissing sounds. The mimic reacted, then settled down as Santa tucked him under one arm.

"Ticktock will be assisting me this year, along with Death. We have quite the mess to clean, don't we?"

"The toaster is Santa's brother?" Lily stared in disbelief, then threw her hands in the air. "What the absolute fuu…" She noticed the dirty looks being thrown in her direction already. "You know what? Fine, I'm with Romeo. This doesn't even shock me."

"Little does these days." Yuki came to Mike. "I think it's about time we head home, don't you think?"

"Yeah, probably." He looked at Holly. She walked over to him, and he knelt to accept a hug from her. She brushed the hair away from his forehead and planted a kiss on his lips.

"Thank you. For everything," she said.

"You're welcome."

When he stood, Holly took him by the hand and led him over to the fireplace. Once at the flames, she reached into her pocket and threw a handful of glittering powder.

"May I walk you home?"

"You certainly can." Mike allowed her to pull him through the flames, and the slight chill of the North disappeared as he stepped into his home. It was just as he had left it—frozen in time. Seeing Beth on her hands and knees over by the tree, he suddenly felt his throat go dry. In the commotion of everything else, he had forgotten.

"She's pretty." Holly walked over to Beth and hopped onto her butt, using her as a chair. "I have a special present for you."

"You do?"

Holly nodded, then patted Beth's butt. "I do." As if it had been timed, the others came through the gate. Tink swatted Mike on the butt as she walked past, then followed Kisa up the stairs. Yuki winked at Mike on her way out of the room. Lily stopped at the door and pulled a bag of popcorn out of nowhere.

"Hey!" Holly pointed at the succubus. "You all agreed to give them some privacy."

"Technically, you asked if we would all make ourselves scarce and everyone else agreed." Lily tossed a piece of popcorn into her mouth. "I, on the other hand, want to watch him make Beth the mayor of pound town."

Yuki stepped back into the room, grabbed Lily around the waist, and lifted her.

"I'll make sure she stays with me." Yuki tossed Lily over one shoulder and started up the stairs. "Will pin her down if I have to."

"Give her hell, Romeo." Lily licked her lips before disappearing up the stairs.

Holly waited for a moment, then slid off Beth. "When you kiss her, time shall return to normal for all of you, but wait until I leave first. Turns out my promotion actually comes with extra responsibilities." She stopped at the fireplace and turned to face Mike. "Thank you, Caretaker. For everything."

"Merry Christmas, Holly."

"Merry Christmas, Mike." She stepped through the flames and vanished.

Left alone, Mike turned around to look at Beth. With her bent over as she was, he had a perfect look at her ass. Her sweater had come untucked at the back of her pants, revealing the red band of her panties sitting just above her leggings.

"God bless leggings," he muttered. He contemplated Beth's frozen form, taking her in like a work of art. Her legs were toned, as if she'd been regularly exercising. The sweater clung to her body like a second skin, highlighting pendulous breasts. Moving back in front of her, he knelt and took a deep breath.

The last several days had been crazy. With the world stuck in eternal night, he had no idea how long it had been since Holly had crashed into his home. Now here he was, at the moment that had become the finish line. Despite all that he had seen and experienced, this still made him nervous. The women of the house were all beautiful in different ways, yet Beth stood out somehow. It wasn't just a crush or some unrealized love he had for her. The longer he thought about it, the more he realized just how much of himself he recognized in her.

She had no hesitation about her relationships with the others. He had heard the stories about what went down between her and the men at the cabin. The fairies were always sneaking over there to watch and subsequently tell everyone. In a way, she was his opposite, a woman who was having the same experiences he was, just from a different perspective.

Was all this supposed to be hers? He stared at her frozen form, wondering if she had been the original inheritor of this house. It put so many questions and doubts into his head, but he shook them off.

There was no use wondering about what-ifs. He was the Caretaker, and right now, a member of his home needed something from him. His magic came to life and crackled across his knuckles as he leaned forward and planted his lips against Beth's.

There was no disorientation or magical light show as the time lock ended. Instead, it was the soft caress of lips against his own and the slight moan of approval. Beth's tongue sought his, and he touched her face, marveling at how soft her hair was. She jerked back, her eyes suddenly wide.

"What's wrong?" He looked around, half expecting the Krampus to knee drop him from the shadows, or maybe a different sort of extra-dimensional incursion that would result in a battle to the death.

"Is that…is that you?" Beth pondered him, confusion in her eyes. "You feel completely different than you did just a moment ago."

"Um…how do you mean?"

She shook her head as if clearing her thoughts. "You have this sudden presence now. It's almost overwhelming. You feel like a different person, somehow."

He nodded, realizing her instincts were sharp. "It's actually a pretty long story. I'm happy to tell you, but this…" He gestured between the two of them. "…will get put on hold for a bit."

Beth frowned and sat back on the floor. "How much do I need to hear?"

"Probably all of it."

"Was anyone else involved?"

He nodded.

"Did everyone come home okay?" Her eyes were suddenly soft. "Did you come home okay?"

"Honestly?" He pondered his answer for a moment. "I think everyone came back better than they went in."

"So…can it wait?" She bit her lip seductively. "If it's important, I want to hear it all, but I absolutely have something else in mind."

He chuckled and moved toward her. The uncertainty from before was gone, the mental barrier erased. Beth was no longer this mythical, unattainable figure in his head. The line between them had always felt blurry, but now he crossed it without hesitation. "I think that maybe this has already waited long enough."

She was suddenly all over him, pressing herself against his body, her lips on his face and neck. He kissed her back, his magic surging in recognition of the nymph magic she carried. When he slid his hand under her sweater and cupped her breast, their magic resonated, causing the lights around the room to flicker.

"That's new," Beth muttered.

"There's always something new," he replied, pushing her onto her back by the fire. With both hands, he pushed her sweater up to reveal breasts trapped beneath a cotton bra. He almost laughed; he couldn't remember the last time he had seen normal undergarments.

She was fumbling with his pants, distracted by the tiny sparks of light that danced along his knuckles and teased her nipples. He discovered that he could control them now—instead of wandering off, they danced along her sensitive flesh.

"You're making it hard to concentrate," she muttered, and he felt her summon her own magic. Suddenly, a wave of lust washed over him, and he gasped in surprise as his cock became so hard it shoved its way free of his pants.

"It's even bigger in person," Beth muttered, then frantically pulled off her pants and underwear. A thin line of auburn pubic hair pointed like an arrow to her clitoris, which was engorged in such a manner that it looked like a tiny replica of Naia's pearl.

"I assume that's a recent development," he said.

She giggled. "Had to wear skirts for a few days to adjust, but yes. The more in tune I become with water, the more nymphlike I become."

He paused. "And you're happy with the changes?"

Beth nodded. "These are changes I enjoy. As Naia explained once, the magic is helping me become who I truly am on the inside."

He smiled. "I'm happy for you."

When he leaned forward to kiss her, he let his magic dance along her skin as he rubbed his cock against her belly. She moaned in delight, her arms wrapping around his waist as her hands squeezed his ass. Her skin was hot against his, and he could feel her magic twist itself around him, filling him with lustful thoughts.

Beth's magic was like a diluted version of Naia's, but that was to be expected. If his magic hadn't evolved so early on, it would probably be very similar.

"I want you on your back," she said, reaching between them to squeeze his cock. "Mind if I take charge?"

"By all means." He rolled off her, allowing her to scramble on top. Her swollen labia rubbed against his erection. She moaned, then sat up so she could hump him.

"I've been wondering what this would be like for so long," she admitted, the thick nub of her clitoris pressing against his glans.

"Um, same." He laughed. "I'm sorry, it's just…I'm not sure I can compare to your other lovers, outside of my magic. I'm competing with a Minotaur, a dullahan, and a guy who can expand his body."

"That's not true." Her hips rolled, and he realized she was using her clitoris to massage his shaft, sending waves of heat through his pelvis. "It's not a competition, and I'm not playing a game. I'm embracing who I am. I don't imagine the women you're with ask you who's better or who feels tighter."

"I live with Lily." He snorted. "If you can think of an embarrassing question about sex, then she's asked it."

Beth laughed, then groaned as she moved higher on his shaft. He could feel the lips of her pussy part around him, the head of his cock now in that perfect spot for penetration.

"I just wanted to be…clear is all." She stared down at him, her hands on his belly. "I have my own life, but I want you to be a part of it. I would have made my move earlier, but I never wanted you to think I was trying to lock you down. I worked hard, making sure that I would be worthy of this."

"You've always been worthy."

Beth rolled her eyes. "I know that now. But it's no different from your comment about my other lovers."

"I see you're still a good lawyer." He put his hands on her hips, marveling at how soft her flesh was. "Is this the part where we try to reach a settlement?"

"Ugh, no lawyer role-play." She pinched his stomach playfully. "But if you wanna play sexy wizards, I'm game."

They both laughed, which caused Beth to shift her weight. Mike slid inside her less than an inch, and she gasped, her eyes now locked on his.

"I want to ride the lightning," she whispered. "That's what the others call it. I have to know what it feels like, to feel it washing over me and—"

She never got a chance to finish. Mike grabbed her by the hips and thrust himself balls-deep, then commanded the magic to take her from the inside. Beth tensed up, her arms curling up at her sides as tiny sparks emerged from her pores and crawled across her skin.

Beth growled, then leaned forward and put her hands on his shoulders. Her eyes were glowing blue now, and a wave of her sexual energy rolled across him. For just a moment, all he could think about was the weight of her body on his, those perfect thighs wrapped around his waist while his cock was buried inside her pussy.

Smiling, he pushed her magic back onto her. Beth gasped, her mouth opening wide as she was forced to endure her own magic on top of his. Her cheeks and chest turned a deep crimson as each breath became a struggle. Digging her nails into his skin, Beth screwed up her face in concentration, then lifted her hips and slammed herself onto him.

That was all it took. When Beth came, the lights in the room flickered dangerously, and it felt like she might crush him between her legs. Her whole body was so tense now that she had become a statue, and a small pool of fluid filled the space between them.

"Holy shit," she whispered, her voice filled with awe.

"That's only the beginning." Mike winked at her. "If you think you can handle it, that is."

Growling, Beth leaned forward and planted her lips on his. When her tongue entered his mouth, he could feel the magic attempt to claim him, to drive him insane with lust. The force was surprisingly easy to manipulate, but he allowed it to drive him wild. His hard cock was already throbbing for release.

Still, this was Beth, and this moment had been over a year in the making. He wasn't ready to let her off the hook so easily. Mike pushed the magic back into her, and her legs sprang free from beneath him, going straight back as another orgasm struck, causing her to topple forward. Even with her hair in his face, he could still see her soul, visualizing it in his mind's eye as a swirling mass of light-filled water. With each thrust of his body, he could see the ripples he caused, watching in delight as his magic sank into her core and made her tremble.

Beth groaned as she rose to a sitting position, his lap now sticky with her fluids. "How are you doing that?" she asked. "It's like my whole body is one giant nerve!"

"You mean this?" He flexed his cock inside her, then teased her with the magic once more, concentrating on the ripples. They were his to command, and Beth cried out in sweet agony as she rode him to yet another orgasm. The humidity in the room had increased drastically. Little clouds of water vapor appeared around them as her magic spiraled out of control. Every time it threatened to claim him, he pushed it back, watching in delight as Beth lost control.

This was the woman that had held it together during a fight with the horsemen of the Apocalypse. She'd battled an evil spirit with a powerful grimoire without so much as a complaint, had been sucked into his strange world without even blinking. He had never seen her rattled or knocked off-kilter.

But now she was a mess. Her skin glistened with sweat, and her hair was now tangled. Magical sparks danced across her exposed skin, coalescing around her nipples as her eyes went unfocused. The moisture-laden air hummed with magic, Beth openly drooling as he took full control of her orgasms. Sometimes he would hold her on the very edge, while other times, he would make her have them back-to-back. Her magic only served as fuel for his own, and he poured all that energy straight back into her until she finally let out a groan and collapsed on top of him.

"Holy…shit…" Her eyes fluttered, and she turned a dreamy gaze on him. "Is that what it always feels like?"

"No." He pushed the hair out of her face. "You haven't seen the real sparks fly yet."

"I want to see them, Mike." She giggled. "But I'm too tired to be on top anymore."

That was all the permission he needed. He slid out from beneath her, and she moaned as a copious amount of liquid formed a pool beneath her belly. She let out a raspy laugh as she looked over her shoulder at him.

"I may be tired, but I like it rough," she said. "Don't go easy on me."

Mike stared at her body, contemplating the magnificent orbs of her ass. He had seen it so many times through skirts and pants, and now that it was in front of him, all he could do was stare. It had always been a great ass, but now that a nymph's magic was helping to perfect it? It was truly a masterpiece.

He gave it a playful swat and was delighted to see that this caused ripples both along Beth's skin and on the outside of her soul. When he swatted it again, she cried out in pleasure.

"Like what you see, Caretaker?" She wiggled her ass for him. The movement itself was borderline hypnotic, and he didn't bother fighting the stupid grin that appeared. Things had changed between them, but in a lot of good ways, they had stayed the same. They just happened to be two really close friends with sex powers who fucked from time to time.

Well, at least he hoped there would be a next time.

"I'm about to show you how much I like it." He straddled her legs, teasing her labia with the head of his cock. She whimpered, her fingers picking at the Christmas tree skirt that was within reach.

When he slid inside, she let out a full-throated groan. Her magic rushed up to meet his once more, but this time, he let it in. His heart raced as he built a steady tempo, pounding her from behind. Whenever his body slammed against the meat of her ass, tiny lights appeared in the air all around them.

"Ah, yeah, give it to me!" Beth tried to push herself up on her hands and knees, so he put his legs inside hers so she could move. A string of curses came out of her as he proceeded to pound her even harder. She paused just long enough to demand that he pull her hair, and he saw no reason not to obey.

He could feel it building within him, a monstrous orgasm. The air was saturated with the smell of sex and ozone, and sweat ran down his forehead in rivers. The runes were drawing themselves on her soul, and he watched as his magic began to gather in what little space separated them. His cock was so slippery now that he would occasionally pull out just to wipe some fluid off with his hands.

Beth was practically incoherent at this point. He didn't know if she was just enjoying herself or if he had blown her mental fuse. Either way, his own orgasm was approaching, and he couldn't help but stare at her soul. Everything she had achieved, she had done on her own terms, in her own way. Her magic was something she had nurtured on her own, carefully cultivating its growth. They may be alike in a lot of ways, but where he was chaos, she was order.

"I'm about to come," he said.

"Wait," she whimpered, catching her breath. "Not there."

He bit his lip, forcing the fire in his belly down as he slid out of her. "Where do you want it?" he asked.

"Right here." She reached back and pulled her ass cheeks apart. "Come inside my ass, Mike."

His mouth was suddenly dry, and he licked his lips in anticipation. When he placed the head of his cock at the entrance to her ass, she arched her back to give him a better angle. The runes on her soul turned to mist and disappeared.

"I'll try to go slow—" he began.

"Like hell you will. If I can take Bigfoot back there, I can take you." She grabbed onto the tree skirt again. "Now fuck me like you mean it!"

He started slow but was surprised to discover that her ass had no problem accommodating his girth. Her ass was phenomenally tight but stretched without any problems. His cock was still soaking wet, so lube wasn't a problem in the slightest. When he was halfway into her ass, his trepidation vanished as his magic guided his actions. This wasn't just the ass of a beautiful woman. This was the ass of a beautiful woman with nymph magic running through her body.

Mike grabbed Beth's hair and pulled her head back as he slammed himself the rest of the way in.

"YES!" Beth cried, her hands now frantically grabbing for anything as he rammed himself into her. The lightning gathered between them anew, crawling across the hemispheres of her buttocks like a miniature aurora borealis.

It was too much. Between Beth's screams of pleasure and the tightness on his shaft, he exploded inside her. Copious amounts of cum blasted her insides, and his magic took no prisoners, washing over both of them. Several of the lights in the room brightened, and then a few burned out as his magic took them both over.

Beth pulled several ornaments off the tree when she came. Her magic fed into his own, those tiny sparks of his gobbling up her aura like it was food. When it came back to him, he came inside her ass again, hollering in ecstasy as he pushed himself deep inside her. More lights blew out, and Beth collapsed to the ground beneath him, her whole body twitching as she lost control.

He had no idea how much time passed or how many orgasms they exchanged. By the time he finally pulled himself out of Beth, there was a massive pool of their combined fluids all over the floor. The fairies had arrived some time ago, all four of them rolling around in the puddle while they feasted. Mike went limp on top of Beth, his hand going down to her ass and giving it a squeeze.

"They really could base a religion on this ass," he muttered.

Beth snorted, her eyes barely visible through her hair. "So I've been told."

They lay there, exchanging small talk for quite some time. Eventually, Carmina tried to bury herself in the crack of Beth's ass, so she pulled the trespasser free and sat up.

"The others lied to me," she said, looking around the room for her clothes.

"Oh?"

"Yeah. They undersold the experience." Beth winked at him as she stacked up her clothes. "I'm just gonna walk of shame my way home, if you don't mind."

"Still a place for you here if you want it." Mike paused. "Whatever bed you want, honestly."

She knelt and caressed his face. "Thank you for the offer, but I'm still enjoying my own space. I thought I had it all figured out, but it looks like I've got some catching up to do."

"It's not a race," he said.

"Oh, I know. But it doesn't mean I don't want to keep pace." She planted a kiss on his lips, her eyes sparkling. "And, Mike?"

"Yeah."

"Thanks for letting me just be me." Beth kissed him one more time. "I'll be back in the morning. Merry Christmas."

"Merry Christmas, Beth." He watched her go and let out a sigh. Lying back on the floor, he chuckled as the fairies swarmed his lap, eager to lick him clean. It had been a really good Christmas.

THROUGH THE FRONT WINDOW OF THE LIVING ROOM, LILY watched as the others started another one of their silly snowball fights. She had her arms crossed beneath a bright-red sweater Tink had knitted her for Christmas and was holding a mug of hot cocoa with her tail. It was Christmas Day, and she was feeling miserable.

She sighed, contemplating the battle outside. It looked like there were now three groups. Beth, Mike, and Cecilia had teamed up against Tink, Kisa, and Jenny while Yuki and Abella rained icy terror on all from above. There was no keeping score or moments of anger. In fact, Cerberus, in human form, was absolutely mesmerized by the snow and kept chasing after the snowballs that were thrown her way. It was just some good old-fashioned family fun.

Lily caught sight of her scowling reflection in the window and turned away. She plopped down onto the nearest chair and winced. Leaning forward, she pulled what looked like a Monopoly hotel from underneath her butt. One end had been melted into a fine point.

"I should really start coming to game night," she muttered, flicking the hotel across the room. It bounced off the wall and vanished behind the couch.

"Well, you seem full of Christmas cheer." The voice was soft but powerful. Lily turned around in her seat to see Christmas Present standing by the fireplace. Her once red hair was now flecked with white, and she had crow's-feet in the corners of her eyes.

Lily slid out of her seat and moved to the spirit, her mouth open wide. "You…what happened?"

"You refer to my appearance?" Christmas Present smiled. "I think you forget that today is my special day. When it is over, I shall become the Ghost of Christmas Past, just as my predecessors have."

"It's not fair." Lily wrapped her arms around the spirit and inhaled her scent. Christmas Present smelled like peppermints. "Your life is so short!"

"On the contrary. I am the spirit of the season! For wherever there is celebration this day, I am there. As the day progresses, I shall bear witness to hundreds of years' worth of celebration. It will pass much faster for you, but for me? It will become everything." Christmas Present hugged Lily. "Weep not for me, dear friend. I will have lived plenty when the night is over and shall have this day forevermore."

Lily sniffed, rubbing her face against the spirit's robe. "So what? Just thought you'd make a special appearance to make me cry or whatever?"

"Nay!" The fireplace ignited, sending flames up the chimney as Death stepped out. His robes and body were decorated with garland, glitter, and all things Christmas. "For she hath brought with her tidings of joy and good cheer! Me!"

Even Death's scythe had been decorated, wrapped up in red-and-white ribbon. A fur-lined stocking with his name hung from the far end of it, bulging with candy and small gifts. He turned around toward the fireplace and waved at the flames.

Christmas Present chuckled. "Santa wanted me to bring him back. He's been a great help, but he should spend the day with his family." She looked out the window. "As should you."

Lily snorted and stepped away from the giant. "Please. If you think you're just going to waltz into my day with that hot body and some dommy-mommy vibes in order to make me change my stripes, you are sorely mistaken. I can't be fixed."

"Shame." The giant stroked Lily's cheek with an oversize hand. "Regardless, I heard from my sibling Christmas Future that Mike will be getting a very special present from you sometime around three o'clock. Something about a hot elf role-play fantasy?"

Lily smirked. "Please. I'm going to set the bar for hot elf role-play."

"Do you think he'd mind if I join in?" The spirit's eyes sparkled.

Lily laughed. "He's gonna need a new bed, isn't he?"

"Perhaps." Christmas Present ran her hands through Lily's hair. "Until later, then. Just remember, this is my day. I'm always watching." With that, the ghost transformed into silver specks of light that floated through the floor and disappeared.

"Watching me the whole day? That's kinda hot," Lily muttered, turning her attention outside. "Bet she's been getting worked up all day staring at Romeo. Probably watched that romp he had with Beth last night too."

"Lily, my dear friend!" Death wrapped his arm around Lily's shoulder and held up a cell phone. The grim reaper snapped a selfie of the two of them and tucked the phone away in his pocket. "I had the most amazing time at the North Pole! Santa said I can come with him every year to deliver presents if I wish! I'm going to meet so many children in the years ahead. Isn't that great?"

"Sounds kinda dark when you put it that way," she said with a frown. "But I'm glad you're happy. And who gave you a phone?"

"Santa did, of course. It's so we can stay in touch. I can even send him emojis! It took us quite some time to get the North Pole put back together, and we are very good friends now." Death pulled a cloth bag from his robes that Lily recognized as the one they had lost to the Krampus. "By the way, Santa taught me how to do woodworking. Would you like to see?"

Lily fought the urge to roll her eyes. "Okay, what did you make in woodshop? Is it a birdhouse?"

Death held out a rectangular package wrapped in green paper. "There are no birds at the North Pole, my friend. Here, this is for you."

Lily took it with a frown. "What is it?"

"If I told you, then why bother wrapping it?" Death chuckled, the blue fire in his sockets shedding tiny sparks. "Open it!"

She slid her finger along the edge, using her nail to cut the paper. With one quick movement, she unwrapped the gift, revealing an ornate frame with decorative inlays made of sea glass.

"I collected those on our trip together," Death said, touching the different stones. "If you are interested, I can tell you where each one came from."

"Not right now." She stared at the frame for a moment, contemplating its beauty. It looked to be made from a single piece of wood, and she had no idea how he had embedded the sea glass inside it. "It's beautiful, Death. Thank you."

"I made it from oak because you're the strongest person I know." Death pulled some more gifts from his bag and set them under the tree for the others to find later. "And it is the perfect size for that drawing Reagan made for you."

A chill ran down Lily's spine, and she glanced at the reaper.

"You don't have to put that in there if you don't want to," Death continued, paying no special attention to her. "And I know what you're thinking. I would like to reassure you that this frame is just a gift and that I still owe you many favors."

"Very many," she added, narrowing her eyes.

Death nodded sagely. "Indeed. And should you ever wish to collect, you know where to find me. Ah!" He knelt by the tree and picked up a package with his name on it. He gave it a shake and grinned. "This must be a new tea I haven't tried yet!"

"You can tell just by shaking it?" Lily asked.

Death nodded. "It's a trick I picked up on the road with Santa. If you'll excuse me, I am very excited to try it."

She watched the reaper leave, then turned her attention to the picture frame. With trembling hands, she summoned Reagan's drawing and slid it into place. It was a perfect fit.

It felt like the room was spinning. She set the picture down on the table and contemplated it for a moment, hot tears filling her eyes. Outside, she heard the others laughing. The woman in the picture frame looked like she would fit right in with the festivities, unburdened by a shameful past.

"Damn it, Death." Grinding her teeth, she walked toward the front door, a coat and snow pants appearing on her body. She casually dodged the snow, crossing the yard to where Mike and Beth had built a small snow wall.

The snowball fight continued right up until Lily took Mike by the hand. He looked at her in surprise, then melted in her arms when she put her lips to his. She clutched his face in her hands, as if afraid he might disappear. The battle came to a standstill as her wings popped free behind her back. It was an involuntary reaction, but Mike didn't seem to care. When she broke the kiss, she stared into those beautiful eyes of his.

"I want my own room," she told him. "Here. For Christmas. A place that's just mine. I have a picture I want to put up in it."

"Uh, yeah! Sure!" He looked surprised but genuinely excited. "Here, let's go inside and figure somethi—"

"No, not right now." She grabbed a generous quantity of snow with her tail and curled it up behind her. "I'm on Yuki's team."

With that, she smashed the snow into Mike's face, whitewashing him until he fell over backward with a laugh. Beth grabbed Lily from behind, pinning her wings so she couldn't get away as Tink and Kisa pelted the succubus with snowballs. Abella swooped down and pulled Lily free, the succubus loudly vowing revenge on her attackers. When she looked down, it was to see that Tink was mooning her from atop her own fort.

The snowball fight was still stupid, childish at best. Laughter echoed across the yard, filling Lily for the first time with a different kind of warmth.

There was no place she would rather be.

The Jabberwock sat at attention, its serpentine neck elevated so Yuki could sit on the end of his snout with a thermos full of hot chocolate. The others had gotten too cold hours ago, but she was content to sit outside and gaze out over the neighborhood.

A storm had blown in overnight, painting the world anew in a fresh white coat. Other than a couple of people out for a Christmas walk, the world was relatively untouched. Tomorrow, the streets would be plowed, and trash would start to pile up by the curb, mostly boxes and wrapping paper. But for now, it was perfect.

The front yard was a mess. Large chunks of yard had been revealed by displacing the snow, but even those looked small in comparison to the structures that had been built for the fight. She smiled, thinking about how happy everyone was to see a fresh blanket of the good stuff after waking. The fight had been Tink's idea, which surprised nobody.

With a thought, Yuki commanded the yard to reset itself. Walls of ice fractured into soft powder that filled in the gaps, and a snowman with a giant carrot for a penis turned into three balls that unrolled themselves all over the yard. Within minutes, the yard looked as if nobody had ever been there, a blank canvas once more.

A chill breeze tousled Yuki's hair, and she felt a presence behind her.

"Nice trick." Freyja sat down next to Yuki, causing the Jabberwock to snort. Yuki patted the beast, settling it down with her will. "Where'd you learn that?"

"Picked a few things up in the arctic. You know how it goes." She offered her thermos to Freyja. "Do you want some? It's not as good as the stuff Santa has, but it's pretty close."

"No, but thank you." The goddess looked tired, her white hair longer than it had used to be. "I thought I would drop by and see how you were doing."

"Me?" Yuki leaned back and smiled. "I'm doing great."

"I'm grateful to hear that." Freyja looked down at the yard. "I saw your snowball fight earlier. It looked like fun."

"You should have joined us." Yuki looked over at Freyja. "In fact, why didn't you join us? We didn't see you after the big fight. What happened?"

"I paid a rather large price for our victory." Freyja held out her hand. Curious, Yuki took it. "It took me some time to come to terms with it, but I finally have."

"Are you okay?" Yuki held the goddess's hand for a moment before realizing how warm it felt. "Freyja, what happened?"

"The world has changed, Yuki. As all things do." She gazed over at the house. "Have you ever wondered why the gods abandoned humanity?"

"Who hasn't? I know for a fact that gods exist, which kind of makes it worse. But who am I to question the will of the gods?" She opened up the thermos and drank straight from it. "You sure you don't want some?"

"We had no choice." Freyja let out a sigh. "During the battle for the North Pole, more of my memories returned. Disturbing ones. The gods didn't abandon this world on a whim or even for self-preservation. We were forced to flee from predators."

"Predators?" Yuki frowned. "Who would challenge the gods?"

Freyja's face twisted up. "We called them the Others. We used to call them the outsiders, but that isn't entirely accurate. They came through the cracks in this world, attacking the gods where they lived.

"What you don't know is that these Others surpassed us in strength and numbers. They couldn't be killed, at least not in a manner we were aware of. Many of us were slain, and the rest of us scattered. We didn't abandon mankind to save our own skins though. I don't ever want you to think that." The goddess took her hand back from Yuki. "They were attracted to our power. That's how the Others found this world in the first place. We went into hiding to make this place harder to find, but that meant losing ourselves in the process."

"I see." Yuki looked over at the goddess. "So what does that mean for you now?"

"I'm not sure. But I had to make a choice. You see, as a goddess, I was the embodiment of many things. In a way, I have lost a right to many of those claims. There are those out there who still have faith in me, and it's time I do right by them. They deserve a reason to believe."

"So you're gonna be Freyja officially? Make a comeback?"

"In a way." Freyja grinned. "When the Others broke into this world, there was a man who had an insane idea on how to hold them back. He wanted to build something that would hold the cracks shut, like driving a screw into the edges of reality. It would be some of the most powerful magic that the world had ever seen, but it came at a heavy cost. He built several legendary artifacts, structures tied strongly together by our love of games. As long as these structures exist, the Others cannot come through and claim this world.

"Knowing this, I can't be the only one who survived. The other gods are out there somewhere, and I plan to find them. While the Others are locked away, we have the chance to build our strength anew for when they inevitably return. But we can't come back as we once were. This world is too different. New gods must rise to replace those who have fallen. Surely this you understand."

"I do." Yuki's tails twitched behind her. "And I assume some of these new gods will be less than desirable?"

"Indubitably. I will need those I can trust to have humanity's interests at heart. Which is why I want to be the first to recognize you formally as the new goddess of winter." Freyja turned toward Yuki and bowed low with her hands together over her heart.

Yuki felt something shift inside her and gasped. "What did you do?"

"Recognized you and relinquished my title. During my fight at the North Pole, I was forced to choose. I couldn't be the goddess of so many things when my power was weak. My followers have prayed to me all these decades and never received an answer. And so I let certain things go. My divinity lives on inside you, Yuki. I can feel it, like a distant heartbeat. I can no longer command the ice and snow as I once did. This power is now yours."

"But...that can't be right? I can't be a god. I don't even have all my tails!" Yuki touched her chest. "It's not like I feel any different."

"And you won't. None of us became gods overnight. You now have a legacy to live up to as Old Man Winter." Freyja smirked. "Or you could always go by a cute name like Jack Fox."

"Ugh, no." Yuki wrinkled up her nose. "I don't want to be a god. I just want to stay here and be with my family."

"As you should." Freyja stood. "But now that I have recognized you as such, you are officially on the path. Your powers will grow, their boundaries set only by your determination. I will need others like you, someday. To become new beacons of light for the world, ready to stand and defend it when the time comes. And I shall become stronger too. The age of miracles is about to return."

Down below, the front door of the house opened, and Mike stepped out. He slipped something into his pocket and contemplated the fresh appearance of the front yard. He rubbed at his lower back and did a couple of stretches. Yuki noticed that Freyja watched him with a smile.

"You have plans for him too." Yuki shook her head. "I can promise you that godhood isn't something he wants."

"I know. Some people chase greatness. Others have it thrust upon them."

"He wants what I do. A quiet life for his family."

"I know." Freyja grinned. "And that's what makes him so special." The wind picked up, ruffling Yuki's fur. Down below, Mike adjusted the collar of his jacket and zipped it up, oblivious that he was being watched.

"And what if I say no?" Yuki scowled at Freyja. "What if I don't want any part in this fight?"

"You don't have a choice. For you see, my dear kitsune, that man has become the Caretaker of several of these magical structures. Should he ever fall, it is possible that the world shall fall with him." Freyja's whole body became translucent as the wind carried her into the sky, and her voice became a whisper in Yuki's ears.

Go forth, child of winter. Know that Freyja watches over you.

Stunned, Yuki stared into the empty sky. She heard the crunching of footsteps below as Mike made his way through the hedge maze to where the sundial sat. It looked like he was getting ready to reset it.

Eager to tell him what she had just learned, Yuki leaped from the Jabberwock's snout, commanding the snowbank below to catch her. Mike looked in her direction, then waved. He waited for her in the center of the maze.

"Hey," she said. "Freyja was just here."

"Oh, really? How is she?"

"Fine, I guess. Gonna go out and find her followers and some of the other gods." Yuki gave Mike a brief summary of what she had learned.

"I see." He sighed. "Well, I quit expecting things to be quiet after our first Apocalypse."

"Our *last* Apocalypse," she corrected him.

"Probably not. The end of the world is relative, after all." He reached into his pocket and pulled out Tink's goggles.

"What are you doing with those?"

Mike grinned. "It's a surprise. Want to see?"

"Sure." She stood back as he pulled a small vial from his pocket. "Is that blood?"

"Sure is. A single drop of Santa's blood." Mike put his hands on the sundial, the lenses flicking into place. "I spent a lot of time in bed last night going over things in my head."

"From what I heard, you spent a lot of time in bed last night turning Tink into an air-raid siren."

Mike winced. "Yeah, sorry about that. She was being a bit loud."

"More than a bit. And why does she call you her special hammer?" Yuki actually knew the answer to this but absolutely loved seeing Mike turn beet red and squirm. "Also, I'm sure you both know this, but you never need to lube a hammer. It's a safety hazard."

Mike stared straight ahead. "God loves you," he muttered.

"What?"

"Just checking that you're not a certain succubus. Anyway, I was thinking about some stuff. Did you know that a drop of Santa's blood was what originally established the geas?"

Yuki shook her head. "Nobody knew where the geas had come from. We always just accepted that it was here."

He nodded. "Well, Santa informed me that I could use this to strengthen the geas even further. I talked it over with Ratu, and I think we might be able to upgrade it. Make it even better than before."

"How are you going to do that?"

He turned and looked up at the house. "I've wondered more than once if the house is alive. On a few occasions, I've even spoken with the spirit that inhabits it. The North Pole has one, and so does the cabin. All part of some game I don't really care that much about, to be honest. All I want is to protect my home and my family from harm."

Mike held up the vial of Santa's blood. "Its rooms are already there but forgotten. It changes shape before our eyes, reality rewriting itself to accommodate. Remind you of anything?"

"You think the house was built out of…an Ancient One?"

"No. The spirit of this home is definitely grounded in our reality, but it makes me wonder: was it designed to mimic one? And for what purpose? Every time I get answers, it just creates more questions. Truthfully, the most important question I can ask is how to keep everybody safe." Mike set the vial down on the sundial and watched the stone timer click through its final minute. Once time ran out, a chill wind blew across the yard, making Yuki shiver. "So I'm going to do what the house does. We're going to hide in plain sight."

Mike looked at her, then back up at the house. "I will protect everyone," he said, raising his voice. "They say that home is where your heart is, but guess what? It doesn't have to be a place. It can be a friend, a lover, or a child. So if a geas can wrap itself around a piece of land, why not the people inside? And don't think for a moment that I'm doing it for you. I don't give a damn about your Architect or your game." He picked up the vial and pulled the stopper free. Yuki's ears popped, and the fading light of day bent and warped around the opening of the vial.

"I'm doing this because I'm the Caretaker," he declared. "And these are the people I love." He dumped the single drop of blood onto the sundial, then summoned lightning into his hands. The air around him sizzled as he grabbed the sundial and gave it a twist.

The drop of blood became mercurial, coating the sundial in a silver gloss that Yuki could see her reflection in. Mike's magic was carried along with it, dancing across the ground and causing the earth beneath the snow to glow blue and purple. Mike's attention was on the sundial at first, and then he spun around and stared at the house.

Before their eyes, the house changed colors. Multiple variations of the home appeared, as if it was trying on different appearances. The Victorian home was suddenly a quaint cottage, then a stone fortress, followed by what looked like a fishing hut. It expanded rapidly, eventually settling on a proper manor with at least four floors. The structure had at least doubled in both length and depth, and large portions of the building had been replaced with intricate stonework. The turret over his bedroom was now matched in height only by the observatory on the opposite corner, and the placement of the windows indicated his room was now a private fifth floor. Balconies had protruded from numerous windows, which would allow their occupants to sit outside should they choose. Up above, thick stony ridges had formed, perfect for a certain gargoyle who enjoyed lurking.

"I knew it," Mike whispered, his eyes on something Yuki couldn't see. The sundial sent a beam of blue light into the sky where it collided with a spherical barrier. Motes of light floated down from above and winked out of existence before they could touch anything.

A ring of light emerged from the house and washed over both of them. When it passed through Yuki, she became light-headed and grabbed Mike's hand for support. He squeezed her hand firmly but didn't look away from a spot above the home. She squinted in the same direction but still couldn't see what he had.

After several minutes, the blue light faded. Cecilia appeared on her swing, her face composed as she surveyed the much larger front porch that had appeared. Through the closed windows, Yuki could hear the shouts of surprise as everyone realized the house had expanded once again.

"C'mon," he said, pulling Yuki toward the door. "Let's see what our magical home has in store for us today."

With a smile, she obliged. She would follow him anywhere.

The cemetery behind St. Andrew's was quiet, most of the markers buried under a thin blanket of snow. It was late in the afternoon, and other than some light traffic out on the street, the world was quiet. In the distance, the skyscrapers of New York stood watch like slumbering giants.

Kisa knelt, brushed the ice and snow off the marker, and let out a sigh when she read the name.

Yuriy Petrov

She brushed away some more snow. The small headstone had been paid for by his church, so other than his name and the year of his death, it was blank.

"I should have come to your funeral," she began. "I mean, maybe I did, but I can't remember. Some bad stuff went down, but you should know that I'm sorry I forgot who you were," she said, apologizing to the grave of the man who had saved her from the streets. "Would you like to hear about it?"

A distant car honked at someone crossing the street. Kisa waited a few moments before she continued. She told Yuriy all about how she had gone on a hunt to remove the cursed collar on her neck and ended up trapped by Emily. The details for that period weren't necessary, but if his spirit was somehow listening, she wanted him to know how and why she had forgotten all about him.

From there, she talked about how she had ended up with Mike, both in his house and as his familiar. The words poured out of her like water as she spilled years' worth of pent-up feelings. It no longer mattered if anyone was there; these were words that needed to be said.

She told Yuriy all about the horsemen of the Apocalypse, and that time she'd been possessed by a spirit. Tink and Mike both came up, but she left out the sexy parts. After rambling for nearly an hour, she let out a heavy sigh.

"You're probably wondering how I found you." Kisa reached into her coat and pulled out the packet of adoption papers. "For my most recent adventure, I went to the North

Pole and ended up finding these in Santa's Undeliverables Warehouse. Turns out you died of a heart attack right before Christmas, and Santa has to jump through the same legal bullshit we all do. That's so stupid, right? Jolly old fat guy has to plan his Christmas miracles months or even years in advance. I was supposed to wake up on Christmas Day and find these under the tree."

The papers trembled in her hands. "When Holly first told me all about it, I'll admit I cried. It took me a few days to wrap my head around how such a stupid thing as a heart attack had changed my life completely. If not for that cursed collar, I would have gone back to being an orphan. Nobody even missed me when I disappeared. How messed up is that?"

She laughed sadly, then set the papers down by the grave. "I signed them, just so you know. Not that it matters, considering I'm legally dead now. Regardless, I would have been happy to be your daughter, would have traded everything for it, in fact. I looked up my family, or what's left of them. Mom was an addict who dropped off the radar. No dad on file. My grandmother took me in but died from a stroke when I was eleven. I spent a couple years on the street before you found me and taught me to dance. I had nobody, was nobody, yet you saw worth in me, convinced me I could be something. You were a dancer who fled the fall of the Soviet Union; you knew all about starting your whole life over and about putting faith in others.

"I guess for the longest time, I was worried that my life was full of people who abandoned me because of who I was. My mom, if she's still alive, doesn't have an address. Grandma is in an unmarked grave somewhere, so I can't even visit her. You were the only connection to my old life. Maybe these papers couldn't bring me the happily ever after that I wanted, but they helped me find the closure to chase the one I deserve. Once upon a time, you were my whole family. The one I have now though?" She chuckled and looked over her shoulder. Death and Mike stood several headstones over, sharing a large thermos of hot chocolate. The grim reaper had a large pad of paper and was using a crayon to take rubbings from the graves, a trick Mike had taught him.

"They're pretty great." She stared up into the sky and sat with her feelings for a bit. Once she was ready to go, she pulled a black marker from her pocket and wrote the word *father* below Yuriy's name. Leaning forward, she placed a kiss on the cold marble and then stood. When she walked back over to Mike, he stopped talking to Death and gave her his full attention.

"How are you feeling?" he asked.

"Good, I guess." She shrugged. "Not really sure. Dead father issues and all that jazz."

Death nodded sagely. "Indeed. The loss of a parent is a difficult situation, no matter—"

Kisa stood on her tiptoes and placed her hand over Death's mouth. "Shush." Some moments were simply better when less was said.

"We can stay longer if you'd like. Whatever you need." Mike ran his hand between her ears in a way that made her shiver in delight.

"Nah, I'm good. We can go whenever."

They turned and walked toward the edge of the cemetery where a gnarled tree stood. Once nearby, Mike stopped and looked out at the city.

"Oh, by the way. I sort of accidentally promised Death we could go see Times Square."

"He did, Kisa Radley." Death was busy folding up his gravestone rubbings to tuck them away into his robes. "But it is your day, and I do not wish to intrude."

She laughed at this. "I guess we can go check it out. But aren't you worried you might scare the shit out of someone?"

Death shook his head. "This is New York, my feline friend.

Even if someone is able to see me, I doubt I shall even be noticed."

"Well, I guess we'll see about that." Kisa slid her hand into Mike's, feeling his magic rub against hers. With just a thought, she willed her magic to extend over his body, hiding him in plain sight. To anybody watching, everything else in the cemetery would suddenly be far more interesting. "Shall we?"

"We shall." Mike put his hand on the tree, and the portal opened. The three of them stepped through, finally leaving Kisa's past behind.

SUNLIGHT STREAMED THROUGH THE DINING ROOM WINDOW, illuminating the tray of bacon that had been set to cool on the counter. Sofia hummed to herself, swaying her hips from side to side as Mike came up from behind. She jumped when he put his hands on her hips, then turned around to swat him with a spatula.

"Don't sneak up on me!" She gave him another playful swat.

"You said you didn't want me smacking your butt anymore." He winked at her. "But that cancels out your early warning system, now doesn't it?"

"Silly man. I didn't expect you to listen." She pushed her fingers through his hair. "It's getting long again. You should cut it."

Mike sighed and looked out the window at Naia. She was busy doing her princess bit with some birds who had stuck around for the winter. Her fountain was heated, and the local fauna treated his enlarged backyard like a sanctuary of sorts. Currently, she was singing to a group of finches who did little circles over her head.

"Yeah," he replied, watching the nymph. "I was planning on it today, actually."

Distracted, he didn't notice when Sofia wound her arm back and swatted him in the ass with the spatula. He jumped and rubbed at his backside, giving her a frown.

"I thought I was supposed to see that coming," he muttered.

"Perhaps." Sofia's cheeks were flushed pink. "You should stop by the Library later. Come see me in the Head Librarian's office. We have some stuff to go over." She pulled her apron off and hung it on a nearby hook. "Breakfast is ready for anyone who wants it, but I'm off to organize a new shipment. See you later?"

"Of course. Need me to bring anything?"

The cyclops grinned, then handed Mike the spatula. "Maybe that. And the apron."

Intrigued, he swung the spatula experimentally, cracking it on the palm of his other hand. "I mean, you could just stick around if you wanted."

"I could, but I do actually have a shipment of books coming in that require special handling. Some stuff Eulalie helped me procure." She licked her lips. "Don't disappoint me, Caretaker."

"I don't plan to." He watched Sofia saunter off, then turned his attention to the coffee maker. Moments later, Yuki ducked through the door in a pink terry-cloth robe.

"Thank gods, I thought you two were going to fuck in front of the bacon." The kitsune grabbed a few pieces off the pan and turned her attention to the nearby platters of eggs, sausage, and toast. While she was loading her plate, others arrived. The kitchen became busy as anyone capable of eating food made a plate for themselves. Mike leaned against the counter and watched everyone with a smile, then made his own plate and went out to the dining room.

The dining room was larger than ever, but the massive table was the same as before. It was one of the rooms in the house that had changed the least after the last transformation.

His own bedroom now had a sitting area and had become large enough that the windows overlooked the entire property. The observatory was on the opposite side of the manor and was more tower than turret. Dana had been surprised to see that the house had changed, but immediately took the room that had appeared just outside the observatory. It was almost as if it had been built just for her.

Lily's room was just down the hall from Mike's. Other than a very decadent bed that she would never sleep in, the only piece of furniture was the beautiful picture frame that Death had made for her. Mike had noticed that she dodged any questions about who drew that wonderful picture of her, but figured he would learn who Reagan was eventually.

Mike sat and ate breakfast, then took care of his dishes and wandered toward the front of his manor. The front room of the house had expanded into a large open space with a double staircase that went up to the second floor. A beautiful mosaic had been built into the wooden floor using different types of hardwood. The pattern was intricate and shimmered in the daylight, scattering colors like a prism. Some of the larger windows higher up had been replaced with stained glass that Mike was certain would be a bitch to repair.

Reggie and Jenny sat at one of the couches, locked in yet another battle of wills. This time, it was over a game of Connect Four. Mike was surprised that it hadn't lost any pieces yet.

He stepped out front and took a deep breath. The cold air entered his lungs, and he let it all out in a single burst.

"Mike." Cecilia appeared next to him and laid her head on his shoulder. "Good morning, *mo stór.*"

He put a hand around her waist and squeezed, his fingers sliding along the cool fabric of her eternal dress. When he planted a kiss on her head, he noticed that the red streak of hair was thicker than it had been.

His manor now sat atop a small hill, the plot of land

around his home nearly triple in size. The distances between the home, garage, and greenhouse were easily three times bigger, and he guessed his property was probably around twenty acres now, all enclosed by formidable stone walls that were several feet thick. He had no idea how large his home would get but had decided that it was never something he would worry about. The people already here were the important ones.

"How are you?" he asked.

"I am well." She sighed, her empty gaze fixed on the distant road. "How did you sleep?"

"I slept okay." In fact, it hadn't been great. There had been a lot on his mind, and he had spent a good chunk of his time in the Dreamscape having a heated debate with all the personalities living there. "Anything to report?"

Cecilia shook her head as Abella landed in front of the house.

"Nothing new," Abella said. "Though, more people are driving by and looking at the house."

Mike nodded. To the rest of the world, his home had always been a magnificent manor. It was likely that his neighbors were suddenly curious and probably wondered why they didn't drive by more often. "As long as none of them come into the yard, we should be fine."

Abella nodded her agreement. "And even if they do, we will be ready."

Mike glanced over at the corner where the Jabberwock was asleep beneath the snow. On the other side of the yard was a small structure they had built for Cerberus. Now that the hellhound was free of the Underworld, she chose to sleep the day away and come out mostly at night. Even so, any sign of trouble would bring her out.

The stone lions on the perimeter of the house stared out at the street. There were six of them now, with several smaller iterations ensconced across the exterior of the manor. Now that the sundial was permanently activated, he knew the home's defenses would never be better.

"Are you okay?" Abella asked.

"Yeah. Just gearing up for something I'm a bit nervous to do is all." He wasn't going to lie to them, but he couldn't afford to say the truth until he was certain. "Wanted to take in the calm of the morning."

Abella looked concerned but said nothing. Cecilia took Mike's hand and gave it a squeeze.

"Call us if you need us," she whispered, then faded away.

"Always." He stepped down the stairs and kissed Abella's forehead. "I have the egg later today and was thinking of taking her for a walk in the greenhouse. You want to come?"

Her obsidian eyes sparkled. "I wouldn't miss it," she declared, then stepped back and leaped into the sky, her wings flapping as she spiraled around the manor and eventually landed on a ledge just above his bedroom window. She settled into a crouch, her eyes landing on the front gate, his family's protector.

Mike took a walk in the garden to clear his head, pausing at the sundial. The smooth stone surface sparkled now, as if crushed diamonds had been laid into the stone. It no longer rotated, frozen in a single moment of time by the drop of Santa's blood.

"What husband doing?" Tink stepped from behind him and examined the sundial. "Find way to fix?"

He chuckled to himself. After he'd reset the sundial, Tink had informed him that its final position was actually a couple degrees off, meaning it was only accurate within a few minutes. Though it didn't actually matter, she liked to tease him about it every chance she got.

"Nope." He ran his hand along the gnomon of the dial, feeling a brief connection to the ancient power that ran beneath the land. "Figured I would wait until my favorite goblin fixed it for me."

Tink pinched him, and he flinched.

"Not favorite goblin. Favorite. One word." Tink sounded dead serious, but there was a mischievous look in her eye.

"Favorite wife, maybe?"

Tink snorted, then took him by the hand. "Only wife," she reminded him, then bit his wrist.

"Ow!" He jerked his hand back. "Didn't you eat enough breakfast?"

"Tink always hungry for husband." She let out a sigh and turned her head toward the house. "But busy today. Dead girl need internet, have to install wires. Ugh."

"I'm sure Dana will appreciate it," he reminded her.

"Dead girl said husband pay price." She sashayed away from him, then looked over her shoulder directly. "Husband get ambushed later, this only warning."

"I have been warned." He followed her back to the house and walked inside. A roll of Ethernet cable was sitting at the bottom of the stairs, and Tink picked it up and held it over her head as she grumbled to herself.

"Stupid fucking stairs," she muttered.

Mike watched her go, then walked around the stairs and down the long hallway that would take him to the backyard. There were two new sitting rooms along the hall, and one of them was already accumulating children's toys. Callisto would need somewhere to play on days he visited, after all.

The back door now exited to a sunroom. Mike walked across it and through the final gold-trimmed door that led outside. The temperature in his backyard was roughly twenty degrees warmer than out front, and he didn't even question it. He was fairly certain it was partially due to Naia's fountain running hot water this time of year to help the creatures who came to visit her.

Naia was watching a pair of finches bathe in the uppermost tier of her fountain with a smile on her face. Her blue eyes focused on him as he approached the edge of her fountain.

"Good morning, lover." Naia melted into the water, reappearing a moment later on the edge. She twisted her body so she was sitting on the ledge, her hands still connecting her to the fountain's basin. "It's so good to see you this morning."

"Good morning, Naia." He didn't come any closer. "How are you today?"

"I am well. It's pretty quiet, but I rather enjoy it." Her eyes narrowed. "Your hair is getting long again. You should let me cut it for you."

"Yeah, about that. I sure could use a haircut, but that kind of depends on something else. There's a question I want to ask, but I don't know that you're going to like it."

Naia's smile faded. "I don't understand. Mike, I can feel your emotions from here, is something wrong?"

He shrugged. "I don't know yet. It's just us back here, right?"

She nodded. "That I'm aware of. Well, and the birds."

"Good. Because the question I'm about to ask is for your ears only." He walked around the edge of her fountain. "Do you remember Christmas Day? When I used that drop of blood to strengthen the geas?"

"Of course." Naia's body slid along the edge of the fountain, keeping Mike facing her. "My fountain got a bit bigger, and my bathtub now has a window with a view!"

Mike nodded. "There were so many changes all at once, and it seems like we're still discovering some of them. But that's not what this is about. It's actually about something I learned from the North Pole, and a little bit about the cabin."

"What's that?" She tilted her head to one side, her blue-and-green locks tumbling down her shoulder.

"Well, let's start with the cabin. I was only there a couple of days, and the entity that resides there made direct contact with me. Sure, it was in a dream, but I was actually speaking with her."

"Uh-huh."

Mike frowned. "And when I went to the North Pole, the entity that resides there spoke with me directly. He also spoke with Holly. I checked with her later on. Came right out and said hello."

Naia blinked, confusion on her face.

"However, my own home seems to be more mysterious. The spirit who lives here has contacted me but never directly, not in a face-to-face manner. I've occupied her body, or heard her voice in my head. I thought that was really weird, right?"

She shrugged. "I guess. But two out of three doesn't necessarily mean anything."

"You're right, it doesn't." Mike stopped at a stone bench and sat down. "But it was the North Pole that gave it away. I got to see Freyja's memories, you know, was floating around in her head quite a bit. Some of it didn't make sense to me, but Yuki filled me in on Freyja's visit, and a lot of things clicked into place."

"Oh? Like what?" Naia blinked at him with those beautiful sapphire eyes. She was the first one Mike had met, this beautiful creature who had pulled him into an exciting, unexpected adventure. For a while, she had been his everything, and then the others had come. As the house expanded, she was ever there, his Naia, maybe even his first real love.

"I'm not going to pretend to understand the rules of the great game, or even its true purpose. But I have learned why it demands secrecy and what is at risk if the truth of the matter ever got out. For example, I know now that the Architect built all these locations using the bodies of the gods." Mike sat forward on the bench, his magic wrapping around him like a shield. "A simple Google search pretty much confirms that the North Pole is Cronus, or maybe Janus—it seems like there's quite a bit of overlap in regard to who is in charge of time."

Naia nodded, waiting for him to continue.

"Now the cabin is likely Artemis, or a similar counterpart." He paused, half expecting to be struck down by lightning. When it didn't happen, he continued. "But it makes sense in hindsight. The Architect made their bodies into physical locations, then bound their souls to the property. The gods are hiding in plain sight, protecting this world from outside forces…somehow."

The nymph shrugged. "I guess that makes sense."

Mike sighed. "Well, that brings us to now. You see, ever since dealing with Artemis and Cronus, I've wondered why the spirit of this home isn't more directly involved. How come I've never seen her face?"

"Maybe she's shy?" Naia looked at him, her face the picture of innocence.

"Or maybe she's been hiding in plain sight." Mike stood and let out a sigh. "So my question is this: Were you ever planning to tell me that you're not actually Naia?"

There was a long pause as Naia stared at him, her features frozen in shock. The birds behind them continued to bathe in her fountain, singing cheerfully to themselves despite the sudden shift in atmosphere.

Naia didn't respond, her eyes glistening as the fountain gurgled behind her. She eventually blinked. When her eyes opened once more, they had become golden in color.

"Well done, lover." Naia stretched her arms over her head, then stood and stepped out of the fountain. Streamers of water connected her to the basin as she walked toward Mike across the cobblestones. "Though I don't know why you're suddenly so defensive."

"Because you lied to me." Mike took a step forward, closing the distance. "From the very beginning."

"That's not true at all. Naia has never lied to you. She doesn't know I'm in here." She reached out and touched his face. "So did the all-powerful Google tell you who I am too?"

"Maybe. A quick search for gods and goddesses who represent the home gave me a fairly solid option, but I have my doubts." He fought the urge to push her hand away. "For example, if you are who I think you are, it's more than a little strange that you chose a nymph as your guardian."

"Naia was one of the only survivors when Olympus fell. I consider her and Amymone to be family so had the Architect save them. I was forced to choose between one of them as my guardian. I couldn't use Amymone because she sleeps in the winter, which left Naia. Though her sexual proclivities fall outside my domain, she is pure of heart. Neither of them remember any of this, by the way. Not because of the geas but due to becoming pawns in the great game." She winked at him. "So are you going to guess, or do you plan on keeping a lady waiting?"

"Then you are Hestia, goddess of the hearth and home." If he was wrong, he honestly didn't know who she could be.

Her golden eyes shimmered in relief as the goddess took a step back. "You have no idea how long it's been since someone has spoken my own name to me. Yes, I am Hestia, one of the last gods of Olympus, and you are living inside what remains of my body." Hestia put her hands over her heart. "You have found me at last."

"Why play hide-and-seek with me, then? The other gods, they showed up pretty quick."

Hestia's eyes shimmered. "I have always been here, looking out through her eyes. You see, Caretaker, though I was careful in who I chose, your predecessor's mistakes almost cost me everything. You see, after Emily died, Naia… didn't make it." Her shoulders drooped. "Or at least, she wouldn't have, had I not intervened. The fountain was cut off, and she was dying. Not only do I think of her as my own child, but losing my guardian means I would become little more than another piece to be collected. So, in her final moments, I initiated the soul swap with her so my magic could be used to force enough water through her spring to keep her alive. But, as you know, some souls are indivisible."

"So Naia didn't know? She hasn't been lying to me?" Mike let out the breath he had been holding. It was the one thing he had been worried about. She had been the first person he had ever truly trusted, and the knowledge that she had been lying to him this whole time had nearly made him sick to his stomach.

"No, she hasn't, never knowingly. Nor could I casually reveal myself, not without potentially harming her." Hestia sighed. "The rules of the game, as it were. But I must ask—how did you figure it out?"

"I can see souls now." He could picture it again, that magnificent fractal pattern above the house as the geas took a stronger hold. It rotated in place like a distant galaxy, marked with golden streaks of divinity. The house itself was alive, and it was a pattern he recognized as the runes on Naia's ribs. "That, and I discovered something interesting in the Dreamscape."

"Oh?" Hestia cocked her head.

"Naia doesn't have her runes there. Which means they aren't technically a part of her soul. For the longest time, I thought they were what shackled her to this place, but when I saw them on Holly, I realized it was part of the soul-swapping magic."

The goddess clapped her hands and laughed, a magical sound that caused the nearby birds to burst into song. "Oh my. You are quite the detective."

"So is that why I haven't been able to reach you when I wanted to? Because you're part of her?"

Hestia nodded. "An unforeseen consequence, I assure you. On occasion, I have tried to lead the way through Naia's words or have impressed visions upon you in the hopes you would understand. Though you have found me, I am still bound by the rules of the great game and can only offer so much assistance."

Mike stared into her eyes, wondering if the goddess was being truthful with him. Every interaction he had ever had with Naia was now under scrutiny, and he hated it. Either he would have to accept that Hestia had his best interests at heart or he could choose to forever doubt a woman he loved.

"From now on, I would prefer we speak like this. Visions are fine or whatever, but no putting words into Naia's mouth for her. She deserves better."

Hestia gave him a little bow. "I find these terms agreeable. Now that you have found me, I shall reveal my presence to her later tonight and let her know that she is my vessel. She will be like the priestesses of old, allowing me to use her body to speak with my chosen."

Mike contemplated the goddess for several more moments. Hestia was the house itself, but knowing how to reach her directly changed everything. Would he use this knowledge to make an honest attempt to further his progress in the great game? Or would he continue as he had, simply enjoying the time he had with the others? He felt like the choice was clear but wanted to be sure.

"So what happens now?"

Hestia giggled, then stepped backward until she was standing in the fountain.

"That's just it, Caretaker. Your agenda has ever been your own, and I would not seek to change it in any way. The choice is forever yours."

"Can I tell the others about you?"

She smirked. "Refer to my last answer."

"Oh good." He chuckled. "You gods sure do enjoy walking the line between mysterious and annoying."

"And we wouldn't have it any other way. But know this, child—when you were lost, I gave you a home. You became the bond that tied our family together and allowed it to grow.

You have seen success where others have failed and have yet to lose sight of what is important to you. As far as I'm concerned, you have already succeeded."

Hestia closed her eyes. When she opened them, the crystalline blue pupils had returned, and he realized Naia was standing before him once more. She shook her head and looked around as if puzzled.

"I'm sorry, I must have tuned you out. Were we talking about something?"

"I'll explain later." He moved to the fountain's edge and stuck out his hand. When she took it, he gave her a squeeze. "Have I ever told you how lucky I was to find you?"

"You mean you got lucky when you found me." She winked. "Twice, if I remember correctly."

He laughed, then slid his arm around her waist. "So about that haircut—"

"Mike!" The back door of the sunroom burst open, the glass in the door shattering. It was Eulalie, her eyes wider than he'd ever seen. Clutched in her hands was Velvet's egg, the swirled gemstone lines sparkling in the limited light of winter.

"What is it, what's wrong?" By the time Mike stood, Eulalie was standing over him. She held the egg down where he could see it.

"Put your hands on it, quick!"

Mike pressed his hands to the hard surface of the egg and was surprised at how hot it felt. Some of the others came out the back door to see what the commotion was, and Abella landed next to them, her wings curling against her body.

"What is happening?" Abella demanded.

"She's moving!" Eulalie grabbed Abella's wrist and put the gargoyle's hand on the egg. "Can you feel her? She's never been so active!"

Mike stood in awe, feeling his daughter shift around beneath the egg's surface. All around the egg, he could see the swirling, magical colors of her soul as it shifted about like a flower in a storm. The others gathered nearby, eagerly waiting their own turns. Two more hands appeared, and Mike looked up to see that Lily and Dana had pushed their way through to touch it.

The new soul turned to regard each of them but eventually focused on Mike. He could feel his daughter's attention now, as if she was studying him through her shell. He had felt her shift a couple of times while watching her in the past but never like this. She was present, fully aware now.

"I'm your daddy," he said, rubbing his palm across the top of the egg. "And I really can't wait to meet you."

The soul sparkled with light, something that only he could see. Gossamer strands drifted away from it and brushed against everyone, as if inspecting them. Beneath his palm, he felt something scratch the interior of the egg, then tap it a couple of times.

A crack appeared.

END

AFTERWORD

This story started as a dare. What began as a story about a man finding a nymph in his bathtub exploded into six books and three spinoffs.

I'd like to thank my Patrons. This story and the world it exists in simply would not exist without them. You can find some of the cool kids at https://annabellehawthorne.com/hall-of-caretakers/

Second, an author is only as good as their readers. I have a bunch of enthusiastic readers who would love to chat about the story and other things that they like! Come meet the monster family over on my Discord channel at https://discord.gg/gWjTY8D

A special thanks to my beta team who give up a ton of free time to help me get the story straight. There are many, but special thanks to Tj Skywind, the Mikes, Pastor, Artvr and Zing. A big thank you to all the others who have helped here and there, I appreciate all that you've done.

Lyss Em is my editor and she is simply the best.

Last, but most important, thank you. Please make sure you leave a review, they have quickly become the lifeblood of online publishing.

"No one is useless in this world who lightens the burdens of another." - *Charles Dickens*

Ingrid sat in the conference room with other members of the Order, her eyes on the projector screen. The images clicked by every few seconds, displaying the grisly scene of hundreds of beached merfolk, many already in a state of decomposition.

They had been boiled alive.

The room was silent as the other operatives contemplated the images. The merfolk colonies of Maui had never seen a loss this bad before. Typically, merfolk deaths were attributed to accidents that occurred with boats or even the occasional misplaced submarine. This time, however, it had taken an enormous amount of effort to conceal the loss from the public because the cause was only partially known.

Her partner, Wallace, was leaning back in his seat with his hands behind his head. If he were to close his eyes, he could easily be sleeping.

At last, somebody asked the question everyone was waiting for.

"Are there any leads?" This was from a local mage who had flown in from the big island.

"We've got one." Master Eamon, who was leading the meeting, turned toward the projector. "We found tracks all along the beach that we were able to trace back up the mountain. Whatever attacked the merfolk was big."

"How big?" Wallace leaned forward in interest.

"Big enough that it flash boiled the entire bay." Eamon crossed his arms. "Preliminary reports indicate it might be reptilian, or even serpentine. We aren't sure, because it triggered several mudslides on its way down."

"Ah." Wallace leaned back. "Okay, then."

"Point of origin?" Ingrid studied the images of the

monster's tracks, which were poor in quality. Did they use the cheap drones to take these?

"And that's where you come in." Eamon turned back to the display, which now showed a topographical map of Maui. "You see, we were able to get a rough estimate of where the creature came from, and this is where things get interesting." He pointed at a spot near the top of Haleakalā. "We believe the creature emerged from somewhere by the Big Bog."

"How big is it?" asked Wallace. Ingrid elbowed him in the ribs.

Ignoring Wallace, Eamon continued. "This area is largely a state park, but there's a small plot of land that is privately owned. I shouldn't have to explain to you all why this is so unusual. Anyway, all signs point to that as our target's point of origin. I need your team to head out to the east coast and make contact with its owner."

"Which billionaire are we going to meet with?" Wallace looked over at Ingrid. "I've always wanted to punch a billionaire."

"Nobody you've heard of." The slides shifted to show a man with brown hair in his late 20s. "In fact, he just inherited this property a few years back."

"Name?" asked Ingrid.

"Mike Radley."

ABOUT THE AUTHOR

Annabelle Hawthorne lives in a top secret location somewhere in the Rocky Mountains with a loving family and potentially a dog or two. The mysterious Hawthorne can usually be found with coffee and a good horror novel.

Find Annabelle on Twitter @authorannabelle

Support Annabelle's Patreon to get exclusive access to art and more!

www.Patreon.com/sexyannabelle

Official website at https://www.annabellehawthorne.com

Chat with other readers at https://discord.gg/gWjTY8D

Thanks for reading!

ABOUT THE PUBLISHER

Wet Leaf Press is a small press dedicated to providing high-quality erotica to discerning readers.

You deserve smart.
You deserve sexy.
You deserve quality erotica.

ALSO BY ANNABELLE HAWTHORNE

Stories in the Horny Monsters Series (Chronological)

The Last of Her Kind

Radley's Home for Horny Monsters

Radley's Labyrinth for Horny Monsters

Radley's Wardrobe for Horny Monsters

Dead and Horny

Radley's Underworld for Horny Monsters

Radley's Apocalypse for Horny Monsters

Other Series

Master Class: A Slice of Life LitRPG Harem (w/ Virgil Knightley)

Succubus Summoner (w/ Virgil Knightley)

Made in the USA
Middletown, DE
29 August 2024

59995486R00398